Squire Arden by Margaret Oliphant

In Three Volumes

Margaret Oliphant Wilson was born on April 4th, 1828 to Francis W. Wilson, a clerk, and Margaret Oliphant, at Wallyford, near Musselburgh, East Lothian.

Her youth was spent in establishing a writing style and by 1849 she had her first novel published: Passages in the Life of Mrs. Margaret Maitland.

Two years later, in 1851 Caleb Field was published and also an invitation to contribute to Blackwood's Magazine; the beginning of a life time business relationship.

In May 1852, Margaret married her cousin, Frank Wilson Oliphant. Their marriage produced six children but, tragically, three died in infancy. When her husband developed signs of the dreaded consumption (tuberculosis) they moved to Florence, and then to Rome where, sadly, he died.

Margaret was naturally devastated but was also now left without support and only her income from writing to support the family. She returned to England and took up the burden of supporting her three remaining children by her literary activity.

Her incredible and prolific work rate increased both her commercial reputation and the size of her reading audience. Tragedy struck again in January 1864 when her only remaining daughter Maggie died.

In 1866 she settled at Windsor to be closer to her sons, who were being educated at near-by Eton School.

For more than thirty years she pursued a varied literary career but family life continued to bring problems. Cyril Francis, her eldest son, died in 1890. The younger son, Francis, who she nicknamed 'Cecco', died in 1894.

With the last of her children now lost to her, she had little further interest in life. Her health steadily and inexorably declined.

Margaret Oliphant Wilson Oliphant died at the age of 69 in Wimbledon on 20th June 1897. She is buried in Eton beside her sons.

Index of Contents

VOLUME I
CHAPTER I
CHAPTER II
CHAPTER III
CHAPTER IV
CHAPTER V
CHAPTER VI

CHAPTER VII
CHAPTER VIII
CHAPTER IX
CHAPTER X
CHAPTER XI
CHAPTER XII
CHAPTER XIII
CHAPTER XIV
CHAPTER XV
CHAPTER XVI
CHAPTER XVII
CHAPTER XVIII
CHAPTER XIX
CHAPTER XX
CHAPTER XXI
CHAPTER XXII
CHAPTER XXIII
CHAPTER XXIV
CHAPTER XXV
CHAPTER XXVI
CHAPTER XXVII
CHAPTER XXVIII
VOLUME II
CHAPTER I
CHAPTER II
CHAPTER III
CHAPTER IV
CHAPTER V
CHAPTER VI
CHAPTER VII
CHAPTER VIII
CHAPTER IX
CHAPTER X
CHAPTER XI
CHAPTER XII
CHAPTER XIII
CHAPTER XIV
CHAPTER XV
CHAPTER XVI
CHAPTER XVII
CHAPTER XVIII
CHAPTER XIX
CHAPTER XX
CHAPTER XXI
CHAPTER XXII
CHAPTER XXIII
CHAPTER XXIV
CHAPTER XXV

CHAPTER XXVI
CHAPTER XXVII
CHAPTER XXVIII
VOLUME III
CHAPTER I
CHAPTER II
CHAPTER III
CHAPTER IV
CHAPTER V
CHAPTER VI
CHAPTER VII
CHAPTER VIII
CHAPTER IX
CHAPTER X
CHAPTER XI
CHAPTER XII
CHAPTER XIII
CHAPTER XIV
CHAPTER XV
CHAPTER XVI
CHAPTER XVII
CHAPTER XVIII
CHAPTER XIX
CHAPTER XX
CHAPTER XXI
CHAPTER XXII
CHAPTER XXIII
CHAPTER XXIV
CHAPTER XXV
CHAPTER XXVI
CHAPTER XXVII
CHAPTER XXVIII
CHAPTER XXIX
MARGARET OLIPHANT – A SHORT BIOGRAPHY
MARGARET OLIPHANT – A CONCISE BIBLIOGRAPHY

CHAPTER I

"What are the joy bells a-ringing for, Simon?" said an old woman, coming briskly out to the door of one of the pretty cottages in the pretty village of Arden, on a pleasant morning of early summer, when all the leaves were young, and the first freshness of the year was over the world. "There's ne'er a one married as I knows on, and it aint Whitsuntide, nor Holmfirth fair, nor—"

"It's the young Squire, stoopid," said the old clerk, gruffly, leaning his arms upon the little paling of the tiny garden and looking at her. "He's come home."

What he really did say was "he's coom whoam;" but the reader will be so kind as take it for granted that Simon Molyneaux was an old Lancashire man, and talked accordingly, without giving a pen not too familiar with the dialect the trouble of putting in all the o's that are necessary. Simon said coom, and he said loove, and moother; but as there is no moral meaning in the double letter, let us consent to leave it out.

"The young Squire!" said the old woman, with a start.

She was a tidy fresh old woman, with cheeks of a russet colour, half brown half red, yet soft, despite all their wrinkles—cheeks that children laid their little faces up to without feeling any difference of texture; and eyes which had stolen back during these years deeper into their sockets, but yet were bright and full of suppressed sunshine. She had a little shawl pinned over her print gown, and a great white apron, which shone in the sun, and made the chief light in the little picture. Simon's rugged countenance looking at her was all brown, with a deep dusky red on the tops of the cheekbones; his face was as full of cross-hatching as if he had been an old print. His eyes were deeper than were hers, but still at the bottom of the wrinkled caves they abode in had a spark of light in each of them. In short, there was sufficient resemblance between them still to show that Simon and Sarah were brother and sister. A young woman of four and twenty came to the door of the next cottage at the sound of his voice, and opening it, went in again, as if her duty was done. She was Simon's daughter and housekeeper, who was not fond of gossip, and the two kindred households were next door to each other. It was a very pretty village, much encouraged to keep itself tidy, and to cultivate flowers, and do everything that is proper in its condition of life, by the young lady at the Hall. The houses had been improved, but in an unobtrusive way. They were not painfully white-washed, but showed here and there a gleam of red brick in a thin place. The roses and the honeysuckles were not always neatly trained, and there was even an old shawl thrust into a broken pane in the window of Sally Timms, who was so much trouble to Miss Arden with her untidy ways. Old Simon had nothing but wallflower and southernwood (which was called lad's love in that region), and red and white daisies in his garden. But next door, if you came at the proper season, you might see picottees that were exhibited at the Holmfirth flower show, and floury auriculas, such as were the height of the fashion in the floral world a good many years ago. In short there was just that mixture of perfection and imperfection which kept the village of Arden a natural spontaneous village, instead of an artificial piece of luxury, cultivated like any other ornament, in consequence of the very close vicinity of the Hall gates.

"The young Squire!" said old Sarah again, who had been shaking her head all the time we have taken to interpolate this bit of description; and she did it still more emphatically now when she repeated her words, "Poor lad—poor lad! Eh, to think the joy bells should be rung in Arden Church along o' him! He never came home yet that I hadn't a good cry for't afore the day was done. Poor lad!"

"Thee needn't cry no more," said Simon, "along of him. He's come to his own, and ne'er one within twenty miles to say him nay. He came home last night, when folks were a' abed; but he's as bright as a May morning to look at him now."

"He was allays bright," said Sarah, wiping her eyes with her apron, an action which disturbed the whole picture, breaking up the lights, "when he was kepp like the lowest in the house, and 'ad the nose snapped off his face, he'd cry one minute and laugh the next, that's what he'd do. He never was long down, wasn't Mr. Edgar. Though where he got that, and his light hair, and them dancing eyes of his, it's none o' us that can say."

"It was off his mother he got 'em, as was natural," said the old clerk. "I saw her when old Master he brought her home first, and she was as fair as fair. But, Squire or no Squire, I'm going to my breakfast. Them bell-ringing boys they're at the Arden Arms already, drinking the Squire's sovereign, the fools, instead of laying it up for a rainy day. If they had the rheumatiz as bad as me they'd know what it was to have a penny laid by; but I don't know what young folks is coming to, I don't," said Simon, opening his own gate, and hobbling towards the open door. He had a large white handkerchief loosely tied about his shrivelled brown throat, and an old black coat, which had been an evening coat of the old Squire's in former days. Simon preferred swallowtail coats, chiefly because he thought they were more dignified, and became his position; but partly also because experience had taught him that coats which were only worn in the evening by their original proprietor had a great deal more wear in them than those which the Squire or the Rector walked about in all day.

Sarah went in also to her own cottage, where for the moment she was all alone. She spread down her white apron, and smoothed out the creases which she had made when she dried her eyes; but, notwithstanding, her eyes required to be dried again. "Poor lad," she said at intervals, as she "tidied" her already tidy room, and swept some imperceptible dust into the fireplace. The fire was made up. The cat sat winking by it. The kettle feebly murmured on the hob. It was not the moment for that kettle to put itself in evidence. It had made the breakfast, and had helped in the washing of the solitary cup and saucer, and it was only just now that it should retire into the background till the afternoon, when tea was again to be thought of. Its mistress was somewhat in the same condition. She walked round the room two or three times, trying apparently to find some piece of active work which required to be done, and poked into all the corners. "I done my scouring only yesterday," she said to herself in a regretful and plaintive tone; but, after a little interval, added energetically, "and I cannot settle down to plain sewing, not to-day." She said this as if somebody had commanded her to take to her plain sewing, which lay all ready in a basket on the table, and the command had roused her to sudden irritation. But it was only the voice of duty which gave that order. Even after this indignant protest, however, Sarah took her work, and put in three stitches, and then picked them carefully out again. "I think I'm losing of my seven senses," she said to herself plaintively. "It aint no use a struggling." And with that the old woman rose, tied on her big old bonnet, and set out through Arden village in the sunshine on her way to Arden Hall.

To see that pretty rural place, you would never have supposed it was within a dozen miles of the great, vulgar, bustling town of Liverpool—nay, within half a dozen miles of the straggling, dreary outskirts of that big beehive. But yet so it was; from the tower of Arden Church you could see the mouth of the Mersey, with all its crowds of ships; and, but for the haughty determination of the old Squire to grant no building leases on his land, and the absence of railway communication consequent thereupon, no doubt Arden would have been by this time full of villas, and would have sent a stream of commercial gentlemen every morning out of its quiet freshness by dint of a ten o'clock train. But there was no ten o'clock train, and no commercial gentlemen, and no bright shining new villas; but only the row of houses, half whitewash half red brick, with lilac bushes all in flower, and traveller's joy bristling over their porches, and all the little gardens shining in the sun. The Church was early English; the parsonage was red brick of Queen Anne's time. And there was a great house flush with the road, disdaining any petty interposition of garden between it and the highway, with white steps and a brass knocker, and rows upon rows of brilliant dazzling windows, which was the doctor's house. The parson and the doctor were the only gentlemen in Arden village; there was nobody else above the rank of an ordinary cottager. There was a little shop where everything was sold; and there was the post office, where stationery was to be had as well as postage stamps; and the Arden Arms, with a little green before it, and a great square sign-post standing out in the midst. A little way beyond the Church, which stood on the other side of the road, opposite but higher up than the Arden Arms, were the great Hall gates. They had a liberal hospitable breadth about them which was suggestive somehow of guests and good cheer. Two carriages could pass, the village folks said, with natural pride, through those wide portals, and the breadth of the great splendid old avenue, with its elms and limes, was in proportion. There were two footpaths leading on either side of the avenue, like side aisles in a great cathedral, under the green-arched splendour of meeting trees; and so princely were the Ardens, with all their prejudices, that not only their poor neighbours, but even Liverpool folks pic-nicing, had leave to roam about the park, and take their walks even in the side aisles of the avenue. The Squire, like a great monarch, was affable to the populace—so long as it allowed that it was the populace, and kept in its right place.

Up one of these side walks old Sarah trudged, with her white apron disturbing all the lights, and with many homely musings in her old head, which had scarcely a right to the dignified title of thoughts. She was thinking to herself—"Eh, my word, but here's changes! Master o' all, him that was never made no more of nor a stranger in his own father's house; nor half so much as a stranger. Them as come on visits would get the best o' all, ponies to ride, and servants to wait upon 'em, and whatever they had a mind for:—and Mr. Edgar put into that bit of a room by the nursery, and never a horse, nor a penny in his pocket. I'd just like to know how it was. Eh, my word, what a queer feel it must have! You mind me, he'll think he hears oud Squire ahind him many and many a day. And an only son! And I never heard a word against Madam, and Miss Clare always the queen of all. Bless him! none on us could help that; but I was allays one as stood up for Mr. Edgar. And now he's master o' all! I wonder is she glad, the dear? Here's folks a coming, a man and a maid; and I canno' see who they are with my bad eyes. Eb, but I could once see as good as the best. I mind that time I was in Cheshire, afore I came home here—Lord bless us, it's Miss Clare and the young Squire!"

The young pair were coming down under the trees on the same path, and Sarah stopped short in her thinkings with a flutter, as if they must have divined the subject of them:—Two young people all in black, not lighting up the landscape as they might have done had their dress been as bright as their faces. The first thing that struck the observer was that they were utterly unlike; they had not even the same little family tricks of gait or gesture, such as might have made it apparent that they were brother and sister. The young lady was tall and slight, with a great deal of soft dignity and grace; dignity which might, however, grow imperious on occasion. Her face was beautiful, and regular, and full of sweetness; but those fine lines could set and harden, and the light young figure could erect itself, if need were, into all the severity of a youthful Juno. Her hair was very dark, and her eyes blue—a kind of beauty which is often of the highest class as beauty, but often, also, indicates a character which should attract as much fear as love. She was soft now as the opening day, leaning on her brother's arm with a certain clinging gesture which was not natural to her, lavishing upon him her smiles and pretty looks of affection. Old Sarah, looking on, divined her meaning in a moment. "Bless her!" the old woman said to herself, with a tear in the corner of her eye, which she dared not lift the apron to dry. Hard injustice and wrong had been Edgar's part all his life. His sister was making it up to him, pouring upon him all the sunshine she could collect into her moist eyes, to make him amends for having thus lived so long in the dark.

Clare Arden might have stepped out of one of the picture frames in the hall, so entirely was her beauty the beauty of her family; but her brother was as different as it is possible to imagine. He was scarcely taller than she was, not more than an inch or two, instead of towering over her as her father had done. He had light brown, curly, abundant hair, frizzing all over his well-shaped, well-poised head; and brown eyes, which sparkled, and danced, and laughed, and spoke, and defied you not to like them. They had laughed and danced in his worst days, irrepressibly, and now, notwithstanding the black band on his hat, they sent rays about like dancing fauns, all life, and fire, and active energy. He looked like one whom nobody could wrong, who would disarm the sourest critic. A stranger would have instantly taken it for granted that he was the favourite child of the house, the one whose gay vagaries were always pardoned, and whose saucy ways no father or mother could well withstand. How such a being could have got into the serious old-world house of Arden nobody could make out. It was supposed that he was like his mother; but she had been in delicate health, poor lady, and had lived very little at Arden Hall. The village folks did not trouble their head with theories as to the cause of the old Squire's dislike to his only son, but the parson and the doctor had each a very decided opinion on the subject, which the reader shall learn further on, and make his own conclusions from. For, in the meantime, I cannot go on describing Edgar Arden. It is his business to do that for himself.

"Who is coming?" he said. "Somebody whose face I know; a nice old woman with a great white apron. But we must go on to see the village, and all your improvements there."

"There are no improvements," said his sister. "Oh, Edgar, I do hope you hate that sort of thing as I do. Let us keep it as it was. Our own people are so pleasant, and will do what we want them. The only thing I was afraid of you for was lest you should turn radical, like the rest of the young men. But then you have not been in the way of it—like the Oxford men, you know."

"I don't know about the Oxford men," said Edgar, "but I am not so sure I haven't been in the way of it." He had the least little touch of a foreign accent, which was very quaint from those most Saxon lips. He was just the kind of young man whom, anywhere abroad, the traveller would distinguish as an undeniable Briton; and yet his English had a touch of something alien in it—a flavour which was not British. He laughed as he spoke, and the sound startled all the solemn elms of Arden. The Ardens did not laugh much; they smiled very sweetly, and they liked to know that their smile was a distinction; but Edgar was not like the Ardens.

"How you laugh," said Clare, clinging a little closer to his arm, "It is very odd, but somehow I like it. Don't you know, Edgar, the Ardens were never people to laugh? We smile."

"So you do," said Edgar, "and I would rather have your smile than ever so much laughing. But then you know I am not half an Arden. I never had a chance. Here is our old woman close at hand with her white apron. Why, it is old Sarah! You kind old soul, how are you? How does it go?" And he took both her hands into his and shook them till old Sarah lost her breath. Then a twinkle like a tear came in to Edgar's laughing eye. "You gave me half-a-crown when I left Arden last," he said, still holding her hands, and then in his foreign way he kissed her first on one brown cheek and then on the other. "Oh, Master Edgar!" cried old Sarah, out of breath; while Clare looked on very sedately, not quite knowing what to say.

CHAPTER II

"It was kind of you to come and see my brother," said Clare at length, with something of that high and lofty sweetness which half implies—"it was kind, but it was a piece of presumption." She meant no harm to her old nurse, whom she was fond of in her heart, and who was besides a privileged person, free to be fond of the Ardens; but Edgar had been badly used all his life, and his sister was more proud on his behalf than if he had been the worshipped heir, always foremost. She drew herself up just a little, not knowing what to make of it. In one way it was right, and she approved; for even a king may be tender to his favoured dependents without derogation—but yet, certainly it was not the Arden way.

"Miss Clare, you don't think that, and you oughtn't for to say it," said old Sarah, with some natural heat; "but I've been about the house ever since you were born: and staying still to-day in my little place with my plain-sewing was more nor I could do. If there had been e'er a little maid to look to—but I ain't got none in hands now."

"I beg your pardon, Sarah," said Clare promptly; "and Mrs. Fillpot has something to say to you about that. If you will go up to the house and speak to her, now that you have seen Edgar, it will be very nice of you. We are going down to the village to see some of his old friends."

"The young master don't know the village, Miss Clare, as he ought to have done," said old Sarah, shaking her head. She had said such words often before, but never with the same result as now; for Clare was divided between allegiance to the father whom she loved, who was dead, and whom she could not now admit to have ever done any wrong—and the brother whom she loved, who was there by her side, and of whose injuries she was so keenly sensible. The blood rushed to her cheek—her fine blue eyes grew like steel—the lines of her beautiful face hardened. Poor old Sarah shrank back instinctively, almost as if she expected a blow. Clare's lips were formed to speak when her brother interrupted her, and probably the words would not have been pleasant which she was about to say.

"The more reason I should know it now," he said in his lighthearted way. "If it had not been so early, Sarah, you should have come back and made me some tea. What capital tea she used to make for you in the nursery, Clare, you lucky girl! It is Miss Arden's village I am going to see, Sarah. It shall always be hers to do what she likes with it. You can tell the people nothing is changed there."

"Edgar, I think we should go," said Clare, restraining him with once more that soft shade of possible haughtiness. "Stay till we come back, Sarah;" and with a little movement of her hand in sign of farewell, she led her brother away. "You must not tell your plans to that sort of person," she said with a quick breath, in which her momentary passion found relief.

"What! not your old nurse, Clare?" he cried. "You must not snub the old woman so. We had better make a bargain in time, we who are so different. You shall snub me when you please for my democratic ways, but you must not snub the others, Clare."

"What others?"

Edgar made no direct answer. He laughed and drew his sister's arm close within his own. "You are such a pretty picture with those great-lady looks of yours," he said; "they make me think of ruffs and hoops, and dresses all covered with pearls. What is a farthingale? I am sure that is what you ought to wear."

"You mean it is out of fashion to remember that one is well born, and of an old family," said Clare with energy, "but you will never bring me to see that. One has enough to do to keep one's proper place with all those encroachments that are going on, without one's own brother to take their part. But oh! forgive me, Edgar; I forgot: I will never say another word," she said, with the tears rushing to her eyes.

"What did you forget?" he said gently—"that I have been brought up as never any Arden was before me, and am not an Arden at all, so to speak? Perhaps on the whole it is better, for Arden ways are not the ways of our time. They are very splendid and very imposing, and, in you, dear, I don't object to them, but—"

"Oh, Edgar, don't speak so!" said his sister, with a certain horror.

"But I must speak so, and think so, too," he said. "Could not you try to imagine, Clare, among all the many theories on the subject, that this was what was meant by my banishment? It is as good a way of accounting for it as another. Imagine, for instance, that Arden ways were found to be a little behind the generation, and that, hard as it was, and, perhaps, cruel as it was—"

"Edgar—I don't say it is not true; but oh, don't say so, for I can't bear it!"

"I shall say nothing you can't bear," he said softly, "my kind sister! you always did your best for me. I hope I should not have behaved badly anyhow; but you can't tell what a comfort it is that you always stood by me, Clare."

"I always loved you, Edgar," she cried, eagerly; "and then I used to wonder if it was my fault—if I got all the love because I was like the family, and a girl—taking it from you. I wish we had been a little bit like, do you know—just a little, so that people should say—'Look at that brother and sister.' Sometimes one sees a boy and a girl so like—just a beard to one and long hair to the other, to make the necessary difference; and then one sees they belong to each other at the first glance."

"Never mind," said Edgar with a smile, "so long as we resemble each other in our hearts."

"But not in our minds," said Clare, sorrowfully. "I can see how it will be. You will always be thinking one thing when I am thinking another. Whatever there may be to consider, you and I will always take different views of it. You are for the present, and I am for the past. I know only our own Arden ways, and you know the ways of the world. It is so hard, Edgar; but, dear, I don't for a moment say it is your fault," she said, holding his arm clasped between her hands, and looking up with her blue eyes at their softest, into his face. He looked down upon her at the same time with a curious, tender, amused smile. Clare, who knew only Arden ways, was so sure they must be right ways, so certain that there was a fault somewhere in those who did not understand them—but not Edgar's fault, poor fellow! He had been brought up away from home, and was to be pitied, not blamed. And this was why her brother looked down upon her with that curious amused smile.

"No," he said, "it was not my fault; but I think you should take my theory on the subject into consideration, Clare. Suppose I had been sent off on purpose to inaugurate a new world?"

Clare gave a little shudder, but she did not speak. She was troubled even that he could joke on such a matter, or suggest theories, as if it had been a mere crotchet on the part of her father, who was incapable of anything of the kind; but she could not make a direct reply, for, by tacit mutual consent, neither of them named the old Squire.

"Let us think so at least," he answered gaily, "for the harm is done, I fear; and it would not be so bad to be a deserter from Arden ways, if one had been educated for that purpose, don't you think? So here we are at the village! Don't tell me anything. I remember every bit of it as well as if I had been here yesterday. Where is the old lathe-and-plaster house that used to stand here?"

"To think you should recollect it!" said Clare, her eyes suddenly lighting up; and then in an apologetic tone—"It was so old. I allow it was very picturesque and charming to look at; but oh, Edgar, you would not blame me if you knew how dreadfully tumble-down and miserable it was inside. The rain kept coming in, and when the brook was flooded in winter it came right into the kitchen; and the children kept having fevers. I felt very much disposed to cry over it, I can tell you; but you would not have blamed me had you seen how shocking it was inside."

"I wonder if Mistress Arden, in a ruff and a farthingale, would have thought about the drainage," he answered, laughing. "Fancy my blaming you, Clare! I tell you it is your village, and you shall do what you like with it. Is that Mr. Fielding at his gate? Let us cross over and shake hands with him before we go any further. He is not so old, surely, as he once was."

"It is we who are old," said Clare, with the first laugh that had yet come from her lips. "He is putting on his gloves to go and call on you, Edgar. The bell-ringers must have made it known everywhere. Mr. Fielding and Dr. Somers will come to-day, and the Thornleighs and Evertons to-morrow, and after that everybody; now see if it does not happen just as I say!"

"Let us stop the first of these visits," said Edgar, and he went forward holding out his hand, while the parson at the gate, buttoning his grey gloves, peered at him through a pair of short-sighted eyes. "It will be very kind of you to name yourself, Sir, for I am very short-sighted," the Rector said, looking at him with that semi-suspicion which is natural to a rustic of the highest as well as the lowest social position. The newcomer was a stranger, and therefore had little right and no assignable place in the village world. Mr. Fielding, who was short-sighted besides, peered at him very doubtfully from the puckered corners of his eyes.

"Don't you know me?" said Edgar; and "Oh, Mr. Fielding, don't you know Edgar?" came with still greater earnestness from the lips of Clare.

"It is not possible!" said Mr. Fielding, very decidedly; and then he let his slim umbrella drop out of his fingers, and held out both his hands. "Is it really you, my dear boy!" he said. "Excuse my blind eyes. If you had been my own son I would not have known you. I was on my way to call. But though this is not so solemn or so correct it will do as well. And Clare: Will you come in and have some breakfast? It cannot be much past your breakfast hour."

"Nor yours either," said Clare; "it is so naughty of you and so wrong of you to sit up like that, when you might just as well read in daylight, and go to bed when everybody else does. But we don't follow such a bad example. We mean to have breakfast always by eight o'clock."

Mr. Fielding gave a little sigh, and shook his venerable head. "That is all very pretty, my dear, and very nice when you can do it; but you know it never lasts. Anyhow, don't let us stand here. Come in, my dear boy, come in, and welcome home again. And welcome to your own, Edgar," he added, turning quickly round as he led them into his study, a large low room, looking out upon the trim parsonage garden. He put out both his hands as he said this, and grasped both those of Edgar, and looked not at all disinclined to throw himself upon his neck. "Welcome to your own," he repeated fervently, and his eyes strayed beyond Edgar's head, as if he were confronting and defying some one. And then he added more solemnly, "And God bless you, and enable you to fill your high position like a man. Amen. I wonder what the old Doctor will say now."

"What should he say?" said Edgar, fun dancing in his bright brown eyes; "and how is he? I suppose he is unchangeable, like everything here."

"Not unchangeable," said Mr. Fielding, with a slight half-perceptible shake of his head at the levity, one of those momentary assumptions of the professional which most old clergymen indulge in now and then; "nothing is unchangeable in this transitory world. But old Somers is as steady as most things," he added, with a responsive glance of amusement. "We go on quarrelling, he and I, but it would be hard upon us if we had to part. But tell me about yourself, Edgar, which is more interesting. When did you get home?"

"Late last night," said Edgar. "I came straight through from Cologne. I began to get impatient as soon as I had settled which day I was to reach home, and came before my time. Clare was in bed, poor child; but she got up, fancy, when she heard it was me."

"Of course she did; and she wants a cup of chocolate now," said the old parson, "when her colour changes like that from red to white, you should give her some globules instantly, or else a cup of chocolate. I am not a homœopathist, so I always recommend the chocolate. Mrs. Solmes please, Miss Clare is here."

"Shall I make two, sir?" said the housekeeper, who had heard the unusual commotion, and put her head in softly to see what was the matter. She did not quite understand it, even now. But she was too highly trained a woman, and too good a servant to take any notice. The chocolate was her affair, while the identity of the new comer was not.

"Don't you know my brother, Mrs. Solmes?" cried Clare. "He has come home. Edgar, she takes such good care of dear Mr. Fielding. I don't know how he managed without her before she came."

Edgar was not failing in his duty on the occasion. He stepped forward and shook hands with the radiant and flattered woman, "as nat'ral as if I had known him all his life," she said in the kitchen afterwards; for Mrs. Solmes was a stranger and foreigner, belonging to the next parish, who could not but disapprove of Arden and Arden ways, which were different from the habits of Thornleigh parish, to which she belonged. Edgar made her quite a little speech as he stood and held her hand—"Anybody who is good to Mr. Fielding is good to Clare and me. He has always been so kind to us all our lives."

"He loves you like his own children, sir," said Mrs. Solmes, quickly; and then she turned and went away to make the chocolate, not wishing to presume; while her master walked about the room, rubbing his hands softly, and peering at the young man from amid the puckers of his eyelids with pleased and approving satisfaction. "It is very nicely said," cried Mr. Fielding, "very nice feeling, and well expressed. After that speech, I should have known him anywhere for an Arden, Clare."

"But the Ardens don't make pretty speeches," said Clare, under her breath. She never could be suite sure of him. Everything he did had a spontaneous look about it that puzzled his sister. To be in Arden, and to know that a certain hereditary course of action is expected from you is a great advantage, no doubt, yet it sometimes gives a certain sobriety and stiffness to the external aspect. Edgar, on the contrary, was provokingly easy, with all the spontaneousness of a man who said and did exactly what he liked to do and to say. Clare's loyalty to her race could not have permitted any such freedom of action, and it puzzled her at every turn.

"We must send for old Somers," said Mr. Fielding. "Poor old fellow, he is very crotchety and fond of his own notions; but he's a very good fellow. We are the two oldest friends you have in the world, you young people; and if we might not get a little satisfaction out of you I don't know who should. Mrs. Solmes," this was called from the study door in a louder voice, "send Jack over with my compliments to Dr. Somers, and ask him to step this way for a minute. No, Edgar, don't go; I want to surprise him here."

"But no one says anything about Miss Somers," said Edgar; "how is she?"

"Ah, poor thing," said Mr. Fielding, shaking his head, "she is confined to bed now. She is growing old, poor soul. For that matter, we are all growing old. And not a bad thing either," he added, pausing and looking round at the two young figures so radiant in life and hope. "You children are sadly sorry for us—but fading away out of the world is easier than you think."

Edgar grasped Mr. Fielding's hand, not quite knowing why, with the compunction of youth for the departing existence to which its own beginning seems so harsh a contrast, and yet with a reverential sympathy that closed his lips. Clare, on the contrary, looked at him with something almost matter-of-fact in her blue eyes. "You are not so old," she said quietly. "We thought you looked quite young as we came to the door. Please don't be angry, but I used to think you were a hundred. You have grown ever so much younger these last three years."

"I should be very proud if I were a hundred," said Mr. Fielding, with a laugh; but he liked the grasp of Edgar's hand, and that sympathetic glance in his eyes. Clare was Clare, the recognised and accustomed princess, whom no one thought of criticising; but her brother was on his trial. Every new look, every movement, spoke for or against him; and, so far, everything was in his favour. "Of course, he is like his mother's family," the old Rector said to himself, "more sympathetic than the pure Ardens, but with all their fine character and best qualities. I wonder what old Somers will think of him. And here he comes," he continued aloud, "the best doctor in the county, though he is as crotchety as an old magician. Somers, here's our young squire."

CHAPTER III

Dr. Somers came in, with a pair of eagle eyes going before him, as it seemed, like pioneers, to warn him of what was in his way. The Rector peered and groped with the short-sighted feeble orbs which lurked amid a nest of wrinkles, but the Doctor's brilliant black eyes went on before him and inspected everything. He was a tall, straight, slim, but powerful old man, with nothing superfluous about him except his beard, which in those days was certainly a superfluity. It was white, and so was his hair; but his eyes were so much darker than any human eyes that were ever seen, that to call them black was not in the least inappropriate. He had been the handsomest man in the county in his youth, and he was not less so now—perhaps more, with all the imposing glory of his white hair, and the suavity of age that had softened the lines in his face—lines which might have been a little hard in the fulness of his strength. It was possible to think of the Rector as, according to his own words, fading away out of the earth, but Dr. Somers stood like a strong tower, which only a violent shock could move, and which had strength to resist a thousand assaults. He came into the sober-toned rectory, into that room which was always a little cold, filled with a soft motionless atmosphere, a kind of abiding twilight, which even Clare's presence did not dispel—and filled it, as it seemed, swallowing up not only the Rector, but the young brother and sister, in the fulness of his presence. He was the light, and Mr. Fielding the shadow in the picture; and, as ought always to be the case, the light dominated the shadow. He had taken in every thing and everyone in the room with a devouring glance in the momentary pause he made at the door, and then entered, holding out his hand to the newcomer—"They meant to mystify me, I suppose," he said, "and thought I would not recognise you. How are you, Edgar? You are looking just as I thought you would, just as I knew you would. When did you come home?"

"Last night, late," said Edgar, returning cordially the pressure of his hand.

"And did not wait to be waited on, like a reigning monarch, but came to see your old friends, like an impatient good-hearted boy? There's a fine fellow," said the Doctor, patting him on the shoulders with a caress which was quite as forcible as it was affectionate. "I ought to like you, Edgar Arden, for you have always justified my opinion of you, and done exactly what I expected you would do, all your life."

"Perhaps it is rash to say that I hope I shall always justify your opinion," said Edgar, laughing, "for I don't know whether it is a good one. But I don't suppose I am very hard to read," he added, with a warm flush rising over his face. He grew red, and he stopped short with a certain sense of embarrassment for which he could scarcely account. He did not even try to account for it to himself, but flushed all over, and felt excessively hot and uncomfortable. The fact was, he was a very open-hearted, candid young fellow, much more tempted to wear his heart upon his sleeve than to conceal it; and, as he glanced round upon his three companions, he could see that there was a certain furtive look of scrutiny about all their eyes: not furtive so far as the Doctor was concerned, who looked through and through him without any concealment of his intention. But Mr. Fielding had half-turned his head, while yet he peered with a tremulous scrutiny at his young guest; and Clare's pretty forehead was contracted with a line of anxiety which Edgar knew well. They were all doubtful about him—not sure of him—trying to make him out. Such a thought was bitter to the young man. His colour rose higher and higher, and his heart began to beat. "I do not think I am very difficult to read," he repeated, with a forced and painful smile.

"Not a bit," said the Doctor; "and you are as welcome home as flowers in May: the first time I have said that to you, my boy, but it won't be the last. Miss Clare, my sister would be pleased if you told her of Edgar's return. She will have to be prepared, and got up, and all sorts of things, to see him; but, if you were to tell her, she would think it kind. Ah, here's the chocolate. Of course in this house everything must give place to that."

"I will go over to Miss Somers for ten minutes," said Clare, "thank you, Doctor, for reminding me; and, dear Mr. Fielding, don't let Edgar go till I come back."

"I should like to go too," said Edgar. "No? Well, I won't then; but tell Miss Somers I will come to-morrow, Clare. Tell her I have brought her something from Constantinople; and have never forgotten how kind she used to be—how kind you all were!" And the young man turned round upon them—"It is a strange sensation coming back and feeling myself at home among the faces I have known all my life. And thank you all for being so good to Clare."

Clare was going out as he spoke, with a certain shade of reluctance and even of pride. She had been told to go, and she did not like it; it had been implied that she had forgotten a duty of neighbourship, and to Miss Somers, too, who could not move about, and ascertain things for herself; and Clare did not like to be reminded of her duties. She turned round, however, at the door, and looked back, and smiled her acknowledgment of what her brother said. These two old men had been very kind to her. They had done everything that the most attached old friends could do at the time of her father's death. That was a whole year ago; for old Squire Arden had made a stipulation that his son was not to come back, nor enter upon the possession of his right, till he was five-and-twenty—a stipulation which, of course, counted for nothing in the eye of the law, but was binding on Edgar, much as he longed to be at his sister's side. Thus, his father oppressed him down to the very edge of his grave. And poor Clare would have been very forlorn in the great house but for her old friends. Miss Somers, who was not then so great an invalid, had gone to the Hall, to be with the girl during that time of seclusion, and she had been as a child to all of them. A compunction smote Clare as she turned and looked round from the door, and she kissed her hand to them with a pretty gesture. But still it was with rather an ill grace that she went to Miss Somers, which was not her own impulse. Compulsion fretted the Arden soul.

"I brought Clare into the world, and Fielding has been her head nurse all his life," said the Doctor, "no need for thanking us on that score. And now all's yours, Edgar. I may say, and I'm sure Fielding will say, how thankful we both are to see you. You could not have been altogether disinherited, as the property's entailed; but I never was easy in my mind about it during your father's lifetime. The old Squire was a very peculiar man; and there was no telling—"

"Doctor," said the young man, once more with a flush on his cheek, "would you mind leaving out my father's name in anything that has to be said?—unless, indeed, he left any message for me. He liked Clare best, which was not wonderful, and he thought me a poor representative of the Ardens, which was natural enough. I have not a word to say against him. On the whole, perhaps, I have got as much good of my life as if I had been brought up in England. I have never been allowed to forget hitherto that my father did not care for me—let me forget it now."

"Exactly," said the Doctor, looking at him with a certain curious complacency; and he gave a nod at Mr. Fielding, who stood winking to get rid of a tear which was in the corner of his eye. "Exactly what I said! Now, can you deny it? By Jove! I wish he had been my son! It is what I knew he would say."

"Edgar, my dear boy," said the Rector, "every word does you credit, and this more than all. Your poor father was mistaken. I say your poor father, for he evidently had something on his mind just before he died, and would have spoken if time had been allowed him. I have no doubt it was to say how sorry he was. But the Ardens are dreadfully obstinate, Edgar, and he never could bring himself to do it. It is just like you to say this. Clare will appreciate it, and I most fully appreciate it. It is the best way; let us not dwell upon the past, let us not even try to explain. Your being like your mother's family can never be anything against you—far from it. I agree in every word you say."

This speech, flattering and satisfactory as it was, took the young man a little by surprise. "I don't know what being like my mother's family has to do with it," he said, with momentary petulance; but then his brighter spirits gained the mastery. "It is best never to explain anything," he continued, with a smile. "There is Clare calling me. I suppose I am to go to Miss Somers, notwithstanding your defence, Doctor." And he waved his hand to Clare from the window, and went out, leaving the two old men behind him, following him with their eyes. He was glad to get away, if truth must be told; they were fighting some sort of undisclosed duel over his body, Edgar could see, and he did not like it. He went across the village street, which was very quiet at that end, to the Doctor's great red brick house, and as he did so his face clouded over a little. "They have got some theory about me," he said to himself; "am I never to be rid of it? And what right has any one to discuss me and my affairs now?" Then the shade gradually disappeared from his face, and in spite of himself there glided across his mind a sudden comparison between the last time he had been at Arden and the present. Then he had a boy's keen sense of injustice and unkindness eating into him. It had not cut so deeply as it might have done if his temperament had been gloomy; but still it had galled him. He had felt himself contemned, disliked, thrust aside—his presence half clandestine—his wishes made of no account—his whole being thrust into a corner—a thing to hide, or at least to apologise for. Now, he was the master of all. The bells had rung for his home-coming; everything was changed. The thought made his head swim as he walked along in the serene stillness, with the swallows making circles about, and the bees murmuring round the blossomed trees. He had been living an uncertain wandering life, not always well supplied with money, not trained to do anything, an innocent vagabond. Now there was not a corner of his life upon which some one interest or another did not lay a claim. He had the gravest occupations on his hands. He might make for himself a position of high influence and importance in his county; and could scarcely be insignificant if he tried. And all this had come to him without any training for it. His very habits of mind were not English; even in the midst of these serious thoughts the village green, which was at his left hand, beyond the Church and the Rectory, caught his eye, and a momentary speculation came across him, whether the village people danced there on Sundays? whether the fairs were held there, or the tombola, or something to represent them? and then he stopped and laughed at himself. What would Mr. Fielding say? Thus Edgar had come to be Squire Arden without even the habit of being an Englishman. The sense of injustice which had weighed upon him all his life might have embittered his beginning now, had his mind been less elastic. But nature had been so good to him that he was able to toss these dreary thoughts aside, as he would have tossed a ball, before he went in to see Miss Somers. "Things will come right somehow," he said to himself. Such was his light-hearted philosophy; while Clare stood grave and silent at the door to meet him, with a seriousness which would have been more in accordance with his difficulties than with hers. What troubled her was the question—Would he be a radical, and introduce innovations, ignore the mightiness of his family, conduct himself as if his name were anything else than Arden? This sufficed to plant the intensest seriousness, with almost a cast of severity in it, upon the brow of Clare.

"Didn't I tell you exactly how it would happen?" said the Doctor, when Edgar was gone; "no sentiment to speak of—utter absence of revengeful feelings: settling down as if it was the most natural thing in the world—bygones to be bygones, and a fair start for the future. Didn't I tell you? That boy is worth his weight in gold."

"You certainly told me," said Mr. Fielding, faltering, "something very like what has come to pass; but I don't receive your theory, for all that. No, no; depend upon it, the simplest explanation is always the best. One can see at a glance he is like his mother's family. Poor thing! I don't think she was too happy; and that must have intensified old Arden's remorse."

"Old Arden's fiddlestick!" said the Doctor. "I wouldn't give that for his remorse. He had his reasons you may be sure. Character has been my favourite study all my life, as you know; and if that frank, open-hearted, well-dispositioned boy ever came out of an Arden's nest, I expect to hear of a dove in an eagle's. He has justified every word I ever said of him. I declare to you, Fielding, I am as fond of him as if he were my own boy."

"Poor fellow!" said Mr. Fielding, shaking his head, as if that was not so great a compensation as might have been desired. "He will get into dozens of scrapes with these strange ways of thinking; and he knows nothing and nobody—not a soul in the county—and probably will be running his head against some stone wall or other before he is much older. If I had been twenty years younger I might have tried to be of use to him, but as it is—"

"As it is we shall both be of use to him," said the Doctor, "never fear. Of course, he will get into a hundred scrapes; but then he will struggle out again, and no harm will come of it. If he had been like the

Ardens he might have escaped the scrapes, but he would have missed a great deal besides. I like a young man to pay his way."

"It appears to me, Somers, that you are a radical yourself," said the Rector, shaking once more his feeble old head.

"On the contrary, the only real Tory going. The last of my race,—the Conservative innovator," said Dr. Somers. "These old races, my dear Fielding, are beautiful things to look at. Clare, for instance, who is the concentrated essence of Ardenism—and how charming she is! But that order of things must come to an end. Another Squire Arden would have been next to impossible: whereas this new-blooded sanguine boy will make a new beginning. I don't want to shock your feelings as a clergyman: but the cuckoo's egg sometimes comes to good."

"Somers," said the Rector, solemnly, "I have told you often that I knew Mrs. Arden well. She was a good woman; as unlikely to go wrong as any woman I ever knew. You do her horrible injustice by such a supposition. Besides, think: he was always with her wherever she went—there could not have been a more devoted husband; and to imagine that all the while he had such a frightful wrong on his mind—it is simply impossible! besides, she was the mother of Clare."

"That covers a multitude of sins, of course," said the Doctor, "but you forget that I know all your arguments by heart. I don't pretend to explain everything. It is best never to explain, as that boy says—wise fellow! Half the harm done in the world comes of explanations. But to return to our subject. I never said he found it out at once; perhaps—most likely—it was not discovered in her lifetime. Her papers might inform him after her death. It is curious that when there is anything to conceal, people do always leave papers telling all about it. If you will give me any other feasible explanation I don't stand upon my theory. Like his mother's family—bah! Is that reason enough for a man to shut his heart against his only boy? Besides, he is not like any one I know. I wish I could light upon any man he was like. It might furnish a clue—"

"When you are on your hobby, Somers, there is no stopping you," said the Rector, with a look of distress.

"I am not alone in my equestrian powers," retorted the Doctor, "you do quite as much in that line as I do; but my theory has the advantage of being credible, at least."

"Not credible," said Mr. Fielding, with gentle vehemence. "No, certainly not credible. Nothing would make it credible—not even to have heard with your ears, and seen with your eyes."

"I never argue with prejudiced persons," answered the Doctor, with equal haste and heat; and thus they parted, with every appearance of a quarrel. Such things happened almost daily between the two old friends. Dr. Somers took up his hat, gave a vague nod of leave-taking, and issued forth from the rectory gate as if he shook the dust from his feet; but all the same he would drop in at the rectory that evening, stalking carelessly through an open window as if, Mrs. Solmes said, who was not fond of the Doctor, the place belonged to him. He went across the street with more than his usual energy. His phaeton stood at his own door, with two fine horses, and the smartest of grooms standing at their heads. Dr. Somers was noted for his horses and the perfection of his turn-out generally, which was a relic of the days when he was the pride of the neighbourhood, and, people said, might have married into the highest family in the county had he so willed. He was still the handsomest man in the parish, though he was no longer young;

and he was rich enough to indulge himself in all that luxury of personal surroundings which is dear to an old beauty. Edgar, who was standing at one of the twinkling windows, watched the Doctor get into his carriage with a mixture of admiration and relief. On the whole, the young man was glad not to have another interview with his old friend; but his white hair and his black eyes, his splendid old figure and beautiful horses, were a sight to see.

CHAPTER IV

"I am not quite in a state to receive a gentleman," Miss Somers was saying when Edgar went in, with a little flutter of timidity and eagerness. "But it is so kind of you to let me know, and so sweet of dear Edgar to want to come. I told my brother only last night I was quite sure—But then he always has his own way of thinking. And you know why should dear Edgar care for a poor creature like me? I quite recognise that, my dear. There might be a time in my young days when some people cared—but as my brother says—And just come from the Continent, you know!"

"May I come in?" said Edgar, tapping against the folding screen which sheltered the head of the sofa on which the invalid lay.

"Oh, goodness me! Clare, my love, the dear boy is there! Yes, come in, Edgar, if you don't mind—But I ought to call you Mr. Arden now. I never shall be able to call you Mr. Arden. Oh, goodness, boy! Well, there can't be any harm in his kissing me; do you think there can be any harm in it, Clare? I am old enough to be both your mothers, and I am sure I think I love you quite as well. Of course, I should never speak of loving a gentleman if it was not for my age and lying here so helpless. Yes, I do feel as if I should cry sometimes to think how I used to run about once. But so long as it is only me, you know, and nobody else suffers—And you are both looking so well! But tell me now how shall you put up with Arden after the Continent and all that? I never was on the Continent but once, and then it was nothing but a series of fétes, as they called them. I was saying to my brother only last night—; for you know you never would visit the Pimpernels, Clare—"

"Who are the Pimpernels? and what have they to do with it?" said Edgar. "But tell me about yourself first, and how you come to be on a sofa. I never remember to have seen you sitting still before all my life."

"No, indeed," said Miss Somers, her soft pretty old face growing suddenly grey and solemn, "that is what makes old Mercy think, it's a judgment; but you wouldn't say it was wicked to be always running about, would you now? It's wrong to follow one's own inclinations, to be sure, but so long as you don't harm anybody—There are the Pimpernel girls, who play croquet, from morning till night—not that I mean it's wicked to play croquet—but poor Mr. Denbigh gets just a little led away I fear sometimes; and if ever there was a game intended for the waste of young people's time—"

"Never mind the Pimpernels," said Clare, with a slightly imperative note in her voice. "It is Edgar who is here beside you now."

"Oh, yes—dear fellow; but do you know I think my mind is weakened as well as my body? Do I run on different from what I used, Edgar? I was talking to my brother the other night—and he busy with his paper—and 'how you run on!' was all he said when I asked him—You know he might have given me a civil answer. I fear there is no doubt I am weakened, my dear. I was speaking to young Mr. Denbigh yesterday, and he says he said to the Doctor that if he were him he would take me to some baths or other, which did him a great deal of good, he says; but I could not take him away, you know, nor give anybody so much trouble. He is such a nice young man, Edgar. I should like you to know him. But, then, to think when I ask just a quiet question, 'how you do run on!' he said. Not that I am complaining of him, dear—"

"Of young Mr. Denbigh?" said Clare.

"Now, Clare, my love—the idea! How could I complain of young Mr. Denbigh, who is always the civillest and nicest—Of course, I mean my brother. He says these German baths are very good; but I would not mention it to him for worlds, for I am sure he would be unhappy if he had to leave home only with me."

Edgar and Clare looked at each other as Miss Somers, to use her own expression, ran on. Clare was annoyed and impatient, as young people so often are of the little follies of their seniors; but Edgar's brown eyes shone with fun, just modified by a soft affectionate sympathy. "Dear Miss Somers," he said, half in joke half in earnest, "don't trouble yourself about your mind. You talk just as you always did. If I had heard you outside without knowing you were here, I should have recognised you at once. Don't worry yourself about your mind."

"Do you think not, Edgar?—do you really think not? Now that is what I call a real comfort," said Miss Somers; "for you are not like the people that are always with me; you would see in a moment if I was really weakened. Well, you know, I could not make up my mind to take him away—could I? For after all it does not matter so much about me. If I were young it would be different. Dear Edgar, no one has been civil enough to ask you to sit down. Bring a chair for yourself here beside me. Do you know, Clare, I don't think, if you put it to me in a confidential way, that he has grown. He is not so tall as the rest of you Ardens. I was saying to my brother just the other day—I don't care for your dreadfully tall people; for you have always to stoop coming into a room, and look as if you were afraid the sky was falling. And oh, my dears, what a long time it is since we have had any rain!"

"Any rain?" said Edgar, who was a little taken by surprise.

"What the farmers will do I can't think, for you can't water the fields like a few pots of geraniums. That last cutting you sent me, Clare, has got on so well. Do you mean to keep up all the gardens and everything as it used to be, Edgar? You must make her go to the Holmfirth flower show. You did not go last year, Clare, nor the year before; and I saw such a pretty costume, too, in the last fashions-book—all grey and black—just the very thing for you. You ought to speak to her, Edgar. She has worn that heavy deep mourning too long."

"Don't, please," said Clare, turning aside with a look of pain on her face.

"My dear love, I am only thinking of your good. Now is it reasonable, Edgar? She looks beautiful in mourning, to be sure; but it is more than a year, and she is still in crape. I would have put on my own light silk if I had known you were coming. I hate black from my heart, but it is the most useful to wear, with nice coloured ribbons, when you get old and helpless. I don't know if you notice any change in my appearance, Edgar? Now how odd you should have found it out! I have plenty of hair still—it is not that; but one gets so untidy with one's head on a pillow without a cap. Mrs. Pimpernel has quantities of hair;

but a married lady is quite different—they can wear things and do things—Did you observe, Edgar, if ladies wear caps just now abroad?"

"They wear a great many different things," said Edgar, "according to the different countries. I brought Clare a yashmak from Constantinople to cover her head with, and an Albanian cap—"

"My dear," said Miss Somers, sitting upright with horror, "the idea of Clare wearing a cap at nineteen! That shows one should never speak to a man about what is the fashion. Just look at her lovely hair! It will be time enough for that thirty years hence. I cannot think how you could like to live among the Turks. I hope you did not do as they do, Edgar. It may be all very nice to look at, but having a quantity of wives and that sort of thing must be very dreadful. I am sure I never could have put up with it for a day; and then it goes in the very face of the Bible. I hope you are going to forget all that sort of thing now, and settle down quietly here."

"Miss Somers," said Edgar, with mock solemnity, "if I had left a quantity of wives at Constantinople, is it possible that you could calmly advise me to forget them, and marry another here?"

Miss Somers sat up still more straight on her sofa, and showed signs of agitation. "I am sure I would not advise you to what was wrong for all the world," she said. "Oh, Edgar, my poor boy, what a dreadful position! You might ask the Rector—But if they were heathens, you know, in a Christian country do you think it would be binding? Clare, dear, suppose you step into the drawing-room a minute, till we talk this dreadful, dreadful business over. Oh, you poor boy! It seems wicked for me, an unmarried lady, even to think of such things; but if I could be of any use to you—Edgar! that kind of poor creatures," said Miss Somers, putting her face close to his, and speaking in a whisper, "people buy them in the market, you know, as we read in books. Listen, my dear boy. It is not nice, of course, but—"

"What?" said Edgar, bending an eager ear.

"You could sell them again, don't you think? Poor souls, if they are used to it, they wouldn't care. Good gracious, how can you laugh, with such a burden on your mind? I am thinking what would be the best, Edgar, for you."

The old lady was so anxious that she put her soft wrinkled old hand upon his, holding him fast, and gazing anxiously into his face. "You young men have such strange ways of thinking," she said, looking disapprovingly at him; "you treat it as if it was a joke, but it is very, very serious. Clare, my love, just go and speak to old Mercy a moment. I cannot let him leave me, you know, until we have settled on something to do."

"He is only laughing at you," said Clare, with indignation. "How can you, Edgar? Dear Miss Somers, do you really believe he could be so wicked?"

"Wicked, my dear?" said Miss Somers, with a look of experience and importance on her eager old face, "young men have very strange ways. The less you know about such things the better. Edgar knows that he can speak to me."

"But Clare is right," said Edgar, smothering his laugh. "I did not mean to mystify you. I brought nothing more out of Constantinople than pipes and embroideries. I have some for you, Miss Somers. Slippers that will just do for you on your sofa, and a soft Turkish scarf that you might make a turban of—"

"What should I do with a turban, my dear boy?" said the invalid at once diverted out of her solemnity, "though I remember people wearing them once. My mother had a gorgeous one she used to wear when she went out to dinner—you never see anything so fine now—with bird of paradise feathers. Fancy me in a turban, Clare! But the slippers will be very nice. There was a Mr. Templeton I once knew, in the Royal Navy, a very nice young man, with black hair, like a Corsair, or a Giaour, or something—That was in my young days, my dears, when I was not perhaps quite so unattractive as I am now. Oh, you need not be so polite, Edgar; I know I am quite unattractive, as how could I be otherwise, with my health and at my age? He was a very nice young man, and he paid me a great deal of attention; but dear papa, you know—he was always a man that would have his own way—"

Here Miss Somers broke off with a sigh, and the story of Mr. Templeton, of the Royal Navy, came to an abrupt conclusion, notwithstanding an effort on the part of one of the listeners to keep it up. "Was Mr. Templeton at Constantinople?" Edgar asked, bringing the narrator back to her starting-point; but it was not to be.

"Oh, what does it matter where Mr. Templeton was?" said Clare. "Edgar has come down to see the village, Miss Somers, and all the poor people; and I must take him away now. Another time you can tell us all about it. Edgar, fancy, it is nearly twelve o'clock."

"It is so nice of you to come and chatter to me," said the invalid. She was a little fatigued by the conversation, the burden of which she had taken on herself—by Edgar's (supposed) difficulties about the wives, and by that reference to Mr. Templeton of the Royal Navy. "You may send old Mercy to me," she said with a sigh as she kissed Clare; for old Mercy was the tyrant whom Miss Somers most dreaded in the world. It was a sad change from the presence of the young people to see that despot come into the room, in the calm confidence of power. "Now, lie down a bit, do, and rest yoursel'," Mercy said, peremptorily, "or we'll have a nice restless night along o' this, and the Doctor as cross as cross. Lie down and rest, do."

Meanwhile the brother and sister went downstairs, she relieved, he much softened, and full of a tender compassion. "If that would do her any good, you and I might take her to the German baths some day," said the soft-hearted Edgar, "if she is able to go. Such a restless little being as she was, it is hard to see her lying there."

"I hope I am not hard-hearted," said Clare, "but I think she is very well where she is. It is not as if she suffered much. We have lost almost an hour with her chatter. We shall never get back in time for luncheon if we talk to other people as long."

"But there are not many other people like Miss Somers," said Edgar, with a passing shade of gravity. He in his turn was grieved now and then by something Clare did or said. But in a few minutes they returned to their interrupted stream of talk, and began to discuss the village, and the plans for the new cottages, and the enlargement of the schools, and the restoration of the Church, and many other matters of detail. The two went from house to house, the village gradually becoming aware of them, and turning out to all the doors and the windows. The women stopped in their cooking and the men, jogging home for their early dinners, ranked themselves in rows here and there, and stood and gaped; the children formed themselves into little groups, and looked on awestricken. Such was Edgar's first entry as master into the hereditary village. He made himself very "nice" to all the bystanders, and was as cordial as if he had been canvassing for their votes, Clare thought, who stood by in her position as domestic critic, and noted everything. It was odd to see what trifles he remembered, and what a memory he had for names and places. If he had been canvassing he could not have been more ingratiating, more full of that grace of universal courtesy which, in a general way, is only manifest at such times. And yet, it was not as a candidate for their favour, but as their sworn hereditary sovereign, that he came among them. Clare, her mind already in a tumult with all the events and all the talk of the morning, could not but acknowledge to herself that it was very strange.

Edgar Arden had lived hitherto, as we have said, a very desultory wandering sort of life. He had been at school in Germany during his earlier years, and afterwards at Heidelberg, at the University, where he had seen a great many English afar off, and vaguely found out the difference between their training and ways of thinking and those in which he had himself been brought up. When he had first come to the age when a boy begins to inquire into his own position, and when it no longer becomes possible to take everything for granted, he had been told first that it was for his health that he had been sent away from home; and when he had fully satisfied himself that his health could no longer be the reason, other causes had been suggested to him equally unsatisfactory. It was his father who was in bad health, and could not be troubled with a lively boy about him; but then there were schools in England as well as in Germany, which would have settled that matter: or the German education was superior, which was a theory his tutor strongly inclined to, but which did not seem to Edgar's lively young intelligence quite justified by the opinion visibly entertained by the English travellers whom he met. His first visit to England, after he was old enough to understand, made matters a great deal more clear to him. Injustice and dislike are hard to conceal from a young mind, even under the most specious disguises—and here no disguise was attempted. The Squire received his boy with a coldness which chilled him to the heart, saw as little of him as he possibly could, endured his presence with undisguised reluctance, and made it quite apparent to poor Edgar that, unlike all the other sons he had ever seen in his life, he was only a vexation and trouble to his father. The fact that his father was his enemy dawned vaguely upon him at a much later period; for it is hard in extreme youth to think that one has an enemy. A vague sense of being hustled into corners, and shut out of the life of the family, such as it was, had been the cloud upon his earlier days. He had felt that only in Clare's nursery did he hold that position of chief and favourite to which surely the only son of the house was entitled. And little Clare accordingly became the one bright spot in the house which he still by instinct called home.

He had returned when he was seventeen, and again after he came of age—though not to be received with any rejoicings at that later period, as became the birthday of the heir. His birthday was over when he came home, and Clare, a girl of sixteen, thrust her little furtive present into his hand with a full sense that her brother was not to the Squire what he was to her. But at this period something occurred which enlightened Edgar as to his father's feelings towards himself in the cruellest way; it enlightened him and yet it threw a confusion darker than ever over his life. The day after his arrival Mr. Arden sent for him, and elaborately explained to him that he wished for his aid in breaking the entail of certain estates, of which the young man knew nothing. It was the longest interview that had ever taken place between the two; and the Squire made very full explanations, the meaning of which was but indistinct to the youth. Edgar had all the impatient and reckless generosity which so often accompanies a buoyant temperament; his sense of the sweets of property was small; and he knew next to nothing about the estates. Had he known much there is little doubt that he would have done exactly as he did; but, however, he had not even that safeguard; and the consequence was that he took his father's word at once, responded eagerly and promptly to the proposal, and gave his consent to denude himself of the property which had been longest in the family, the little estate from which the name of Arden first came, and which every Arden acquainted with his family history most highly prized. Edgar, however, knew very little about his family history; and with the foolish disinterestedness of a boy he acquiesced in all his father suggested. But after the necessary arrangements in respect to this were concluded Edgar caught a glance from his father's eye which went to his heart like an arrow. It was in the hunting-field, where, untrained as he was, he had acquitted himself tolerably well; and he was just about to take a somewhat risky fence when he saw that look which he never forgot. The Squire had reined in his own horse, and sat like a bronze figure under a tree watching his son. And as plain as eyes could tell Edgar read in his father's look a suppressed inappeasable enmity, which it was impossible to mistake; his father was watching intently for the spring—was it possible he was hoping that a fall would follow? How it was that Edgar got over the fence he never could tell; for to his hopeful, all-believing temper such a sudden glimpse into the darkness was like a paralysing blow. He kept steady on his saddle, and somehow, without any conscious guidance on his part, the horse accomplished the leap; but Edgar turned straight back, and went home with such a sense of misery as he had never experienced before. He was too wretched to understand the calls sent after him—the questions with which he was assailed. He could not even reply to Clare's wondering inquiries. His father hated him—that was the discovery he had made. To suspect that anybody hated him would have given Edgar a shock; but to know it beyond all doubt, and to feel that it was his father who regarded him with such fierce enmity, made his very heart sink within him. He went away next day, giving no explanation of his desire to do so. Nor did the Squire make any inquiries. It was a mutual relief to them to be free of each other. Before his departure his father informed him that he would henceforward receive a much more liberal allowance—an intimation which Edgar received without thinking what it meant—without caring what sense was in the words. And that was the last he had seen of the Squire. Nobody but himself knew of this incident. It was nothing—an impression—a fancy; but in all Edgar's life nothing had happened that was so bitter to him. The effect had not lasted, for his mind was essentially elastic, and he was young, and free to amuse himself as he would. Fortunately, the kind of amusements he preferred were innocent ones; for he had no guide, no one to control or restrain him, and not even the shadow of parental authority. His father hated him—a horrible freedom was his inheritance—nobody cared if he were to die the next day—nay, on the contrary, there was some one who would be glad.

This impression, which had been swept out of his mind by years and changes, came back upon him with singular force as all at once his eye fell on the great portrait of old Squire Arden, painted when he was Master of the Hounds, in sporting costume, which hung in the hall. He stopped short before it as he went in with his sister on the first day of his return, and felt a shudder come over him. Perhaps it was the costume and attitude which moved his memory; but there seemed to lurk in his father's face, as he entered the house of which that father had been unable to deprive him, the same look which once had fallen upon him like a curse. He stopped short and grew pale, in spite of all his attempts to control himself. "Would you think it cruel, Clare," he said suddenly in his impulsive way, "if I were to ask you to transfer that portrait to some other place? It has a painful effect upon me there."

"This is your house, Edgar," answered Clare. On this point her sweetness abandoned her. She knew he had been badly used; but she knew at the same time that her father had been all love and kindness to herself. Therefore, as was natural, Miss Arden took it for granted that somehow it must be Edgar's fault.

"That is not the question," he said. "I can understand by my own what your feelings must be on the subject. But it cannot harm him to remove it, and it does harm me to have it stay. If you will make this sacrifice to me, Clare—"

"Edgar, I tell you this is your house," she said, with the tears rushing to her eyes; and ran in and left him there, in a sudden passion of grief and anger. Her brother, left alone, looked somewhat sadly round him. He was very destitute of those impulses of self-assertion which come so naturally to most young men; on the contrary, his impulse was to yield when the feeling of anyone he loved ran contrary to his own: he was a little sorrowful at Clare's want of sympathy, but it did not move him to act as master. "What harm can it do me now?" he said, going up and looking closely at the portrait. It came natural to him to reason himself out of his own fancies, and to give place to those of others. "It would be wounding her only to satisfy my caprice," he added after a while; "and why should I be indulged in everything, I should like to know?" Poor boy! up to this moment he had never been indulged in anything all his life. He stayed a long time in the hall, now walking about it, now standing before the portrait. It haunted him so that he felt obliged to face it, and defy the look; and he could not but think with a sigh what a comfort it would be to get quit of it, to take it down and turn it somewhere with its face to the wall. But then he remembered that though he was the master he was more a stranger in the house than any servant it contained; and what right had he to cross his sister, and go in the face of every tradition, and offend every soul in the place, by taking down that picture, which looked malevolent to nobody but him? "God forgive you!" he said at last, shaking his head at it sorrowfully as he went slowly upstairs. He could not feel himself free or safe so long as it remained there. If anything happened to him—supposing, for instance (this grim idea crossed his mind in spite of himself)—supposing it might ever happen that he should be carried into that hall, wounded or mangled by any accident, would the painted face smile at him, would the eyes gleam with a horrible joy? And it was his father's face. Edgar shuddered, he could not help it, as he went slowly up the great stairs. As he went up, some one else was coming down, making a gleam of reflection in the still air. It was old Sarah, with her white apron, making a curtsey at every step, and finding that mode of progress difficult. Edgar's mobile countenance dressed itself all in smiles at the appearance of this old woman. Clare would have thought it strange, but it came natural to her brother; though, perhaps, on the whole, it was Clare, her own special charge and nursling, who was most fond of old Sarah, as, indeed, it became her to be.

"Have you been waiting for us?" he said. "My sister has gone to look for you, I suppose."

"Not gone to look for me, Mr. Edgar," said Sarah, petulantly; "run upstairs in one of her tantrums, as I have seen her many a day. You'll have to keep her a bit in hand, now you've come home, Mr. Edgar."

"I keep her in hand!" cried Edgar, struck with the extreme absurdity of the suggestion; and then he tried hard to look severe, and added—"My dear old Sarah, you must recollect who Miss Arden is, and take care what you say."

"There's ne'er a one knows better who she is," said old Sarah, "she's my child, and my jewel, and the darlin' of my heart. But, nevertheless, she's an Arden, Mr. Edgar. All the Ardenses as ever was has got tempers—except you; and for her own good, the dear, you should keep her a bit in hand; and if you say it was her old nurse told you, as loves her dearly, it wouldn't do no harm."

"Am I the only Arden without a temper?" said Edgar, gaily; "it's odd how I want everything that an Arden ought to have. But my sister is queen at Arden, Sarah; always has been; and most likely always will be."

"Lord bless you, sir, wait till you get married," said Sarah, nodding her head again and again, and beaming at the prospect. "Eh! I'd like to live to see that day!"

"It will be a long day first," said Edgar, with a laugh, meaning nothing but a young man's half-mocking, half-serious denial of the coming romance of his existence; "though I promise you, Sarah, you shall dance at my wedding—but at Clare's first, which is the proper arrangement, you know."

"If he was a good gentleman, Sir, and one as was fond of her, I shouldn't care how soon it was," she said. "Eh, my word, but I'll dance till I dance you all off the floor!"

"But you must not go without something to remind you of your first visit to us," he said; and he took out his purse from his pocket with the lavish liberality of his disposition. "Look, there is not very much in it. Buy something you like, Sarah, and say to yourself that it is given you by me."

"No, Mr. Edgar; no, Sir. Oh, good Lord, not a purse full of money, as if that was all I was thinking of! I didn't come here, not for money, but to see Miss Clare and you."

"It is because it is your first visit to us," repeated Edgar, and he gave her a kind nod, and went lightly past to his rooms. All his gloomy thoughts and superstitions had been driven out of his mind by this momentary encounter. His light heart had risen again like a ball of feathers. The glooms and griefs that lay in his past he shook off from him as lightly as thistledown. He thought no more of his father's grim face in the hall—did not even look at it when he went downstairs. Was it that his mind was a light mind, easily blown about by any wind? or that God had given him that preservative which He gives to those whom He has destined to bear much in this world? At so early a moment, when his life lay all vague before him, this was a question which nobody could answer. There was one indication, however, that his elasticity was strength rather than weakness, which was this—that he had not forgotten what had moved him so strongly, but was able, his sunny nature helping him, to put it away.

CHAPTER VI

The first day at Arden had been play; the second, work began again, and the new life which was so unfamiliar to the young Squire came pouring in upon him like a tide. In the morning he had an appointment with the family solicitor, who was coming, full of business, to lay his affairs before him, and to inaugurate his curiously changed existence. In the evening, his old friends in the village were coming to dine with this equally old friend, and Edgar felt that he would, without doubt, have a great deal of good advice to encounter, and probably many reminiscences which would not be pleasant to hear. None of these very old friends knew in the least the character of the young man with whom they had to do. They saw, as everybody did, his light-heartedness, his cheerful oblivion of all the wrongs of the past, and quiet commencement of his new career; but they did not know nor suspect the thorns that past had left in his mind—the haunting horror of his father's look, the aching wonder as to the meaning of treatment so extraordinary, which had never left him since he caught that glance, coupled with a strange consciousness that some time or other he must find out the secret of this unnatural enmity. Edgar, though he was so buoyant as almost to appear deficient in feeling to the careless observer, kept this thought lying deep down in his heart. He would find it out some time, whatever it was; and though he could not frame to himself the remotest idea what it was, he felt and knew that the discovery, when it came, would be such as to embitter if not to change his whole existence. No one had any clue to the cause of the Squire's behaviour to his son. To Clare it had seemed little more than a preference for herself, which was cruel to her brother, as shutting him out from his just share in his father's heart, but not of any great importance otherwise; and at least one of the theories entertained on the subject outside the house of Arden was such as could not be named to the heir. Therefore, he had not a single gleam from without to assist him in resolving this great question; yet he felt in the depths of his heart that some time or other it would be resolved, and that the illumination, when it came, could not but bring grief and trouble in its train.

"I never saw this Mr. Fazakerley," he said, as Clare and he sat alone over their breakfast on that second morning. Already it had become natural to him to be the master of the great house, of all those silent servants, the centre of a life so unlike anything that he had known. His mind was very rapid, went quickly over the preliminary stages, and accustomed itself to a hundred novelties, while a slower fancy would but have been having its first gaze at them; but the absolutely New startled him to a greater degree than it ever could have startled a more leisurely imagination. "I don't know him a bit," he repeated, with a half laugh, in which there was more nervousness than amusement. "What sort of a man is he? I always like to know—"

"Mr. Fazakerley!" said Clare, with a soft echo of wonder, "why, all the Ardens have known all the Fazakerleys from their cradles. He must have had you on his knee a hundred times, as I am sure he had me."

"I don't think so," said Edgar, suppressing, because of the servants, any other question, "or, if I ever saw him I have forgotten. Why must we have business breaking in upon us at every turn? I am afraid I like play."

"I am afraid you have had too much play," Clare said, looking at him with those eyes of young wisdom, utterly without experience, which look so soft yet judge so hardly; "but, Edgar, you must remember you are not a wanderer now. You have begun serious life."

"I wonder if life is as serious as you are, Clare," he said, looking at her with that half-tender, half mocking look, which Clare did not quite understand nor like; "or whether this lawyer and his green bag will be half as alarming as those looks of yours. I may satisfy him; but I fear I shall never come up to your mark."

"Don't speak so, please," said Clare. "Why shouldn't you come up to my mark? I like a man to be very high-minded and generous, and that you are, Edgar; but then I like people to have proper pride, and believe in their own position, and feel its duties. That is all—and I like people to be English—, and it would be so nice to think you were going to show yourself a true Arden, in spite of everything." This was said at a fortunate moment, when Wilkins, the butler, was at the very other end of the great room, fetching something from the sideboard, and could not hear. She leant across the table hastily, before the man turned round, and added, in a hurried tone, "Don't discuss such things before the servants, Edgar; they listen to everything we say."

"I forgot," he said; "I never had servants before who knew English. You don't recollect that English has always been a grand foreign language to me."

"The more's the pity!" said Clare, with a deep sigh. This sentiment made her beautiful face so long, and drooped the corners of her mouth so sadly, that her brother laughed in spite of himself.

"But it is possible to live out of England for all that," he said; "and I know people in Germany that would have the deepest sympathy with you. The Von Dummkopfs think just the same of themselves as the Ardens do, and look down just as much upon outsiders. I wonder how you would like the Fraulein Ida? They have twenty quarterings in their arms, and blood that has been filtered through all the veins worth speaking of in Germany for ever so many centuries; but then the Von Dummkopfs are not so rich as we are, Clare."

"As if I ever thought of that!" she said. "Who is Fraulein Ida? I have no doubt I shall like her—if she is nice. But, Edgar, though I would not say a word against your German friends, it would be so much nicer if you would marry an English girl. I should be able to love her so much more."

"Softly," said Edgar; "don't go so fast, please. I have not the least intention of marrying any one; and I don't admire the Fraulein Ida. I want nobody but my sister, as long as she will keep faithful to me. Let us have the good of each other for a little now, without any one to interfere."

"Edgar, no one can interfere," said Clare hurriedly. "Now that man is gone, oh, Edgar! I must say one word for poor papa. I know he was hard upon you, dear; but he never interfered—never said a word—never tried to keep me from loving you. Indeed, indeed, he never did! I know I was cross yesterday about that picture. If you don't like it, it shall come down; it is only right it should come down. But oh, Edgar, he was so kind, he was so good to me!"

Edgar had risen before the words were half said, and stood by her, holding her tenderly in his arms. "My dear little sister!" he said, "you have always been the one star I had to cheer me. You shall hang all the house with his picture if you like. I forgive him all my grievances because he was good to you. But, Clare, he hated me."

"No, Edgar, not hated," cried Clare, raising to him her weeping face. "Oh, not hated; but he loved mamma so, and you were so like her, he never could bear—"

Her voice faltered as she spoke. It was all she could say, but she did not believe it. As for Edgar, he shook his head with a smile that was half bitter half sad.

"I know better," he said; "but it is a question we need not discuss. Believe the gentle fiction, dear, if you can. But I will never say a word again about any picture. Let it be. It would be hard if your brother could not put up with anything that was dear to you. Now tell me about Mr. Fazakerley, and what he is going to say."

"Edgar, it all belongs to the same subject," said Clare, drying her eyes. "I am glad you have spoken. I should not have had the courage to begin. There is something about the Old Arden estate; they told me, but I would not listen to them—would not hear anything about it till you came back. They said it was your doing as well as his; I don't understand how that can be. They said you wanted it to be settled on me; but why, Edgar, should it be settled on me? It is neither right nor natural," said Clare, her blue eyes lighting up, though tears still hung upon the eyelashes. "Arden, that gave us our name—that was the very beginning of the race—why should you wish to give it to me?"

"Is it given to you?" said Edgar, with a certain sense of bewilderment creeping over him. "I am afraid I have been like you—I have not understood, nor thought on the subject indeed for that matter. There was something about breaking the entail between him and me; but I did not understand anything about it. I never knew—Clare, I can't make it out," he said, suddenly sitting down and gazing at her. "Why did he hate me?"

Then they looked at each other without a word. Clare's great blue eyes, dilated with grief and wonder, and two big tears which filled them to overflowing, were fixed upon her brother's face. But she had no elucidation to give. She only put out her hands to him, and took his, and held it close, with that instinctive impulse to tender touch and contact which is more than words. She followed her brother with her eyes while he faced this new wonder. "Well," he was saying to himself, "of course you must have known he meant something by breaking the entail. Of course it was not for your sake he did it. What could it be for? You never asked—never thought. Of course it could only be to take it from you. And why not give it to Clare? If not to you, of course it must go to Clare; and but for that she could not have had it. It is very well that it should be so. It is best; is it not best?" Thus he reasoned according to his nature, while Clare sat watching him with wistful dilated eyes. While he calmed himself down she was rousing herself. Her agitation rose to the intolerable pitch, while his was slowly coming down to moderation and composure. The sudden cloud floated away from him, and the light came back to his eyes. "I begin to see it," he said slowly. "Don't be vexed, Clare, that I did not see it all at once. It is not that I grudge you anything; he might have given you all, and I don't think I should have grudged it. It is the mistrust—the preference. It is so strange. One wonders what it can mean."

"Yes," said Clare, impulsively, "I wonder too. But, more than that, Edgar; you did not know—you did it in ignorance; and I will never, never, take advantage of that! I was bewildered at first; but it is your right, and I will never take it from you—"

Then it was he, who had been robbed of his birthright, who had to exert himself to reconcile her to his loss. "Nay, that is nonsense," he said. "It is done, and it cannot be done over again. The will must not be interfered with: it is my business to see to that. No, Clare; don't try to make me do wrong. Nothing we can say will change it, nor anything you can do either. What has been given you is yours, and yours it must remain."

"But I will not accept it," said Clare; "I will give it all back the moment I come of age. What! rob you and your children, Edgar—all the Ardens that may come after you! That is what I will never do."

"It is time enough to think of the Ardens who may come after me," said Edgar, with an attempt at a laugh. But Clare was not to be pacified so easily. He drew closer to her side, and sat down by her, and took her hand, and spoke softly in her ear, arguing it out as if the question had not been a personal one. "It startled me at first," he said; "it was strange, very strange, that he should think of taking this, as you say, Clare, not only from me, but from all the Ardens to come; but then you were the dearest to him, and that was quite natural. And it must have been my fault that he did not tell me. I never asked any questions about it—never thought of inquiring. He must have taken me for a kind of Esau, careless of what was going to happen. If I had shown a little more interest, no doubt he would have told me. Of course, he must have felt it would have been for your advantage had I known all about it, and been able to stand by you. I am so glad you have told me now. You may be sure he would have done so had I behaved myself properly. So, you see, it was my fault, Clare. I must have been ungracious, boorish, indifferent. It is clear it was my fault."

"Mr. Fazakerley, sir, is in the library," said Wilkins, opening the door. There was a certain breath of agitation in the air about the two young people which the servants had scented out; and the eager eyes of Wilkins expressed not only his own curiosity, but that of the household in general. "He was a patting of her and a smoothing of her down," was the butler's report downstairs, "and Miss Clare in one of her ways. I daresay they have quarrelled already, for she is her father's daughter, is Miss Clare." The brother and sister were quite unconscious of this comment; but though they had not quarrelled, the conflict of feeling had risen so high that Mr. Fazakerley's arrival was a relief to both. "I must go and see him," Edgar said, loosing his sister's hand, and laying his own tenderly upon her bowed head. "Don't let it trouble you so much. You will see it as I do when you think of it rightly, Clare."

"Never!" Clare cried among her tears. Edgar shook his head, with a soft smile, as he went away. Of course, she would come to see it. Reason and simple sense must gain the day at last. So he thought, feeling perfectly persuaded that such were his own leading principles—calm reason and sober sense. Edgar rather prided himself upon their possession; and thus fortified with a conviction of what were the leading characteristics of his own mind, went to meet the family lawyer, and hear all about it in a sober and business-like way.

CHAPTER VII

Mr. Fazakerley was a little brown man, with a wig—a man who might have appeared on any stage as the conventional type of a crafty solicitor. He was very much like a fox, with little keen red-brown eyes, and whiskers which were grizzled, yet still retained the reddish colour of youth. His wig, too, was reddish-brown, and might have been made out of a foxskin, so true was it to the colour and texture of that typical animal. As may be divined from the fact of his outward appearance, he was not in the very least like a fox or a conventional solicitor, but was a good, little, kind, respectable sort of man, chiefly distinguished for his knowledge of Lancashire families—their intermarriages, and the division of their properties and value of their land; on which points he was an infallible guide. He came forward to meet the young Squire with both his hands extended, and a smile beaming out of every wrinkle of his brown face. "Welcome home, Mr. Edgar," he said; "welcome home, welcome to your own house," with a warmth and effusion which betrayed that there was more than the usual occasion for such a welcome. He shook the young man's hand so long, and so energetically, swaying it between both of his, that Edgar felt as if it must come off. "You don't remember me, I can see," said Mr. Fazakerley. "I never happened to be at home while you were at Arden; but I know you well, and how nobly you have behaved. So you must think of me as your old friend, and one always ready to serve you—me and everybody belonging to me—you must indeed."

"Thanks," said Edgar, taken by surprise; "a thousand thanks. I never knew how rich I was in friends till now. Clare has just been telling me I ought to have known you all my life."

"So you ought, and so you should, but for—ah—circumstances, Mr. Edgar," said the lawyer, "circumstances of a painful character—over which we had no control. Miss Clare said that, did she? And quite right too. Your sister is a very sweet young lady, Mr. Edgar. You may be proud of her. I don't know her equal in Lancashire, and that is saying a great deal, for we are proud of our Lancashire witches. I have two daughters of my own, pretty girls enough, and I am very proud of them, I can tell you; but I don't pretend that they come within a hundred miles of Miss Arden. You must not think me an impudent old fellow to talk of her so, for, as she says, I have known her all her life."

In this way Mr. Fazakerley chatted on, doing, as it were, the honours of his own house to Edgar, inviting him to sit down, and gradually beginning to arrange before him on the table a mass of papers. Then he changed the subject; gave up Clare, whose trumpet he had blown for about half-an-hour; and began a disquisition upon "your worthy father," at which Edgar winced. And yet there was nothing in it to hurt him; it was not full of inferences which he could not understand, like the sayings of Mr. Fielding and Dr. Somers. It had not a hidden meaning, like so much that Clare said on the same subject. Mr. Fazakerley was in his way very straightforward. "I won't attempt to disguise either from myself or from you that there was much in his conduct that was very extraordinary," said the lawyer, "very extraordinary—so much so, that monomania is the only word that occurs to me. Monomania—that is the only explanation, and I don't know that it is a satisfactory explanation; but it is the best we can make. We need not enter into that matter, Mr. Edgar, for it is very unintelligible; but the question is—Why did you give in to any arrangement about breaking the entail without my advice?"

"I did what my father wished me to do," said Edgar, with a deep colour rising over his face. "It appeared to me that in so doing I could not but be right."

"You were very wrong, Mr. Edgar," said the lawyer. "What! rob your children because it pleased your father! Your father was a very worthy man—an excellent landlord—a good staunch Tory—everything a country gentleman need wish to be; but he was only one of the family, Mr. Edgar, only the head of it in his time, as your son will be. You had no more right to consult the one than the other. I don't want to hurt your feelings, but you were wrong."

"My son is not born yet, nor, so far as I can see, any chance of him," said Edgar, laughing, "so he could scarcely be consulted."

"That is all very well," said Mr. Fazakerley, bending over his papers. "I do not object to a laugh; but at the same time it was very foolish, and worse than foolish—wrong. I don't blame you so much, for of course you were taught to be generous, and magnanimous, and all that; but your worthy father, Mr. Edgar, your worthy father—it was more than wrong."

Mr. Fazakerley shook his head for at least five minutes while he repeated these words; but Edgar made no reply. If he could have found the shadow of an excuse for the old Squire, or even perhaps if it had not been for that look which he remembered so distinctly, he would have said something in his defence. But his mouth was closed, and he could not reply.

"If it had been any other part of the estate, or if Miss Clare had not been well provided for already, I could have understood it," the lawyer continued; "but she is very well provided for. Monomania, Sir, it could be nothing but monomania; and to give up Old Arden was quite inconceivable—permit me to say it, Mr. Edgar—on your part."

"I did not know much about old Arden," said Edgar, shyly putting forth this excuse for himself, almost with a blush. It was not his fault; but he looked much as if it had been a voluntary abandonment of his duty.

"The more shame to—ah," said Mr. Fazakerley, with a frown, feeling that his zeal had led him too far; and then he paused, and coughed, and recovered himself. "The thing to be done now is to set it right as far as possible," he went on. "We may be quite sure that Miss Clare, as soon as she knows of it, will be but too eager to aid us. She is only a girl, but she has a fine spirit, and hates injustice. What I would suggest to you would be to effect an exchange. Old Arden lies in the very centre of the property, besides being the oldest part of it, and all that. I don't insist upon the sentimental reasons; but the inconvenience would be immense—especially when Miss Clare marries, as of course she will soon do. I advise you to offer her an equal portion, by valuation, of some other part of the estate—say the land between this and Liverpool—which she could make untold wealth of—"

"I don't think we must interfere with the existing arrangement," said Edgar. "Pray don't think of it. My father must have had some reason. I can't divine it, nor perhaps any one; but some reason he must have had."

"Reason—nonsense! Caprice, monomania," said Mr. Fazakerley, getting excited. "That was the reason. He indulged himself so that at the last every impulse became irresistible. That is my theory. I don't ask you to accept it, but it is my way of explaining the matter. One day or other he looked at Miss Clare, and perceived how like she was to the family portraits (she is an Arden all over, and you are like your mother's family), and he said to himself, no doubt, 'Old Arden must be hers.' Some such train of ideas must have passed through his mind. And nobody ever opposed him. You did not oppose him, not knowing any better. He had come to take it for granted that he must have his own way. It is very bad for a man, Mr. Edgar, to have everything his own way. It led your worthy father on to a great piece of injustice and even folly. But, now that the time has come when the folly of it is apparent—if we give her acre for acre of the land near Liverpool—"

"Why should you take so much trouble?" said Edgar. "If such was his desire, it is my duty to see it carried out. And I do not insist on the compactness of the property. Why should I? I who am the one who knows least about it. If this division pleased my father—"

"Tut, tut," said the lawyer, "pleased a man who was a monomaniac and had a fixed idea! I had formed a higher opinion of your good sense and judgment; but to stand out for a piece of nonsense like this! Miss Clare herself would be the first to say otherwise. When dead men do justly and wisely by those they leave behind them, I am not the man ever to interfere. I hold a will sacred, Mr. Edgar, within fit bounds; but when a dead man's will wrongs the living—"

"He is dead, and cannot stand up for it," said Edgar, who was very pale; "and it was his own to do as he liked."

"There's the fallacy," cried Mr. Fazakerley triumphantly, "there is just the fallacy. It was not his own. He had to get you to help him, and cheated you in your ignorance. Besides, even had he not required your help, which convicts him, it still was not his own. He was but one in the succession. What is the good of an old family but for that? Why, it is the very bulwark and defence of an aristocracy. I ought to know, for I see enough of the reverse. You may say the money these fellows make in Liverpool is their own—they may do what they like with it; and so they do, and the consequences are wonderful. But Squire Arden, good heavens, what was the good of him, what was the meaning of him, if he dismembered his property and broke it up! My dear Mr. Edgar, you are a charming young fellow, but you don't understand—"

"Well," said Edgar, warming under the influence of the lawyer's half-whimsical vehemence, "perhaps you are right, but it does not matter entering into that now. Before Clare marries—"

"There is no time like the present," said Mr. Fazakerley. "When she marries she will have other things in her mind, and her husband, that is to be, might interfere. Besides, that land near Liverpool is the most valuable part of the property. You have nothing to do but build villas upon it, or let other people build villas, and you will make a fortune. Your worthy father would never hear of it; but it really was a prejudice, and a waste of opportunity—"

"Do you want me to fly in his face in everything, and do just what he did not wish to be done?" said Edgar, with a smile, which he tried to suppress.

Mr. Fazakerley shrugged his narrow brown shoulders. "New monarchs, new laws," he said. "I don't see why you should be bound by his fancies. He did not show much respect for yours, if you had any. No, I mean to suggest very important modifications, if you will permit me, in the management of the estate. Perhaps, if we were to have up Tom Perfitt and the map, and go over it—"

Edgar consented with a sigh, which he also suppressed. It was not that he disliked the initiation into his real work in life, or objected to throw off the idleness in which he had spent all these years. On the contrary, he had chafed again and again over the inaction—the wretched aimlessness of his existence. But there was something in this sudden plunge into all its new responsibilities and trials, and, more than all, in this posthumous conflict with the will and inclinations of the father who had hated him, which sent a thrill through his mind, and moved his whole being. And in this life which was about to begin there was a mystery concealed somewhere—the secret of his own existence, which some time or other would have to be found out. Nobody seemed to feel this, not even those who were the most fully conscious that an explanation was wanted of the old Squire's ceaseless enmity to his son. They all took it for granted that it was over; that the Squire's death had ended everything; and that the heir who had succeeded so tranquilly would reign in peace in his unkind father's stead. But Edgar's mind was not so easily satisfied. It seemed to him that on this road which he was entering there stood a great signpost, with a shadowy hand pointing to the secret, and he shrank, knowing that secret would bring him trouble. However, to oppose this visionary sense of risk and danger to Mr. Fazakerley and his papers or to Perfitt and his map would have been folly indeed. So Perfitt, who was the Scotch steward, came, and the young Squire was drawn unconsciously within the charmed circle of property, and began to feel his heart beating and his head throbbing with a certain exhilarated sense of importance and responsibility. When he heard of all that was his, he, who never up to this moment had possessed anything but his personalities, a curious feeling of power came over him. He was young, and his mind was fresh, and the emotions of nature were still strong in him. He had seen a great deal of the world, but it had not been that phase of the world which makes a young man blasé. He sat and listened to the discussion of rents and boundaries, of what ought to be done with one farm and another, of the wood that ought to be cut, and the moor that ought to be reclaimed, with a puzzled yet pleasant consciousness that, discuss as they liked, they could not decide without him. He knew so little about it that he had to content himself with listening; but the talk was as a pleasant song to him, pleasing his newborn sense of importance. "You'll understand fine, Sir, when once you've been over the estate with me," said Perfitt, with a certain condescension which amused Edgar mightily. They seemed to him to be playing at government, suggesting so many things which they had no power to carry out, which must wait for his approval. All his graver anticipations floated away from him in his sense of the humour of the situation. He made mental notes in his mind as they settled this and that, saying to himself, "Wait a little; I will not have it so" with a boyish delight in the feeling that he could put all their calculations out by any sudden exercise of his will. If this was very childish in Edgar, I don't know what excuse to make for him. It was so amusing to him to feel himself a great man, with supreme power in his hands—he who had never been master of anything all his life.

That day was a long day. Just before luncheon the Thornleighs called, as Clare had expected. The Thornleighs were next neighbours to the Ardens in the county; and in the general estimation they were more fashionable than the Ardens, in so much that Mr. Thornleigh had married Lady Augusta Highton, a daughter of the Duke of Grandmaison; whereas the late Mr. Arden had married a wife whose antecedents were very little known, and who had been dead for years. So that while the Thornleighs had a house in town, and went a great deal into society, the Ardens had not budged for years from Arden Hall, and were very little known in the great world. This, however, was counterbalanced by the fact that while Clare was quite fresh and unworn, the five Thornleigh girls were rather too well known, and were talked about with just that shade of ennui which so speedily creeps over a fashionable reputation. "One sees them everywhere," said the fastidious rulers of that capricious world; and as there were five of them, it was not easy to invite them to those choicest little gatherings in which Fashion is worshipped with the most perfect rites, and distinctions are granted or withdrawn. None of the Thornleigh girls were yet married, and many people were disposed to censure Lady Augusta for bringing out little Beatrice, who was just seventeen, while she had still Ada, and Gussy, and Helena, and Mary on her hands. How could she ever expect to be able to take them all out—people said?—which was very true.

But, however, the thing was done, and could not be mended. Lady Augusta was not a matchmaker, in the usual sense of the word; neither were her daughters trained to the pursuit of elder sons or other eligible members of society, as it is common to suppose such young women to be. But it cannot be denied that as a reasonable woman, much concerned about the wellbeing of her children, Lady Augusta now and then allowed, with a sigh, that if Gussy and Ada were comfortably married it would be a very good thing, and a great relief to her mind. "Not to say that they could take their sisters out," she would sometimes say to herself, with a sigh reflecting upon all the cotillions to which little Beatrice, in the fervour of seventeen, would no doubt subject her mother. And it would be vain to attempt to deny that a little thrill of curiosity was in Lady Augusta's mind as she drove up the avenue to Arden. Edgar was their nearest neighbour, he was young and "nice," so far as anybody knew—for, of course, he had been met abroad from time to time by wandering sons and cousins, and reports of him had been brought home—and just a suitable age for Gussy, or, indeed, for any of the girls, should the young people by any chance take a fancy to each other. I cannot see why Lady Augusta should be condemned for having this speculation in her mind. If she had been quite indifferent to the future fate of her daughters she would have been an unnatural woman. It was her chief business in the world to procure a happy life for them, and provide them with everything that was best; and why—a good husband being placed, by common consent, foremost in the list of those good things—a mother's efforts towards the securing of him should not be thought the very highest and best of her occupations, it is very hard to say. As a matter of fact, everywhere but in England it is her first and most clearly recognised duty. And I for one do not feel in the least disposed to sneer at Lady Augusta. She went with her husband to look at this young man with a sense that one day he might be very important to her. It is possible that Edgar might not have liked it had the idea occurred to him that he was thus already a subject of speculation, and that his tenderest affections—the things which belong most exclusively to a man's personal being—were already being directed, whether potentially or not, by the imagination of another, into channels as yet totally unknown to him. I believe such a thought is not pleasant to a young man. But still it was quite natural—and, indeed, laudable—on the part of Lady Augusta, and demands neither scorn nor condemnation. She had made Mr. Thornleigh give up a morning's consultation with the keeper on some interesting young moorland families and the general prospects of the game, in order that no time might be lost in making this call. Of course, she said nothing to him as he sat rather sulkily by her side, thinking all the time of the young pheasants; but on the whole, perhaps, the mother's were not the least elevated thoughts.

"I am so very glad to be the first to welcome you home, Mr. Arden," she said. "We don't know each other yet—at least we two individuals don't know each other; but the Ardens and the Thornleighs have been friends these hundreds of years. How many hundreds, Clare? You girls are so dreadfully well-informed now-a-days, I never dare open my lips. And I hope now your sister will go out a little more, and come to us a little more. She has been such a little hermit all her life."

"She shall not be a hermit now, if I can help it," said Edgar. And he was pleased with the kindness of the elder woman, who was still a handsome woman, and gracious in her manner, as became a great lady. He sat down by her, as was his duty, but without thinking it was his duty—another sign of the spontaneousness which puzzled Clare, and gave Edgar's simple ways their greatest charm.

And the fact was that Lady Augusta, without in the least meaning it, was captivated by the young man. "He is not the least like an Arden," she said to her husband, as they drove away; "he has not their stiffness, any more than their black hair. I think he is charming. There is something very nice in a foreign education, you know. One would not choose it for one's own boys; but it does give a certain character when you meet with it by accident. Young men in general are so frightfully like each other," she added, with a sigh. Mr. Thornleigh gave a half articulate grunt, being full of calculations about the partridges; besides, the young men did not trouble him much. He was not called upon to remember which was which, and to hear them say exactly the same things to his girls ball after ball. Lady Augusta's sigh turned into a half yawn as she glanced back upon all her experiences. He was just about the age and about the height for Gussy. Gussy was a small, little thing, and Edgar was not tall. He would not answer at all for the stately Helena, who was five feet ten. And then, if the mother had a weakness, it was for little Gussy of all her children. And it would be so nice to have her settled so near. "But just because it is so nice, and would be so desirable, of course it will never come to pass," she said to herself, with another sigh. She had left an invitation behind her, and had made up her mind it should not be her fault if it came to nothing. Thus Edgar was assailed by altogether unexpected dangers the very day after his return.

And then there was the dinner in the evening, which was not so pleasant to think of as the dinner to which the brother and sister had been invited at Thorne. There were only three gentlemen—the Rector, and the Doctor, and Mr. Fazakerley—all twice as old as Edgar, and all patronising and explanatory. They knew his affairs so much better than he did, that it was not wonderful if they alarmed him. So long as Clare sat at the other end of the table her brother did not mind, for she was used to them, and used to having her own way with them; but Edgar felt it would be hard upon him when he was left to their tender mercies. He was very anxious to detain Clare, so as to shorten the awful hour after dinner. "Why should you go away?" he said, "wait till we are all ready. Are we such bears in England that ladies can't stay with us for an hour? We don't mean to smoke; that is the only thing that need send you away."

"Smoke!" said Mr. Fielding, with horror. "Edgar, I hope you don't mean to introduce these new-fangled foreign ways. I shall have to retire with the ladies if you do. I detest smoke, except in the open air."

"That is one of his old-fashioned notions," said Dr. Somers, "but you must have a smoking-room fitted up: then the ladies can't object. The old Squire resisted such an innovation. He was of the antique school, like Fielding here, and hated everything that was new."

"Just the reverse of our young friend," said Mr. Fazakerley. "I and Tom Perfitt have been giving him a great many ideas to-day. You will find Tom a very satisfactory fellow, I am sure. He is broad Scotch, and he is fond of having his own way, but he knows every inch of the land, and what is best for it. If you do any amateur farming you could not have a better man. If that sort of thing ever was anything but ruinous, Tom is the man to make it pay."

"I must take a little time to think what I am going to do," said Edgar, "and to make acquaintance with the place. You forget that I don't know Arden, though you all do. Clare, why should you go away?"

"I am going to make you some tea," said Clare, with a smile, as she went away. And she took no notice of his appealing look. She was half vexed, indeed, that he should have suggested such an innovation. It was a bad symptom for the time to come. Why should not Edgar be content, as everybody else was, with the usual customs of society? She was annoyed that he should show his foreign breeding even before his old friends. It seemed to her that Dr. Somers' keen eye launched a gleam of mockery at her as she went out. They would laugh at him, even these old gentlemen; and of course other people would laugh still more.

"Let her go," the Doctor said, as the door closed behind the young mistress of the house. "Don't disturb the customs of your country, Edgar. It is all very well just now when you are young; but the time will come, my boy, when you will prefer having an hour's serious talk, without any women to interfere with it. And they like it themselves, my dear fellow; they like a moment to put their hair straight and their ribbons, and have their private gossip. Don't train Clare into evil ways."

"I think they are much pleasanter ways," said Edgar; but he was put down by acclamation. To suggest an innovation in Arden of all places in the world! the three old men looked at him as if he were a natural curiosity, and studied his unusual habits with a mixture of amusement and alarm.

"I don't object to young men being fond of ladies' society," said Mr. Fielding, in his gentle voice; "it is a great preservative to them; but still not too much, not too much, my dear boy. Your sister, of course, will be a kind of guardian angel to you; but you know there are a great many Liverpool people about with large families—nice people enough, and of course they will be very friendly, if you will let them; and pretty girls, and all that. But you must be careful, you must be very careful. You must remember a great deal depends on the circle you collect round you at first."

"I don't see how I can collect a circle round me," said Edgar, laughing. "I have always supposed it was the great ladies who did that—Lady Augusta, for instance, who called here to-day—"

"My dear fellow," said Dr. Somers, "take care of that woman. She has five daughters, and she will play the pretty comedy of the spider and the fly with you for the amusement of the county, if you don't mind. If you let yourself be drawn into her net, you will have to marry one of the girls, and that is a severe price to pay for a few dinners. You must take care what you are about."

"The Miss Thornleighs are nice girls," said Mr. Fazakerley, "but they will have very little money. Young Thornleigh has been dreadfully extravagant at Oxford. I know for certain that his father has paid his bills three times. Of course they have so much under the marriage settlements; but when there are five, and only a certain sum to be divided, there can't be very much for each."

"She has Edgar booked for one, you may be sure," said the Doctor, "and a very nice thing, too—for them. Next neighbours, and a fine old place, and a nice young fellow. For my part, I think Lady Augusta is quite right."

"If you don't mind," said Edgar, "I'd rather not have myself suggested as the subject of anybody's calculations. Suppose one of the Miss Thornleighs should do me the honour to marry me hereafter, do you think I should like to remember how you talked of it? I am aware I have ridiculous notions—"

Dr. Somers laughed; Mr. Fazakerley chuckled, interrupting the young man's speech; but Mr. Fielding, who was of a gentler nature, peered at him through his short-sighted old eyes with kindly sympathy. "Edgar, I think you are quite right," he said. "We all talk about women in a most unjustifiable way. The Miss Thornleighs are very nice girls, and never gave any one reason to speak of them without respect—nor their mother either, that I know of; but we all talk as if they were put up to auction, and you might buy which you please. You are quite right."

"I do not know whether I am right or not," said Edgar, with some vehemence; "but I know I should punch any man's head who spoke so of Clare."

"Clare! Ah, that's different," said the Doctor; "where Clare is concerned, I give you full leave to punch anybody's head—"

"Miss Clare is an heiress," said Mr. Fazakerley. "She is as great a prize in the matrimonial market as her brother. If I took the liberty to speak on such a subject at all, I should represent her, not as the huntress, but the hunted. Penniless girls are in a very different position; and why should we blame them? It is their natural way of providing for themselves, after all."

"Then, money is everything," said Edgar, "and to provide for one's self one's first duty. I have not been very well brought up, you know, but I thought I had heard something better than that."

"Don't be too severely virtuous, my boy," the Doctor said, pushing back his chair. "You may be sure that, from the savage to the swell (two classes not so far apart), to provide for one's self is one's highest duty. Love, &c., are very nice things, but your living comes first of all. Now, come, we are getting metaphysical; let us join Clare."

CHAPTER IX

"Tell me something about the Thornleighs," Edgar said on the morning of the day they were to dine at Thorne. "I like to know what sort of people I am about to make acquaintance with. Are they friends of yours, Clare?"

"Pretty well," Clare answered, with just that little elevation of her head which Edgar began to know. "What is the use of describing them when you will see them to-night, and then judge for yourself? Ada is nice. She is the eldest of all, and she talks very little. I like her for that. Gussy is short, with heaps of light hair; and Helena is very tall, and rather dark, like her father. They are not at all like each other—not much more like each other than you and me."

"That is a consolation," said Edgar, with a smile.

"Not so much as you think, for they are like in their ways; and then you can tell in a moment which side of the house they belong to," said Clare, with a shade crossing her face. "Whereas, Edgar—don't be vexed with me for saying so—but you are not even—like mamma."

"How do you know?" said Edgar, a little sharply; for that he was like his mother had been one of the established principles of his life.

"I have a little miniature in a bracelet. Nobody knows of it, I think, but myself. She must have been fair, to be sure; but you are not very like her, Edgar. You are not vexed? Of course, you must be like her family. But Helena Thornleigh is like her father, and Ada and Gussy are like Lady Augusta. You can't mistake it; and then they all have little ways of speaking, and little movements: if you are going to like any of them, I wish it may be Ada. She is really nice. But Gussy is a chatterbox, and Helena is superior; and as for Mary and Beatrice—"

"Is it certain that I must like one more than another?" said Edgar. "I mean to like them all, as they are our next neighbours. Is there any reason why I should confine myself to one?"

"Oh, I suppose not," said Clare, with a suppressed laugh; "only somehow one always thinks where there are girls—Look! Edgar; here is some one coming up the avenue. Who can it be? The servant is in livery, and I don't recognise the carriage, nor anything. It can't be the Thorpes, or the Mandevilles, or the Blundells; and it can't be the Earl, for he is in town. Look! they don't see us and I do so want to make them out."

"The servants are in purple and green, and there is an astounding coat of arms on the panel," said Edgar. "You must know that—arms as big as a saucer—and somebody very big inside." The two were in a little morning room which opened from the great drawing room, where they could see the avenue and even the flight of steps before which the carriage stopped. Clare uttered an exclamation of horror as she stood gazing out at the new comers. She seemed to her brother to shiver with sudden dismay. "It cannot be possible!" she said. What could she mean? Perhaps it was some secret enemy whom she recognised but he did not know; somebody, perhaps, connected with the secret which more or less weighed on Edgar's life.

"Who is it?" he said, in serious alarm, coming close to her. "Any one we have reason to be afraid of? Don't tremble so. Nobody can harm you while I am here."

"On the contrary, they would never have ventured had not you been here!" said Clare, with vehement indignation. "They never could have had the presumption—Edgar, it is an insult! We ought to send and say we are not at home. There are some things one ought not to bear—"

"Who are they?" he asked, beginning to perceive that there was no serious cause for fear.

But Clare's flushed and indignant countenance showed no signs of softening. "I knew they were presuming, but I never could have imagined anything so bad as this," she cried. "Edgar, it is the Pimpernels!"

"The Pimpernels?" Edgar repeated, confused and wondering; but before he could ask another question the door was thrown open, and Wilkins appeared in front of the invading party. Wilkins' face was a study of suppressed consternation and dismay. He did his office as if he were going to the stake, stern necessity compelling him in the shape of those three solid figures behind. "Mr., Mrs., and Miss Pimpernel," said Wilkins, with a voice in which the protest of a martyr was audible behind the ordinary formality. Edgar did not know anything about the Pimpernels. He saw before him a large man, made larger by light summer costume, which magnified his breadth and diminished his height, with sparkling jewelled studs in his shirt, and a great coil of watch-chain spreading across his buff waistcoat; and a large lady, enveloped in black silk and lace, which somehow, though so totally different, seemed to have the same effect of enlarging and setting forth her amplitude of form. Behind these two there appeared, seen by intervals, the slim figure of a tall girl, with a pretty blushing face. Nothing could have made Edgar uncivil—not even the terrible fact, had he known it, that Mr. Pimpernel was a Liverpool cotton-broker, such a man as had never before made his appearance in the capacity of visitor within the stately shades of Arden. But he was not aware of that awful fact. He knew only that Clare had been moved by horror at the sight of them, and that she stood now at as great a distance as possible, and made a very solemn curtsey, and looked as if she were assisting at a funeral. The Pimpernels, who had produced this melancholy effect, were themselves so utterly unlike it, at once in manners and appearance, that the situation affected Edgar rather with comic than with solemn feelings.

"I am very glad to see you, and to welcome you home, Mr. Arden," said Mr. Pimpernel, when they had all sat down in the form of a semicircle, of which Edgar and Clare formed the base. "I can't pretend to be an old neighbour, but we have been here long enough to take an interest in the county. I have always taken a great interest in the county, as my wife knows."

"Yes, indeed," said that ample woman. "Since ever we settled here Mr. Pimpernel has quite thrown himself into Arden ways. We were so very lucky in getting the Red House—the only one in the neighbourhood. It is wicked to say so, but I felt so much obliged to poor Mr. Dalton when he died and let us have it—I did indeed. It was quite obliging of him to die."

Upon this Miss Pimpernel laughed shyly, and Mr. Pimpernel smiled; and Edgar, seeing it was expected of him, would have smiled too had he not encountered Clare's stormy countenance, without a gleam of light upon it. It embarrassed him sadly, poor fellow; for of course he did not want to wound his sister, and yet he could not be uncivil. "I am such a stranger in my own country," he said, "that I really don't know where the Red House is. I know only the village, and nothing more."

"It is the sweetest village," said Mrs. Pimpernel. "We were so glad to hear that there were no building sites to be given, though, of course, in one way it must have been a sacrifice. It is selfish of us, because we have been so fortunate as to secure the only house; but the moment you begin to build villas you spoil the place. It never would have been the same sweet old place again. Mr. Pimpernel drives over every morning to Farnham Green, the station. Of course, he could not do it unless he was able to afford horses; but we are able to afford them, I am glad to say. I don't know if you have ever remarked his Yankee waggon, with two beautiful bright bays? I hope I am not horsey, which is very unladylike, but I do like to see a fine animal. It is next to a pretty girl, my husband always says."

"The only thing wanting in Arden is a little society," said Mr. Pimpernel; "and I hope, Mr. Arden, that your happy return, and the new life you must bring with you, will change all that. We hoped you would perhaps dine with us on Monday week? Young Newmarch is coming, the Earl's eldest son, a very nice young fellow—quite a man of his century; but of course you must know him better than I do; and we expect some young Oxford men with my son, who is at Christchurch. My wife wanted to write, but I think it is always best to settle such things by word of mouth."

"I am afraid Miss Arden may think all this a little abrupt," said Mrs. Pimpernel, taking up the strain when her husband paused. "Of course, if it had not been for the change, and Mr. Arden coming, as it were, fresh to the place, it was not our part to call first; but all this last year I have done nothing but think of you, so lonely as you must have been. I have said to Alice a hundred times—'How I wish I could go and call upon that poor dear Miss Arden.' But I never knew whether you would like it. I am sure, many and many a time, when I have seen all my own young ones so merry about me, I have thought of you. 'If we could only have her here, and cheer her up a little,' I used to say—"

"It was kind of you to think of my sister. I am very much obliged to you," said Edgar, warmly. Clare made a little bow, and after her brother had spoken murmured something vaguely under her breath.

"I know what it is to have no mother," continued the large lady, "and to be left alone. I was an only daughter myself; and when I looked at all mine, and me spared to them, and thought 'Oh, that poor dear girl, all by herself!' I could have cried over you; I could, indeed."

"You were very kind," said Edgar once more, and Clare uttered another faint murmur, as if echoing him, unable to originate any sentiment of her own.

"But I fear Miss Arden has poor health," Mrs. Pimpernel continued, fixing her eyes, which had been contemplating the company in general, upon Clare. And Mr. Pimpernel, who had been inspecting the room with some curiosity, looked too at the young lady of the house; and the slim daughter gave her a succession of shy glances, so that she was hemmed in on every side, and could no longer meet with silence, or with her haughty little bow, those expressions of friendly interest.

"Indeed I am very well—quite well," she said. "I must have been getting sympathy on false pretences. There is no lack of society had I wanted it. It was my choice to be alone."

"Oh, my dear, that I have no doubt of," said Mrs. Pimpernel; "in your position, of course, you can pick and choose; but still, when you are not in good spirits, nor feeling up to much exertion—However, I do hope you will waive ceremony, and come in a friendly way with your brother to dine at the Red House on Monday. It would give me so much pleasure. And Alice has been looking forward to making your acquaintance for so long."

"Oh, yes; for a very long time," said pretty Alice, under her breath. She was as pretty as Clare herself, though in a different way; and sat a little behind her mother, looking from one to the other of her parents, like a silent chorus, softly backing them with smiles and sympathy. When she caught Edgar's eyes during this little performance, she blushed and cast down her own, and played with the fringe of her parasol; and with a certain awe now and then, her looks strayed to Clare's beautiful, closed-up, repellent face. She was shy of the brother, but downright frightened for the sister; and besides these two sentiments, and a faith as yet unbroken in her father and mother, showed no personal identity at all.

"I do not go out at present," said Clare, looking at her black dress; upon which Mrs. Pimpernel rushed into remonstrance and entreaty. Edgar sat looking on, feeling almost as much bewildered as Alice; for, notwithstanding her black dress, Clare had shown no particular unwillingness to go to Thorne.

"For the sake of your health you ought not to shut yourself up," urged Mrs. Pimpernel; "a young creature at your age should enjoy life a little; and for the sake of your friends, who would be so glad to have you—and for your brother's sake, my dear, if you will let me say so—I speak freely, because I have daughters of my own."

"Thanks, you are very kind," said courteous Edgar; while his sister shut her beautiful lips close. And then there was a pause, which was not comfortable. Mrs. Pimpernel began to smooth the gloves which were very tight on her plump hands, and Mr. Pimpernel resumed his inspection of the room.

"That is a Turner, I suppose," he said, pointing to a very poor daub in a dark corner. "I hope you are fond of art, Mr. Arden. When you come to the Red House I can show you some rather pretty things."

"It is not a Turner; it is very bad," said Edgar. "We have no pictures except portraits. I don't think the Ardens have ever taken much interest in art."

"Never," said Clare, with a little emphasis. She said so because she had heard a great deal about Mr. Pimpernel's pictures, and felt it her duty to disown all participation in any such plebeian taste; and then she recollected herself, and grew red, and added hurriedly—"The Ardens have always had to think of their country, Edgar. They have had more serious things to do."

"But I am not much of an Arden, I fear, and I am very fond of pictures," said Edgar carelessly, without perceiving the cloud that swept over his sister's face.

"Then I assure you, though I say it that shouldn't, I have some pretty things to show you at the Red House," said Mr. Pimpernel. Thus it came to be understood that Edgar had accepted the invitation for Monday week, and the party rose,—first the mother, then Alice, obedient to every impulse, and finally Mr. Pimpernel, who extended his large hand, and took into his own Clare's reluctant fingers. "I hope we shall soon see you with your brother," he said, raising his other hand, as if he was pronouncing a blessing over her. "Indeed, I hope so," said Mrs. Pimpernel, following him with outstretched hand. Alice put out hers too, but withdrew it shyly, and made a little curtsey, like a school girl, Clare thought; but to her brother there was something very delicate, and gentle, and pretty in the girl's modest withdrawal. He went to the door with them to put Mrs. Pimpernel in her carriage, and came back to Clare without a suspicion of the storm which was about to burst upon his head.

CHAPTER X

Clare was standing by the table with her hands clasped tightly, her mouth shut fast, her tall figure towering taller than usual, when Edgar, all unconscious, returned to her. She assailed him in a moment, without warning. "Edgar, how can you—how could you?" she said, with an impatient movement, which, had she been less fair, less delicate, less young, would have been a stamp of her foot. Her tone and look and gesture were so passionate that the young man stood aghast.

"What have I done?" he asked.

"What have you done? You know as well as I do. Oh, Edgar, you have given me such a blow! I thought when you came home, and we were together, that all would be well; but to see you the very first day—the very first opportunity—throw yourself into the arms of people like these—people that never should have entered this house—"

"Who are they? What are they? Have they done us any harm?" said the astonished Edgar. "If they are enemies you should have told me. How was I to know?"

"Enemies!" said Clare, with increasing indignation; "how could such people be our enemies? They are a great deal worse—they are the vulgar rich, whom I hate; they are trying to force themselves in among us because they are rich; they are trades-people, pretending to be our equals, venturing to ask you to dinner! Oh, Edgar, could not you see by my manner that they were not people to know?"

"I saw you were very rude to them, certainly," he said. "But, Clare, that goes against me; even—may I say it?—it disappointed me. I do not understand how a lady can be rude."

Once more she repeated his last word with a certain contempt. "Rude! The man is a tradesman. They have thrust themselves into the village; and now they have seized an opportunity—which was in reality no opportunity—to thrust themselves into the house. Edgar, I have no patience; I ought not to have patience. They have been impertinent. And you as civil as if they were the best people in the county—and going to dine with them! I did not expect this."

"I am sorry, Clare, if it hurts you," he said. "They seemed very kind; and how could I help it? Besides, you made them very uncomfortable, and I owed them amends. And you know I am but an indifferent Arden; I have not any horror of trade."

"You told them so!" said Clare—"you took people like these into your confidence, and confessed to them that you were not an Arden like the rest of us! Oh, please, Edgar, don't! you might think how unhappy it makes me. As if it was not enough—"

"What, Clare?"

"Oh, can't you understand?" she cried. "Is it not enough to see that you are not a thorough Arden; that you don't care for the things we care for, nor hate the things we hate. But to have to hear you say so as if it did not matter!—it is the grief of my life."

And she threw herself into a chair, and cried—weeping a sudden shower of passionate tears, which were so hot and rapid that they seemed to scorch her, yet dried as they fell. Her brother came and stood by her chair, putting his hand softly on her bent head. Edgar was sorry, but not only because she wept. He was grieved, and perplexed, and disappointed. A half smile came over his serious face at her last words. "My poor Clare—my poor Clare," he repeated softly, smoothing the dark glossy locks of her hair. When the thunder shower was over he spoke, with a voice that sounded more manly and mature and grave than anything Clare had heard from him before.

"You must take my character and my training a little into consideration," he said. "If I had been brought up like you I might have thought with you. But, Clare, though I love you more than anything in the world, and would not vex you for all Arden, still I cannot change my nature. Arden is only a very small spot in England, dear, not to speak of the world; and I can't look at the big world through Arden spectacles. You must not ask it of me; anything else I will do to please you. I will give up dining with these people if you wish it. Of course I don't care for their dinner; but they looked as if they wanted to be kind—"

"They wanted to come to Arden, to know you and me, and get admittance among the county families," said Clare in one breath.

"Well, perhaps. I suppose we are all mean wretches more or less," he said. "Suppose we give up the Pimpernels; but you must not ask me to avoid everybody who has anything to do, or to content myself with the old groove. For instance, I like pictures, though you say the Ardens don't—"

"That is not what I meant," said Clare, with a blush; "I meant—"

"You meant opposition, and to snub that fat, good-tempered man; and you only made me uncomfortable—he did not feel it. But I like pictures, Clare, and the people who paint them. I have known a great many in my life; and when I like any man I cannot pause to ask what is his pedigree, or what is his occupation. Putting aside the Pimpernels, you must still make up your mind to that."

"But you will put aside the Pimpernels?" said Clare, with pleading looks.

"I will see about it," said Edgar. It was the first time he had not yielded, and Clare felt it. She felt too that a shade of real difference had stolen between them—almost of separation. She had been unreasonable, and had put herself in the wrong; and he had set up a principle of action, erected as it were his standard, and made it clearly apparent what he would and what he would not do. She went away to her own room with a certain soreness in her heart. She had committed herself. Certain words of her own and certain words of his came back to her with the poignant shame of youth—what she had said about the pictures, and what Edgar had said of her rudeness, and of the antagonism which only made him uncomfortable. She had made herself ridiculous, she thought—that worst of all offences against one's self. It seemed to the proud Clare as if neither she nor any one else could forget how ridiculous she had made herself; and more than ever with tenfold force of enmity she hated those unlucky Pimpernels.

It was brilliant daylight, the sun was setting, and the air full of light and sweetness, when they set off upon their drive to Thorne. Clare was all black, as her mourning demanded—black ornaments, black gloves—everything about her as sable as the night—a dress, which was not perhaps so becoming to her dark hair and pale complexion as it would have been to pretty Alice Pimpernel, or the fair-haired Gussy, whom Edgar was going (though he did not know it) expressly to see. Probably Clare did not waste a thought on the subject, for she was young and entirely fancy free, a condition of things which frees a girl from any keen anxiety in respect to her appearance. She was wrapped in a large white cloak, however, which relieved the blackness, and brought out the delicate pale tints of her face as only white can do; and Edgar, as he took his place by her side, found himself admiring her as if he had seen her for the first time. The high, proud features, so finely cut, the perfect roundness of youth in the cheek, the large, lovely blue eyes, were of a kind of beauty which you may like or dislike as you please, but which it is impossible to ignore. Clare was beautiful, there was no other word for it. Not pretty, like that pretty Alice; and her proud looks and air of reserve enhanced her beauty, just as the sweet wistful frankness of the simpler girl added a charm to hers. "I don't suppose I shall see any one like my sister where we are going," Edgar said, with that admiring affection which is so pleasant in a brother.

"No, indeed, they are all quite a different style," Clare answered with a laugh, turning aside the compliment, which nevertheless pleased her. This did much to restore the former delightful balance of affairs between them. About half-a-mile from the village they came upon a house, just visible through the trees, a very old solid mass of red brick, shining with a subdued glow in the midst of the green wealth of foliage, which looked the greener for its redness, and heightened its native depth of colour. There was a fine cedar on the lawn, and many great old trees within the enclosure, which was so arranged that it might be taken for a park. Edgar gave an inquiring glance at his sister, who answered him by shaking her head, and putting up her hands as if to shut out the hateful vision.

"So that is the Red House?" said Edgar. "I had forgotten all about it. It is a nice house enough. If I should ever happen to be turned out of Arden, I should like to live there."

"What nonsense you do talk!" said Clare. "Who can turn you out of Arden, unless there was a revolution, as some people think?"

"I don't think there will be a revolution. But have we no cousins who might do one that good turn?" he said, laughing. "How? Oh, I can't tell how. It is impossible, I suppose."

"Simply impossible," said Clare with energy. "We are the elder branch. The Ardens of Warwickshire were quite a late offshoot. You are the head of the name."

"I am glad to hear it," said Edgar; "and I am sure it is a very proud position. Does that Red House belong to us, Clare? But if it had belonged to us, I suppose you would not have let it to those respectable—I mean objectionable—Pimpernels?"

"Don't speak of the Pimpernels," she said. "Oh, Edgar, if you only knew how much I dislike those sort of people—not because they are common people—on the contrary, I am very fond of the poor; but those presumptuous pushing nouveaux riches—don't let us speak of them! We have got a cousin—only one; and if you were not to have any children, I suppose the estates would go to his son. But I hope they never will."

"Why?" said Edgar. "Is there any reason to suppose that his son would be less satisfactory than mine? I hope he is less problematical. Tell me about him—who is he—where is he? I feel very curious about my heir."

"And I hate to hear you speak in such a careless way," said his sister. "Why should you show so much levity on so serious a subject? Arthur Arden is a great deal older than you are. I dislike him very much. Pray, don't speak of him to me."

"Another subject I must not speak of!" said Edgar. "Why do you dislike him? Is it because he is my heir? You need not hate a man for that."

"But I do hate him," said Clare, with a clouded brow; and the rest of the way to Thorne was gone over in comparative silence. The jars that kept occurring, putting now one string, now another out of tune, vibrated through both with an unceasing thrill of discord. There was no quarrel, and yet each was afraid to touch on any new subject. To be sure, it was Clare who was in the wrong; but then, why was he so light, so easily moved, so free from all natural prejudices, she said to herself? Men ought not to run from one subject to another in this careless way. They ought to be more grave, more stately in their ways of thinking, not moved by freaks of imagination. Such levity was so different from the Arden disposition that it looked almost like something wrong to Clare.

Thorne was a great house, but not like Arden. It stood alone, not shadowed by trees, amid the great green solitude of its park; and already lights were glimmering in the open windows, though it was still day. The servants were closing shutters in the dining-room, and the table gleamed inside under the lamplight, making itself brightly visible, like a picture, with all its ornaments and flowers. It was Lady Augusta's weakness that she could not bear to dine in daylight. In the very height of summer she had to support the infliction; but as long as she could she shut out the intrusive day. Edgar felt his head swim as he walked into the cool green drawing-room after his sister into the midst of a bevy of ladies. He was fond of ladies, like most well-conditioned men; but the first moment of introducing himself into the midst of a crowd of them fluttered him, as was quite reasonable. There was Ada, the quiet one, on a sofa by herself, knitting. Edgar discriminated her at once. And that, no doubt, was Gussy, with the prettiest tiny figure, and a charming little rose-tinted face, something between an angel and a Dresden shepherdess. "That will be my one," he said to himself, remembering with natural perversity that Ada was Clare's favourite. That little indication was enough to raise in the young man's mind a certain disinclination to Ada. And he did not know that Lady Augusta had already decided upon the advisability of allotting to him her second daughter. He could not see the others, who were busied in different corners with different occupations. It was the first English party of the kind he had ever been at, and he was very curious about it. And then it was so perfectly orthodox a party. There was the nearest squire and his wife, one of the great Blundell family; and there was a younger son of the Earl's, with his young wife; and the rector of the parish, and a man from London. Such a party is not complete without the man from London, who has all the news at his finger-ends, and under whose manipulation the biggest of cities becomes in reality that "little village" which slang calls it. "Will you take in my daughter, Mr. Arden?" said Lady Augusta; and Edgar, without any thought of his own dignity, was quite happy to find Gussy's pretty curls brushing his shoulder as they joined the procession into the dining-room. He thought it was kind of his new friends to provide him with such a pleasant companion, while Clare was making herself rather unhappy with the thought that he should have taken in, if not the Honourable Mrs. Everard, at least Mrs. Blundell, or, at the very least, Ada, who was the Princess Royal of the House of Thorne. "I am so glad all the solemn people are at the other end of the table," Gussy whispered to him, as they took their places. "Mr. Arden, I am sure you are not solemn. You are not a bit like Clare."

"Is Clare solemn?" asked Edgar, with a half sense of treachery to his sister; but he could not refuse to smile at Gussy's pretty up-turned face.

"I love her dearly; she is as good as gold," said Gussy, "but not such fun as I am sure you are. If you will promise never to betray me to mamma, I will tell you who everyone here is."

"Not if I went to the stake for it," said Edgar; and so his first alliance was formed.

CHAPTER XI

"You know mamma, of course," said Edgar's pretty cicerone. "I suppose I need not enter into the family history. You know all us Thornleighs, as we have known you all our lives."

"I am ashamed of my ignorance; but I have never been at home to have the chance of knowing the Thornleighs," said Edgar. "Don't imagine it is my fault."

"No; it is quite romantic, I know," said Gussy. "You have been brought up abroad. Oh yes; I know all about it. Mr. Arden nearly died of losing your mother, and you are so like her that he could not bear to look at you. Poor dear old Mr. Arden, he was so nice. But I thought you must have known us by instinct all the same. That is Ada sitting opposite. I must begin with us young ones, for what could I say about papa and mamma? Everybody knows papa and mamma. It would be like repeating a chapter out of Macaulay's history, or that sort of thing. Harry is the eldest, but he is not at home. And that is Ada opposite. She is the good one among us. It is she who keeps up the credit of the family. Poor dear mamma has plenty to do with five girls on her hands, not to speak of the boys. And Ada looks after the schools, and manages the poor people, and all that. All the cottagers adore her. But she is not fun, though she is a dear. There is not another boy for ever so long. We girls all made a rush into the world before them. I am sure I don't know why. As if we were any good!"

"Are not you any good?" said Edgar, laughing. He was not used to advanced views about women, and he thought it was a joke.

"Of course, we are no good," said Gussy. "We are all very well so long as we are young—and some of us are ornamental. I think Helena is very ornamental for one; but we can't do anything or be anything. You should hear what she says about that. Well, then, after Ada there is nothing very important—there is only me. I am the chattering one, and some people call me the little one, or the one with the curls. I have not any character to speak of, nor any vocation in the family, so it is not worth while considering me. Let us pass on to Helena. That is Helena, the one who is so like papa. I think she is awfully handsome. Of course, I don't mean that I expect you to think so, or to say so; but all her sisters admire her very much. And she is as clever as a dozen men. All the boys put together are not half so clever as she is. She ought to have been in Parliament, and that sort of thing; but she can't, for she is a girl. Don't you think it is hard? Well, I do. There is nothing she could not do, if she only had the chance. That is the Rector who is sitting beside her. He is High, but he is Broad as well. He burns candles on the altar, and lets us decorate the church, and has choral service; but all the same he is very philosophical in his preaching. Helena thinks a great deal of that. She says he satisfies both the material and intellectual wants. Do you feel sleepy? Don't be afraid to confess it, for I do myself whenever anybody uses long words. I thought it was my duty to tell you. For anything I know, you may be intellectual too."

"I don't think I am intellectual, but I am not in the least sleepy," said Edgar; "pray go on. I begin to feel the mists clear away, and the outlines grow distinct. I am a kind of Columbus on the shores of a new world; but he had not such a guide as you."

"Please wait a little," said Gussy, shaking her pretty curls, "till I have eaten my soup. I am so fond of white soup. It is a combination of every sort of eatable that ever was invented, and yet it does not give you any trouble. I must have two minutes for my soup."

"Then it is my turn," said Edgar. "I should like to tell you all my difficulties about Arden. Clare is not such an able guide as you are. She does not tell me who everybody is, but expects me to know. And when one has been away from home all one's life, instinct is a poor guide. Fancy, I should never have known that you were the chattering one, and Miss Thornleigh the good one, if you had not told me! I might have supposed it was the other way. And if you had been at Arden I never should have made such a dreadful mistake as I made this morning."

"Oh, tell me! what was it?" said Gussy, with her spoon suspended in her hand, looking up at him with dancing eyes.

"I hope you will not think the worse of me for such a confession. I was so misled as to say I would go and dine with a certain Mr. Pimpernel—"

"Oh, I know," said Gussy, clapping her hands, and forgetting all about her soup. "I wish I could have seen Clare's face. But it is not at all a bad house to dine at, and I advise you to go. He is a cotton-merchant or something; but, you know, though it is all very well for Clare, who is an only daughter and an heiress, we can't afford to stand on our dignity. All the men say it is a very nice house."

"Then I have not behaved so very badly after all?" said Edgar. "You can't think what a comfort that is to me. I rather thought I deserved to be sent to the Tower."

"I should not think it was bad at all," said Gussy. "I should like it of all things; but then I am not Clare. They have everything, you know, that can be got with money. And such wine, the men say; though I don't understand that either. And there are some lovely pictures, and a nice daughter. I know she is pretty, for I have seen her, and they say she will have oceans of money. Money must be very nice when there are heaps of it," Gussy added softly, with a little sigh.

Edgar paused for a moment, taken aback. He had not yet met his ideal woman; but it seemed to him that when he did meet her, she would care nothing for money, and would shrink from any contact with the world. A woman was to him a soft, still-shadowy ideal, surrounded by an atmosphere of the tenderest poetry, and celestial detachment from earth and its necessities. It gave him a gentle shock to be brought thus face to face with so many active, real human creatures, full of personal wants and wishes, and to identify them as the maiden-queens of imagination. Clare had not helped him to any such realisation of the abstract woman. There was no sort of struggle in her being, no aspiration after anything external to her. It was impossible to think of her as capable of advancement or promotion. Edgar himself was by no means destitute of ambition. He had already felt that to settle himself down with all his energies and powers into the calm routine of a country gentleman's life would be impossible. He wanted more to do, something to aim at, the prospect of an expanding existence. But Clare was different. She was in harmony with all her surroundings, wanted nothing, was adapted to every necessity of her position—a being totally different from any man. It seemed to Edgar that so all women should be—passive, receiving with a tender grace, which made their acceptance a favour and honour, but never acquiring, never struggling; regarding, indeed, with horror, any possibility of being obliged to struggle and acquire. Gussy, though she charmed him, gave him at the same time a gentle shock. That it should be hard for Helena not to be able to go into Parliament, and that this fair creature should sigh at the thought of heaps of money, sounded like sacrilege to him. He came to a confused pause, wondering at her. Gussy was as keen as a needle notwithstanding her chattering, and she found him out.

"Do you think it is shocking to care for money?" she said.

"N-no," said Edgar, "not for some people. I might, without any derogation; but for a lady—You must remember I don't know anything about the world."

"No," said Gussy, "of course you don't; but a lady wants money as much as a man. We girls are dreadfully hampered sometimes, and can't do what we please because of money. The boys go and spend, but we can't. It is a little hard. You should hear Helena on that. I don't mind myself, for I can always manage somehow; but Helena gives all sort of subscriptions, and likes to buy books and things; and then she has to keep it off her dress. Papa gives us as much as he can afford, so we have nothing to complain of; for, fancy five girls! and all to be provided for afterwards. Of course, we can't go into professions like the boys. I don't want to change the laws, as Helena does, because I don't see how it is to be done; so then the only thing that remains is to wish for heaps of money—quantities of money; and then everybody could get on."

Edgar was very glad to retire into an entrée while this curious statement of difficulties was being made. It seemed so strange to him, with all his own wealth, to hear any of his friends wish for money without offering his purse. Had Gussy been Gus, he would have said—"I have plenty; take some of mine," with all the ready goodfellowship of youth. But he dared not say anything of the kind to the young lady. He dared not even suggest that it was possible: this wonderful difference was beyond all aid of legislation. Accordingly, he was silent, and ate his dinner, and was no longer the agreeable companion Gussy expected him to be. She did not like her powers of conversation to be thus practically undervalued, nor was she content, as her sister Helena would have been, with the feeling that she had made him think. Gussy liked an immediate return. She liked to make her interlocutors, not think, but listen, and laugh, and respond, giving her swift repayment for her trouble. She gave her curls another shake, and changed the subject, having long ere this got done with her soup.

"I have not half finished my carte du pays," she resumed; "don't you want to hear about the other people, or have you had enough of Thorne? I feel sure you must be thinking about your new friends. If I ride over to see Clare the day after your dinner, will you tell me all about the Pimpernels? I do so want to have a credible account of them, and the Lesser Celandine, and all—"

"Who is the Lesser Celandine?"

"Oh, please, do not look so grave, as if you could eat me. I believe you are a little like Clare after all. Of course it is the pretty daughter: they say she is just like it; peeps from behind her leaves—I mean her mamma—and never says a word. Don't you think all girls should do so? Now, confess, Mr. Arden. I am sure that is what you think, if you would allow yourself to speak."

"I don't suppose all girls should follow one rule any more than all boys," said Edgar, with polite equivocation; and then Gussy returned to her first subject, and gave him sketches of everybody at the table. Mr. Blundell, who was stupid and good, and his wife, who was stupid and not very good; and the Honourable pair, who were close to their young historian—so close, that she had to speak half in whisper, half in metaphor. "They have both been so dreadfully taken in," Gussy said. "She thought his elder brother was dying; and he thought she was as rich as the Queen of Sheba; whereas she has only got a little money, and poor Newmarch is better again. Hush, I can't say any more. Yes, he is better; and they say he is going to be married, which would be dreadfully hard upon them. How wicked it is to talk like this!—but then everybody does it. You hear just the same things everywhere till you get to believe them, and are so glad of somebody fresh to tell them to. Oh yes, there is that man. If you were to listen to him for an hour, you would think there was not a good man nor a good woman in the world. He tells you how all the marriages are made up, and how she was forced into it, and he was cheated; or how they quarrelled the day before the wedding, and broke it off; or how the husband was trapped and made to marry when he did not want to. Oh, don't you hate such men? Yet he is very amusing, especially in the country. I don't remember his name. He is in some office or other—somebody's secretary; but there are dozens just like him. We are going to town next week, and I shall hate the very sight of such men; but in the country he is well enough. Oh, there is mamma moving; do pick up my glove for me, please."

Thus Gussy was swept away, leaving her companion a little uncertain as to the impression she had made upon him. It was a new world, and his head swam a little with the novelty and the giddiness. When the gentlemen gathered round the table, and began to talk in a solid agricultural way about steady-going politics, and the state of the country, and the prospects of the game, he found his head relieved a little. Clare had given him a glance as she left the room, but he had not understood the glance. It was an appeal to him not to commit himself; but Edgar had no intention of committing himself among the men as they drank their wine and got through their talk. He was far more likely to do that with Gussy, to make foolish acknowledgments, and betray the unsophistication of his mind. But he did not betray himself to Mr. Blundell and Mr. Thornleigh. They shook their heads a little, and feared he was affected by the Radical tendencies of the age. But so were many of the young fellows, the Oxford men who had distinguished themselves, the young dilettante philanthropists and revolutionists of the time. If he sinned in that way, he sinned in good company. There was Lord Newmarch, for instance, the Earl's eldest son, and future magnate of the county, who was almost Red in his views. Edgar got on very well with the men. They said to each other, "Old Arden treated that boy very badly. It is a wonder to see how well he has turned out;" and the ladies in the drawing-room were still more charitably disposed towards the young Squire. There was thus a certain amount of social success in Edgar Arden's first entrance into his new sphere.

CHAPTER XII

After the dinner at Thorne there was nothing said between Edgar and Clare about that other humbler invitation which had caused the first struggle between them. She took Mr. Fielding into her confidence, but she said nothing more to her brother. As for the Rector, he was not so hard on the Pimpernels as was the young lady at the Hall. "They are common people, I allow," he said. "They have not much refinement, nor—nor education perhaps; and I highly disapprove of that perpetual croquet-playing, which wastes all the afternoons, and puts young Denbigh off his head. I do not like it, I confess, Clare; but still, you know—if I may say exactly what I think—there are worse people than the Pimpernels."

"I don't suppose they steal," said Clare.

"My dear, no doubt it is quite natural, with your education and habits—but I wish you would not be quite so contemptuous of these good people. They are really very good sort of people," said Mr. Fielding, shaking his head. She looked very obdurate in her severe young beauty as the Rector looked at her, bending his brows till his eyes almost disappeared among the wrinkles. "They find us places for our boys and girls in a way I have never been able to manage before; and whenever there is any bad case in the parish—"

"Mr. Fielding, that is our business," said Clare, almost sharply. "I don't understand how you can talk of our people to anybody but Edgar or me."

"I don't mean the people here," said Mr. Fielding meekly, "but at the other end of the parish. You know that new village, which is not even on Arden land—on that corner which belongs to old Stirzaker—where there are so many Irish? I don't like to trouble you always about these kind of people. And when I have wanted anything—"

"Please don't want anything from them again," said Clare. "I don't like it. What is the good of our being lords of the manor if we do not look after our own people? Mr. Fielding, you know I think a great deal of our family. You often blame me for it; but I should despise myself if I did not think of our duties as well. All that is our business. Please—please don't ask anything of those Pimpernels again!"

"Those Pimpernels!" said Mr. Fielding, shaking his head. "Ah, Clare! they are flesh and blood like yourself, and the young lady is a very nice girl; and why should I not permit them to be kind to their fellow-creatures because you think that is your right? Everybody has a right to be good to their neighbours. And then they find us places for our boys and girls."

"I have forgotten about everything since Edgar came," said Clare, with a blush. "I have not seen old Sarah since the first day. Please come with me, and I will go and see her now. What sort of places? They are much better in nice houses in the country than in Liverpool. The girls get spoiled when they go into a town."

"But they get good wages," said Mr. Fielding, "and are able to help their people. I have not told you of this, for I knew you were prejudiced. Old Sarah has a lodger now, a relation of Mr. Perfitt—an old Scotchwoman—something quite new. I should like you to see her, Clare. I have seen plenty of Scotch in Liverpool, both workmen and merchants; but I do not understand this old lady. She is a new type to me."

"I suppose being Scotch does not make much difference," said Clare, discontentedly. "I do not like them much for my part. Is she in want, or can I be of any use to her? I will go and see her in that case—"

"Good heavens!" cried Mr. Fielding, in alarm, "Want! I tell you she is a relation of Perfitt's, and they are all as proud as Lucifer. I almost wonder, Clare," he added more softly, dropping his voice, "that you, who are so proud yourself, should not have more sympathy with the pride of others."

"Others!" cried Clare, with indignation, and then she stopped, and looked at him with her eyes full. If they had not been in the open air in the village street she would have eased herself by a burst of tears. "I am all wrong since Edgar came home," she cried passionately out of the depths of her heart.

"Since Edgar came home? But my dear child—my dear child!" cried Mr. Fielding, "I thought you were so proud of your brother."

"And so I am," said Clare, hastily brushing away the tears. "I know he is good—he is better than me; but he puts me all wrong notwithstanding. He will not see things as I do. His nature is always leading him the other way. He has no sort of feeling—no—Oh! I don't know how to describe it. He puts me all wrong."

"You must not indulge such thoughts," said the Rector, with a certain mild authority which did not misbecome him. "He shows a great deal of right feeling, it appears to me. And we must not discuss Edgar's qualities. He is Edgar, and that is enough."

"You don't need to tell me that," cried Clare, with sudden offence; and then she stopped, and controlled herself. "I should like to go and see this old Scotchwoman," she added, after a moment's pause. What she had said was true, though she was sorry for having said it. Edgar, with his strange ways of thinking, his spontaneousness, and freedom of mind, had put her all wrong. She had been secure and certain in her own system of life so long as everybody thought with her, and the bonds of education and habit were unbroken. But now, though she was still as strong in her Ardenism as ever, an uneasy, half-angry feeling that all the world did not agree with her—nay, that the person of most importance to her in the world did not agree with her—oppressed Clare's mind, and made her wretched. It is hard always to bear such a blow, struck at one's youthful convictions. It is intolerable at first, till the young sufferer learns that other people have really a right to their opinions, and that it is possible to disagree with him or her and yet not be wicked. Clare could not deny that Edgar's different views were maintained with great gentleness and candour towards herself—that they were held by one who was not an evil-minded revolutionary, but in every other respect all that she wished her brother to be. But she felt his eyes upon her when she said and did many little things which a few weeks ago she would have thought most right and natural; and even while she chafed at the tacit disapprobation, a secret self-criticism, which she ignored and struggled against, stole into the recesses of her soul. She would not acknowledge nor allow it to be possible; but yet it was there. The natural consequence was that all her little haughtinesses, her airs of superiority, her distinctions between the Ardens and their class and all the rest of the world, sharpened and became more striking. She was half-conscious that she exaggerated her own opinions, painted the lights whiter and the shadows more profound, in involuntary reaction against the new influences which began to affect her. She had not noticed the Pimpernels, though she knew them well by sight, and all about them; but she had no active feeling of enmity towards them until that unfortunate day when they ventured to call, and Edgar, in his ignorance, received them as if they had been the family of a Duke. Since then Clare had come to hate the innocent people. She had begun to feel rabid about their class generally, and to find words straying to her lips such as had struck her as in very bad taste when old Lady Summerton said them. Lady Summerton believed the poor were a host of impostors, and trades-people an organised band of robbers, and attributed to the nouveaux riches every debasing practice and sentiment. Clare had been disgusted by these opinions in the old days. She had drawn herself up in her youthful dignity, and had almost reproved her senior. "They are good enough sort of people, only they are not of our class," Clare had said; "please don't call them names. One may be a Christian though one is not well-born." Such had been her truly Christian feeling while yet she was undisturbed by any doubt that to be well-born, and especially to be born in Arden, was the highest grace conceded by heaven. But now that doubt had been cast upon this gospel, and that she daily and hourly felt the scepticism in Edgar's eyes, Clare's feelings had become as violent as old Lady Summerton's. The sentiment in her mind was that of scorn and detestation towards the multitude which was struggling to rise into that heaven wherein the Ardens and Thornleighs shone serene. "The poor people" were different; they made no pretences, assumed no equality; but the idea that Alice Pimpernel came under the generic title of young lady exactly as she herself did, and that the daughter of a Liverpool man might ride, and drive, and dress, and go everywhere on the same footing as Clare Arden, became wormwood to her soul.

Mr. Fielding walked along by her side somewhat sadly. He was Clare's godfather, and he was very proud of her. His own nature was far too mild and gentle to be able to understand her vehemence of feeling on these points; but he had been grieved by it often, and had given her soft reproofs, which as yet had produced little effect. His great hope, however, had been in the return of her brother. "Edgar must know the world a little; he will show her better than I can how wrong she is," the gentle Rector had said to himself. But, alas, Edgar had come home, and the result had not been according to his hope. "He is young and impetuous, and he has hurried her convictions," was the comment he made in his grieved mind as he accompanied her along the village street. Mr. Fielding blamed no one as long as he could help it; much less would he blame Clare, who was to him as his own child. He thought within himself that now the only chance for her was Life, that best yet hardest of all teachers. Life would show her how vain were her theories, how harsh her opinions; but then Life itself must be harsh and hard if it is to teach effectual lessons, and it was painful to anticipate any harshness for Clare. He went with her, somewhat drooping and despondent, though the air was sweet with honeysuckle and early roses. The summer was sweet, and so was life, at that blossoming time which the girl had reached; but there were still scorching suns, as well as the winds of autumn and the chills of winter, to come.

Old Sarah had more ways than one of gaining her homely livelihood. The upper floor of her cottage, on which there were two rooms, was furnished out of the remains of some old furniture which an ancient mistress had bequeathed to her; and there at distant intervals the old woman had a lodger, when such visitors came to Arden. They were homely little rooms, low-roofed, and furnished with the taste peculiar to a real cottage, and not in the least like the ideal one; but people in search of health, with small means at their disposal, were very glad to give her the ten or twelve shillings a week, which was all she asked. Down below, in the rooms where Sarah herself lived, she was in the habit of receiving one or two young girls, orphans, or the children of the poorest and least dependable parishioners, to train them to household work and plain sewing. It was Clare's idea, and it had worked very well; but for some time past Clare had neglected her protégées. Edgar's arrival and all the dawning struggles of the new life had occupied and confused her, and she had left her old nurse and her young pupils to themselves. She could scarcely remember as she went in who they were, though Sarah's pupils were known in the parish as Miss Arden's girls. There were two on hand at the present moment in the little kitchen which was Sarah's abode. One stood before a large white-covered table ironing fine linen, while the old nurse sat by in her big chair, spectacles on nose, and a piece of coarse needlework in hand, superintending the process, with many comments, which, added to the heat of the day and the irons, had heightened Mary Smith's complexion to a brilliant crimson. The other sat working in the shady background, the object of Mary's intensest envy, unremarked and unreproved. It was the unfortunate clear-starcher who had to make her bob to the gentlefolks, and called forth Miss Arden's questions. "I hope she is a good girl," Clare said, looking at Mary, who stood curtseying and hot, with the iron in her hand. "She is none so good but she might be better, Miss Clare," said old Sarah; "I don't know none o' them as is; but she do come on in her ironing. As for collars and cuffs and them plain things, I trust her by herself."

"I am very glad to hear it," said Clare, "and I hope Jane is as satisfactory; but we have not time to talk about them to-day. Mr. Fielding says you have a new lodger, whom he wishes me to go and see. Is she upstairs? Is she at home? Does she like the place? And tell me what sort of person she is, for I am going to see her now."

Sarah got up from her chair with a bewildered look, and took off her spectacles, which she always did in emergencies. "I beg your pardon, Miss Clare," she said with a curtsey, "but—She ain't not to say a poor person. I don't know as she'd—be pleased—Not as your visit, Miss, ain't a compliment; but—"

"The Scotch are very proud," said Mr. Fielding, in his most deprecating tone; "they are dreadfully independent, and like their own way. And, besides, she does not want anything of us. She is not, as Sarah says, a poor person. I think, perhaps, another day—"

"Then why did you bring me here to see her?" said Clare, with some reason. Was it to read her a practical lesson—to show her that she was no longer queen in Arden? A flush of hasty anger came to her pale cheek.

"I only meant—" Mr. Fielding began; "all that I intended was—Why, here is Edgar! and Mr. Perfitt with him. About business, I suppose, as you two are going together. My dear boy, I am so glad you are taking to your work."

"We have been half over the estate," said Edgar, coming in, and putting down his hat on Mary Smith's ironing table, while she stood and gaped at him, forgetting her curtsey in the awe of so close an approach to the young Squire; "but Perfitt has some one to visit here, and I have come to see Sarah, which is not work, but pleasure. I did not expect to find you all. Perfitt, go and see your friend; never mind me. Oh, I beg your pardon," said Edgar, standing suddenly aside. They all looked up for the moment with a little start, and yet there was nothing to startle them. It was only Sarah's Scotch lodger, Mr. Perfitt's relative, who had come into the little room.

CHAPTER XIII

She was a woman of about sixty, with very dark eyes and very white hair—a tall woman, quite unbent by the weight of her years, and unshaken by anything she could have met with in them; and yet she did not look as if she had encountered little, or found life an easy passage from the one unknown to the skirts of the other. She did not look younger than her age, and yet there was no sentiment of age about her. She was not the kind of woman of whom one says that they have been beautiful, or have been pretty. She had perhaps never been either one or the other; but all that she had ever been, or more, she was now. Her eyes were still perfectly clear and bright, and they had depths in them which could never have belonged to them in youth. The outline of her face was not the round and perfect outline which belongs to the young, but every wrinkle had its meaning. It was not mere years of which they spoke, but of many experiences, varied knowledge, deep acquaintance with that hardest of all sciences—life. Not a trace of its original colour belonged to the hair—slightly rippled, with an irregularity which gave a strange impression of life and vigour to it—which appeared under her cap. The cap was dead white too, tied under her chin with a solid bow of white ribbon; and this mass of whiteness brought out the pure tints of her face like a picture. These tints had deepened a little in tone from the red and white of youth, but were as clear as a child's complexion of lilies and roses. The slight shades of brown did but mellow the countenance, as it does in so many painted faces. The eyes were full of energy and animation, not like the eyes of a spectator, but of one accustomed to do and to struggle—acting, not looking on. The whole party assembled in old Sarah's living-room turned round and looked at her as she came in, and there was not one who did not feel abashed when they became conscious that for a moment this inspection was not quite respectful to the stranger. So far as real individuality and personal importance went, she was a more notable personage than any one of them. The Rector, who was the nearest to her in age, drew a little aside from before the clear eyes of this old woman. He had been a quiet man, harboured from all the storms, or almost all the storms of existence; but here was one who had gone through them all. As for Edgar, there was something in her looks which won his heart in a moment. He went up to her with his natural frankness, while the others stood looking on doubtfully. "I am sure it is you whom Perfitt has been talking to me about," he said. "I hope you like Arden. I hope your granddaughter is better. And I trust you will tell Perfitt if there is anything than can be done to make you more comfortable; my sister and I will be too glad—"

Here Clare stepped forward, feeling that she must not permit herself to be committed. "I am sure Sarah will do her very best to make you comfortable," she said, with great distinctness, not hurrying over her words, as Edgar did—and not disposed to permit any vague large promises to be made in her name. She was not particularly anxious about the stranger's comfort; but Edgar was hasty, and would always have his way.

"I am much obliged to ye both," said the newcomer, her strong yet soft Scotch voice, with its broad vowels, sounding large and ample, like her person. She gave but one glance at Clare, but her eyes dwelt upon Edgar with curious interest and eagerness. No one else in the place seemed to attract her as he did. She returned the touch of his hand with a vigorous clasp, which startled even him. "I hear ye're but late come hame," she said, in a deep melodious tone, lingering upon the words.

"Yes," said Edgar, somewhat surprised by her air of interest. "I am almost as much a stranger here as you are. Perfitt tells me you have come from the hills. I hope Arden will agree with the little girl."

"Is there some one ill?" said Clare.

"My granddaughter," said the stranger, "but no just a little girl—little enough, poor thing—the weakliest I ever trained; but she's been seventeen years in this world—a weary world to her. Her life is a thread. I cannot tell where she got her weakness from—no from my side."

"Na; not from your side," echoed Perfitt, who had been standing behind. "But Mr. Arden has other things ado than listen to our clavers about our family. I'll go with you, with his leave, up the stair."

"Has Dr. Somers been to see her?" said Clare. "If she is Mr Perfitt's relation, perhaps we could be of some use; some jelly perhaps, or fruit—"

"I am much obliged to the young lady, but I'll not trouble anybody," was the answer. "Thank ye all. If I might ask the liberty, when Jeanie is able, of a walk about your park—"

She had turned to Edgar again, upon whom her eyes dwelt with growing interest. Even Mr. Fielding thought it strange. "If she wants anything, surely I am the fit person to help her," Clare could not help saying within herself. But it was Edgar to whom the stranger turned. He, too, was a little surprised by her look. "The park is open to everybody" he said; "that is no favour. But if you would like to go through the gardens and the private grounds—or even the house—Perfitt, you can arrange all that. And perhaps you might speak to the gardener, Clare?"

"Whatever you wish, Edgar," said his sister, turning away. She was displeased. It was she who ought naturally to have been appealed to, and she was left out. But the new-comer evidently was honestly oblivious of Clare's very presence. She had no intention of disrespect to the young lady, or of neglecting her claims; but she forgot her simply, being fascinated by her brother. It was him whom she thanked with concise and reserved words, but a certain strange fulness of tone and expression. And then she made the party a little bow, which took in the whole, and turned and led the way up the narrow cottage stair—Perfitt following her—leaving them all considerably puzzled, and more moved than Clare would have allowed to be possible. "If this is your Scotchwoman," she said, turning to the Rector, "I don't wonder you found her original;" and Clare went hastily out of the cottage, without a word to Sarah, followed by the gentlemen, who did not know what to say.

"Listen to her story before you begin to dislike her," said Edgar. "Perfitt told me as we came along. It appears she had her daughter's family thrown on her hands a great many years ago. She has a little farm in Scotland somewhere, and manages it herself. When these children came to her, she set to work as if she had been six men. She has brought up and educated every one of them,—not to be ploughmen, as you would think—but educated them in the Scotch way; one is a doctor, another a clergyman, and so on. If you don't respect a woman like that, I do. Perfitt says she never flinched nor complained, but went at her work like a hero. And this is a granddaughter of another family whom she has taken charge of in the same way."

"I felt sure she was something remarkable," said Mr. Fielding, "I told Clare I had never seen any one quite like her; now, didn't I? Scotch, you know—very Scotch; but to me a new type."

"I think I prefer the old type," said Clare, with a feeling of opposition, which she herself scarcely understood; "one knows what to do with them; and then they are civil, at least. I am going to see some now," and she turned back suddenly, waving her hand to her companions, and went on past Sarah's cottage to pay her visits. The people she was going to see were quite of the old type. They had no susceptibilities to menagér, no over-delicate feelings to be studied. They were ready to accept all that could be procured, and to ask for more. Clare knew, when she entered these cottages, that she was about to hear a long list of wants, and to have it made apparent to her that the comfort, and health, and happiness of her pensioners was entirely in her hands. It was more flattering than the independence of the stranger, who wanted nothing; but yet the contrast confused the mind of the girl, who had never had anything of the kind made so clearly apparent to her before. One of her old women had an orphan granddaughter too; but her complaints were many of the responsibility this threw upon her, and the trouble she had in keeping her charge in order. "Them young lasses, they eats and they drinks, and they're never done; when a cup o' tea would serve me, there's a cooking and a messing for Lizzy; and out o' evenings when I just want her; and every penny a going for nonsense. At my time o' life, Miss, it ain't bother as one wants; it's quiet as does best for ou'd folks."

"But she has nobody to take care of her except you," said Clare, pondering her new lesson.

"Eh, Miss! They ben't good for nothing for taking care o' young ones ben't ou'd folks."

Clare turned away with a little disgust. She promised to supply all the wants that had been indicated to her, and they were many. But she did it with less than her usual kindness, and a sensation of indignation in her mind. How different was this servile dependence and denial of all individual responsibility from the story she had just heard! She was wrong, as was natural; for the old egotist was in reality very fond of her Lizzy, and only made use of her name in order to derive a more plentiful supply from the open hand of the young lady. Had there been no young lady to depend on, probably old Betty would have made no complaint, but done her best, and grudged nothing she had to her grandchild. Clare, however, was too young and inexperienced in human kind to know that what is bad often comes uppermost, concealing the good, and that there are quantities of people who always show their worst, not their best, face to the world. She went away in suppressed discontent, revolving in her mind without knowing it those questions of social philosophy with which every alms-giver must more or less come in contact. It was right for the Ardens, as lords of the manor, to watch over their dependents; of that there could be no doubt. Clare would have felt, as one might imagine a benevolent slaveholder to feel, had there been any destitution or unrelieved misery in her village: but the question had never occurred to her whether it was good for the people to be so watched over and taken care of? Supposing, for instance, such a case as that of Mr. Perfitt's relative, Sarah's lodger. Was it best for a woman in such circumstances to toil and strive, and deny herself all ease and pleasure, and bring up the children thus cast upon her with the sweat of her brow, according to that primeval curse or blessing which was not laid upon woman? Or would it be better to appeal to others, and make interest, and establish the helpless beings in orphan schools and benevolent institutions? The last was the plan which Clare had been chiefly cognisant of. When any one died in the village, it had been her wont to bestir herself instantly about their children, as if the responsibility was not upon the widow or the relatives, but upon her. She had disposed of them in all sorts of places—here one, and there another; and she had found, in most cases, that the villagers were but too willing to transfer their burdens to the young shoulders which were so ready to undertake them. But was that the best? If Edgar had enunciated this new doctrine in words, no doubt she would have combated it with all her might, and would have been very eloquent about the duties of property and the bond between superiors and inferiors. But Edgar had not said a word on the subject, probably had not thought at all about it. He was as liberal as she was, even lavish in his bounty, ready to give to anybody or everybody. He had said nothing on the subject; but he had told the story of that strange new-comer, who was (surely) so out of place, so unlike everything else in the little Arden world.

Clare passed by Sarah's house again as the thoughts went through her mind. The window of the upper room was a broad lattice window with diamond panes, half concealed by honeysuckles, which were not in very good trim, but waved their long branches in sweet disorder over the half-red half-white wall, where the original bricks, all stained with lichens, peered through the whitewash. The casement was open, and against it leaned a little figure, the sight of which sent a thrill through the young lady's heart. The face looked very young, and was surrounded by softly curling masses of hair, of that ruddy golden hue which is so often to be seen in children's hair in Scotland, and which is almost always accompanied by the sweetest purity of complexion. It was a lovely face, like an angel's, with something of the half-divine abstraction about it of Raphael's angel children. She had never seen anything so strangely visionary, fair, and wild, like something from another world. Clare stood still and gazed, forgetting everything but this strange beautiful vision. The stranger's eyes were turned towards Arden, to the great banks of foliage which stood up against the sky, hiding the house within their depths. What was she thinking of? whom was she looking for? or was she thinking of, looking for no one, abstracted in some dream? Clare's heart began to beat as she stood unconscious and gazed. She was brought back to herself and to the ordinary rules of life by seeing that the old woman had come to the window, and was looking down upon her with equal earnestness. Then she went on with a little start, trembling, she could not tell why. Was it a child or a woman she had seen? and why had she come here?

CHAPTER XIV

The next day after these events occurred the dinner at the Pimpernels. Miss Arden had made no further allusion to it in her brother's presence. He had said he would stay away if she exacted it, but Clare was much too proud to exact. She stood aside, and let him have his will. She was even so amiable as to fasten a sprig of myrtle in his coat when he came to bid her good night. "That is very sweet of you, as you don't approve of me," he said, kissing the white hand that performed this little sisterly office. They were two orphans, alone in the world, and Edgar's heart expanded over his sister, notwithstanding the many doubts and difficulties which he was aware he had occasioned her.

"Why should I disapprove?" she said. "You are a man; you are not so easily affected as a girl; but only please remember, Edgar, they are not people that it would be nice for you to see much of. They are not like us."

"Not like you, certainly," said light-hearted Edgar. "I rather liked to see you, do you know, beside them; you looked like a young queen."

Clare was pleased, though she did not care to confess it. "It does not require much to make one look like a queen beside that good, fat Mrs. Pimpernel," she said, with more charity than she had ever before felt towards her recent visitors. "If you are not very late, Edgar, perhaps I shall see you when you come home."

And she watched him as he drove his dogcart down the avenue with a less anxious mind. "He is not like an Arden," she said to herself; "but yet one could not but remark him wherever he went. He has so much heart and spirit about him; and I think he is clever. He knows a great deal more than most people, though that does not matter much. But still I think perhaps he would not be so easily carried away after all."

Edgar, for his part, went away in very good spirits. He liked the rapid sense of motion, the light vehicle, the fine horse, the swiftness which was almost flight. He rather liked making a dive out of the formal world which had absorbed him, into another hemisphere; and he even liked, which would have vexed Clare had she known it, to be alone. He would not suffer himself to think so, for it seemed ungrateful, unbrotherly, unkind; but still a man cannot get over all the habits of his life in three weeks, and it was a pleasure to him to be alone. He seemed to have thrown off the burden of his responsibilities as he swept through the village and along the rural road to the Red House. He expected to be amused, and he was pleased that in his amusement he would be subject to no criticism. Criticism is very uncomfortable, especially when it comes from your nearest and dearest. To feel in your freest moments that an eye is upon you, that your proceedings are subject to lively comment, is always trying. And Edgar had not been used to it. Thanks to the sweetest temper in the world, he took it very well on the whole. But this night he certainly did feel the happier that he was free. The Pimpernels greeted him with a cordiality that was almost overpowering. The father shook both his hands, the mother pounced upon him and introduced him to a dozen people in a moment, and as for poor Alice, she blushed, and smiled, and buttoned her gloves, which was her usual occupation. When the business of the introduction was over Edgar fell back out of the principal place, and took a passing note of the guests. A dozen names had been said to him, but not one had he made out, except that of Lord Newmarch, who was a tall, spare young man in spectacles, with a thin intellectual face. There were two men of Mr Pimpernel's stamp, with vast white waistcoats, and heads slightly bald—men very well known upon 'Change, and holding the best of reputations in Liverpool—with two wives, who were ample and benign, like the mistress of the house; and there were two or three men in a corner, with Oxford written all over them, curiously looking out through spectacles, or as it were out of mists, at the other part of the company. Lord Newmarch did not attach himself to either of these parties. It was not very long indeed since he had been an Oxford man himself, but he was now a politician, and had emerged from the academical state.

There was one other among the guests who attracted Edgar's attention, he could not tell why—a tall man about ten years older than himself, with black hair, just touched in some places with grey, and deep-set dark-blue eyes, which shone like a bit of frosty sky out of his dark bearded face. The face was familiar to him, though he felt sure he had never seen this individual man before; and though he kept himself in the background there was an air about him which Edgar recognised by instinct. Among the old merchants and the young Dons—men limited on one hand within a very material universe, and on the other by the still straiter limitations of a purely intellectual sphere—this man looked, what he was, a man of the world. Edgar came to this conclusion instinctively, feeling himself drawn by an interest which was only half sympathy to the only individual in the party who deserved that name. Chance or Mrs. Pimpernel arranged it so that this man was placed at the opposite end of the table at dinner, quite out of Edgar's reach. Mr. Arden of Arden had to conduct one of the most important ladies present to dinner, and was within reach of Mrs. Pimpernel with Alice on his other hand; but the stranger who interested him was at the foot of the table, being evidently a person of no importance. It was only Edgar's second English party, and certainly at this moment it was not nearly so pleasant as the dinner at Thorne, with pretty Gussy telling him everything. Mrs. Buxton, who sat between him and Lord Newmarch, was too anxious to attend to her noble neighbour's conversation to give very much attention to Edgar. Now and then she turned to him indeed, and was very affable; but her subject was still Newmarch, and they were too near to that personage to make the discussion agreeable. "You should hear Lord Newmarch on the education question," the lady said; "his ideas are so clear, and then they are so charmingly expressed. I consider his style admirable. You don't know it? How very strange, Mr. Arden! He contributes a good deal to the Edinburgh. I thought of course you must have been acquainted with his works."

"I never read any of them," said Edgar; and I trust I never shall, he felt he should have liked to have said; but he only added instead, "I have spent all my time wandering to and fro over the face of the earth, which leaves one in the depths of ignorance of everything one ought to know."

"Oh, do you think so?" said Mrs. Buxton. "For my part, I think there is nothing like travelling for expanding the mind. Lord Newmarch published a charming book of travels last year—From Turnstall to Teneriffe. Turnstall is one of his family places, you know. It made quite a commotion in the literary world. I do think he is one of the most rising young men of the age."

"Do you admire Lord Newmarch very much?" Edgar whispered to Alice, who was eating her fish very sedately by his side. Poor Alice grew very red, and gave a little choking cough, and put down her fork, and cleared her throat. She looked as if she had been caught doing something which was very improper, and dropped her fork as if it burned her. And it was a moment before she could speak. "Oh yes, Mr. Arden," was the reply she made, giving a shy glance at him, and then looking down upon her plate.

"But don't you think he looks a little too much as if the fate of the country rested on his head?" said Edgar, valiantly trying again. "Tell me, please, is he a bore?"

"Oh no, Mr. Arden!" said Alice, and she looked at her plate again. "Does she want to finish her fish, I wonder?" Edgar asked himself; and then he turned to Mrs. Buxton, to leave his younger companion at liberty. But Mrs. Buxton had tackled Lord Newmarch, and they were discussing the question of compulsory education, with much authoritative condescension on the gentleman's part, and eager interest on the lady's. Edgar was not uninterested in such questions, but he had come to the Red House with a light-hearted intention of amusing himself, and he sighed for Gussy Thornleigh and her gossip, or anything that should be pleasant and nonsensical. Alice had returned to her fish, not that she cared for the fish, but because it was the only thing for her to do. If Edgar had but known it, she was quite disposed to go on saying, "Oh yes, Mr. Arden," and "Oh no, Mr. Arden," all the time of dinner, without caring in the least for the entrees, or even for the jellies and creams and other dainties with which the banquet wound up. But then he did not know that, and could not but imagine that her fish was what she liked best.

In his despair, however, he caught Mrs. Pimpernel's eye, who was looking bland but disturbed, saying "There is no doubt of that," and "Education is very necessary," and "I am sure I am quite of Lord Newmarch's opinion," at intervals. She was amiable, but she was not happy with that wise young nobleman at her right hand, and such an appreciative audience as Mrs. Buxton beside him. Edgar glanced across at her, and caught her look of distress. "I do not care anything about education," he said, firing a friendly gun, as it were, across her bows. "I hate it when I am at dinner." And then Mrs. Pimpernel gave him a look which said more than words.

"Oh, fie," she said, leaning across the corner, "you know you should not say that. Do you think we English are behind in light conversation, Mr. Arden? For more important matters I know we can defy anybody," and she gave Lord Newmarch an eloquent look, which he returned with a little bow; "but I daresay," said Mrs. Pimpernel, with that cloud of uneasiness on her brow, "we are behind in chitter-chatter and table-talk."

"I like chitter-chatter," said Edgar; "and besides, I want to know who the people are. Who is that pretty girl on Mr. Pimpernel's left hand? You must recollect I know nobody, and am quite a stranger in my own place."

"Oh, Mr. Arden, that is Miss Molyneaux, Mrs. Molyneaux's eldest daughter," said the gracious hostess, indicating the lady on her left hand, who smiled and coloured, and looked at Edgar with friendly eyes. "She is pretty—such a complexion and teeth! Did you notice her teeth, Mr. Arden? They are like pearls. My Alice has nice teeth, but I always say they are nothing to compare to Mary Molyneaux's. And that's Mr. Arden, your namesake, beside her. He is considered a very handsome man."

"Do you approve of personal gossip, Mr. Arden?" said Mrs. Buxton, breaking in; but Edgar was too much interested to be stopped, even by motives of civility.

"Mr. Arden, my namesake! Then that explains it." He said these last words, not aloud, but within himself, for now he could see that the face which this man's face recalled to him was that of his own sister, Clare. It gave him the most curious sensation, moving him almost to anger. A stranger whom he knew nothing of, who was nothing to him, to resemble Clare! It looked like profanity, desecration. After all, there was something evidently in the Arden blood—something entirely wanting to himself—a secret influence—which he, the first of the name, did not share.

"Not only your namesake," said Lord Newmarch, in his thin voice, much to Mrs. Buxton's disgust. The young lord was very philosophical, and full to overflowing with questions of political importance, and the progress of the world, and all the knowledge of the nineteenth century; but still he was patrician born, and could not resist a genealogical question. "Not only your namesake. He is old Arthur Arden's son, who was your father's first cousin. He is the nearest relative you have except your sister; and, as long as you don't have sons of your own, he is the next heir."

"Ah!" said Edgar, as if he had sustained a blow. He could not explain how it was that he received the information thus. Why should he object to Arthur Arden, or be anything but pleased to see the next in the succession—the man who, of all the men in the world, should be most interesting to him? "The same blood runs in our veins," he tried to say to himself, and gazed down curiously at the end of the table, raising thereby a little pleasurable excitement in the bosom of Mrs. Molyneaux, who sat opposite to him. "He is struck with my Mary," the mother thought; and Edgar was so good a match that it was no wonder she was moved a little. Fortunately, Mary knew nothing about it, but sat by the other Arden, and chattered as much as Gussy Thornleigh had done, and could not help thinking what a pity it was so handsome a man, and one so like the family, should not be the true heir. "I have been over Arden Hall, and you are so like the portraits," Mary Molyneaux was saying at that very moment, while Lord Newmarch explained who her companion was to Edgar. "The present Mr. Arden is not a bit like them. I can't help feeling as if you must be the rightful Squire."

"I have got only the complexion, and not the lands," said Mr. Arthur Arden. "It is a poor exchange. And this is the first time I ever saw my cousin. He does not know me from Adam. We are not a very friendly race; but I know Clare."

"Oh, Miss Arden? Don't you think she is quite beautiful—but awfully proud?" said the girl. "She will not know the Pimpernels; though all the best people have called on them, she will never call. Don't you think it is horrid for a girl to be so proud?"

"She has the family spirit," said her kinsman, with a look which Mary, in her innocence, did not comprehend. The talk at the table at Thorne was more amusing, but perhaps there was a deeper interest in what was then going on at the Red House.

CHAPTER XV

It was impossible for Edgar not to look with interest upon this other Arden, who was so like his family, so like his own sister, with the very same air about him which the portraits had, and in which the young man felt he was himself so strangely wanting. Perhaps if Gussy Thornleigh had been by his side, or even that pretty Miss Molyneaux, who was entertaining his unknown relation, his eyes and thoughts would not have been so persistently drawn that way. But between Alice Pimpernel, who said, "Oh no, Mr. Arden," and "Oh yes, Mr. Arden," and Mrs. Buxton, who was collecting the pearls which dropped from the lips of Lord Newmarch, the dinner was not lively to him; and he caught from the other end of the table tones of that voice which somehow sounded familiar, and turns of the head full of that vague family resemblance which goes so far in a race, and which recalled to him not only his sister whom he loved, but his father whom he did not love. How strange it was that he should have been so entirely passed over amid all those family links that bound the others together! It proves, Edgar said to himself, that it is not blood that does it, but only association, education, the impressions made upon the mind at its most susceptible age. He reasoned thus with himself, but did not find the reasoning quite satisfactory, and could not but feel a mingled attraction and repulsion to the stranger who was his nearest relation, his successor if he died, and surely ought to be his friend while he lived. When the ladies left the room, and the others drew closer round the table, he could no longer resist the impulse that moved him. It was true that Clare had expressed anything but friendly feelings for this unknown cousin; but anyhow, were he bad or good, it was Edgar's duty, as the chief of the family, to know its branches. It did not seem to him even that it was right or natural to ask for any introduction. After a little hesitation he changed his place, and took the chair by Arthur Arden's side. "They tell me you are of my family," he said, "and your face makes me sure of it—in which case, I suppose, we are each other's nearest relations, at least on the Arden side."

The landless cousin paused for a moment before he replied to the young Squire. He looked him all over with something which might have seemed insolence had Edgar's nature led him to expect evil. "I suppose, of course, you are my cousin the Squire," he said, carelessly, "though I certainly should never have made you out to be an Arden by your face."

"No; I am like my mother they tell me," said Edgar; but for the first time in his life he reddened at that long understood and acknowledged fact. There was nothing said that insulted him, but there was an inference which he did not understand, which yet penetrated him like a dagger. It was unendurable, though he had no comprehension what it meant.

"I never knew rightly who Mrs. Arden was," said Arthur; "a foreigner, I believe, or at least a stranger to the county. I don't think I should like my eldest son to be so unlike me if I were a married man."

"Mr. Arden, I don't pretend to understand your meaning; but if you wish to be offensive perhaps our acquaintance had better end at once," said Edgar, "I have no desire to quarrel with my heir."

Another pause followed, during which the dark countenance of the other Arden fluctuated for a moment between darkness and light. Then it suddenly brightened all over with that smile for which the Ardens were famous. "Your heir!" he said. "You are half a lifetime younger than I am, and much more likely to be my heir—if I had anything to leave. And I don't want to be offensive. I am a bitter beggar; I can't help myself. If you were as poor as I am, and saw a healthy boy cutting you out of everything—land, money, consideration, life—"

"Don't say so," cried open-hearted Edgar, forgetting his offence; "on the contrary, if I can do anything to make life more tolerable—more agreeable—I am just as likely to die as any one," he continued, with a half comic sense that this must be consolatory to his new acquaintance; "and I have my sister to think of, who in that case would want a friend. Why should not we be of mutual use to each other? I now; you perhaps hereafter—"

"By Jove!" cried the other, looking at him keenly. And then he drank off a large glass of claret, as if he required the strength it would give. "You are the strangest fellow I ever met."

"I don't think so," said Edgar, laughing. "Nothing so remarkable; but I hope we shall know each other better before long. There is not much attraction just now in the country, but in September, if you will come to Arden—"

"Do you know Miss Arden can't bear me?" said his new friend.

"Can't bear you!" Edgar faltered as he spoke—for as soon as his unwary lips had uttered the invitation he remembered what Clare had said.

"Yes; your sister hates me," said Arthur Arden. "I cannot tell why, I am sure. I suppose because my father and yours fought like cat and dog—or like near relations if you choose, which answers quite as well. I am not at all sure that he did not send you abroad to be out of our way. He believed us capable of poisoning you—or—any other atrocity," he added, with a little harsh laugh.

"And are you?" said Edgar, laughing too, though with no great heart.

"I don't think I shall try," said his new kinsman. "My father is dead, and one is less courageous than two. By Jove! just think what a difference it would make. Here am I, a poor wretch, living from hand to mouth, not knowing one year where my next year's living is to come from, or sometimes where my next dinner is to come from, for that matter. If ever one man had an inducement to hate another, you may imagine it is I."

This grim talk was not amusing to Edgar, as may be supposed; but, as his companion spoke with perfect composure, he received it with equal calm, though not without a secret shudder in his heart. "I think we might arrange better than that," he said. "We have time to talk it over later; but, in my opinion, the head of a family has duties. It sounds almost impertinent to call myself the head of the family to you, who are older, and probably know much more about it; but—"

"You are so," said Arthur Arden, "and fact is incapable of impertinence. Talking of the country having no attractions, I should rather like to try a June at Arden. I suppose you bucolics think that the best of the year, don't you? roses, and all that sort of thing. And I happen to have heaps of invitations for September, and not much appetite for town at the present moment. If it suits you, and your sister Clare does not object too strenuously, I'll go with you now."

This sudden and unexpected acceptance of his invitation filled Edgar with dismay. September was a totally different affair. In September there would be various visitors, and one individual whom she disliked need not be oppressive to Clare. But now, while they were alone, and while yet all the novelty of his situation was fresh upon Edgar, nothing, he felt, could be more inappropriate. Arthur Arden swayed himself upon his chair, leaving one arm over the back, with careless ease, while his cousin, suddenly brought to a stand-still, tried to collect himself, and decide what it was best to do. "Ah, I see," Arthur said, after a pause, still with the same carelessness, "I bore you. You were not prepared for anything so prompt on my part; and Madam Clare—"

"I cannot allow my sister's name to be mentioned," cried Edgar angrily, "except with respect."

"Good heavens, how could I name her with greater respect? If I said Madam Arden, which is the proper traditionary title, you would think I meant your grandmother. I say Madam Clare, because my cousin is the lady of the parish: I will say Queen Clare, if you please: it comes to about the same thing in our family, as I suppose you know."

"As I suppose you don't know," was in this arrogant Arden's tone; but it was lost upon Edgar, whose mind was busy about the problem how he could manage between Arthur's necessities and Clare's dislike. The party was in motion by this time to join the ladies, and Lord Newmarch came up to the two Ardens in the momentary breaking up.

"I want very much to see more of you," he said, addressing himself to Edgar. "I see you two cousins have made acquaintance, so I need not volunteer my services; but I am very anxious to see more of you. I daresay there are many things in the county and in the country which you will find a little puzzling after living so long abroad; and I hope to get a great deal of information from you about Continental politics. My father is in town, so I cannot ask you to Marchfield, as I should like to do; indeed, I am only off duty for a week on account of this great social assembly in Liverpool. How shall I manage to see a little of you? I go back to Liverpool with the Buxtons to-night."

"I cannot promise to go to Liverpool," said Edgar; "but if you could come to us at Arden—"

"That would be the very thing," said the young politician, "the very thing. I could spare you from the 1st to the 5th. I must be back in town before the 7th for the Irish debate. My father has Irish property, and of course we poor slaves have to come up to the scratch; though, as for justice to Ireland, you know, Arden—"

"I fear I don't know much about it; shall we join the ladies?" said Edgar, a little confused by finding his hospitality so readily embraced.

"I shall be very happy to give you the benefit of my experience," said Lord Newmarch; "there are some things on which it is necessary a young landed proprietor should have an opinion of his own. Yes, by all means, let us go upstairs. There is a great deal in the present state of the country that I should be glad to talk to you about. We have become frightfully empirical of late; whether the Government is Whig or whether it is Tory, it seems a condition of existence that it should try experiments upon the people; we are always meddling with one thing or another—state of the representation—education—management of the poor—"

Such were the words that came to Arthur Arden's ears as his cousin disappeared out of the dining-room under the wing of Lord Newmarch, being preached to all the way. The kinsman, who was a fashionable vagabond, looked after them with a smile which very much resembled a sneer. "Thank heaven, I am nobody," he said to himself, half aloud. He was the last in the room, and no one cared whether he appeared late or early in Mrs. Pimpernel's fine drawing-room; no one except, perhaps, one or two young ladies, who thought "poor Mr. Arden" very handsome and agreeable, but knew he was a man who could never be married, and must not even be flirted with overmuch. If he was bitter at such moments, it was not much to be wondered at. He was more mature, and much better able to give an opinion than Edgar, better educated, perhaps a more able man by nature; but Edgar had the family acres, and therefore it was to him that the politician addressed himself, and whom everybody distinguished. Arthur Arden persuaded himself, as he went his way after the others to the drawing-room, that it was almost a good bargain to be quit of Lord Newmarch and his tribe, even at the price of being quit of land and living at the same time; but the attempt was rather a failure. He would have appreciated political power, which Edgar was too ignorant to care for; he would have appreciated money, which Edgar evidently meant to throw away, in his capacity of head of the family, on poor relations and other unnecessary adjuncts. What a strange mistake of Providence it was! "He would have made a capital shopkeeper, or clerk, or something," the elder Arden said to himself, "whereas I—; but, at all events, we shall see what effect his proceedings will have upon saucy Clare."

CHAPTER XVI

It would be difficult to imagine anything more uncomfortable than were Edgar's feelings as he drove home that evening. He had tried with much simplicity to avoid his kinsman Arden, thinking, in his inexperience, that if he did not repeat his invitation, or if no further conversation took place between them as to that visit in June, that the other would take it for granted, as he himself would have been quick to do, that such a visit was undesirable. Edgar, however, had reckoned without his guest, who was not a man to let any such trifling scruples stand in the way of his personal comfort. He was on the lawn with some of the other gentlemen when Edgar got into his dogcart, and shouted to him quickly, "I shall see you in a few days," as he drove past. Here was a pleasant piece of news to take back to Clare. And Lord Newmarch was coming, who, though a stranger to himself, was none to his sister, and might possibly be, for anything Edgar knew, as distasteful to her as Arthur Arden himself. He laughed at his own discomfiture, but still was discomfited; for indifference to the feelings of anybody connected with him was an impossibility to the young man. "Of course, I am master, as people say," he suggested to himself, with the most whimsical sense of the absurdity of such a notion. Master—in order to please other people. Such was the natural meaning of the term according to all the laws of interpretation known to him. It was Clare who was queen at the present moment of her brother's heart and household; but even if there had been no Clare, Edgar would still have been trying to please somebody—to defer his own wishes to another's pleasure, by instinct, as nature compelled him. It is a disposition which gives its possessor a great deal of trouble, but at least it is not a common one. And the curious thing was that he did not blame Arthur Arden for pushing his society upon him, as anybody else would have done. It was weakness on his own part, not selfishness on that of his kinsman. Had he been driven to reason on the subject, Edgar would have indeed manifested to you clearly how his own yielding temper was the greatest of sins, as tempting others to be selfish. "Of course it is my own fault" had been his theory all his life.

But he was very uncomfortable about it in this case. Up to this time, when he had been injudiciously amiable he alone had been the sufferer; but now it was Clare who must bear the brunt. When he reached the village he threw the reins to the groom, and jumped out of the dogcart. "If Miss Arden is downstairs let her know that I have gone for an hour's chat to Dr. Somers'," he said; and so started on, with his cigar, in the moonlight, feeling the stillness and solitude a relief to him. How free his old life had been! and yet he had felt himself wronged and injured to be left in enjoyment of so much freedom. Now he was hampered enough, surrounded by duties and responsibilities which he understood but dimly, with one of those terrible domestic critics by his side who had the power which only love has to wound him, and who subjected him to that terrible standard of family perfection which in his youth he had known nothing of, and the rules of which even now he did not recognise. Edgar sighed, and took his cigar from his lips, and looked at it as if he expected the kind spirit of that soothing plant to step forth and counsel him; but receiving no revelation, sighed and put it back again, and thrust his hands into his pockets, and passed along the silent village street with his disturbed thoughts. All was silent in Arden: the doors closed which stood open all day long, and only here and there a faint light twinkling. One in John Horsfall's cottage, in the little room where Lizzie, his eldest daughter, was dying of consumption; one in old Simon the clerk's window, downstairs, where his harsh-tempered but conscientious Sally was busy with the needlework which she did, as all Arden knew, "for the shop." "The shop" meant a certain famous place for baby-linen in Liverpool, which demanded exquisite work—and Sally alone of all the neighbourhood was honoured with its commissions. In her aunt Sarah's cottage, next door, the upper window showed a faint illumination, and stood open. These were all the signs of life which were visible in Arden. The old people, and the hard-working out-door people who began the day at five in the morning, were all safe in bed, enjoying their well-won repose. The moon was shining brightly, with all the soft splendour of the summer—shining over Arden woods, which looked black under her silver, and making the little street, with its white lines of broken pavement before each door, as bright as day. Edgar's footsteps rang upon the stones as he crossed those little strips of white one by one. The sound broke the silent awe and mystery of the night, and with his usual sympathetic feeling he did his best to restrain it. He had thrown away his cigar, and had taken off his hat to refresh himself with the cool sweet air, when he heard a cry from the window above. It was the window of old Sarah's Scotch lodger. He looked up eagerly, for her aspect had awakened some curiosity in his mind. But what he saw was a little white figure leaning out so far that its balance seemed doubtful, spreading out its hands, he thought, towards himself as he stood looking up. "My Willie! my Willie!" cried the voice; "is it you at last? Oh, he's here, he's here, whatever you may say. Willie! Willie! How could he rest in his grave, and me pining here?"

Edgar rushed forward in the wildest alarm. The little creature leaned over the window-sill, with arms stretched out, and hair streaming about her, till he felt that any moment she might be dashed upon the pavement below. The cry of "Willie!" rang into the stillness with a wild sweetness which went to the listener's heart. It sounded like the very voice of despair. "Take care, for God's sake," he cried, instinctively rushing into the little garden below the window and holding out his arms to catch her should she fall. Just then, however, she was caught from behind. The grandmother's face looked suddenly out, ghastly pale and stern in its emotion. "I have her safe, sir, thanks to you," said the serious

Scotch voice, every word of which sounded to Edgar like a chord in music full of a hundred mingled modulations. "Willie, my Willie!" cried the younger voice, rising wilder and shriller; and then there followed a momentary rustle, as of a slight struggle, and then the sharp decisive closing of the window. He could see nothing more. But it was not possible to pass on calmly after such an incident. After a moment's indecision, Edgar tapped lightly at old Sarah's window, which was dark. The sounds upstairs died into a distant murmur of voices, and downstairs all was still. Old Sarah, if she heard, took no notice of his summons; but young Sarah, her niece, who was working in the next cottage, roused herself and came to the door. "It's best to take no notice, sir, if you'll take my advice," said Sally, with a piece of white muslin wrapped round her arm, which shone in the moonlight. "It's nought but the mad lass next door."

"Mad! is she mad?" said Edgar eagerly.

"Poor lass! they do say as it's a brother; but I don't hold for making all that fuss about brothers," said Sally. "T'ou'd dame, she's a proud one, and never says nought she can help; and the poor wench ain't dangerous or that, but as mad as mad, in special when the moon's at the full. Don't you take no notice, sir, for there never was a proud un like t'ou'd dame. T' poor lass had an only brother as died, and she's ne'er been hersel' since. That's what they say."

"But she looks like a child," said Edgar, not knowing what to do; for already complete silence and darkness seemed to have fallen over the cottage. Old Sarah did not wake, or if she waked, kept still and made no sign, and the light had disappeared from the upper window. It was hard to believe, to look at the perfect stillness of the summer night, that any such interruption had ever been.

"She do, Squire," said Sally; "but seventeen they say, and some thinks her mortal pretty—t'ou'd Doctor for one, as was awful wild in his own time, I've heerd say. But Mrs. Murray she watches her like a dragon. It's t'ou'd lady as is my sort. I don't hold with prettiness nor fuss, but them as takes that care of their own—"

Sally jumped aside with a sudden cry, as the door of the next house softly opened, and Mrs. Murray herself suddenly appeared. In the moon-light, which blanched even Sally's dingy complexion, the old woman looked white as death; but probably it was as much an effect of the light as of the scene she had just gone through. She laid her hand very gently, with a certain dignity, upon Edgar's arm.

"Sir," she said, "you'll excuse my poor bairn. Willie was her brother, that we lost a year back. He was lost at sea, and the poor thing looks for him night and day. He was in a Liverpool ship; that's why we're here. She took you for him," the grandmother continued, and then made a pause, as if to recover her voice. Tears were glistening in her eyes. Her voice thrilled and changed even now, it seemed to Edgar, like chords. She touched his arm again with her hand, a soft, yet firm, momentary touch, which was like a caress. And then, all at once, "You're like him. Good night," she said.

It was as if she could not trust herself to say more. And Edgar stood gazing at the vacant spot where she had stood, while Sally peered round the porch of her own house, straining to see and hear. "She's a queer 'un, t'ou'd dame," said Sally, with a little gasp of disappointed excitement; and she stood at her door with the muslin twisted about her hand, and gazed after him when he went away up the village with a hasty good night. Edgar heard her close and bolt her door as he hurried on to the Doctor's. Poor rural fastenings, what could they shut out? not even a clever thief, did any such care to enter—much less pain, trouble, sorrow, madness, or death.

Dr. Somers' study was a great contrast to the splendour and silence of the night. It was lighted by a green reading-lamp, which threw its illumination only on the table, and it was full of smoke from a succession of cigars. The Doctor was seated in a large old-fashioned elbow-chair, with a high back and sides, covered with dark leather, against which his handsome head stood out. On the table stood a silver claret-cup, and a rough brown bottle of seltzer-water—such were his modest potations. He had a medical magazine before him on the table, but it was a novel which was in his hand, and which he pitched away from him as Edgar entered. "Some of Letty's rubbish," he explained, as he threw it on the sofa in the shade, and welcomed his young guest. "Bravo, Edgar! Now this is what I call emancipating yourself from petticoat government. These sisters of ours are as bad as half-a-dozen wives."

"You don't seem to have suffered much under yours," said Edgar; "and mine, I assure you—"

"Oh, yes; yours, I assure you," cried the Doctor, "is exactly like the rest—would not curtail any of your pleasures for the world; in short, would entreat you to amuse yourself, and be heartbroken at the thought of keeping you at home for her; but once let her find out that you have wings and can fly, and see what she says. I know them all."

Edgar sat down, and cast a hurried glance round the room as the Doctor spoke. He asked himself quite involuntarily whether, after all, a cigar in Dr. Somers' study was so much more delightful than Clare's society and her pretty surroundings, and was not by any means so certain on that point as the Doctor was. But if he smiled within himself he suffered no evidence of it to escape, and for this night, at least, he had a definite object in his visit. "I did not know if I should find you," he said. "What has become of the old whist party, of which I used to hear so much?"

"Ah, the whist party," said the Doctor, with a sigh. "Poor Letty made an end of that. She was always willing to do her best, though she never was anything of a player; and she bore abuse like an angel. But that won't do now, you know. And young Denbigh is the most abject spoon I ever saw. When he is not dangling after Alice Pimpernel, he is writing verses to her, I believe. The boy is capable of any folly, and revokes as soon as look at you. Croquet is the food of love; and that is what the degenerate cub has abandoned whist for. No wonder the race deteriorates day by day."

"That is just what I wanted to speak to you about," said Edgar; "I have just come from the Pimpernel's."

CHAPTER XVII

"Let us be correct and categorical," said Dr. Somers. "That is just what you wanted to talk to me about? Which? Love, or croquet, or the Pimpernels?"

"Neither," said Edgar, with a little impatience. "These are things altogether out of my way; and I must ask you to be serious, for what I have to ask is grave enough. Can you tell me anything about my cousin Arthur Arden? and why my sister dislikes him? and why—"

"Whew!" said Dr. Somers, with a prolonged whistle. "You might well tell me to be serious. Why, and why, and why? Have you met Arthur Arden? And if so, did nobody warn you that he was the worst enemy you ever had in your life."

"He might very easily be that, and not scare me much," said Edgar, with his careless, almost boyish, smile.

"You silly lad!" said the Doctor. "You simpleton! You think you never had an enemy in your life, and feel as if this would be something new. I wonder if I ought to enlighten you? You remember your father, Edgar? Which was he, enemy or friend?"

"Dr. Somers," said Edgar, gravely, "I have already told you that nothing shall induce me to discuss my father."

Dr. Somers said "Humph!" with sudden confusion, and filled himself out a large bumper of wine and seltzer water. "That shows a fine disposition on your part," he said; "but whether it is safe or expedient to ignore such things you must judge for yourself. Perhaps I know more about it than you do, and it seems to me you have had an enemy or two. But, anyhow, take care of Arthur Arden, for he will be the worst."

"I don't think I am afraid."

"No; I don't suppose you are," said the Doctor, looking at him between two puffs of his cigar; "but whether that is wise or not is a different matter. Why does Clare hate him? Why, I suppose, because he once made love to her, and offered 'his hand,' as people say, with nothing in it. Was not that enough?"

"Surely not enough to make her hate him," said Edgar, "but enough to make it horribly embarrassing. Was that all? Don't people say it is the highest compliment, &c. I am sure I have read something like that in books."

"And so have I," said the Doctor; "and I suppose it is the highest compliment, &c. Women don't generally hate us because we love them, or think we love them. Clare has been petted and spoiled all her life. But still Arthur Arden is a handsome fellow—"

While Dr. Somers went on thus philosophically, Edgar winced and shifted about in his chair. He was not susceptible about himself, but he was intensely sensitive in respect to his sister. Clare was not to him an abstract woman, to be discussed by general rules, but an individual whom he would fain have drawn curtains of profoundest respect about, and veiled from every vulgar gaze. There is no doubt that this is one of the first primitive instincts of love. The Turk is the truest symbol of humanity so far, and there is no man, worth calling a man, who would not be satisfied in his inmost heart if he could shut up his womankind from every rash look or doubtful comment. Edgar beat a tune on the table with his fingers, blew clouds of smoke about him in his restlessness, shuffled and swayed himself about in his chair; but what could he do to stop the disquisitions of the man who had known Clare all her life?

"Arthur Arden is a handsome fellow, and a clever fellow," continued Dr. Somers. "If he had impressed a girl's imagination, I for one should not have been surprised. My own theory is that he did, and that it was her liking for him, combined with her sense of his enmity to you—"

"Good heavens! what has that to do with it?" cried Edgar, thankful of some means of expressing his impatience. "How could he show enmity to me when he had never seen me? and what did it matter if he had? That has nothing to do with Clare."

"It had a great deal to do with Clare," said the Doctor. "If I tell you what my theory is, of course you will understand I don't mean to hurt your feelings, Edgar. I think he must have proposed some sort of compromise to your father to exclude you quietly—"

"To exclude—me!" Edgar stopped him with an impatient gesture. "Dr. Somers, you speak in riddles. How could I be excluded? What compromise was possible? This is something so astounding that I must ask what it means in so many words—"

"Oh, of course it was absolute folly," said the Doctor, with confusion. The truth was, he had taken Edgar for a fool, and it seemed to him as if anything could be said to so amiable, so good-tempered, so unsuspicious a simpleton. He paused and grew red, notwithstanding his ordinary composure and knowledge of the world. "I speak of the mad notions of a self-willed man, who thought persistence would overcome everything," he went on, embarrassed. "Of course there was no compromise possible. You were the only son, and the undoubted heir. But, going upon some notion of his own that the Squire hated—I mean was not fond of you—In short, Edgar, I warned you you were not to think I wanted to wound your feelings—and that Arthur Arden was the worst enemy you ever had in your life."

"You have given me a glimpse of something worse still," said Edgar. "You have insinuated the possibility that his enmity might have been of importance—that there was some harm possible. What could he do? What could—since you force me to speak of that—my father have done? The estates were entailed. If he could have cut me off by will, I am not so simple as to doubt that he would have done it. But being, as I am, heir of entail—"

"Yes, yes," said Dr. Somers eagerly; "of course you are heir of entail; of course it was all nonsense; you can't imagine for a moment—But then there are such very curious things in law and family history. Men sometimes take an unaccountable aversion—Did I ever tell you the story of the Agostinis, a very strange thing that excited everybody when I was at Rome?"

Edgar gave a little wave of his hand in impatience. What were the Agostinis or their story to him?

"That was almost a case in point," said the Doctor. "There was supposed to be no heir, and the estates had gone to the daughter (of course there was no law of entail to complicate the matter), when all at once starts up a young man, who had been bred in a public hospital, and yet was proved beyond dispute to be the Duchess Agostini's son. She was living, though her husband was dead, and could not deny it. The proof, indeed, was so strong that he won his suit, and is now the Duke, and head of one of the oldest houses in Italy. Brought up in an orphan hospital, and just as nearly shut out from all inheritance for ever—just as near—"

"But I suppose there was some explanation," said Edgar, interested in spite of himself; "mere aversion of a father could not surely go so far as that?"

"Oh, yes, there was a reason given," said the Doctor, more and more confused, "something about the mother—some little speck, you know, on her character: one must not inquire too closely into those family stories. But he won his suit, and now he is Duke Agostini—the hospital boy! You may imagine what a sensation it made in Rome."

"Something about his mother," Edgar repeated vaguely, under his breath, with eyes in which a strange light suddenly sprang up. Then he bit his lip, and restrained himself. Dr. Somers, watching closely, saw that he had made an impression much more serious than he intended. He did not, indeed, intend to make any impression. He meant only, in the wantonness of fancied power, to make an experiment, to pique Edgar's curiosity, to give him, perhaps, a passing thrill of alarm and wonder, such as an operator might give, half in jest, to curious spectators round an electric machine; but, unfortunately, the operation had been too successful, the shock overmuch. The young man said nothing farther, but sat moody, with the cigar between his fingers, and let the Doctor talk. Dr. Somers said a great deal more, but with the sense that Edgar was not listening, and that he might as well have been a hundred miles off for any companionship there was between them. And though he had in general a very good opinion of himself, for once in his life the Doctor was abashed, and felt that he had gone too far. He tried to draw the young man's attention to other matters—to local interests—to Lord Newmarch and his enlightened views. "I may be a Radical myself," said the Doctor, "but I do not belong to that school of Enlightened Youth. Newmarch is very appalling to me; and if you don't mind, Edgar, you'll find he wants to make up to Clare too."

"Too! is there any other?" said Edgar, with a certain languid haughtiness which was more like the Ardens than anything that had ever been seen in him before, and which gave Dr. Somers a thrill almost as sharp and sudden as that he had produced in the young Squire. "Could it be possible, at this moment, of all others, that his theory was to prove itself wrong?"

"I should think there were others," he said, with an attempt at carelessness. "Flowers like Clare do not grow in every garden, not to speak of the dot which you and your father endowed her with. I suppose nothing has been done about that as yet; or have you been so wise as to take old Fazakerley's advice?"

"I think I shall go home," said Edgar abruptly, and he got up, and lighted his cigar by the Doctor's candle. "There was something I wanted to speak to you about, but it has gone out of my head."

"Nothing about your health, I hope," said the Doctor anxiously. "You look quite well—"

"Oh, no, nothing about my health," he said, with a short laugh, and went out, leaving Dr. Somers in a state of great discomfort, saying to himself that he had not meant it, and that he could not have imagined such a good-tempered careless fellow would have taken anything up so quickly. "It was nothing," he said to himself. "I did not even imply that his circumstances were the same; in short, I did not say a word to offend—any one; nonsense! Who is Edgar Arden, I wonder, that one should study his feelings to such an extent? Good heavens, didn't he insist upon being told?" Thus the Doctor excused and accused himself, and felt extremely uncomfortable, and at last went to bed, not feeling able to drown his remorse either in his seltzer water or his novel. "If Fielding had done anything as idiotic," was his comment as he went upstairs, "or poor Letty—but I, that pretend to some sort of discretion!" His folly had at least this salutary effect.

Meanwhile Edgar walked home very fast, as if some one were pursuing him. It was his thoughts which were pursuing him, rushing and driving him on. The avenue had never looked so stately in the moonlight, nor the woods so mysteriously sweet. All the soft perfumes of the night were in the air; the smell of the fresh earth and the dew, the fragrance that breathed out of here and there an old hawthorn, still covered with blossom, beginning to brown and fade in the daylight, but still sweet in the darkness. The front of the house lay in a great shadow made of its own roof and the big trees behind; but lights were twinkling about, as they ought to be in a house which expects its master. Was it possible that Arthur Arden could have turned him out, could have replaced him there? Could it be that Clare knew such a thing was possible? "Something about his mother." Edgar did not himself realise what horror it was which had thus breathed across him. What could it be about his mother? Could there be anything about her which gave to any man the right of a possible insinuation? He did not remember her, and had not even a portrait of her, but was like her, people said. And therefore his father had hated him. Edgar's brain burned as this strange thought whirled and fluctuated about him; he was its victim, he did not entertain it voluntarily. His father hated him because he was like her; but yet, was not she the mother, too, of the beloved Clare?

CHAPTER XVIII

It was perhaps fortunate for Edgar that he did not see his sister that night. She had waited for him till the return of the groom with the dogcart, and then she had gone upstairs. Probably she had gone with a little irritation against him for delaying his return, Edgar felt; and a momentary impatience of all and everyone of the new circumstances which made his life so different came upon him. What if Dr. Somers' suggestion had come true, and he had been shut out of the succession? Why, then, this bondage on one side or other, this failure in satisfying one and understanding another, this expenditure of himself for everybody's pleasure, would not have been. "I should have been brought up to a profession, probably," he said to himself, "or even a trade;" and for the moment, in his impatience, he almost wished it had been so. But then he looked out upon the park, lying broad in the moonlight, and the long lines of trees which he could see from his open window, and felt that he would be a coward indeed who would give up such an inheritance without an effort. The lands of his fathers. Were they the lands of his fathers? or what did that terrible insinuation mean?

Clare was cloudy, there could be no doubt of it, when she met her brother next morning. She thought he might have come back earlier. "What is Dr. Somers to him?" she said to herself, and concluded, like a true woman, that he must have fallen in love with Alice Pimpernel. "If he were to marry that girl I should certainly keep Old Arden," she said to herself; for it seemed almost impossible to imagine that, seeing Alice was the last girl in the world who ought to attract him, he should have been able to resist falling in love with her. And thus she came down cloudy, and found Edgar with a face all overcast by the events of the previous night, which confirmed her in all her fears. "Of course, he does not like to speak of her," Clare said to herself. Poor Alice Pimpernel! who was too frightened for Mr. Arden even to raise her eyes from her plate.

"Had you a pleasant party?" she said, with a half angry sound in her voice.

"Not very pleasant," said Edgar. "I suppose that is why I am so tired this morning; but yet I met some people who interested me."

"Indeed!" said Clare, with polite wonder. "Tell me who you took in to dinner? and who was next you? and in short all about it? One would think it was I who had been at a party last night, and you who had stayed at home."

"I took in Mrs. Buxton, whoever she may be—and I sat next Miss Pimpernel—and the one was philosophical, and the other was—Is there not some word that sounds pretty, and that means inane?

She is a very nice girl, I am sure. She said, 'Oh, yes, Mr. Arden,' and then, 'Oh, no, Mr. Arden.' If I had not kept up the proper alternations I wonder what the poor girl would have said?"

"But you did?" said Clare, with all her cloud removed. Had she but known who was at that party beside Alice Pimpernel!

"Oh, yes, I did. And there was Lord Newmarch, who is coming here on the 1st to make my acquaintance. I hope you don't mind. He was so anxious to see me, poor fellow, that I could not deprive him of that pleasure. I hope, Clare, you don't mind."

"Not in the least," she said, in her most genial mood. "If you will not be shocked, I rather like him, Edgar. He means well; and then if he is a Radical, it is in a kind of dignified superior way."

"So it is," said Edgar; "very superior, and very dignified—not to say instructive—but we might get too clever, don't you think, if we had too much of it? There was some one else there, about whom you must pardon me, Clare. I was led into giving him an invitation—without thinking. It did not occur to me till after—"

Edgar grew very red making his excuses, and Clare grew pale listening. She made a great effort over herself, and clasped her hands together, and looked at her brother with a forced smile. "Why should you hesitate?" she said. "Edgar, you are master; I wish you to be master. Whoever you choose to ask ought to be welcome to me."

"I do not wish to be master so long as I have my sister to consult," he said; "but this was a mistake, an inadvertence, Clare. You can't guess? It was Arthur Arden whom I met at the Pimpernels!"

"Ah!" Clare said, growing paler and paler. But she made no observation, and kept listening with her hands clasped fast.

"I asked him to come in September, remembering you had said you did not like him much; but he offered himself for June. I did not accept his proposed visit; but from what I saw and what I hear it seems likely he will come."

"No doubt he will come," said Clare; and then her hands separated themselves. She had heard all that she had to fear. "If I hate him it is not for myself," she added hurriedly, "but for you Edgar. He did all he could to injure you."

"So I have heard. But how could he injure me?" said her brother, feeling that it was now his turn.

"Edgar, I hate to speak of it. You can't understand my love for poor papa. Arthur tried to set him against—It was—his fault. No; Edgar, no, I don't mean that—it was not his fault; but he tried to make things worse. That is why I hate—no, I don't hate. If you don't mind Edgar—You kind, good, sweet-tempered boy—!"

And here, in a strange transport, which he could not understand, Clare took his hand, and held it close, and pressed it to her heart, which was beating fast. She looked up at him with tears in her eyes, with a curious admiration. "You are not like us other Ardens," she said. "We ought to learn of you; we ought to look up to you, Edgar. You can forgive. You don't keep on remembering and thinking over everything that people have done and said against you. You can put it away out of your mind. Edgar, dear, I hate myself, and I love you with all my heart."

"Do you, Clare; do you, indeed, Clare?" he said, and went to her side, and kissed her with brotherly tenderness. "God do so to me and more also," he said to himself, if I ever forget her good and her happiness; or, at least, if he did not say the words, such was the sentiment that passed through his mind. He was so much moved that he felt able to ask a question he had been hesitating over all the morning. "Clare," he said softly, bending over her, and smoothing her dark hair. His voice had a certain sound of supplication in it which struck her strangely. She thought he was about to ask something hard to do—perhaps a renunciation, perhaps a sacrifice. "Clare, can you tell me anything about our mother? Do you know?"

"About mamma?" said Clare, with a sense of disappointment. "Edgar, you frighten me so; I thought you were going to ask me something that was very hard. About mamma? Of course I will tell you all I know."

"And there is a portrait—you said there was a portrait—I should like to see that too."

"Yes, Edgar, I will run and get it. Oh, I wonder if you would have been very like her—if she had lived? I sometimes think it would have been so much better for us all."

"Do you think so?" said Edgar, with a sadness which he could not control. Would it have been better? But, at all events, Clare knew of nothing evil that concerned their mother. He walked about the room slowly while she went to seek the portrait, and finally paused at the great window, and gazed out. It had the same view over the park which he had looked at last night under the moon-light. Now, in the morning, with a certain ache of strange doubtfulness, he looked at it again. The feeling in his mind was that it might all dissolve as he looked, and melt away, and leave no sign—that, and the house, and the room he stood in, with all their appearance of weight and reality. Such things had been; at least, surely that was what Dr. Somers' story meant about those Agostini. What was it? "Something about the mother." A mist of bewilderment had fallen over him, and he could not tell.

Clare's entrance with a little case in her hand roused him. She came up, and put her arm within his where he stood, and, thus hanging on him, opened the case, and showed him the miniature, which formed the clasp of a bracelet. It was the portrait of a face so young that it startled him. He had been thinking and talking of his mother, which meant something almost venerable, and this was the face of a girl younger, ever so much younger, than himself. "Are you sure this is her?" he said in a whisper, taking it out of his sister's hand. "Of course it is her; who else could it be?" she answered, in the same tone. "She is so young," said Edgar, apologetically. He was quite startled by that youthfulness. He held it up to the light, and looked at it with wondering admiration. "This child! Could she be my mother, your mother, Clare?"

"I suppose everybody is young some time. She must have looked very different from that when she died."

"Will it ever seem as strange, I wonder," said Edgar, still little above a whisper, "to somebody to look at your portrait and mine? How pretty she must have been, Clare. What a sweet look in her eyes! You have that look sometimes, though you are not like her. Poor little thing! What a soft innocent-looking child."

"Edgar," said his sister, half horrified, for she had little imagination, "do you remember you are speaking of mamma?"

He gave a strange little laugh, which seemed made up of pleasure and tears. "Do you think I might kiss her?" he said under his breath. Clare was half scandalized half angry. He was always so strange; you never could tell what he might do or say next; he was so inconsistent, not bound by sacred laws like the Ardens; but still his sister herself was a little touched by the portrait and the suggestions it made.

"She would not have been old now if she had been living, not too old for a companion. Oh, Edgar, what a difference it would have made! I never had a real companion, not one I was thoroughly fond of; only think what it would have been to have had her—"

"With that face!" Edgar said, with a sigh of relief, though Clare could not guess why he felt so relieved. Then—"I wonder if she would have liked me," he said, softly. "Clare, there has been a kind fiction about my mother. I am not like her. I don't think I am like her. But she looks as innocent as an angel, Clare."

"Why should not she be innocent?" said Clare, wondering. "We are all innocent. I don't see why you should fix upon that. What strikes me is that she must have been so pretty. Don't you think it is pretty? How arched the eyebrows are and dark, though she is so fair."

"But I am not like her," he said, shaking his head. How strange it was. Was he a waif of fortune, some mere stray soul whom Providence had made to be born in the house of Arden, quite out of its natural sphere? It gave him a little shock, and yet somehow he could feel no sharp disappointment on the day he had made acquaintance with this innocent face.

"Do you think not?" said Clare, faltering. "Oh, yes; you are like her. See how fair she is, and you are fair, and the Ardens are all dark; besides, you know, poor papa—Don't change like that, Edgar, when I mention his name. He was the only one who knew her, and he said—"

"Did he ever say I was like my mother?" said Edgar, while the sweetness and softness had all gone out of his voice.

"I am not sure that he ever said it in so many words. But, Edgar! Why, everybody here—What could it be but that? And see how fair she is, and you are fair—"

Edgar Arden shook his head. The face in the miniature was not sanguine and ruddy, like his, but a pensive face; locks too fair to be called golden surrounding it, and soft blue eyes. Everything was soft, gentle, tender, composed, in the young face. Even Clare's grave beauty, though in itself so different, was less unlike her than Edgar's warm vitality, the gleams of superabundant life, which showed as colour in his hair and as light in his eyes. "I am not like her," he said to himself, as he closed the little case and gave it back to his sister; but the shadow which had been upon him all the morning had disappeared for ever. Whatever was the secret of his story, it was not like the story of the Agostini. Once and for ever he dismissed that dread from his breast.

CHAPTER XIX

It was, however, some time before Edgar got over the painful impression made upon his mind by what Dr. Somers had said. He had known very well for the greater part of his life that his father did not love him; but the idea that doubt had ever fallen upon his rights, that there had been a possibility of shutting him out from his natural inheritance, had never entered his mind. Of course there was really no such possibility; but still the merest suggestion of it excited the young man. It seemed to hint at a deeper secret in his own existence than anything he had yet suspected. He had been able to take it for granted with all the carelessness of youth that his father disliked him. But why should his father dislike him? What reason could there be? And then that story of the Agostini returned to him. Edgar pondered and pondered it for days, and rejected the suggestions conveyed in it, feeling from the moment he had seen his mother's picture a certain fierce sentiment of rage against Dr. Somers as her maligner. But yet this explanation being evidently a false one, and his mother cleared of all shadow of shame or wrong, there remained the strange thought that there must be some clue to the mystery; and what was it? If it had been within the bounds of possibility that the Squire could have doubted his wife's faithfulness, that of course would have explained a great deal. But the evidence of the portrait was quite conclusive that any such suspicion was out of the question. Edgar was young and fanciful, and ready to accept the evidence of a look, and every natural sentiment within him rose up in defence of his mother. But he could not help asking himself, even though the question seemed an injury to her—what if it had been possible? Had she been another kind of woman and, capable of wickedness, what in such horrible circumstances would it have been a man's duty to do? He had of course heard such questions discussed, like everybody else in the world, as affecting the husband and wife, the immediate parties. But imagine a young man making such a discovery, finding himself out to be a spurious branch thus arbitrarily engrafted upon a family tree; in a position so frightful, what would it be his duty to do? Edgar roamed about the woods which were his, putting to himself in every point of view this appalling question. A man could take no single step in such circumstances without taking upon him the responsibility of heaping shame upon his mother, and giving up her cause. It would be her whom he would cover with disgrace, much more than himself. He would have to decide a question which nobody but she could decide, and to give it against her, his nearest and dearest relation. Could any one willingly assume such an office? And, on the other hand, how could he retain a name, an inheritance, a position to which he had no right, and probably exclude the rightful heir? "Thank heaven," said Edgar fervently, "that can never be my case. The son of the woman to whom God gave so angelic a countenance can never have to blush for his mother. Whatever records came to light, she never shall be shamed." He gave up whole days to this question, pondering it again and again in his mind. The sight of the portrait gave him for that one day an absolute certainty that such was not his position: and this force of conviction carried him through the second and even the third day; but then as the first impression waned a horrible chill of doubt stole slowly over him. That hypothesis, terrible as it was, could it but be believed, explained so much. It explained the Squire's dislike to himself at once and vindicated the unhappy old man. It explained why he was kept at so great a distance, brought up in so strange a way; and oh, good God! if such could be the case, what was Edgar's duty? His brain began to whirl when he got so far; and then he would work his way back again through all the arguments. Dr. Somers had calculated when he threw abroad this winged and barbed seed that Edgar was too easy-minded, too careless and good-natured and indifferent to let it rest in his thoughts; and to hide his consciousness of it, to be blank as a stone wall to any allusion which might recall it, was clearly now the first duty of Mrs. Arden's son. If he could but be absolutely sure of it one way or other; if he could put it utterly out of his mind, on the one hand, or—a horrible alternative, which nevertheless would be next best—know absolutely that it was true! But neither of these things seemed possible to Edgar. He had to submit to that doubt which was so fundamental and all-embracing—doubt as to his own very being, the foundations upon which his life was built—and never to breathe a whisper of it to any creature on the face of the earth. A hard task.

It may be thought that Clare must have observed her brother's abstraction, his silent wanderings and musings, and the look of thought and care which he could not banish from his face; but the truth was that Clare herself was occupied by a hundred reflections. She had told her brother she hated Arthur Arden, and at the moment it was true; but now that Edgar, for whose sake she hated him, had condoned his offences, and asked him to the house, Clare, if her pride would have let her, might have confessed that she loved Arthur Arden, and it would have been equally true. He had exercised over her when she had seen him last that strange fascination which a man much older than herself often exercises over a girl. She had been pleased by the trouble he took to make himself agreeable, flattered by the attentions which a man of experience knows how to regulate according to the age and tastes of the subject under operation, and had felt the full charm of that kindred not near enough to be familiar, but yet sufficiently near to account for all kinds of mysterious affinities and sympathies which he knew so well how to make use of. He was a true Arden—everybody said so. And Clare, who was an Arden to the very finger tips, felt all the force of the bond. She had sighed secretly, wishing that her brother might have been like him. The tears had come into her eyes with affectionate pity that such a genuine representative of the family should be so poor; and again a little glow of generous warmth had followed, as a faint dream of how it might be made up to him stole across her mind. A man of such excellence and such grace—so distinguished by blood and talent, and all the qualities that adorn a hero, who could doubt that it would be made up to him? Honour would fall at his feet for the lifting up, and if wealth should be wanting, why then somebody whom Clare would try to love would endow him with everything that heart could desire, and herself best of all. She had nourished these notions until she had heard from Arthur himself, with one of the inadvertencies common to men whose consideration for others, however elaborate outside, does not come from the heart, of his opposition to her distant brother. He had taken it for granted that she must share her father's opinion on the subject. "Why, you do not know him!" he had said, in his astonishment, when he became aware of his mistake. "I love my brother with all my heart," was all the answer Clare had made. Something of the magniloquence of youth was in this large assertion; but the poor girl's heart was very sore, and the struggle she had with herself in this wild sudden revulsion of feeling was almost more than she could bear. He was Edgar's enemy, this man who had been too pleasant, only too tender to herself and she hated him! She had walked away from him at that painful moment, and when they met afterwards had only looked at him from behind the visor of cold pride and icy stateliness which the Ardens knew so well how to use. But the feeling in her heart was only hatred because it had been so nearly love.

And now that the tables had been so strangely turned, now that Arthur was coming to Arden as Edgar's guest, Clare was seized with a sudden giddiness of mind and heart, which made the outer world invisible to her, or at least changed, and threw it so awry that no clear impression came to her brain. As Edgar's friend—She could not feel quite sure whether her feelings were those of excited expectation and delight or of alarm and terror. And she was not sure either what to think of her brother. Was he magnanimous beyond all the powers of the Arden mind to conceive, as had been her first idea; or was he simply careless, insensible—not capable of the amount of feeling which came natural to the Ardens? This second thought was less pleasant than the first, and yet in one way it was a kind of relief from an overpowering and scarcely comprehensible excellence. "He does not feel it," Clare said to herself; but surely Arthur would feel it; Arthur would be moved by a forgiveness so generous. Even now, when Edgar was fully aware what his kinsman had done against him, it did not occur to him to withdraw his invitation or forbid his enemy to the house. Such a sublime magnanimity could not fail to impress the mind of the other. But yet, Clare recollected that Arthur was a true Arden, and the Ardens were tenacious, not addicted to forgiving or giving up their own way, as was her strange brother. Arthur might come, concealing his enmity, watching his foe's weak points and the crevices in his armour, and laying up in his mind all these particulars for future use. Such a proceeding was not so foreign to the Arden mind as was that magnanimity or indifference—which was it?—that made Edgar a wonder in his race. If her cousin was to do this, what horrible thing might happen? Between Arthur's watchfulness and Edgar's unwariness, Clare trembled. But then, would not she be there to guard the one and keep the other in check?

Thus, Clare was so fully occupied with thoughts of her own that she did not notice the change in her brother's looks, nor his sudden love of solitude. When Mr. Fielding expressed to her his fear that Edgar was ill, the thought filled her with surprise. "Ill! Oh, no, there is nothing the matter with him," she said. "Here he comes to speak for himself: he looks just the same as usual. Edgar, you are not ill? Mr. Fielding has been giving me a fright."

"I am not ill in the least," he said, "but I wanted to see you. Are you going into the village? I will walk there with Mr. Fielding, Clare, and you can pick me up on your way."

"You see there is not much the matter with him; he is always walking," said Clare, waving her hand to the Rector. "I will call for you, Edgar, in half-an-hour;" and she went away smiling to put on her riding-habit. The brother and sister were going to Thornleigh to pay their homage before Lady Augusta should go away.

"Of course I understand you don't want to alarm Clare," said the Rector, when they were on their way down the avenue; "but, my dear boy, you are looking very poorly. I don't like the change in your look. You should speak to the Doctor. He has known you more or less all your life."

"The Doctor! I do not think he knows much about it," said Edgar, with vehemence. "But I am not ill. I am as well as ever I was." Then he made a little pause; and then, putting his hand on his old friend's arm, he said impulsively, yet trying with all his might to hide the force of the impulse, "Mr. Fielding, you have always been very good to me. I want you to help me to recollect what happened long ago. I want you to tell me something about—my mother."

Old Mr. Fielding's short-sighted eyes woke up amidst the puckers which buried them, and showed a diamond twinkle of kindness in each wrinkled socket. He gave a look of benign goodness to Edgar, and then he turned and sent a glance towards the village which might almost have set fire to Dr. Somers' high roof. "Yes, Edgar," he said quickly, "and I am very glad you have asked me. I can tell you a great deal about your mother."

"You knew her, then?" cried the young man, turning upon him with eager eyes.

"I knew her very well. She was quite young, younger than you are; but as good a woman, Edgar, as sweet a woman as ever went to heaven."

"I was sure of that!" he cried, holding out his hand; and he grasped that slim hand of the old Rector's in his strong young grasp, till Mr. Fielding would fain have cried out, but restrained himself, and bore it smiling like a martyr, though the water stood in his eyes.

"Somers never saw her," said Mr. Fielding, waving his hand towards the village. "He was in Italy at the time; but ask his sister, or ask me. Ah, Edgar! in that, as in some other things, the old parson is the best man to come to. Why, boy, it is not you I care for! How do I know you may not turn out a young rascal yet, or as hard as the nether millstone, like so many of the Ardens? but I love you for her sake."

"Your mother was very young," Mr. Fielding continued, "and early matured as marriage makes a girl. She was a little old-fashioned, I think, as well as I can remember, through being driven into maturity before her time. When a girl is married, not over happily—"

"Was her marriage not happy?" Edgar interrupted, with a cloud on his face.

"I should not have said that. I mean, you know, her being so young. Why, I don't think she was as old as Clare when they came back here with you a baby—"

"I was born abroad," said Edgar, half in the tone of one making an inquiry, half as asserting a fact.

"If you would try not to interrupt me, please," said Mr. Fielding, piteously. "You put me off my story. Yes, you were born abroad. They came home in October, and you had been born in the end of the previous year. They took everybody a good deal by surprise. In the first place, few people knew there was a baby; and no one knew when your father and mother were coming. There were no bells rung for you, Edgar, when you came home first, and the old wives have a notion—but never mind that."

"Tell me the notion," said Edgar.

"Oh, nothing—about mischief to the heir for whom no bells are rung. That's all; and heaven be praised, no mischief has come to you, Edgar. They came quite suddenly and the baby. Your father never made a fuss about babies. That is to say, my dear boy," said the old Rector, lowering his voice, "if it will not grieve you; from the very beginning that had begun."

Edgar gave a little nod of his head, sudden and brief, understanding only too clearly; and Mr. Fielding stopped to grasp his hand, and then went on again.

"If I could have helped it, I would not have mentioned it; but, of course, it must be referred to now and then," continued the Rector. "Instead of being proud of you, as a man, if he is good for anything, always is, he never seemed able to bear the fuss. To be sure, some men don't. They will not be made second even for their own child. Your mother—"

"My mother was fond of me at least?" said Edgar, turning away his head, and cutting at the weeds with the light cane in his hand, doing his best to conceal his excitement and emotion.

"Your mother, poor child!—but that of course, that of course, Edgar; how could she be otherwise than fond of her first-born? Your mother's entire life was absorbed in an attempt to satisfy her husband. I saw the whole process; and it made my heart bleed. She was a passive, gentle, little creature—not like him. She shrank from the world, and all that was going on in it. She liked melancholy books and sad songs, and all that—one of the creatures doomed to die young. And he was so different! She used to strain and strain her faculties trying to please him. She would try to amuse him even in her innocent way. It was very hard upon her, Edgar. You are an active, restless sort of being yourself; but, for heaven's sake, don't worry your wife when you get one. Let her follow her own constitution a little. She tried and tried till she could strive no longer: and when Clare was born, I think she was quite glad to be obliged to give in, and get a little rest in her grave. Of course, she was not here all the time. They used to come and go, and never stayed more than a month or two. You were left behind very often. The Doctor never saw her," Mr. Fielding added pointedly, "till just before she died. He had newly come back and got settled in his house. He never saw her but on her death-bed. He knew nothing about her; but I—you may think I am bragging like a garrulous old talker as I am—but I saw a great deal of her one way or another. I think she felt she had a friend in me."

"Thanks!" Edgar said below his breath. He was too deeply moved to look at his old friend, nor could he trust himself to speak.

"I buried her," said the old clergyman in his musing way. "You know the place. It was all I could do to keep from crying loud out like a child. I lost my own wife the same way; but the child died too. That is one reason, perhaps, why I am so fond of Clare. When you come to think of it, Edgar, this world is a dreary place to live so long in. A year or two's brightness you may have, and then the long, long, steady twilight that never changes. They are saved a great deal when they die early. What with her natural weakness, and what with you, it would have been hard upon her had she lived. However, it is lucky for us that life and death are not in our power."

"I hate myself for thinking of myself when you have been telling me of—her," said Edgar. "But—my fate, it appears, was the same from the beginning. It could not arise from anything—found out?"

"There was nothing that could be found out," Mr. Fielding answered, almost severely. "Your mother was as good a woman as ever lived—too good. If she had been less tender and less gentle it would have been better for her—and for her son as well. Yes, there is such a thing as being too good."

"Am I like her?" said Edgar suddenly, looking for the first time in the Rector's face.

Mr. Fielding looked at him with critical gravity, which by-and-bye melted into a smile. "If black and white put together ever produced red," he said, "I should be able to understand you, Edgar. But I can't somehow. It must be one of the old Ardens asserting his right to be represented; that sometimes occurs in an old family; some great-grandfather tired of letting the other side of the house have it all their own way; for you know that dark beauty came in with the Spanish lady in Queen Elizabeth's time. You must be like your mother in your disposition—for you are not a bit of an Arden. The difference is that you don't take things to heart much—and she did."

"Don't I take things much to heart?"

"My dear boy, you ought to know better than I do. I should not think you did. The world comes more easily to you; and then, a man—and a young man in your position—can't be kept down as she was. I am not blaming your father, Edgar. He meant no harm. To him it seemed quite proper and natural. Men should mind when they have a life and soul to deal with; but they never do until it is too late. Yes, of course, you are like her," Mr. Fielding added; "I can see the marks of her bonds upon you. She taught herself to give in, and submit, and prefer another's will to her own; and you do that same for your diversion, because you like it. Yes, my boy, you carry the marks of her bonds—you are the son of her heart."

"That is a delusion," said Edgar. "I always please myself." But he was soothed by the kind speech of the old man, who was a friend to him, as he had been to his mother, and her story had moved him very deeply. She, too, had suffered like himself. "Thanks for telling me so much," he added, humbly. "I never heard anything about her before. And Clare has a little picture, which she showed me. I have been thinking a very great deal about her for the last two or three days."

"What has made you think of her more than usual?" asked Mr. Fielding, with some sharpness. Edgar paused, unwilling to answer. It seemed to him that the Rector knew or divined how it was. He had made several allusions to the Doctor, as if contradicting beforehand an adverse authority. But Edgar felt it impossible to allow that he had heard of any suspicion against his mother. He made a dash into indifferent subjects—the management of the estate, the building of the new cottages. Mr. Fielding was not deceived: but he was judicious enough to allow the conversation to be turned into another channel, and on this subject to ask no more.

CHAPTER XXI

Clare rode down the avenue about ten minutes later, the groom behind her leading Edgar's horse, and her own thoughts very heavy with a hundred important affairs.

The immediate subject in her mind, however, was one which was very clearly suggested by the visit which she was about to make; and when her brother joined her at the Rectory Gate, she led him up to it artfully with many seeming innocent remarks, though it was with a little timidity and nervousness that she actually introduced at last the real matter which occupied her thoughts.

"You will laugh, I know," she said, "but I don't think it at all a laughing matter, Edgar. Please tell me, without any nonsense, do you ever think that you must marry—some time or other? I knew you would laugh; but it is not any nonsense that is in my mind."

"Shouldn't I return the question, and ask you, 'Do you ever think that you must marry, Clare?'" said Edgar, when his laugh was over. Clare drew up her stately head with all the dignified disapproval which so much levity naturally called forth.

"That is quite a different matter," she said, impatiently. "I may or may not; it is my own affair; but you must."

"Why must I? I do not see the necessity," said Edgar, still with a smile.

"You must, however. You are the last of our family. Why, because it is your duty! Arden has not gone out of the direct line for two hundred and fifty years. You must not only marry, but you must marry very soon."

"There remains only to indicate the lady," said Edgar. "Tell me that too, and then I shall be easy in my mind."

"Edgar, I wish you would not be so teasing. Of course, I don't want to indicate the lady; but I will tell you, if you like, the kind of person she ought to be. She must be well born; that is quite indispensable; any other deficiency may be taken into consideration, but birth we cannot do without. And she must be young, and handsome, and good—but not too good. And if she had some money—just enough to make her feel comfortable—"

"This is a paragon of all virtues and qualities," said Edgar; "but where to be found? and when we find her, why should she condescend to me?"

"Condescend! Nonsense!" cried Clare. "You are just as good as she is;—so long as you are not carried away by a pretty face. It is so humbling to see you men. A pretty face carries the day with you over everything. Can you fancy anything more humiliating to a girl? She may be good, and wise, and clever, and yet people only want to marry her because her cheek has a pretty colour or her eyes are bright. I think it is almost as bad as if it were for money. To be married for your beauty! Every bit as bad—or even worse; for the money will last at least, and the beauty can't."

"But, my dear Clare, I don't want to marry—either for beauty or anything else," said Edgar.

"But you must marry," repeated his sister, peremptorily. "If you had set your heart upon it, Edgar, I would not mind Gussy Thornleigh. I should like Ada a great deal better; but of course they have the same belongings. I think she is rather frivolous, and a great chatterbox; but still if you like her best—"

"I don't like her best," said Edgar. "I don't like anybody best, except you. When you marry, then perhaps it will be time to think of it; but in the meantime I am very happy. I think, Clare, you should let well alone."

"But it is not well," said Clare, with her usual energy. And then she added, under her breath, "Arthur Arden is your heir-presumptive. He will be the one who will be looked up to; and if you don't marry soon, people will think—Edgar, you had much better make up your mind."

This was said very rapidly, and with great earnestness. Was it a last attempt to stand by her brother, and resist the influence of the other, who, whether visibly or not, was her brother's antagonist? Edgar turned round upon her with tranquil wonder, entirely unmoved. She was excited, but he was calm. Arthur's pretensions, it was evident, were nothing to him.

"Well?" he said. "Of course Arthur Arden is my heir; and probably he would make a much better Squire than I. The only thing for which I have a grudge at him is that he is like you. I confess I detest him for that. He may have my land when his time comes and I am out of the way; but I don't like him to be nearer than I am to my sister. He is an Arden, like you."

"He is like the old Ardens," said Clare, with a faint smile; and then the conversation dropped. She did not care to prolong it. They went across the cheerful country, still in the glory of the fresh foliage. The blossoms were beginning to fall, the first flush of spring verdure was past, but still the road was pleasant and the morning fine. Whether it was that Clare found enough to occupy her thoughts, or that she did not wish to disclose the confused state of feeling in which she was, it would be difficult to say; but, at all events, she gave up the talk, which it was her wont to lead and direct. And Edgar, left to himself, ran over his recent experiences, and, for almost the first time since he had seen her, thought of Gussy Thornleigh. She was very "nice;" she was a very different person to have at your elbow from that pretty Alice Pimpernell, whom Clare held in such needless terror. If a man could secure such a companion—so amusing, so pretty, so full of brightness, would not he be a lucky man? Edgar let this question skim through his mind, with that sense of pleasant exhilaration which moves a young man who is sensible of the possibility of power in himself, the privilege of making choice, before any real love has come in to change the balance of feeling. He had not been made subject by Gussy, had not set his heart on her, nor transferred to her the potential voice; and it half amused, half disturbed him to think that he probably might, if he chose, have for the asking that prettiest, liveliest, charming little creature. He did not enter so deeply into the question as to realize that it was his position, his wealth, his name, and not himself which she would be sure to marry. He only felt that it was a curious, amusing, exciting thought. He was not used to such reflections; and, indeed, had he gone into it with any seriousness, Edgar, who had a natural and instinctive reverence for women, would have been the first to blush at his own superficial mixture of pleased vanity and amusement. But, being fancy free, and feeling the surface of his mind thus lightly rippled by imagination, he could not think of the young women with whom he had been brought into accidental contact since he came home without a certain pleasant emotion. They moved him to a sort of affectionate sentiment which was not in the least love, though, at the same time, it was not the kind of sentiment with which their brothers would have inspired him. Probably he would have been utterly indifferent about their brothers. With a sensation of pleasure and amusement he suffered his thoughts to stray about the subject: but he had not fallen in love. He was as far from that malady as if he had never seen a woman in his life; and, with a smile on his lip, he asked himself how it was that they did not move him simply as men did—or rather, how it was that they affected him so differently? not with passionate or irreverent, far less evil thoughts, but with a soft sense of affectionateness and indulgent friendship, a mingling of personal gratification and liking which was quite distinct from love on the one hand, and, on the other, from any sentiment ever called forth by man.

Lady Augusta was at home, with all her girls, but on the eve of starting. They were going to town for the short season, which was all Mr. Thornleigh meant to give them that year. "Don't you think it is hard," Gussy said, confidentially, to Edgar, "that because Harry has got into debt we should all be stinted? If any of us girls were to get into debt, I wonder what papa would say. This is the last day of May, and we must be back in July—six weeks; fancy only six weeks in town, or perhaps not quite so much as that."

"But Clare does not go at all," said Edgar, "and I don't think she suffers much."

"Oh, Clare! Clare is a great lady, and not dependent upon anybody's pleasure. When one is mistress of Arden, and has everything one's own way—" Here, apparently, it occurred to Gussy that she was expressing herself too frankly, for she stopped short, and laughed and blushed. "I mean, when one is one's own mistress," she said, "and not one of many, like us girls—it is quite different. If Clare chose to go to Siberia, instead of going to town, I think she would have her way. I am sure you would not oppose."

"I never oppose anybody," said Edgar; and it was curious how strongly inclined he felt to laugh and blush just as Gussy had done, and to ask her whether she would like to be mistress of Arden? "Why shouldn't she, if she would like it?" he felt himself asking. It seemed absurd not to give her such a trifle if it really would make her so much more comfortable. Edgar, however, felt a little disposed to reason with her, to demonstrate that the position was not so very desirable after all. "But it is not so easy as you think," he said, "for Clare finds it very difficult to manage me. I don't think she ever had so hard a task. She has no time to think of town or the season for taking care of me."

Gussy's eyes lighted up with fun and mischief. "I wonder if I could manage you—were I Clare," she said, laughing, and not without a little faint blush of consciousness. Perhaps Lady Augusta heard some echo of these last words, for she came and sat down by Edgar, entirely breaking up their tête-à-tête. Lady

Augusta was very kind, and motherly, and pleasant. She inquired into Edgar's plans with genuine interest, and gave him a great deal of good advice.

"If I were you, I should take Clare to town," she said. "I think it would do her good. To be sure, she is still in mourning, but she ought to be beginning to think of putting her mourning off. What is the use of it? It cannot do any good to those who are gone, and it is very gloomy for the living. To be sure, it suits Clare; but I think, Mr. Arden, you should take her to town. Besides, you ought not to shut yourself up at your age in the country all the year through; it is out of the question. My girls are grumbling at the short season we shall have. I daresay Gussy has told you. You must not mind her nonsense. She is one of those who say not only all, but more than they really mean to say."

"Then I wish there were more of such people in the world, for they are very charming," said Edgar heartily; and he thought so, and was quite sincere in this little speech. Lady Augusta was very friendly indeed as she shook hands with him. "Don't forget that we expect to see you in town," she said, as he went away. "He will be with us before ten days are over," she said to Mr. Thornleigh, in confidence, with a nod of satisfaction: but her conclusion was made, unfortunately, on insufficient grounds.

CHAPTER XXII

The first of June was very bright and warm. The summer had set in with great ardour and vehemence, not with the vacillation common to English summers. There had been no rain for a long time, and the whole world began to cry out for the want of it. A long continuance of fair weather, though it fills an Englishman with delight out of his own country, is very embarrassing to him at home. He gets troubled in his mind about the crops, about the grass, about the cattle, and tells everybody in the most solemn of voices that "we want rain;" whereas when he has crossed the Channel it is the grand subject of his self-congratulations that you need not be always speculating about wet days, but can really believe in the weather. The weather had been thoroughly to be trusted all that month of May, and all the rural world was gloomy about it; but Edgar had not yet acquired English habits to such an extent, and he was glad of the serene continuous sunshine, the blue sky that made a permanent background to his fine trees. It was the first time that he had been able to give hospitality, and it pleased him. When he had made sure that his sister did not object, he anticipated Lord Newmarch's visit with a certain pleasure. There would be novelty in it, and some amusement; and it was natural to him to surround himself with people, and feel about him that flow and movement of humanity which is necessary to some spirits. The Ardens could do without society as a general rule. They had stately feasts now and then, but for the greater part of their lives the stillness of the park that surrounded them, the gambols of the deer, or the advent of now and then the carriage of a county neighbour coming to pay a call, was all that was visible from their solemn windows. This was not at all in Edgar's way; and accordingly he was glad somebody was coming. It would have been a pleasure to him to have filled his house, to have put himself at everybody's service, to have felt the tide rising and swelling round him. To Clare it might be a bore, but it was no bore to her brother. Lord Newmarch drove out from Liverpool, where he had been attending the great social meeting, between five and six in the afternoon. Edgar saw him from a distance, and hurried home to meet his guest. "Newmarch is coming, Clare," he cried as he came into the little drawing-room in which Clare sat very demurely, with the silver and china shining on the little tea-table beside her, and her embroidery in her hand. It was not an occupation she cared for, but yet it was good for emergencies, and especially when it was necessary to take up that dignified position as the lady of the house. "Very well, Edgar; but you need not be excited about it," said Clare. What was Lord Newmarch that any one should care about his coming? She sat in placid state to receive her brother's visitor, secretly fretting in her heart to see that Edgar was not quite as calm as she was. "Can it be because he is a lord?" she said to herself, and shrank, and was half ashamed, not being able to realise that Edgar's fresh mind, restrained by none of the Arden traditions, would have been heartily satisfied to receive a beggar, had that beggar been pleasant and amusing. To be sure Lord Newmarch was not amusing; but he was instructive, which was far better—or at least so some people think.

Clare's placidity, however, vanished like a dream when she raised her astonished eyes and saw that two people had come into the room, and that one of them was Arthur Arden. The sudden wonder and excitement brought the blood hot to her cheeks. She gave Edgar a rapid angry look, which fortunately he did not perceive, and then her cousin's voice was in her ear, and she saw dimly his hand held out to her. She had known, of course, that they must meet, but she had expected to have time to prepare herself, to put on her finest manners, and receive him in such a way that he should feel himself kept at a distance, and understand at once upon what terms she intended to receive him. But there he stood all at once before the dazzled eyes which were so reluctant to believe it, holding out his hand to her, assuming the mastery of the position. Clare's high spirit rose, though her heart fluttered sadly in her breast. She got up hastily, stumbling over her footstool, which was an admirable excuse for not seeing his offered hand. "Mr. Arden!" she exclaimed. "Forgive me for being surprised; but Edgar, you never told me that you expected Mr. Arden to-day."

"I did not know," said Edgar, with anxious politeness; "but he is very welcome anyhow, I am sure. We did not settle anything about the day."

"Newmarch drove me over," said Arthur. "I have been at Liverpool too, going in for science. At my age a man must go in for something. When one ceases to be interesting on one's own merits—But Miss Arden, if I am inconvenient, send me off to the Arden Arms. There never was man more used to shift for himself than I."

"It is not in the least inconvenient," said Clare, with her stateliest look; and she seated herself, and offered them tea. But she did not look again at her cousin. She addressed herself to his companion, and asked a hundred questions about his meeting, and all that had been discussed at it. Lord Newmarch was not in the least disinclined to communicate all the information she could desire. He sipped his tea, and he talked with that surprised sense of pleasure and satisfaction which the sudden discovery of a good listener conveys. He stood over her, his tea-cup in his hand, with the light, which was not positive sunshine, but a soft reflection of the blaze without thrown from a great mirror, glimmering on his spectacles as it did on the china—and expounded everything. "It was a very inconvenient time," he said, "but fortunately nothing very important was going on, and I was so fortunate as to secure a pair. So I do not feel that I have neglected one part of my duty in pursuing another. This was the most convenient moment for our foreign friends. The fact is, all great questions affecting the people should be treated internationally. That has long been my theory. Politics are a different thing; but social questions—questions which affect the morality and the comfort of the entire human race—"

"But the measures which suit one portion of the race might not suit another," said Clare, who was intensely British. "I don't think I have any confidence in things that come from abroad."

"Except brothers," said Arthur Arden, almost below his breath.

Nobody heard him but Clare. It was said for her, with the intention of establishing that private intercourse which can run on in the midst of the most general conversation. But Clare had set herself stoutly against any such indulgence.

"Except brothers," she said calmly, as if the observation had been her own.

"That is exactly my own way of thinking," said the social philosopher, "but are not we all brothers? Am not I identical with my cousin in France and my brother in America so far as all social necessities are considered? I require to be washed, and clothed, and fed, and taken care of exactly as they do. We will never have a thorough and effectual system till we all work together. Though I am a Liberal in politics, I am not at all against the employment of force in a legitimate way. If I will not keep myself clean of my own accord, I believe I ought to be compelled to do it—not for my own sake, but because I become a nuisance to my neighbours. If I do not educate my children as I ought, I should be compelled to do. There are a great many things, more than are thought of in our philosophy, which ought to be compulsory. The individual is all very well, and we have done a great deal for him; but now something must be done for the race."

"If a man eats garlic, for instance, he should be compelled to give it up," said Arthur Arden. "I was in Spain last year, and I would give my vote for that. Insects ought to be abolished, and all that. If you get up a crusade on that subject, I will give you my best support. And then there are duns. To be asked to pay money is a horrible nuisance. I don't know anything that makes a man more obnoxious to his neighbour—"

"I don't see what advantage is to be gained by laughing at a serious subject," said Lord Newmarch, over his tea-cup. "There are a great many things that can scarcely be discussed in general society; though indeed ladies are setting us a good example in that respect. They are boldly approaching subjects which have hitherto been held unfit—"

"Edgar, you will remember that we dine at half-past seven," said Clare, rising. Her usual paleness had given way to a little flush of excitement. It was not Lord Newmarch and his questionable subjects that excited her. Lord Newmarch was a politician and a Social Reformer, and, as he himself thought, a man of intellect; but Clare was perfectly able to make an end of him should it be necessary. It was the other man standing by, who made no pretension to any kind of superiority, who alarmed her. And he did more than alarm her. She was confused to the very depth of her being to see him standing there by her brother's side. Was he friend or foe? Had he come back to Arden in love or in hatred; for herself or for Edgar? Arthur Arden had powers and faculties which were the growth of experience, and which are rarely possessed by very young men. He could look so that nobody could see him looking except the person at whom he gazed. He could express devotion, almost adoration, without the bystanders being a bit the wiser. He could flatter and persuade, and make use of a thousand weapons, without even addressing the object of his thoughts. And Clare, how she could not tell, had come to understand that strange language. She knew how much was meant for herself in all he said. She felt the charm stealing over her, the sense that here were skill and strength worthy a much greater effort brought to bear upon her, as if her approbation, her love, were the greatest prizes to be won upon earth. There is something very captivating to the imagination of a young woman in this kind of pursuit; but this time she was forewarned, and had the consciousness of her danger. She hurried away, and took refuge in her own room, feeling it was her only stronghold. Then she tried to ask herself what her feelings really were towards this man, the very sight of whom had made her heart flutter in her bosom. He was poor, and she was rich; he had passed the limits of youth, and she was in its first blossom. He had no occupation, nothing to do by which he could improve or advance himself. It was even suspected that he had not passed through the troubles of life without somewhat tarnishing his personal character. The history that could be made of him was not a very edifying history, and Clare was aware of it. But yet—All these things were of quite secondary importance to her. The question that really absorbed her mind was—Had he come here for her? Was she his object? and if so, why? Clare knew well what everybody would say—that he came "to better himself;" that her fortune was to fill up the gap in his, and her young life to be absorbed in order to give sustenance and comfort to his worn existence. Could it be so? Could anything so humbling be the truth? Not merely to love and soothe, and make him happy; but her money to maintain, herself to increase his personal comfort. Clare tried very hard to consider the matter fully in this light. But how difficult it was to do it! Just when she tried to remember how penniless he was, and how important her fortune would be to him, a certain look rushed back on her mind which surely, surely could have nothing to do with her fortune! And then Clare upbraided herself passionately for the gross and foul suspicion: but yet it would come back. Was he a man to love generously and fondly, as a woman likes to be loved? or would he think but of himself in the matter, not of her? If he loved her, it would not matter to her that he had nothing, or even that his past was doubtful, and his life half worn out: all that was nothing if it was true love that moved him; but—Old Arden was hers, and she was an heiress capable of setting him up again in the world, and giving to him honour and position such as in reality had never been his. And she felt so willing to do it. True, she had assured Edgar that she would not take Old Arden from him. But anyhow she would be rich, able to place her husband, when she married, in a position worthy of her name. If—

It may be supposed that to dress for dinner while these thoughts were buzzing through her brain was not the calm ceremony it usually is. And all this commotion had arisen from the first glance at him, the mere sense of his presence. What would it be, then, when he had found time to put forth all his arts?

The reader will probably think it very strange that Clare Arden should not have been utterly revolted by the thought that it was possible her kinsman could mean to make a speculation of her, and a mere stepping-stone to fortune. But she was not revolted. She had that personal objection to being married for her money which every woman has; but had not she herself been the heroine of the story, she would rather have felt approval than otherwise for Arthur Arden. What else could he do? she would have said to herself. He could not dig, and begging, even when one is little troubled with shame, is an unsatisfactory maintenance. And if everything could be put right by a suitable marriage, why should not he marry? It was the most natural, the most legitimate way of arranging everything. For the idea itself she had no horror. All she felt was a natural prejudice against being herself the subject of the transaction.

CHAPTER XXIII

"May I walk with you, if you are going to the village?" said Arthur Arden, when Clare met him in one of the side walks, two or three mornings after his arrival. She had not seen him until he was by her side, and all this time had avoided him strenuously, allowing herself to be deluged with Lord Newmarch's philosophy, and feeling by instinct that to keep out of her cousin's way as long as she was able would be her soundest policy. She would have abandoned her walk had she known that he was in the park waiting for her; but now it was too late to escape. Clare gave him a little bow of assent, feeling that she could not help herself; and she did not take any trouble to conceal her sentiments. The pucker came to her brow which Edgar knew so well, and the smile that just touched her lips was merely a smile of civility—cold and reluctant. She was, indeed, so far from disguising her feelings that Arthur, who was learned in such matters, drew a certain encouragement from her frank discontent. He was clever enough to know that if this reluctance had been quite genuine, Clare would have taken some pains to restrain it. Her faint smile and only half-suppressed frown were the best warrants to him that she was not so perfectly indifferent as she had attempted to appear.

"You don't want me?" he said, with a plaintive intonation. "I can see that very clearly; and you will never give me a chance of saying a word. But, Miss Arden, you must not be angry with me, if I have schemed for this moment. I am not going to say anything that will offend you. I only want to beg you to pardon me for what I once said in ignorance. I did not know Edgar then. What a fine fellow he is! I came disposed to hate him, and find fault with everything he did and said. But now I feel for him as if he were my younger brother. He is one of the finest young fellows I ever met. I feel that I must say this to you, at whatever cost."

The blood rushed to Clare's cheek, and her heart thumped wildly in her breast, but she did all she could to keep her stiff demeanour. "I am glad you acknowledge it," she said, ungraciously; and then with a little rush of petulance, which was more agitation than anger—"If that was how you thought of my brother—if you intended to hate him—why did you come here?"

A pause followed upon this hasty question—a pause which had the highest dramatic effect, and told immensely upon the questioner, notwithstanding all her power of self-control. "Must I answer?" said Arthur Arden, at last, subduing his voice, and permitting a certain tremulousness to appear in it—for he had full command of his voice; "I will, if I must; but in that case you must promise not to be angry, for it will not be my fault."

"I do not want any answer," said Clare, seeing her danger. "I meant, how could you come with that opinion of Edgar? and why should you have formed such an opinion of Edgar? He has done nothing to make any man think ill of him—of that, I am very sure. An old prejudice that never had any foundation; because he did not resemble the rest of us—"

"Dear Miss Arden, do not I confess it?" said her cousin, humbly. "The echo of a prejudice—that was all—which could never stand for a moment before the charm of his good nature. If there are any words which will express my recantation more strongly teach them to me, and I will repeat them on my knees."

"Edgar would be much surprised to see you on your knees," said Clare, who felt the clouds melting away from her face, in spite of herself.

"He need not see me," said Arthur; "the offence was not committed in his knowledge. I am in that attitude now, though no one can see it. Will not the Lady Clare forgive her poor kinsman when he sues—on his knees?"

"Pray—pray, don't be ridiculous!" said Clare, in momentary alarm; but Arthur Arden was not the kind of man to go the length of making himself ridiculous. Emotion which is very great has not time to think of such restraints; but he was always conscious of the limitations which it is wise to put to feeling. His homage was spiritual, not external; but still, he allowed her to feel that he might at any moment throw himself at her feet, and betray that which he had the appearance of concealing so carefully. Clare went on, unconsciously quickening her steps, surrounded by an atmosphere of suppressed passion. He did not attempt to take her hand—to arrest her in any way; but yet he spread round her that dazzling web which was woven of looks and tones, and hints of words that were not said.

"It is not anything new to me," she said, hurriedly. "I always knew what Edgar was. It is very sad to think that poor papa would never understand him; and, then, his education—One cannot wonder that he should be different. My grand anxiety is that he should marry suitably," Clare added, falling into a confidential strain, without knowing it. "He has so little knowledge of the world."

"Does he mean to marry? Lucky fellow!" said Arthur Arden, with a sigh.

"It does not matter much whether he means it or not," said Clare. "Of course he must. And then, he has such strange notions. If he fell in love with any girl in the village, I believe he would marry her as soon as if she were a Duke's daughter. It is very absurd. It is something wanting, I think. He does not seem to see the most ordinary rules of life."

"Lucky fellow, I say!" said Arthur Arden. "Do you know, I think it is angelic of me not to hate him. One might forgive him the houses and lands; but for the blessed power of doing what he pleases, it is hard not to hate him. Of course, he won't be able to do as he pleases. If nobody else steps in, Fate will, and baulk him. There is some consolation to be got out of that."

"It does not console me to think so," said Clare. "But look—here is something very pretty. Look at them, and tell me if you think the girl is a great beauty. I don't know whether I admire her or not, with those wild, strange, visionary eyes."

The sight, which was very pretty, which suddenly stopped them as they talked, was that of Mrs. Murray and her granddaughter. They were seated under a hawthorn, the whiteness of which had begun to tarnish, but which still scented the air all round. The deeper green of the elms behind, and the sweet silken greenness of the limes in the foreground framed in this little picture. The old lady sat knitting, with a long length of stocking depending from her hands, sometimes raising her head to look at her charge, sometimes sending keen glances up or down the avenue, like sentinels, against any surprise. Jeanie had no occupation whatever. She lay back, with her eyes fixed on the sky, over which the lightest of white clouds were passing. Her lap was full of flowers, bits of hawthorn, and of the yellow-flowered gorse and long-plumed grasses—the bouquet of a child; but she was paying no attention to the flowers. Her eyes and upturned face were absorbed, as it were, in the fathomless blue of the sky.

"I hope she is better," said Clare, in her clear voice. "I am very glad you can bring her out to enjoy the park. They say the air is so good here. Do you find it much milder than Scotland? I suppose it is very cold among the hills."

"Cold, oh, no cold," said Mrs. Murray, "but no so dry as here among your fine parks and all your pleasant fields. Jeanie, do you see the young lady? She likes to come out, and does nothing, the idle thing, but look up at the sky. I canna tell what she finds there for my part. She tells me stories for an hour at a time about all the bits of fleecy clouds. Ye may think it idle, Miss Arden, and a bad way to bring up a young thing; but the doctors a' tell me it's the best for the puir bairn."

"I don't think it idle," said Clare, who nevertheless in her mind highly disapproved. "When one is ill, of course one must seek health first of all."

"Jeanie, do ye no see the young lady?" whispered the grandmother; but neither of them rose, neither attempted to make that curtsey of which Clare felt herself defrauded. When the girl was thus called, she raised her head and looked up in Clare's face with a soft child-like smile.

"I am better, thank you," she said, with a dreamy sense that only a question about her health could have been addressed to her. "I am quite better, quite better. I canna feel now that it's me at all."

"What does she mean?" said Clare, wondering.

"That was the worst of all," said Jeanie, answering for herself. "I never could forget that it was me. Whatever I did, or wherever I was, it was aye me, me—but now the world is coming back, and that sky. Granny! do ye mind what you promised to say?"

"It was to tell you how thankful we are," said Mrs. Murray, looking up from her knitting, yet going on with it without intermission, "that ye let us come here, Miss Arden. It is like balm to my poor bairn. When it's no the body that's ailing, but the mind, it's hard to ken what to do. I've tried many a thing they told me to try—physic and strengthening meat, and all; but there's nothing like the sweet air and the quiet—and many, many thanks for it. Jeanie, Jeanie, my darlin', what has come to you?"

The girl had gradually raised herself upright, and had been seated with her eyes fixed in admiration upon Clare, who was as a goddess to the young creature, thus dreaming her way back into life; but there had been a rustle by Clare's side which had attracted her attention. It was when she saw Arthur Arden that she gave that cry. It rang out shrill and wild through the stillness, startling all the echoes, startling the very birds among the trees. Then she started up wildly to her feet, and clutched at her grandmother, who rose also in sudden fright and dismay. "Look at him, look at him!" said Jeanie—"that man! it's that man!"—and with every limb trembling, and wild cries bursting from her lips, which grew fainter and fainter as her strength failed, she fell back into the arms which were opened to support her. Arthur Arden started forward to offer his assistance, but Mrs. Murray waved him away with an impatient exclamation.

"Oh, if you would go and no come near us—oh, if you would keep out of her sight! No, my bonnie Jeanie—no, my darlin'! it's no that man. It's one that's like him, one ye never saw before. No, my bonnie bairn! Oh, Jeanie, Jeanie, have ye the courage to look, and I'll show ye the difference? Sir, dinna go away, dinna go away. Oh, Miss Arden, keep him still till my darling opens her eyes and sees that he's no the man."

Clare stood silent in her consternation, looking from one to the other. Did it mean that Arthur knew these strangers? that there was a secret, some understanding she had not been meant to know, some undisclosed wrong? She suspected her cousin; she hated that old, designing, artful woman; she feared the mad girl. "I can do nothing," she said hoarsely, with quivering lips, drawing apart, and sheltering herself behind a tree. And then she hated herself that her first movement was anger and not pity. As for Jeanie, her cries sank into moans, her trembling increased, until suddenly she dropped so heavily on her grandmother's shoulder as to draw Mrs. Murray down on her knees. They sank together into the deep, cool grass—the young creature like one dead, the old woman, in her pale strength and self-restraint, holding her fast. She asked no help from either of the two astonished spectators, but laid the girl down softly, and put back her hair, and fanned her, with the gentleness of a nurse to an infant, murmuring all the while words which her nursling could not hear. "It's no him, my bonnie bairn; oh, my Jeanie, it's no him! It's a young gentleman, one ye never saw—maybe one of his kin. Oh, my poor bairn, here's it come all back again—all to do over again! Why did I bring her here?"

"What has here to do with it? what do you mean by calling Mr. Arden that man? what is the meaning of it all?" said Clare, coming forward. "I must know the meaning of it. Yes, I see she has fainted; but you are used to it—you are not unhappy about her; and I am unhappy, very unhappy, to know what it means."

The three women were by this time alone, for Arthur Arden had gone for help from the Hall, which was the nearest house, as soon as Jeanie fainted. Clare came forward, almost imperious, to where the poor girl was lying. It was a thing the grandmother was used to, she said to herself. The old woman made no fuss about it, and why should she make any fuss? "I don't want to be cruel," she said, almost crying in her excitement; "if you are anxious about her, tell me so; but you don't look anxious. And what, oh, what does it mean?"

"It means our ain private affairs, that neither you nor any stranger has aught to do with," said Mrs. Murray, looking up with an air as proud as Clare's own. And then she returned in a moment to her natural tone. "I am no anxious because she has fainted. She will come out of her faint, poor bairn; but it's sore, sore work, when you think it's all passing away, that the look of a man she never saw before should bring it back again. I canna tell ye my private history, Miss Arden. I may have done wrong in my day, and I may be suffering for it; but I canna tell it a' to a stranger; and that is what it means—no an accident, but our ain private affairs that are between me and my Maker, and no one beside."

"But she knew Mr. Arden!" said Clare.

"The man she took him for is dead; he was a man that did evil to me and mine, and brought us to evil," said the grandmother, solemnly. "The life is coming back to her; and oh, if ye would but go away, and keep yon gentleman away! If we were to bide here for a year, I could tell ye no more."

Wretched with suspicion, unbelieving and unhappy, Clare turned away. Had she been capable of feeling any additional blow to her pride, that dismissal would have given it; but her pride was in abeyance for the moment, swallowed up in wonder and anxious curiosity. "The man she took him for is dead"—was that true, or a lie invented to screen one who had betrayed poor Jeanie. The girl herself could not surely be deceived. And if Arthur Arden had wrought this ruin, what remained for Clare?

CHAPTER XXIV

Mrs. Murray was left alone with her grandchild, and she was glad. Though she was old, she was full of that patient strength which shows itself without any ostentation whenever the emergency which requires it arises. She was not sorry for herself, nor did she think much of her own age, or of what was due to her. She had long got over that phase of life in which a woman has leisure to think of herself. And there was no panic of alarm about her, such as might have come to the inexperienced. She knew her work, and all about it, and did not overwhelm herself with unnecessary excitements. She laid her child down in the grass, in the shade, laying her head upon a folded shawl. Jeanie had come out of her faint, but she lay in a state of exhaustion, with her eyes closed, unable to move or speak. The grandmother knew it was impossible to take her home in such a state of prostration. She seated herself so as to screen her charge from passers by, and resumed her knitting—a picture of calm and thoughtful composure—serious, yet with no trace of mystery or panic about her. What had happened to Jeanie was connected with their own affairs. It was a thing which nobody but themselves had anything to do with. She sat and watched the young sufferer with all that grave power of self-restraint which it is always so impressive to witness, asking neither help nor pity, knitting on steadily, with sometimes a tender glance from her deep eyes at the young fair creature lying at her side, and sometimes a keen look round to guard against intrusion. The work went on through all, and those thoughts which nobody knew of, which no one suspected. What was she thinking about? She had a breadth of sixty years to go back upon, and memories to recall with which nothing here had any connection. Or could it be possible that there might be a certain connection between her thoughts and this unknown place? Sometimes she paused in her work, and dropped her hands, and turned her face towards the house, which was invisible from where she sat, and fell into a deeper musing. "Would I do it over again if it were to do?" she said half aloud to herself, with an instinctive impulse to break the intense stillness; and then, making no answer to her own question, sat with her head dropped on her hand, gazing into the shadowy distance. What was it she had done? It was something which touched her conscience—touched her heart; but she had not repented of it as a positive wrong, and could yet, it was clear, bring forth a hundred arguments to justify herself to herself. She paused, and leant her head upon her hand, and fixed her eyes on the distance, in which, unseen, lay the home of the Ardens. Her thoughts had strayed away from Jeanie. She mused, and she sighed a sigh which was very deep and long drawn, as if it came from the depths of her being. "The ways of ill-doers are hard," she murmured to herself; and then, after a pause, "Would I do it again?" It was not remorse that was in her face; it was not even penitence; it was pain subdued, and a great doubt which it was very hard to solve. But there was no clue to her musing, either in her look or her tones. She took up her knitting with another sigh, when she had apparently exhausted, or been exhausted by that thought, and changed the shawl under Jeanie's head, making her more comfortable, and looked at her with the tenderest pity. "Poor bairn!" she said to herself; "Poor bairn!" and then, after a long pause, "That she should be the first to pay the price!" The words were said but half aloud, a murmur that fell into the sound of the wind in the trees and the insects all about. Then she went to work again, knitting in the deepest quiet—a silence so intense that she looked like a weird woman knitting a web of fate.

It was a curious picture. The girl with her bonnet laid aside, and her hair a little loosened from its smoothness, lying stretched out in the deep cool grass which rose all round her, and shaded by a great bough of hawthorn, laden with the blossom which was still so sweet. The white petals lay all about upon the grass, lying motionless like Jeanie, who was herself like a great white flower, half buried in the soft and fragrant verdure; while the old mother sat by doing her work, watching with every sense, ear and eye on the alert to catch any questionable sound. The girl fell asleep in her weakness; the old woman sat motionless in her strength and patience; and the trees waved softly over them, and the summer blue filled up all the interstices of the leafage. This was the scene upon which Arthur Arden came back as he returned from the house with aid and promises of aid. He had been interested before, and now, when he perceived that Clare was not to be seen, his interest grew more manifest. He came up hurriedly, half running, for he was not without natural sympathy and feeling. "Is she better?" he asked. "Miss Arden's maid is coming, and the carriage to take her home; and, in the meantime, here is something." And he hastily produced a bottle of smelling-salts and some eau-de-cologne.

"She is better," said Mrs. Murray, stiffly. "I thank ye, sir, for all your trouble; but there's no need—no need! She is resting, poor lamb, after her attack. It's how she does always. But I would fain be sure that she would never see you again. Dinna think I'm uncivil, Mr. Arden; for I know you are Mr. Arden by your looks. You are like one that brought great pain and trouble to our house a year or two since. I would be glad to think that she would never see ye more."

"But that is a little hard," said Arthur Arden. "To ask me to go away and make a martyr of myself, without even telling me why. I must say I think that harsh. I would do a great deal for so pretty a creature," he added, carelessly drawing near the pretty figure, and stooping over her. Mrs. Murray half rose with a quick sense of the difference in his tone.

"My poor bairn is subject to a sore infirmity," she said, "and for that she should be the more pitied of all Christian folk. A gentleman like you will neither look at her nor speak to her but as you ought. I am asking nothing of you. It's my part to keep my own safe. All I pray is that if you should meet her in the road you would pass on the other side, or turn away your face. That's little to do. I can take care of my own."

"My good woman, you are not very complimentary," said Arthur; and then he went and gazed down once more upon the sleeping figure in the grass. His gaze was not that of a pure-minded or sympathetic spectator. He looked at her with a half smile, noting her beauty and childish grace. "She is very young, I suppose?" he said. "Poor little thing! What did the man who was like me do to frighten her so? And I wonder who he was? The resemblance must be very great."

"He brought grief and trouble to our house," said Mrs. Murray, who had risen, and stood screening her child with a jealous mother's instinct. "Sir, I am much obliged to you. But, oh! if you would be kinder still, and go on your way! We are complaining of nothing, neither my bairn nor me."

"Your 'bairn,' as you call her, is mighty pretty," said Arthur Arden. "Look here, buy her a ribbon or something with this, as some amends for having frightened her. What, you won't have it? Nonsense! I shall probably never see her again. You need not be afraid of me."

"I am no afraid of any man," said Mrs. Murray; "if you would leave us free in this spot, where we're harming nobody. Good day to you, sir. Give your siller to the next poor body. It's no wanted by me."

"As proud as Lucifer, by Jove!" said Arthur Arden, and he put back his half-sovereign in his pocket, perhaps not unwillingly, for he had not many of them; and then he stood still for a minute longer, during which time the old woman resumed her knitting, and went on steadily, having dropped him, as it were, though she still watched him keenly from under her eyelids. He waited for some other opportunity of speech, but at length, half amazed half annoyed, swore "by Jove!" once more, and turned on his heel with little courtesy. Then he began to bethink himself of Clare, who had gone down the avenue, and whom he had missed. He was a man used to please himself, used to turn aside after every butterfly that crossed his path, and it was so long since he had engaged in the warm pursuit of anything that he had forgot the amount of perseverance and steadiness necessary for it. He had been almost, nay quite glad, when he saw that Clare was gone, and felt himself free for the moment to find out something about the pretty creature who lay in the grass like a Sleeping Beauty; but now that the careful guardian of the sleeping beauty had sent him away, his mind returned to its original pursuit. Would Clare be angry; would she consider his desertion as a sign of indifference, an offence against herself? He chafed at the self-denial thus made necessary, and yet he was as anxious to secure Clare's good opinion as any man could be, and not entirely on interested motives. She was very dignified and Juno-like and stately. She would condemn him and all his ways did she know them. She would be intolerant of his life, and his friends, and his habits; and yet Clare attracted him personally as well as pecuniarily. He would be another man if he could succeed in persuading her to love him. It would make him rich, it would give him an established position in the world—and it would make him happy. Yes, there could not be any doubt on that subject, it would make him happy; and yet he was ready to be led astray all the same by any butterfly hunt that crossed his path.

As he hastened down the avenue, he met a little procession which was coming up, and which consisted of an invalid chair, drawn by a man, who paused every ten minutes to speak or be spoken to by the patient within, and followed by an elderly maid, who walked with a disapproving air under a huge umbrella. Arthur Arden was sufficiently acquainted with the population of Arden to know at once who this was, and the voice which immediately addressed him was one which compelled his attention. "Mr. Arden, Mr. Arden," said the voice, "do stop and look at this beautiful chair; a present from Edgar. I was saying to my brother just the other day—Ten minutes in the open air—only ten minutes now and then, if there was any way of doing it! And to think of dear Edgar recollecting. And the handsomest—Now, is not he a dear fellow? All padded and cushioned, and as easy as a bed—And the very best temper in the world, Mr. Arden, and always thinking of others. You will think me an old fool, but I do so love that boy."

"He is very lucky, I am sure, to inspire so warm a feeling," said Arthur, with mock respect.

"Lucky indeed! he deserves it, and a thousand times more. Of course I would not speak of such a thing as loving a gentleman," said Miss Somers, with a soft blush stealing over her pretty faded old face, "if it was not that I was so old and helpless. And dear Edgar is so nice and so kind. Fancy his coming to see me the very first day he was at home: a young man you know, that might have been supposed—and, then this beautiful chair. I was saying to my brother just the other day—but then some men are so different from others, and never take the trouble even to give you an answer. To be sure, there are many things that put a gentleman out and try his temper that we ladies have not got to bear; but then, on the other hand—And, as I was saying, it arrived all at once, two days ago, in a big packing-case—the biggest packing case, you know. My brother said, 'It is for you, Lucy;' and 'Oh, good gracious, is it for me? and what is it, and who could have sent it? and how good of them to think of me;' and then, when one is in the midst of one's little flutter, you know, he tells you you are a little fool, and how you do run on!"

"That was unkind," said Arthur, when she paused to take breath; "but will you tell me, please, have you seen Miss Arden? I left her going down the avenue."

"Oh, Clare! she's in the village by this time, walking so quick. I wonder if it is good to walk so quick, especially in the sun. When I was a young girl like Clare—And then they say it brings illnesses—She was in such a hurry; not a bit like Clare to walk so fast; and it makes you look heated, and all that. Mr. Arden, you will make me so happy if you will only look. It can draw out, and I can lie all my length when I get tired. The Queen herself, if she were an invalid—but I'm so glad she is not an invalid, poor dear lady; with all those horrible death warrants to sign, and everything—Don't you think there should be somebody to do the death warrants when there is a lady for the Queen—I mean, you know, when there is a Queen? But if I were the Queen I could not have anything better. Isn't he a dear fellow! And the springs so good, and everything so light and nice and so pretty. You have not half seen yet how nice—"

"There is somebody a little in advance who will appreciate it a great deal better than I can," said Arthur. "I must overtake Miss Arden. Yes—there; just a little further on."

"Now, I wonder what he can mean by somebody a little in advance," said Miss Somers, as Arthur went hastily on. "Can it be Edgar, I wonder—the dear fellow! or the Rector? or whom, I wonder? Mercy, please, if you don't mind the trouble, do you see anybody coming? Not that I mind who I meet. I am sure I should like to show dear Edgar's present everywhere. I wonder if it is Lady Augusta? I am sure, Mercy, you know I have always thought well of Lady Augusta—"

"I don't see nobody, mum," said Mercy, cutting her mistress remorselessly short, "but them Scotch folks as lives in the village, and ain't no company for the quality; set them up, them and their pride! John, Miss Somers wants to go a little quicker past them tramps and folks; for they ain't no better, a poking into our parish," muttered Mercy, under her breath.

"Oh, no, John; please, John—I want so much to see them," remonstrated Miss Somers. Fortunately, John wanted to see them too, and after a struggle with Mercy, who ruled her mistress with a rod of iron, the procession paused opposite to where Mrs. Murray sat. Mercy herself could not be more unwilling for any colloquy. The old Scotchwoman kept on her knitting, with her eyes steadily fixed upon it, as long as that was possible. She only moved when the invalid's eager voice had called her over and over again, "Oh, please, come and speak to me. I am Dr. Somers' sister, and a great invalid, and I have heard so much about you; and just yesterday I was saying to my brother—Oh, please, do put down your knitting for a moment and come to me. I am so helpless, I cannot put my foot to the ground."

Mrs. Murray rose slowly at this appeal, and came and stood by the invalid's chair.

CHAPTER XXV

"I have heard so much about you," said Miss Somers, eagerly. "I am so glad to have met you. The Doctor is always so busy he never gives me any answer when I speak; and you know when one is helpless and can't budge—I should have been in my room for ever but for Edgar, you know—I mean Mr. Arden—the dearest fellow!—who has sent me—I don't know if you understand such things; but look at it. This is the first time I have been out for two years. Such a handsome chair! the very best, you may be sure, that he could get to buy. And I know he is so interested in both—Which is your grandchild? Goodness gracious me? Are not you frightened to death to leave her? She might catch cold; she might have something go up her ear—lying right down in the grass."

"She'll take no harm," said the old woman, "and it's kind, kind of you to ask—"

"Oh, I am always asking," said Miss Somers; "but people are so very impatient. 'How you do run on!' is all my brother says. I hear your child is so pretty; and I am so fond of seeing pretty people. Once, when I was young myself—but that is such a long time ago, and, of course, you would not think it, and I don't suppose any traces are left—but people did say—Well, well, you know, one ought never to be vain. She lies dreadfully still; are you not frightened to see her like that—so pale, you know, and so still? It always frightens me to see any one lie so quiet."

"She is sleeping, poor bairn," said Mrs. Murray. "She has had a fright, and a bit little attack—and now she's sleeping. The Doctor has been real kind. I canna say in words how kind he has been—and Mr. Arden. You're fond of Mr. Arden? I do not wonder at that, for he's a fine lad."

"There can't be anything wrong in saying I am fond of Edgar. No; I am sure there can't be anything wrong," said Miss Somers: "he is the dearest fellow! We were brought up so very strict, I always feel a little difficulty, you know, in saying, about gentlemen—But then at my age, and so helpless as I am—I have him up to my room to see me, you know, and I can't think there is any harm, though I would not for the world do anything that was considered fast, or that would make any talk. Why, I have known him from a baby—or rather I ought to have known him. The Doctor was not here then. When one thinks of such a while ago, you know, everything was so very different. I was going to balls and parties and things, like other young people. Five and twenty years ago!—there was a gentleman that had a post out in India somewhere—but it never came to anything. How strange it would have been, supposing I had been all these five and twenty years in India! I wonder if I should have been helpless as I am now?—but probably it would have been the liver—it would have been sure to have been the liver. Poor dear Edgar, he never was like the Ardens. That was why they were so unkind."

"Unkind!" said Mrs. Murray, with a sudden start.

"Oh, you must not say anything of it now," said the invalid, frightened. "He is the Squire, and there is no harm done. The old Squire was not nice; he was that sort of hard-hearted man—and poor dear Edgar was never like an Arden. My brother has his own ways of thinking, you know, and takes things into his head; and he thinks he understands: he thinks it was something about Mrs. Arden. But that is all the greatest wickedness and folly. I knew her, and I can say—He was so hard-hearted—not the least like a father—and that made him think, you know—"

Mrs. Murray, who was not used to Miss Somers, and could not unravel the maze, or make out which him was the Squire and which the Doctor, gazed at her with wondering eyes. She was almost as much moved as Edgar had been. Her cheeks grew red, her glance eager. "I have no right to be asking questions," she said, "but there's a cousin of mine here that has long been in their service, and I cannot but take an interest in the family. Thomas Perfitt has told us a' about the Ardens at home. If I was not presuming, I would like to know about Mr. Edgar. There's something in his kind eyes that goes to the heart of the poor. I'm a stranger; but if it's no presuming—"

"Yes; I suppose you are a stranger," said Miss Somers, who was too glad to have any one to talk to. "But I have heard so much about you, I can't think—Oh, dear, no, you are not presuming. Everybody knows about the Ardens; they were always a very proud sort of stiff people. The old Squire was married when I was a young lady, you know, and cared for a little attention and to be taken notice of; though I am sure why I should talk of myself! That is long past—ever so long past; and his wife was so nice and so sweet. If she had been a great lady I am sure I should never have loved her so—And the baby—but somehow no one ever thought of the baby—not even his mamma. She had always to be watching her husband's looks, poor thing. On the whole, I am not sure that one is not happier when one does not marry. The things I have seen! Not daring to call their souls their own; and then looking down upon you, as if you were not far, far—But poor dear Edgar never was petted like Clare. One never saw him when he was a child; and I do believe his poor dear papa hated him after—I ought not to talk like this, I know. But he has come out of it all like—like—Oh, he is the dearest fellow! And to be sure, he is the Squire, and no one can harm him now."

"Maybe the servants should not hear," said Mrs. Murray, whose face was glowing with a deep colour. The red was not natural to her, and seemed to burn into her very eyes. And she did not look at Miss Somers, but stood anxiously fingering the apron of the little carriage. John and Mercy were both close by—perhaps out of hearing, but no more.

"Oh, my dear woman, the servants know all about it," said Miss Somers. "They talk more about it than we do; that is always the way with them. I might give a hint, you know; but they speak plain. No; he was not happy when he was a boy; he went wandering all about and about—"

"But that was for his education," said the anxious inquirer, whose interest in the question did not astonish Miss Somers. To her it seemed only natural that the Ardens should be prominent in everybody's horizon. She shook her head with such a continuous shake, that Mercy was tempted to interfere.

"You'll have the headache, Miss, if you don't mind," said Mercy, coming forward; "and me and John both thinks that it ain't what the Doctor would like, to see you a-sitting here."

"It's only for a minute," said the invalid, humbly, "I want a little breath, after being so long shut up. You may think what it would be if you were shut up for two years. Would you tell John to go and gather me some may, there's a dear good creature? I am so interested in these nice people; and my brother says—Some may, please, John; not the brown branches that are going off—I think I saw some there. Mercy, you have such good eyes, go and show him, please. There, now they are gone, one can talk. Old servants are a great blessing, though sometimes—But it is all their interest in one, you know. His education was the excuse. I remember when I was young, Mary Thorpe—They said it was to learn Italian; but if that young man had not been so poor—It is such a strange, strange world! If people were to think less of money, don't you think it would be happier, especially for young girls? I hope it is not anything of that kind with your poor little grandchild; but then she is so young—"

"You were speaking of Mr. Arden," said Mrs. Murray, with a sigh; and then she added—"But he is the only heir, and all's his now."

"Oh, yes, all is his—the dear fellow; but he is not the only heir; there is Clare, you know—Don't you hate entails, and that sort of thing, that cut off the girls? We may not be so clever, though I am sure I don't know—But we can't live without a little money, all the same. I say to my brother sometimes—but then he is so impatient. And Clare is wonderfully superior—equal to any man. I think, though I have seen her every day for years, I get on better with Edgar. It makes my poor head ache, I am such a helpless creature, not good for anything. If you could have seen me a few years back you would not know me. I was always running about: the 'little busy bee;' when I was young that is what they always used to call me. There was a gentleman that used to say—a Mr. Templeton, of the Royal Navy—but there were difficulties, you know—Oh, yes; I remember, about Arden—I do run on, I know; my brother is always telling me I lose the thread, but why there should be a thread—Yes, there is another Arden—Arthur Arden; you must have seen him pass just now."

"The man that was so like—" said Mrs. Murray; and then she stopped, and shut up her lips tight, as if to establish even physical safeguards against the utterance of another word.

"He is very like his family—just the reverse of poor dear Edgar," said Miss Somers; "but I don't like him at all, and he is such a dear fellow—If there had been no son, Arthur would have succeeded, and poor dear Clare would have been cut off, unless they were to marry. I sometimes think if they were to marry—Was that your daughter stirring? I can't think how you don't die of fright to see her lying there so still. Do bring her to see me, please. I am never out of my room—except now, in this fine new chair, of course, I shall be going out every day. But it is so dreadful to have to be carried, and not to put your foot to the ground. Mercy says it is a judgment; but, you know, I cannot believe—Of course, you must be a Calvinist, I suppose?"

"There's many a judgment that never shows," said the Scotchwoman; "you feel it deep in your heart, and you ken how it comes, but nobody in this world is any the wiser. Of that I am well aware."

Miss Somers was a little frightened by the gravity of her companion's tone, and did not quite understand what she meant, and was alarmed by the sight of Jeanie lying still and white in the grass. She gave a little cough, which was an appeal to Mercy, and was seized with a sudden flutter of nervousness and desire to get away.

"Yes, yes; I have no doubt you know a great deal better," she said; "if one was to do anything very wicked—I say to my brother sometimes—I am on my way to Arden, you know, to show Edgar—And Clare passed just now; did you see her? I mean Miss Arden, but it comes so natural to say Edgar and Clare. Oh, yes, I must go on; my brother might think—And then Mercy does not like to be kept—and John's work—Good-bye. Please come and see me. If there was any room, I should offer to take your grandchild home, but a chair, you know—I am so glad to have seen you. And do you think you should let her sleep there in the grass? Earwigs is the thing that frightens me; they might creep up, you know, and then—Yes, Mercy, I am quite ready; oh, yes, quite ready. I am so sorry—Please come to see me—and the grass, and the earwigs—Oh, John, gently! Good-bye, good-bye!"

With these fragmentary words Miss Somers was drawn away, looking behind her, and throwing her good-byes after her with a certain guilty politeness. This Scotchwoman was superior, too, she said to herself, with a little shudder, and made her head ache almost as much as Clare did. Mrs. Murray, for her part, went back and sat down by Jeanie, who still slept, but began to move and stir with the restlessness of waking. The grandmother did not resume her work. She let her hands drop on her knees, and sat and pondered. The sound of the wheels which slowly carried the invalid along the path grew less and less, the air sank into quietness, the bees hummed, and the leaves stirred, murmuring in that stillness of noon, which is almost greater than the stillness of night. But the old woman sat alone with another world about her, conscious of other times and other things. She was in the woods of Arden, with the unseen house near at hand, and all its history, past and present, floating about her, as it were, an atmosphere new and yet old, strange yet familiar, of which she knew more and knew less than any other in the world. How and what she knew was known to nobody but herself; yet this very conversation had opened to her a mass of unsuspected information, and new avenues of thought, each more painful than the other. She had to bring all the powers of her mind to bear upon the new questions thus set before her, and it was with a doubly painful strain that she brought herself back when the young creature at her feet opened her bright eyes, and with a confused gaze, slowly finding out where she was, came back to the life of dreams, which was her portion in this world so full of care.

CHAPTER XXVI

While Miss Somers was discoursing thus with Mrs. Murray under the trees, Arthur Arden had pursued Clare to the village. He had lost the best possible opportunity, he felt. Just as he had been beginning to make an impression! He sped after her between the long lines of trees, swearing softly under his breath at the intruders. "Confound them!" he was saying; and yet in his secret thoughts there was a lurking determination to see that pretty little thing again, although the pretty little thing was nothing to him in comparison with Clare. He skimmed along, devouring the way, planning to himself how he should recover the ground he must have lost by his benevolent errand. "Putting one's self out of the way for other people is a deuced mistake," he said to himself. It was not a habitual weakness of his, so that he could identify the moment and recognise the results with undoubting accuracy, and a clear perception of the weakness and folly which had produced them. He must get over this kind of impulse, he thought, and prove himself superior to all such frivolous distractions. A mere pretty face! with probably nothing in it. Arthur Arden remembered Clare, who was not pretty, but beautiful; whose face had a great deal in it, not to speak of her purse; who was to have Old Arden, the cradle of the race. If he could but secure Clare everything would come right with him; and accordingly no pretty face—nothing frivolous or foolish—must be allowed to intercept or block up his way.

Clare was going towards the village school when Arthur overtook her. She had been walking very fitfully, sometimes with great haste, sometimes slow and softly, losing herself in thought. He came up to her when she had fallen into one of these lulls of movement, and Arthur was satisfied to see that he was recognised with a start, and that the little shock of thus suddenly perceiving him brought light to her eyes and colour to her face.

"You, Mr. Arden!" she said, with a kind of forced steadiness. "I thought you were still occupied about—that—girl. I am so sorry, it seems uncivil, but I don't really know her name. Was she better? It was good of you to interest yourself so much."

"I did no more than any man must have done," said Arthur. "Your maid promised to go, and gave me salts, &c. But she was better, I think. The old woman seemed quite used to it. She was lying asleep in the grass—a very pretty picture. But the old woman is an old dragon. She fairly drove me away."

"Indeed!" said Clare feebly, with white lips, feeling that the crisis of her fate might be near.

"I only looked at the child—pretty she is, you know, but a little dwarf—when the mother got up and drove me away. I dared not stay a moment longer; and she gave me my orders, to turn my head away if I met them, and never to show my face again. Droll, is it not? One surely should be permitted a little property in one's own head and face."

"Yes; but it is not every head and face that have the same effect." And then Clare paused a little to collect her energy. She had the fortitude of a young princess and ruling personage, accustomed (for their good) to speak very freely to the persons under her, and even to ask questions which would have covered her with confusion had she looked at them in another point of view; but the queen of a community, however small, is not permitted to blush and hesitate like other girls. She made a pause, and collected all her energies, and looked her cousin in the face, not with any shyness, but pale, with a passionate sense of her duty. She was so simple at bottom, notwithstanding all her stateliness, that she thought she could assume over him the same authority which she had over the lads of the village. "Mr. Arden," she said, with tremulous firmness, "you may think it is a matter with which I have nothing to do—you may think even that it is unwomanly in me to ask anything about it," and here a sudden violent blush covered her face; "but I have always considered myself responsible for the village, and—and entitled to interfere. One's position is of no use unless one can do that. I wish to know what you have to do with these people—what is—your business—with that poor girl?"

Clare's courage almost gave way before she concluded. She faltered and stumbled in her words; her face burned; her courage fled. If she could have sunk into the earth she would gladly have done it. This was very different from a village lad. She felt his eye upon her; she imagined the curious gleam that was passing over his countenance; she was almost conscious of putting herself in his power. And yet she made her speech, going on to the end, though her excitement was such that she felt quite incapable of paying any attention to the answer. She did not look at him, and yet she divined the look of mingled wonder and offence and partial amusement that was in his face. There was something else besides—a look of less innocent meaning—the significant glance which such a man gives to the woman who has committed herself; but Clare was too innocent, too void of evil thought to divine that.

"My dear Miss Arden, you surprise me very much," he said. "What could be my business with the girl? What could I have to do with such people? Your imagination goes more quickly than mine. I do not know what connection there could possibly be between us. Do you? I am at a loss to understand—"

Poor Clare felt herself ready to sink to the ground with shame and mortification; and then her pride blazed up in sudden fury. "How can you ask me? How dare you ask me?" she said, at the height of passion; and he was so quiet, so entirely in command of himself.

"Why should not I dare?" he said softly. "My cousin has always been very good to me, except once, when she mistook my meaning, as she does now. There is nothing I dare not tell you about myself at this moment." He winced a little when he had said this, not intending to make so explicit a declaration; but yet went on courageously. "About these poor people, there is really nothing in the world to say. I never saw them in my life before. The old woman said so, if you remember. I was like somebody who had disturbed their peace—very unlucky indeed for me, for I feel I shall be subject to all manner of false construction. But my cousin Clare can understand me, I think. Should I be likely to venture into her presence while carrying on a vulgar—Such things should never so much as be mentioned in her hearing. I am ashamed to seem to imply—"

Clare had been driven to such a pitch of shame and passion that she could no longer endure herself. "I did not imply," she said, "I asked—plainly—I am the protector of everybody here. It is not for me to shut my eyes to things, though they may be a horror and shame to think of. I asked you—plainly—what you had been doing—why the sight of you had such an effect upon that poor girl?"

"I will answer the Princess, not the young lady," said Arden, with mocking calm. "Your young subject has taken no scathe by me. I never saw her until this morning in your presence. I never should have known of her existence but for you; is that enough? or shall I appear in your Highness's Court and swear to it? Such a question could scarcely be put by you to me; but from a Sovereign to a stranger is a different matter. Have I cleared myself to the Princess Clare of Arden? Then let me be acquitted, and let it be forgotten. It wounds me to suppose—"

"You are to suppose nothing," said Clare, with averted face. "I have asked you because I thought it was my duty, Mr. Arden, in my position—I have spoken quite plainly—and—I am going to visit the school. You will not find it at all amusing. I am sorry to have said anything—I mean I am sorry if I have been unjust. I am grieved—Good morning. I will not trouble you more just now—"

"Mayn't I wait for you?" said Arthur, in his gentlest tone. "If you could know how much higher I think of you for your straightforwardness, how much nobler—No, please don't stop me; there are some things that must be said—"

"And there are some things that cannot be listened to," said Clare, waving her hand as she entered the porch. She escaped from him without another word, plunging into the midst of the children and the monotonous hum of their lessons with a sense that everything about it was simply intolerable, that she could bear no more, and must fall down at his feet or their feet, it did not much matter which. She could not see the trim little schoolmistress, her own special protegée and pupil, who came forward curtesying and smiling. A haze of agitation and bewilderment was about her. The rows of pinafored children rising and bobbing their little curtseys to the young lady of the manor were visible to her as through a mist. "My head aches so," she said faintly. "Let me sit down for a little in the quiet; and oh, couldn't you keep them quite still for two minutes? The sun is so hot outside."

"Won't you go and sit down in my room, Miss Clare?" said the schoolmistress. "The children will be moving and whispering. It is so cool in my room. You have never been there since you had it built for me; and the jasmine has grown so, you would not know it. Please come into my room."

Clare followed mechanically into the little sitting-room, a tiny cottage parlour, with jasmine clustering about the window, and some monthly roses in a little vase on the table. "It is so sweet and so quiet here. I am so happy in my little room," said the schoolmistress; "and it is all your doing, Miss Clare: everything is so convenient. And then the garden. I am so happy here."

"Are you, indeed?" said Clare, sitting down in the little wickerwork chair, covered with chintz, which creaked under her, but which was at once soft and splendid in the eyes of her companion. "Never mind me, please; go on with your work, and as soon as I am rested I will follow you to the school. Please leave me by myself, I want nothing now."

And there she sat for half an hour all alone in that little homely quiet place. The window was open, the white curtain fluttered in the wind, the white stars of the jasmine gleamed—just one or two early blossoms—among the darkness of the foliage. And the roses were faintly sweet, and the atmosphere warm and balmy; and in the distance a faint hum like that of the bees betrayed the neighbourhood of the school. Clare, who had all Arden at her command, and to whom the great rooms and stately passages of her home were a matter of necessity, felt grateful for this balmy, homely stillness. She took off her hat, and pushed her hair off her forehead, and gradually got the mist out of her eyes, and saw things clearly. Oh, how foolish she had been! She, who prided herself upon her good sense. Edgar would not have committed himself so, she thought, though she was continually finding fault with him; but she, who had so good an opinion of her own wisdom, she who was so proudly pure, and above the breath of evil, that she should have thus betrayed and made apparent her evil suspicions and wicked thoughts! What must anyone think of her? "Your imagination goes faster than mine;" that was what he had said. And her imagination had jumped at something which should never be named in maidenly ears. Clare's confusion and self-horror were so great that the longer she mused over them the more insupportable they grew. Her cheeks blazed with a hot permanent blush, though she sat alone. What could he think of her? what could anybody think of her? Such thoughts would never have entered Miss Budd's head, whose life was spent between the noisy school and this quiet parlour, who was a good little creature, never interfering with anybody, doing her work and smiling at the world. "Why cannot I do that?" Clare said to herself, with the wild shame of youth, which feels its little sins to be indelible. She, Clare, did not seem to be able to help interfering with her brother, who knew better than she did—with everybody, down to this little Scotch girl, and even with Arthur Arden! Oh, how she hated herself, and what a fool she had been!

Clare was very lowly in her tone when she went into the school, with a bad headache and a pale face, and a spirit more subdued probably than it had ever been in her life before. It is very dreadful to make one's self ridiculous, to show one's self in a bad light, when one is young. The sense of shame is so intense, the certainty that nobody will ever forget it. She passed a great many false notes in the singing, and big stitches in the needlework, and was altogether so subdued and gentle that Miss Budd was filled with astonishment. "She must be going to be married," sighed the schoolmistress, with a glow of sympathy and admiration in her eyes; for she was romantic, like so many young persons in her position, and full of interest, and a wistful, half-envying curiosity what that state of mind could be like. Miss Budd had seen a gentleman lingering about the school door; she had seen him pass and repass when she came back from the little parlour in which she had left Clare. She could not but volunteer one little timid observation, when Miss Arden's duties were over, and she attended her to the door. "The gentleman went that way, Miss Clare," said the schoolmistress, timidly stealing a glance from under her eyelashes. "What gentleman?" said Clare, with a start; and her self-control was not sufficient to keep the telltale blush from her cheeks. "Oh, my cousin, Mr. Arden," she went on, coldly. "He has gone back to the Hall, I suppose." And she pointedly went the other way when she left the school, taking a path which could only lead to Sally Timms' cottage, a woman who was quite out of Clare's good graces. "Can it be a quarrel?" Miss Budd asked herself anxiously, as she went back to her scholars. And Clare went hurriedly, seeing there was nothing else for it, to visit Sally Timms. Nothing could well be imagined more utterly unsatisfactory than Sally Timms's house, and her children, and her personal character. She was the favourite pest of the village, though she did not originally belong to it, or even to the neighbourhood. Her boys thieved and played tricks, and took every malady incident to boys, and were generally known to have brought measles and whooping-cough, not to say small-pox, into Arden. The two former maladies had passed through all the children of the place, in consequence of the wandering propensities of Johnny and Tommy, and their faculty for catching everything that was going. And the latter had been only kept off by the prompt removal of Sally herself to the hospital in Liverpool, from whence she had come back white and swollen, and seamed and scarred, to the utter destruction of the remnant of good looks which she had once possessed. She was a widow, as such people always manage to be, and had no established means of livelihood. She took in washing when she could get it. She would go messages to Liverpool when her boys were doing something else, always ready for any piece of variety. She had some boxes of matches and bunches of twigs in her window for lighting fires, by which she sometimes turned a penny. Now and then she had been seen with a basket furnished with tapes and buttons, which she sold about the country, enjoying that, too, as a relief from the monotony of ordinary existence. In short, she was one of those wild nomads to be met in all classes of society, who cannot confine themselves to routine—who must have change and movement, and hold in less than no estimation the cleanliness and good order and decorums of life. She was very fond of gadding about, not very particular as to the laws of property, and utterly indifferent to ordinary comfort. It would be impossible for one person to disapprove more entirely of another than Clare disapproved of Sally Timms. And yet she was on her way to see her—there being only her cottage at the end of the village street which could lead her in an opposite direction from that taken by Arthur Arden—which was only too clear a sign, had she but known it, how important Arthur Arden was becoming to Clare.

How long the conversation lasted Miss Arden could not have told any one—nor indeed what it was about. Sally was saucy and she was penitent; but she was not hopeful; and Clare shook her head as she went away. She gave a little nod to John Hesketh's wife, who was the model woman of the village, as she passed her cottage. "I have been talking to Sally Timms, but I fear there is nothing to be done with her," she said, stopping a second at the garden gate. "She's a bad one, Miss Clare, is Sally Timms," said Mrs. Hesketh, disapprovingly. But neither of them were aware that Clare's visit was totally irrespective of Sally's welfare, spiritual or bodily; and was only a pretext to avoid Arthur Arden, who, nevertheless, was patiently waiting for her all this time at the great gate.

The conversation which Arthur Arden thrust upon Clare by persistently waiting for her in the avenue was not a satisfactory one. Though she could not refuse to accept his explanation that he knew nothing about the strangers, yet a sense of uneasiness and discomfort remained in her mind. When once it is suggested that such secrets exist in a world which looks all fair and straightforward, it is difficult for a young mind to throw off at once the shock of the suggestion. Clare looked at her cousin, who was so much older than herself, and who had been so much in the world, acquiring, no doubt experiences of which she knew nothing, and shrank just a little aside, closing herself up, and putting on all her defences. "How do I know what his life has been, what things may have happened to him?" she said to herself. With a certain mingling of attraction and repulsion, she glanced at him from under her eyelashes. He had lived a man's life, which is so different from a woman's; he had been abroad in the world, swept along in the great current, driven from one place to another, from one society to another. And Clare felt that she could never tell what recollections he might have brought out of that great ocean in which he had been sailing, which was so unknown to her, and doubtless so distinct and clear to him. He might have left cares and sorrows behind him—nay, was it not certain that he must have left many a trace behind him, being such a man as he was? As she walked on beside him this feeling came over her so strongly that it swallowed up all other sentiments. She too had a little line of memories, innocent recollections, pangs of childish suffering, unjust reproofs, wounded self-love, and one great natural grief. It was like a little rivulet running under the bushes, hiding only the softest blameless secrets. But his must be like the sea, full of sunny islands and dark cliffs, with calms and storms in it, and havens and shipwrecks—things she could not possibly know of, except by some chance word now and then, and never could fully enter into. A certain admiration grew unconsciously in her mind, along with a great deal of dread and shrinking. What a fine thing it would be to be such a man! How wide his horizon in comparison with hers! How extended and varied his knowledge! Poor Clare! she shrank with a chilled sense that she never could partake or share this vast extent of experience; but it never occurred to her to inquire what kind of knowledge of the world is acquired at German gaming-tables. Clare's imagination was utterly ignorant of the Turf, and the coulisses, and the Kursaal. She had an idea much more elevated than reality of the Clubs, and took it for granted that a man who was an Arden, even though he was poor, must have entrance always into the best society. He for his part walked by her side with the real recollections bubbling in his mind of which she formed so flattering a vision. He was remembering various things that would not have borne telling, even to ears much less innocent than those of Clare. The girl, who knew nothing about it, surrounded him with a bright and wide and noble world, swelling higher and greater than her unassisted thoughts could penetrate—with tragedies in it, no doubt, and sins, but all on so large a scale; whereas the meanest matters possible haunted Arthur's mind, the narrow stifling atmosphere of commonplace dissipation, the "Life" which is a round of poor amusements, varied only by the excitement of gain or loss, with now and then a flavour of vice, the only piquant element in the poor mixture. Thus Imagination and Fact went side by side, unable to divine each other; and Clare shrank, yet wondered, secretly inclining towards the man who was so little known to her, painfully attracted and repelled, averting her face for the moment, but drawing near in her heart.

Lord Newmarch could only spare three days to the Ardens, one of which was a Sunday. And he walked dutifully to church, carrying Clare's prayer-book, and placing himself by her side. "This is what I like," he said. "The only real remnant of anything worth preserving in the feudal system. Here are your brother and yourself, Miss Arden, at the head of your people, to take their part or plead their cause, or redress their wrongs; here they can see you, and pay their homage; they have the advantage of feeling that you too worship God in the same place; they have the benefit of your example. This is the beautiful side of a country gentleman's life."

"But they see us, I assure you, on other days besides Sunday," said Clare.

"That I do not doubt. Forgive me, Miss Arden, but it is very charming to see your sense of duty. Women seem to me generally to be deficient in that point. I see it in my sisters. They will be wildly charitable whenever their feelings are touched, and that is easily enough done, heaven knows. Any cottager on the estate—or off the estate, for that matter—who has a story to tell can accomplish it. But they have not that sense of duty to all, which is more or less impressed upon men who have dependents. Allow me to pay my tribute of admiration to one who is an exception to the rule."

Clare made him a little curtsey in reply to his elaborate bow, and did not laugh, partly because she was wanting in the sense of humour, and partly because, to tell the truth, she agreed with him, and was so far conscious of her own excellence. And then he had suggested another line of reflection. "But your sisters"—she said, and hesitated, for it was not quite polite to say what she was going to say, that his sisters were young women of no family, with no feudal rights, and very different from a daughter of the house of Arden. It does not answer, however, to make this sort of speech to the son of an Earl, and Clare caught herself up.

"My sisters are comparatively little at Marchfield?" he suggested. "That is what you would say; and no doubt it is quite true; but still there is a deficiency in this point. There is no sense of duty. And I find it common among women. They do things from emotional motives, or because they like to do them, but not from that manly, serious sense—I am not one of those who sneer at what are called women's rights. For my part, I should be but too happy, for instance, to have the assistance of your fine instincts and administrative powers in public business; but, still, there are characteristic differences which cannot be overlooked—"

"Pray, don't think I care for women's rights," said Clare, with a blush of indignation. "I hate the very name of them. Why should we be jested and sneered at for the sake of two or three here and there who make a talk? Let us alone, please. I would rather suffer a great deal, for my part, than hear all this odious, odious talk!"

"Ah, you feel it in that way?" said Lord Newmarch, impartially. "I cannot say I quite agree with you there, Miss Arden. You at present suffer nothing. You are young and rich, and—and every one you meet with is your slave," the young philosopher added gallantly, after a pause. "But that is not the case with all women. Some of them are oppressed by unjust laws, some feel the necessity of a career—"

"Helena Thornleigh, for instance," said Clare. "I have no patience with her. Thornleigh village is in pretty good order, thanks to Ada; but only fancy a girl wanting a career, and all those dreadful cottages within a mile of her father's house! Don't you know Chomely and Little Felton, on the way to Thorne? They are frightful places. If the poor people were pigs, they could not be more uncomfortable. And what does Helena ever do to mend them? Why, there is a career ready to her hand."

"But what could she do to mend them?" said Lord Newmarch, "I don't suppose she has any money of her own."

"She has her father's," said Clare indignantly, and walked on, elevating her head, her heart swelling with a recollection of all the power her father accorded to her, and all the revolutions she had made.

"Ah," said Lord Newmarch, shaking his head, "there are fathers and fathers; and besides, Miss Thornleigh probably thinks that to gain a thing by wheedling her father, which her brother could do independently, is but a sign of bondage. She has a fine intellect, and a great deal of energy—"

"Then I would go and build them with my own hands!" said Clare, with that fine mixture of unreasoning Conservatism and Revolutionism which so often distinguishes a woman's politics. She was the strictest Tory in the world: a change of law or custom was a horror to her. She scorned the idea of a career for Helena Thornleigh with the intensest inconsiderate disdain. But she would have backed her up about the cottages to the fullest extent that enthusiasm could go, and helped her to work at them had that been needful. Lord Newmarch put his head a little on one side and took a close view of her, which was not without meaning. Strong sense of duty, good fortune, enthusiasm in a certain way which might be most usefully trained, excellent old family, great personal beauty, youth. These were qualities most worthy of consideration. He could not feel that he had encountered any one yet who was quite so well endowed. She would do credit to the choice even of an Earl's son; she might further even a high political career. He made a mental note in his mind to this effect as they arrived at the church door.

Mr. Fielding was not very much of a preacher. He looked venerable in his surplice, with his white hair, and he read the service with a certain paternal grace, like a father among his children. He had baptised the great majority of his hearers, married them, had some share in all the great events of their life, and had given them all the instruction they had in sacred things. Accordingly, there was no one so appropriate as he to conduct their prayers, to read them the simple lesson of love to God and aid to man. His teaching seldom went any further. His was not the preaching which insists upon the authority of the Church, or the extreme importance of the divisions of the ecclesiastical year. And though there were one or two points of doctrine which he held very strongly, it was only on very urgent pressure that he preached on them. His audience knew, or, at least, the instructed among his audience knew, that the Rector had been holding a very hot discussion with Dr. Somers when he produced one of his discourses upon Faith or Predestination. On such occasions Dr. Somers would himself be present, with his keen eyes confronting the gentle preacher in an attitude of war, and noting all the flaws in his armour; and it was well for Mr. Fielding that he was short-sighted and could not see his adversary. But on this Sunday there had been nothing to excite him. The June day was soft and balmy, and through the open door the peaceable blue sky and green boughs looked in to cool and lighten the atmosphere. A grave or two outside but made the sense of home more profound. The rustics worshipped with their dead around them, almost sharing their prayers, and eyes that wandered found nothing worse to look upon than the green grassy turf with its pathetic mounds below, and the deep blue, leading their thoughts to the unutterable, above. The line of educated faces in the Squire's pew, and Dr. Somers, like a humanised eagle, seeing everything, were the only breaks in the usual audience. Here or there a farmer or two, with an ample wife more brilliant than her humble neighbours, headed a row of ruddy boys and girls—but these were as much rustics as the ploughmen round them. At the big door of the church, the west end, sat Perfitt and Mrs. Murray, two faces of a very different type. She looked on, rather than joined in the service, half disapproving, half interested; while he, with a certain matter-of-fact superiority, patronised and initiated the stranger, finding the places in the prayer-book for her, and thrusting it into her hand at every change. No one noted the two thus strangely introduced into a scene foreign and strange to at least one of them, except Edgar, who, perhaps, was not so attentive as he ought to have been to Mr. Fielding's sermon, and to whom the changes on the old Scotchwoman's face were interesting, he could not tell why. It seemed to him that he could divine what was passing through her mind, and he looked on with almost affectionate amusement at the listener, who was perhaps Mr. Fielding's only attentive hearer in all the congregation. The good folks about were dropping asleep in the unaccustomed quiet, or else looking straight before them with complacent composure, hearing the words addressed to them as they heard the bees and insects, which made a slumberous pleasant hum about the place. That sound was natural to church, as the hum of bees and twitter of birds are natural which come so sweetly from the outer world. The hush, the warmth, the stray breath of air, now and then, the Sunday clothes, the hum of parson and bees together, the scent of the monthly rose laid on the prayer-book—all this was pleasant to the simple folk. They were doing their duty, and their hearts were at rest. But Mrs. Murray looked and commented, and sometimes softly shook her handsome Scotch head, and wondered if this was all the spiritual fare vouchsafed to the inhabitants of Arden. Edgar divined her thoughts as if he had known her all his life, and was more interested than if Mr. Fielding had been a much better preacher, though it would have been hard to tell why.

CHAPTER XXVIII

After this Sunday, and the thoughts it awoke in his mind, Lord Newmarch found that he could stay another day, and during that day he sought Clare's company with great perseverance. And it was not so difficult as might have been expected to secure it. Miss Arden, indeed, found her noble companion tiresome sometimes, but yet she agreed in a good many of his ways of thinking. His Radicalism did not jar upon her as did the Radicalism of other people. For Lord Newmarch was clear as to the duty of the upper classes to head and guide the new movement in which he devoutly believed. He had no desire to lessen the influence of his own order, or withdraw a jot of position or power from them. And Clare did not laugh at the social reformer, as her brother was tempted to do. She was even angry with Edgar for his amusement, and could not understand what called it forth. "He is serious, of course; but a man whose mind is full of such subjects ought to be serious," she said, with a little displeasure. "I don't know what you find to laugh at in him." And she did not object to being talked to about the improvement of the country, and how the people could best be guided for their own good. Clare knew, no one better, that the people took a great deal of guiding. She had not the least objection to make their social existence the subject of laws, to condescend to minute legislation, and ordain how often they were to wash, and what clothes they were to wear. Why not? It was all for their own comfort, and not for anybody else's advantage. Thus Lord Newmarch and she had a good many topics of mutual interest. They squabbled over the question of education, but that only increased the interest of their talk; and it is not to be denied that his position as an actual legislator, a man not discussing an abstract question, but seeking information on a matter he would have personally to do with, increased his importance in her eyes. She battled stoutly against the impression which sometimes forced itself upon her mind that he was a bore, and did not decline to talk to him, nor show any desire to avoid him all through the following Monday. Arthur Arden looking on was dismayed. Even he was not clever enough in his own case to perceive, what he would have perceived in any other, that Clare's avoidance of himself was the strongest argument in his favour. She did not avoid Lord Newmarch; and Arthur was in dismay. He took Edgar dolefully to the other end of the terrace, upon which the drawing-room windows opened, that Monday evening. Lord Newmarch had engaged Clare upon some of their favourite subjects, and the other two were thrown out, as people so often are by one animated dialogue going on in a small society.

"That Newmarch has plenty to say," Arthur ejaculated, sulkily; and pulled his moustache, and secretly murmured at Clare, whose presence prevented even the consolation of a cigar.

"Yes; he will not soon exhaust himself I fear," said Edgar. "Clare will be too much accomplished with all this flood of information poured upon her. It is a triumph of good manners on her part not to look bored."

"Do you think she is bored?" said Arthur Arden, eagerly. "I fear she is not. See how interested she looks. Confound him! The fellow's father was a cheesemonger, or his grandfather—it comes to the same thing—and to see him sitting there! If I were you, Arden, I should not stand it. Being as I am, you know, only a poor cousin, it goes against me."

"Why would not you stand it?" asked Edgar, calmly.

"Because—why, look at your sister. He is a nobody—a prig, and the son of a man who has no more right to be an Earl than Wilkins has. But can't you see he is making up to Clare? I can't help saying Clare. Why, she is my cousin, and I have known her all her life. She is rich, and she is handsome, and she has the air of a great lady, as she ought to have. But, mark my words, the fellow is making up to her, and if you don't mind something will come of it."

"I suppose he is what people call a very good match," said Edgar. "If Clare is not to be trusted to refuse the honour—though I think she is quite to be trusted—we shall have nothing to reproach each other with. He is a bore, but if she should happen to like him, you know—"

"Oh, confound your coolness!" said Arthur, between his teeth; and he left Edgar standing there astonished, and made the round of the house, and came back to him. During that round various thoughts and calculations had passed through his mind. Should he tell Edgar of his love for Clare? Should he thus commit himself without knowing in the least whether Clare cared for him or not? It might secure him a powerful auxiliary, and it might lay him open to a rebuff which he could ill bear. The pause looked like a start of impatience, but it was in reality a most useful and important moment of deliberation. He had decided that boldness was the best policy by the time he came back to his cousin's side.

"You think me a strange fellow," he said, "making off from you like this, and showing so much temper about a matter which really does not seem to concern me in the least. But—I may as well make a clean breast of it, Arden—I am in love with Clare myself. Yes, you may well start—a penniless wretch like me, that am twice her age! But these things don't go by any rule. I don't ask you to approve of me; but I can't stand by calmly, and see other people using opportunities which I fear to use. That's enough. I am glad I have told you. I ought perhaps to have done so before I came into your house; but I thought I had got the better of it. Forgive me; I have no other excuse."

Edgar stood and looked at his cousin with unfeigned surprise. He watched him as he got through his speech with a wonder which was soon mingled with other emotions. He was not prejudiced either for or against him; but the more he said the less and less favourable became Edgar's countenance. "Does Clare know of this?" he inquired coldly, in a tone which suffered surprise to be seen under a veil of indifference. Such a sentiment was the very last which Arthur had imagined possible. He could conceive his cousin angry, or he could conceive, what in his superficial eyes seemed equally probable, that Edgar would have embraced his cause at once with the impulsive readiness with which he had invited him to his house. But this chilling calm was utterly unexpected. Notwithstanding all his self-command, he stammered and faltered as he replied—

"No, I don't suppose she does. She looks on me as an uncle, I have no doubt. Arden, you young fellows are lucky fellows, I can tell you, who know what you are born to. And you don't know what injury you did me by not coming into the world ten years sooner. The foundations of my education were laid on the principle that I was the heir."

"I beg your pardon, I am sure, for being born at all," said Edgar, with a laugh in which there was not much mirth; "I could not help it, you know. But I cannot see how that can have done you much harm at ten years old. However, this is a very useless discussion. I don't quite know what you expect me to say to you. Am I to make any decision? Is this a confidence that you make to me privately, or am I to consider that my consent is asked?"

"Confound it!" said Arthur Arden, "you look at me as cool as a judge, without a bit of sympathy in you. I did not look for this, at least. Flare up, if you please—treat it any way you like. I was driven to it by my feelings; if yours are so calm—"

"Were you?" said Edgar, gravely. "Perhaps I am wrong. I have no right to make light of any man's feelings; but naturally it is my sister I must think of, not you. You talk of Newmarch as something not to be supported; but do you really think, Arden, that you yourself would be a better match for Clare?"

"I am a gentleman, at least, though I am not the son of a pasteboard Earl," said Arthur, angrily. To tell the truth, it was hard upon him. Up to this moment it was he who had held the superior position, as the man of most age, and experience and knowledge of the world. But now he felt that he stood at the bar before this boy, and the change galled him. And then his resentment impaired at once his dignity and judgment, as may be supposed.

"He is a gentleman also, whatever his father may be," said Edgar; "and though he is a bore he has a great many advantages to offer. He is rich and he has a good position, and some reputation, such as it is. I should not like to marry him myself, if the question were put to me; but Clare has her own ambitions, and might choose to influence the world as the wife of a statesman. Why shouldn't she? These are all substantial advantages, whereas—"

"Whereas I am a miserable beggar, twice her age, with not even much to brag of in the way of reputation," said Arthur Arden. "Say no more about it; I perceive the contrast sufficiently as it is."

Edgar did not say any more; but looked so serious and unmoved by his cousin's impatience, that he occasioned Arthur a new sensation. To be set down by this boy, whom he had believed to be a simpleton and enthusiast! To meet the gravity of a look which became penetrating and keen the moment it was roused with such an interest—all this was utterly unexpected. He had feared Clare, but he had said to himself, with the contempt of a man of the world for Edgar's open temper and liberal heart, that he could twine her brother round his finger. Indeed, there had not seemed any particular credit in so doing. Anybody could do it, even a novice. The young man could be persuaded out of or into anything, and was not in reality worth considering at all. But now Arthur Arden paused, and changed his mind. The tables were turned—the simpleton had seen through the whole question at once, and had calmly snubbed him, Arthur Arden, and put him back in his proper place. By Jove!—a fellow who had taken his inheritance from him, and who probably had no more real right to it than—. What a drivelling fool old Arden was to put up with it, and how hard a case for himself! All this fermented so strongly in Arthur's mind that he flung off the restraints which had hitherto confined him. He had been, by way of being very civil to Edgar since he came to the house, deferring to his wishes and consulting all his tastes; but if this was all that was to come of it! Accordingly, he left Edgar abruptly, and went and joined himself to Clare and her supposed admirer. "Here is Frivolity come to the rescue, in case my young cousin should become too wise," he said. "We don't want to have her made too wise. She is cleverer than all the rest of us by nature; and, Newmarch, I can't have her made more dangerous still by your art."

"Miss Arden instructs instead of needing to be instructed," said Lord Newmarch. "What astonishes me is the breadth of her views. She does not go into detail, as women generally do, but takes a broad grasp. I assure you, her feeling about the education of the people and the knowledge of their wants is marvellous. She knows the poorer classes as well as I flatter myself I know them, and her knowledge can only come by intuition, whereas mine is the result of careful study and—"

"You ought to know them better, certainly," said Arthur, with suppressed insolence. "As a race advances in the world it forgets the sentiments of the common stock it sprang from—and we Ardens are a long way off the original root."

"Yes, very true," said Lord Newmarch, with a little bow, "very much what I was saying. I am going to persuade your brother to make a run up to town with me," he added, turning to Clare, and rising from his seat—into which Arthur threw himself without loss of time.

"Mr. Arden, how could you speak to him so? You were rude to him," said Clare, the moment they were left alone.

"I meant to be," said Arthur Arden, carelessly. "What right had he, I should like to know, to monopolise you? What right had he to cross his legs, and sit here talking to you all the evening? Besides, it is perfectly true; and why should I be expected to eat humble pie, and loiter at a distance, and see you appropriated? You might have a little pity on your kinsman, Lady Clare."

"My kinsman ought not to be rude," said Clare. But that was all the punishment she inflicted. Something warped her judgment and blinded her clear eyes. She was not even angry at this piece of incivility, much as she prided herself upon the stateliness of the Arden manners, which Edgar could not acquire. And she sat on the terrace for ever so long after, and let him talk to her, compensating herself for the severity of the morning. And her brother looked on with a grave countenance, wondering much what he could or ought to do.

VOLUME II

CHAPTER I

Up to this time it had been Clare who had made herself anxious about her brother, worrying herself over his ways and his words, and all the ceaseless turns of thought and expression and perplexing spontaneousness which made him so unlike the Ardens; and Edgar had been conscious of her anxiety with a sense of amusement rather than of any other feeling. But now that their positions were reversed, and that it was he who was anxious about Clare, the matter was a great deal more serious. Edgar Arden felt but lightly the slights or the censures of fortune; he was not specially concerned about himself, nor prone to consider, unless on the strongest provocation, what people thought of him, or if he was taking the best way to obtain their suffrage. But this easy mind, which Clare sometimes took as a sign of levity of disposition, forsook him completely when his own duties were in question. He took them not lightly, but seriously, as Mr. Fazakerley, and Perfitt the steward, and everybody connected with the estate already knew. And not even the estate was so important as Clare. He asked himself, with a puzzled sense of ignorance and incapacity, what in such circumstances a brother ought to do. He had all the theories of a young man against any restraint or contradiction of the affections; but held them much more strongly than most young men, who it must be admitted are apt to see very clearly the necessity of interference in the love affairs of their sisters, however much they may dislike it in their own. Edgar had no family training to help him, and he was aware that English habits in such matters were different from those foreign habits which were the only ones with which he had any acquaintance, and which transferred all power in the matter into the hands of parents. Poor Clare! who had no mother to sympathise with her, no father to guide her—was it not his business to be doubly careful of all her wishes, to watch over her with double anxiety, and anticipate everything she would have him to do? But then, supposing she should wish to marry this landless and not very virtuous cousin, this man whose prospects were naught, whose character was so unsatisfactory, and with whom he himself had so little sympathy—would it be right to let her do it? Should he acquiesce simply without a word? Should he remonstrate? Should he speak of it to her? Or should he wait until she had first consulted him? Edgar found it very hard to answer these questions. He took to watching his sister, and her manner to Arthur Arden, her ways and her looks, and every passing indication; and got hopelessly bewildered, as was natural, in that maze of fluctuating evidence, which sometimes seemed to him to go dead against, and sometimes to be entirely in favour of his cousin.

For Clare did not let herself go easily down that dangerous slope. She stopped herself now and then, and became utterly repellant to Arthur; now and then she relapsed into softness. Sometimes she would ask, wonderingly, when he meant to go? "Is he to stay on at Arden for ever? Did you ask him to stay as long as he liked?" she would say with a frown on her brow, expending upon her innocent brother the excitement and restless agitation of her own mind. "Should you like him to stay as long as he wished?" Edgar asked on one of these occasions, with a look which he tried hard not to make too anxious. "I think we were far happier before anybody came," Clare answered, with curious heat, and a tone almost of resentment. What did it mean? Did she want really to get rid of the visitor? Did she really hate him, as she had once said she did? When Edgar recollected that his sister had said so, and that Arthur Arden had confirmed it, he was quite staggered. And thus June ran on amid difficulties, which much confused the relations between the brother and sister. Lord Newmarch too left traces of himself in the field. He had started a correspondence with both, according to his opportunities—that is, he wrote long letters to Edgar upon the state of the political world, and sent messages and brochures to Miss Arden, who sent him messages in return. If she was to marry either of them, surely Lord Newmarch was the more appropriate of the two. He was younger as well as richer, and, though he was a prig, had the reputation of being a good man. He was galantuomo, as well as my lord; and, alas! it was quite uncertain whether Arthur Arden was galantuomo. Poor Edgar felt like an anxious mother, and laughed at himself, but could not mend it, until at last it occurred to him that the best way was to ask advice. Accordingly, he set out very solemnly one day about the end of June to consult his chief authorities. He meant to conceal his personal trouble under the guise of a fable. He would ask Mr. Fielding what a brother (in the abstract) ought to do in such a position, and he would ask Miss Somers. Miss Somers was not a very wise counsellor; but no doubt her brother must have interfered in her affairs one time at least, and she would have some practical knowledge. He went to lay his case before them with a little trepidation, wondering whether they would find him out at all, and what they would say. Dr. Somers probably would have been the best counsellor of all, but Edgar had no confidence nor pleasure in the Doctor since their last interview. So he chose Mr. Fielding in his study, and Miss Somers on her sofa, two people whose lives had not come to much; but surely they were old enough to know.

Mr. Fielding was in his study writing his sermon. It was the day after one of his grand discussions with the Doctor, and the good man was excited. He was engaged in the manufacture of a polemical sermon, culling little bits out of the polemical sermons which had gone before, but combining them so with links of the new that his adversary might not perceive the antiquity of some of his arguments. It was a relief to him to lay down his pen and clear his mind from the fumes of controversy. "I am very glad to see you, Edgar," he said. "You find me in the midst of my troubles. Young Denbigh, you know, ought to take the preaching more than he does, but I have no confidence in him in a doctrinal point of view. He would be bringing up some of the new notions, and setting our good folks by the ears—though it is rather hard upon me to preach so often myself."

"But you are the best able to instruct us, Sir," said Edgar, who to tell the truth did not often derive a great deal of instruction from Mr. Fielding's good little sermons. And then the excellent Rector coughed modestly, and blushed a little, and put his paper away from him with a gently deprecating air.

"I suppose, when one lives to be seventy, one must have learned a little—if one has made a right start," he said, "at least I hope so, Edgar, I hope so; though some of us unfortunately—The thing that startles me is that Somers should take the Calvinist view. I would not judge him—I would be, indeed, the very last to judge any one; but how a man who has lived, on the whole, rather a careless sort of life—not culpable, I don't say that—but careless, as, indeed, the best of us are—should stand up for hell and torture, and all that, is more than I can guess. If he had taken another view—more lax instead of more strict—"

"Do you think he cares at all?" said Edgar, still under the prejudice of his last interview.

"God bless us, yes; surely he must care; don't you think he cares, Edgar? Why, then, he must be sniggering in his sleeve at me. No, no, my dear boy, of course he must be in earnest; no man could be such a humbug as that. But if it was Mrs. Murray, who is Scotch, it would seem more natural. I hear she was in Church on Sunday, looking very serious. But, bless me, Edgar, you are very serious too. Is there anything wrong—with Clare?"

"There is nothing wrong—with anybody," said Edgar. "The fact is, I want your advice. At least, it is not I that want it, but—a very intimate friend of mine. He has got a sister, just like me, very pretty, and all that; but he does not know what to do—"

"About his sister?" asked Mr. Fielding, with a smile. "What does he want to do?"

"Did I tell you there was some one who—wanted to marry her?" said Edgar. "Yes, to be sure, that was it; somebody I—he don't approve of—not a proper match. And he doesn't know what to do, whether to speak to her, or to wait till she speaks, or whether he has any right to interfere. He is not her father, of course, only her brother, and he is in an utter muddle what to do. And of all the people in the world," said Edgar, with a little hysterical laugh which sounded like a giggle, "he has asked me."

"Well, that was a very curious choice, though the circumstances so much resemble your own," said the Rector, with a smile; "what do you think you would do if it were Clare?"

"That is just the question I have been asking myself," said Edgar, embarrassed. "Supposing, for the mere sake of argument, that it was Clare—I have not the remotest conception what I should do."

"With such a suitor as Arthur Arden, for instance? Edgar, never try to take in anybody, for you cannot do it. I feel for you sincerely—"

"But stop," said Edgar; "I never said Arthur Arden had anything to do with it. I never implied—"

"You have been perfectly wary and prudent," said Mr. Fielding; "but I knew Arthur Arden long before you did, and I am quite sure he means to mend his fortune, if he can, by means of Clare. I knew it before you did, Edgar, and that was why I was so grieved to see him here. Now you know it, my dear boy, send him away."

"Why did not you warn me, if you knew?" asked Edgar, surprised.

"What was the good? He might have changed his mind, or you might have thought me mistaken, and I did not know Clare's feelings, or even yours, Edgar; if you had liked him, for instance—But, my dear fellow, now you have found it out, send him away."

"I know as little about Clare's feelings as you do," said Edgar, almost sullenly, feeling that this was really no solution of his difficulties. "Clare, I suppose, is the chief person to be consulted. Should I speak to her? Should I bring matters to a conclusion? Perhaps it might come to nothing if they were let alone."

"Edgar, my advice to you is to make short work," said the Rector, solemnly, "and send him away."

"That is very easy to say," said Edgar, "but it takes more trouble in the doing. What, my nearest relative, my heir if I die! How can I turn him out of the house which is almost as much his as mine? So long as I am unmarried, which I am likely to be for some time, he is my heir."

"Then you like him?" said the Rector; "that was what I feared. Of course, if you like him, and Clare likes him, nobody has any right to say a word."

"But I never said I liked him," said Edgar, pettishly. "Neither love nor hatred seems necessary so far as I am concerned; but could not something be done that would be just without being disagreeable? I don't like to treat him badly, and yet—"

The Rector shook his head. "I think I would have courage of mind to do what I advise," he said; "he is too old for Clare, and he has not a good character, which is a great deal worse. He will make love to her one day, and then the next he will come down to the village—Faugh! I don't like to soil my lips with talking of such things. He is not a good man. I love Clare like my own child, and I would fight to the last before I would give her to that man. He ought never to have come here, Edgar, never again."

"Did anything happen when he was here before; do you know anything?" said Edgar, eagerly.

"He is your enemy, my dear boy, he is your enemy," said Mr. Fielding; and that was all that could be elicited from him. Edgar remembered that Clare had used the very same words, and it did not make him more comfortable. But yet, an enemy to himself was of so very much less importance; in short, it mattered next to nothing. He smiled, and tried to persuade Mr. Fielding that it was so, but produced no result. "Send him away" was all the Rector would say: and it was so easy for one who had not got it to do to give such advice to Edgar, who was a man incapable of sending any stranger away who claimed his hospitality, and whose sense of that virtue was as keen as an Arab's. He would have taken in the worst of enemies had he wanted shelter, with a foolish, young, highminded scorn of any danger. Danger! Let the fellow do his worst; let him put forth all the powers he had at his command, Edgar was not afraid. But then! when Clare was in question, the importance of the matter increased in a moment tenfold, and he could not make up his mind what to do.

CHAPTER II

From Mr. Fielding Edgar went to Miss Somers, to whom he told his story under the same disguise, but who unlike the Rector believed him undoubtingly, and gave him her best sympathy, but not much enlightenment, as may be supposed. And he returned to Arden very little the wiser, asking himself still the same question, What should he do? Must he go home and be patient and look on while Arthur Arden, quite unmolested and at his ease, laid snares and toils for Clare? Clare had no warning, no preparation, no defence against these skilful and elaborate plots. She might fall into the net at any moment. And was it possible that her brother's duty in the matter was to sit still and look on? Would not his very silence and passive attitude embolden and encourage the suitor? Would it not appear like a tacit consent to his plans and hopes? He was walking up the avenue while these thoughts were passing through his mind, when all at once there came to Edgar a suggestion which cleared his whole firmament. I call it a suggestion, because I do not understand any more than he himself did how it happened that all at once, being in utter darkness, he should see light, and perceive in a moment what was the best thing to do. If some unseen spirit had whispered it all at once in his ear it could not have been more vivid or more sudden. "I must go to town," Edgar said to himself. He did not want to go to town, nor had the idea occurred to him before; but the moment it came to him he perceived that this was the thing to do. Arthur could not stay when he was gone; indeed, to take him away from Clare he did not object to his cousin's company in London. "Poor fellow! after all I have the sweet and he has the bitter," Edgar thought; and to share his purse with his kinsman was the easiest matter, so long as the kinsman did not object. After he had made this sudden decision his heart sat lightly in his breast, and everything brightened up. He even grew conceited, the simple fellow, thinking on the whole it was so very clever of him to have thought of so beautiful and simple a solution to all his troubles, though, as I have said, he did not think of it at all, but had it simply thrown into his mind without any exertion of his.

"I have taken a great resolution," he said that evening after dinner before Clare left the table. "I have made up my mind to take the advice of all my good friends, and to betake myself to town."

"To town!" said Clare and Arthur, in a breath—she with simple astonishment, he with dismay. "To town, Edgar? but I thought you hated town," added Clare.

"I don't know anything about it—I don't love it," he said; "but one must not always mind that. There is Newmarch, who writes me—and—why, there are the Thornleighs. With such inducements don't you think it is worth a man's while to go?"

"The Thornleighs; oh, they are cheap enough. You will meet them everywhere," said Arthur, with a sneer. "If that is all you go to town for—"

"The Thornleighs!" said Clare; and she made a rapid feminine calculation, and decided that though it was very sudden it must be Gussy, and that a new mistress to Arden was inevitable. It did not strike her so painfully as it might have done, in the tumult of her personal thoughts. "Everything will be strange to you," she said. "And then you are so fond of the country, and have to make acquaintance with everything. Don't you think, Edgar—that might wait?"

"What might wait?" said Edgar, laughing; but he kept firm to his proposal. "Yes, I must go as soon as it is practicable," he said to Arthur when they were alone. "I have got to make acquaintance with my own country. I don't know London any more than I know Constantinople; I have been in it, and gazed at it, but that is all. And Newmarch is a very sensible fellow," he added, abruptly. "By the way, Arden, what do you say to coming with me? You might share my rooms. If you have not any pressing engagements—"

"I have nothing at all to do," said Arthur. "Of course, I should rather have stayed here. I need not tell you that, after all I have told you. Arden is to me the most captivating place in England. But if you are going, of course I must go too." And he sighed a profound sigh.

"Of course," said Edgar, with quiet calmness; and then there was an uncomfortable pause.

"That is what I object to," said Arthur Arden; "You give me to understand you won't interfere, and then you as good as turn me out of the house by going away yourself. By Jove! I believe that is the reason why—"

"If you think I am to give up all control over my movements because you happen to be in the house—" said Edgar, with a laugh. "No, Arden, that will never do. And I never said I would not interfere. It might be my duty. I am Clare's brother, and the head of the house."

"Clare can take care of herself, and so can the house. Fancy you—"

"I am all it has for a head," said Edgar, keeping his temper with an effort. "But this is very unprofitable sort of talk."

And then there was a gloomy pause, all conversation being arrested. Arthur Arden had been making, he thought, considerable progress with Clare, which was a thing that made Clare's brother much less important. She and Old Arden seemed almost within reach of his hand, and what should he care for the Hall and the Squire if he were Mr. Arden of Old Arden, with a beautiful wife? But to be thus sent away at the most critical moment! Arthur was sullen, and did not think it worth his while to conceal it. He asked himself, Should he risk the final effort—should he put it to the test, and know at once what his fortune was to be? in which case he might scorn the spurious Arden and all his efforts; or should he be wary, and flatter him, and wait?

He had not yet resolved the question when they joined Clare on the terrace, which was her summer drawing-room. But Arthur's mind was not relieved by seeing the lady of his hopes take her brother's arm, and lead him away along the front of the house, talking to him. "Has anything happened that makes you want to go?" Clare asked. "Have you heard anything—have you had any letter—is it about—Gussy? I am the only one that has a right to know, Edgar; you might tell me."

"Tell you what?"

"Why you are going to town: there must be some reason. I am sure it is not caprice. Edgar, don't you know, I care for everything that concerns you; but you speak as if your affairs were of no consequence, as if they were nothing to me."

"I am not so ungrateful nor so silly," said Edgar: "but look here. I can't tell you why I'm going, Clare; and yet I am going for a good reason, which is quite satisfactory to myself. Can you allow me as much private judgment as that?"

"Of course, your private judgment is all in all," said Clare, affronted. "How could any one attempt to dictate to you? But one might wish to know without thrusting in one's opinion—Tell me only this one thing, Edgar. Is it about Gussy Thornleigh?"

Edgar laughed in the fulness of his innocence. "No more about Gussy Thornleigh than about—"

"Me?" said Clare. "You are quite sure? If it is business, that is quite a different thing. I hope I am not so foolish as to think of interfering with business. But I do feel so concerned—so anxious, Edgar dear, about—"

"About what?" said Edgar, meeting her troubled look with his habitual smile.

"About your wife," said Clare, solemnly. She only shook her head when he laughed, disturbing all the quiet echoes. "Ah, yes, you may laugh," she said, "but it is of the greatest importance. I assure you our—cousin thinks so too."

Edgar made a profane exclamation. "I am infinitely obliged to him, I am sure," he said, after the objectionable words had escaped his lips. "Our cousin thinks so too!" What was "our cousin" between these two, who ought to be everything to each other? And then it occurred to him, with a softening sense of that comic element which runs through human nature, that while Arthur Arden so kindly interested himself in his (Edgar's) hypothetical interests, he, on his side, was taking a good deal of trouble wholly and solely on Arthur's account. His kinsman was not aware how much he was influenced by this consideration; and the thought of this mutual regard amused Edgar, even in the midst of his displeasure. "We all take an interest in each other," he said, laughing, half jestingly, yet with a sense of fun which was very odd to Clare.

And then she went, all unconscious, to her little table, and sat down, and took her work. She did not work very much, her hands being full of things more important—the affairs of the parish and estate; but to her, as to most other women, it was a welcome occasional refuge. It was true, quite true, that she was anxious about Edgar's wife, and ready to believe in the attractions of Gussy Thornleigh, or any one else who came in his way; but other feelings confused her mind at the same time. When Edgar went away of course Arthur must go also; and Arthur had managed to twine himself up with her life in the strangest subtle way. How should she bear the blank when they were gone? It would be like the time before Edgar's return—the silent days when she was alone in Arden. But these days had not been quickened by any new touch of life as the present time had been; and it made her shudder to think how such grey days would look when they came back.

"This is fatal news to me," said Arthur, softly sitting down opposite to her. "I thought I might have stayed here at Arden, and for once kept out of the racket of town."

"I thought you liked town," said Clare, "and I thought my brother hated it. I must have been mistaken in both."

"Do not be so hard upon me. I have liked town more than I ought. When there are a good many things in a man's life that he is very glad to forget, and not many that are much pleasure to think of, town is a resource to him; but when there comes a balmy time like this, when it almost looks as if the gates of heaven might open once in a way—"

"You are very poetical," said Clare, forcing herself to smile, though her heart began to flutter and beat with the sense of something more to come.

"Am I?" he said, and then began to mutter between his teeth, the first line faintly, the second more audible—

"If Maud were all that she seemed,
And her smile were all that I deemed,
Then this world were not so bitter
But a smile might make it sweet."

Clare heard, but she did not smile. She kept her eyes on her work, and her lips shut close. And after he had discharged this little arrow, he sat and looked at her and wondered. She gave him no encouragement—not the least. She would not even let it be apparent that she understood, or that there was any meaning whatever perceptible to her in what he said. The only thing that could give him any hope was a subdued consciousness about her, a thrill of suppressed excitement—something which made her fix her eyes upon her work and restrain her breath. Arthur saw this, and it made his heart beat. She was expectant—waiting for other words which she foresaw were coming—words which he would have given a great deal to be allowed to speak. For one moment he hesitated, and had almost gone on. But again a cold dread came over him. Was it according to nature that a proud girl like Clare should thus wait for her lover's declaration if she meant to answer it favourably? Was it not a stately, reluctant kindness on her part, to get over a crisis which she felt to be coming, and spare him as much pain as possible? He shrank back into himself with a sense of suffering greater than he could have considered possible when this idea took possession of him. Would she have given him this gracious opportunity, waited for him in such stillness and consciousness, had any word but "No" been on her lips? He did not think that Clare felt herself like a sovereign princess, one whom men dare not woo unless when signs and tokens to justify the daring are supplied. She sat motionless, expecting, meaning to give him courage. And he took from this indication of royal readiness to listen only an intimation of despair.

"Yes, it is fatal news to me," he said, with a deep sigh; and he got up, and stood over her, reluctant to go, too unhappy to stay. "When shall I see Arden again, I wonder, and what will have become of us all by that time?" he added, taking momentary courage; but just then Edgar came up to them, and it was too late.

Clare's thoughts had travelled very far during Arthur Arden's visit at the Hall. When he arrived she had made up her mind to endure him, to have as little to say to him as possible, to watch anxiously all his relations with her brother, and keep all her wits about her to counteract his schemes against Edgar, if he had any. But all these original intentions had floated away from her, she could not tell how. The whole condition of affairs was changed. He had no schemes against Edgar: on the contrary, he heartily liked and thought well of the strange, generous, open-hearted soul, who was so very unlike all the Ardens had ever been, and yet was the head of the Ardens, and master of the family destiny. Arthur did not understand him any more than Clare did, but had given in his declaration of loyalty and support. So that the great obstacle—was it the only obstacle between them?—was swept away at once. And then there had been the doubt of her cousin's motives, the uncertainty as to his meaning, whether he loved her for herself, or whether—but this Clare had been very reluctant to think of—he had contemplated enriching himself by her means. It would have been quite natural that he should have done so by means of any other lady. It was not the mere mercenary pretence at love which revolted his young kinswoman, but simply a personal aversion to be herself the subject of such a commercial transaction. This dread had also floated away. How could it withstand the influence of his presence—of his looks and words, and the absolute devotion he threw into his manner towards her? They had been together for long days, spending, with little meetings and partings, hours in each other's society—not alone, indeed, but almost better than alone; for a skilful and experienced hunter like Arthur Arden has it in his power to isolate his victim, and to make her feel herself the one object of interest—the one being in the room and in the world, with almost a more subtle certainty than could be given by downright words. All this Clare had come through, and it had wrought a great change upon her. She had been penetrated with Arthur Arden's influence through and through. She had grown to feel that everything she had, or anybody else had, would be better spent in his service than in any other—that it was natural to devote her possessions to him—that he had a right to appropriate what he would. This was never breathed into words, even in her own mind, but it had come to be her fixed, half-conscious principle. Mercenary!— how could it be mercenary? The world had done him the huge injustice of leaving him, a born prince, without any due provision, and was it not some one's duty—every one's duty—to neutralise that horrible injustice? Clare no longer thought of it as a desire on his part, but as a necessity on her own. And now he must go away, as poor, as unfriended, as lonely as ever, without either money in his purse, or companion to make his life go easier! She too grew furious with Edgar as she thought it all over. For a caprice! It must be a caprice. He said it was not for Gussy Thornleigh, which would have been a feasible reason, though frivolous. And what then was it for? A foolish boyish fancy, an inclination towards pleasure-seeking and the follies of London society. Nothing more! And to risk two lives for that! To break up all the combinations that were daily growing into shape and becoming practicable—all for a vulgar fancy to go to town! Clare was very angry with her brother. She thought more meanly of him than she had ever done before. "It is his education," she said to herself. "He must have been used to all kinds of junketing, as people are abroad, and he has tried to get into our quiet English ways without effect. And he feels he must get back to his natural element. Oh, heavens, my brother!" This was how poor Edgar was judged in the midst of his self-denial—the usual fate of those who think more of others than of themselves.

It was not till the very day before her brother's departure that Clare acquired a clearer light upon the subject. She had gone to visit Miss Somers, which was a duty she had much neglected of late. The village too had been neglected; she could scarcely tell why. "I have been so busy," she said, "with visitors in the house. Visitors are so rare in Arden, one gets out of the way of them; but now Edgar is going away, of course I shall be quiet enough."

This she said with a sigh; but Miss Somers was not quick enough at the first moment to understand that Clare had sighed. She was full of other subjects, and anxious for information on her own account.

"Dear Edgar, he is so nice," she said. "A young man, you know, who must have so many things—but just as pleased—Do you know, I think he is—a little—fond of me, Clare! Of course I don't mean anything but what is right. I am old enough to be—And then to think he should ask in that nice way—Fancy, Clare, my advice! If it had been my brother, you know—or anybody—but my advice!"

"Did Edgar ask your advice?" said Clare, with a smile; and she said to herself what a deceiver he is—he will do anything to please people. As if anybody could be the better of Miss Somers's advice!

"It was not for himself, my dear. Of course it can't be very—I may tell you. That friend of his, Clare, and the sister, you know—And then somebody that was fond of her—and what was he to do? It was as good as a novel—indeed, I think it was rather better. Don't you remember that story where there was—Oh, my dear child, I am sure you remember! There was such a sweet girl—Helena was her name—or no—I think it was Adela, or something—and she had a lover. Just the same—And then the good brother in such distress. Clare, why do you turn so red? I am sure you know—"

"About a brother and a sister and a gentleman who loved her," said Clare, colouring high. "Oh, no—I mean yes—I think I do recollect. And did you say the brother wanted your advice?"

This was said in a tone which chilled poor Miss Somers through and through to her very heart.

"I told him so," she said, faltering. "Of course I never pretended to set up to be very—And how could I give advice? But then the poor dear brother was so—And I suppose he thought a lady, you know—and old enough to be—or perhaps it was only to please me. I told him oh, no! never, never! And I told him some things that were too—Dear Edgar was quite affected, Clare."

"Did you advise him to go away?" asked Clare, with a smouldering fire in her eyes.

"Oh, my dear, could I take upon me to—And then he never said anything about—It was the poor girl I was thinking of. I said oh, no! never, never!—rather anything than that. You know what I have said to you so often, Clare? When a girl has a disappointment, you never can tell. It may be consumption, or it may be—oh, my dear, the unlikeliest things!—bilious fever I have known, or even rheumatism. I told dear Edgar, and he was so nice; he was sure his friend would never think—And fancy, dear, of its being my advice!"

"It must be very flattering to you," said Clare; but she rose instantly, and took a very summary leave, avoiding Miss Somers's kiss. She went home, glowing with anger and mortified pride. It was but too easy to see through so simple a veil. Edgar, who met her on the way home, could not understand her glowing cheek and angry eye. He turned and walked with her, feeling quite concerned about his sister. "What has happened?" he said. "Something disagreeable at the village? Can I set it right for you, Clare?"

"No," she said; "it is nothing disagreeable in the village. It is much nearer than the village. Edgar, I have found out why you are going away. You are going for my sake; you think I am not able to manage my own affairs—to take care of myself. You think so poorly of your sister as that!"

"What do you mean?" he said. "I think anything that is disagreeable or distasteful to you? You cannot believe it for a moment—"

"It is that Arthur Arden may go," she said firmly, but with flaming cheeks. And Edgar looked at her confused, not knowing what to say. But after the first moment he recovered himself.

"I think he has paid us a sufficiently long visit, I confess," he said. "I think, as it cannot be his while I live, that perhaps he had better not remain longer at Arden. But why should this be a matter of offence to you?"

Clare was silent; her blush grew hotter, her eyes were glowing still, but she faltered, and drooped her head as she went on.

"If that was all! if you had no other meaning! Edgar, do you think I am so frivolous, so lightly moved, so—"

"Clare," he said seriously, "do not let us discuss a subject which has not yet been put in our way. I think of you as the creature I love best in the world. I prize your happiness, and comfort, and welfare more than anything in the world. What would you have me say? I do not think I am wronging any one by going for a few weeks to London. I neither reproach nor restrain by so simple a step. Don't let us talk of it any more."

"You do both," said Clare, under her breath; but Edgar was kind, and would not hear. He was sorry for her, seeing her emotion, and he was half ashamed besides that his immaculate sister—the Princess whom everybody served and honoured—should suffer herself to be thus moved. It gave him a little pang to think that anything connected with Arthur Arden, or, indeed, with any man, could thus disturb her stately maidenly serenity. A man may be very respectful of love in the abstract, but the sight of his sister in love is a sight which is not pleasant to him. He tried to shut it out from himself by rushing hurriedly into other matters of conversation, and did a great deal of talking by way of covering her silence. Clare recovered her composure by degrees, and then had to recover from the shame which followed, and the feeling of having betrayed herself, so that Edgar's monologue was of infinite value to her, though, perhaps, she was scarcely grateful enough to him for keeping it up; and it was then that she fully found out that her brother, who was so weakly considerate of everybody's feelings, and anxious to save everybody pain, was nevertheless very firm when he thought it necessary, and did not give in, as many people supposed he would be sure to do. This discovery had a great effect upon his sister. It bewildered her, as going entirely against her preconceived notions, and it also moved her to a little alarm. For she, too, had supposed he would yield, being so tender of giving pain, and he had not yielded nor budged a step. And Clare, high-minded and high-spirited and proud as she was, grew frightened, as she glanced with furtive eyes at her gentle brother, who, she knew well, would not hurt a fly.

But if Clare was frightened, the effect upon Edgar was still more serious. He felt that his flight was too late to do any good. She loved this man whom he thought so unworthy of her. So much older, poorer, less true and good than herself; a man, with so many soils of the world upon him, whom even Edgar felt to possess experiences of which he would rather know nothing; but Clare loved him! Nothing else could account for her agitation. It was too late to banish him from the house, too late to build up defences round her—the stronghold was gone. Edgar's quick mind jumped from that conclusion to an instant and final summary of Arthur Arden's character. He was a man who might mend, as so many men might mend, if prosperity smiled upon him. If he had love, and money, and an established position, he might settle down, as so many have settled down, all his wild oats sown, and himself a most virtuous member of society—"a sober man among his boys," giving them the best advice and example. Had he been the Squire, he would have fitted the place beautifully. This idea came to Edgar in spite of himself. He would have made an admirable Squire, and the little process of wild oats-sowing would have been no social disadvantage to him. Even now, if he became Mr. Arden, of Old Arden, in right of his wife—this was one of the things that annoyed Edgar, but he tried to look it in the face. His sister had said no more about giving that possession up, and Edgar did not find it within the limits of his powers to make a proposal to her on the subject—and accordingly the chances were that Arthur would be Arden, of Old Arden, while Edgar was only the young Squire. It galled even his sweet temper to think of this transference. But, putting feeling aside, and thinking only of justice, he did not doubt that his cousin would mend. He had reached the age when men often mend, when dissipation becomes less sweet, and reputation more dear, and when comfort comes in as a powerful auxiliary to virtue. To have only such satisfaction as could be given by these thoughts when he was considering Clare's future husband, and her hopes of happiness, was poor enough; but still it was better than the thought that he was giving her over to the charge of a man who would ruin her and break her heart.

The household at Arden was an uneasy one that night; the three kept together, making each other uncomfortable, but with a vague sense of safety in company. Edgar was anxious to prevent any definite explanation; Arthur was afraid to risk the words he would be sure to say if Clare and he were alone; and she, not knowing what she feared, not knowing what she wished, afraid of her brother, afraid of her cousin, uncertain of herself, kept between them, with such a painful attempt at ordinary talk as was possible. They were to separate to-morrow—the two men into the world, the woman into the stillness which had been familiar to her so long. "I am used to it, but it will be different," she said, almost pathetically, strong in the presence of both, and feeling that what she said could produce no agitating response. "It will be very different for all of us," said Arthur Arden. "Will there ever come days like these again?"

CHAPTER IV

It would be difficult to conceive anything more strangely lonely and bleak than Arden seemed to Clare the day after her brother and cousin left it. She wandered about the vacant rooms and out upon the terrace, and kept thinking that she heard their voices and steps, and caught glimpses of them turning the corners. But they were gone—Edgar to come back again shortly, so that could scarcely be counted a calamity. But Arthur—would he come at all? Would he be years of coming, as he had been before? It seemed to Clare that it was years instead of weeks since she had dwelt thus alone and tranquil, waiting for Edgar's return. She had been alone, but then her loneliness had seemed natural. She took it as a matter of course, scarcely pausing to think that she was different from others, or, if she ever did so, feeling her isolation almost as much a sign of superiority as of anything less pleasant. She was the Chatelaine—the one sole lady of the land, in her soft maidenly state; and the visits of the kind friends who offered themselves on all sides to come and stay with her, out of pity for her solitude, had been more a trouble than a pleasure to her. But now it seemed to Clare that she would be thankful for any companionship—anything that would free her from her own thoughts. She felt like a boat which had drifted ashore, like something which had been thrown out of the ordinary course of existence. Life had gone away and left her; and yet she was more full of life than she had ever been before, tingling to the very finger points, expecting, hoping, looking for a thousand new things to come. Once it had not occurred to her to look for anything new; but now every hour as it came thrilled her with consciousness that her life might be changed in it, that it might prove the supreme moment which should decide the character and colour of all the rest.

And yet what hope, what chance, what possibility was there that this auspicious moment should come now? Had not "everybody" been driven away? This was how she phrased it to herself—not one person, but every one. Who could approach her now in the solitude which was a more effectual guard than twenty brothers? If "any one" wished to come, if any one had anything to say, why, the visit must be postponed, and the words left unsaid, until—how could she tell how long? Three years had passed between Arthur Arden's two last visits. What if three years should come and go again before Chance or Fate brought him back? It could only be Chance that had done it this time, not Providence; for if Providence had come the agent, then the visit must have come to something, and not ended without result. Thus Clare mused, as it were, in the depths of her being, concealing even from herself what she was thinking. When Arthur Arden's name flitted across that part of her mind which lay, so to speak, in the light, she blushed, and started with a sense of guilt; but in the shadowy corners, where thought has no need of words, and where a hundred aimless cogitations pass like breath, and no sense of responsibility comes in, she put no bridle upon her dreaming fancy. And it was all new to her; for dreams had never been much in Clare's way. Hers had been a practical intelligence, busied with many things to do and think of—the village and her subjects in it; the legislation necessary for them; the wants of the old women and the children—a hundred matters of detail which deserved the consideration of a wise ruler, and yet must be kept subordinate to greater principles. Even the larger questions affecting the estate had come more or less into Clare's hands. She had been allowed no time to dream, and she had not dreamt; but now idleness and loneliness fell upon her both together. She was weary of the village and its concerns. She had nothing else to occupy her. And, indeed, she had no desire for other occupations, but preferred this new musing—this maze of fancies—to anything else in earth and heaven.

But the evenings were dreary, dreary, when darkness fell, and the wistful shadows of the summer night gathered about her, and no one came to break the silence. She tried to follow her brother in imagination, and to picture to herself what he might be doing—hanging about Gussy Thornleigh, perhaps—letting himself drift into the channel indicated by Lady Augusta. Ah!—and then, while she thought she was still thinking of Edgar and Gussy, Clare's fancies would take their flight in another direction to another hero. When this, however, had gone on for a few days and nights, she was seized with a sense that it must not continue—that such a way of passing her time was fatal. It was much too like the girls whom Clare had read of in novels, whom she had indignantly denied to be true representatives of womankind, and whom she had scorned and blushed for in her heart. Was she to become one of that maudlin, sentimental band, to whom love, as novel-writers and essayists said, was everything, and to whom the inclinations of one man in this world conveyed life or death? Clare's modesty, and her pride, and her good sense, all rose in arms. She had given up all her former pursuits for these first dreamy days; but now she woke up, and tied on her hat, and forced herself down the avenue to the village. There something was sure to be found to do—whatever might be the state of her own mind or its fancies. She walked straight to Sarah's cottage, where Mary Smith and Ellen Jones were still busy with their needlework and their clear-starching. Sarah was sitting out in her cottage doorway, enjoying the evening calm. The sun had not yet set, but it had fallen below the line of the trees; and Sarah's doorway was shadowy and cool. The old woman had many grumbles bottled up for Clare's private enjoyment, which had been aggravated by keeping. Mary was "the thoughtlessest lass." She had burned a big hole in Miss Somers' muslin dressing-gown with an iron that was too hot. She had torn Mrs Pimpernel's lace; and then, instead of trying to do her best for the future, she had cried her eyes out, and become hysterical, and could do nothing at all. Nor was Ellen a great deal better. Sally, next door, had got a piece of work clean spoiled in her hands; and some things as she was making for Mrs Solms, the Rector's housekeeper, had just got to be unpicked on the spot. "The back was put to the front, and the wrong side to the right side—as if she had tried!" said old Sarah. "It couldn't be accident, Miss Clare; and the sleeves put in bottom up. It's enough to break a body's heart, after all the trouble I've took." The two culprits stood curtseying with their aprons to their eyes while this dreadful picture was being drawn; and Clare put on her most solemn face, and told them she was very sorry. "I hope I shall never hear anything of the kind again," she said, in her most serious tones; and then stopped, and sighed with a weariness which had never before moved her. "Am I to go on all my life," she said to herself, "looking after Mary's clear-starching and Ellen's sewing? Is this all I am to have out of the existence which is so rich and full to some people?" And for the moment Clare thought she understood Helena Thornleigh and the rest of the young women who wanted something to do. But this, the reader will perceive, was not really because she wanted anything to do, or was dissatisfied with the conditions of her own life, but only because she was in that state of suspense which turns existence all awry, and demands excitement of some kind outside to neutralise the excitement within.

Clare's mind, however, was suddenly diverted from herself when she looked into old Sarah's living-room, and saw another figure, which she had not before remarked, seated in the background. When Sarah perceived her keen look inside, she approached Clare with nods and significant glances. "Yes, Miss," she said in a whisper, "she's there, and as sensible as you or me, and the sweetest little thing that ever was, though she's Scotch, and I don't hold with Scotch, not in general. Just you go in and say a word to her, Miss Clare."

"I don't think she ought to be left by herself," said Clare, drawing back with a certain repugnance. Jeanie was seated in a low chair, and looked like a child—her pretty head, with its golden hair closely braided about it, bent over her work. She looked so serious, so absorbed in her occupation, so far removed from the feverish regions in which Clare felt herself to be wandering, that the dislike she had felt for this mysterious child suddenly warmed into a certain curiosity and interest. She paused on the threshold, looking in, feeling as if the step she was about to take was much more important than an innocent every-day entrance into Sarah's cottage; but after that momentary hesitation she went in, causing the little recluse to raise her head. When she saw who it was Jeanie rose, and gave Miss Arden a chair—not as Mary or Ellen would have done, but with simple courtesy. She stood until her visitor was seated, and then sat down again. But still she did not give to Clare that curtsey which she felt to be her due.

"I am glad to see you are better," Clare said, with a little stiffness; and then she was melted in spite of herself by the soft wistful look in little Jeanie's eyes. "Has your mother left you alone?" she said. "It must be strange to you to be left alone in such a place as this."

"They are all kind, kind," said Jeanie. "I'm no lonely, as if it was new to me; and then I have something to do. My head has been so strange, I have never had a seam for so long. And now it is as if I was coming back—"

"Poor child!" said Clare, "does it make you suffer much? Do you feel ill when—I mean when—your head has been strange, as you say—?"

"I canna think about it," said Jeanie, softly; "I mustna think about it; the world begins to swim and swim, and the light to go out of my eyes—I will sew my seam, if ye please."

And then there was a little pause, and everything was still. Old Sarah and her pupils stayed outside, and the murmur of their voices sounded softly in the summer air; but within the clock ticked, and the white ashes from the half-dead fire fell now and then faintly on the hearth, and Jeanie's "seam" rustled as she worked; that was all. Though there was that ghost of a fire, the room, with its tiny window and thick walls, was cooler than many a much better ventilated house; and the light was cool and green and shadowy, coming through the tall woody branches of a geranium trained upon a fanshaped framework, which answered instead of a curtain to the little window. Clare sat embarrassed, not knowing how to address this creature, who was so unlike anything she had known or encountered before.

"Do you remember your home? I suppose it is a place very different from Arden?" she said at last.

"Home! oh it's bonnie, bonnie!—bonnier than Arden," cried Jeanie, and then she paused with instinctive courtesy. "But Arden is beautiful," she said. "It's a' so beautiful that God has made. I canna' bide towns and streets and places that are built—but Arden—and the green grass and the bonnie trees—"

Where had the child learned to think of other people's sentiments—was it natural to her nation—or only to her individual character? Clare felt that the Marys and Ellens of the village would not have thought of any such refinement. "Do you live among the hills?" she said.

"On Loch Arroch side. The trees are very bonnie, and so are all the parks and pleasant fields," said Jeanie; "but if you were to see the hills up among the clouds, and the bonnie water at their feet! and then when you live always there, and your heart gets full—"

"Poor child!" said Clare again, growing more and more interested in spite of herself. "You are too young to have felt your heart grow full as you say."

"I am seventeen," said Jeanie. "Plenty folk have learned trouble before that. Granny says she had nobody to take care of her when she was seventeen—neither father nor mother, nor—And I have always her—Oh, if you had seen my Willie!" she said suddenly, "he was aye so bright and so kind. Miss Arden, you have a brother too—"

"My poor child!" cried Clare. "Jeanie, Jeanie, if that is your name, don't think of that. For your poor grandmother's sake don't do anything to bring it on."

"I cannot bring it on," said Jeanie; "it comes when I am not thinking of Willie, if there is ever a time I am not thinking of him. It's best to let me cry. Oh my bonnie boy! and in the sea, Miss Arden; think of that! no a grave under the sod, where I could go and greet, but in yon great, great, wild stormy sea—it is that I cannot bear."

"Let us talk of something else," said Clare, trembling. "Do you like old Sarah? I hope she is very attentive to you and does everything you want. You must come to the hall some day and see me; I am all alone in the hall."

"Where has he gone that you are your lane?" said Jeanie; and she raised her head with a look of anxiety which startled Clare.

"He! whom?" cried Miss Arden; she drew herself up and looked at Jeanie from her altitude, feeling all her prejudices reawaken. Jeanie, for her part, put down her work in her lap, and crossed her hands softly with a smile and a sigh.

"I am meaning your bonnie brother, Miss Arden. Oh, I wish he was my brother! We dinna know him, but we're awfu' fond of him, both grannie and me."

"Fond of him!" exclaimed Clare, more and more bewildered. "Do you know what you say?"

"Oh aye, real fond," said innocent Jeanie; "he has such a bonnie light in his eyes."

And while Clare sat in a state of partial stupefaction wondering what this might mean, there was a little stir at the door, and Mrs. Murray came in, as it were to the rescue, before her child could commit herself more.

CHAPTER V

"I am speaking of Miss Arden's brother," said Jeanie, introducing her grandmother into the conversation without a moment's pause. "Granny, tell Miss Arden. He's like faces we ken, and his voice is like a kent voice. If I was in trouble I would go and ask him. I would trust him, and I would be safe. Granny!"

"She speaks as others of her age would scarcely speak," said the grandmother, quietly. "She's no like others, Miss Arden. Her trouble is like a shield about her, like an angel o' the Lord. You think she should not name like that a gentleman that's far, far above her, but it's in her innocence she speaks. She has taken a fancy into her head that your brother is like her brother—"

"So he is," said Jeanie, softly. "She would have thought so too, if she had seen my Willie; no like yon grand, dark, hard man that comes and troubles me with his e'en; but oh, so friendly and so kind, and like a real brother. The other gives me a thrill at my heart. I'm feared still, though it's no him!"

"What other?" said Clare in some amazement. Except the Rector and the Doctor there was no gentleman in Arden of whom Jeanie could have spoken, and neither of them could be so described—a grand, dark, hard man! Her heart began to flutter painfully, and no one answered her question. Perhaps it was because there was a rustle and movement outside, and Sarah appeared on the threshold. "Mrs. Pimpernel's acoming, Miss Clare, with her daughter and the gentlemen," said Old Sarah. "T'ou'd lady's awful pushing, and you're not one as likes that sort; and Mrs. Murray, it's best for you and for me as Jeanie should go upstairs."

"I will go upstairs too," said Clare, hurriedly; and she rose and went hastily up the narrow staircase, forgetting that any invitation was necessary. But Mrs. Murray did not forget. She made a little ceremonious speech to the unceremonious young lady of the manor. "It's a poor place," she said, "but such as it is Miss Arden is very welcome." Clare, however, was far too deeply convinced of her own importance to see any reproof in these words.

"Come and sit here," said Jeanie, softly, stealing a little hand, which was like a child's, into Clare's. "I see all the folk passing from this window. Granny says no to do it; but I say what harm? And there he is, that dark man. I saw him with you, and once since then, and he spoke soft and kind; but oh, Miss Arden, I'm feared for that man! You canna see into his heart; whiles I think, has he a heart at all? And what does he want coming here?"

Clare's curiosity, or rather her anxiety, was great. She allowed herself to be drawn to the lattice window, which stood half open, all embowered in honeysuckle. She kept Jeanie's soft hand in hers with a sense of clinging to it, as if there was help in its soft childlike pressure. The new-comers were walking down the village street, filling the breadth of the road—Mrs. Pimpernel full-blown and gorgeous as usual; her pretty daughter half smothered in her finery; at one hand the young curate, Mr. Denbigh, whose head was supposed to be turned by croquet and Alice; and on the other—Clare said to herself she had known it all along. She had divined it from the first moment when Jeanie spoke. She stood leaning one arm against the half-opened window, and with the other hand holding Jeanie fast. Yes, of course, it was he; she had known it all along. The scene looked so familiar to her that she seemed to have seen it somewhere in a picture ages ago. Pretty Alice Pimpernel, blushing, and saying two words by intervals now and then—"Oh, no, Mr. Arden," and "Oh, yes, Mr. Arden" (was not that the sort of conversation Alice Pimpernel kept up? somebody, she could not remember who, had once told Clare)—and stooping over her, doing his best to entertain her, smiling that smile she knew so well—Clare grasped Jeanie's hand so hard that it hurt the girl, who gave a half-suppressed cry; and then the young Princess of Arden dropped suddenly into the nearest chair. Her heart seemed to sink somewhere into unimaginable depths. It was no surprise to her. She had known it all along. And yet—

Jeanie stood by her, unaware of what was passing through her companion's mind; or was she somehow aware, though Clare said not a word? "He thinks little, little of her he's speaking to," said Jeanie, softly. "He thinks nothing of her. If it was me, I would not let a man speak to me and look at me like that, and scorn me, Miss Arden. They're rich and grand, but he thinks he's better than them—"

"And he is better than them," said Clare, under her breath. "He is an Arden. Better than them! They are nobody. You are better. Hush! you don't understand—"

And she held the little hand clasped tight, and almost leaned upon Jeanie, not knowing it. The party came nearer; their voices became audible from the window, and it annoyed Clare to hear sounds behind her, Mrs. Murray moving about, which prevented her hearing what was said. She uttered an imperative "Hush!" and turned round, half angrily, to command silence; but still she could hear nothing but the well-accustomed tones—the voice she knew so well. "You must see her. She is the prettiest creature," she heard him say just as they passed into the room below; and then Clare loosed Jeanie's hand, and looked at her with a new inspiration. It was not for Alice Pimpernel; it was for Jeanie this visit was made.

"You pretended to be afraid of him when you met him with me," she said sharply, and then turned to the grandmother. "She fainted or something at the sight of him, and now he brings people to make a show of her. How is this?" she cried. "Do you know that this village is mine, and I have the charge of it? I must know what it means. You must explain this to me."

"Miss Arden," said Mrs. Murray, "you mistake me and mine, I canna tell why. I have lived sixty years in this world, and nobody has bidden me humble myself as you have done—though it is justice upon me, but you know nothing of that. I owe ye no explanation. I am not of your parish nor in your charge; but out of courtesy, and because of something ye never heard of, I'll satisfy you this time. The man is nothing to her nor to me. He was like a man that once we knew, as I told you. But he came here three days ago, and I was glad, for the poor bairn saw it was another face and another voice, and got over her fear. He's clever and soft-spoken, as ye ken; but he should never speak to my Jeanie more, never with my will. That is all I have to say. You should not be here, spying on your kinsman, you that's such a proud lady. You should not watch at that window, nor catch his words unawares. I would do more for you than for anybody in the world that's not my ain—"

"Why do you talk such nonsense to me," cried Clare, angrily. "Am I such a fool as to be deceived by it? What reason have you to care for me? I thought you were proud and gave yourself airs, but I did not think you would make false pretences like this. Why should you care for me—"

"I canna tell ye why, and ye will never ken," said Mrs. Murray with a sigh, "though I would give my life for you or your brother, if that would serve you. But you say well, I have no right to make pretences. You're young and I'm old, Miss Arden, and when your kinsman is below you should not be watching him here."

"I am not watching him," said Clare; and she sat with an obstinate stateliness by the window, her face deeply flushed, her heart beating high. It was not her fault. She would not have stolen here into this coign of 'vantage had she thought of Arthur. It was but to avoid the Pimpernels, not to watch him. But, even had she known he was coming, would it not have been better in any case to keep out of his way? Had not Edgar left home on purpose to send him away from Arden?—Edgar, whose fault it was, who had thus thrown his cousin into the arms of the Pimpernels, into the way of temptation. Clare was unreasonable, as was natural. She forgot—as it is so easy to forget—that Arthur Arden was much older than her brother, far more experienced, a man doubly learned in the ways of the world. The first thing that occurred to her had been to suspect poor little Jeanie, to blame Mrs. Murray; and now her imagination fell upon Edgar, putting all the responsibility on his shoulders. He had sent his cousin away. It was a new beginning which poor Arthur was making—an attempt, poor fellow, at that pure domestic life which had never been within his reach before. And Edgar, who had all the lands and all the prosperity, had refused to this other Arden even the poor shelter of his roof—the chance of learning to love something that was better than his past had been. And thus he had been thrown back upon the Pimpernels. To look at these good people in the mirror of Clare's fancy, one would have supposed they were everything that was disorderly and improper, instead of being the most respectable of households, correct in every possible point, and domestic to a degree only possible to a British nature with commercial associations. Clare sat and listened to the hum of voices down-stairs with the strangest emotion. What was he doing there? What had he come for? Why was he making himself the attendant of Alice Pimpernel? He had no money, and her father was rich—was he, thwarted in his affections, intent upon marrying and indemnifying himself by securing money at least? All these thoughts passed through Clare's mind with the rapidity of lightning. Very different would have been her brother's thoughts, even of Arthur Arden; but Clare's mind was more sophisticated than Edgar's, and leapt in a moment at this vulgar danger, which to her felt so real. And, as we have said, the idea of marrying for money did not in itself revolt her. If he could not secure the woman he loved, and her fortune, what could he do but at least attempt to secure another fortune?—something he could live on, and which would give him something to live for. Alice Pimpernel! How much would she have? Clare wondered, in her feverish suspense. Something, surely, not worth the sacrifice—a share of her father's money only—not an estate or ancient barony in her own right.

And then it occurred to her suddenly, she could not tell why, that Old Arden was the seat of an ancient barony. It had dropped away from the family in some of the civil wars; but the Squires had once been

Barons, and Lord Arden was a title that might easily be renewed in a generation unfriendly to attainders, and which had a respect for old memories. Should it be Edgar who would bear the recovered title? Edgar, Lord Arden! The idea was absurd somehow. And then, Old Arden was not Edgar's, but hers—hers to bestow. Good heavens!—that it should be so! And all the time, Arthur Arden—he who was the truest representative of the family, in look, and thought, and disposition—he who would be the ideal Lord Arden—was wasting his time upon a cotton-broker's daughter—a Liverpool girl, with a little paltry money—down-stairs! These may have been deemed strange thoughts for a girl who had just seen her lover absorbed in attendance upon another. She had been miserable enough—angry enough for the first moment. She had loathed the innocent Jeanie, and hated the stupid Alice; but while she thus sat waiting and listening, it was another channel into which her thoughts flowed. It was because he had been sent away from her own side that he was driven to "amuse himself"—poor fellow! And she could give him all that was needful, and the higher life along with it! Clare's heart beat high with impatience as she heard the sound of the voices. Should she go down and reveal herself? Should she wait? What should she do? It was while her excitement thus gradually grew stronger—after she had risen and seated herself again twice over, and felt herself almost carried away by the torrent of her thoughts—that the stir down-stairs took a definite form; there was a sound of approaching footsteps and voices, which came nearer and nearer. Mrs. Murray divined what it meant sooner than Clare did; and hastily taking Jeanie's hand, led her into the inner room. "Take your seam, my bonnie lamb, and never you mind what they say or what they do," said the grandmother; and she closed the door upon her charge, and drew a chair to the table, and took up her own knitting. The room grew suddenly a place full of protection and safety, Clare could not tell how. The first sensation of fright, and horror, and excitement, at the sound of their approach, died out of her mind. "Thanks," she said, under her breath. And then there came a sudden knock and flutter of voices close by; and Arthur Arden, smiling and introducing the pretty figure of Alice Pimpernel, suddenly appeared at the door.

CHAPTER VI

Clare, who knew what was coming, had instinctively changed her position. She had subdued her excitement, as perhaps only a woman could do, and adopted, with the speed of thought, her ordinary air of stately composure. Her look was that of one paying a dignified, yet friendly, visit to a cottage acquaintance, below her in rank, yet not beyond the range of her sympathy. And Mrs. Murray, with feminine skill so natural that it was unconscious, supported her visitor in the emergency. Not a word of explanation passed between them; but yet, they instinctively fell into their parts. Arthur Arden, however, was not in the least prepared for the sight which met his eyes as he opened the door. Partly as making an experiment, to see if it was possible to rouse her, and partly out of sheer idleness and indifference, he had suddenly suggested to Alice Pimpernel to "visit the little beauty" upstairs. "I know the mother; and I want your opinion," he had said. "Oh, Mr. Arden!" had been Alice's reply, as she buttoned the second button of her gloves; and thus they had come upstairs. But it would be impossible to describe in words how small Arthur Arden felt when he opened the door and found himself suddenly in the presence of his cousin Clare. Though he was a man of experience, and not easily daunted, the sudden sight of her covered him with confusion. Instead of introducing Alice into the room as he had intended, he stumbled into it before her, and changed colour and hesitated like a boy of sixteen. "Miss Arden!" he stammered forth, not knowing what he said; and forgot all about Alice Pimpernel behind him, who tried to peep over his shoulder, and mentally sank upon her knees before the majesty of Clare.

"Yes," said Clare; and then, after a little pause—"Do you want me, Mr. Arden, or Mrs. Murray? Please tell me, and I will go away."

"I wanted—it is nothing—I did not know," Arthur stammered. "Miss Pimpernel was interested—that is, I told her of—I think you know Miss Pimpernel."

And then, much confused, he stood aside, and made visible Alice, who preferred her shy obeisance, and once more buttoned her glove, too shy to venture to speak. Clare rose, and bowed in her stately way. She was mistress of the situation; and no one could have told how violently her heart was beating against her side.

"I have paid Mrs. Murray too long a visit," she said. "I must go now. I did not know you were in the neighbourhood, Mr. Arden. You are at the Red House, I suppose?"

"Yes," said Arthur, meekly. "I meant to have let you know—but—Mrs. Pimpernel is down-stairs. I intended to have continued my walk to the Hall to ask how you were—"

"Oh! I am always very well," said Clare; and then there was a pause in the hostilities, and the two armies stopped and looked at each other. Mrs. Murray had taken no notice of the belligerents up to this moment. She had gone on quietly with her knitting, aware that her own charge was in safety. Now she looked up from her work, though without rising from her seat, and turned to the new-comers with a grave face.

"If ye were wanting me, Sir, I would like to know what it was for? I am no used to the ways of the place, and I cannot think I could be of any use."

"Oh, Miss Arden!" said Alice Pimpernel, driven to her wits' end, and feeling that it was now her turn to say something. The girl gave Clare a supplicating glance. "Would she knit something for mamma—or—Oh, I don't know what to say!"

And Arthur Arden gave no assistance. He stood speechless among them, cursing his own folly. Clare had all the advantage, whereas he had only the comfort of feeling that he had made himself look like a fool in everybody's eyes.

"I think the young lady has come to see Jeanie," said Clare.

"But Jeanie is no a show, that folk should come to see her," said the grandmother. "She is as much thought of and as precious to her own folk as any young lady. It's no that I would be uncivil to them that mean no harm, but my Jeanie is as sacred to me as any lady's bairn."

"Oh, Mr. Arden!" said poor Alice Pimpernel.

At this moment there was heard in the distance the sound of rustling robes and heavy feet upon the stair, a sound which carried confusion to all bosoms except that of Alice, whose relief when she heard the approach of her maternal guardian was great. Mrs. Pimpernel's cheerful voice was heard before she could be seen. "Well," she said, "have you seen her, and is she as wonderful as you thought? Poor thing! I am sure I am sorry for her, with this stair to go up and down; and the poor old lady—"

The poor old lady stood confronting Mrs. Pimpernel, who came in very red and heated, and almost fell into her arms. "My good woman, do give me a chair," she cried. "I am nearly suffocated. Oh, Alice and Mr. Arden, what are you doing here? Give me a chair, please. Miss Arden, I declare! How nice it is to meet like this, when one is trying to do the little good one can among the poor! It is so charming of you to take such trouble with your people, Miss Arden. There is really next to nothing left for any one else to do. Might I ask you for a glass of water, my good woman? and wipe the glass first, please. Everything looks very clean, but one never can get quite rid of dust in a cottage. Wipe it well, please."

Clare stood looking on with consternation while these ejaculations were uttered. She had very little sympathy with Mrs. Murray, but yet there was something about her which made Mrs. Pimpernel's easy "my good woman" sound extraordinary enough. "What will she do? Will she scold, or turn her out?" was Clare's question to herself. What Mrs. Murray did was to laugh—a low, soft laugh—which brightened her face as Clare had never seen it, and to bring from a side-table a bottle of water, a glass, and a snow-white napkin. She rubbed the glass for full three minutes, always with a smile upon her face. "Do you think it clean now?" she said, holding it up with amused demonstration. "If I were at home I would give you better than water; and if you should ever come to Loch Arroch I will be glad to see you—you and yours. Miss Arden, the lady means no harm," the old woman added, turning to Clare, "and she's simple and kind. Why should I no make clean the glass and serve her to drink? She kens no better. I take that easy, easy; but them that would make an exhibition of my poor bairn—"

"I don't think any one meant to offend you," said Clare; and then she turned and bowed to Mrs. Pimpernel, who started from her seat to detain her. "I must go, thank you; I am busy," she said, with another stately gesture of leave-taking to where Arthur and Alice stood together. "Bring Jeanie to see me to-morrow," she added, pausing as she went away. It was an impulse she could not restrain, though Jeanie's part in it was very small. She lingered that there might be a chance for some one else to say something—a possibility. And then she made that chance impossible. "Come up as early as twelve o'clock, please, if she is well enough. I have a great deal to talk to you about." And with these words she hurried away. She would not look at him, or permit any sympathetic glance to open the way for a word. And yet she had lingered that a look or word might come. Strange inconsistency! She ran downstairs, leaving them above, leaving them together, and went out alone, without saying a word to Sarah or her myrmidons, feeling so lonely, so sad, so solitary, so deserted by heaven and earth! It was right, quite right, of Arthur Arden to make some provision for himself; she had no fault to find with him, not a word to say. But she was very solitary, and very sad. If she only had been spared the sight of it! But no; all her fortitude would be required. He would probably live here in the neighbourhood somewhere after he had married Alice Pimpernel; and he would be well off at least, if not happy! Oh! surely not happy with that insipid creature, who buttoned her gloves and trembled to hear her own name.

Clare hurried along the village street at a pace quite unusual to her; but she had not gone far when she found that she was pursued. She would not look back for the first moment; but, notwithstanding the repugnance in her own mind to turn and speak to him, it was inconsistent to her dignity to be thus followed by her cousin, whom everybody knew. She turned round with the best grace she could muster, and addressed him with her usual manner. "Did you want me?" she said, and slackened her pace that he might come up.

"It seems so strange that you should ask," said Arthur, "Want you? As if I dared tell you half how much—But never mind! I went to the Pimpernels' thinking I should be at hand and might have opportunities—I did not know you were so prejudiced against them. May not I even come to see you while I am there?"

"Being there does not matter much," said Clare, hastily, and then she corrected herself. "Of course, you think me prejudiced and disagreeable," she said; "but I am as I was brought up. Edgar thinks me dreadfully prejudiced. I dare say they are very nice, and all that; but perhaps it would be as well that you did not come to Arden while you were there."

"Why?" said Arthur, in a low voice.

"Why? Oh, I can't tell why. Because I don't like it. Because I am cross and testy, and like to contradict you. Because—But you know it is no use asking. If a woman is not to chose who she will call on, she must be oppressed and trampled down indeed."

"You are concealing your real objection," said Arthur; and I, who went because I thought—Why, I met Edgar there! But never mind; of course, it must be as you please. I said I would stay a fortnight. Must I never come near you all that time? It is very hard. And it is harder still that Edgar should have gone away as he did, breaking all our party up. Do you know, I have never been so happy, not all my life?"

"I am sure you must be quite as happy now," said Clare; "and I hope you will be prosperous in everything you may undertake. Edgar, I am sure, would be very glad to hear, and I—I do so hope, Mr. Arden, that everything you wish will thrive—as you wish—" And here Clare stopped short, breathing quickly, almost overcome by mixture of despite, and self-restraint, and sorrow for herself, which was in her mind.

"Do you, indeed?" he said. "That is very, very kind of you. It would be kinder still if you knew—but you don't care to know. If I should ever remind you of your good wishes—not now, because I dare not, but afterwards—some time—if I should pluck up courage—"

"I don't think there is any great courage required," said Clare. "Trust me, I shall always be glad to hear that you have done—well for yourself. There could be no more agreeable news. Neither Edgar nor I could have any desire but to see you—happy. Excuse me, I am going to see Miss Somers. I should ask you to come in too, but she is such an invalid, and I am keeping you from your friends. You may be sure you have my very best wishes—good-bye—"

And Clare held out her hand to him, and smiled a smile which was very proud and uncomfortable. She had not in the least intended to visit Miss Somers, but it would have been utterly impossible for her (she thought) to have walked up all the length of the avenue by Arthur Arden's side. Most likely he would have told her of his progress with Alice. And how could she bear that? It was better to part thus abruptly as long as she was capable of smiling and uttering those good wishes which, she had some faint perception, were gall and wormwood to the recipient. She could see that her benevolent hopes and desires were bitter to him, and it pleased her to see it. Yet, notwithstanding, she still believed in Alice Pimpernel. Why should he be there otherwise? He might not like it to be known until everything was settled—it might be galling to his pride. But still, why should he be there but for that? It was the only possible attraction. And no doubt it was a very sensible thing to do. She hurried across to the doctor's house without looking back, eager to be rid of him—to get away—to forget all about it. And yet not without a thought that perhaps he would refuse to be dismissed—perhaps would insist upon explaining—perhaps—But the door opened and closed upon her, and not a word was said to prevent her visit to Miss Somers. When she looked out of the invalid's window Arthur was walking very slowly and quietly down the street to rejoin his friends. This was how it was to be. Well! he had been driven out of Arden, poor fellow! he had been discouraged in his dearer hopes. She herself had been unkind to him; and Edgar had been, oh, how unkind! And he was poor, and must do something to re-establish himself in the world. Was he to blame? Clare clasped her two hands tightly together, and set her lips close that no sigh might escape from them. What alternative was there for him but to act as he was doing; and what for her but to wish him well? And Edgar, too, no doubt, would wish him well—Edgar, who had done it all.

CHAPTER VII

Arthur Arden went back to the Pimpernels' with no very comfortable feelings. He had gone to the Red House, he said, in order to be near Arden, and that he might make frequent visits to the central object of his pursuit; but he had not been aware how far Clare carried out her principles, and that she really declined to know the people whom she did not think her equals. Arthur was accustomed to people who sneer yet visit and take advantage of all the wealth and luxuries of the nouveaux riches. Make use of them: was not that what all the world did, accepting their costly dinners and fine carriages, and laughing at them behind their backs? How was it that Clare refused to do this like other people? Her kinsman could not tell. He thought it foolish of her, if Clare could do anything foolish, and in his own mind quoted the example of a great many very fine people indeed who did it freely. Why should one be so much better than others? he thought to himself; and so went back disconcerted to join the Pimpernels.

Clare was wrong in the conclusion she had jumped at, and still she was not altogether wrong. Alice was pretty and quite inoffensive, and she would have thirty thousand pounds. When a young man of good family without any money or any profession has arrived at the borders of forty, various questions present themselves to him in a very decided way, and demand consideration. What is to become of him? You may keep time at bay if you have all the aids and preventives at hand for doing so; but when that is not the case, when you have, on the other hand, anxieties instead of cosmetics, and increase your wrinkles by every hour's thought, the crisis is a very formidable one. Arthur Arden had been brought up, like so many young men, with vague thoughts of an appointment which was to do everything for him. This expectation had quieted the consciences of everybody belonging to him. He had been waiting for an appointment as long as he could recollect, and he was still waiting for it now. To tell the truth, the progress of years did not make it more likely or bring it any nearer; but still, he knew a great many people who had in their hands the giving of appointments, and it was not impossible that such a thing might drop from the skies at any moment. What he would have done with it when it came, after so many years' lounging about the world without anything definite to do, is a different question. But, in the meantime, Alice Pimpernel, as a pis aller, was as good as an appointment, and Clare a great deal better, and it seemed only natural that the best should claim his devotion first. He had not attempted to exercise upon Alice the full force of those fascinations which he had poured forth upon Clare; but he kept her in hand, as it were, ready for an emergency. He cleared the cloud off his face as he approached the door of old Sarah's cottage, where the ladies had just appeared. Young Denbigh, the curate, had left them when they went in, so that Arthur was their sole escort. He arrived in time to hear Mrs. Pimpernel's parting words.

"Don't think any more about the loss. It was not very expensive lace, you know, and I have plenty. Thank heaven, I am not in circumstances to be obliged to consider every trifle. I was annoyed at first, of course, and it was dreadfully careless of the girl. What does she expect is to become of her, I wonder, if she takes no more pains? I have known a girl just simply ruined by such carelessness. Oh, you need not cry—crying does very little good. I assure you I have, indeed."

"It's what I'm atelling 'em morning, noon, and night," said old Sarah, while the culprit retired into her apron, and sobbed, and curtsied, being past all power of speech.

"Simply ruined," said Mrs. Pimpernel with solemn iteration; "but I trust you will think what you are doing, and never be so wicked again. I am very much interested in your lodgers, Sarah. What a very nice old woman, and so clean! Mr. Arden did you observe? But there is no use speaking to you gentlemen—you are always thinking of something else. So very clean! If anything should ever be wanted for her or for the sick girl, you may send to me freely. We are never without some little delicacy, you know—something that would tempt an invalid. Mr. Pimpernel is so very particular about what he eats. All you gentlemen are. I dare say you want it more after being out in the world all day knocking about. Well, Mr. Arden, and so you went and made your peace with your cousin? I hope everything is right now."

"Nothing was wrong," said Arthur hastily. "I had no peace to make. I was only anxious to ask Miss Arden about—Edgar. I don't know where he is, and I wanted his address."

"She does not half like your staying with us," said Mrs. Pimpernel. "Oh, don't speak to me! I know better. I don't know what we have ever done to her, but she hates us, does Miss Arden. She is quite spiteful because you are staying with us."

"Oh, mamma, dear!" said Alice, in gentle deprecation.

"You may say what you please, Alice, but I know better. That child is always standing up for Miss Arden. I don't know why she should, I am sure, for she never is barely civil. Not that we want anything from her; we visit quite as much as I wish to visit; but if I were ever so anxious to increase my list, Arden Hall, you know!—It never was very amusing, I believe. It is not that I care for the airs she gives herself—"

"You forget that my cousin has been brought up very quietly," said Arthur. "Her father was very peculiar. He never saw any society unless he could not help it. You know, indeed, that poor Edgar, his only son—But that is a painful subject to us all."

"Please, tell me!" said Mrs. Pimpernel. "One hears hints, you know; but it would be so much more satisfactory from one of the family. Do, please, tell me. He snubbed him dreadfully, and never educated him, nor gave him any allowance nor anything. Fancy, his own father! But there must have been some cause."

"He was a very peculiar man," said Arthur Arden. "There are things in families, you know, which don't bear discussion. If I was more hard-hearted than I am, or more indifferent to the credit of the name—But never mind—it is a question I would rather not discuss."

"Oh, Mr. Arden!" cried Alice Pimpernel, clasping her hands, and looking up at him with unfeigned admiration. Yes, he was more interesting than Mr. Denbigh, with that fine family face, and all its romantic associations—and sacrificing himself, too, for the good of the family. How grand it was! The Pimpernels, too, had certain features which were peculiar to them; but oh! how different from the Ardens. Mr. Denbigh was interesting too—he was very nice and attractive, and second cousin to the Earl of Tintagel. But he had not a story to attract the imagination like this.

"I would never insist upon confidence," said Mrs. Pimpernel; it is against my principles, even with my own child. If it's about money, I always say, 'Speak to your papa—he is the one to manage all that;' and, between ourselves, he is a great deal too liberal; he never knows how to say 'No' to any of them. But if it's their feelings, I never exact anything. I am always ready to do my best, but confidence is a thing I would never exact."

"It is a thing I should be most ready to give," said Arthur Arden, with a bow and a smile, "if the secret were only mine. But my poor cousin Edgar—he is a most worthy fellow—an excellent fellow. I confess I was prejudiced against him, which is not unnatural, you know, considering that he stands, between me and—But really it is a question I must not enter on."

"Anything you may say to us will be sacred, you may be sure," Mrs. Pimpernel said, with breathless interest; and Alice looked up appealingly in his face. They were quite tremulous with expectation, looking for some romance of real life, something more exciting than gossip. Arthur Arden could scarcely restrain the impulse to mystify them at least; but he remembered that it might be dangerous, and refrained.

"No," he said, with a sigh, shaking his head, "not even to you. If it were my own secret you should have it fast enough; but I must not betray another's. No, no. And poor Edgar is an excellent fellow—as good a fellow as ever breathed."

Mrs. Pimpernel shot a lively glance across him at her daughter, who replied to it quickly enough, though she was not over-bright. "Depend upon it, there is some flaw in Edgar Arden's title," was Mrs. Pimpernel's comment that evening when she repeated the conversation to her husband. "Depend upon it, all's not right there. I never saw anything written more plainly on a man's face."

"Then you must have seen fool written after it," said Mr. Pimpernel. "Stuff and nonsense! This fellow Arden is very well up to most things. He knows what he's about, does Arden; and so he should, if he's making up to your daughter, Mrs. Pimpernel."

"I wish you would not be so coarse," said the lady. "Making up! There is nothing of the sort. He is an agreeable sort of man, and knows everybody; though, if there was anything in this story, Alice might do worse. It would be very nice to have her settled so near us. And Arden is a good name; and I must say, if there is one thing I am partial to, it is a good family. Though you never will acknowledge it, or give any weight to it, it is well known my grandmother was a Blundell—"

"I don't know anything about your grandmother; but I shan't give your daughter, if I can help it, to a fellow who has nothing. Why don't he get his appointment? Or, if he wants to marry, let him marry his cousin, and get her share of the property. That would be the sensible thing to do."

"He would not look at his cousin, take my word for it," said Mrs. Pimpernel. "He has more sense than that at least. A proud, stuck-up thing, as vain of her family—As if it was any virtue of hers to belong to an old family! She wasn't consulted about it. For my part, I'd rather be like Alice, well brought up, with a father and mother she has no reason to be ashamed of, than Clare Arden, with all her mysteries and nonsense. I should indeed; and that is a deal for me to say that am partial to old families. But, if you had a chance, you might just question Arthur Arden a little, and see what he means by it. I don't see why he should sacrifice himself. And if there should be anything in it, to have Alice settled so near us, on such a pretty property—"

Thus Mrs. Pimpernel showed an inclination not only to count her chickens before they were hatched, but even before it was quite certain that there were eggs for the preliminary ceremony. The husband did not say very much, but he thought the more. He had money to back any claimant, and would not hesitate to do so. And as for any folly about self-sacrifice or fine family feeling, the cotton-broker felt that he would make very short work with that. "Rubbish and nonsense!" he said to himself. "What were all the feelings in the world in comparison with a fine property like Arden—a property that might almost double in value if it were in proper hands. Why, in building leases alone, he could undertake to add five thousand a-year to the property. There might be dozens of Arden Villas, Pimpernel Places, &c., which would pay magnificently, without interfering in the least with 'the amenities.' And if nothing was wanted but money for a lawsuit, why he himself would not mind providing the sinews of war.

"I understand there is some uncertainty about your cousin's title to Arden," he said next morning, in his uncompromising way.

"Good heavens! who said so?" said Arthur, in consternation; for to do him justice he had meant only to be interesting, and knew that, as respected Arden, his suspicions, and those of other people, did not value a brass farthing. "Pray be cautious of repeating such a thing. It is quite new to me—"

"Why, why, why!—I thought you gave a little colour to it at least, by something you said yourself—so I heard," said Mr. Pimpernel. "I am a practical man, Arden, and I never have any time to beat about the bush. Should there be anything in it, and should you be disposed to fight it out, and should you have evidence and all that, why, I should not mind standing by you, as a matter of business, you know. I don't understand fine feelings, but I understand what an estate's worth; and if you can prove to my solicitor you have ground to go upon, why, I shouldn't mind backing you up. There, I never make mysteries about anything, and you will follow my example, if you take my advice—"

"My dear sir, how can I thank you for your confidence in me?" said Arthur. "The truth is, there has always been something very odd; but I fear that so far as evidence goes—You may depend upon it, if I ever should find myself in a position to prove anything, yours would be the first aid I should seek."

"Well, well, you know your own affairs best," said Mr. Pimpernel. And so there was no more said about it; but Arthur's brain was set to work as it had never yet been. What if there might be evidence after all—something the old Squire had made up his mind not to use? Arden was worth a great deal of exertion, even a little treachery; and, of course, if Edgar was not a real Arden, it would be a duty to the race to cast him out—a duty to the race, and a duty to himself. Duty to one's self is a very prevailing principle; there is not much about it in the canons of Christianity, but there is a great deal about it in the practical laws which govern the world. Arthur was vaguely excited by this unexpected proposal. He was not lawyer enough to know much of the possibilities or impossibilities of the matter. But it was worth thinking about, worth inquiring into, surely, if anything ever was.

CHAPTER VIII

It was with this idea strong in his mind that Arthur marked out for himself a certain scheme of operations during his stay at the Red House. He had still ten days to remain there, and time, it must be allowed, hung sometimes heavy on his hands. To play croquet with devotion for several hours every day requires a mind free from agitation and innocent of scheming—or, at least, not burdened with schemes which are very important—or any warm personal anxiety in the bigger game of life. Alice Pimpernel was good for two hours in the morning, with her little sisters, when they had done their lessons; and Arden felt that it was a very pretty group on the first day of his visit, when he looked up from his newspaper, and let his eyes stray over the well-kept lawn, with its background of trees, and all the airy figures in their light dresses that were standing about. But, then, Alice was good also for four hours in the afternoon, when there was nothing better going on—namely, from half-past two, when luncheon was just over, till half-past six; when it was time to dress for dinner. Young Denbigh, by right of his youth, was equal to this long continued enjoyment; but Arthur was not equal to it. And, as at that moment there were no other visitors at the Red House, time was hard to kill. He felt that if he had been a little younger he would have been driven, in self defence, to make love to somebody—Alice or her mother, it did not much matter which—but it was too great a bore, with all his anxieties on his mind, and with the amount of real feeling he had in respect to Clare. Accordingly, it was rather a godsend to him when Mr. Pimpernel threw this suggestion into his mind. He did not take it up with any active feeling of enmity to Edgar, nor even with any great hope of success. If it were as he thought, the Squire had either been uncertain to the last of his wife's guilt, or he had been sufficiently infatuated to accept the consequences, finally and irredeemably—in which latter case, no doubt, he must have destroyed any evidence that existed against her; while, in the former case, there could have been no evidence sufficiently strong to convict her. In either point of view, it was madness, after all this lapse of time, to attempt to make any discoveries. Yet Arthur made up his mind to try to do so, with a resolution which grew stronger the more he thought of it. And from this moment he thought of little else. He had believed his own hypothesis steadily for so many years; and it was so much to his interest to believe it, if proof of any description could be found. He strolled down to the village next morning, not knowing exactly what he wanted, and stopped at old Sarah's cottage, and beguiled her into conversation. Jeanie, he noted, had been sent away at his approach, and this fact alone determined him to see Jeanie. He went upstairs, again, undaunted by the experience of yesterday, and knocked softly at the door of the little parlour. "Mrs. Murray," he said from the landing, not even presuming to enter, "I have something to say to Sarah, and I cannot manage it below, with these two girls listening and staring. Would it disturb you to let us come up here?" There was a pause, and a little rustle, as of movement and telegraphed communications, before any answer was made to him; and then Arthur smiled to find that his appeal to Scotch politeness was not made in vain. "Come in, sir," Mrs. Murray said, gravely. Jeanie was seated at the open window with her needlework, and her grandmother in her usual place by the table, engaged in her usual occupation of knitting. "Take a seat, sir; we'll leave you to yourselves," said Mrs. Murray. But this did not suit Arthur, who, even in the midst of a new interest, loved to have two strings to his bow.

"By no means," he said; "what I have to say may be said quite well before you. I have to put a question or two about my cousins at the Hall. Here is a chair for you, Sarah; sit down, and don't be frightened. Nothing is going to happen. I want you to tell me what you know about Mrs. Arden, that is all."

"How could I know aught about Mrs. Arden, Mr. Arthur," said Sarah, wonderingly, "when she died afore I come? I took Miss Clare from a baby, but her poor dear mamma was dead and gone. My brother Simon he knows, and so do the Rector, and poor Miss Letty, at the Doctor's; but I don't know no more than this good lady, as is a stranger to the place. There's her name on the stone, top of t'oud Squire's pew in t'church, and that's all as I know."

"Are there none of the old servants about that knew her?" asked Arthur.

At which point a very strange interruption ensued.

"I canna tell, sir, why you are asking, or if it is for good or evil," said Mrs. Murray. "I dinna belong to the place, as Sarah says, nor I'm no one that ought to ken; but I have seen Mrs. Arden, if its about her ye want to ken—"

"You have seen Mrs. Arden!" said Arthur, in amazement; and old Sarah echoed his exclamation.

"Yes, I have seen her; no often, but more than once. If that is all, I can tell you what like she was, and all I ken about her; or, if not all—She was ill in health and troubled in spirit, poor thing, when I saw her. I cannot think she was ever either strong or gay."

"Was that after her—children were born?" asked Arthur, eagerly.

"It was before she had any bairn. It was thought she never would have one, and her husband was sore disturbed. But, ye see, the doctors turned out fools, as they do so often," Mrs. Murray added hastily, turning and fixing her eyes upon him. She made a pause between the two sentences, and changed her tone completely. The first was mere reminiscence, the other had a certain defiance in it; and Arthur felt there was some meaning, though one he could not read, in the suddenly watchful expression of her eyes.

"Yes," he said, thoughtfully, "so it appears." And as he spoke the watchfulness went off Mrs. Murray's face, and she evidently (though why he could not think) calmed herself down. "So it appears," he repeated vaguely. "She was some time married, then, I suppose, before my cousin Edgar was born?"

"I have heard say five years," said the old woman, once more rousing up, with a watchful light in each steady eye.

"Ah, then, that's impossible," he said to himself. An idea had been growing in Arthur's mind that the Squire's wife might have been a widow with an infant child—an explanation which would make everything clear, yet save her from the imputation of a capital crime in respect to her husband. That was impossible. He mused on it for a minute or two, and then he resumed his questions.

"Who was Mrs. Arden? I am anxious to know," he said, and then corrected himself, for his tone had been peremptory. "I am thinking of the family history," he added. "She was a stranger, and we don't know even where she belongs to. That will explain my curiosity to you. I am anxious to know."

"She was Mrs. Arden when I saw her, and I ken nothing more," said the Scotchwoman, shortly; and again he noted that her interest had failed. Evidently she knew something which it might possibly concern him much to know, but what kind of knowledge it was remained a mystery to him. He had not even light enough on the subject to guide him as to what questions he ought to put to her. Old Sarah sat gazing, open-mouthed and full of wonder. Only little Jeanie took no interest in the inquiry. She sat at the window, now dreaming, now working, sometimes playing with a long tendril of the honeysuckle, sometimes pausing to look out from the window. The talk was nothing to her. And Arthur's interest flagged as this pretty figure caught his eye. Why should he attempt to find out anything about Edgar's mother? What difference could it ever make to him? Whereas, here was a human plaything which it would be pleasant to toy with, which would amuse and distract him in the midst of his cares. What a pretty little thing she was! much prettier than Alice Pimpernel—in some things even more attractive than Clare. Ah, Clare! This thought brought him back to his original subject; but yet the other thought was in his mind, and found expression first.

"Your daughter seems better," he said. "I don't think she is frightened for me now; are you, Jeanie? You know I am a friend now. The man must have been a wretch who frightened such a sensitive sweet little creature. I don't think he can have been like me."

"Sir, did ye speak?" said Jeanie, with a start. And she turned to him an innocent, unconscious face, moved with a little wonder only at the sound of her name.

"No; the gentleman did not speak to you," said her grandmother. "Go ben the house, my darling, where you will be quiet, and away from all clashes. Sir, my bairn is Jeanie to her own folk," she added, as the docile girl withdrew into the inner room, "but no to every stranger that hears her innocent name. It will be kindest of you not to speak to her. The attack might come again."

"I suppose you know your own business best," said Arthur, shrugging his shoulders; "but you seem very foolish about the child. How can I hurt her by speaking to her? To return to Mrs. Arden. She was Scotch, I suppose, as you knew her so well?"

"She was not Scotch that ever I heard; and I did not know her well," said Mrs. Murray, and then there was a pause. "If you'll tell me what you have to do with it, and what you want to know, I will answer you—if I can give you any information," she said with decision. "I may not know what you want to hear, but if you'll tell me what you have to do with it—"

"I am only the nearest relation that Mr. Arden and his sister have in the world," said Arthur, in spite of himself shrinking from her eye.

"And the heir if this bonnie lad should—die—or fail—" This was spoken with an eagerness which puzzled him more and more. He felt that he was put on his defence. And yet there was no indignation in her look. It was guilt of conscience that startled him, and brought the colour to his cheek.

"Well," he said, crimson and angry with consciousness, "what then? My cousin is much younger, and more likely to live than I am. Nothing can be more unlikely than that I should be his heir. That has nothing to do with what I want to know."

"Aye, he's younger than you, and far liker to live. He's strong, and he's got a constitution that will bear trouble. I should ken," she said under her breath, whispering to herself. And then she too coloured, and faced him with a certain gleam of fear in her eyes. "Aye," she repeated, "Mr. Edgar's a bonnie lad, bless him, and real well and strong. It's no likely you'll ever live to be his heir."

"It is unnecessary to remind me of that; haven't I just said it?" said Arthur, hastily. "I trust he'll live a hundred years. That has nothing to do with the matter."

"A hundred years!" said old Sarah. "That's a great age. I know'd an ou'd man up Thornleigh way—but, bless you, Mr. Edgar's young and strong—as like as not he'll live to a hundred. I never heard as he'd anything the matter all his life. It would be a credit to the family, I do declare—"

"And so it would," said Arthur, with a smile of disdain. "No, you need not be afraid," he went on, turning again to Mrs. Murray. "I am ten years older than he is. I am a poor devil without a penny, and he has everything. Never mind. I am going to write a book about the family, and that will make me rich. I can't do your favourite any harm—"

"Has he everything?" said the Scotchwoman, earnestly. "You'll no think me presuming, Mr. Arden, but I would like to hear. It's no fair to the rest when everything goes to one. I canna think it is fair. He should share with you a bit of the land, or some of the siller, or one thing or another. And you as sib to the race as he? I would like well to ken—"

"It is very good of you to take my interest so much to heart," said Arthur, with a certain contempt which was not unmixed with bitterness. "No, nothing comes to me. One cousin is a prince and one is a beggar. That's the way of the world. So you can't tell me Mrs. Arden's name, nor anything about her friends or her family? Had she any one with her except her husband when you made her acquaintance? What kind of a woman did you take her to be?—"

"I ken neither her name nor her kin, nor nought about her. They were travelling, and no a creature with them, no even a maid—but there might be reasons. She was a young sorrowful thing, sore broken down with a tyrant of a man. That is all I can tell; and whatever was done, good or evil, was his doing, and not hers. It was him that did, and said, and settled everything. I have nothing more to say—"

"It does not sound much," said Arthur, with an accent of discontent; and then it seemed to him that a certain gleam of relief shot across her face. "And yet you look as if you could tell me more," he added, with a suspicion which he could not explain. She eyed him as a man fighting a duel might regard his adversary who had just fired upon him, but made no reply.

"With ne'er a maid?—now that's strange!" cried old Sarah. "That is the strangest of all, saving Mr. Arthur's presence. And them very words clears it all up to me, as I've wondered and wondered many a day. If madam as was, poor soul, had been a lady like the other ladies, there would have been a deal more things for Miss Clare. She ain't got anything of her mother's, the dear. Most young ladies they have their mamma's rings, or her jewels, or something. They tell you this was my mamma's, or this was my grandmamma's, or such like. But Miss Clare, she hasn't a thing—And travelling with ne'er a maid? She wasn't a lady born, wasn't Madam Arden; that's as clear as clear—"

"I canna tell ye who she was—she was a broken-hearted thing," said Mrs. Murray, with some solemnity; "and what was done in her life, if it was good or if it was evil, it wasna her blame."

This was all Arthur Arden made of his first investigation. He was working in the dark. He went away a short time after, leaving Sarah full of excited questions, to which she received very scanty response. He was a little excited himself, he could not tell why. This woman was a relation of Perfitt's, which, of course (he supposed), explained her acquaintance with his cousin's mother. But still she was a strange woman, and knew something he was sure that might be of use to him, if he could only find out what it was. What could it be? Could she have been Mrs. Arden's maid, and in her secrets; or had the proud Squire married some one beneath him—some one probably connected with this stranger? It was all quite dark, and no thread to be found in the gloom. Was it worth his while to try to penetrate that gloom? And he would have liked to see little Jeanie before he left, the pretty creature. He would rather have questioned her than her grandmother. What could the old woman mean by keeping her so persistently out of his way?

Arthur Arden strayed through the village street in the stillness of the summer afternoon after this bewildering interview. He did not know what he was to do to carry on his researches. Probably he might light upon some chance information in one of the cottages where there were people old enough to have known Edgar's mother, but this was utterly uncertain, and he might be committing himself for no use in the world. If he went to the Rector or the Doctor he might commit himself still more, and rouse their curiosity as to his motives in an uncomfortable way. What he had to do was to find out accidentally, to discover without searching, a secret, if there was a secret, which must have been carefully hidden for twenty-five years. The chance of success was infinitesimal, and failure seemed almost certain. Probably everything that could throw any light on the subject had been destroyed long since. And then, if he injured Edgar, what of Clare? Was Mr. Pimpernel's support worth Clare's enmity? This, however, was a question he did not dwell on, for Arthur satisfied himself that Clare had no need to know, unless by some strange chance he should be successful. And if he were successful, she was not one to stand in the way of justice. But there was not the very slightest chance that he would be successful. It was simply impossible. He laughed at himself as he strolled along idly. If there had been anything better than croquet to do at the Red House he would have gone back to that, and left this wild-goose chase alone; but, in the meantime, there was nothing else to do, and at the worst his inquiries could do no harm.

The church was open, and he strolled in. Old Simon, the clerk, was about, heavily pattering in a dark corner. It was Saturday, and Sally had been helping her father to clean the church. She had gone home to her needlework, but he still pattered about at the west end, unseen in the gloom, putting, as might be supposed from the sound, his dusters and brooms away in some old ecclesiastical cupboard. He had clogs on, which made a great noise; and the utter stillness and shady quiet of the place was strangely enhanced by the sound of those heavy footsteps. Arthur walked down the length of the church, which echoed even under his lighter tread. The light in it was green and subdued, coming through the foliage and the dim small panes which replaced the old painted glass in the windows. Here and there a broken bit of colour, a morsel of brilliant ruby out of some saint's mantle, or a warm effective bit of canopy-work, interrupted the colourless light. Arden Church had been a fine church in the ancient days, and there were tombs in the gloom in the corners near the chancel which were reckoned very fine still when anybody who knew anything about it came to see them. But knowledge had not made much inroad as yet in the neighbourhood. The old Squire had not been the kind of man to spend money in restoring a church, and Mr. Fielding had not been the kind of man to worry his life out about it. Should young Denbigh survive the croquet and succeed the Rector, it was probable that Edgar would not have half so easy a time in this respect as his father had been allowed to have; but, in the meantime, there had been no restoration, and there were even some high pews, in which the principal people hid themselves on Sundays. The Squire's pew was like a box at the theatre, with open arches of carved oak, and a fireplace in it behind the chairs, and a private passage which led into the park. The impression which the church made upon Arthur Arden, however, was neither sacred nor historical. He did not think of it as associated for all those hundred years with the fortunes of his race; neither (still less) did he think of it as for all this time the centre of prayer and worship—the place where so many hearts had risen to God. All he thought was, what a curious ghostly look all those unoccupied seats had. The quiet about was almost more than quiet: it was a hush as if of forced stillness—a something in the air that made him feel as if all the seats were full, though nobody was visible, and some unseen ceremonial going on. And the old man in his clogs went clamping, clattering about in the green dimness under cover of the organ gallery. Simon's white smock was visible now and then, toned down to a ghostly grey by the absence of light. Arthur Arden felt half afraid of him as he walked slowly up the aisle. He might have been the family Brownie—a homely ghost that watched over the graves and manes of the Ardens, which Arthur, though an Arden, meditated a certain desecration of. These, however, were sentiments not long likely to move the mind of such a man. He walked slowly up until he found himself opposite the Squire's pew. It was quite near the chancel, close to the pulpit, which stood on one side, and opposite the reading desk, which stood on the other, like two sentinels watching the approach to the altar. On the wall of the church, almost on a parallel with where the Squire's head must have come when he sat in his pew, was the white marble tablet that bore his wife's name. It was a heavy plain square tablet, not apt to attract any one's attention; and Arthur, who when he was in Arden Church had always been one of the occupants of the stage box, had scarcely remarked it at all. He paused now and read it as it glimmered in the dim silence. "Mary, wife of Arthur Arden of Arden." That was all. The Arden arms were on the tablet, but without any quartering that could have belonged to the dead woman. Evidently she was the Squire's wife only, with no other distinction.

While he stood thinking on this another step entered the church, and looking round Arthur saw Mr. Fielding, who after a few words with old Simon came and joined him. "You are looking at the old pew," the Rector said in the subdued tone that became the sacred place. "They tell me it ought not to be a pew at all if I took a proper interest in Christian art; but it will last my time, I think. I should prefer that it lasted my time. I never was brought up in these new-fangled ways."

"I was not looking at the pew, but at that," said Arthur, pointing to the wall.

"Yes; it is very bad, I suppose," said Mr. Fielding. "We are very far behind, I know, in art. It's ugly, I confess; but do you know I like it all the same. When the church gets dark in a wintry afternoon, these white tablets glimmer. You would think there were angels holding them up. And after all, to me, who am far advanced in life, such names are sweeter than the finest monuments. It is different, of course, with you younger folks."

"I was not thinking of art," said Arthur, "but of the curt way the name is put. 'Mary, wife of Arthur Arden.' Was she nobody's daughter? Hadn't she got a name before she was married? Dying so young, one would think some one must have been living who had an interest in her; but there is neither blazon nor name."

"Eh? What? I don't see anything remarkable in that," said Mr. Fielding. "The others are just the same. Aren't they? I don't remember, I am sure. 'Mary, wife of Arthur Arden.' Yes; that is all. Now that I think of it, I don't remember Mrs. Arden's name. I never knew what family she belonged to. They were married abroad."

"And their son was born abroad. Was not that strange?" said Arthur. "There seems to have been a great deal of mystery about it one way and another—not much like the Arden ways."

"You have been listening to Somers," said Mr. Fielding, hotly; "pestilent old cynic as he is. He has taken up his notion, and nothing will make him give it up. If you had known Mrs. Arden as I did, you would have scouted such an idea. I never knew a better woman. She had dreadfully bad health—"

"Was that the reason why they were so much abroad?"

"I can't tell why they were so much abroad," said the Rector, testily. "Because they liked it, I suppose; and let me tell you, it would have been better for all the Ardens had they been more abroad. I suppose there never was a more bigoted, self-opinionated race. To be sure you are one of them, and perhaps I ought not to say it to you; but you have knocked about the world, and you know them as well as I do—"

"I knew only the old Squire," said Arthur, "and my own father, of course; but he had knocked about the world enough. There was not much love lost between them, I think—"

"They hated each other, my dear sir—they hated each other," said the Rector; and then he paused and wiped his forehead, as if it had been too much for him. "I beg your pardon, I am sure, for calling up family matters. I am very glad to see you on such different terms with the young people here—"

"Yes," said Arthur, with a half sigh. "What is the use of keeping up rancour? The old Squire on the whole was rather kind to me. I suppose it was enough for him to have one Arden to hate. And as he transferred the feeling from my father to his own son—"

"Hush—hush—hush," said the Rector, anxiously. "Don't let us rake up old troubles. Thank heaven poor Edgar is very comfortable now. His father couldn't do him any tangible injustice, you know; though that business about Old Arden was very shameful, very shameful—there is no other word for it. To take advantage of the boy's ignorance to break the entail, and then to settle the very oldest of the property on Clare! I love Clare dearly—if she was my own child I could not love her more; but rather than take that from my brother, I would strip myself of every penny if I were in her place. It was shameful—there is no other word—"

"My cousin is much more of an Arden than her brother," said Arthur. "I don't see why she should strip herself of every penny? Surely he has enough. She is twice as much of an Arden as he."

"And what is an Arden, I should like to know," said Mr. Fielding, "to be kept up at such a cost? Edgar is not much of an Arden, poor boy! He is worth a dozen of any Ardens I ever knew—"

"You forget I am one of that unfortunate race," said Arthur, with a forced laugh. "Oh, no harm! I know you don't love us less, but only him more. And my cousin Clare is an Arden," he added, after a pause; "for her I must make a stand. Even beside her brother's excellence, you would still allow her a place, I hope."

"I love Clare dearly," said the Rector, with abrupt brevity. And then there was a pause. Arthur Arden smiled to himself—a smile which might very well have been a sneer. What did it matter what the old parson's opinions were? The Ardens could stand a harder judgment than his.

"But about this poor lady," he said. "She was a perfect creature, you say, and I don't want to contradict you. Probably she was everything that was good and lovely; but I suppose a woman of no family, from the evidence of this record here?"

"I don't know anything about her family," said Mr. Fielding, shortly. "It never occurred to me to think what her family was." This he said with some heat and energy, probably because it was—and alas! the good Rector knew it was—a considerable fib. Time was when he had asked a great deal about Mrs.

Arden's family—as, indeed, everybody in the county had done; but without gaining any information. The Rector was angry with himself for the fib; but still maintained it, with a certain irritation, as it was natural for a man to do.

"It is a pity there should be so much mystery," said Arthur, quietly. Of course, he saw through the fiction with the utmost distinctness; but civility required that he should take no further notice. And then the two stood together for a minute or, perhaps, two, in the narrow aisle, pretending to look round them, and making a critical survey of the church. "That tomb is fine, if one could see it," Arthur said, pointing to a recumbent figure of an old Arden; and Mr. Fielding assented with a little nod of his head. And all this time old Simon, in his clogs, with the smock that looked grey-green in the dimness, was clamping slowly about, stirring the slumbrous, silent echoes. How strange it was—so real and living and full of so many seeds of excitement; yet all the time like something in a dream.

The Rector, however, accompanied Arthur out with pertinacity, seeing him, as it were, "off the premises"—as if there could have been anything to find out in the little innocent church, which all the world was free to inspect. Was it to keep him from talking to old Simon?—who, however, knew nothing—or was it from mere wantonness of opposition? The latter was really the case, though it was difficult even to make out how Mr. Fielding was stimulated into opposition. He must have felt it in the air, by some curious magnetic antipathy, for Arthur had not said a word, so far as he was aware, to betray himself. They walked together as far as the Hall gates, talking of various indifferent matters. "Living at the Red House!" said Mr. Fielding, with a smile of strange satisfaction. "Does Miss Arden know?" The Rector was pleased with this bit of information. He was glad of anything which would set their kinsman wrong with the brother and sister. It was a highly unchristian sentiment, but so it was.

"Yes, she knows," said Arthur, quietly. "I met her yesterday; and I am going to call there now. I suppose, as Clare is my cousin, and I am old enough to be her father, I may be permitted to call—"

"Yes, I suppose you are old enough to be her father," Mr. Fielding said, with most provoking acquiescence. Arthur could have knocked the Rector down, had he given way to his feelings. After all, though there was a good deal of difference in point of age, it would have been difficult for him to have been Clare's father. And he did not feel like her father in the smallest degree. The Rector paused at the Hall gates, and looked at his watch to see if he had time also to pay a visit to Clare; but, to Arthur's intense relief, the man-of-all-work came running across from the Rectory as Mr. Fielding hesitated. Some one who was ill had sent for the Rector—some one who lived two miles off—and who had sent so urgent an appeal that Jack had already put the saddle on his master's sturdy old cob. "I shall have to put it off till to-morrow," Mr. Fielding said, with a sigh. "Tell Clare I shall see her to-morrow." But alas! (he thought to himself) an antidote given twenty-four hours after the poison, what good is it? And he could not forbid her own cousin to pay her a visit. So Mr. Fielding turned away with a bad grace to visit his sick parishioner; and Arthur, much relieved, opened the little postern gate, and took his way under the great elms and beeches to the Hall.

CHAPTER X

Clare was all alone when Arthur reached the Hall. She had been all alone the whole day. She had not even received a letter from anybody, to help her through its long hours. She had looked after her accounts, and arranged something for the schools, and answered an application which some one in

Liverpool had made in respect to one of the girls whom old Sarah had trained. And then she sat down and read for half-an-hour, and then rose and stood for ten minutes at the window, and then had taken her tapestry-work, and then gone to the window again. From that window the view was very fair. It would have lightened the burden off the shoulders of many a careworn man and woman only to have been able to go and look at it from time to time in the midst of their work. There were the woods, in all their summer wealth, stretching as far as the eye could see; and under their shade a gleam of water catching the sunshine—water which was one of the charms of Arden—a series of old fish-ponds threaded upon the thin silvery string of a little stream. It glimmered here, and it glimmered there, through the rich foliage—and now and then the elms and beeches stood apart, as it were, drawing their leafy skirts about them, to open a green glade, all brightened up with a flash of that fairy water; and between the window and the wood was the great wealthy stretch of immemorial turf, the park, with here and there a huge tree standing with modest consciousness by itself—a champion of the sylvan world. People had been heard to say that the mere sight of all that lordly, silent scene—so profuse in its verdure, so splendid in its space and freedom—was enough to drive care and pain far from Arden. Nothing knew Nature there of pain or evil. She lay and contemplated herself, wrapped in a holy, divine content, listening to the rustle of the leaves, taking thought for the innumerable tiny lives that buzzed and fluttered in the air, watching the grasses grow and the little fish leap. It was all very lovely, and to Clare it was dear, as only such a home can be. But when she went to the window her heart grew sick of the silence and the calm. Oh, only for a little movement and commotion! A storm would have been better than nothing; but still a storm would only have moved these great, strong, self-sufficing, unsympathetic trees. It could not have given the secousse she wanted to Clare herself, who, for the first time in her life, had ceased to be self-sufficing. No, not self-sufficing—longing for anything, it did not matter what, to disturb the stagnation about her. How different it had been before Edgar came home! Even when she was absorbed by her first grief for her father, time did not hang heavy on her hands. Once before, it is true, a similar feeling had come over her—after Arthur Arden went away the first time. Clare clasped her hands together and blushed crimson, with sudden shame, when she identified the previous moment at which she had felt lonely and weary of everything as she was now: violent shame seized upon her—though there was nobody to see, even if any one could have seen into her mind and surprised the unspoken thought. And then she turned her back upon the weary window, and represented to herself that the misery of that former time had passed away. Time had gone on, and other thoughts had come in, and it had passed away. A little patience, and again it would pass away now. Everything does in this world.

Clare's experience was not great, but yet even she knew something of that terrible tranquillising force of time. How wretched she had been about Edgar, again and again, during those years when he had been absent, and her father never mentioned his name. But these wretchednesses had all floated away, one after another. And when the Squire died, it had seemed to Clare that she never could get beyond that sense of desolation which filled the house and all the familiar scenes in which he had been the first figure. But she had got over it. She had not forgotten her father; her memory of him was so vivid that she could think she saw him, could think she heard him, so clear in her recollection were his voice and his face. And yet the world was no longer desolate because he was not there. It was a curious train of thought for a girl of her age. But Clare was very reasonable, and she was very much alone, with nobody in the world to whom she could legitimately go for consolation. She had no mother into whose ear she could pour her woes; she had been compelled to be a mother to herself. And thus, as if she had been her own mother, she represented to herself that this pain also would pass away in time. Let her but occupy herself, keep doing something, bear it as patiently, and think as little about it as possible, and in time it would come to an end. This is a hard, painful, inhuman way of consoling one's self; but yet when one is alone, and has nobody else to breathe a word of comfort, perhaps it is as good a way as any. "It will not last," she said to herself. "It is miserable now, and shameful, and I hate myself. To think that I should feel like that! But one has only to be patient and put up with it. It cannot last." And she had just fed herself with this philosophy, and taken what nourishment she could out of it, when all her loneliness, and miserableness, and philosophisings were put to flight in a moment. Arthur Arden was ushered in solemnly by Wilkins, who had half a mind to remain himself, to make sure that the rules of perfect propriety were observed; and all at once the tedium and the unprofitableness departed out of Clare's life.

But she would have given her life, as was perfectly natural, rather than let him see that his arrival was anything to her. "I am taking advantage of Edgar's absence to do quantities of things," she said, looking into his face, "clearing away my old pieces of work. No, perhaps I was never very fond of work; I have always had so many other things to do.—Thanks; I heard from him yesterday; Edgar is quite well."

"I hope he is enjoying himself in town," said Arthur, subduing himself to her tone.

"He talks only of the Thornleighs," said Clare, with that familiar pucker in her brow. Pretending to be anxious about Edgar was so much more easy than adopting that air of absolute calm for herself. "Of course I know I ought to be very glad that he has chosen such nice friends. There is nothing to object to in the Thornleighs. Still, to go to town only to see them, when he can see them as much as he pleases at home—"

"Lady Augusta, I should think, likes to have such a captive at her chariot-wheels," said Arthur. "How much anxiety it must cost you! Poor dear Arden! What a pity he knows so little of the world."

"Oh, my brother will do very well," said Clare, with a sensitive movement of offence; and then it occurred to her that it was safest to carry the war into the other camp. "I should like to know how you get on at the Red House?" she said. "Miss Pimpernel is quite pretty, I think. Is she always buttoning her glove? I hear they play croquet a great deal. Are you fond of croquet, Mr. Arden? If you are, it must have been so dull for you, never having it while you were here."

"I hate croquet," he said, almost rudely (but Clare was not offended). "I hope the man who invented it died a violent death. Miss Arden, I know I have put myself in a false position by going to visit the Pimpernels—"

"Oh, no, indeed no, not at all," said Clare, with majestic suavity; "why should not you visit them if you like them? I object to visiting that sort of people myself, you know. Not that they are not quite as good as I am—but—And then one acts as one has been brought up. I never supposed it was a wrong thing to do—"

"It would not be right for you," said her cousin. "With us men, of course, it don't matter; but you—I should not like to see you at the Red House with a mallet in your hand. I must not tell you my motive in going there, I suppose?"

"Oh, please, do," said Clare, with queenly superiority, but a heart that beat very quick under this calm appearance. "I think I can divine—but you may be sure of my interest—in whatever concerns you. Miss Pimpernel is very pretty; she has the loveliest complexion. And I was not in earnest when I spoke about—buttoning her glove."

"Why should not you be in earnest? She does nothing but button her glove. But I don't know what Miss Pimpernel has to do with it," said Arthur, putting on an air of surprise. He knew very well what she had to do with it. He understood Clare's meaning at once, and he knew also that there was a certain truth in the suggestion. If he was utterly foiled concerning herself, he was by no means sure that Alice Pimpernel was not the next best; but he put on an air of surprise, and gravely waited for a reply. Clare, however, was not quite able to reply. She smiled, and waited till he should say more. It was the wisest and the safest way.

"I think, after what you have implied, I must tell you why I am at the Pimpernels," he said, after a pause. "It was very silly of me, of course; but I never thought—In short, I did not know you were so consistent. I thought you would do as other people did, and that you visited them like the rest of the world. All this, Miss Arden, I told you before; but I don't suppose it was worth remembering. When your brother turned me out—"

"Mr. Arden, you forget yourself; Edgar never turned any one out. Why should he?" said Clare; and then she stopped, and said to herself—"Yes; it was quite true."

"Of course, I could not expect he was to stay here for me; but he did turn me out. And very right too," said Arthur, sadly. "He divined me better than you did. Had I been Edgar, and he me, I should have done just the same."

"I do not understand you, Mr. Arden," said Clare, raising her lofty head. "Edgar is the very soul of courtesy and kindness. You do not understand my brother." She knew so well that she was talking nonsense, and he knew it so well, that here Clare paused, confused, not able to go on with her fiction under his very eye.

"Well," he said, with a sigh, shaking his head, "we must not discuss that question. I could throw light upon it perhaps, but for the present I dare not. And I thought in my stupidity that the Red House was near Arden. I find it is a thousand miles away. Is not that strange? Miss Arden, I am going to do something genealogical, or historical. I think I will write a book. Writing a book, people say, is a very nice amusement when you don't know what to do with yourself, and if you happen to be rather wretched now and then. I am going to write something about the family. I wonder if Edgar and you would let me see the old family papers—if any papers exist?"

"To write a book!" said Clare. Miss Arden had rather a contempt for literature; but to write a book which was not for money, like the books of professional authors, but about "the family," like so many handsome books she had seen—a glorification, not of one's self to be sure, but of one's ancestors—was a different matter. A slight, very slight, rose-tint came upon her pale face. It was not the kind of flush which appeared when Arthur Arden talked of other subjects. It was a thrill of pleasurable excitement—a movement of sudden interest and pride.

"If you will permit me to see what papers there are," said Arthur; "I know there are some which must be interesting, for I remember your father—He was peculiar in some things, Miss Arden; but how full of knowledge and power he was!"

"Oh, was not he?" cried Clare, with sudden tears in her eyes. "Poor papa! Poor dear papa! I think he knew everything. Mr. Arden, it is so kind of you to speak of him. No one ever speaks of him to me. People think it brings one's grief back—as if one would not give the world to have it back! And Edgar and I—poor Edgar!—he can't talk of him as—as most children can. You know why: it is no one's fault. Perhaps if I had been a little more firm—But, oh, it is so kind of you to talk to me of papa!"

"I did not mean to be kind," said Arthur Arden, with a sudden compunction, feeling his own treachery. "But perhaps I knew him better than Edgar could," he added, gently. "And he loved you so—no child was ever more to a father. But I should not say anything to make you cry—"

"I like to cry," said Clare. "I have not cried for months, and it does me so much good. Nobody ever loved me as poor papa did. I am not blaming any one. Edgar is very fond of me, Mr Arden—he is very fond of me and very good to me—but you know—papa—"

"He was like no one else," said the traitor; and, good heavens, he asked himself, am I putting all this on by way of getting possession of her father's papers? What a horrible villain I must be! But he did not feel himself a villain. He went on talking about the Squire with the profoundest seriousness, and feeling what he said, though he was conscious of his own motive all the time. It was frightful to think of, but yet thus it was. And Clare, who had so much emotion pent up within her—so much which she would have been ashamed to trace to its just source, and which nothing in the world would have persuaded her to show—when the fountains of her heart were thus opened, and a feasible occasion given her, Clare's whole being seemed to flow forth. She talked of her father, and felt that of him alone could she thus have talked. And her tears flowed, and were dried, and flowed again. Not all for her father—a great deal for herself, for the complications of her own life—for nameless agitations and trouble. But this one legitimate reason for weeping relieved them all.

"How stupid I am," she said at last, "entertaining you with my silly crying, as if that could be anything to you. Mr. Arden, I don't think you need wait for Edgar's leave. I am sure he would let me give it. I don't know whether the papers are interesting—but there is that old bureau in the library. It was papa's bureau—he always used it as long as he lived. I have never said anything about it, and I have never had the heart to go over them myself: but there are quantities of letters in it. I suppose they ought to be burnt. If you find anything that interests you, I might go over papa's papers at the same time—it would be something to do—"

"And I shall be at hand, if you want anything," said Arthur. Was it possible he was to get his wish so easily? This poor little lamb did not even wait to be asked, she thrust her milk-white head into the wolf's mouth. The papers; not only those old papers which he had pretended to want, but any windfall of modern letters that might fall in his way—and not only this, but Clare's society, and full opportunity to work upon her as he might. He could not believe it was true as he went away. It was his first visit, and he would not stay too long, nor run any risk. He left her, as it were, on the verge of a new world. To-morrow even might bring forth results more important than anything that had yet dawned on his life—to-morrow he might discover something which would put Arden within his reach—or to-morrow's chances might place Clare within his reach, the next thing to Arden. His head throbbed with excitement and his heart with hope.

As for Clare, she too was on the verge of a new world—but it was one of excitement and emotion only. Her dull life quickened into sudden radiance. She looked out again from the window, and saw the silvery water gleaming, and the branches waving, and all the face of nature gay. The day had brightened, the world grown cheery—and to-morrow, with new things in it, new companionship, new work, new interests, smiled and invited her. She did not say even to herself "I shall see him again." On the contrary, she thought of her father and his papers, and the melancholy pleasure of setting them in order. It would be, of course, a melancholy pleasure; and yet she caught herself singing as she ran upstairs to get her hat, and go out for a walk. Could it be this prospect only which made her heart so light and so gay?

CHAPTER XI

The next day was one of excitement for Clare. She began it with feelings so changed from that of the previous morning, when life had seemed nothing but tedium and heaviness to her, that it was difficult to imagine that she was the same creature. The calm composure of her earlier days, when no new incident was wanted to break the pleasant blank of existence, was as different from this new exhiliration as it was from the heavy, leaden dulness of the time which was just over. She had wanted nothing in the first serenity of her youth. She had seemed to want everything in the monotony of her loneliness after her brother and her cousin had left her. And now, again, she wanted nothing—except—

Except—She did not say to herself what it was; or if she did she called it by other names. Something to do—something to interest her—a little society in the midst of her solitude. She did not say, I am happy because he is coming. A girl must have gone a long way on that path before she will say as much to herself; but a sense that he was coming seemed to be in the air—the sunshine was brighter for it, the morning was sweeter, all kinds of lovely lights and gleams of life and movement were upon the park— the very scene which yesterday had been so unbearably still and motionless. The hours did not seem long till he came, but glided past with the softest harmony. She rather felt disposed to dwell upon them—to lengthen them out—for were they not all threaded through with that thread of expectation which made their stillness rosy? It fretted her a little to have this enchanted quiet broken by Mrs. Murray, though she came according to an appointment which Clare had forgotten. The girl's brow clouded over with impatience when this visitor was announced to her. "Yes, I remember," she said sharply to Wilkins. "Let her come upstairs. I told her to come." But it was a little relief to Clare's mind to find that her visitor was alone, which supplied her at once with a legitimate cause of offence.

"You have not brought Jeanie with you?" she said. "Is she ill, or what is the matter? I so particularly wished her to come!"

"I had a reason for no bringing her; and in case it should be made known to you after, and look like a falseness, I have come to tell you, Miss Arden," said Mrs. Murray. "Your house, no doubt, is full of pictures of your father. It is but right. I saw one down the stair as I came in at the door—"

"And what then? What has papa's picture to do with it?" asked Clare in amaze.

"You would think, little enough, Miss Arden," said Mrs. Murray. "That is just what I have to tell you. Ye'll mind that my cousin Thomas Perfitt has been long in the service of your house. And Jeanie has seen your father, and it made her heart sore—"

"Seen my father!" said Clare, with wonder, which was not so great as her visitor expected. "I did not know you had been here before."

"We were never here before. Where we saw your father was at Loch Arroch in our own place. I knew him before you were born, Miss Arden—when I was—no to say young, but younger than I am now; and your mother, poor lady, too—"

This she said sinking her voice, so that Clare with difficulty made it out.

"My mother, too!" she cried, "how strange, how very strange, you should never have told me this before!"

"I canna think you will say it's strange, if ye consider," said the Scotchwoman; "plenty folk here must have seen your mother. It's no as if you were ignorant—and it's no as if I had anything to say but as I've been led to say it to others, I wouldna have you think there was a falseness. She was young, and she was feeble, poor thing, when I saw her. It's more than five and twenty years ago, when him that's now Mr. Arden had but lately come into this weary world."

"You speak in such a strange way," said Clare—"him that's now Mr. Arden! Do you mean my brother Edgar? He is just twenty-five now."

"He was but an infant, and well I mind it," said the old woman, shaking her head with mournful meaning. "It was a sore time to me—death and trouble was in my house; and, oh, the trouble and the deaths I have had, Miss Arden! To hear of them would frighten the like of you. But first I must tell you why I canna bring Jeanie here. Two years ago, or may be more—two months more, for it was in the month of April—your father came to see me. Him and me, I told you, had met before. There were things I kent that were of consequence to him, and things he kent that were of consequence to me. Jeanie and her brother Willie—a bonnie blythe laddie—were both about the house. Willie was a sailor, sore against my will; and, oh, Miss Arden, so bonnie a boy! Your father was real kind. It's been hard, hard to bear—but he meant to be kind. He got my Willie a ship out of Liverpool. The poor laddie went away from us—it's two years this June—as blythe as ony bridegroom; and, Miss Arden, he's never come back—"

"Never come back!" Clare's wonder was so great that she repeated the last words without any real sense of their meaning, as she would have repeated anything that made a pause in this strange narrative. Her father! She seemed to herself to possess his later life—to know its every detail—to hold it, as it were, in her hands. He had never done anything without telling her—without consulting her, she would have said. Yet here was a secret of which she knew nothing. She was not selfish, but her mind was not so readily open to the affairs of others as was that of her brother. She never thought of the young sailor, or of the old mother, who spoke so sadly. She thought only of her father and his secret. What were the others to her? Of course she would have been sorry for them had their sorrows been sufficiently impressed on her imagination. But in the meantime it was her father she was thinking of, with bewildering wonder and pain.

Mrs. Murray, on the other hand, was absorbed with her own part of the tale. "He never came back," she repeated, with a thrill of agitation in her voice. "He was lost in the wild sea, far out of our reach. Oh! it might have happened a' the same. It might have come to the innocentest woman as it came to me. Many a lad is lost, and many a family brought to mourning, and naebody to blame. But when I think of all that's been in my life, and that the like of that should come by means o' the one man!—That is how Jeanie knew your father, Miss Arden. She took your cousin for him, and it made her wild. I daurna bring her here to pain her with his picture. She was aye a strange bairn all her life, and Willie's loss made her all wrong. That's what I came to tell you, to be honest and clear o' reproach. I'm no good or without guilt, that I should say so—but, oh, I hate a lie!"

Clare scarcely heeded this exclamation. She did not realise it, nor occupy herself about what her visitor felt. There was so much in this revelation that concerned herself that she had no leisure for other people's feelings. "I do not see how you could blame papa," she said, almost coldly; "of course, he did it for the best. How was he to know the ship would be lost? I am sorry, but I think it very strange that you should suppose it was his fault. Jeanie ought to be told how foolish it is. Papa would not have hurt any one—he would not have been cruel to—a fly."

Here Clare paused with a good deal of natural indignant feeling. Was the woman trying to make some claim upon her, to establish a grievance? It was a kind thing her father had done. He had taken the trouble to interest himself about it without even telling his daughter. And then they were discontented because the ship was lost. How unreasonable, how preposterous it seemed! "Nothing must be said about my father which I ought not to hear," she said after a pause. "No words can say how fond I was of papa. He was everything to me; he was so good to me. He never had any—secrets from me. No, I am sure he had not! He did not speak of you, because perhaps—For he was not one to blazon his own kindness, or—And then he might forget. Why should he speak to me of you?"

"You think we are humble folk, no worthy to be thought upon," said Mrs. Murray with a half smile. It was not sneering, but pitying, very grave and very sad. "And that's true—that's true. What was a life more or less in a poor farmhouse so long as the grand race ran on? You are very like your father, Miss Arden—that was the very way his thoughts ran—"

"His thoughts were always kind and good," said Clare, hastily; and it was hard, very hard for her in the agitation of the moment to resist a girlish inclination to burst into tears. It was so ungrateful, she would have said—so cruel and unkind. What! because a kind service was done, which brought on painful results, was it the benefactor that was to be blamed? "If Jeanie were to be ill now, you might just as well say it was my doing," she added in her suppressed passion, and felt that she disliked the very looks of this stranger and her monotonous Scotch voice.

Then there was a long pause. Clare turned over all the books on the table before her—took up and put down her work—twisted the wools about her fingers till her anger had somewhat evaporated. Mrs. Murray sat at a little distance from her, saying nothing. Her eyes were fixed on a portrait of Clare, taken a year or two before, which hung on the wall. She looked at it with a wondering interest, growing more and more earnest in her attention. "You are like her, too," she said at length, with a certain astonishment. The portrait was not like Clare at that moment. It was Clare in repose, when gentler thoughts were in her mind. "You are like her, too," Mrs. Murray resumed, with a little eagerness. "I could not have thought it. But you're no one to let your heart be broken without a word, the Lord be praised."

"What do you mean? If it is of mamma you are speaking, it is my brother who is like her," said Clare, haughtily, "and I should be glad if you would not meddle any further with our affairs."

"Eh, if I could but let them alone, and never think of them more!" The Scotchwoman rose as she said this, with a deep and prolonged sigh. Without another word she went to the door. "I will come to you if you send for me, Miss Arden, if I'm ever wanted in this house," she said, "but no for any other reason. I would forget if I could that there ever was man or woman bearing your name. But the past cannot be forgotten, and I'll come if I am ever wanted here."

With these words she went away. Something solemn was in them, something which was incomprehensible, which sounded real, and yet must be absolute folly, Clare thought. Why should she be wanted at Arden? What could she ever do to affect the house? No doubt there were people still living in the world who believed in revenge, and would hunt down (if they could) a man who had injured them. But what revenge could this woman carry out upon the Ardens? It was a piece of folly—a mere dream. Clare laughed at the thought that Mrs. Murray could be wanted—that she could be sent for to Arden. But her laugh sounded harsh to herself. She resented the whole matter, the visit, the uncalled for narrative, the almost threat, the interruption of her pleasant thoughts. And then the question would come back—What had been the tie between her parents and this woman? She remembered so clearly her father's absence from home two years ago. He had told her he had business in London—and he had gone to Scotland instead! How very strange it was! The more Clare thought of it the more angry she grew. If he had secrets—if he did things she was not to know—what right had any one to come and tell her now, when he could no longer explain the matter, and all his secrets were buried with him? She had her hand on the bell, to send for Mr. Perfitt, and question him what sort of woman this was whom he had brought to Arden to perplex and vex everybody. And then she remembered Sally Timms' gossip, and tried to think evil thoughts. To some people it comes natural to think ill of their neighbours; but Clare was too spotless and too proud for such a tendency. She did not believe any harm of Mrs. Murray, and yet she tried to believe it. And then she tried to laugh once more and dismiss the whole matter from her mind; and then—

It was the clock striking two which roused her, and the entrance of Wilkins with the little luncheon tray, which furnished her doleful, solitary, little meal. This roused her out of her resentment and her dreams—not that she was tempted by the chicken's wing, or even the strawberries among their cool green leaves; but that the morning was over, and the second chapter of the day, as it were, about to commence. And that second chapter had the hero in it, and all the nameless sweet agitations that would come with him—the fancies and visions and expectations which distinguish one phase of life, and make it more enthralling than any other. After a while that other step would disturb the silence, and all the world would brighten up and widen, she could not tell why. Not because of Arthur Arden, surely. He was no prince of romance, she said to herself. She entertained (she assured herself) no delusions about him. He was very agreeable to her—a man who pleased her—a true Arden; but she did not pretend to think him a king of men. Therefore, it could not be her cousin whose coming was to change everything. It must be the pleasant work she was about to begin with him—the common family interest—the intercourse with one who almost belonged to her—who was always ready to talk, and willing to discuss anything that caught her interest. Very different from being alone, and worrying over everything, as people do who have no one to confide their troubles to. She would tell her cousin about Mrs. Murray, and thus get rid of the thought. This was what lightened the cloud from about her, and brought back the atmosphere to its original clearness. It was so pleasant to have some one to talk to—one of the family, to whom she could venture to say anything. Of course, this was all; and it was enough for Clare.

CHAPTER XII

Arthur Arden was punctual to his appointment: he had thought of little else since he left Arden the day before. To do him justice, Clare's society, the power of approaching her as he would, was very sweet to him, especially after a severe course of croquet at the Red House, and a few days with the Pimpernels. In short, he was able to disguise to himself his other motive altogether, and to forget he had any clandestine object. "I am going to look over some old family papers with my cousin," he had said to Mrs.

Pimpernel, who, for her part, had not much liked the information. "If he is going to make a cat's-paw of us, and spend all his time running after that proud stuck-up thing!" she said to her husband. "Our Alice is worth two of her any day; and I don't hold with your family papers." "We haven't got any, have we?" said Mr. Pimpernel; "but you wait a bit, Mary; I know what the family papers mean." "I hope you do, Mr. Pimpernel," said his wife, with evident scepticism. And she did not like it when Arthur Arden, instead of joining Alice at her croquet, or attending herself upon her drive, went off again after luncheon to visit his cousin. "If that is the way of it, I don't see the good of having a gentleman in the house," she said to Alice. "But then there is Mr. Denbigh, mamma," said Alice, innocently, for which her mother could have boxed her ears.

And Arthur turned his back upon them and their croquet ground with the intensest satisfaction. It was very heavy work. He had been in a great many country houses, and he had occasionally felt that in his position as a man without any particular means or advantages, a good deal of exertion had been required from him in payment for the hospitality he received. He had seen the justice of it, and in a general way he had not made much objection. But then these were houses full of people where, if a man made himself generally useful, every necessity of the circumstances was satisfied, and he was not compelled to devote himself specially to stupid or wearisome individuals. He had the sweet along with the bitter, and he had not complained. But to be told off for Mrs. Pimpernel's personal service or for croquet was a different matter, and he turned his back upon them with a light heart. And when the door of the old hereditary house opened to him, and Clare, like one of the pictures from the walls, rose with a little tremulous expectation, holding out her hand, the difference was such that it confused his mind altogether, and made him conscious of nothing but intense relief. Look over family papers! oh, yes; or mow the lawn, if she liked, or work in the garden. He said to himself that the one pretext would be just as good as the other. It was a pretext, not any intended treachery, but only a means of being near Clare.

"Would you like to go to the library at once?" she said. "I have just glanced at the papers poor papa arranged on the top shelves of his bureau. All his own letters and things are below. Shall we go to the library at once?"

"I am not in a hurry," said Arthur; "if you don't mind, let me wait a little and breathe Arden. It is so sweet after the atmosphere I have been in. I am not ungrateful; pray don't think so. It was extremely kind of the Pimpernels to give me shelter in my forlorn condition—"

"I don't see why you should ever be in a forlorn condition," said Clare. "Please don't suppose I mean to be rude; but I can't bear to think of an Arden receiving hospitality from people like the Pimpernels."

"My dear cousin," said Arthur, "an Arden, when he is not actually of the reigning family, must do what he can in this world. The sanctity of the race is not perhaps acknowledged as it ought to be; and I am too much obliged to anybody who gives me shelter in this neighbourhood. One ought to be in town, I suppose; but then I am sick of town, and there is nobody to go to yet in the country. Therefore I say long live the Pimpernels. But all the same, one breathes freer here."

"There is not much to amuse any one here," said Clare.

"Amuse! I know how it will be. You will make me speak as—I ought not to speak, and then you will drive me away; and I cannot bear being driven away. There is a little pucker in the brow of the Lady Clare. May I know why?"

"You are like Edgar. He always worries me about that line in my forehead," said Clare; "as if I could help it! Yes; I have been a little annoyed to-day. I think I may as well tell you, and perhaps you can give me some advice. It is that Mrs. Murray—that Scotchwoman. She has just been here to tell me that she knew papa, and that he went to see her in Scotland two years ago. It is very strange, and very uncomfortable. He used to tell me everything—or at least so I thought."

"Nobody ever does tell everything," said Arthur, like an oracle. Clare paused, and gazed wistfully into his face.

"Not what they are thinking, nor what they feel, but surely what they do. How can you conceal what you do? Some one must be taken into your confidence. Common people must see you, in whom you have no confidence; while your very own—"

Here Clare stopped abruptly, feeling that tears were about to come into her voice.

"You don't know what you say," said Arthur, who was secretly touched. "What one thinks and feels is often the best of one. But what we do—Was there ever a man who could venture to show a woman everything in his life—a woman like you?"

"Yes; papa," said Clare, boldly. "I am sure he told me everything—except—Oh! is it not dreadful, is it not horrible, to have this wretched woman coming, when he is no longer here to explain it all, to make me lose my confidence in papa? And then you too!"

"I too!" he said, and he ventured to take her hand; "who am not worthy of your interest at all, and dare not lay my poor worthless life open before you. But listen, I will recant. One could not show you the past, in which one was wandering without any compass. But, Clare—I am your cousin—I may call you Clare sometimes?—if one could be so bold as to believe that you took any interest—I mean—Edgar, for instance, who can be sure you take an interest—I do believe that such a lucky man as he is might tell you everything. Yes; no doubt your father did; but not the past—not all the past!"

Clare drew a little aside, afraid, she could not tell why. She had withdrawn her hand from him at once. She had given him only a little bow of assent when he called her by her name. She had not encouraged him—of that she was certain.

"Perhaps it is best not to discuss it," she said. "But I cannot tell you how that woman vexed me. To come and say she knew things of my own father which I did not know. Fancy, papa! Perhaps it is my pride—I should not wonder; but I could not bear it. And now, you know, if I look into his letters I may find things. Do you think it is likely? He was an old man; he was sixty when he died. He had been forty years in the world before he had any one—I mean before he had me to confide in. Should I read them? Should I look at them? I don't know what to do."

"If you could trust me," said Arthur Arden. The thought flushed him with sudden excitement. This would indeed be delivering the very stronghold into his hands. And then all the remnants of honourable feeling that was left there stirred together in his mind. He blushed for the baseness he had almost meditated. "If you could trust me to look over them," he resumed, with an earnestness which surprised himself, "you may be quite sure that any and every secret—I mean—I am nearest to you after Edgar—it would be safe with me."

And then with the speed of lightning a calculation ran through his mind. Yes, he would be faithful to his word. The secret should be safe with him, safe as in the grave. If even he should find proof of facts which would be damning to Edgar, he would consider himself bound to take no personal action upon it, if he discovered it in such a way. He would let Edgar know and Clare, who were the persons most concerned; and then he would himself withdraw, and never more mention the subject. He would leave the knowledge of it to work in their minds. He himself would win only the reward of honour and virtue. To such a course of procedure the strictest moralist could have no objection. For if anything were found out, though it would be treachery to employ it for his own interest, it could only be duty to reveal it to Edgar and Clare. He looked at his cousin with a certain anxiety, feeling that his fate lay in her hands. It lay in her hands in a great many ways. She was but a child in comparison with his years—a baby in experience, an unreasoning, impulsive girl. And yet she held all his future in her little fingers. Its higher or lower position, even its honour or dishonour, its virtue or ill-doing—a tremendous power to lie in such unconscious hands.

"Thanks!" said Clare, with a certain haughtiness; and then in a moment Arthur felt that this at least was not to be. "No one but myself must do it," she went on firmly; "not even Edgar, who did not love—At least it was not possible he could love much—they were so separated. No; if there is any pain in it, I must bear it as best I can—no one must do it but me."

He made a bow of assent to her decision. It was not for him to say a word, and even in his momentary disappointment there was a certain relief. After all, even had he adopted that path of strict virtue, there would have been something doubtful about the proceeding. Whereas, if he found anything by chance—And then he could not but speculate what Clare would do if she made any such discovery as he hoped. What would she do? Would she, in her innocence, understand what it meant? or if it should be too clear for mistake, would her love for him who would still be her brother, for her dead mother's son, be stronger than abstract justice? Probably she would not understand it all, he thought, and so this fine opportunity, this wonderful chance, would be thrown away. He heard her renewed invitation to him to go to the library like a man in a dream. The issues might be mighty, but it was such a chance—all depending upon how far an innocent girl could understand a record of wickedness, or an injured man have proofs of his own dishonour. "The chances are he destroyed everything," he said to himself, but half aloud, as he followed Clare.

"What did you say?"

"I was not aware I said anything. The thought that passed through my mind was that probably your father, if he had any painful secrets in his life, was so wise as to destroy all trace of them. Nay, don't mistake me. I say if. Probably he had no secrets at all, or only innocent ones—but if—"

"I don't think he destroyed anything," said Clare, almost sharply, as she led the way. Now that she had made up her mind to it, she did not wish to be balked of her mystery. It was very dreadful and painful, and a great shock; but still, if there was anything in it—She went on first into the large, lofty, sombre room which was the Arden library. It was everything that a library ought to be. The books were but little used, it is true; but then the room was so noiseless, so cool, and grey, and secluded, that it seemed the very place for a student. To be sure the Ardens had never been great students, but they had all the books that ought to be in a gentleman's library—an excellent collection of English literature, a fair show of classics, and many books in other living languages. These books were very seldom disturbed behind their wires; but the silence was supreme, and would have lent itself to the deepest study. Edgar had been daunted by the solemn dignity of the place. He had felt that his discussions with Perfitt, and all the business he had to transact, were out of place in this stately, solemn room; and, with his usual indifference to the traditions of the Ardens, had removed himself into a homely, bright, little place, full of impertinent windows and modern papered walls, where he had hung up a great many of his possessions, and where Perfitt could talk above his breath.

After this change, a deepened and still deepening solemnity had fallen upon the library. It had been the old Squire's room, where he had spent all his mornings. The quaint, old-fashioned bureau, which stood in one corner, was full of his papers. He had locked it up himself the last day he was downstairs, and nobody had opened it since. So completely was the room identified with him that the maids in the house began to rush past the door when twilight was coming on, and would not enter it after dark. "I know I'd see t' ou'd man a-sitting in his chair as he used to," the housemaid had said to the housekeeper; and the library was clearly in a fair way for being haunted. It was with a certain solemnity now that Clare opened the door. She had scarcely been in it since her father's death; and though she would have repudiated all superstitious feeling, no doubt there was a certain thrill of awe in her mind when she entered her father's private room, with the intention of investigating into his secrets. What if some spiritual presence might guard these relics of the ended life—what if something impalpable, undiscernible, should float between her and its records! Clare hung back a little, and paused on the threshold. She could almost fancy she saw him seated at the writing-table, not yet feeble, not asking even her sympathy, dearly though he loved her. She had known everything he did or planned; and yet, now she thought of it, how little had she known of him! Nothing except the present; his old age, with all its hushed excitements and interests past. It was (now that she thought of it) a veiled being who had sat there for so many years in her sight. Except that he loved herself, that he dined and rode with her, and sat for hours in this library, and allowed the cottages to be rebuilt, and a great deal of charity to be given, what did she know of her father? That—and that he hated Edgar; nothing more. Her heart gave a jump to her mouth as she entered the room, in which the silence seemed to brood and deepen, knowing a great deal more than she did. Clare owned this strange influence, and it subdued her for the moment; but the next, she raised her head proudly, and shook off the momentary impression. Not now, on the threshold of the mystery, was it possible to withdraw or fail.

CHAPTER XIII

Two or three days elapsed after this commencement of operations, and the Pimpernels had begun to be seriously affronted. Day by day Arden deserted them after luncheon without even taking the trouble to apologise. Now and then it happened that the croquet came absolutely to a stand-still, and once Mrs. Pimpernel drove into Liverpool without any captive knight to exhibit, which was very hard upon her. She was a hospitable woman, ready to invite any well-born, well-mannered individual of the (fashionable) houseless and homeless class; but then, on the other hand, she expected something in return. "Proper respect," she called it; but it meant a good deal of social work—attendance upon her daughter and herself, a sort of combination of the amateur footman and the amusing companion. At this rate she would have given Arthur Arden board and lodging for as long a period as he might desire. So long as she could have it in her power to explain to any of her friends whom she met that he was "one of the Ardens of Arden—indeed, the next heir to the property," she was able to feel that she had something for her money. But to give him the green room, which was one of the nicest in the house, and to feed him with truffles and champagne and all the delicacies of the season, in order that he might spend half the day— the really useful part of the day—with his cousin, was a thing she had not bargained for. She showed her displeasure to the culprit himself in a manner which would have been much more plain to him had he cared more about it; and she complained to her husband, stating her grievance in the plainest terms. "That Arthur Arden is an utter nuisance," she said. "I consider it most impudent of him, Mr. Pimpernel. He comes and stays here, making a convenience of our house, but never thinks of paying proper respect, such as any man who was a gentleman would. He sees Alice and me drive out by ourselves, and actually has the assurance to wave his hand to us, and wish us a pleasant drive. Yesterday I said to him—I really could not help it—'You don't do much to make our drive pleasant, Mr. Arden,' and he simply stared at me. Fancy, having to drive into Liverpool shopping, Alice and I, without a soul!—when everybody knows I like to have a gentleman to do little things for us—and that Arden actually staying in the house!"

"It was cool of him," said her husband. "He is what I call a cool hand, is Arden. I'll speak to him, if you like. I am not one of the men that beat about the bush. Make yourself understood, that's my motto. There is just one thing to be said for him, however, and that is, that it may be business. He told me he was hunting through the Arden papers; confounded silly of that girl to let him; but that is no business of mine."

"Oh, business indeed!" said Mrs. Pimpernel. "Business that takes him to Clare Arden's side every afternoon! I don't much believe in that kind of business. What he can see in her I am sure I cannot divine. A stuck-up thing! looking down upon them that are as good as she is any day! Just fancy a man leaving our Alice hitting the balls about all day by herself, poor child, on the lawn!—a man staying in the house!—and going off to the Hall to Clare Arden! Do you call that proper respect? As for good taste, I don't speak of that, for it is clear he has not got any. And you take my word for it, business is nothing but a pretence."

"I am not so sure of that," said Mr Pimpernel. "You see, if he really is doing anything, it's his policy to make himself agreeable to that girl. She gives him access to the papers, you know. The papers are the great thing. Don't you be too exacting for a day or two. If Alice mopes let me know; by Jove! I won't have my little girl crossed. It's odd if I can't buy her anything she takes a fancy to. But all the same he's an old fellow is Arden, and he hasn't a penny to bless himself with. I can't see much reason why she should set her heart on him."

"Upon my word and honour, Mr. Pimpernel!" said the lady, "if that is all the opinion you have of your own child—Set her heart on Arthur Arden, indeed! She would never have looked at him if it hadn't been for that talk about the property. And if it turns out to be a mistake about the property, do you think I'd ever—? I hope I have more opinion of my girl than that. But when I ask a man to my house, I own I look for proper respect. I consider it's his business to make himself agreeable to me, and not to strangers. My house ain't an inn to be at the convenience of visitors to Arden. If he likes best being there, let him go and live there. I say Arden is Arden, and the Red House is the Red House, and the one don't depend upon the other, nor has nothing to do with the other. If there's one thing I hate it is pride and mean ways. Let her take him in and keep him if she wants him. But I won't keep him, and feed him with the best of everything, and champagne like water, for Miss Clare Arden's sake, or Miss anything that ever was born!"

Mrs. Pimpernel was tying on her nightcap as she spoke, and the act deafened her a little, for the nightcap strings were stiff and well starched—which was perhaps the reason why she delivered the concluding words in so loud a voice. Mr. Pimpernel was a courageous man enough, but when it came to this he was too prudent to do anything to increase the storm.

"I'll speak to him if you like," he said. "It's always best to know exactly what one is about. I'll put it in the plainest terms; but I think we might wait a day or two all the same. Arden's a fine property, and Arthur Arden is a clever fellow. He knows what's what as well as any man I know: and if he's making a cat's-paw of his cousin you can't blame him. If I were you I'd give him a day or two's grace."

"I am sick of him and everything about him. He is no more use than that poker," said Mrs. Pimpernel, seating herself in disgust in a chair which stood in her habitual corner, at the side of the vacant fireplace. The poker in question gleamed in brilliant steel incongruity from amid the papery convolutions of an ornamental structure which filled the grate. Nothing could well be more useless: it was a simile which went to her husband's heart.

"To think that I was poking the fire with that identical poker not six weeks ago!" he said, "and now the heat's enough to kill you. If you had felt it in the office at three o'clock to-day! I can tell you it was no joke."

"Do you think I didn't feel it?" said his wife; "driving into Liverpool under that broiling sun, without a soul to amuse you, or offer you his arm, or anything; and that Arden quite comfortable, enjoying himself in the big cool rooms at the Hall. Ah, fathers little know what one has to go through for one's children. All this blessed afternoon was I choosing sleeves and collars and things for Alice, and summer frocks for the children. The way they grow, and the number of changes they want! And we had to allow half-an-inch more for Alice's collars. She is certainly getting stout. I am stout myself, and of course at my age it don't matter; but the more that child takes exercise the more she fills out. I don't understand it. You might have drawn me through a good-sized ring when I was her age."

"It must have been a very good-sized ring," said Mr. Pimpernel. "And I don't like your maypoles of girls. I like 'em nice and round and fat—"

"Good heavens, Mr. Pimpernel, you speak as if you were going to eat them!" said his wife.

"If they were all as nice, healthy, plump, red and white as my Alice," said the indulgent father. And then there followed a few parental comments on both sides on the comparative growths of Jane, Eliza, and Maria-Anne. Thus the conversation dropped, and the danger which threatened Arthur Arden was for the moment over. But yet he felt next morning that something explosive was in the air. It was his interest to stay at the Red House as long as possible, to have his invitation renewed, if that was possible; and he felt instinctively that something must be done to mend matters. It was a great bore, for though he had discovered nothing as yet, he had been living in the closest intercourse with Clare, and had been making, he felt, satisfactory progress in that pursuit—indeed, he had made a great deal more progress than he himself was aware; for the fact was that his own feelings (such as they were) were too much engaged to make him quite so clear-sighted on the subject as he might have been. A bystander would probably have seen, which Arthur Arden did not, that everything was tending towards a very speedy crisis, and that it was perfectly apparent how that crisis would be decided. Had he himself been cool enough to note her looks—her tremulous withdrawals and sudden confidences—her mingled fear of him and dependence upon him, he would have spoken before now, and all would have been decided. But he was timid, as genuine feeling always is—afraid that after all he might be deceiving himself, and that all the evidences which he sometimes trusted in might mean nothing. Things were in this exciting state when his eyes were opened to see the cloudy countenance of Mrs. Pimpernel and the affronted looks of Alice. He was late at breakfast, as he always was—a thing which had been regarded as a very good joke when he first came to the Red House. "Papa has been gone for an hour," Alice had been wont to say, looking at her watch; and Mrs. Pimpernel would shake her head at him. "Ah, Mr. Arden, it is just as well you have no house to keep in order," she would say. "I can't think whatever you do when you are married, you fashionable men." But now the comments were of a very different character. "I am afraid the coffee is cold," Mrs. Pimpernel said, looking hot enough herself to warm any amount of coffee. "It is so unfortunate that we cannot make our hours suit; and I must ask you to excuse me—I must give the housekeeper her orders before it is quite the middle of the day—"

"Am I so very late—I am dreadfully sorry," said Arthur, appealing to Alice, who sat at the end of the table looking shyly spiteful, and who remained for a moment undecided whether to follow her mother or to put on an aspect of civility and stay.

"Oh no, Mr. Arden—I mean I can't tell—mamma thinks we see so very little of you now—"

"Do you see little of me? Ah, yes, I remember, you were in Liverpool yesterday shopping, and I found the house all desolate when I came back. You can't think how dreary it looks when you are away. This suggestion of your father's gives me so much work in the afternoon—"

"Oh, Mr. Arden! a suggestion of papa's?"

"Did you not know—did you think it was by my own inclination that I was at work all day long?" said Arthur. "How much higher an opinion you must have of me than I deserve! Does Mrs. Pimpernel think it is all my doing? No, I am not so good as that. I am going over the family papers on your papa's suggestion—trying to find out something—Most likely I shall write a book—"

"Oh, Mr. Arden!" cried Alice Pimpernel.

"Yes; most likely I shall write a book. You can't think how many interesting stories there are in the family. Should you like me to tell you one this morning before the children are ready for their croquet? I don't know if I can do it well, but if you like—"

"Oh, Mr. Arden, I should like it so much!"

"Then, come out on the lawn," said Arthur. "I know a spot where it will be delicious this warm morning to lie on the grass and tell you about our Spanish lady. Did you ever hear of our Spanish lady? It was she who gave us our olive complexions and our black hair."

"Oh, Mr. Arden!" Alice cried, dazzled by the prospect; "only wait, please, till I fetch my work;" and she hurried away into the drawing-room, leaving him to finish his breakfast. Alice ran across her mother in the hall, as she crossed from one room to the other. Her pretty complexion was heightened, and her eyes shining with pleasure and interest. "Oh, mamma! I am going out to the lawn to hear Mr. Arden tell a story," she cried, "about the Spanish lady—a family story; and, oh! he says he does not go away for his own pleasure, but because of something papa put into his head. Fancy—papa!"

"That is all very well," said Mrs. Pimpernel. "Your papa, indeed!—but I happen to know better. Your papa only told him, if he could find a flaw in the title—Your papa is a great deal too liberal, Alice—offering to help people that have not a penny to bless themselves with—as if it could ever be anything to us!—or, as if there was such a thing as gratitude in the world."

"Oh, mamma—hush!" whispered Alice, pointing to the open door of the dining-room, through which Arthur heard every word that was said; and then she added, plaintively, with ready tears gathering in her eyes, "Mayn't I go?"

"I suppose he thinks we are all to be ready as soon as he holds up his little finger," said the indignant mother. And then she paused, and calmed herself down. "I don't want you to be uncivil, Alice," she added, still much to Arthur's edification, who heard every word. "As long as he is your father's guest, of course you must be polite to him. Oh, yes, you can go. But mind you don't stay too long, or expose yourself to the sun; and don't forget that I expect my daughter to show a little proper pride."

Poor Alice lingered for a long time in the hall before she had courage to rejoin the guest, who must have heard everything that was said. She made believe to return to the drawing-room to look for something else which she had forgotten. And it was not till Arthur himself—who was much more amused than angry—had leisurely ended his breakfast, and strolled out into the hall, that she ventured to join him. "Oh! Mr. Arden—I am so sorry to have kept you waiting," she cried. "Never mind. I had nothing to do but wait," he said, smiling, and took the basket with her work out of her hand. He took her to the very shadiest seat, brought her a footstool, arranged everything for her with an air of devotion which went to the heart of Alice, and then he threw himself on the grass at her feet, and prepared to tell his tale.

CHAPTER XIV

Mrs. Pimpernel considered that she did well to be angry. It was all very well for her husband to put off and give him time; but a man who did not show proper respect to herself and Alice was certainly not a man to be encouraged in the house. She was glad she had had the opportunity of throwing that arrow at him from the hall, and letting him see that she was not so short-sighted as other people. But, as the morning went on, she cast several glances from more than one window upon the scene on the lawn, which was a very pretty scene. Alice was seated quite in the shade, with her worsted work and her basket of wools, the wools so bright, and her dress so light and cool, against the shady green background. And on the grass at her feet lay Arthur Arden, so fine a contrast in his dark manhood to her fairness. He was a little too old, perhaps, to make the contrast perfect. But he was still very handsome, and had about him a certain air of youth such as often clings to an unmarried vagrant. He lay looking up at Alice, telling his story; and Alice, with her head dreamily bent over her work, sat rapt and listened. As the narrative went on, her interest became too great for her work. She dropped the many-coloured web on her knee and clasped her hands, and fixed her eyes upon the teller of the tale. "Oh, Mr. Arden!" she exclaimed by intervals, carried away by her excitement. Mrs. Pimpernel took views of this group from all the bedrooms on that side of the house, and then she went downstairs and seated herself at the drawing-room window, and studied it at her leisure. Her thoughts changed gradually as she gazed. Arden looking up at Alice, and Alice shyly gazing down at Arden, were arguments of the most convincing character. After all, probably he had been making a sacrifice of himself. That stuck-up cousin of his could not possibly be so charming as Alice, who was open to every new interest, and made such a flattering absorbed listener. "That is what the men like," Mrs. Pimpernel said to herself. "She is not clever, poor love; but they never like women to be clever." And then, after a long interval, she added, still within herself, "I shouldn't wonder a bit if he was frightened for the stuck-up cousin." Yes, no doubt that was it. He had to conciliate her, and pretend to be fond of her society. "After all, he is always here all the evening," she went on, softening more and more; and the result was that at length she took down a broad hat which hung in the hall, and stepped out herself to join the garden party. "You look so comfortable, and there is evidently something so interesting going on, that I should like to have a share," she said, in a voice so softened that Arthur instantly felt his device had succeeded. "Oh, go on, please. I can always imagine what has gone before. Don't go over it again for me."

"Oh, mamma, it is so exciting," cried Alice; "it was one of the Ardens, you know, that was a sailor, and went abroad; and then he took a town out in South America; and then the Governor's daughter, the most beautiful creature in the whole place—Oh, mamma! and that is why all the Ardens have black hair and blue eyes."

"Mr. Arden of Arden has not black hair and blue eyes," said Mrs. Pimpernel.

"No," said Arthur, very distinctly and emphatically. He did not add another syllable. The very brevity of his reply was full of significance, and told its own story. And Mrs. Pimpernel looked upon him with more and more favourable eyes.

"Do you find out all this in the papers at Arden?" she resumed. "How nice it must be. I do respect an old family. My grandmother—though Mr. Pimpernel will never hear of it; he says he has enriched himself by his own exertions, and he is not ashamed of it, and won't have any pretensions made—just like a man's impetuosity—but my own grandmother was a Blundell, Mr. Arden. I often think I can trace a resemblance between my Alice and the Blundells. Does Miss Arden go over the papers with you, may I ask, when you are at the Hall?"

Arthur was so much taken by surprise that he was afraid he blushed; but his looks were less treacherous than he thought them to be, and it did not show. "Sometimes—No. I mean, the first day she gave the old bureau up to me," he said, faltering a little, "she showed a little interest too; but my cousin Clare—I am sorry you do not know Clare a little better, Mrs. Pimpernel. It would do her good to come under your influence. She wants a little womanly trifling and that sort of thing, you know. She is always full of such high designs and plans for everybody. She is—"

"A little tiresome sometimes and high-flown. Oh, I see exactly," Mrs. Pimpernel replied, nodding her head. Too clever for him evidently; men all hate clever women, she said inwardly, with a smile; while Arthur, with a savage desire to cut his own throat, or fly at hers, after his treachery to Clare, got hold of the basket of wools and scattered them wildly about the grass. He broke the basket, and he was glad. It would have been a satisfaction to his mind if he could have trampled upon all the flower-beds, and thrown stones at the windows of the peaceful house.

"Oh, Mr. Arden, never mind," said Alice. "The basket does not matter; it was not a dear basket. Oh, please, never mind. Go on with the Spanish lady. I do want so much to hear."

"It was a Spanish lady, and she loved an Englishman," said Arthur, making an effort, and resuming his tale. He did not dislike Alice. There was no impulse upon him to fly upon her and shake her, or do anything but be very civil and gentle to the pretty inoffensive girl. In short, he was like all coarse-minded men. The young fresh creature exercised a certain influence over him by reason of her beauty; but the elder woman was simply an inferior being of his own species—a weaker man in disguise, whom he dared not treat as he would a man, and accordingly hated with a double hatred. Mrs. Pimpernel perhaps would scarcely have objected to the sentiment. She had as little refinement of the heart as he had, and was ready to use all the privileges of her sex as weapons of offence to goad and madden with them any man who was any way obnoxious to her. "He knows he cannot take me in. I am not a simpleton to be deceived by his fair talk; and I know he hates me," she would have said, with real triumph. But in the meantime he was obliged to keep the peace. So he resumed his story. The hour of luncheon was approaching, and after that would come the welcome hour when for three or four days back he had been able to escape from all the Pimpernels. But he did not dare to make his escape that day; and while he told his romantic tale he was painfully contriving how he should manage to send word to Clare, and wondering if she would miss him! It would be a dreary business for himself, giving up the day to croquet and Pimpernels. Would Clare feel the disappointment too? Would the house be lonely to her without him? His heart gave a leap, and he felt for a moment as if he was certain it would be lonely. Curiously, this thought did not sadden but exhilarate his mind; and then he returned anxiously to the question— How could he, without exciting suspicion, have a note sent to Clare?

The ladies were so interested that they neglected the sound of the luncheon bell, and did not even perform that washing of hands which gives a man space to breathe. They did not budge, in short, until the butler came out, solemn in his black clothes, to intimate that their meal awaited them; and Arthur, in dismay, had nothing for it but to offer his arm to his hostess. It was a hot day, and the luncheon was hot too. How he loathed it!—and not a moment left him to write a word, explaining how it was, to Clare!

"Positively, Mr. Arden, you have been so interesting that one forgot how the time had gone," cried Mrs. Pimpernel. "It is an idle sort of thing amusing one's self in the morning; but when one has such a temptation—it was quite as good as any novel, I declare!"

"Oh, mamma! Mr. Arden said he was perhaps going to write a book," said Alice, who had grown bolder after this whole long morning which had been given up to herself.

"That would be very nice," said Mrs. Pimpernel, with affable patronage. "Mr. Pimpernel would take half-a-dozen copies at once, I am sure. How I envy talent, Mr. Arden. It is the only thing I covet. And to find all your materials in your own family—"

"Talking of that," said Arthur, "I must make a run up to the Rectory, after luncheon, to see Mr. Fielding. I have a—question to ask—"

At this he could see Mrs. Pimpernel's brow cloud over at once, and the look of suspicion and angry distrust come back to her face. Alice was better advised. She looked down on the table, and broke a piece of bread in little pieces, which answered nearly as well as a glove to button. "Oh, Mr. Arden," she said; "I thought this day you were going to stay with us. I thought we were really to have had a game at croquet to-day?"

"Oh, my dear! don't attempt to interfere with Mr. Arden's engagements," said Mrs. Pimpernel, with a forced laugh. "Gentlemen are always so much happier when they have their own way."

"And do ladies dislike their own way?" said Arthur; but he was in the toils, and could not escape. "I am looking forward to my game of croquet," he said; "and I have no engagements. I will do my business with Mr. Fielding while you are putting on your hat. It will not take me twenty minutes. He is a good old soul. He is as fond of the Ardens as if they were his own children; but not all the Ardens. I think he does, not approve of me."

"Oh, Mr. Arden!—nonsense!" cried Alice, decidedly. Her mother did not say anything, but a rapid calculation ran through her mind. If the Rector did not like Arthur he could not be going to meet Clare at the Rectory; and Mr. Fielding had been quite civil—really very civil to herself. She did not see any reason to fear him.

"If you are in a hurry for your croquet, Alice," she said, graciously, "the only thing is to send the carriage to take Mr. Arden there and back."

"Oh! that would be so nice!" cried Alice, with transport. But Arthur was of a very different frame of mind. "Confound the carriage," he said within himself; but his outward speech was more civil. He had not the least occasion for it. He would so much rather not give trouble. A walk would be good for him—he should like it. At last his earnestness prevailed; and it is impossible to describe his sense of relief when he walked out into the blazing afternoon, along the dusty, shadeless road that led to the village. He had got free from them for the moment; but he could not rush to Arden in the half-hour allotted to him. He could not secure for himself a peep at Clare. He did not even feel that he could trust the Rector to deliver his note for him; and where was he to write his note? And what would Clare think? Would she despise him for his subserviency to the Pimpernels? And why should he be subservient to them? Arthur knew very well why. He would have to abandon his researches altogether, and leave to chance the furtherance of his designs upon Clare, if he had to leave the Red House. "Everything is lawful in love and in war," he said to himself. It was both love and war he was carrying on. Love to the sister, war to the brother; and, with such a double pursuit, surely a little finesse was permissible to him, if to any man in the world.

But he did not reach the Rectory nor run the risk of Mr. Fielding's enmity that day. He had not gone half way up the village when he bethought himself of a much safer medium in the shape of old Sarah. Sarah's cottage was very quiet when he reached the door. Neither Mary, the clear-starcher, nor Ellen, the sempstress, were visible in it, and Sarah herself was not to be seen. He gave a glance in at the door into the little living room, which looked cool and green—all shaded with the big geranium. The place was quite silent, too; but in the corner near the stair sat a little figure, with bright hair braided, and head bent over its work. "Jeanie, by Jove!" said Arthur Arden; and he forgot Clare's note; he forgot Alice Pimpernel, who was waiting for him. He went in and sat down by her, in that safe and tempting solitude. "Are you all alone?" he said; "nobody to keep you company, and nothing but that stupid work to amuse you? I am better than that, don't you think, Jeanie? Come and talk a little to me."

"Sir!" said Jeanie, with a little start; and then she looked him steadily in the face. "I'm no feared for you now. I see you're no that man; but I cannot believe you when you speak. Eh, that's dreadful to say to one like you!"

"Very dreadful," said Arthur, laughing, and drawing closer to her. "So dreadful, Jeanie, that you must be very kind to me to make up for having said it. You don't believe me—not when I tell you are the loveliest little creature I ever saw, and I am very fond of you? You must believe that. I should like to take you away to a much prettier house than this, and give you all kinds of beautiful things."

Jeanie looked at him with steadfast eyes. Not a blush touched her face—not the slightest gleam of consciousness came into her quiet, steady gaze. "It's a dreadful thing to say of a man," she said; "a man should be a shelter from the storm and a covert from the tempest. It's in the Bible so; but you're no shelter to anybody, poor man. You're growing old, and yet ye never learn—"

"By Jove!" said Arthur, rising up. He had forgotten both Clare and Alice for the moment, and this little cottager was avenging them. But yet the reproof was so whimsical that it diverted him. "Do you know you are a very uncivil little girl," he said. "Are you not afraid to speak to me so, and you quite alone?"

"I'm no feared for you now," said Jeanie. "I was silly when I was feared. There is nothing you could do to me, even if ye wanted; and ye're no so ill a man as to want to harm me."

"Thank you for your good opinion," said Arthur; "but there are a great many things I could do. I could give you pretty dresses and a carriage, and everything you can think of; and if you were very sweet and kind to me—"

"Mr. Arden," said a voice over his shoulders, "if you have business with Jeanie, maybe it would be mair simple and straightforward if ye would settle it with me."

Arthur turned round with a mixture of rage and dismay, and found himself confronting Mr. Perfitt, who stood stern and serious in the doorway. He had need of all his readiness of mind to meet such an emergency. He paused a moment, feeling himself at bay; but he was not the man to lose his head even in so disagreeable a crisis.

"My business is not with Jeanie," he said, briskly. "My business is with old Sarah, who is not to be found; but you will do quite as well, Perfitt. I want to send a note to Miss Arden. If Jeanie will get me some paper? Do you understand me, little one? Could you give me some paper to write a little letter? Poor child; do you think she understands?"

Thus he got the better of both the protector and protected. Jeanie, who had been impervious to all else, blushed crimson at this doubt of her understanding; and so did Perfitt. "She's no like an innocent or a natural. She's been well brought up and well learned," the Scotchman said, with natural and national indignation. "Indeed! I thought she was an unmistakable innocent," said Arthur; and thus it came about that Clare's note was written after all.

CHAPTER XV

These days of mutual study had been very sweet to Clare. They had soothed her out of her agitation, without, however, stilling it altogether. She had acquired a new habit, and it was pleasant. While Arthur sat at the great table with the old MSS., which her father had partially arranged and prepared, she sat at the bureau, going over hosts of letters, which sometimes amused, sometimes interested her, but which were for the greater part quite unimportant—old bills and receipts and invitations, the broken fragments and relics of social life. If there had been any excitement in her mind to begin with—as it was natural there should be when she felt herself thus standing, as it were, on the edge of any secrets which her father might have had—it all died away on the first day. How innocent the life must have been of which only such harmless evidences remained! There were letters from some of his old friends—some with dead jokes in them, and dead pieces of news, embalmed and preserved, as if they were worth preserving. Clare took a pleasure in these, because it was to her father they were addressed; and she would look up now and then, and read a few words aloud to her fellow-student, who, on his side, had many things to communicate to her out of his MSS. Sometimes Arthur was obliged to get up and bring them to her that she might help him with a difficult sentence. Sometimes it was she who had to call him.

They were such near relations, their interest in the family was almost the same, and it was very natural that they should constantly refer to and consult each other. Sometimes a momentary compunction crossed Clare's mind when she thought of her brother. Would he like it? Would not he prefer to go over these papers himself, and be the first to discover his father's secrets—if there were any secrets? But he would not care for them, Clare thought to herself. He confessed openly that his interest in the Ardens was limited; whereas her own interest was without limits. If she felt sometimes a more lively compunction still at the thought that she was absolutely foiling all Edgar's precautions, and making his unwilling absence from home ridiculous by receiving thus, if not secretly, still without avowal, the visits of her cousin, her natural pride arose and put the whisper down. "Why should I give in to Edgar?" she asked herself. "It is my life, not his, that is concerned. It is my happiness that is concerned. I took care of myself before Edgar came; and why do I need his guardianship now?"

This view of the matter made it almost a duty to balk him. Had she foreseen that Arthur was going to remain in the neighbourhood, of course she would have told her brother; but she did not know. Nobody could be more surprised than she was to find him with the Pimpernels; and it was no pleasure to her, but quite the reverse, that he should be with the Pimpernels. Besides, it might justify and strengthen Edgar in his democratic ways if he heard that his cousin, so much more true an Arden than himself, was staying at the Red House. Accordingly, she wrote to her brother less frequently than usual, and said nothing about Arthur, which was not perhaps quite what Edgar might have expected from his sister. Probably, if he heard of it, he would manage in some insidious way to get her carried off to town, which Clare detested; or he would return himself, which, in present circumstances, Clare did not desire. So she let the days run on, finding a subtle sweetness in them. There was nothing said between her kinsman and herself which all the world might not have heard—except, perhaps, by times, a tone, an inflection of voice, an almost imperceptible inference. Arthur was skilful in such ways of making himself secretly understood; but he said nothing to agitate or alarm her. And thus they went on with their respective pursuits, side by side. What could be more sober, more grave, less like any sentiment or romance or nonsense? But Clare lived in those hours, which were thus sensibly and seriously spent. All the evening she remembered, all the morning she looked for them. She had not been into the village for a week; she had not seen the Rector except at church, nor any of her old friends. She took her evening ramble through the park all alone, and happy to be alone. "It is just as it used to be," she said to herself; but Clare knew very well that it was not as it used to be. Even now a dread of the arrival of some friendly visitor, bent upon taking care of her, would sometimes overcloud her mind. If they but knew how she detested being taken care of—if they but understood how happy she could be alone!

And thus it was with her on the morning of that day which Arthur spent playing croquet and telling stories to Alice Pimpernel. She had got safely over the post and her letters. There was not one from old Miss Arden at Escott, proposing a visit, such as, from day to day, she trembled to receive; neither did Clare's old governess, Mrs. Seldon, throw herself upon her pupil's hospitality; and though Edgar begged her again to reconsider her decision, and join him for at least a week or two "to see the pictures," there was no violence of urgency in his letter. She was safe for another day, and the sunny hours were drawing on, bringing the afternoon and its visitor. "I shall finish that first drawer to-day," Clare said to herself, with a half-conscious exaggeration of the importance of her work. She went into the library more than once to see that all was ready—that the shutters were closed to keep out the noonday sun, and the waste-paper basket cleared of all the fragments that had been thrown into it. "It is odd how pleasant such an occupation can grow," she said to herself; "I don't so much wonder at the passion for old papers that some people have." She liked to keep this thought well before her mind. Her new study was so curious and full of interest. Such a lesson, too, in life, the smallest details of which were so absorbing as long as it lasted, so sadly, amusingly insignificant now. "Some day or other some one will read my letters like that," she would add, with an incredulous smile. It was impossible, and yet no doubt it would come to pass; but would any one ever know how full and strong the blood was running in her veins—how vigorous life was, and warm and intense? Never before in her life had she so felt the power of the present—the moment that was hers, whatever might be taken from her. The clock was about to strike, and by this time no doubt he was coming up the avenue—her fellow-student—and the pleasantest work she had ever tried was about to begin.

Clare sat down to her tapestry to occupy the moment till he should arrive—he was very exact generally, punctual to his hour. It surprised her when the little French clock chimed a quarter-past. It was strange—it gave her a little chill in the midst of her expectation—but of course it could only be accidental. Another chime, and her heart began to beat—what if he should not be coming! Clare had known little of the vicissitudes to which such intercourse as this is specially subject. Except the few days of utter loneliness which she had passed after Edgar's departure, none of the heats and chills of wooing had ever been hers. She had been mistress of the situation. It had been in her power to send him away, to discourage him, and remind him that he was utterly at her mercy; but it had never occurred to her that such power is mutual, and that she, too, was at his mercy. As she waited and listened and heard nothing, her heart began to beat high and loud. Not only or even in the first place was it mere disappointment. A certain angry amazement and wild pride sprang up along with it. What, slight her! neglect to come when she expected him! It was an enormity which startled Clare, and shook her mind to its foundations. She could not understand nor believe it, and yet she could not believe either the suggestions of accident which she tried to make to herself. Could it be intentional neglect, discourtesy—and to her! Then there came another chime, and then the hour; he was a whole hour behind time. Clare bent her head over her tapestry as she heard a footstep approaching, and laboured as if she were labouring for her daily bread. A hot steady flush of angry excitement came to her cheek. She would not raise her head to see who it was. Had he broken his leg it might have been some excuse; but if it was he who was walking into the room, as she supposed, of course he had not broken his leg. The first thing she saw, however, was Wilkins' hand suddenly appearing before her, holding a silver tray with a letter upon it. She took it with a sense that some one had given her a blow. "Is this all?" she said mechanically. "Mr. Perfitt is waiting downstairs to see you, Miss Arden, if you will please to receive him," said Wilkins. Perfitt! what could he have to do with—"I hope nothing has happened," said Clare, holding, as if it were a serpent, the letter in her hand.

"I don't think so, Miss Arden; only he would like to speak a word to you if you are not too busy."

"I am much too busy," said Clare, in her anger. "I mean, let him come up in five minutes," she added, waving her hand to the alarmed servant. Then she tore open Arthur's note.

"My dear Cousin—A cursed chance (forgive the adjective, I can't help it) keeps me from Arden to-day. I have been fighting and struggling all the morning, but I cannot get off. Imagine how I hate the day and everything round me! To have to stay and be bored to death, instead of going on with the work most interesting to me in the world! Please postpone yours till to-morrow. I shall go crazy if I think you are at it without me.—In the deepest wretchedness and devotion, ever yours,

"A. A."

Clare read it twice over, and then put it from her. She stopped herself for the first moment from all expression even in her own mind. She took up her needle, and went on again furiously. Ye know, ye youths and maidens, how the air all darkened round her, how the day became odious! "Does he think it matters to me, I wonder?" she said at length aloud, and laughed; and then threw her work down, and covered her face, and burst into violent tears. They must have been lying very near the surface, they fell so hot and so suddenly, and were over so soon. When Mr. Perfitt was ushered in five minutes later, he found Miss Arden seated with her usual dignity, a little flushed, but showing no other traces of that sudden tumult. Mr. Perfitt himself was considerably disturbed; he crushed his hat in his hand, and seated himself, when she graciously invited him to be seated, on the very edge of his chair.

"Miss Arden," he said, "I've come to make a bit complaint—tho' indeed it's no a complaint; it's rather that you might maybe speak a warning word—You're young to meddle or trouble with such things; but you're no like other young ladies. You aye were the grand authority in old Mr. Arden's time; and so ye are with the present lad—I mean with the present Squire."

"Would you please tell me what it is? I am very busy," said Clare. "Has anything happened, Mr. Perfitt? Of course I am the only person to refer to in my brother's absence, whatever it may be."

"It's no just that anything has happened," said Perfitt, crushing his hat, and then anxiously examining its wounds. "It's a thing I would ask nobody about, but soon settle, if it was not a gentleman connected with the house. You see it's me that brought Mr. Arthur Arden's note; but I got it like by chance, turning in as I was passing to see little Jeanie Murray. You'll see what I'm meaning now. He's a gentleman that has always behaved gentlemanly to me; but a bit lassie, Miss Arden, and no just right in her mind—no mad, I'm no meaning that—but scarce wise enough to understand it's a a' nonsense that such a gentleman says."

"Is Mr. Arthur Arden with Jeanie now?" said Clare, in her most distinct chill tones. She had been frozen suddenly where she sat—frozen to her very heart; but the shock had brought her back to perfect possession of herself.

"Na, na! trust me for that," said Perfitt, with a laugh. "Before I left the house I saw my lord off the premises—ye may trust me for that. And there's nae harm done, Miss Arden. I do not for a moment suppose there's any harm. But Mr. Arthur was aye a thought wild, saving your presence—"

"I will take care," said Clare, steadily, "that it does not occur again." Her voice was frozen too. In the shadowy warmth of the room, in the heat of the summer afternoon, it went like a touch of ice through Perfitt's bones. How will she manage that, I would like to know? he said to himself, but was so chilled that he only gasped audibly, and had no other answer to make.

"I will take care it does not occur again," said Clare. "You were quite right to tell me. If there is anything else you want to say, pray go on."

"Nothing else—nothing else, Miss Arden," said Perfitt, stumbling to his feet; and then he stood awkwardly clasping his hat for a minute more. "And I have no fear on my mind that any harm's been done," he added. "There's no harm done, Miss Arden. I wouldna give you a wrong idea. But only Mr. Arthur—"

"I have told you," repeated Clare, still more and more coldly, "that it shall not occur again."

Perfitt went away from Arden, as, indeed, he had gone to the house, in a very perplexed and uncomfortable state of mind. "I have great doubts in my mind if I should have spoken," he said to himself as he went away; and then all at once there flashed upon him a report he had once heard which connected Arthur Arden's name with that of Clare. When he recalled this, he slapped himself upon the thigh with supreme self-contempt. "My man, you've gone and put your foot in it now," he thought; "could you no have taken care of your ain flesh and blood yourself, without bothering that poor lassie? Dash ye! and dash him, the ne'er-do-weel!" This was how Mr. Perfitt contemplated his own conduct as he went away; but it was a very different kind of self-discussion that he left behind.

Clare was absolutely stunned by the blow which had just fallen upon her. Had she taken time to think, no doubt she would have seen that she was unjust—but she did not take any time to think. It was the first great slight she had ever received in her life—a slight greater than any other kind of disrespect that could be shown to a woman. A man who had been devoting himself to her, who had caught at every opportunity for showing his devotion since the moment he reappeared at Arden—that he should venture to go and excuse himself to her on the ground of inevitable engagements, and then be discovered hanging about a village girl, recommending himself so potently that her friends interfered! Oh, how glad she was, how grateful to Perfitt for bringing that complaint to her! She might never have known; she might have believed that he was worthy, and that he loved her, but for that revelation. She was grateful to Perfitt, and yet how she hated him! But for him she might still have been partially happy. She would have received the excuse, and to-morrow all might have been well; that was to say, she would have allowed herself to be deceived, which, of all fates, was surely the meanest and most humiliating. And then to think how much good she had intended to her cousin! In this moment of bitter humiliation Clare ceased to trifle with herself. She tore off the veil which she had wrapt so willingly over her eyes, and admitted to herself that she had meant to bestow everything upon her kinsman. She had even gone the length of being quite content to despoil her brother for his sake. She had made up her mind that Old Arden should be his, and that if she could not make him the head of the family she would at least secure to him its oldest possessions. All this she admitted to herself in the tumult of rage and shame which filled her mind. She was ready to do all this, and he—He could not sacrifice to her a passing fancy for the pretty face of a girl; for there could be nothing more than that in it. And where was the mother who should have taken charge of the girl? Clare tried hard to persuade herself that it was Jeanie's fault, or that the grandmother had some artful design upon Arthur. She tried very hard to believe that she believed this, but it was a difficult attempt. The thought came back to her with renewed bitterness that it was he—he only—who was in fault, he to whom she would have given everything! Then her mind took a sudden leap, as the mind will sometimes do at its own will and pleasure, and pictured for her what might have happened had she actually done what she had been willing to do. The future, which had been so likely an hour ago, which was so impossible now, opened up upon her with a great flash and glow. She saw herself his wife, dependent upon him for all her happiness, pledged to him for ever and ever; his honour hers, his credit hers; the burden of any scandal, of any shame that might come upon him, to be borne by her equally; and it seemed to her as if she were gazing into a mirror, in which she saw herself seated alone and neglected in the house which she had bestowed upon him, while he himself roamed about the world, finding at every turn some facile love—some Jeanie, she said to herself—and yet was so just that she paused and blushed, knowing she did an innocent creature wrong.

This extraordinary revulsion of feeling shook Clare to the very depths of her being. She had been floating so smoothly down the stream that she was not aware how very fast she had been going; and now this sudden and terrible obstacle seized her and maddened her, and enveloped her in a whirlwind of wild thoughts, as a sudden Niagara might seize and rend a pleasure-boat. She had been prepared for some dangers. He might have got "involved," as people say, with Alice Pimpernel, and been compelled by honour to marry her for her money's sake. Such a catastrophe, Clare thought, she could have borne. And he might have been a treacherous enemy to her brother; for that she had been afraid, and had prepared herself. But for this she was unprepared. False to her, false to his own interests, wooing ruin instead of prosperity, giving up his reputation and his life, as well as slighting the true love she had waiting for him. Oh, how miserable, how mean, how wretched it was! Was it possible that he could hold life so cheap as to spend it thus? And he not a boy—no longer a boy who might be tempted and led astray. She made an effort to calm the wild misery in her own breast, by forgetting herself, and making believe that pity for him was the only sentiment that moved her. He was a fool, he was mad, she said to herself; and then the something that burned within her, the terrible pain that gnawed and gnawed at her heart, came uppermost. It was the first slight she had ever received—and such a slight! The Princess had found that a beggar might be preferred to her. The proud, upright, spotless Clare had discovered an attempt to deceive her. The thought made her writhe, as any poor living creature might writhe against the spear that pinned it to the earth. Oh, if she could but escape it, forget, throw Arthur Arden out of her thoughts! But that was impossible. She had to bear it, and get the better of it if she could.

And underneath there existed a still deeper feeling, at which Clare almost trembled. She would be avenged on him one way or other. She would punish him for his inconstancy and, for what was worse, his deception. This incident should not, could not, must not pass over as if it had happened to any common milk-and-water girl. The intensity of her passion dismayed even herself. She would bear it, so that no man should ever have it in his power to say he had broken Clare Arden's heart; and she would not bear it, so that no man should dare believe it was possible to slight her or treat her as a nobody. She took up his letter, crushing it as if it were a real enemy, and her eye caught the entreaty that she would postpone her work, as he was obliged to postpone his. It was a satisfaction to her to be able to contradict him practically and at once. She tore his letter up into little pieces, and then she went with a rapid step to the library. To do instantly and energetically what he had begged her not to do, was in its way a consolation to Clare.

She had but just entered the library when a timid knock came to the door. It was repeated again, even after she had said languidly, "Come in—" "Come in," she repeated, with that impatient irritability which is natural to a disturbed and excited mind. Then, after a little pause, the head of Mrs. Fillpot, the housekeeper, appeared timidly at the half-opened door. "May I speak a word with you, Miss Clare?" said Mrs. Fillpot in a tone of fright. "Come in!" repeated Clare, this time imperiously. The housekeeper at Arden was an old servant. She had been supreme in the house ever since Clare was born. And though Miss Arden's decided character had quietly shorn her of all transferable authority, yet Clare herself had sufficient sense of the woman's value to be respectful of Mrs. Fillpot's opinions. The housekeeper had not given in without a struggle, and she had a great awe of Clare: but at the same time she was conscientious, and had an opinion of her own; so that there was now and then a little skirmishing between the two, always ending in a victory for Clare, but yet never without a certain effect upon her. Mrs. Fillpot came in with the air of a woman who had made up her mind to something desperate. She gave a frightened glance round the room, and then approached her young mistress. "I beg your pardon, Miss Clare," she said, "for disturbing you; but I thought Mr. Arthur Arden was here—"

"Mr. Arthur Arden is not here, you perceive," said Clare, feeling as if his name choked her; "and I should be very glad to know what you want at once, for I am busy. It can wait till to-morrow if it is anything about the house."

"It is nothing about the house," said Mrs. Fillpot, breathing hard with alarm and excitement; and then she made another pause, which drove Clare wild with impatience.

"For heaven's sake say what it is," she cried, "and leave me; don't you see I have something to do?"

"Miss Clare," said Mrs. Fillpot, solemnly, "I've been about you since you were a baby. When your poor dear mamma died, though it was Sarah as took you from the month, I had all the responsibility. When you was a little girl with governesses and that sort, it was always me as was referred to—"

"Please to tell me what all this is about," said Clare, coldly. "You see I am engaged; I have a great many things to think of. I don't want to go over all my childish days now—"

"Miss Clare, it's not my wish to make myself disagreeable—it never was," said Mrs. Fillpot, growing breathless, "but when I see things going on as are not what they should be, and gentlemen's visits which it's not nice for a young lady to be known as one that would put up with them, and going on day after day, and the Squire not here, nor no lady companion, nor even a servant a-setting in the room—"

"What do you mean?" said Clare sharply, stopping her in the midst of this harangue.

"I mean just what I am saying, Miss," said Mrs. Fillpot, in her excitement; "it's not nice for no young lady—it's a thing as no young lady should do, Miss. I've held my tongue as long as I could, and I won't no longer. I'll write to Master, Miss—I'll speak to Mr. Arthur—I must do something. Not so much as a maid a-setting in the room and ne'er a lady in the house—and him coming and coming. I will say of Mr. Arthur as I thought he had more sense."

Clare had chilled and hardened into stone as she was thus addressed. A deep blush had covered her face at first, but that had faded, leaving her more pale than usual; and her blue eyes shot glances that were like arrows of ice into the good woman's heart. Those blue eyes, which were sometimes so sweet, how cold, how blighting, how withering they could be! She pointed her hand to the door before she could speak. She made a spasmodic effort to retain her composure and dignity. "Do precisely what you please," she said, "but do not let me see you again."

"Miss Clare!" said the woman. "Oh, Miss Clare, it's your good I am thinking of. What could I want but your good?—me that has nursed you, and loved you, and took an interest—"

"Go away, please," said Clare, with a choked voice. "Go away; I don't wish to see you again."

"Oh, Miss Clare!—"

"Go. Don't you see I am—occupied? Can't you see? Good heavens! are you a woman, and have no more sense than to stand and drive me frantic there?"

"But Miss Clare—"

"I have no more to say to you. Go, please," said Clare, falling back into her seat. She leaned her head against the old bureau, which had been her father's. He had sat there a thousand times bending over it as she was doing now. Would he have been any aid to her in this terrible emergency! Shame, too, as well as everything else! She had been no better than Jeanie—less maidenly than Alice Pimpernel. She had cared too much for him to remember the maidenly decorums in which she had been brought up. She had laid herself open to the comments of this woman, and probably of every servant in the house. No doubt they had found her out, and laughed to see how she, too, indulged herself when her own feelings were touched, indifferent to all proprieties—she who had made so many indignant remonstrances on that very subject, and so often bidden the village girls to have a due respect for themselves. She sat with her face turned away, pretending to search among the drawers of the bureau, while Mrs. Fillpot stood explaining and protesting behind. Clare did not even know when the housekeeper retired, weeping and wondering. She sat absorbed in her own misery, drawing to herself such pictures of her own conduct as the most guilty could scarcely have exceeded. She did not know how long she sat opening and shutting mechanically the drawers of the bureau, idly examining, without seeing what she was doing, its inner corners. Half in abstraction, half in determination to prove to herself that she was pursuing the researches which Arthur had begged her not to pursue, she had opened a little door which was locked, and which shut in a nest of smaller drawers which had not as yet been examined. It was these she was now playing with unconsciously, not thinking or seeing what she did. One of them, however, was very stiff, and the little material obstacle roused her up almost against her will. She pulled at it in her confusion of mind, growing angry over the difficulty. Was everything to resist her, even such a thing as this? Then she perceived there was a bundle of papers within which kept it from opening. Clare woke up, and took pains when she felt herself, as it were, held at bay. She took a great deal of trouble over it, and at last succeeded in opening the drawer. That was all she wanted—her interest failed as soon as the bundle fell out. It was a packet of letters enclosed in a piece of paper sealed at the ends and endorsed. She had found twenty such already, all of the most ordinary description—"Poor Howard's letters," "Applications for leases," "Papers about the woods." This was the sort of endorsing she had generally found. The new packet, doubtless, was no more important than the others. She took it into her hand and threw it down again into the open pigeon-hole which was nearest to her. And then only for the first time she perceived that it was growing dark, and that the day was almost over. The shutters had never been opened which she had closed in the morning to keep out the sun. To keep out the sun! would the sunshine ever come in again? She locked up the bureau slowly, and went wandering out, not knowing where she went. Sunshine and light had departed from Arden. Was it for evermore?

CHAPTER XVII

Clare's condemnation of her cousin was, of course, unjust. He had not done anything to deserve so harsh a judgment. At least, what he had really done to deserve it was unknown to her. He had not attempted to deceive her in that special point. His note was true to the letter: the fault he had committed was but of two minutes' duration, and was simply the result of a sudden temptation, which probably he would have avoided had he been at all prepared for it—avoided, be it understood, not out of any distaste for the pleasant folly, but for prudential motives. But he had not been prepared for it; and he had seen a pretty, defenceless creature in his way, poor enough and of sufficiently small consideration to have violent pseudo-love made to her, and an attempt at least at familiarity; and he had not been able to resist the opportunity. Arthur Arden would not have ventured to address Jeanie so had she been even Perfitt's daughter. He was not cowardly in the ordinary sense of the word; but there was so much of the craven in him, as in most men moved by similar impulses, that his passions were only irrestrainable when the object of them could be safely assailed. Even with all this, and allowing that could he have done it he would have tried his best to make a victim of Jeanie, still there had not been time enough, nor opportunity enough, to raise any such purpose seriously in his mind. When he spoke to her, he only half meant, or perhaps did not mean at all, what he said. It was mere levity and spontaneous, instinctive, not intentional, wickedness. How far this would have mended matters with a really just critic I will not pretend to ask; but it would have mended matters with Clare. She, however, had formed a very different opinion of the whole transaction. It was most serious, and full of elaborate plan and purpose in her eyes—the basest purpose of which man could be guilty, and the most mortifying to herself. She made the fact which Perfitt had disclosed to her into a whole drama of evil intention. She did not know in what self-denial her kinsman had spent the morning, in what self-sacrifice he was about to spend the afternoon. She did not know how much he was suffering in order chiefly to prolong his stay in her neighbourhood. It is true that his other sins richly deserved the condemnation she had pronounced. He was employing her as a shield, while he attempted to do the greatest possible injury to her brother. He was plotting secretly under her protection and in her very shadow against the honour and good fame of the family, and even against herself personally; for her own fortune was involved in Edgar's, so far, at least, as Old Arden was concerned. For all this she could have better pardoned him than for the supposed deception he had just practised upon her. Thus his doom was just, but it was not given on just grounds.

But it happens often enough, as many women could testify, that the doom pronounced by virtue upon vice, by the true upon the false, bears very often much more heavily upon the judge than upon the condemned. The culprit bears up under the blow, while she who sits on the throne of Justice is shaken to pieces by the reverberation. Clare, who felt herself both judge and executioner in one, and whose mind was full of wild plans of vengeance, was herself at the same time the immediate victim. Drearily, more dreary than ever before, the day closed upon her, leaving her all alone in the solitude of those stately rooms, dimly lighted and all so silent. Night was coming—night which, if it brought forgetfulness, would be her best comforter; but it seemed utterly impossible that it could bring forgetfulness, or that sleep should ever come again to her burning, weary, yet wakeful eyelids. She could not read, she could not work; she could think but of one subject, and that was not one which she could exercise any free will about, discussing it reasonably with herself; but one which pursued her, forcing itself into supremacy, driving her thoughts wildly into one channel, whether she would or not. She sat by the table, with her head supported in her two hands, and gazed into the white flame of the lamp till her eyes were almost scorched, while a thousand wild fancies pursued each other through her mind. The moths circled about and about the light, and so did her thoughts about the fatal centre which they had formed for themselves; until the flimsy suicides wove themselves in with her imaginations, and became somehow a part of her and them. She had not energy enough left to save them. "There is another," she would say to herself; "are they all mad, I wonder? Can't they feel that it kills them? I wonder where he is now. Oh, I hope he is beginning to feel what a false step he has taken! There is many a woman that will put up with being deceived, but not me—never me. To think he should have known me so little, and he an Arden! I wonder what Edgar will say when he knows: he shall never know. I hate him, but I will never, never betray to any one—And yet I promised I would interfere. I said it should never occur again. There is another, and another. I wonder why they like it so much. It can't be for the warmth, for it is warm everywhere to-night. I said it should never occur again—I was a fool to take any part; what have I to do with—with—that girl? She is not even a village girl, to have a claim upon me. If she likes to be ruined and shamed, that is not my affair. Perhaps she thinks he—loves her, forsooth! Oh, what fools, what fools people are—people and moths! The lamp is choked up with them; what strange, strange, silly creatures! I can't stop them; and how can I stop her? And why should I!—it is her business, it is not mine. If she had been a girl in the village—But then I said it should not occur again."

Thus Clare mused: and as the slow moments went on, her musing grew into a kind of rhythm of broken fancies, all bound together by the continued burden—"I said it should not occur again." It was like a song which she thus murmured to herself, or rather which murmured in her ears without any will of hers, rising and falling, with its refrain—"I said it should not occur again." At length the refrain gained upon the rest, and repeated and repeated itself till her brain grew dizzy. At all events she had to keep her word—and what should she do? Should she interpose authoritatively, as was her right as the natural protectress of every girl in Arden? Should she write to him herself, and warn him that his evil designs were known, and she, the champion and shield of her maidens, in arms against him? Should she act imperiously and with a high hand, by sending Jeanie and her grandmother out of her territory? She was so used to think as well as act en princesse that neither of those plans seemed quite impracticable to Clare. They were, on the contrary, quite natural, things which had she been less concerned she would not have hesitated to do. But, alas, she was intimately concerned, and her arm seemed paralysed. She gave forth the sentence without hesitation, but as for the manner of executing it, she seemed only capable of thrusting the sword into herself.

Then a sudden thought struck her. As it came to her all at once, so she executed it all at once, with the impatient and irritable haste of suffering. Half the mad things that people do when they are in trouble are done in this way. Their brain grows dizzy over deep-laid plans and long-nursed impossible conceptions, and then a sudden suggestion comes across them and they obey it on the moment. She started up and brought her blotting-book from the writing-desk where it was, to the ring of light round the lamp. And she wrote the following note hastily, without even pausing to draw breath:—

"DEAR MR. FIELDING,—I have just heard, to my great pain, that your little friend Jeanie has been annoyed by my cousin Arthur Arden. There are difficulties in the way of my direct interference which I need not explain. One ought to be above all secondary motives, but unfortunately one is not. I do not know who is most to blame, if she has been trying to attract him, thinking, perhaps, he was less experienced in such matters than he is, or if it is entirely his fault. He is staying at the Red House with the Pimpernels, which of itself, of course, is a reason why I do not desire to have more intercourse with him than I can help; and, of course, this affair is a double reason. I do not advise you to communicate with him, for gentlemen, I believe, do not like to be called to account for their actions; but I think you should do something at once in respect to the girl. You might put her on her guard, that he is not at all the sort of man to be made a victim of, or taken in in any way. He must either be simply amusing himself, or his object cannot be a good one. I speak freely, because you know I have always felt that in my position false delicacy would be a crime. I have always considered myself responsible for the girls in the village, and my motive is, I think, quite enough to justify me. I think if I were in your place—not being able to act in my own—that I should have the girl removed at once from Arden. There seems no reason why she and her grandmother should have chosen this place to live in. And there is nothing particular that ever I heard of in Arden air. Any other fresh country air would, no doubt, do quite as well.

"I should be glad if you would let me know what you do, and as soon as possible. Edgar being away makes one feel it all the more.

"Yours affectionately, "CLARE ARDEN."

Poor Clare! she wrote this at a stretch, scarcely lifting her head from the paper, with a philosophy which surprised herself, and which was not in the least philosophy, but only the very highest strain of excitement. But she could not help hanging up that one little flag of distress at the end—"Edgar being away makes one feel it all the more." She had not said a word about feeling it till then; but now her head fell upon her clasped hands, and she wept a few very bitter, very scalding tears, hiding them even from herself, so to speak, in the handkerchief which she crushed against her hot, scorched eyes. And then she rose up and put her note in an envelope, and sent it off—for it was only about nine o'clock still, though it felt to Clare as if it must have been the middle of the night.

Immediately after she went upstairs, and went to bed, to the great amazement of her maid, for Clare did not usually keep early hours. She wanted the darkness, the stillness, the quiet, she said to herself; but the fact was, she wanted a change—anything that would be different from what she had been before doing. She could not sleep, of course; and when she had borne that as long as it was possible to bear it, she got up and partially dressed herself, and went down in her dressing-gown to the library, to see if some novelty or distraction could be found there. By this time the whole house was asleep—dark, motionless, and silent, like a house of the dead. Her candle was ghostly beyond description in the great, dim library. It even occurred to Clare's mind, as a kind of hope, that she might see something unearthly, and thus be driven legitimately mad, and a reason given to herself and others for the change in her, which no doubt others would see. But nothing unearthly was to be seen—nothing but a vast expanse of darkness—her father's chair standing by the table—the walls clothed with books, glimmering faintly in the corner nearest the light, from out the tarnished brass of the lattice-work which enclosed them. Nothing to see, nothing to hear, nothing but herself—the one thing of which no change could rid her. Clare sat down at the bureau in her misery, and opened it with the key which she had left in it. The little inner door which she had unlocked in the morning, and which now it suddenly occurred to her she had never seen unlocked before, swung in her face as she opened the outer enclosure. In mere sickness of heart she thrust her hand into the corner where that afternoon she had thrown the bundle of letters which had prevented one of the drawers from opening. Indifferently she had thrown it down; indifferently she took it up. One end of it was singed and brown, as if it had been thrown into the fire, and the outside corner was slightly torn, with a black mark on it of something by which it had evidently been fished out again. Somebody's letters which her father had almost made up his mind to burn, and then had repented. This did her a little good. A languid interest—too languid almost to be called interest—came into her mind—a faint wonder breathed across her why he who burned nothing should have thought of burning that. She turned it over indifferently to read the endorsing. And even after she had read it, it was some time before the words produced any effect upon Clare's mind. "Papers concerning the boy." Papers concerning the boy! "Who is the boy? What does it mean? she said to herself. Then she came, as it were, to life, as she gazed at it. Through the broken envelope two or three words caught her eye. She raised herself quite upright, seized it tremulously, and put her hand upon the seals. But even while she did so her mind changed. Instead of breaking open the packet, she snatched up another piece of paper, and hastily re-covered it, then taking her handkerchief, which was the first thing she could find, tied it round the parcel. Then she sat for half the night stupefied, with a new subject for her thoughts.

CHAPTER XVIII

Clare's proceedings next day were the cause of absolute consternation to everybody concerned. In the morning she was very restless, roaming about from floor to floor—from the library to the dining room, and then to her bed-chamber, carrying with her something tied up in her handkerchief. "Can I carry it for you, Miss Arden?" her maid had asked, meeting her suddenly on the stair. "Carry it! what?" Clare had answered, sharply, dropping her hand, with the little bundle in it, among the folds of her dress. Had it been perceived how often she changed the place in which she had this parcel locked up the wonder of the household would have been still further roused. She had sat up half the night at least doing nothing, staring into the candle; and when finally she went up stairs, she had carried her mysterious bundle with her, placing it under her pillow. When she came down, weary and pale, in the morning, she had carried it to the library, and locked it into the bureau. Then, prompted by some sudden change of mind, she had transferred it from the bureau to a drawer in the writing table in the morning room, where she chiefly sat; then she carried it off to her wardrobe; and, finally, about noon, restored it to its original place in the bureau. She put it back into its own original drawer, which would scarcely contain it—locked the inner door, and hung the key round her neck on a ribbon; and then locking the outer part of the bureau, shut up the key of that in her desk. She was very pale, and yet now and then would grow hot and flushed without any reason. She employed herself all the morning in feverish movement from one place to another. At twelve she called her maid Barbara and told her to make ready to go out. "I am going up to the Three Beeches," she said; "take something with you to eat, for it may be late before we get home again." "Shall I take any luncheon for you, Miss Arden?" said the girl, "and shall I order the carriage?" "I don't want anything to eat, and I prefer to walk," Clare said abruptly; and, accordingly, at twelve o'clock of a blazing summer morning, she set out for a three miles' walk, attended by her unwilling maid with a parcel of books. "If any one calls you can say I have gone out for the day," she said to Wilkins, who was no less amazed. She had not gone a hundred yards from the house when Barbara interrupted her progress. "Please, Miss Arden, I see the Rector coming up the avenue." "Never mind," said Clare, with an impatient gesture, and hurried on.

The Rector had come up in a state of great trouble and excitement—first, to remonstrate with Clare for her injurious suspicions in regard to poor little Jeanie; secondly, to warn herself against Arthur Arden; and, thirdly, to ask her advice what he should say to Mrs. Murray on the subject, which was a part of the business which frightened him much. He was not an early man at any time, and Clare's note had much discomposed him, and the parish business had taken him up for at least an hour. When he was turned back from the door of Arden his astonishment knew no bounds. "Gone out!" he said, "gone out for the day! What is the meaning of that, Wilkins? Has she gone to pay a visit! But I did not meet her in the avenue, and she has not passed through the village this morning, so far as I could hear."

"No, sir; she has not gone upon a visit," said Wilkins; "she's about somewhere in the park, I do believe. Not as I knows that o' my own knowledge," he added, hurriedly. "Miss Clare may have gone—bless you, she might have gone anywhere—to Lady Augusta's, maybe, only they're all away, or to Miss Somers's, or to the village. Miss Clare is the independentest young lady, as you know—"

"Yes, yes, she may be independent, but she does not rush out like this without any reason. Has she had any letters about Business—anything to call her abroad—"

"I don't know, sir, no more than Adam," said Wilkins, shaking his head; and then he sank into mystery. "If you'll step in for a moment, sir, I'll call Mrs. Fillpot. I think she'd like to say a word; and she has a kind of a notion she knows why."

Mr. Fielding went into the hall, shaking his head, and then he passed into Clare's morning room, where everything was painfully tidy, and there was no appearance of any occupation about. The Rector shook his head still as he peered into the corners with his short-sighted eyes. "She has taken it to heart; she has taken it to heart!" he said to himself, and shook his head more and more.

Then Mrs. Fillpot came in, with a white apron, the corner of which she held in one hand, ready for instant action. Wilkins lingered near the door, with the view of being one of the party, but the Rector promptly closed it upon him. "You have something to tell me from Miss Clare?" he said; for to be sure he was jealous of being thought to come and ask questions of the servants at the Hall.

"Nothing from Miss Clare, sir; worse luck," said Mrs. Fillpot; "but I come to tell you what's to do with her this morning. Mr. Arthur, sir, has been a-coming day after day. He's been here, has Mr. Arthur, since last Monday, every afternoon of his life; and Miss Clare and he a-sitting in the library, as none of us likes to go in no more nor we can help, a-working with their papers. It's hurt me to see it, Mr. Fielding, like as if she had been my own child. A young lady and no mother, and the Squire away as should take care of his sister. So I up and told her yesterday. It took a deal of screwing up to give me the courage; but bless you, sir, if a woman hasn't that courage for one as she's brought up—So I up and told her. I said—'It ain't right, Miss, and it ain't nice, nor what your poor dear mamma, if she'd have lived, would have approved.' I said it plain out as I'm saying it to you, though I was all of a tremble. Bless you, thinking of it, I'm all of a tremble now."

"And what did she say?" asked Mr. Fielding.

"She didn't say much, sir. Miss Clare was never one to say much. She waved me to go, and I went, without even a 'Thank you, Mrs. Fillpot,' or 'I know you means well,' nor nothing. But when Barbara came to me this morning asking for a bit of lunch, and saying as her young lady was a-going out to spend the day, bless you, I saw it all in a moment. She didn't say nothing, but she's acted upon it, has Miss Clare."

"And did nothing else happen besides what you tell me?" said Mr. Fielding, still shaking his head.

"Nothing as I can think on. Well, Mr. Arthur he didn't come yesterday, and Mr. Perfitt he brought a bit of a letter, and he went in and saw her for five minutes or so, did Perfitt; but that's all."

"Oh, Perfitt saw her, did he?" said the Rector.

"Yes, sir. But I don't see what difference that could make," said Mrs. Fillpot, jealous of her power.

"No, no, I don't suppose so," said Mr. Fielding; but in his mind he allowed that it might make a great deal of difference, and went away very thoughtfully, shaking his head. "She has taken it to heart, poor child; she has taken it to heart," he said to himself as he went home, shaking his head with that mingled pity and sense of superiority which an affectionate bystander feels in such a case. Better that she should suffer a little now than afterwards, when it would be too late, was Mr. Fielding's thought, and in his aged mind this "suffer a little" was all that was comprehensible of Clare's passion and agony. She would get over it after a while, of course, and no particular harm would be done. Such was his conception of the state of affairs.

There was, however, another visitor to Arden, whose consternation was still greater. Arthur came at his usual hour in the afternoon, with all his energies refreshed by his temporary absence, and with a determination in his mind to know his fate at once, so far as Clare was concerned. He loved her, he said to himself. It was true that he was quite capable of being momentarily drawn aside from his allegiance, and that his recent pursuit of her had been complicated by other motives. But yet he loved her. If Edgar were unmasked to-morrow, and himself in Edgar's place, it would still be his cousin Clare whom he would prefer to all others to sit upon his throne with him. And why should he delay speaking to her on the subject? If things remained as they were—which was probable—then she would share what she had with him; and if he could make any discovery and better his own position, why then of course he would share everything with her.

"If you are not the heiress born,
And I, he said, the lawful heir,
We two will wed to-morrow morn,
And you shall still be Lady Clare."

This rhyme ran in his head as he went up the avenue, with many a softer thought. He had made himself very agreeable to Alice Pimpernel the day before—so much so as to leave little doubt on her mother's mind as to what would follow "if anything came of that Arden business;" and he had shown an inclination to make himself more than agreeable to Jeanie. But neither of them so much as touched his determination, if it were possible, to wed Clare Arden, whatever might happen. Accordingly, he went with his mind made up to see her, and open his heart. And there was so much natural feeling in the matter that he was more excited by it than he had been for years. Really it was something which he could with justice call his happiness which was involved. It would make the most material difference to him if she refused him. He felt that he might return to the Red House an altered man—either happy and serene, or discouraged beyond all conception. He feared a little, because he was in earnest; but he hoped a great deal more than he feared. These days of uninterrupted intercourse had been much in his favour, he felt. He had done everything he could to gain his cousin's confidence; he had refrained from love-making in any of its distincter fashions. He had shown himself anxious for her approval, conscious of the improprieties of his past life. In short, he knew he had made progress; and now with a thrill of excitement he came to seek his fate.

"Out!" he said blankly, stricken dumb with amazement, and gazing at Wilkins as if he had been a prodigy; and then he recovered himself. "Ah! out in the garden, I suppose," he added. "Be so good as to let Miss Arden know that I am here, and ask if I may join her."

"She is not in the garden," said Wilkins, with a solemn enjoyment of the other's disappointment. Arthur Arden was not liked by the servants; and Wilkins lingered over every word by way of tantalising him more. "Miss Arden has gone out, sir, for the day. For the day—them were her very words. 'Wilkins,' she says, 'if any one calls, I have gone out for the day.' Nothing, sir, could be more exact than Miss Arden was."

Arthur was so completely taken aback that he stood aghast for a moment gazing at the man who confronted him with the ghost of a smile on his face, blocking up the door. Wilkins stood like one who felt his own supremacy, in an easy attitude upon the threshold, forbidding all comers as effectually as if he had been a squadron of cavalry. "Them were the very words," he said, rubbing his hands; and Arthur stood below, expelled as it were from Paradise. The catastrophe was so sudden and so unlooked for that he did not in the least know how to meet it. He could not even for the moment hide his own discomfiture and dismay.

"I suppose Miss Arden intends me to go on with my work and await her coming," he said at length. "I am very sorry to miss her, but I suppose that is what I must do."

"She didn't say nothing about it, sir," said Wilkins; "and what is more, she's been and locked the library door."

Then Arthur perceived that things were really going against him. He would not betray himself to the servant's all-penetrating eyes. "Ah, I suppose something must have happened," he said, with as light a tone as he could summon up. "Tell Miss Arden I was very sorry to find her gone. I suppose she has changed her mind about the papers. Tell her if she wishes me to go on with them that she must send me word to the Red House. I shall be there for some days longer. I shall pay my respects to her whether I hear from her or not before I leave; but if I am to do any more work ask her to let me know."

"I'll give her your message, sir," said Wilkins, with ill-concealed satisfaction; and then, before he was conscious what it meant, before he could half realise the position, Arthur found himself with his back to the house, making his way once more down the avenue. Could it be possible? Was he dreaming? He was so completely taken by surprise that he had lost all his readiness of reason and promptitude in an emergency. Nothing so overwhelming, so sudden, so mysterious, had ever happened to him before. It was not only a disappointment, it was an insult. Dismissed by a servant; turned away from the door which, it might be, was legally his; sent off without a word of explanation! Arthur paused when he had gone half-way down the avenue to say to himself that he must be dreaming, that he must go back and laugh at the hoax that had been played upon him, and find Clare, in the full satisfaction of a successful trick, laughing too. But then there came in the chill thought that Clare was not at all the sort of person to perform a trick of any kind, and that what she did was generally in deadly earnest, relieved by no practical jokes. His amazement was so profound that he scarcely said a word to himself all the way down. Had she found out anything? Was there anything to find out? His meaning in that raid upon the papers was known to no one but himself. Nobody could say a word against his motives; nobody could be offended with him because he had a zeal for his family. To write a book about them even was a perfectly justifiable, not to say laudable, idea. What could she have had to find fault with? Arthur was as much surprised as dismayed. He went home feeling as if he had been beaten corporeally as well as mentally—feeling more absolutely small, and mean, and contemptible than he had ever done in his life—humiliated before Wilkins, even—made the laughing-stock of the servants. This was the manner in which he was sent away from Arden on the day which he had selected to decide his fate.

CHAPTER XIX

It is comparatively easy to make a sudden and rapid decision which is (one says to one's self) final, and settles in a moment some great question which affects a whole existence. As soon as the uncertainty is over, and the decision absolutely made, everything will come easy, the sufferer thinks. And such had been Clare's feeling when she set out upon that wretched ramble, with Barbara toiling after her. She would cut herself off at once, and for ever, from all possibility of being remonstrated with, talked over, moved by any argument. She would cut the knot by one arbitrary action, and free herself. And when that was once successfully done she could live without sympathy, without any desire to cast herself upon the aid of others; she would be self-sufficing, self-contained, self-restraining all the rest of her life. Had not she already tried every relationship, and found it wanting? He who had made himself most dear to her—he who had pretended to love her, had deceived her. Every friend she had, in all probability, would disapprove of the encouragement she had given to Arthur, and would equally disapprove of the summary and insulting way in which she had cast him off. Her father—Clare's whole being surged up into excitement as she thought of him—excitement produced by two words which she had spied through a torn envelope, and which, perhaps, meant nothing in the world. Her brother—Clare's heart sank again into a sickness and miserable failing of all strength and composure. She was alone, absolutely alone, on the face of the earth. She had no one to fall back upon, to consult on such a terrible dilemma as never surely woman was placed in before. Walking under that blazing sun was fortunately of itself confusing and exhausting enough; but when she reached the Three Beeches, and sat down under their shadow, all the excitement in her mind seemed to meet and clash, filling up her brain with a buzz and sound which almost drove her mad. Not one great battle only, but two or three were raging within her, exploding now from one quarter, now from another, like a network of storms. The Three Beeches stood upon an elevated point, not very high in itself, but possessing all the importance of a hill in that level country. The trees were very fine old trees, with great gnarled trunks, and such a wealth of shadow under them as made the traveller rejoice. Seated on the thick mossy turf, Clare looked down and saw her home among its trees, and the bright white street of the village, and the Red House, burning in the sunshine. Even Thornleigh Church, which was seven miles off, was visible in the sunny distance. Almost every individual involved in the dim and confused drama which was weaving itself about her was at present, could she but see under those roofs, within her range of vision. She let her books, which she had brought with the intention of working hard at a translation, and thus making thought impossible, lie beside her, without so much as remembering their existence. Thinking! How could she help thinking? As long as there is nothing particular in your mind it is, of course, easy enough to occupy it with external matters; but when it is full—full to overflowing—So Clare thought and thought till her mind felt on the eve of giving way. Arthur Arden had done her a great wrong—she thought he had done her such a wrong as a woman can never forgive to a man—not only preferred another to her, but made false pretences of love to her in order to enjoy that other's society. Injury and contempt could go no further. He had wounded her heart, and struck a deadly blow at her maidenly dignity and pride. It was the bitterest wrong, and as such she had resented it.

And yet perhaps Arthur Arden had been wronged as bitterly; perhaps he had unconsciously suffered all his life, and Providence had thrown the means of avenging him into her hands. Edgar, too, had been wronged, not in the same way, but by being made an instrument of injury. But from the thought of Edgar she shrank as if it hurt her. And her father, whom she had held in such reverence, whom she had worshipped as the very embodiment of all the Ardens, whom she had loved so much, and who had loved her—Clare shrank as if a shower of blows were hailing upon her head. She had thrust herself into his secrets, and now she must bear the burden. If she had pried over his shoulder while he was living, how poor, how dishonourable she would have felt herself; but she had done worse than that. She had stolen a surreptitious glance at his secrets after he was dead. Then she tried to calm herself down. Perhaps the words she had read did not mean what they seemed to mean. Perhaps they referred to something perfectly innocent, some piece of generosity on her father's part of which he had said nothing to any one. But Clare felt that even were this the case she must bear the penalty of her prying. She dared not examine further. Her half-secret, which perhaps was no secret, must be the burden of her existence. Never would she breathe it to any one, never allow she knew it; never, never escape from its burning presence. If there was wrong involved, she must allow that wrong to go on; she must not even permit herself to see or approach the man who was the sufferer. And then, all at once, in the midst of her rage and indignation against him, and while she still felt that no punishment was too great to requite his treachery, there suddenly came upon poor Clare, in her inexperience and ignorance, a fit of such yearning for him as rent her very heart. What! with her injury so fresh, with all that anger and bitterness in her mind? Dismayed, bewildered, torn asunder, she thus found out that love will not go out of the heart at any formal bidding. It turned and rent her, like the demon, convulsing her very soul with pain. She opened her heavy eyes after the struggle with a despairing amazement in them. Could it be? Was her judgment to go for nothing, and the bitter wound which he had inflicted to be no argument against him? Nothing but this sudden, appalling, unlooked-for experience could have convinced her. She felt so weak and miserable that she dropped her face into her hands, and wept, she who had been so indignant and so strong.

"Miss Arden, I'm afraid you're feeling poorly," said Barbara. "Do now, there's a dear young lady, take this glass of wine. I made Mrs. Fillpot give it me for you, and I've kept it cool in the bottom of the basket. Do, Miss, there's a dear."

"I don't want anything, Barbara," said Clare; and in the greatness of her misery, she who had made up her mind for the rest of her life to be self-sufficing, to hide her secret in the depths of her being, and ask no one for sympathy, had all the difficulty in the world to keep from throwing her arms round Barbara's neck, and weeping on her breast. She restrained the impulse, however, and kept her head away, and preserved her pride for the moment. This was, alas, how her heart treated Clare, after she had made up her mind that one decision was all that was necessary. She made her decision, expecting henceforward everlasting sadness, but calm; whereas, on the contrary, she was a prey to shock after shock, her heart melting, her resolution giving way, a hundred struggles going on within her. Her very determination made everything worse instead of better. "If you had not thrust everybody from you, if you had not condemned unheard, if you had not come away, and insulted, and abandoned him, all might yet have been well," said the traitor within. And thus poor Clare waded in the very deepest of waters all that long miserable day.

It was nightfall when she returned to the house. Time had gone imperceptibly, as it goes when there is nothing tangible in it. Long threads of reverie linked themselves into each other, going on and on as if they need never end, and coming back after all manner of digressions to the same central subject. "Don't you think it's time to be going, Miss?" the maid would say timidly from time to time. "Presently," Clare would reply, hopelessly opening or shutting the book she had taken into her hands; but at length the sun began to sink, and it was evident they must begin their walk if they were to reach Arden before night. Clare swallowed Barbara's glass of wine, and then set out upon the weary way. "It has been a nice quiet day," she said, mechanically, fibbing with the instinct of good society, as she got up. "I hope it has done you good, Miss," said Barbara, doubtfully. "Oh, all the good in the world," said Clare. And with this forlorn fiction she walked home again; so much less sure of her own constancy; so much more doubtful of the possibility of shutting up secrets in a silence as of the grave, and living a perpetual life of sacrifice, without hope or call for sympathy, than she had been in the morning. She was very weary when she got home, weary in body and mind, and could only answer with a faint smile to the message which Wilkins gave her from her cousin. Jeanie had not kept him back to-day; only one day had he been kept back by all the united influences which could be brought to bear upon him. Had not she been hard upon him, sending him summarily away from her for one offence, he who perhaps all his life had been wronged so bitterly? Had he been wronged? Or was it a dream? And had he wronged her—or was this but a cloud that might pass away? When Clare had got rid of the servants, who worried her, and had also got rid of the poor pretence of dining which she went through in order not to reveal to them too clearly the commotion in her mind, she had another struggle with herself. Whether he had wronged her or had been wronged, surely it was best now to keep him at arm's length. Better not to see him again, never to attempt to lean her cares upon him, to confide her difficulties to him. Oh, no, no! He must never come again. And Clare said to herself that she must live and die alone.

When the servants had gone to bed she went into the library once more in her dressing-gown with her candle, and unlocked all its fastenings, and took out the bundle of papers to look at it. The words she had seen, which had woke her out of one dream of pain into another, and which had shaken her being so profoundly, were covered over now by the envelope into which she had thrust them. She took it out and weighed it in her hands—the neat harmless little packet, which looked as if it could harm nobody! What right had she to think it would harm any one? Clare took it out as if it had been something explosive, and weighed it, and gazed at it. All the house was silent. There was not one creature in it who was not sleeping or seeking sleep. Her own light and the dim one which awaited her in her chamber upstairs were the only signs of life in the great, silent, locked-up place. It was guarded without from every kind of assault; but who could ward off the enemies who existed insidious within?

Clare sat revolving this problem until the night was far gone. She did not seem able to leave it; and yet her thoughts made no progress. Was she the guardian of Arden, watching over that secret, unable to give it up, keeping the house and the family from harm? She thought it was some demon which kept tempting her to open the packet, and discover all. Most likely it would be the best thing to do. Most likely what she would find out on a closer examination would altogether clear up those words which had thrilled her through and through as with an electric touch. They were her father's papers. Was it not her duty to find out what was in them, to be ready to vindicate her father's memory should anyone ever assail it? She sat and weighed the papers in her hand, and listened to all the mysterious sounds and mutterings of the night, till at last her mind became incapable of any personal action, and she felt it grow into a furious battle-field of the two opinions which charged and encountered and were repulsed, and rallied again, and tore her in sunder. It was more weariness than anything else which prompted her at last to the step she took. She was reluctant to think of Edgar at all in the present state of her mind, and yet it was he who was most deeply concerned. After she had discussed it with herself for hours she rose up from the bureau at the bidding of a sudden impulse, and sat down in her father's chair. It was a chair which nobody ever occupied, which the servants were afraid of—and Clare could not but feel with involuntary superstition that her father himself was somehow superintending this action of hers. She drew towards her the blotting book he had used, and which contained his paper—paper which no one had made any use of since his death. Was it he who was dictating to her, holding her pen, guiding her in this tardy justice? Her letter was very short, concise, and restrained. Before she began to write she did not feel as if she could address him again, or could know what to say; but old use and wont came to her aid.

"DEAR EDGAR (this is what Clare wrote)—I have found something among my father's papers which seems to me very important—important to everybody, and to you above all. I have not read it—only just seen a word or two, which have made me very unhappy. I thought I would try to keep it from you, but I find I cannot. Come, then, and see what it means. It is of more importance than anything you can be doing. Come immediately, if I may ask that much of you. Come without any delay.

C. A."

This was all the subscription she could bring herself to put. When she had read it over and placed it in an envelope, she put it down on the Squire's blotting book in front of his seat. It was a kind of test which she felt herself to be applying. If the letter disappeared before morning she would accept it as a supernatural intimation that it ought not to be sent. If not—To such a pass her mind had come, which was in general so free from any fear or consciousness of the supernatural. When she had done this she took up her packet again and went upstairs, and replaced it under her pillow. And thus worn out with all she had gone through Clare slept. She had not expected it, but she fell asleep like a child. Fatigue, excitement, and that long conflict had been of use to her in this one way from which she could derive any help or consolation. And then she had done something which must be decisive, and settle the matter without any further action of her own.

While all these schemes and dreams were going on at Arden Edgar was learning to accustom himself to the life of a young man about town—a thing which it was almost as hard for him to do as it would have been for any of the male butterflies whom he was attempting to emulate to settle down to work. Edgar found it very hard work to adapt himself to the systematic diversions of society—to portion out his hours and engagements on the theory of killing time, and getting through as much amusement as possible. To him the world was full of amusement taken simply by itself, or else of something more satisfactory, more important, which made amusement unnecessary. He did not know what it was to be vacant of interest either in his own affairs or those of his neighbours, and consequently a system which is built upon the theory that Time is man's enemy, and must be killed laboriously, did not at all suit him—but yet his mind was so fresh that he found it possible to shift his interest, to get concerned about the new people round him and their new ways, which were so wonderful. Not the German professors, with their speculations, their talk, their music, and their bier-garten, nor their wives and daughters, at once so notable and so sentimental, nor the English farmers and peasants of Arden, were really so wonderful to Edgar as the ways of Mayfair in June. He would sit and listen with eyes which shone with fun and wonder while the people about him went gravely on making and re-making their engagements, promising to go there, promising not to go here, rising into wild excitement about a difficult invitation, dining, dancing, driving, riding, sauntering at flower shows, at Zoological gardens, at afternoon teas, at garden parties, counting the Row and the Park as sacred duties, considering as serious occupation the scribbling of half-a-dozen notes, and considering the gossip about Lord This and Lady That to be matter of European interest. And how seriously they did it all! How important they felt themselves with all that mass of engagements on hand—every hour of every day forestalled! Edgar looked on laughing, and then gradually got beyond laughing. It was difficult for so sympathetic a spirit to live long in such an atmosphere without beginning to feel that there must be some intrinsic value in the system which was held in such high esteem by all around him. He was bewildered in his great candour. He laughed, and then, growing silent, only smiled, and then began to ponder and wonder and ask himself questions. Perhaps it was well on the whole that as the apex of a great social system founded upon a vast basis of labour and suffering and pain, there should be this human froth, or rather those bubbles sparkling in the sun—those snowy foam-wreaths and gleaming surface ripples to cover and beautify the depths below. Was it well? He could not come to any very satisfactory conclusion with himself. It was easy to laugh, and easy to condemn, and equally easy, when one was trained to it, to take it as the natural condition of affairs; but here, as in all other cases, it was the attempt to discriminate what was good and what was bad—what was mere frivolity and what had some human use in it, which was the difficult matter. The puzzle brought a look of wonder to Edgar's brown eyes. "Are you going to Lady Thistledown's to-night?" Harry Thornleigh would say to him; "it is a horrible bore." "Why should you go then?" Edgar would answer. "My dear fellow, everybody will be there." "And everybody will be bored," said Edgar; "and if everybody survives it, will do the same to-morrow, and to-morrow, and to-morrow. Why don't you do something that interests you, all you fellows?" "That would be a still more confounded bore," said Harry. And what could the new man do but shrug his shoulders and give up the discussion?

He himself was the only one perhaps among them who was not in the least bored. There was something even in Lady Thistledown's party that occupied Edgar. Sometimes he was interested, sometimes amused, and sometimes very much saddened by what he saw. And then personal risks surrounded him, which he did not in the least understand or realise. "Lady Augusta is to be there, I suppose, and your sisters, so that I don't think I shall be bored," he had said to Harry Thornleigh in reference to this very party; and Harry said nothing, but opened his eyes very wide at this plain speaking. "Which of them is it, I wonder?" he mused to himself as he went off. "Gussy, I hope;" for Gussy was her brother's favourite, and he felt it would be very pleasant, as Lady Augusta did, to have the pleasantest and brightest and most sweet-tempered of the girls settled so near as Arden. But in point of fact Edgar had no intention of settling any one at Arden. He was still quite faithful to his sister's sway. If Clare were to marry and go away, then indeed he would no doubt feel the loneliness uncomfortable; but at present it would have seemed something like high treason to Edgar to dethrone his sister. Such an idea had never entered into his mind. But he was fond of Lady Augusta, who was like a mother to him, and he was fond of her daughter—indeed, of all her daughters—whom he regarded with the freshest and most cordial sentiment. He was always ready to get their carriage, to do anything for them. He was not afraid, as so many men were, to afichér himself; and, therefore, as society does not understand brotherly affection on the part of a young man towards young women, everybody decided that one of the Thornleigh girls was to be his lawful owner. There was some difficulty in the common mind as to which was the fortunate individual; but Gussy was so distinctly indicated by the family for the post that naturally no one else had a chance against her. And this conclusion was really the most natural that could be drawn. Edgar, though he was so friendly and so frank, was yet in some respects a shy man, and he clung to the people he knew best. When he was with the Thornleighs he was free from every shade of embarrassment—he knew them all so well (he thought); they were so kind to him—they understood him and his ways of thinking so completely (he believed). When he went to them it was like going home—entering into his family—a more genial family, and one more apt to understand, than he had ever known.

And it was to the Thornleighs that Edgar allowed himself to speak most freely of his own wonderments and perplexities. "I look at you all with amazement," he said. "I don't disapprove of you." ("How very nice of him," interrupted Gussy.) "You look very pretty ("Thanks," said Beatrice, making him a curtsey), and you are very pleasant. Of course, I don't mean ladies in particular ("Oh, you savage," ejaculated Mary, the second youngest, who was a little disposed to hold Helena's views, but did not understand them in the very least), I mean everybody. All this is very nice. It is charming never to take any thought for the morrow, except which invitation one will accept, or rather which place one will go to, of all that one has accepted. The only thing is, what is the good of it all? It tires you so that you require nine months' rest to refresh you, and get you up to the point of doing all this over again; and while you are doing it, you call heaven and earth to witness what a bore it is. Would it not be better to try some other kind of useful exertion now and then? Three months' work in the fields, for instance, or as poor needlewomen, or even in one of those pretty shops—"

"Oh, a shop! that is worse and worse; that is more frightful than ever. I should prefer the fields," said Beatrice and Mary in a breath.

"The fields are exposed to a great deal of rain and cold, drought and wet, frost, and all kinds of perils," said Edgar; "and then they would spoil your complexions. Ask Lady Augusta; she would never let you do that. But these beautiful shops, you know, such as that you took me to—Smallgear or something; and then that one in Regent Street. Why, they are palaces; soft carpets under your feet, and great mirrors to display you in, and beautiful things to handle. I should think it rather nice to belong to one of those shops."

"You can't possibly mean it?" cried Gussy, concerned for the credit of the man who was so generally assigned to her. "Fancy what an occupation it must be, turning over things to be pulled about by ladies who don't know what to do with themselves otherwise, and never mean to buy."

"Well," said Edgar, "we are not criticising, we are merely taking facts as we find them. If it amuses the ladies to turn the things over, the men in the shops are really more useful to them than the other men who go to their five o'clock tea. And now and then there comes a bona fide purchaser. Whereas for you young ladies what could be better? trying on pretty shawls and things (I saw them), exercising the highest qualities of self-denial, making your prettiness and gracefulness of use to others, and yet having your time to yourselves say after six or seven o'clock. You would see the best of company all the same, par dessus la marché. Don't you think it would be a very pleasant change?"

"If you would treat it seriously, and really consider how little women are allowed to do, Mr. Arden," cried Helena Thornleigh, who was too much in earnest to encourage mere chatter like her sisters. "I am sure you might be a great help to us. You see what a desert our lives are, with no object in them. You see what vapid, aimless, useless creatures the most of us are—"

"I beg your pardon," said Edgar. "I feel that it is frightfully selfish, but all my sympathies, in the first place, are for my own class. Stop till I have made that out. I will come to the ladies by-and-bye. We never have a moment's time for anything; we are always pursued by work which has to be done, whether it is riding in the park, or going to the opera, or dining at Richmond. How stern duty runs after your brother, for instance, always reminding him of some engagement or other. Poor Harry finds it a dreadful bore. He says so, and he ought to know best. He is always bemoaning his hard fate, and yet he always goes on obeying it. I don't object to routine, and I don't object to suffering. They are both good things enough; but to suffer and be a slave to routine all for nothing is very hard—I confess I think it is very hard. To be sure, Harry need not do it unless he likes; but that he should like, and should go on doing it, and should not be able to find something better, that is what puzzles me."

"I say," said Harry, who was half-dozing over a book, "what is that about me? I don't want to be made to point a moral in this house. The girls turn me to that use fast enough. What is Arden saying now?"

"Nothing that is very remarkable," said Edgar; "only that we poor fellows, or you poor fellows, don't get half enough credit for the hard life you lead. You give yourselves as much trouble as if you were founding a state or reforming society, and all the time you are doing nothing. I don't object to it. If a man likes to spend his life so, why, of course, he is free to do it: he is a British subject like the rest of us. But I want to know who invented this theory of existence, and how men were got to give in to it—that is all."

"It is all they are good for," said Helena Thornleigh. "It is partly education and partly nature. Boys are brought up to think that they are to have everything they want. They are never obliged to deny themselves or think of others. However silly or frivolous a thing may be, they are free to do it if they like. And they have everything open to them; they go where they like, they live as they please—"

"And a very fine thing they make of it," said Edgar, reflectively, as the young reformer paused for breath. "Miss Thornleigh, when you begin to work upon the young ladies, I think I ought to have a try at the men. We might go halves in a crusade. We should disagree in this, though—for I am quite satisfied with the ladies. You are all very nice; you are just what you ought to be."

"Mr. Arden, I hate compliments," said Helena, growing red with indignation. "When you make those sort of speeches I should like to do something disagreeable. We are not in the least nice. Oh, I don't believe in your crusade; you are not half earnest enough. You laugh and jibe and then you ask us to believe that you have a serious meaning. That is not how I should take it up. You don't half understand, you don't realise how serious it is—"

"Then I may not share in the missionary work?" said Edgar; and he was a little surprised when Gussy interposed, with a slight flush on her face.

"If you were working with Helena, people would not believe much in your seriousness," said Gussy; "they would not give you much credit, either one or the other. Missions á deux are not understood in society—or I suppose they are too well understood," said Gussy, with a laugh. She had been aggravated, as everybody may perceive. Edgar was her special property, allotted to her by the world in general, and what had Helena to do with him, cutting in like this with her missionary work and her nonsense? Gussy felt that she had very good reason to be put out.

And Helena, though she was a missionary, was woman enough to see the justice of the irritation and to cover her sister's retreat. "I hate missions á deux," she said. "We had much better go on in our own way. And then, what Mr. Arden wants and what I want are two very different things. He is only amused, but it goes to my very heart—"

"What, Miss Thornleigh?"

"To look round upon all the women I know, and see them without any occupation," said Helena; "dressing and dancing, that is about all we do. And when we make an effort after something better we are snubbed and thrust down on every side. Our people stop us, our friends sneer at us; they tell us to go and amuse ourselves. But I am sick of amusing myself. I have done it for three years, and I hate it. I want something better to do."

"But Harry does not hate it," said Edgar, turning his eyes once more upon the eldest son. Harry was not at all a bad fellow. He tossed the book he had been reading away from him, and twisted his moustache, and pulled his snow-white cuffs. "I think it's a confounded bore," said Harry, and then he got up and strolled away.

This conversation took place in a house which had shuddered from garret to basement at the thought of not being able to get cards for Lady Bodmiller's ball. Harry had roused himself up for that occasion, and had shown an energy which was almost superhuman. He had rushed about London as if his mission had been to stop a war or save a kingdom. His scheme of operations was as elaborate and careful as if it had been a campaign. And even Helena had forgotten all about the injuries of women, and had rushed to meet her brother at the door and to ask "What news?" with as much eagerness as if she thought dancing the real employment of life. Such relapses into levity may be pardoned to a young philosopher; but they were very strange to Edgar who, with the wondering clear mystified eyes of a semi-savage, was looking on.

CHAPTER XXI

It was not, however, Edgar Arden's intention to preach any crusade. On the contrary, the first impulse of his friendly and neighbour-loving soul was to find out some reason for the existence which seemed so strange to him. He tried to approach, in a great many different ways, and evoke out of it, as it were, or surprise out of it, its secrets. It could not exist, he said to himself, without a meaning. Edgar was not very profound in his philosophy, but still he had a way of thinking of what he saw, and his amused interest in everything led him into a world of questions. Besides, he was not merely conversant with Harry Thornleigh and his class, but also with various other divisions of society. He saw a good deal of Lord Newmarch, for instance, who was entirely a different kind of man; and he renewed his acquaintance with some men whom he had met abroad in his earlier days, one of whom was a great cricketer, and another who was of the Alpine Club, and whose soul dwelt habitually in the sacred recesses of the Matterhorn or Jungfrau. Except Lord Newmarch and his set, these men were all utterly disinterested, pursuing their favourite amusements, not for any purpose to be gained, but for the mere sake of the pursuit itself. The Alpine Club man had no curiosity about the view from the mountain-head, and cared nothing for the formation of the glaciers, or any other subject connected with his mountains: all his object was to get to the top; and he did get to a great many tops, and distinguished himself, and acquired various bits of practical knowledge, which, having no connection of purpose or interest in his mind, were of little use to himself, and none to others. And so likewise the men who devoted themselves to society did not expect to be amused, or instructed, or to meet people they liked, or to find in it any of those solaces which theorists pretend. They went because everybody went—because it was the right thing to do—just for the sake of going, and no other reason. This disinterestedness was the great thing that struck Edgar. He himself was aware that he did not at all possess it. He was continually desiring some result—pleasure or advantage of some description, which, when you come to think of it (he reflected), is a mean way of treating existence after all. Whereas, society was grand in its indifference to any issue. It lived, it assembled, it talked, it went to and fro, and gave itself a great deal of trouble; and from all this exertion it expected nothing to come. This was the first discovery Edgar made, or thought he made; and it staggered him much in the contempt for society which he had been settling into. Was not this in reality a higher principle than his own? It bewildered him, and he could not make it out; and Lord Newmarch, though he was a social philosopher of much greater experience than Edgar, did not seem capable of giving him any aid.

"I don't know what you mean by disinterestedness," Lord Newmarch said. "There is nobody who is disinterested. We have some selfish object in whatever we do. I think, for my own part, that I desire sincerely the good of the country, and make it the grand object of my life; but I know that I want the country to be benefited in my way, not in any one else's. We are all like that. There is my brother Everard, do you see, making himself very agreeable to that great fat woman. He hates fat women, and that one in particular, I know; but he is being so very civil to her because he wants her to ask him to her garden party, which is coming off next week. He is going to call her carriage for her, like a humbug as he is—but all with the most selfish and interested motives."

"I allow that," said Edgar. "I allow that anybody will do anything for an invitation; but why should he wish to go to her garden party? That is what I want to know."

"My dear fellow," said Lord Newmarch, shrugging his shoulders, "why, even I am going! everybody will be there."

"Does he want to meet everybody?" said Edgar. "He does continually, and he is sick of them. Does he want to see any one in particular? Does he think he will enjoy himself? Is it for the pleasure of it he is going? When he has got his invitation he will say, what a confounded bore! He knows exactly beforehand what it will be like. Well, then, I say he is utterly disinterested. He is going for the sake of going. It is not to make him happier, or amuse him, or benefit him. And everybody is going just for the same reason. Surely something might be made of this wonderful disinterestedness! It cannot be meant to be wasted upon garden parties and Lady Bodmiller's ball."

"My dear Arden, you mistake completely," said Lord Newmarch, with even a little irritation. "Disinterestedness! nonsense! Don't you see they want it to be known they have been there; everybody will be there. And out of the list, if one name was wanting, don't you see that the owner of it would lose a certain position. He would feel himself left out. Of course, you have a card. You are one of the most eligible young men of the season. There is no telling what fears and hopes you are exciting in some gentle breasts. Disinterested! That shows how little you know."

And even Lord Newmarch laughed—a refined little laugh—not much like him. He was drawn out of his usual rôle for the moment by the exceeding simplicity of his friend—a thing he could not help laughing at. "Why, there is no saying how many fair huntresses will go there in search of you," he said. "These are the happy hunting-grounds where every woman is permitted to shoot, and none of the men dare run away."

"I was not speaking of women," said Edgar, sharply, for he had a kindness for women. "I was talking of your brother and the rest. These are not happy hunting-grounds for them. There is nothing there for them except the mere fact that they are there. They go for the sake of going. The other is poor enough, but still it is a motive if it exists. The question is, which is finest, my stupid search for a motive, or your brother's grand disinterestedness. There is something splendid, don't you think, in seeing a man throw away his life like this?"

"What do you mean by throwing away a man's life?" cried the social philosopher. "You have become dreadfully highflown. An hour or two in an afternoon, in a pretty garden, with well-dressed people about, and a band, and all that—I don't understand what you mean."

To this Edgar made no reply. His antagonist had the best of it; and yet he was right, and his theory was just. As for the poor ladies who went to those happy hunting-grounds—if there was any truth in it—that was a branch of the subject more melancholy and more intricate still. Edgar preferred not to enter into it. He thought of Helena Thornleigh and her visions, poor girl—visions which, perhaps, were only evidences of a spasmodic state of conflict against the happy hunting-grounds. Fancy Clare going out with her bow and her spear like the other young Dianas! Edgar thought to himself. But then Clare was rich: she had no need to become a huntress. She, like himself, would be the pursued and not the pursuer. This thought made the young man faint and sick. What a ghastly light it threw upon all these pretty parties and assemblies of pleasure! Even the men who sought nothing were better than this.

"Women are so much more practical than we are," said Lord Newmarch. "I see it constantly Now that I think of it, there is some truth in what you say. The young fellows are singularly without motive. I don't see the beauty of it as you do. They do what other people do; but the women always have an object— they are trying to marry their daughters or to marry themselves, or to rise in the social scale, or something which is definite. They are practical, but not in a large way. That is what prevents them from being so useful in the way of public work as they ought to be. They won't or they can't take a broad view. They fasten upon some matter of fact, and stick to that. It is all very well, you know, for a girl with Helena Thornleigh's notions to talk as she does, in that grand, vague way. But observe how women will pick up a subject—probably a nasty subject—and harp upon it. I could give you a hundred instances. They are not nasty women, that is the odd thing. I suppose it is from some feeling of duty not to shrink from what is most repugnant to them—so instead of shrinking they make a pounce upon it, and hold by it in the most aggravating way. I don't know a woman who takes a really large view except your sister, Arden. She is the sort of girl that would help a man, that would be of real use—"

"She is much obliged to you, I am sure," said Edgar, interrupting him; "but we were not talking of my sister—nor, indeed, of women at all. Let us settle with the others first. You don't seem to understand that I want information. I want to know why these sons of piratical land-acquiring Saxons, and conquering Normans, and robber Danes, and marauding Celts—every one of them getting and taking as much as ever they could—should have got into this habit of spending their lives for nothing, neither gain nor honour, nor pleasure nor advantage to others, nor profit to themselves—that is what I can't make out."

"This sort of thing only lasts for three months or so," said Lord Newmarch; "then there is grouse, and so forth. Never mind them—they can take care of themselves. But, Arden, I wish you would make up your mind to go into Parliament, and give your attention to more serious matters. We have too many of those young fellows who mean nothing, and we have too many who mean just one thing in particular, your rich cotton-spinners, and so forth. They are not bad so far as they go, but they are like women—they never take a broad view. They think themselves Radicals, but some of them are as narrow and limited as old wives in a village. And then there are our old squires, who are narrow in another way. They don't understand things as this century understands them. The most enlightened of them will turn short round upon you all at once, and join in some insane cry. We want young men, Arden—men of independent minds, who have been used to think for themselves. If you were a Tory of the old Arden type you would have been the last man I should have made overtures to. And what is odd about it is, that your sister is out-and-out of the old Arden type, and yet, for the best kind of reform I should trust her instincts. She is not one of those who would be afraid of such words as liberty or despotism. Liberty means something more than giving a man a vote, and the people never like you any the worse for using a little dignified force. It must be real force, however, not sham, and it must be used with dignity. Your sister fully understands—"

"Never mind my sister," said Edgar, with some impatience.

"But I must mind your sister," said Lord Newmarch. "My dear Arden, I wish so much you would give me your ear for a little. I never met anyone who entered into all my views like Miss Arden. I cannot tell you—for anything I could say would sound exaggerated—how much I admire her. I have too great a respect for her to venture to approach herself till I have your approval. If you should know any obstacle, any difficulty—you must know better than anyone what a treasure she is."

Edgar was disposed to be angry, and then he was disposed to laugh, but he did neither, feeling himself in too grave a position to permit any levity. "Confound the fellow!" he said to himself. "You take me very much by surprise," he said when he had composed himself a little. "I had not the least expectation of any such proposal from you—"

"Why not from me?—from any other, then?" asked Newmarch with anxiety. "I thought you could not fail to remark before I left your house. Ah, Arden, that never-to-be-forgotten visit! I had known her before, of course, for years—but there are moments when a woman's existence bursts upon you like a revelation, however long you may have known her. Such a revelation then happened to me. So beautiful, so dignified, so truly liberal in her views, so full of real insight! I have every reason to believe that such a match would receive the most complete sanction of my family, and I trust it would not be disagreeable to you."

"I am sure you do Clare and myself great honour," said Edgar, "but you must pardon me for being quite unprepared. I don't know in the least what my sister's feelings may be; of course it is for her, and for her alone, to decide. You know I have been little at home. I know of no difficulties, no—; but my opinion on this point is really of very little importance," he continued, pausing with a recollection of Arthur Arden which was anything but comforting. "It is Clare only who can decide."

"But if such a happiness should be in store for me," said Lord Newmarch, always correct in his expressions, "I might hope that I should meet with no disapproval from you?"

"Whatever my sister's decision should be, you may be sure I shall do my best to carry it out," said Edgar, who was confused by this sudden attack; and they stood together for five minutes in an embarrassed silence, and then separated, to the great relief of both. This sudden declaration was to Edgar what a bomb suddenly falling without any warning would be to the inhabitants of a peaceful town. He was quite unprepared for it; his mind was full of other things, occupied with a hundred novelties quite detached for the moment from Arden and its concerns. He had even half forgotten the original cause which made him leave home, and his fears for his sister. He walked to his rooms that evening from the house where this conversation had taken place, and found himself thrown back at once to his home and its more intimate concerns. He had left Clare alone—much to his annoyance—but she assured him she preferred being alone; and Arthur Arden had given him the slip, and declined his invitation to spend the remainder of the season with him in town. Clare had not mentioned Arthur in any of her letters. No doubt he must be at the end of the world, forming new plans, perhaps pursuing some new love. It was folly to think of him as Edgar felt himself doing the moment Clare's affairs were thus brought before his mind. He had been so easily able to dismiss Arthur that he had ceased thinking of him as dangerous— but now he kept presenting himself like a spectre wherever Edgar turned his eyes. "I wonder where the fellow is. I wonder how those fellows manage. He ought to have a secured income," he said to himself; and yet could not make out why it was that when he ought to be thinking of Clare it was Arthur Arden he began to think of—Arthur, who had divined Lord Newmarch, and hated him. Edgar's mind was full of excitement. It is so much more easy to philosophise about things which don't affect ourselves personally. He had been amused and quite calm when he discussed with himself the doings of Mayfair, but when it was Arden that was the subject of his thoughts he was not calm. Thus it was the most steady and serious among all his friends and acquaintances who threw this sudden barb into Edgar's life.

CHAPTER XXII

"I don't think you are happy in town, Mr. Arden," said Gussy Thornleigh the next time Edgar presented himself in Berkeley Square; "and when we saw you last at home you said you were not coming. What made you resolve to come after all?"

The truth was that Gussy supposed it was herself who had made him come: this had been taken for granted by all the family, and Gussy naturally had believed it, or at least had tried to believe it—a point on which, however, her good sense made a feeble conflict with that happy girlish vanity, which as yet had not experienced many rebuffs. Privately in the retirement of her own chamber she had already disclosed her scepticism to her sister Helena. "I don't believe he came after me," she said. "Mamma thinks so, and Harry thinks so, but I believe it is only their innocence. They don't understand Edgar

Arden. He is fond of me and he is fond of you, and he does not care a bit for either of us. That is my opinion. He wants to make friends of us all the same as if we were not girls."

"And why shouldn't he?" asked Helena with some indignation; not that she cared for Edgar Arden, but for the principle. "His being a man does not make any difference to me; and why should it make a difference to him that I am a girl?"

"Ah, but it does make a difference," said wiser Gussy. "Perhaps not when people are older; but I don't know any except fast girls who go and afficher their friendship with men. I don't think he came for me. I think I shall ask him some day, quite promiscuous, that he may not be put on his guard—and I shall soon see if it is for me."

It was in accordance with this resolution that she spoke, and her question was "quite promiscuous," as she said, interjected into the midst of a conversation with which it had nothing to do. Edgar bore the test with a composure which satisfied Gussy's intellect at once, though it somewhat depressed her in spite of herself.

"I could not help it," he said quite seriously, "It seemed a way out of a difficulty. I am not quite sure now that it was a wise way, but then it seemed the best."

Gussy looked at him with a little surprise. He was so perfectly composed and unmoved, evidently quite unaware of the interpretation that had been placed on his change of purpose. She was not in love with him in the very least, and yet it was a shock to her vanity to see how unconscious he was of the supposed reason. "He might have complimented and made belief a little," she said to herself; "there is no need for being so deadly sincere."

"How odd that you should have to do anything like that," she said aloud; "it is like one of our expedients; but you can do just as you like, at least Helena tells us so, and I suppose men can—"

"I don't think men can," said Edgar, laughing; "at least not men like myself. The fact was, I had a guest whom I did not wish to keep any longer. You must be kind, and not betray me."

"Certainly," said Gussy with promptitude, opening her eyes wide at the same time in wonder at such a confession. "Don't be angry with me," she resumed; "I do so like to know everything about my friends. Do tell me! Was it Arthur Arden? Mamma would scold me dreadfully for asking; but I should so like to know. There, don't tell me any more. I can see it was by your eyes. I know some people don't like him; but he is very nice. I think you might have let him stay."

"Do you think he is very nice?" said Edgar, who was, as she had divined, very fond of Gussy, though not (according to her own dialect) in that way.

"Yes," said Gussy, jumping by instinct into the heart of the question. "The thing is, you know—but you serious people cannot understand—that he never means anything. He is very attentive, and all that. It is his way with girls. He makes you think there never was any one like you, and that he never had such an opinion of anybody before, and all that; but he never means anything. Even mamma says so. A very young girl might be taken in; but we all know that he means nothing, and I assure you he is very nice."

"I don't understand how such a man can be very nice," said Edgar, with subdued annoyance, for he did not quite like the idea that Gussy herself should have gone through this discipline or made such a discovery. "I like people who mean more and not less than they say."

"That is all very well, Mr. Arden, in most matters," said Gussy, with a little hesitation and a momentary blush. ("I wonder if he means anything?" she was asking herself; but Edgar was looking at her with the simplest straightforwardness and making no pretences.) "But, you know, when it is only just the common chatter of society—Well, why should everybody be so dreadfully sincere? People may just as well be agreeable. I am not standing up for flirting or that sort of thing. But still, you know, when you are quite sure that nothing is meant—"

"Don't confuse my mind altogether," said Edgar. "I am bewildered enough as it is. You go to places not to be amused, but because everybody is going; you do things you don't care for because everybody does them; and now you tell me men are very 'nice' because they never mean anything. My brain is going very fast, but I think this last doctrine is the most confusing of all."

"You would see the sense of it if you were in our position," said Gussy, shaking her pretty head. "Now, for instance, Arthur Arden—suppose, just for the sake of argument, that he was really in love with one of us. It sounds ridiculous, does it not? What do you suppose papa and mamma would say? They would send him out of the house very quickly you may be sure; and the poor girl, whoever it was, would be scolded to death. Oh, there would be such a business in the house! Worse than there was when poor Fred. Burton wanted to marry Ada. Perhaps you never heard of that?"

"No, indeed," said Edgar, to whom Ada, who was the quiet one, had always appeared the least interesting of the family.

"He was the curate at Thorne," said Gussy; "and, of course, he ought never to have dreamt of such a thing; but Harry had been at college with him, and he was very nice, and came to us constantly. I liked him myself—indeed, we all liked him; and if he only had had two thousand or so a-year, or even less, as he was a clergyman—But he had only about twopence," said Gussy, with a sigh; "and what was poor papa to do?"

"And Miss Thornleigh?" asked Edgar, with all the impulsive interest in a love story which comes natural to an unsophisticated mind. Ada was sitting at the other end of the room with a great basket before her full of pieces of coloured print. She was making little frocks for her poor children—a work in which by fits and starts the other girls would give her uncertain aid.

"O Ada!" said Gussy, with a little shrug of her shoulders; and then she glanced at her sister, and a glimmer of moisture came into the corners of her bright eyes. "She is the greatest darling that ever was! I don't think there is anybody so good in the whole world!" she said, under her breath, and dashed away that drop of dew from her eyelashes. "It is so absurd to make any fuss," she added a moment after. "One knows it must be, but one cannot help being sorry sometimes when one sees—" and here Gussy's voice failed her, and she bit her lip, that she might not be proved to have broken down.

"You are a dear, kind girl to feel for her so," cried Edgar, putting out his hand to give her a grasp of sympathy; and then he remembered suddenly that he was a man and she a woman, and that an invisible line was stretched between them. "It is very hard," he said, checking himself with a half laugh, "that you are not your brother, or I my own sister for the moment, because I must not say (I suppose) how sorry I am, nor how I like you for it; but I do all the same. Don't you think if we were to lay our heads together and get him a living—"

"Oh, hush," said Gussy, growing paler, and this time quite unable to conceal the tears that rushed to her eyes. "Did you really never hear about him? He died a year ago. It was not our fault. He went to the East-End of London, you know, and worked dreadfully hard, and caught a fever. Oh, will you take that chair between me and Ada, please! Don't you see she always wears black and white—nothing else—but you men never notice what any one wears."

Edgar made the change as he was desired, and this time all the etiquettes that ever were invented would not have kept him from taking Gussy's soft hand into his, and holding it kindly, tenderly, as a sympathising brother might have done. He would have taken her into his arms, had he dared, in affectionate kindness and sympathy. He was too much moved to say a word, but he held her hand fast, and looked at her with his heart in his eyes.

"Thanks," said Gussy, crying softly; "what a kind, friendly boy you are! Oh, I am sure I never meant to talk of this any more. I was in a fury with papa and mamma at the time, and said a great many things I ought not to have said; but, of course, one knows that it had to be—they could not have done anything else."

"Couldn't they?" said Edgar. "Is money everything then? I am a stranger in this sort of a world, and I don't know."

"If it is not everything, it is a great deal," said Gussy. "And now, can't you understand what I mean when I say a man is nice who can make himself nice, without meaning anything? Why, there is you," she added, with a spice of malice. "You don't do it in Arthur Arden's way; but you are very kind to one, and very pleasant; and it makes one so much at one's ease when one sees you don't mean anything. There! That is a bold argument; but now you will understand what I mean to say."

Gussy got up when she had delivered this shot, and ran over to the other side of the room to get her work, as she said, leaving Edgar very silent and considerably bewildered. It was a new sensation to him. Was he supposed to mean anything, he wondered? He felt that he had received an arrow, but he did not quite understand how or why it came; and he was a little sore, it must be confessed, to hear himself classed with Arthur Arden as one of the men who meant nothing. In his own consciousness he meant a great deal—he meant the most cordial brotherliness, affection, and sympathy. He had "taken to" the Thornleighs, as people say. He liked to go to their house; he liked to talk to them all, one almost as much as the others, and Lady Augusta as much as any of her girls. This was what he meant; but could it be that some other meaning was expected of him? Then he noticed with some surprise that Lady Augusta was quite cognisant of the fact that Gussy had left him, and that he was sitting all alone and silent, pondering and confused. Why should she note so very unimportant a transaction? And she called him to her side immediately on a most transparent pretext.

"Mr. Arden, come and tell me your last news from Clare," she said. "It is very hard-hearted of her not to come with you to town. And it must be very dull for her at Arden, all by herself. Has she got old Miss Arden from Escott, or good Mrs. Seldon with her? What, nobody! that must surely be dull even for Clare—"

"So I thought," said Edgar; "but she will not come—"

"And she has so rooted a prejudice against those good people the Pimpernels—it is a pity," said Lady Augusta. "I suppose you know your cousin Arthur Arden is staying there?"

"There?" cried Edgar, "at Arden?" and he half rose to go off at once and guard his sister, whose imprudence it seemed impossible to understand.

"I mean he is at the Pimpernels;" said Lady Augusta. "Alice, I suppose, will have a good deal of money. I have known the day when Arthur Arden could have done a great deal better than that. But neither men nor women improve their case matrimonially by growing older. It will be curious to see him as the husband of Alice Pimpernel."

"But is it certain that because he is her father's guest the other must follow?" said Edgar, who asked the question at random, without thinking much about it. The answer was a little pointed, and it found a lodgment in his mind.

"Oh dear no, Mr. Arden. But yet the world is apt to ask why does he go there? What does he want in that house? It is a question that is asked whenever a young man visits a great deal at a house where there are girls."

"I did not know that," said Edgar, with a simplicity which went to Lady Augusta's heart. "I believe he is as innocent as a baby," she said afterwards when she was telling the story. "He may be as innocent as he pleases, but he shan't trifle with Gussy," said Harry, putting on a very valiant air. Gussy, for her own part, did not know what to think. "He likes me very well, but that is all," she said to her mother. "I am sure he means nothing. Indeed, mamma, I am quite sure—"

"I don't think you know anything at all about it," said Lady Augusta, with some irritation; for Edgar was her own protegé—it was she who had vouched for him, and settled how everything was to be—and not only her pride but her feelings were concerned. She thought she had never met with any one she could like so well for a son-in-law. He was so thoughtful, so considerate, and (a matter which is well worth noting) had the air of liking her too, for herself, as well as for her daughter. "One could really make a son of him," the poor lady said to herself with a sigh; for to tell the truth she was sometimes sadly in want of a good son to help her. The girls were very good, but they were only girls, and could not be of all the use a man could—and Harry was quite as much trouble as comfort—and Mr. Thornleigh left everything to his wife. Therefore she was reluctant to give up the idea of Edgar, which was, as we have said, her own idea. It was so seldom that everything that could be desired was to be found united in one person, as in his case. When a man was very "nice" and a comfort to talk to, the chances were he was poor and had to be snubbed instead of encouraged. But Edgar was everything that was desirable, even down to his very local position. So Lady Augusta spoke very sharply even to her favourite daughter when she insinuated that Edgar was indifferent. "You don't know anything at all about it," was what she said; and she clung to the idea with a certain desperation. Arden was so near, and the family was so good, and the rent-roll so satisfactory, and the man so nice. It was impossible to improve the combination which she found in him; and Lady Augusta's mind was fully made up to brave a great deal, and do a great deal, before she relinquished the prize which Providence had thrown in her way.

CHAPTER XXIII

Edgar left the Thornleighs that day with several quite new subjects of thought. His heart was touched to the very quick by that little revelation which Gussy had made to him of her sister's history. It stopped him quite suddenly in the current of his previous reflections. He had been so full of the unprofitableness and unmeaningness of the new existence into which he found himself thrown, that the discovery of a tragedy so simple and so hopeless, just one step out of it, upset once more all his conclusions. The idea he had been forming was, that within the range of "Society" strong feeling of any kind, much less passion, was impossible—even suffering and death seemed things too great and too human to penetrate within that artificial ring. He could have imagined the same routine going on for ever and ever, without any novelty in it, or touch of the real. Yet here, upon the very edge of the eternal dance, here was a single silent figure who had suffered (as Edgar felt, in the fervour of youthful sympathy) the extremity of human woe. How strange it was! The contrast confused him, and gave another turn, as it were, to his whirling brain. They were then human creatures after all, those people of fashion, whirling on and on in their everlasting round. Sometimes pain, passion, disappointment, tragical rending asunder of hearts and lives, proved their real nature. Perhaps even the man who was trying to take all the use out of his life by means of engagements twenty deep, had been pierced through and through with some such shaft as that which had killed poor Ada's lover. Perhaps some of those women who hurried from one assemblage to another as fast as hours and horses could carry them had suffered in silence all that Ada had done, and lost all savour and sweetness in life like her. Edgar felt himself pulled up short, and paused in his wholesale criticisms. How could he tell—how could any one tell—what lay underneath the surface of the stream? He paused, and then he went off at a tangent, as young philosophers are apt to do, and asked himself whether this flutter and crowding and universal buzz of amusement was not a vast pretence, adopted by common consent, to hide what everybody was suffering underneath? outside an attempt to appear as if they were having things their own way, enjoying to the height of their capacity all the good the world could give; but underneath a deep universal conviction that life was naught, and happiness a dream! Was this the true theory of life? The question occupied him a great deal more perhaps than the readers of this history will sympathise with; but then, it must be remembered that it was all very new to him, and that every novel phase of life strikes us more strongly than that to which we are accustomed. To Arthur Arden, for instance, the course of existence which startled Edgar was too common to call for a single question. It was the ordinary state of affairs to him. But Edgar knew the other forms so much better. He understood those conditions under which a man labours that he may live. That theory was familiar to him which makes the day's work necessary to the day; but to exist in order to get rid of your existence—to bend all your faculties to the question, not how you are to provide for, but how you are to spend and dispose of your days, that was new to him. And therefore he puzzled over it in a way which a man of fashion to the manner born could not possibly understand. The man of fashion would probably have been quite as much astonished and amazed by Edgar's prejudices in favour of something to do. Something to do! Why, Harry Thornleigh had a hundred things to do, and never a moment to spare, and yet had never been of use either to himself or any other living creature all his life!

And then this new theory—about what was expected of young men who visited in houses where there were girls—troubled Edgar much. The other question occupied his intelligence, but this one disturbed him in a tenderer point. It hurt his amour-propre in the first place; for to suppose you have been a favourite in a house on your own merits, and then to find that you are only encouraged with a view of providing for a daughter, is sadly humbling to a young man's vanity; and it hurt him in the affectionate respect he had for women in general and the Thornleighs in particular. He liked them all so kindly and so truly, and had been so pleased to believe that they liked him; whereas, apparently, it was only on the chance that he should bestow what he had upon one of them that they admitted him so freely. What a disenchantment it was! Instead of being their friend, whom they had confidence in, he was a man who meant nothing like Arthur Arden—a man whose inclinations were speculated upon, and his indifference despised. Edgar asked himself with a certain bitterness which of them it was whom he was expected to address. Perhaps the stately Helena, notwithstanding her views about the occupations of women, had been given to understand that it was her duty to accept Arden instead; perhaps Gussy—But Edgar could not help feeling sore on this subject. He was fond of Gussy, he said to himself; she was so frank, and so friendly, and so sympathetic, so ready to respond, so willing to communicate. He could not bear the idea that she had been making merchandise of him, and calculating upon Arden—for, of course, it is Arden, not me, he thought. I for myself am nobody—less a great deal than the poor fellow who died, whom they seem to have had a kind of human feeling for. She cried over him even—and laughed, and said I meant nothing, Edgar added, in a sudden flush of pique and dissatisfaction. What meaning, I wonder, did she intend me to have? From this it will be seen that Edgar Arden was not in love—was not the least in love; but yet did not care that Gussy should think of him as an article of merchandise—a creature representing settlements and a house of her own. It is a humiliating position for a man to find himself in. It is pleasant (perhaps) to be the object of pursuit, and to feel that mothers and daughters are fluttered by your entrance or exit, or by any silly word it may be your pleasure to address to the young women who are being put up to market. But even to those young women who are put up to market the transaction is scarcely so humbling as it is to the man, who is reckoned among them not as a man at all, but as so much money, so many lands, so many luxuries. Edgar was cast down by this revelation—down to the very depths. What a fool he had been to think they liked him. Was he worth liking by anybody? Was he not rather an insignificant, common-place wretch, unworthy the least notice on his own merits? And he did not in the least desire to be noticed for the sake of Arden. It seemed to him the very last depth of contempt.

For a few days after this Edgar went about very sadly, abstaining from everybody, and feeling very much like a culprit. He kept away from Lady Augusta's pleasant house, and that did not make him any the happier; and then it suddenly occurred to him that he might be thought, in the odious jargon of "society," to be "behaving badly" to Gussy, a thought which stung him so that he seized his hat and rushed out to call, meaning he knew not what—perhaps to ask her piteously if she really wanted Arden, and to offer it to her acceptance. But the room was full of visitors, and Gussy took very little notice of him, and it would be impossible to say how small he felt, how impertinent and presumptuous; but still the thought came back.

It is usual to take it for granted that only one or two of the greater and more primitive sentiments are concerned in that great act of marriage, which is so important a matter for good or for evil in human life. People marry for love, which is the natural motive; or they marry for money or money's equivalent—comfort, advancement, and advantageous development of life. And, no doubt, it is very true that in the majority of cases these are the feelings which are most involved. But yet it is astonishing how many secondary motives come in to determine the most momentous of personal decisions. Edgar Arden had never experienced a grande passion. He had thought himself in love two or three times in his life, and he knew that he had got over the feeling. It was a thing he was ashamed of when he came to think of it, but nevertheless it was quite true that he had got over it. He had just skimmed the surface of those emotions which culminate in the kind of love which is for ever. At the moment he had thought himself deeply moved, but afterwards, with mingled amusement and shame, he had confessed to himself that it was nothing but a passing ripple which had gone over him. Perhaps he was not of a passionate nature, nor one who would be subject to any tragic force of feeling. His love would be tender and deep and true, but it would not be wild or all-absorbing, and he was a man who would be capable of considering the interests of the woman he loved apart from himself, which is a kind of generosity sometimes not at all appreciated by the object of such affection. Perhaps, on the whole, the most real lover, the one most attractive to a woman, is the selfish man who wants her for his own happiness, and will have her, whatever the obstacles may be, rather than the disinterested man who prizes her happiness most, and sacrifices himself and lets her go—not sufficiently realising, perhaps, that he has sacrificed her too. But the absence of this impassioned selfishness on Edgar's part laid him open to the action of all the secondary motives. Never did there exist a more friendly affectionate soul. He would have put himself to trouble to procure what it wanted for any child he heard crying by the way. It came natural to him, as it comes natural to some men, by hook or by crook, to secure their own advantage. And if it really should be the case that he himself, or rather Mr. Arden of Arden, was a thing that Gussy Thornleigh wanted very much, and would be the happier for, why should not she have it? The idea was a little absurd, and yet he could not bring forward a single sufficient reason why it should not be so. Actually, when he considered the matter fully, he had no personal objections. She would be a very sweet, very bright little companion—not a fault could be found with her in any way—Nay, Edgar was too chivalrous to discuss Gussy or any other woman in this irreverent manner—What he meant to himself was rather that any man might be proud and happy to have such a wife. And he had no other love to stand between him and her; no; no other love—except that visionary love whom every young man looks to find somewhere, the Una of imagination, the perfect woman. She only, and no other—and she was no woman's rival. No doubt she would fold her wings and drop down out of the skies, and shadow over and melt into the being of Edgar's wife. Therefore if Gussy chose—Why should not this be—

But perhaps he was just as glad that he had not been allowed a possibility of committing himself. It was not his fault; he would have done it had he been alone with her, or even had he been able to get her to himself in a corner of the drawing-room, apart from immediate observation. But that had been impossible; and consequently it was Providence, not Edgar, which had kept it from coming to pass. Yet he was not sorry; he reflected philosophically that there was plenty of time. She was not in love with him, he felt sure, any more than he was in love with her. She was not in any hurry. She was a dear, good, reasonable girl. In short, the more he thought of it, the more he came to see that (apart from romance, which was always absurd) nothing could be more appropriate in every way. They were made for each other. They were neither of them solemn, passionate people—they were both lively, cheerful, fond of a little movement and commotion, and yet fond of the country and of a reasonable life, with duty and responsibility in it. Gussy, alas! thought very little, had he but known it, of duty and responsibility; but this was how the matter shaped itself in Edgar's mind. Of course, there was no need for anything being decided in a hurry. Clare would probably marry first—or, if not, Clare's wishes must be supreme, whatever they were. She would live with them at Arden—she would still be mistress—no, that was perhaps impossible. At all events, she would still be—Here Edgar found himself in deep waters and stuck fast, not quite making out how this was to be settled. Clare in Arden, and not mistress of Arden was impossible. No doubt, had his feelings been very deeply concerned, he would not have been deterred by such a thought—but as it was chiefly for other people's satisfaction that he was planning the arrangement, it was a very serious drawback. What! please Gussy at the cost of Clare? This was the most grave obstacle to the plan which had yet come in his way.

He was still in this perplexity, and not without a consciousness of its whimsical character, when he received Clare's letter. There was something strained and strange in its expression which struck him curiously. Why should she write to him so? Of course she might ask anything of him—call him to her as she pleased. To make a journey from London to Lancashire was not much—a great deal farther, to the end of the world had she wished it, he would have gone willingly for his sister. He wrote her a little note, full of affectionate playful reproach. "Though I have a hundred things to do," he said; "though I am engaged to go to twenty balls, and ten dinners, and three concerts, and seventeen afternoon teas, in the course of the next four days, yet I will hurry through the most pressing of my engagements, and come home on Saturday." But the meaning of the letter was not in the least the thing that struck him—she wanted to consult him about something, that was all he made of it. And as for the manner of expression, Clare was in haste, or she was annoyed about something, or perhaps a little out of temper. Now and then Clare could be a little out of temper, he knew. Perhaps the village people had been troublesome— perhaps it had vexed her that Arthur Arden should be staying with the Pimpernels. But, on the whole, haste was the most natural explanation. Thus he settled the matter with himself with very little difficulty; and on the whole he was very glad to be called home. And then it occurred to him all at once that the Thornleighs were going on Monday—and then—

Surely, and beyond all question, fate must have decided this matter for him. His summons had come to him at such a moment and in such a way that he must be supposed to be following the Thornleighs home, as he had been supposed to follow them to town. He could not but laugh as he perceived this new complication. Now, indeed, unless he took pains to show that he did mean something, there could be no doubt that it would be said Gussy was badly treated. When he went into the solemn shades of the Minerva to seek Lord Newmarch, with whom he had some business, he felt already sure what would be said to him. "Going home on Saturday!" said the politician; "what, before the education debate, which I so much wanted you to hear! Arden, I suppose it is clear enough to see what that means. But must you go because they go? Though you are not in Parliament, you have a duty to the public too—"

"I go because I am called home on business," said Edgar, "for no other reason, I assure you. I have heard from Clare to-day—"

"Oh, ah," said Lord Newmarch; "of course, we all understand urgent private affairs. But, Arden, though it does not become me to speak, I wish you had not meant to marry immediately. I should be more happy to congratulate you as member for East Lancashire than as Benedict the married man."

"The chances are you will never congratulate me as either," said Edgar, with a certain wayward pathos which puzzled himself; "I am not going to marry, and I don't intend to go into Parliament. I should not be much credit to you in that way; I should go in for impracticable measures, and call a spade a spade. Let me tame down first, and get used to parliamentary language and all the other fictions of life—"

"My dear fellow, I wish you were not so bitter about the fictions of life," said Lord Newmarch, shaking his head.

"Bitter!" said Edgar, with a laugh.

"Well, if not bitter, cynical—cynical—perhaps that is a better word. I have been thinking a great deal about what you said the other day, and I don't think there is much in it. Society must be kept up—some sacrifice must be made to keep up that fine atmosphere—that air so sensitive to everything that comes into it—that brilliant, witty, refined—"

"Newmarch," said another young man, lounging up, "where were you that one couldn't see you at the Strathfeldsays' dance the other night? Awful bore! Never was at anything much worse all my life—the women all frights and the men all notabilities. Ah, Arden, I never see you anywhere now. Where has the t'other Arden gone—Arthur Arden—that one used to meet about? He used to be always with the Lowestofts. Lowestoft wouldn't stand it at the last. Deuced bore! Some men are insufferable in that way. Pull you up short, whether you mean anything or not, and spoil the whole affair. Been doing anything in the House?—Education Bill, and that sort of thing. Hang education! What is the good of it? What has it ever done for you or me?"

"What, indeed!" cried Edgar—a backing which was received with the warmth it merited.

"Eton and Christchurch are reckoned pretty well," said their new companion; "but I don't know what they ever did for me. And as for those confounded fellows that never wash and have votes, what do they want with it? Depend upon it, they are a great deal better without. Teaches them to be discontented; then teaches you to humbug and tell lies for them to read in the newspapers. By the way, where are you going to-night? I've got some men coming to dine with me. Will you make one—or, rather, will you make two, if Arden likes? Then there is that deuced affair on at the Bodmillers' which I suppose I shall have to look in upon; and the Chromatics are giving a grand concert, with Squallini and Whiskerando. Little Squallini is worth listening to, I can tell you. There are heaps of things I never attempt, and one is, going to musical nights promiscuous, not knowing what you're to hear. But the Chromatics know what is what. Going? I shall look out somebody, and have a rubber till five. These concerts and things are a confounded bore."

"Is that your brilliant, witty, refined—is that the sort of thing we should make a sacrifice to keep up?" said Edgar, as they went out together. "What an amount of trouble it has taken to produce him! And now he has to be kept up at a sacrifice. I should prefer to make a sacrifice to get rid of him, Newmarch. He is not so witty as his own groom, nor half so useful as that crossing sweeper—"

"You would find the crossing-sweeper dull, too, if you met him every day," said Newmarch. "The fact is, it is not a very good world, but it is the best we can get; and if a man does as much as he can with it—You must get into the House, Arden. I don't mean to say society is enough for an energetic man, with a great deal of time on his hands: but my occupations I hope are solid enough. I have had three or four hours of committees already; and I am going down to Westminster straight. Of course, it is pleasant to sit over that little table in the corner of the Thornleighs' drawing-room. Ah!—that sort of thing is not for me," said the legislator, with a sigh.

And Edgar laughed—partly at his friend, partly at himself, partly at the universal vanity. Lord Newmarch was no Solomon. The country could have gone on all the same had he, too, gossiped over a tea-table as so many of the youth of England were doing at that moment with relish as great as though they had been so many washer-women, and tongues sharpened at the clubs. England would not have suffered had Lord Newmarch gossiped too. And Edgar was not much more genuine as he walked with him as far as Berkeley Square, and then dropped off "to say good-bye to the Thornleighs," leaving the liveliest certainty on Lord Newmarch's mind as to what were his relations with the family. Nor, perhaps, was Gussy more true, as she sat and filled out the tea, and saw, with a little thrill, the man coming in who was to fix her fate. She did not love him any more than he loved her, and yet, in all likelihood, her life was in his hands. What a strange, aimless whirl it was in which everybody moved, or seemed to move, as some blind fate required, and could not stop themselves, nor change the current which kept drifting them on! The crossing-sweeper was the braver and the more genuine personage. The mud cleared away before his broom; the road grew passable where he moved; he had it in his power to make a new passage wherever he was so minded. At least, so one supposed looking at his mystery from outside. Perhaps within, the guild of crossing-sweepers has its tyrannical limitations too.

It was a quiet hour when Edgar made his appearance in the drawing-room at Berkeley Square. Why this afternoon should have been so still and domestic and the last so noisy and full of visitors, it is difficult to say. The girls had been riding in the Park in the morning, "their last ride," as the younger ones informed him, with voluble regret. The horses were going off that evening; the whole house was, as it were, breaking to pieces. Already half the pretty things—the stands of books and of flowers—had disappeared from the tables. The girls looked somehow as if their very dresses were plainer, which was not actually the case. The cloud upon them was only a moral cloud, consequent upon the knowledge that on Monday they were all going home.

"And fancy, the opera will go on all the same, and Patti will sing, though we are away," said Mary, who was musical.

"There will be just as many dances every night, and all night long, and we at Thorne!" cried Beatrice. Gussy, who looked down upon them both from the altitude of two and twenty, shook her head with a certain grandeur of superior experience.

"Oh, you silly girls! if you had seen as much of it as I have! The opera is all very well, and so are the dances; but you don't know how tiresome they get when you go on and on. Yes; it is my fourth season, Mr. Arden, and I think I have a right to be tired."

Lady Augusta gave her daughter a warning look. "The more seasons you can count the less disposed you will be to speak so very frankly of them," she said; "but Mr. Arden has been too much with us not to know what a chatterbox you are."

"Yes," said Edgar; "how good it has been of you to let me be so much with you. It has made town so much more pleasant to me than it could have been otherwise; and now I have come to bid you good-bye, though I am glad to think it will not be for long."

"To bid us good-bye!" they all cried, with surprise. And Lady Augusta cast another significant glance over the heads of Mary and Beatrice, who were too heedless to take any notice, at the daughter whose interests were more specially concerned.

"Yes," said Edgar; "Clare has written begging me to go to her directly. I am going on Saturday. I had no idea of it when I saw you yesterday; and after all I shall be in Lancashire before you are. I don't even know why it is I am sent for by my sovereign Clare."

Once more a look passed between Lady Augusta and her elder girls. They did not believe one word of this story. They took it quite simply for granted that he was doing this to be near them, to be within reach of Gussy. Gussy herself even was convinced. She had doubted and shaken her head when the entire household had been persuaded of the fact. But now a little flush of gratification lighted up her cheeks. She could no longer resist the conviction that his coming and going depended somehow, as she said modestly to herself, on "us."

"It is strange of Clare to send you such a summons," said Lady Augusta; "but I daresay she is very lonely, poor child. I do hope we shall see a great deal more of her at Thorne when we get home. To tell the truth, I am very glad you are going. I do not like to think of her, still in mourning as she is, and left in that house all alone."

"Yes; I have been a little forgetful of Clare, I fear," Edgar said, without thought; and the girls, who were now very attentive, made another rapid comment within themselves all in a breath. He has been thinking so much of Gussy! How funny it was! How nice to be Gussy, for whose sake a man "forgot all about" his duties! A little thrill of interest ran through the assembled family; and even kind Lady Augusta, who had become, as she herself said, "quite attached" to Edgar, was a little moved by the thought of what might be coming.

"You are never forgetful of anybody, I am sure," she said, "unless with a very strong motive. I don't like to praise people to their faces; but I never saw any one less apt to think of himself than you."

Edgar made no reply to this praise. There was a little pause of expectation, an occasional hush in the room, which one and another attempted to break by snatches of conversation, perpetually interrupted. They can't expect me to make the plunge before them all, Edgar mused to himself, with a sense of fun which was very inappropriate to the gravity of the position. And after all, when he came to think of it, it would be very difficult to make this plunge. What could he say? Gussy and he had been upon the easiest, the friendliest terms. He did not see how he could alter that ground all at once, and assume a vein of high sentiment. There was in reality so little sentiment in his mind. He was not impassioned; and it occurred to him all at once that to ask a girl to marry him in this perfectly calm and humdrum way would not be flattering to the girl. Gussy, no doubt, would expect something very different. She would expect a lover's fervour, the excitement of a man whose happiness for life depended on her Yea or Nay; and Edgar felt that his happiness did not depend upon it. Altogether, it was an embarrassing position. Conversation languished in the Thornleigh drawing-room, and the family gave furtive glances at him, and tried to look indifferent, and betrayed itself. As for Gussy, she never looked at him at all. She had given up her tea-making, though she still sat at the table, with the tray before her, which was a fortunate shield; but her eyes were bent upon her work, and she was as silent as a mouse in her corner, conscious to her finger-points, and expectant too.

It was a relief when old Lady Vere came in, and her daughters, who were much of the same age as Mary and Beatrice, and instantly drew off the attention of those two sharp-eyed young women. Lady Vere, too, kept Lady Augusta in occupation, and had something to say to Helena. So that when Edgar brought her cup back to the tea-table, it was quite natural that he should glide into the vacant chair, and keep Gussy company. "Are you sorry to leave town?" he said; and Gussy gave a shy, blushing, trustful glance into his face, which made him draw his chair a little closer. He was fond of her! not impassioned, but yet—what a dear little girl she was!

"Sorry for some things," Gussy said, "but not so sorry as Mary and Beatrice are. One's first season is always delightful; one feels as if it would all last for ever."

"Do you? I think I have that feeling too, but only because it is so dreary, so flat, so banal, always the same thing over again," said Edgar. "I think life must be waiting for us—real life, not this dull routine—at home."

"Yes, perhaps," said Gussy faintly—for every word he said seemed to be more and more weighted with meaning. He did not say absolutely, "the real life I speak of is our life together, the existence in which we two shall be one," but could anything be more clear than that he meant it so? Her voice sank in spite of herself. Gussy was not in the least impassioned either, but what she thought was—"How dearly he must love me, to be able to give up town and everything for my sake! Poor dear boy, that is all he is thinking of; and oh, I am not so good as he is. I am thinking of a great many other things besides him."

Thus, with the very best motives in the world, they went on deceiving each other. Not much was said over the tea-table except such broken scraps of talk as this—talk which meant next to nothing, and yet was supposed by the listeners on both sides to mean a great deal. "Ada is anxious to get back to her schools and her poor people," Gussy said. "She is so good! She has done nothing but work for the children even here. People ought to be happy, don't you think, that give themselves up like that, and think only of others? They must get to be happy because they are so good."

"I hope so," said Edgar, with a certain doubtfulness; "but, above all, those who are more happy should be good to her. One like her seems a sacrifice for others, securing their happiness. I mean—"

"Oh, I know what you mean," said Gussy, clasping her hands; "and indeed it is no trouble to be good to Ada; we all love her so. Sometimes I feel as if it would be wicked to be very happy while she sits there—"

And they both turned to look at the sister who sat cheerful in the corner making little frocks. She was laughing at the moment, showing one of the Miss Veres how to shape a little sleeve. Gussy, who believed herself to stand on the very threshold of so different a world, felt her heart overflow with love and compassion. "Dear Ada," she said to herself; only schools and poor children's frocks for Ada, while she herself was to have every delight. Edgar's feelings were different. If circumstances were so to arrange themselves as that he should be Ada's brother, he would be very good to her. She would find in him a friend who would never alter, who would stand by her steadily, doing all that brother could do to make her lonely path more easy. Involuntarily there rose before Edgar the vision of an after-life, with new interests in it and new duties; a new race of Ardens curiously different from the old, a warm household place for Ada and for everybody, a centre of domestic kindness. That was what the house of a country gentleman, the natural head of a community, ought to be. He smiled over the imagination, and yet it came naturally and pleasantly to his mind. Gussy, who was not more than a pretty girl now, would be the sweetest, kindest, most charming matron—like her own mother, but younger, and prettier, and more sweet; and the house would be full of pleasant tumult and society. He did not quite clearly identify himself, but that was, perhaps, because of the laugh that gradually broadened in his eyes at the thought. And to think that this arose simply out of Ada's face in the corner, and the impulse of making life brighter for her! Then he roused up, and saw that Gussy was looking the same way, and that her pretty eyes were full of tears. How sweet, and good, and tender-hearted she was! They were women whom a man could trust his honour and happiness to without a doubt or fear. Never surely was there a stranger wooing. When their eyes met, Gussy blushed, and so did Edgar. Had they both been seeing in a vision the house that was not yet, the unborn faces, the unlighted fire? But then more visitors came in, and more tea was wanted, and nothing decisive could be said then and there. "I suppose you are going to the Lowestofts' to-night," Lady Augusta said, as he took leave of her; for she, too, saw clearly that nothing could possibly be settled in the drawing-room, under the eyes of all the family. "So it need not be good-bye yet. Of course we shall see you there."

And thus everything drew on towards the evident termination. If Edgar had been consulted on the subject before hand, he would have said that to enact his love drama, or at least its decisive scene, at a ball, would have been the very last thing in the world he was likely to do—just as it would have seemed absolutely impossible to him, had he foreseen it, to forestall love in the way which he was doing, and put affection in its place. But he did not seem to have any will of his own at all in the matter. He was pleasantly drawn on by a tide which carried him towards Gussy, which made her inevitable, and his position unmistakeable. Not only was it expected of him, but he expected himself to take this step. The only thing he was doubtful of was how to do it. He could not possibly say to a girl so charming and worthy of all homage that he was very fond of her, and yet did not love her in the least as a lover should. If he did, it would be an insult, not such a lovesuit as could be accepted. Therefore, he would be obliged to put aside his true feeling, and produce an utterly false one, out of compliment to her; and how was he to do it? All the rest he could do willingly, pleasantly, with perfect consent of his mind and affections; but how was he to be false to her, to pretend to feelings which were not his? This occupied his mind all the rest of the afternoon, and gave him the greatest possible trouble. And at the same time it was evident that the crisis had come, and that he must speak. He sent her a bouquet as the first step, which was very easy and pleasant. If it had been diamonds and rubies instead of flowers, he would have done it with still greater goodwill. He would give her anything, everything—Arden itself, and his liberty and his life; but how was he to get himself up to a lover's pitch of excitement, and offer her his heart?

CHAPTER XXV

The Lowestofts' ball was a very nice ball, everybody said. There were a great many people there. Indeed, everybody was there: the stairs were crowded and all the passages, and the dancers had scarcely room to move. To make your way up or down was almost as bad as going to Court. The way in which trains were damaged and trimmings torn off would have tried the temper of a saint. Nevertheless, the ladies bore it like heroines, smiling blandly, and protesting that it did not matter, even at the moment when their most cherished lace was being rent under their eyes. The mistress of the house stood at the top of the stairs, ready to drop with exhaustion, but grinning horribly a ghastly smile at everybody who approached her. A Royal Duke had come in for half-an-hour, and a German Prince, whom all the Lowestofts and all their friends treated with supreme contempt when they spoke of him; but yet, vis-a-vis of the Morning Post, were too proud and happy to see at their ball. Edgar Arden was one of those who traversed the crowd with the least ennui; but he could not refrain from making those remarks upon it which he was in the habit of making concerning the natural history and habits of the world of fashion. Edgar remarked that only a very few people looked really happy; and these were either the men and women who had some special love affair, innocent or otherwise, on hand, and had been able to appropriate the individual who interested them with that safety which belongs to a crowd; or else those upward climbers seeking advancement, to whom every new invitation into "the best society" was an object of as much elation as a successful battle. These two classes of persons rejoiced with a troubled joy; but the rest of the guests were either indifferent, or bored, or discontented. They had come because everybody was coming; they had come because they were invited; and it was part of the routine of life to go. Rage was boiling in their souls over their torn lace; or, with a sigh from the bottom of their hearts, they were dreaming of their favourite chair at the club, and all its delights. They said the same things over and over to the same people, whom, probably in the morning in the Row, or in the afternoon at half-a-dozen places, they had met and said the same things to before. Edgar stood for a long time half-way down the stair, and helped the ladies who were pushing their way up. He was waiting for Lady Augusta and her party, who were very late. He was waiting without any excitement, but with a little alarm, wondering if he could say anything to Gussy in the midst of such a crowd, or if still a breathing-time would be given to him. He did not want to elude that moment, but only it was so difficult to do it, so hard to know what to say. "That young Mr. Arden is very nice. I don't think I should ever have got upstairs without him," said more than one substantial chaperon. "He is waiting for the Thornleighs," the daughters would say. Everybody had decided Edgar's fate for him. Some people said it had been all settled before they came up from the country. And there could not be the least doubt that, if Edgar had let the season pass without saying anything to Gussy, he would have been concluded by everybody to have used her very ill.

And a great many speculations passed through Edgar's mind as he stood there and waited. Sometimes he witnessed such a meeting as ought to have been in store for himself. He saw the youth and maiden meet who were to get to the real climax in their romance by means of the Lowestofts' ball, and wondered within himself whether the outside world could see the same glow in his eyes which he could see in those of the other lover, or whether the same delightful atmosphere of consciousness enveloped Gussy as that which seemed to enclose the other girl in a rosy cloud. And he saw other pairs meet, not of youths and maidens; he saw gleams of strange fire which did not warm but burn; he saw the vacant looks of the mass, the factitious flutter of delight with which the dull crowd recognised its acquaintances. Lord Newmarch came up to him when he had occupied this perch for some time. "What are you doing here, of all places in the world? Are you going or coming? Oh, I see; you are waiting for the Thornleighs," he said; "they are generally in good time for a ball—"

"I am waiting because it is amusing here," said Edgar, careful even now that Gussy at least should not be discussed.

"Amusing!—the amusement must be in you, so I will stay by you," said Lord Newmarch; "probably some of it may come my way. What an odd fellow you are, to expect to be amused wherever you go, like a bumpkin at a fair! By the way, that reminds me, Arden, the people have a faculty for being amused which is wonderful; they are ready for it at all times and seasons, you know, not like us. It is a faculty which ought to be made use of for their improvement. I don't see why they shouldn't be educated in spite of themselves. The drama, for instance; now the drama has lost its hold on us—to us the play is a bore. We go to the opera to see each other, not to hear anything. But the people are all agog for anything in the shape of a play. What do you think? If the stage has any vigour left in it, instead of getting up sensation dramas for cads and shopkeepers—"

"But cads and shopkeepers are part of the people," said Edgar.

"No; that is not what I mean; I mean the real lower classes—the working men—our masters that are to be. How could they learn patriotism, not to say good sense, better than by means of Shakespeare? Poetry of the highest class is adapted to every capacity. What is secondary may have to be explained and broken down, but the highest—"

"I think I must ask you to let me pass," said Edgar, seeing the shadow of Lady Augusta's nose (which was prominent) on the wall close to the door. She was bringing in her daughters against a stream which was flowing out, and the struggle was very difficult, and demanded the greatest care.

"Oh, I suppose I am not wanted any longer," said Newmarch; "but, Arden, look here, I hope you mean to let me go to you for a day or two in September—eh? not for the partridges. Wait one moment. I should be glad of a quiet opportunity to speak to you by yourself—"

"Another time," said Edgar, extricating himself as best he could from the crowd.

"Wait one moment! I am free from the 20th of August. I will go to you as soon as you like—you know why I ask. Arden, remember I count upon your good offices—and then if my influence can be of any use to you—"

"Yes, precisely," said Edgar, swinging himself free. Lord Newmarch looked after him with a little metaphorical lifting up of hands and eyes. How simple the boy must be!—falling a hopeless victim to Gussy Thornleigh, his next door neighbour, when he had, so to speak, all England to choose from; for the suit of Arden of Arden was not one which was likely to fail, unless he fixed his fancy very high indeed. Lord Newmarch could not but reflect that in some things Arden had very greatly the advantage even of himself—there were so many people still who had a prejudice in favour of grandfathers, and his own grandfather, though the first Earl, could not, he was aware, bear discussing. Gussy Thornleigh, he reflected, was a very fortunate woman. She would have nothing, or next to nothing. Her sister Helena was one who, under more favourable circumstances, would have attracted Lord Newmarch himself; but he could not afford to throw himself away upon a girl who had nothing, and whose connections even were not of a kind to bring advancement. Nothing could be better than her family, no doubt; but then she had a quantity of brothers who would have to be pushed in the world, and no doubt the sisters' husbands would be called upon for aid and influence. Arden was the very sort of man to suffer himself to be so called on. He would be ready to help them and to get them out of all their scrapes. It was he who would be looked to when anything was the matter. In short, he was just the kind of man to marry a girl who was one of a large family. Lord Newmarch reflected that he himself was not so. He wanted all his influence, all his money, everything his position gave him, for himself or, at least, for his brothers. He even paused to ask himself whether, in case he should marry Clare Arden, he might not be appealed to as a connexion of the family for appointments, &c., for some of those Thornleigh boys. But Clare, he reflected, was not a good-natured fool like Edgar. She was one who knew what was due to a man's position, and that there were few who had anything to spare. Accordingly, he felt easy in his mind respecting that very far off danger. It was Clare who was the proper match for himself; and with a little shrug of his shoulders Lord Newmarch watched Edgar make his way through the crowd to where Lady Augusta, caught in an eddy, with all her train of girls, was struggling to get in, against the almost irresistible force of the torrent going out. Certainly, to come up to town for the purpose of making love to your next neighbour in the country was a waste of means indeed.

Meanwhile, Lady Augusta had seized on Edgar's arm with a sense of relief which made her heart glow with grateful warmth. It was another evidence of what a good son he would be, what a help in need. "I am so thankful to see you," she cried. "We are a little late, I know; but I never dreamt that people would be going so soon. There is a great ball in Eaton Square, I believe, to-night, given by some of those odious nouveaux riches; that is where everybody is flocking to." This was said loud enough to catch the ear of the crowd which was going out, and which had whirled Lady Augusta with it, and disordered the sweep of her train. She held Edgar fast while she made her way upstairs. She could not have done it without him, she said, and mourned audibly over her unfriended condition in the ear of her future son-in-law. "Harry promised to be looking out for us," she said; "but I suppose he is dancing, or something else that amuses him; and Mr. Thornleigh is never any use to us socially. He is always at the House."

"Does he go down to Thorne with you?" asked Edgar, meaning nothing in particular; but at present every word he spoke was marked and noted. No doubt, he wanted to make sure of being able to communicate with Gussy's father at once.

"No, he stays in town," said Lady Augusta, "for a few weeks longer;" and then she added, with an attempt at carelessness, "I am the family business-man, Mr. Arden. We have always one mind about the children and their concerns. He says it saves him so much trouble, and that without my help he could never do anything. It is pleasant when one's husband thinks so, who, of course, knows one's weaknesses best of all. Oh, what a business it is getting upstairs! Gussy, keep close to me, darling. Ada, I hope you are not feeling faint. Dear, dear, surely there must be bad management somewhere! I think I never saw such a crush in a private house."

Lady Lowestoft was nearer the top of the stair than usual, and took this criticism, which she had overheard, for a compliment. "A great number of our friends have been so good as to come to us," she said. "Dear Lady Augusta, how late you are! I fear the dear girls will scarcely get any dancing before supper. Did you meet the Duke as you came in? He is looking so well. It was very kind of him to come so early. I really must scold you for being a little late."

"What a fool that woman is," Lady Augusta whispered in Edgar's ear. "She very nearly compromised herself last season with your cousin Arthur Arden. He was never out of the house. A man without a penny, and whose character is so thoroughly well known! And then for one of those silly women who are really silly, a hundred other women get the blame of it, which is very hard, I think. Helena is always talking of such things, and it makes one think."

Thus Edgar was appropriated for a long time, until he had found a seat for Lady Augusta, and had placed Ada (who did not dance) by her side. When he had time to disengage himself, he saw both Gussy and Helena whirling about among the dancers; for they were popular girls, and always had partners. Thus the whole evening went past, and he found no opportunity for any explanation. Had he been able to monopolise Gussy's attention, and lead her away to a moderately-quiet corner, no doubt he would have delivered himself of what he had to say. But then it was not so very urgent. Had it been very urgent, of course he could have found the ways and means. He had one dance with her, but nothing could be said then; and though he proposed a walk into the conservatory, fate, in the shape of another partner, who carried her off triumphantly, interposed. And what could a man do more? He had been perfectly willing to make the full plunge, and in the meantime he watched over the whole family as if he had been their brother, and put Lady Augusta into her carriage afterwards, never really leaving them all the evening. If this was not to afficher himself, it would be hard to tell what more he could do. He held Gussy's hand after he put her in, and said something about calling next day. "Don't, please," Gussy had whispered hurriedly; "come when we are at Thorne. I know we shall all be at sixes and sevens to-morrow, and no time to talk." She, too, understood now quite calmly and frankly that this next visit must be more important than an afternoon call, and he pressed her hand as he whispered good-bye, feeling disposed to say to her, "What a dear, kind, reasonable girl you are; how well we shall understand each other, even though—" But he did not say this, more especially the "even though—" And he stood on the pavement and watched them drive away with a sensation of relief. He had quite made up his mind by this time, and did not intend to defer the crisis a moment longer than was necessary; but still, on the whole, he was pleased to feel that, whatever might happen afterwards, he was going back to Arden a free man.

CHAPTER XXVI

"Come into my dressing-room before you go to bed," Lady Augusta whispered in her daughter's ear. The sisters were in the habit of holding their own private assemblies at that confidential moment, and the three elder ones were just preparing for a consultation in Ada's room when Gussy received this summons. Of course she obeyed it dutifully, with her pretty hair hanging about her shoulders, in a pretty white dressing-gown, all gay with ribbons and embroidery. "I know mamma is going to ask me ever so many questions, and I have nothing to tell her," she said, pouting, as she left Ada and Helena. But Lady Augusta was very gentle in her questioning. "I think your hair is thicker than it used to be, my darling," she said, taking the golden locks in her hand with fond admiration. "Don't crêper more than you can help, for I always think it spoils the hair. Yours is more like what mine used to be than any of the others, Gussy. Helena's is like your papa's; but my hair used to be just your colour. Alas! it has fallen off sadly now."

"Your hair is a great deal prettier than mine," said Gussy, putting her caressing arm round her mother's neck. "I like that silver shade upon it. Hair gets so sweet when it gets grey—one loves it so. If you had not thought so much about us all, mamma dear, and had so many worries, you would not have had a white thread. I know it is all for us."

"Hush! my dear," said Lady Augusta; "you are all very good children. I have not had half so many worries as most people. It is in the family. The Hightons all grow grey early. You were looking very nice to-night. That blue becomes you; I always like you best in blue. Did you dance with Edgar Arden more than once, Gussy? I could not quite make out—"

"Only once, mamma."

"How was that? He was waiting for us to come in. I suppose you were engaged to half-a-dozen people before you got there. I don't like you to do that. If they don't come for you at the proper moment you are kept from dancing altogether, and look as if you were neglected; and if they do come, probably somebody else has made his appearance whom you would like better. I don't approve of engaging yourself so long in advance."

"But one goes to dance," said Gussy, with humility; "and to tell the truth, mamma, Mr. Arden likes looking after you quite as much as dancing with me. He likes to see that you are comfortable, and have some one pleasant to talk to, and don't want for anything. And I like him for it!" the girl cried, fervently. "He is of more use to you than Harry is. I like him because he is so fond of you."

"Nonsense, dear!" said Lady Augusta, with a pleased smile. "He is good to me on your account. And you must not say anything against Harry. Harry is always a dear boy; but he has a number of friends, and he knows I don't expect him to give up his own pleasure. Yes; Edgar Arden is very nice; I don't deny I am getting quite fond of him. Did he—had you any particular conversation with him, my darling, to-night?"

"No, mamma," said Gussy, with her eyes cast down, and a rising colour on her cheeks.

"Or perhaps he is coming to-morrow? Did he say anything about coming to-morrow?" said Lady Augusta, with a little anxiety in her tone.

"He asked me if he might, but I said no. I thought we would be in such confusion—everything packing up, and all our shopping to do, and so much bother—and then probably when he came nobody at home. And you know, mamma, we shall meet again so soon—next week," said Gussy, apologetically. As she spoke she began to feel that perhaps that little bit of maidenly reluctance had been a mistake; and Lady Augusta shook her head.

"My dear, I don't think putting off is ever good," she said. "When you have lived as long as I have you will know upon what nothings the greatest changes may turn. If he had come to-morrow, one needed no ghost to tell us what would have happened—but next week is a different thing, and the country is a different thing from town. There are seven miles between Arden and Thorne—there is Clare at the other end to hold him back—there are a thousand things; whereas, the present moment, you know—there is nothing like the present moment in all such affairs."

"If he cared so little for me," cried Gussy, indignant, "as to be kept back by seven miles—or even by Clare—"

"My dear, that is not the question," said her mother. "He has been with us here every day, but he can't ride over to Thorne every day. He will find business waiting for him, and his visitors will begin to come, and Clare—without meaning any harm—I am sure Clare would never put herself in opposition to you; she is a great deal too proud for that—but without meaning it she will make engagements for him, she will expect him to attend to her a little—and it is quite natural she should. I am very sorry you did not let him come. For my own part I should have liked to see him again. I am growing quite fond of him, Gussy. He is the sort of young man whom one can put such confidence in. I should have liked to ask his advice about Phil at Harrow. I should have liked—but of course it cannot be helped now. I think I will ask them both to come and spend a week with us at Thorne."

"Mamma!" cried Gussy, with a violent blush. "Oh, don't please; fancy inviting a man—any man—for the express purpose—Oh, please, for my sake, don't do such a thing as that!"

"Such a thing as what?" asked Lady Augusta, gravely. "Because you happen to have a little feeling on the subject, that is not to prevent me, I hope, from doing my duty to my nearest neighbours. Clare Arden has not paid us a visit since she went into mourning. And she really ought not to be encouraged to go on wearing black and shutting herself up in this absurd way. I will write and invite them to-morrow. Don't you see, autumn is approaching, and of course he has asked quantities of people—young men always do the first season, when they feel they have a house all to themselves. No, my dear, don't say anything. I know more of the world than you do, and I know there is nothing so perilous as letting such a thing drag on. He had better either ask you at once, or make it quite plain that he is not going to ask you; and much as I like him, Gussy, if this is not decided directly I shall certainly not invite him any more."

"Mamma, you make me so ashamed of myself," said Gussy. "If you ask him to Thorne for such a purpose I know I shall not be able to look at him. I will not be civil to him—I could not—so it will do more harm than good."

"I am not afraid that you will be uncivil," said Lady Augusta, with a smile, "but it was very foolish of you to say he was not to come. I can't think how you could do it. Sometimes, it is true, it is better for a man not to think he is too distinctly understood. Sometimes—But never mind, my dear, I see it is I who must manage matters now. Go and put up your hair, and go to bed—"

"But, oh, mamma, dear!" cried Gussy, with her arms round her mother's neck. "Don't! How could I ever speak to him when I knew—How could I ever look him in the face?"

"I hope you know how to conduct yourself towards all your papa's guests," said Lady Augusta, with dignity. "If you don't, I should feel that I must have brought you up very badly. I hear your papa's step coming along the corridor. Good night, my darling! Go to bed, and don't think any more of it; and be sure you don't let Angelique crêper your hair."

Thus dismissed, Gussy sped along the passage, and rushed in, breathless and indignant, yet not so indignant as she looked, into Ada's room, where her sisters were waiting for her. "Only fancy!" she cried, throwing herself into the nearest chair. "Only think what mamma is going to do! Because I would not let him come here to-morrow, when we will all be in such confusion, she is going to write and ask the Ardens to Thorne! I shall never be able to look him in the face. I shall feel he knows exactly what is meant—Oh! to think a man should be able to suppose one expects—He will think it is my doing—he will imagine I want him. Oh, Ada! what shall I do—"

"Hush, dear, hush!" said Ada, who was the consoler of the house; while Helena, in her rôle of indignant womanhood, took up Gussy's strain.

"He will think women are all exactly the same—that is what he will think—ready to compass sea and land for the sake of a settlement," cried Helena. If you loved him it would not be so bad—or if he thought you loved him; but it is for the settlement—it is because your trade is to get married. Don't you see, now, the justice of all I have been saying? If you could learn a profession like a man, men would never dare to think so. But the worst is, it is true. All that mamma thinks of is to get you settled at Arden—all she thinks of is to get you provided for—all she cares—"

"Helena!" cried Gussy, with a burst of tears. "I won't hear you say a single word against mamma."

"Hush—hush, both of you children!" said gentle Ada. "Nell, you must not storm; and, Gussy dear, I can't bear you to cry. What mamma does always comes out right. It may not be just what one could desire, nor what one would do one's self. But it always turns out better than one expects. Of course, she wants to see you provided for—isn't it her duty? She wants you to be happy and well off, and have the good of your life as she has. Nobody can say mamma has not done her duty. Sometimes it seems a little hard to others, but we all know—"

"Oh, you dear Ada!" cried both her sisters, taking the comforter between them, and weeping over her. But she, who was the martyr of the family, did not weep. She gave them a kiss, first one and then the other, and smiled at their girlish ready tears.

"I have never said very much about it," she said; "but I think I know Edgar Arden. He will not think anything disagreeable about mamma's invitation, if she sends it. He is not that kind of man; he is not always finding people out, like some of Harry's friends. He would not do anything that is nasty himself; and he would never suspect anybody else. It would not come into his head. And then he is fond of mamma and all of us. I am quite sure, as sure as if I had put it to the proof, that he would do anything for me if I were to ask him—not to speak of Gussy. And if that is really what he means—"

"I don't think you think it is," said Gussy, with a little flush of pride. "I am sure you don't think it is! Don't be afraid to speak quite plainly. You don't suppose I care—"

"But I do suppose you care," said Ada, giving her sister another sympathetic kiss. "We all care. I am fond of him, too. I should like to be quite sure he was to be my brother, Gussy—and I should like, for his sake, to make sure that you too—"

"Oh, it does not matter what a girl feels," said Gussy, pettishly, waving her pretty hair about her face, and concealing her looks behind it. "We have to marry somebody—and then there are so many of us. Mamma says I am not to crêper my hair; but if I don't, how can I ever make a show as everybody does? She would not like to see me different from other girls. Oh, me! I wish I was not a girl, obliged to take such trouble about how I look and what people will think; and obliged to wonder and bother and worry everybody about what some man is going to say next time I meet him. Oh, I cannot tell you how I hate men!"

"I don't hate them," said Helena. "Why should we? Treat them simply as your fellow-creatures. They have got to live in the world, and so have we. The only thing is that we need not try to make each other miserable. There is room enough for both of us. If they will only let me use my faculties, I will take care not to interfere with them. I am not afraid, for my part, to meet them upon equal terms—"

"Oh, I am so tired!" said Gussy. "I don't want to meet any one on equal terms. I never want to see one of the wretched creatures again. I wish somebody would shut them all up, and let us have a little peace. I wish somebody would come and do my hair. Nell, you have got nothing to vex you: if you do not mind a little trouble, please ring for Angelique—"

And then Gussy sat still with tolerable composure, and had her hair plaited up tight, and chattered about the Lowestofts' dance. Her mind, after all, was not seriously disturbed either by Edgar's silence or her mother's threatened invitation. Perhaps, indeed, on the whole, it would be rather pleasant than otherwise to have him at Thorne. He was so nice in a house; he was kind to everybody, always ready to make himself useful—a great deal more serviceable than Harry. And to be sure he had understood perfectly, and so had she, what would have been said if, amidst all the bother of packing, they had met to-morrow. It had not been spoken in words, but in everything else it was decided and settled. Gussy fell into silence after a while, and let the idea of him glide pleasantly, tenderly through her mind. He was not a man who would be like papa, absorbed in his estate, and his sessions, and his game. He would not be selfish, as Harry sometimes was. He could not help being thoughtful of other people, tender of everybody belonging to him. There had been moments when Gussy had entertained a certain harmless envy of Clare's supremacy. But she envied her no longer—though Queen Gussy would be a different kind of ruler from Princess Clare.

CHAPTER XXVII

While all these discussions were going on in Berkeley Square, Edgar was preparing in the most leisurely and easy-minded way for his return home. He had forgotten the urgency of Clare's letter, but he was glad to emancipate himself from the social treadmill which he did not understand, and set his face again towards the fair green country and his duties and his home. It seemed so rational a life in comparison that he had even a higher opinion of himself when he turned his back upon town and its amusements. Not for anything bad he had encountered there; the wickedness had not thrust itself upon him—his own temper and thoughts leaving him out of harmony with it; but the foolishness had struck him with double force. Wickedness itself is better than no meaning, at least it is less contemptible, less bewildering, more comprehensible. He was not only going home, but he was about to change the fashion of his life, to begin who could tell what alterations in everything about him; and a little gentle excitement was in his mind; not any impassioned sentiment, not any whirlwind of fear and hope. He could not even say to himself that the happiness of his life depended on Gussy's reply, or on the chance whether or not she would share the rest of his life with him. But still the thought of so sweet a companion moved him with a little thrill of pleasurable emotion. There was still the chance that he should meet them the next day, a chance which Lady Augusta did not take into consideration; and as the shopping occupied the girls and withdrew them from the usual regions of society, the fact was that he did not meet them anywhere, and found the day hang very heavy on his hands in consequence. When he fell suddenly upon Ada late in the afternoon, returning accompanied by her maid from a visit to some "Sisters" with whom she was allied, Edgar brightened up instantly. He came to her side, and insisted on walking with her across the Park. She had very little to say, except at moments when her sympathy was in forcible requisition, and was not in the least an amusing companion. But he did his best to talk to her, and showed her clearly how glad he was to see her. "I was told I was not wanted at Berkeley Square to-day," he said, "which has been very doleful for me. I shall ride over to Thorne on Tuesday and bid you welcome home." "I am sure mamma will be pleased to see you," said gentle Ada; and she, too, went home a little excited by the encounter. "He said he would ride over on Tuesday to bid us welcome," she repeated to Lady Augusta the moment she entered. "So, perhaps, mamma, you will not require to send that invitation which troubles Gussy so much. It is best when these things come of themselves." "So it is, my dear," said Lady Augusta. "I knew he was the nicest fellow! he shall stay to dinner if he comes." And so that matter was settled. Gussy even made up her mind what dress she would put on to meet him on that eventful afternoon, which probably would decide her fate. Her mother liked her best in blue, and so she decided did he, for had he not once said—So Gussy made a mental memorandum, and felt a warm little thrill of tender kindness at her heart for the man who loved her. Of course he loved her. She might have other inducements to marry him. The charm of Arden, the necessity of being provided for, the trade, as Helena called it, of getting married, would all weigh consciously or unconsciously with her. But with him there could be but one reason—love; and Gussy's heart swelled with that tender gratitude and kindness and half pity with which a woman whose affections are quite free and disengaged often regards the man who has (as people say) fallen in love with her. Pity, she could not tell why, a soft half regret that she could not give him so much as he gave her. "Poor, dear boy!" she said to herself; and then shyly peeping, as it were, behind a veil, found out that she might love him too, could be very fond of him after—when—And she caressed her blue dress with a smile and a little emotion, and looked that the ribbons were fresh that must be worn with it, before Angelique packed it away. "Mamma likes me in blue," she said with a conscious smile. Alas!—But nobody knew nor suspected how little the blue dress would be thought of, or how different the reality and the imagination would be!

Edgar went down next morning to his nearest railway station with an absolute absence of every exciting incident. The groom was waiting with his dogcart, the western sun threw a slanting line on the country, everything looked like home-coming and peace. "Is all right at the Hall?" he asked for mere custom's sake, as he took the reins. "Yes, sir, so far as I know, sir, but Mrs. Fillpot, she thinks there's something to do with Miss Arden," said the groom. "Something to do?" Edgar echoed, unfamiliar with the homely phrase. "Poorly, sir, she thinks, does Mrs. Fillpot," said the man. A headache, I suppose, Edgar thought to himself, and drove on without alarm. How fresh the country was, how green the trees, how restful all those houses, the villagers at their doors, the village patriarchs working leisurely in their little gardens. Even the Red House as he passed it blinked and shone in the sunshine, offering him a certain welcome. Was Arthur Arden there still, he wondered, and how was his suit progressing, and what did Alice Pimpernel think of it? Had she said, "Oh yes, Mr. Arden," to his kinsman's wooing? All these things passed through Edgar's mind as he drove along with a smile upon his face, and the pleasant confidence of a man going home. He was glad to recognise the very trees, much more the familiar faces; glad to think of his sister's welcome which awaited him—full of natural satisfaction and content.

The first shadow that crossed him was at the corner of the road which led to the Red House. There he paused for a moment, hearing behind him a sudden rush and din upon the road, the sound as of horses that had run away. Then they appeared in sight, tearing onward, coming full speed towards him, making his own horse plunge and struggle between the shafts. Edgar flung the reins to his groom, and jumped down instantly to see if he could be of use—but had not touched the ground when they rushed past him—Mr. Pimpernel's bays, a high-spirited, high-fed, excitable pair. The reins were flying loosely about their necks, the horses were half-mad with fright and agitation, and a succession of screams proved, if the gleam of feminine dress had not been enough to do so, that the light waggon had not its ordinary passengers, but was driven by a lady. It swept round the corner like a whirlwind, and Edgar with hopeless horror rushed after. As he did so, he perceived two figures running wildly across a field, in advance, to cut off their progress. It was Mr. Pimpernel and Arthur Arden. Edgar stopped, seeing how hopeless was an idea of being of use, and watched with breathless interest the course of the two men who might yet be in time. Then there was a plunge—a shriek—the appearance as of something falling, like the flight of a bird or an arrow, from the high seat to the ground. Edgar shut his eyes involuntarily with a movement of sympathetic pain. When he opened them again, the horses were standing trembling and panting, with the groom at their heads, who had appeared, he could not tell how or whence; and Mr. Pimpernel and Arthur Arden were standing each by a little particoloured heap on the roadside. A sudden wild fancy that Clare might have been one of the sufferers came into Edgar's mind, and he called to his man to follow him, and hastened up to the scene of the accident. When he reached it, he found Mr. Pimpernel, pale as death and trembling, lifting up his daughter, who had been thrown upon a mossy bank at the foot of the hedge. Alice was ghastly, with little streams of blood trickling down her forehead; but she was conscious, and not apparently severely injured. "It is nothing, papa; I am only scratched and shaken, that is all," she was saying, while her father, too much agitated to understand, dragged her up in his arms and overwhelmed her with incoherent questions. Edgar ran and brought her water from a pool close by, which was not of the clearest, and yet sufficed to wash the trickling drops off her forehead, and lessen her father's apprehensions. And then he produced his travelling flask of sherry, which revived her still more completely. It did not occur to him even that there was another sufferer, nor that his cousin whom he had seen a moment before was lending no assistance here. "See, I can stand—I am not hurt, papa; I am only shaken," Alice was repeating, till Edgar almost loved her for her pertinacity. The father was totally helpless and overcome. "My girl, my child!" he was repeating, with white lips, drawing her into his arms. "I do not think she is hurt, sir," said Edgar, whose impressionable heart was touched. "Let us put her into my dogcart, and my groom will drive her gently home." "Yes, yes, that is best," said Alice. "Papa, you hurt me; but, oh! I am not injured—I am only aching and shaken—and, oh, papa!—"

"What is it?" cried Edgar, seeing her anxious glance round.

"Jeanie!" The name sounded like a cry; and then, all at once, the whole party were aware of Arthur Arden making his way towards the nearest cottage with something in his arms. Even Mr. Pimpernel grew silent in his anxiety. Alice shivered violently, and fell back upon Edgar, who put out his arm to support her with a sudden spasm of pain and terror in his heart. No moan nor cry came from the thing in Arthur Arden's arms. Was it Jeanie who lay thus, in a heap, silent, undistinguishable? Alice shuddered more and more, and fell down on her knees, and began to cry; while old Pimpernel, in his excitement, rose and said—"If anything has happened to her, I will shoot those damned horses, and that damned fool. But for him, curse him, it would never have happened." Edgar felt as if he had been suddenly turned to stone. What was Jeanie to him that her peril should so move him? It was the horror of it, done as it were before his eyes. And then her grandmother—While Alice wept and her father stormed, Edgar felt his very heart grow sick. "Take her home," he said peremptorily to Mr. Pimpernel, who, stilled in his excitement by any sudden voice of authority, humbly obeyed. Between them they lifted Alice, still weeping and moaning, into the dogcart, and slowly and steadily she was driven home to the Red House. Edgar drew a long breath of relief when she was gone; and then he turned with the silent speed of excitement after Arthur Arden to the cottage door.

There, there was nothing but excitement and commotion. One neighbour had gone already for Dr. Somers; another was carrying water to bring the sufferer to herself. One woman shook her head and said—"I saw her face, and it's the face of death; she'll never come round." "Hold your tongue," said another; "she's as like life as you or me; she'll come round fast enough if you'll hold your noise and look after the children." "Little the children's din will hurt her," said a third. Was Jeanie killed? All in a moment, the harmless, gentle little creature, had she been dashed into the unknown world? As this thought went through Edgar's mind, he heard a little stir among the gossips—a silence, and rustle of all their dresses as they stood back instinctively. "It is her grandmother," they said; and immediately after Mrs. Murray, very pale and steadfast, suddenly passed through the crowd. How Edgar's heart yearned over the old woman whom he knew so little of—who was nothing to him! Admiration, pity, something more deep than either, swept over him. This poor woman who had done so much, who had taken upon her so many burdens, was this the reward God was about to give for all her toils and trials?—her child snatched from her in a moment, in the twinkling of an eye. The other was safe, who, herself and all belonging to her, had thought of nothing but their own pleasure and profit, all their lives. And it was this woman who had suffered and toiled, and spent her life for others, who was to open her breast again and receive the cruellest blow. Strange compensation, reward, and encouragement! Edgar attempted to enter two or three times, but was kept back by the crowd. "Lord bless you, sir, you can't do no good," they said to him. "There's one gentleman there already, and better they'd be without him." Somehow it was a kind of comfort to think that Arthur Arden was in the way, and of no use. It made even Edgar more patient as he stood without, waiting for his dogcart, and brooding over those strange imperfections of life. One taken, and the other left. But why Jeanie—why the old mother's one comfort and consolation? When the dogcart arrived he sent it off in search of the doctor. He forgot all about Clare and her anxiety, and thought of nothing but the dead or dying girl.

After a while Arthur Arden came out, very pale, with a tremor and suppressed agitation that was pitiful to see. His mind was not even sufficiently disengaged to be surprised at this sudden appearance of his cousin. He put out his hand to Edgar unconsciously, with a certain appeal to his sympathy. "It was my fault," he said hoarsely. And thus the two stood, almost clinging together till the dogcart rattled past over the bit of causeway, bringing the doctor. Arthur put his arm within Edgar's in the excitement of the moment. "If she dies," he repeated hoarsely, with large drops standing on his forehead, "it will be my fault."

CHAPTER XXVIII

How did it happen?—a question so easy to ask—recalling so often in the midst of the most tragic seriousness a moment of utter levity, gaiety, and carelessness—a light impulse for which never all his life long will some one forgive himself. "It was my fault," Arthur Arden explained, with a voice choked and broken. "I had driven Miss Pimpernel to the station to meet her father, and we met and stopped to talk to Jeanie on the way. We talked to her, and offered her carelessly a drive when we came back. On the way back we found her still on the same spot. I got down to speak to her, and so did old Pimpernel—Heaven knows why! Then there was some talk about this drive. She did not understand us—she had no intention of coming. It was I who almost lifted her into the carriage. I had my foot on the step to mount after her, when Alice seized the reins, and dashed on. Don't ask me any more. And now, God help us, that innocent creature is dying—and it is my fault—"

"It is more Miss Pimpernel's fault," said Edgar, but he turned from his kinsman with a dislike and sense of repulsion which he could hardly explain. Arthur, on the contrary, clung to him with painful anxiety. "Don't leave me until we hear," he cried. He kept his arm within Edgar's, holding him fast, feeling him to be a defence against the Pimpernels, against Mrs. Murray, against even the sour looks of Dr. Somers, when he should come. No doubt, Arthur felt, the whole world would blame him, and consider Jeanie as his victim. The Pimpernels would forsake him, and Clare—"Arden," he said, with sudden weakness, "I have had a great deal to annoy me since you went away. These people, the Pimpernels, invited me after a while, and I stayed, thinking—I don't hesitate to say, for you know—thinking I should be near your sister. And Clare has behaved to me—"

"Hush, for Heaven's sake," said Edgar, angrily. "I will have nothing said of Clare. Let us see what comes of this business in the first place—it is enough for the moment."

"You blame me," said Arthur; "of course I knew you would blame me. But, as you have said yourself, it was that fool of a girl who was to blame. Good God! how could she drive these fiery brutes—I told her it was impossible. If it had only been herself she had killed, and not poor Jeanie—little Jeanie."

"For Heaven's sake, be silent!" cried Edgar, furiously, trying to shake off the hand on his arm. Excitement and apprehension had produced upon Arthur the effect of wine. His nerves were so shaken that he almost wept as he repeated Jeanie's name. Remorse, and anxiety, and pity, which were as much for himself as for any of the others, unmanned him altogether. He was deeply distressed for the girl whom his folly had helped to place in such jeopardy, but he was also distressed for himself, wondering and asking himself what he should do, how he should ever free himself from the consequences of such a misfortune. Clare was lost unless her brother interposed; and though he was innocent, surely, in respect to Alice Pimpernel, she was lost too, with her thirty thousand pounds. And Jeanie, poor little innocent victim, was probably dying. No gratification to himself or his vanity could be got out of further pursuit of her. This selfish compunction was but the undercurrent, it is true. Above that was a stream of genuine grief and distress for the suffering creature; but he had thought of himself too long to be able altogether to dismiss the consideration now.

Half the village had gathered about the door when the dogcart which played so large a part in the scene dashed up again, bringing Dr. Somers. Of all houses in the world it was the cottage of Sally Timms, the one nearest the end of the village, into which Jeanie had been carried. Sally was as prompt and ready of resource as she was thriftless and untidy; but the surrounding villagers did not respect her house sufficiently to keep out of it, or to keep silent. The Doctor dispersed them with a few sharp words. "Take those children away instantly, and keep the place quiet, or I'll bring Perfitt down upon you," he said emphatically. Perfitt's name did what Perfitt's master had not thought of doing. And Edgar immediately bestirred himself to second the Doctor. He partly coaxed, partly frightened the crowd away; while Arthur stood gloomily leaning against the little garden gate chewing the cud of very bitter reflections. Then there was a long pause, a pause of intense expectation. The women who had been sent away watched from the corner and from their own doors for the reappearance of the Doctor. The children slunk away into distant groups, now and then seduced into a shout or gambol, which was instantly put a stop to by some indignant spectator. The very birds and insects seemed to pause, the leaves rustled less loudly. A stranger seeing so many silent spectators all with their eyes turned towards the cottage door, all in such a stillness of suspense, would have found the scene very difficult to interpret. The dogcart stood at the corner of the road with the groom in it gathering up the reins close in his hands, and ready to rush anywhere for whatever might be wanted. Edgar stood in the middle of the dusty road with a sense that if he approached a step nearer the very sound of his step might disturb the patient. And Sally Timms' youngest child, awe-stricken and silent, sat in the dust and gazed up with wide-open eyes at Arthur Arden leaning upon the garden gate.

At length Dr. Somers came out, and everybody made one sudden step forward. He held out his hands warning them off. "No noise," he said; "no excitement. Silence—quiet is everything. Come with me and I will tell you what to do."

She will live if all this care has to be taken, was the thought that past like lightning through Arthur Arden's mind, and he recovered his courage a little. The two cousins followed the Doctor towards the little conclave of women at the corner. "Now, look here," he said, making an address to the community in general, "that poor child is lying between life and death. She may go any moment; but if you will keep everything quiet, and those confounded children of yours, and keep away from the house, and stop all noises, we may bring her through yet."

"God bless you, sir!" cried old Sarah, who was present with her girls, crying and curtseying. The other women were silent, and perhaps not so much impressed. They were ready to give any amount of wondering attentive sympathy, but to keep their children quiet was another matter. One rushed away out of the circle with a baby which was beginning to cry; another administered a private box on the ear to an urchin who had no thoughts of making any noise. But yet they murmured a little in their hearts.

"The Doctor means," said Edgar, "that the poor girl is a stranger, and that all you Arden folks are too friendly and kind to mind a little trouble. You shall send the children to play in the park, and the men will help me to have straw put over the causeway at once. Where is John Hesketh? I know you will all do your very best."

"And that we will, Squire," cried the women. There was nothing in this speech about "confounded children." But the results to the children were more terrible than anything proposed by the Doctor. The mothers made a general rush at them, and put them to bed. "Bless you, it's the only place they're quiet," cried one and another; and Edgar, hurrying to the house of the most respected inhabitant of Arden, got a little party organised at once to lay down straw upon the road. He went with them himself, eager and busy, while Arthur stood at the corner with the Doctor. "Just like him," Dr. Somers said, "and very unlike the Ardens. Was it he that helped on this catastrophe, that he is so anxious and busy now?"

"No," said Arthur, without seeing the full meaning of the question; "he had nothing to do with it. It was I who was to blame."

"Ah! I thought so," cried Dr. Somers, rubbing his hands together with a suppressed chuckle. His professional gravity was over for the moment, having lasted as long as was necessary; and now he was at leisure to indulge in his ordinary speculations.

"Why did you think so?" asked Arthur, coldly.

"Because you are a true Arden, and you are taking no trouble about it," was the reply; and Dr. Somers went on, after he had discharged this shaft, with an inward satisfaction not unnatural in the circumstances. It was not that he was indifferent to poor Jeanie's fate; but he was used to danger, and was not awe-stricken by it, as are the inexperienced. Even while he walked up the side-path into the village street he was turning over with professional seriousness and anxiety what measures it would be best to take—pondering closely which was most suitable; but he could not refuse himself the pleasure of shooting that javelin. It did not do Arthur Arden any great harm, and it relieved him about Jeanie more than a more favourable judgment of her case would have done. In his ignorance he concluded that a doctor could not jibe at other men if his patient was in very great danger; and as for the straw and so forth, that was in Edgar's way, not his. Edgar was the master, and free to order what he pleased; and, besides, was a commonplace being, who naturally thought of such matters of detail. So long as Jeanie was not going to die, that was all that absolutely affected him. And heaven knows, being relieved of that first dread, he had enough on his hands and his mind. There were the Pimpernels, whom he would have to face with the consciousness that he had been instrumental in risking their daughter's life, or, at least, in putting her in circumstances to risk it; and—what was still worse—that he had thought nothing of Alice, done nothing for her, had not even inquired if she was badly hurt or in danger. This last reflection disconcerted him wholly. He could not hasten to the Red House, as he had intended, to show a tardy but still eager sympathy, while still he was unaware what had happened to Alice. He had to hasten after his cousin, who knew all about her, pursuing him to the home-farm and the stacks, where he was loading his volunteer labourers, and losing the precious time which he ought to have spent in smoothing down the Pimpernels. "Wait a little; I have no time to speak to you," Edgar said to him. "I am busy; watch the road that no carts pass till we are ready—" What were all these ridiculous details to him? The girl was not going to die; and how was he to face the Pimpernels?

"Miss Pimpernel? She is not much hurt. I sent her home in the dogcart; but, Arden, don't go—look after the road," Edgar managed to shout to him at last across the farmyard. Arthur took no further thought about keeping Jeanie quiet—except, indeed, that he gave Johnny Timms sixpence to stand and watch at the corner of the road. Edgar, however, was on the spot before he had gone quite away. He saw the work proceeding as he turned in at the gate of the Red House, and asked himself, with a half sneer at his cousin, a half wonder for himself, what made the difference? Edgar had nothing to do with the accident, and yet was taking all this trouble to repair it; whereas he, who was really involved in it, after the first moment, never dreamed of taking any trouble. What was the use, indeed, of thus troubling one's self about others? He had been weakly, foolishly compunctious at the first moment. Why could he not have left Jeanie to Edgar? Why should he have concerned himself at all about her? Why for her sake, a girl who had never even given him a smile, should he have committed himself thus with the Pimpernels? Arthur Arden cursed his own folly, and the impulse which had made him snatch up Jeanie in his arms instead of Alice. Edgar was there, who would have done it, and taken all the responsibility; and such a piece of Quixotism would not harm Edgar. There was the difference—not in the nature, as that insolent Doctor insinuated, but in the fact that Edgar could afford to be helpful, and liberal, and generous—that it could do him no harm. Whereas he, Arthur, dependent upon circumstances—obliged to keep on good terms with this one, to curry favour with that, to consider how everything would affect his own interests—did not venture to be helpful and sympathetic. That was the true explanation of the whole. A man, when he is rich, can afford to be better, kinder, more self-forgetting than a man who is poor; and, above all, the man who lives by his wits, is the man least capable of sacrifices for others. Arthur Arden was very sorry for himself as he went reluctantly, yet quickly, through the shrubberies of the Red House. He knew he had a mauvais quart d'heure before him. However eager or anxious he might manage to look, he knew very well that the father and mother would never forgive him for having left their child to take her chance, while he cared for the little village girl. He cursed his unhappy impulsiveness as he approached the house of the Pimpernels. Taking trouble about other people was always a mistake, unless they were people who could repay that care. Could not he have left Jeanie alone to take her chance? Was not Jeanie somehow at the bottom of Clare's caprice, which had thrown out all his calculations a week ago? And now again, no doubt, she had ruined him with the Pimpernels. Poor Arthur Arden!—if he had been the Squire he would have been above all these miserable calculations—all these apprehensions and regrets. The least sympathetic spectator could scarcely have refrained from a sentiment of pity for the unfortunate schemer as he crossed the threshold of the Red House.

VOLUME III

CHAPTER I

"How is Miss Pimpernel?" Arthur asked as he entered the house. He went in with a great appearance of anxiety and haste, and he repeated his question to a maid who was just preparing to ascend the stairs. The footman had given him no answer—a fact which he did not even observe; and the maid made him a little curtsey, and cast down her eyes, and looked confused and uncomfortable. "My mistress is coming, sir," she said; and Arthur, looking up, saw that Mrs. Pimpernel herself was advancing to meet him. He saw at the first glance that there was to be war, and war to the knife, and that conciliation was impossible. "How is Miss Pimpernel?" he asked, taking the first word. "I was so glad to see she was able to move at once; but I fear she must have been much shaken, at least."

Mrs. Pimpernel came downstairs upon him before she made any answer. She bore down like a conquering ship or a charge of cavalry. Her face was crimson; her eyes bright with anger; her head was agitated by a little nervous tremble. "Mr. Arden," she said, rushing, as it were, into the fray, "I don't think Miss Pimpernel would have been much the better for you, whatever had happened. I don't think from what I have heard, that your kind service would have been much good to her. To tell the truth, when I heard some one asking, I never thought it could be you."

"Miss Pimpernel fortunately, had no need of my services," said Arthur firmly, standing his ground. "I cannot tell you what a relief it was to me to find her unhurt."

"Unhurt, indeed!" said Mrs. Pimpernel. "Who says she is unhurt? A delicate young creature thrown from a high phæton like that, and all but trampled under the horses' feet! And whose fault was it, Mr. Arden? I hope I shall have patience to speak. Whose fault was it, I say? And then to find herself deserted by those that ought to have taken care of her! All for the sake of a designing girl—an artful little cheat and hussy—a—a—"

"I am not the girl's defender," said Arthur Arden. "She may be all you say, and it is quite unimportant to me; but I thought she was killed, and Mr. Pimpernel and my cousin Edgar Arden were with your daughter."

"Ah, Mr. Arden!" said Mrs. Pimpernel, "he is a gentleman—he is a true gentleman, notwithstanding all the nonsense you have been putting in Mr. Pimpernel's head. And I tell you I don't believe a word of it—not a word! Mr. Arden is what he always was, and you are a poor, mean, shabby adventurer, poking into people's houses, and making yourself agreeable, and all that. Yes! I'll make you hear me! that I shall! I tell you you are no better than a—"

"Is it necessary that John and Mary should assist at this explanation?" said Arthur. He smiled, but he was very pale. He said to himself that to attach any importance to the words of such a woman would be folly indeed; but yet shame and rage tore him asunder. A lady would not have condescended to abuse him. She would have treated him with deadly civility, and given him to understand that his room was wanted for another guest. But Mrs. Pimpernel had not been trained to habits of conventional decorum. Her face was red, her head trembled with rage and excitement. She had suffered a great deal in silence nursing her wrath—and now there was no longer any need to restrain herself. Now, Mr. Pimpernel himself was convinced, and Alice was indignant. He had been making use of them, trifling with them, taking advantage of the shelter of their house to carry on first one "affair" and then another. Had it been Clare Arden who had at this last crowning moment led him away from Alice, the affront would have been bitter, but not so unpardonable. But a girl out of the village, a nobody, an artful—Words forsook Mrs. Pimpernel's burning lips. She felt herself no longer able to stand and pour forth her wrath. She made a dash at the door of Mr. Pimpernel's library, and sat down, calling the culprit before her, with a wave of her hand. Arthur went in; but he shut the door, which was not what she had wanted. A certain moral support was in the fact that she stood, as it were, in the open centre of her own house, speaking loud enough to be heard by her husband and daughter above, and by the servants below stairs. But Mrs. Pimpernel, notwithstanding her courage, did not feel so comfortable when she found herself shut into the silence of a separate room, with Arthur Arden, pale and composed, and overwhelmingly gentlemanly, before her, and not even the presence of John or Mary to give her strength. It was a strategical mistake.

"I am glad to say it does not matter to me who hears me," she said. "Let those be ashamed that have acted shabby, and shown themselves what they are. For my part, I couldn't have believed it. To creep into a house, and live on the best of everything, and carriages and horses and all at your command—I should have been ashamed to do it. No man would have done it that was better than an adventurer—a mean, miserable—"

"Mrs. Pimpernel," said Arthur, "you have been very civil and friendly, asking me to your house, and I have done my best to repay it in the way that was expected. Pray don't suppose I am ignorant it was an affair of barter—the best of everything, as you say, and the carriages, &c., on one side; but on my side a very just equivalent. Let us understand each other. What am I supposed to have done amiss? Of course, our mutual accommodation is over, after this scene—but I should be glad to know, before I accept my dismissal, what I am supposed to have done amiss—"

"Equivalent! Accommodation! Oh you!—Without a penny to bless yourself with—and living on the fat of the land—Champagne like water, and everything you could set your face to. And now you brazen it out to me. Oh you poor creature! Oh you beggarly, penniless—"

"Pray let us come to particulars," said Arthur; "these reproaches are sadly vague. Come, things are not so bad after all. You expected me to be your attendant, a sort of upper footman, and I have been such. You expected me to lend the name of an Arden to all your junketings, and I have done it. You expected me, perhaps—But I don't want to bring in the name of Miss Pimpernel—"

"No, don't—if you dare!" cried the mother. "Mention my child, if you dare. As if she was not, and hadn't always been, a deal too good for you. Thirty thousand pounds of her own, and as pretty a girl and as good a girl—Oh, don't you suppose she cares! She would not look at you out of her window, if there was not another man; she would never bemean herself, wouldn't my Alice. You think yourself a great man with the ladies, but you may find out your mistake. Your cousin won't see you, nor look at you—you know that. Oh, you may start! She has seen through you long ago, has Miss Arden—and if you thought for a moment that my Alice—Good gracious!—to think a man should venture to look me in the face, after leaving my child to be killed, and going after a—Don't speak to me! Yes, I know you. I always saw through you. If it hadn't been for Mr. Pimpernel, and that sweet angel upstairs—"

And here Mrs. Pimpernel paused, and sobbed, and shed tears—giving her adversary the advantage over her. She was all the more angry that she felt she had wasted her words, and had not transfixed and made an end of him, as she had hoped—as she had meant to do. To see him standing there unsubdued, with a smile on his face, was gall and wormwood to her. She choked with impotent rage and passion. She could have flown at him, tooth and claw, if she had not put force on herself. Arthur felt the height of exasperation to which he was driving her, and, perhaps, enjoyed it; but nothing was to be made by continuing such a struggle.

"I am sorry to have to take my leave of you in such a way," he said, in his most courteous tone. "I shall explain to Mr. Pimpernel how grieved I am to quit his house so abruptly; but after this unfortunate colloquy, of course there is no more to be said. It is a pity to speak when one is so excited—one says more always than one means. Many thanks to you for a pleasant visit, such as it has been. You have done your best to amuse me with croquet and that sort of thing. Society, of course, one cannot always command. My man will bring over my things to—Arden in the course of the day. I trust that if we meet in the county, as we may perhaps do, that we shall both be able to forget this little passage of arms. Good-bye, and many thanks, Mrs. Pimpernel."

Mrs. Pimpernel gave a little stammering cry of passion and annoyance. She had never calculated upon her prey escaping so easily. She had not even meant to dismiss him entirely, but only to subdue him, and bring him under discipline. After all, he was an Arden, and going to Arden—as he said—and might procure invitations to Arden, probably, notwithstanding her affirmation about Clare. But Arthur left her no time for repentance. He withdrew at once when he had discharged this parting shot, closing the door after him, and leaving the panting, enraged woman shut up in that cool and silent place to come to herself as she best might. He was a little pleased with his victory, and satisfied to think that he had had the best of it. The maid was still standing outside, listening near the door, when he opened it suddenly. "Your mistress is a little put out, Mary," he said to her, with a smile. "Perhaps it would be better to leave her to herself for a few minutes. I hope Miss Pimpernel is not really hurt. Tell her I am grieved to have to go away without saying good-bye." And then he stopped to give John directions about his things, and distributed his few remaining sovereigns among them with fine liberality. The servants had grinned at his discomfiture before, but they grinned still more now at the thought of their mistress weeping with rage in the library, and her visitor escaped from her. "He was always quite the gentleman," Mary said to John, as he left the house; and they laid their heads together over the discomfiture that would follow his departure. Thus Arthur Arden shook the dust of the Red House from his feet, and went out upon the world again, not knowing where he was to go.

And his thoughts were far from cheerful, as he made his way among the shrubberies, which sometimes had looked to him like prison walls. Poor Alice and her thirty thousand pounds had always been something to fall back upon. If Clare did not relent, and would not explain herself, a man must do something—and though it was letting himself go very cheap, still thirty thousand pounds was not contemptible. And now that was over—the hope which after all had been his surest hope—all (once more) from thinking of other people's rather than of his own interests. What was Jeanie to him? She had never given him a kind word or smile. She was a child—a bloodless being—out of whom it was impossible to get even a little amusement. Yet for her sake here was thirty thousand pounds lost to him.

And probably she would go and die, now that she had done him as much harm as possible, leaving it altogether out of his power to do her any harm, or compensate himself in the smallest degree. And in the meantime where was he to go? Arthur's funds were at a very low ebb. All this time which he had been wasting in the country he had been out of the way of putting a penny in his pocket; and for the moment he did not know what he was to do? He had said he was going to Arden, partly to impose on Mrs. Pimpernel, partly with a sudden sense that to throw himself upon Edgar's hospitality was about the best thing on the cards for him. Might he venture to go there at once, and risk welcome or rejection? At the very worst they could not refuse to take him in till Monday. But then it would be better to secure himself for longer than Monday—and Clare was very uncompromising, and Edgar firm, notwithstanding his good nature. Altogether the position was difficult. He had been making great way with the Pimpernels since Clare had shut her doors upon him. There had been nothing to disturb him, nothing to divide his allegiance, and therefore he had been utterly unprepared for this sudden derangement of plans. The Pimpernels, too, were utterly unprepared. His hostess had meant to "set him down," as she said, "to show him his proper place," to "bring him to his senses," but she had never intended the matter to be concluded so promptly. The discomfiture on both sides was equally great. He took a little pleasure in the thought of this, but yet it did not enlighten him as to where he was to go.

The conclusion of the matter was that for that night he went to the Arden Arms. Edgar had disappeared when he returned to the village, and all was quiet and silent. Arthur met Dr. Somers going down to the cottage in which Jeanie still was. The Doctor shook his head, but would not say much. "She is young, and she may pull through, if the place is kept quiet," was all the information he would give. But he asked Arthur to dinner, which was a momentary relief to him, and Arthur recounted to him, with many amusing details, the history of his dismissal by the Pimpernels. The Doctor chuckled, partly because it was a good story, and made the Pimpernels ridiculous, and partly because Arthur Arden, though he put the best possible face upon it, must have been himself discomfited. "Serve him right," the Doctor said within himself; but he asked him to dinner, and saved him from the horrors of a chop at the Arden Arms and a solitary evening in its little sanded parlour, which was a work of true benevolence—for Dr. Somers' dinner and his claret would have been worthy of notice anywhere—much more when contrasted with the greasy attractions of a chop at the Arden Arms.

CHAPTER II

While Arthur went to the Red House, Edgar had been exerting himself to still all the roads and deaden every sound about Sally Timms' cottage. Sally's boys considered the operation as a personal compliment. They tumbled in the straw, and threw it about, and buried each other with cries of delight which had to be suppressed in the most forcible and emphatic way—until at last Edgar, driven to interfere, had to order the removal of Johnny and Tommy. "They can go to the West Lodge for the night," he said, with a hospitable liberality, at which the West Lodge keeper, who was helping in the work, groaned aloud. Sally herself, however, was very indignant at this exercise of despotic authority. She rushed to the front, and demanded to know why her cottage should be taken possession of, and the children carried off for the benefit of a stranger. "A lass as nobody knows, nor don't care to know," said Sally, "as has a deal too many gentlefolks alooking after her to be an honest lass." "Take her away too," said Edgar with benevolent tyranny. And Sally, with a scream of despair, snatched the old petticoat which stuffed her broken window, and fled from the bystanders, who did not attempt to carry out the Squire's command. "I'll go and I'll see what Miss Clare says to it," she cried. Edgar was a great deal too busy to pay any attention. He saw the work completed, and urged the necessity of care upon John

Hesketh and his wife without considering that even they were but partial sympathisers. "I don't hold with no such a fuss," the women were saying among themselves. "If it had been the mother of a family she'd have had to take her chance; but a bit of a wench with a pretty face—" Thus he got no credit for his exertions, notwithstanding the injunctions of Dr. Somers. If Jeanie had been altogether unfriended, the village people would have shown her all manner of care and sympathy; but the Squire's kindness put an end to theirs. They sympathised with Sally in her banishment. "You'll see as Miss Clare won't like it a bit," cried one. "I don't think nothing of Sally, but she has a right to her own place." "She'll be well paid for it all," said another. Sally, and the fuss that was being made, and Miss Clare's supposed sentiments bulked much more largely with the villagers than the thought that Jeanie lay between life and death, although many of them liked Jeanie, and had grown used to see her, so small and so fair, wandering about the street. Only old Sarah stood with her apron to her eyes. "I'm as fond of her as if she was my own. She's the sweetest, patientest, good-temperedest lamb—none of you wenches can hold a candle to her," sobbed the old woman. "She stitches beautiful, though I'm not one as holds with your pretty faces," said Sally, the sexton's daughter; but these were the only voices raised in poor Jeanie's favour throughout the village crowd.

Edgar lingered last of all at the cottage door. John Hesketh's wife, partly moved by pity for the grandmother left thus alone, partly by curiosity to investigate the amount of dirt and discomfort in Sally Timms' cottage—had taken her place in the outer room, to remain with Mrs. Murray until Sally returned or some other assistant came. And Edgar lingered to hear the last news of the patient before going away. The twilight by this time was falling, faint little stars were appearing in the sky, the dew and the peacefulness of approaching night were in the atmosphere. While he stood waiting at the door, Mrs. Murray herself came out upon him all at once. She had an air of suppressed excitement about her which struck him strangely—not so much anxiety, as agitation, highly excited feeling. He put out his hand to her as she approached, feeling, he could not tell how, that she wanted his aid and consolation. She took his hand between both hers, and held it tight and pressed it close; and then surely the strangest words came from her lips that were ever spoken in such circumstances. "He carried her here in his arms—he left the other to save her. You'll no forget it to him—you'll no forget it to him. That is the charge I lay on you."

Edgar half drew away his hand in his surprise; but she held it fast, not seeming even to feel his attempt at withdrawal. "What do you mean?" he said. "I came to ask for Jeanie. Is it of Arthur Arden you are speaking—my cousin? But it is about Jeanie I want to know."

"Ay, your cousin," she said anxiously. "It's strange that I never kent you had a cousin. Nobody ever told me that—But mind, mind what I say. Whatever happens, you'll no forget this. He carried her here in his arms. He forgot all the rest, all the rest. And you'll no forget it to him. That's my injunction upon you, whatever anybody may say."

"This is very strange," Edgar said, in spite of himself. Who was she, that she should lay injunctions upon him—should bid him do this or that? And then he thought to himself that her head too must be a little turned. So startling an event probably had confused her, as Jeanie had been confused by a sudden shock. He looked at her very sympathetically, and pressed the hands that held his. "Tell me first how Jeanie is—poor little Jeanie; that is by far the most important now."

"It's no the most important," said the old woman almost obstinately. "I ken both sides, and you ken but little—very, very little. But whatever you do or say, you'll no forget him for this—promise me that you'll never forget."

"That is easy enough to promise," said Edgar; "but he was to blame, for it was he who put her in the carriage. I think he was to blame. And what am I to reward him for?—for carrying the poor child home?"

"Yes, for carrying her home," said Mrs. Murray, "in his arms, when the other was waiting that was more to him than Jeanie. You'll no please me, nor do your duty, if you do not mind this good deed. They say he's no a good man; but the poor have many a temptation that never comes near the rich; and if he had been in your place at Arden and you in his—or even—"

"My dear, kind woman," said Edgar, trying with a pressure of her hands to recall her to herself, "don't trouble yourself about Arthur or me. You are excited with all that has happened. Think of Jeanie. Don't take any trouble about us—"

"Eh, if I could help troubling!" she said, loosing her hands from his. And then the look of excitement slowly faded out of her face. "I am bidding you bear my burdens," she said, with a deep sigh; "as if the innocent could bear the load of the guilty, or make amends—You must not mind what I say. I've been a solitary woman, and whiles I put things into words that are meant for nobody's ear. You were asking about Jeanie. She is real ill—in a kind of faint—but if she is kept quiet, the doctor says she may come round. I think she will come round, for my part. She is delicate, but there is life in her: me and mine have all so much life." When she said these words Mrs. Murray fixed her eyes upon Edgar keenly and surveyed him, as if trying to fathom his constitution and powers. "I cannot tell for you," she said, with a sudden pause. He smiled, but he was grieved, thinking sadly that her brain was affected, as Jeanie's had been. What was to become of the hapless pair if the mother's brain was gone as well as the child's. The thought filled him with infinite pity, so great as almost to bring tears to his eyes.

"You must try and compose yourself," he said. "I will send Perfitt to see that you have everything you want, and perhaps when she is a little better she may be removed to your own rooms. This is not a comfortable cottage, I fear. But you must compose yourself, and not allow yourself to be worried one way or another. You may be quite sure I will stand by you, and take care of you as much as I can—you who have been so kind to everybody, so good—"

"Oh no, no, no good!" she cried, "not good. I think night and day, but I cannot see what to do; and when a wronged man heaps coals of fire on your head—Oh, you're kind, kind; and I'm no ungrateful, though I may look it. And it is not excitement, as you say, that makes me speak. There's many a thing of which a young lad like you is ignorant. You'll mind this to his credit if ever you can do him a good turn—"

"Yes, yes," said Edgar impatiently; and then he added, "Think of Jeanie. Arthur Arden is very well qualified to take care of himself."

And so he turned away, chafed and disquieted. Arthur Arden had been the cause of his leaving home, and here as soon as he returned Arthur Arden again was in his way, and a trouble to him. He walked through the village street very uneasy about poor Mrs. Murray, and Jeanie, who would be in her sole charge. If the grandmother's mind was unsettled, how could she look after the child, and what would become of two creatures so helpless in a strange place? No doubt it must be in the family, as people say. Jeanie's monomania was about her brother, and Mrs. Murray's was about Arthur Arden. What had he to do with Arthur Arden? He was not his brother's keeper, that he should step in and make of himself a providence for Arthur's benefit. Altogether it was odd and disagreeable and discomposing. As his mind was thus occupied he walked along the village street, pre-occupied and absorbed. When he had nearly reached the Arden Arms he met Dr. Somers, and immediately seized the opportunity to make inquiries. The Doctor held up his hand as if warding him off.

"Not a word, Mr. Edgar, not another word. I have said if she's kept quiet and not excited she'll do. I don't like fuss any more than the villagers. You don't put straw down when a comfortable matron adds to the number of society, and why should you for this girl? You are all mad about Jeanie. She is a pretty girl, I allow; but there is as pretty to be seen elsewhere. You should hear your cousin on that subject. He and his misfortunes are as good as a play."

"What are his misfortunes?" said Edgar, and in spite of himself a certain coldness crept into his voice.

"You don't like him?" said Dr. Somers; "neither do I. I hate a man who lives on his wits. Generally neither the wits nor the man are worth much. But as I say, this time Arthur Arden's as good as a play. He has been turned out of the Red House—the Pimpernels will have no more of him. It is a capital story. He has been sponging upon them for a month (this, of course, is between ourselves), and I daresay they were very glad to get rid of him. You never can tell when such a visitor may go away."

"I thought the Pimpernels liked it," said Edgar; but did not care to enter into any discussion about his cousin; and he walked on in silence for some seconds by the Doctor's side, meaning thus to express his desire to be quit of the subject. He had, on the whole, had quite too much of Arthur Arden. He felt with the Pimpernels that to be quit of him would be a relief.

"Where are you going?" said the Doctor. "It is getting late. Come with me and dine. I have just asked Arden. He is houseless and homeless, you know; and I know what it is to be condemned to the hospitalities of the Arden Arms—"

"Is he at the Arden Arms?" said Edgar. "I suppose only for to-night. He must have plenty of houses to go to—a man who is so well known in the world. Thanks, Doctor; but Clare must have been expecting me for some time. I must go home."

"Clare has not been very well," said the Doctor. "I am glad you have come back. If there ever had been such a thing as brain disease among the Ardens I should have been frightened. Fielding gave me a hint, and I went to see her. The girl has something on her mind. I don't know if it is about Arthur Arden—"

"Confound Arthur Arden!" said Edgar. "What do you suppose he could have to do with my sister Clare?"

"Oh, nothing; nothing, of course," said the Doctor, "except that they were great friends, and now they are friends no longer. And she has not looked well since; there is a look of anxiety and trouble about her. My dear fellow, you and I may not think much of Arthur Arden, but with women he could cut us both out. Some men have that way. There is no genuine feeling about them, and yet they get far before the best. His father was the same sort of fellow; he was my contemporary, and it used to set me on edge to see him. My poor sister, Letty, to this day imagines that he was fond of her. Your cousin is not a man to be despised."

"Doctor, I don't doubt you are very wise and very right," said Edgar; "but you forget you are speaking of Clare. Tell Miss Somers I am coming to see her to-morrow after church. And, Doctor, I think it would be worth your while to examine the old woman, Jeanie's grandmother. I don't think she is quite right. She was speaking wildly. I did not know what to make of her. And if you consider what a helpless pair they would be! What could they do? especially if they were both ill in that way—"

"In what way?—concussion of the brain?" said the Doctor. "Is it Mrs. Murray's brain you are anxious for? My dear boy, you may dismiss your fears. That woman has life enough for half-a-dozen of us cold-blooded people. Her brain is as sound as yours and mine. But it is a very anxious case, and it may well disturb her. Perhaps the accident may be good for the child if she mends. Everything is so mysterious about the brain. Won't you reconsider the matter, and come? I don't want to say too much for my dinner; but it is not bad—not bad, you know—a little better than usual, I think. No? Well, I think it would do you more real good than a long walk in the dark; but, of course, you must have your own way."

And thus they parted at the great gates. The avenue was very dark, and Edgar was not in brilliant spirits. He seemed to himself to be entering a moral as well as a physical obscurity, confused by many mysterious shadows, as he took the way to his own door.

CHAPTER III

The dogcart reached home with news of Edgar's approach before he himself arrived. It passed him in the avenue, and so did Sally Timms, who had rushed to the Hall to carry the news of Jeanie's accident, and to make an appeal on her own account to Clare. Thus his sister had been made acquainted with the cause of his detention—which was a relief to him: for he was fatigued with his recent exertions. He stopped Sally, and recommended her guest to her best care, and gave her a sovereign; and then he went on tired to his own house. His own house! The words were pleasant. The woods rustled darkly about him, concealing everything but the Hall itself, with lights glimmering in its windows; but the sense of secure proprietorship and undisturbed possession was sweet. The sight of Arden brought back the thought of Gussy Thornleigh and of all the new combinations and arrangements that might be coming, which did not excite him, perhaps, so much as they ought to have done, but yet were sweet, and had a soft thrill of pleasure in them. She would be a most genial, gracious little mistress of the house. True, the thought of dethroning Clare was a great trouble to him, an immense obstacle in the way; but probably Clare would marry too, or something would happen. And in the meantime Gussy's image was very pleasant, mingling with that of his sister, giving him a sense of a double welcome, a double interest in his movements. To be loved was very sweet to Edgar. The warm domestic affection, the sense of home enclosing all that was dear, filled his heart with something more tender, almost more delicate than passion. He would never be overpoweringly in love, perhaps; but was that necessary to the happiness of life? With so much as he had he felt that he should be content.

Clare did not come down stairs to meet him, as he expected, which gave him a little chill and check in the warmth of his affectionate pleasure. He had to go up by himself, somewhat startled by the quietness of the house; feeling as if there was nobody in it, or at least nobody to whom his return was an event. And then he bethought himself of what Dr. Somers had said of Clare. He had been so angry about the allusion to Arthur Arden that the report of the state of his sister's health had escaped his attention. When he thought of this he ran hastily up stairs and made his way to the favourite sitting-room, where she had always received him. But there was nobody there. Clare was in the big ceremonious drawing-room—the place for strangers, with many lights, and the formal air of a room which was not much used. He rushed forward as she rose from the sofa at his entrance. He was about to take her into his arms, but she held out her hand. Her cheeks were flushed, her brow cloudy; she did not meet his eye, but averted her face from him in the strangest way. "You are come at last! I had almost given up thoughts of you," she said, and sat down again on her sofa, constrained and cold;—cold, though her hand was burning and her cheek flushed crimson. Could it be possible that she was merely angry at his delay?

"I am late, I know," he said, "but I will tell you why—or, I suppose, you have heard why, as I met Sally Timms coming down the avenue. But, Clare, are you ill? What is the matter? Are you not glad to see me? I lost no more time than I could help in obeying your summons, and this little detention to-night is not my fault."

"I have not blamed you," said Clare. "Thanks—I am quite well. It is rather late, however, and I fear your dinner—"

"Oh, never mind my dinner," said Edgar, "if that is all. I am delighted to get back to you, though you don't look glad to see me. I met Somers in the village, and he told me you had been ill. You must have been worrying yourself while you have been alone. You must not stay here alone again. I begin to think it is bad for everybody. My dear Clare, you change colour every moment. Have I frightened you? I am so grieved—so sorry;" and he stooped over her, and took her hand in his and kissed her cheek. Clare trembled, body and soul. She could not shrink from him—she could not respond to him. She wanted to break away—to shut herself up, never to see him more; and yet she wanted to lay her head down upon his shoulder, and cry, "Oh, my brother! my brother!" What was she to do? The end was that, torn by these different impulses, she remained quite motionless and unresponsive, giving to Edgar an impression of utter coldness and repulsion, which he struggled vainly against. He looked at her for a moment with unfeigned wonder. Then he let her hands drop. He had seen her out of temper, and he had seen her sorrowful; but this was more than either, and he could not tell what it meant.

"I have worried you by being so late," he said quietly; "I am very sorry, Clare. I did not think you would be anxious. But to-morrow I hope you will be all right. Must I go and dine? I am not hungry; but surely you will come too?"

"Yes, I will come, if you want me," said Clare, faintly, and Edgar walked away to his dressing-room with the strangest sense of desertion. What had he done to separate his sister from him? It was obviously something he had done; not any accidental cloud on her part, but something he was guilty of. Poor Edgar put himself in order for dinner with a feeling that the weather had grown suddenly cold, and he had arrived, not in his own but in a strange house. When he went down Clare was in the dining-room, already seated at the opposite end of the great dining-table. "Where is our little round table that we used to have," he asked, with distress that was almost comical. "You forget that we had been having visitors when you went away," said Clare. Was she angry still that he had gone away? Was it the dismissal of the visitors which had made her angry? Was it—Arthur Arden? Edgar was too much distressed and amazed to speak. He told her the story of the accident, feeling as if it was necessary to raise his voice to reach her where she sat half-a-mile off, with her face now pale and fixed into a blank absence of expression, as if she were determined to give no clue to her meaning. But even this history which seemed to him a perfectly innocent and impersonal matter, having nothing to do with themselves, and therefore a safe subject for talk, was received with a certain chill of incredulity which drove poor Edgar wild. Did they not believe him? He said "they" in his mind, because even Wilkins had put on an air incredulous and disapproving, as he stood behind Clare's chair. Finally Edgar grew half amused by dint of amazement and discomfiture. The oddness of this curious tacit disapproval struck him, in spite of himself. He felt tempted to get up and make them a serio-comic speech. "What have I done that you are both sitting upon me?" he felt disposed to say; but after all the atmosphere was terribly chilly and discouraging, and even a laugh was not to be obtained.

After the servants had retired it was worse than ever. Clare sat in the distance and made her little set speeches, with an attempt at indifferent conversation. And when he got up and brought his chair and his glass of claret close to her, she shrank a little, insensibly. Then for the first time he perceived a sealed packet which lay beside her on the table. This is the cause of my offending, Edgar said to himself. Some nonsense verses or letters about my youthful pranks. But these youthful pranks of his had not been at all serious, and he was not much afraid. He smiled to himself, to see how his prevision was verified when she rose from the table.

"I am very tired," said Clare. "I don't know why I should be so stupid to-night. Here are some papers which I found in the bureau—in the library. I have not opened them as you will see. I read one sentence through a tear in the envelope—and I thought—it appeared to me—I imagined—that you ought to see them. I think I shall go to bed now. Perhaps you will take them and—examine them—when you feel disposed. I am so stupid to-night."

"Surely I will examine them—or anything else you like me to do," said Edgar. "My sister ought to know I would do anything to please her. Must it be done to-night? for do you know I am unhappy to see you look so strangely at me—and a little tired too."

"Oh, not to-night, unless you wish—when you think proper. They have never been out of my hands," said Clare, with growing seriousness. "I should like you, please, till you look at them, to keep them very safe."

"Certainly," he said, with the promptest goodwill, and put the parcel into his breast pocket, which was scarcely large enough to contain it, and bulged out. "It does not look very graceful, does it?" he said with a smile as he lighted her candle for her, and then looked wistfully into her eyes. "I hope you will be better, dear, to-morrow," he said tenderly. "I am so sorry to have annoyed you to-night."

"Not annoyed me," Clare said, choking, and made a few steps across the threshold. Then she came back quickly, almost running to him, where he stood holding the door in his hand looking wistfully after her. "Oh Edgar, forgive me. I can't help it!" she moaned; and held up a pale cheek to him, and turned and fled.

Edgar sat down again by the table, very much puzzled indeed. What did she mean? what could be the matter with her? Poor Clare? Could it be this Arthur Arden, this light o' love—this man who was attractive to women, as Dr. Somers said? Edgar's pride in his sister and his sense of delicacy revolted at the idea. And then it occurred to him that the packet she had given him might contain Arden's letters, and that Clare was struggling with her feelings and endeavouring to cast him off. He took the packet out of his pocket, and opened the envelope. But when he found the original enclosure inside, old and brown, and scorched, with yellow letters showing through the worn cover, this idea faded from Edgar's mind. He put them back into the outer cover with a sigh of relief. Of course, had Clare exacted it, he said to himself, he would have read them at once; but they were old things which could not be urgent— could not be of much weight one way or another. And he was anxious and tired, and not in a state of mind to be bothered with old letters. Poor Clare! She had been a little unkind to him; but then she had made that touching little apology which atoned for everything. To console himself, Edgar got up, and, lighting a cigar, strolled out upon the terrace; for as most men know, there is not only consolation, but counsel in tobacco. Clare's window was on that side of the house, and he watched the light in it with a grieved and tender sympathy. Yes, poor Clare! She had no mother to tell her troubles to, no sister to share her life. Her lot (he thought) was a hard one, notwithstanding all her advantages. Her father had been her only companion, and he was gone, and his memory, instead of uniting his two orphan children together, hung like a cloud between them. Perhaps there might even now be memories belonging to the old Squire's time which troubled Clare, and which she could not confide to her brother. His heart melted over her as he mused. Would Gussy, he wondered, take a sister's place, and beguile Clare out of herself? And then he thought he would talk the matter over with Lady Augusta, and ask her motherly advice. As this crossed his mind, he realised more than ever how pleasant it would be to have such people belonging to him. He who had been cast out of his family, and had in reality nothing but the merely natural bond, the tie of blood between himself and his only sister, felt—much more than a man could who had been trained in the ordinary way—how pleasant it would be to be adopted by real choice and affection into a family. Perhaps it seemed to him more pleasant in imagination and prospect than it ever could be in reality—perhaps Gussy's brothers, who were prone to get into scrapes, might, indeed, turn out rather a bore than otherwise. But he had no thought of such considerations now. And, when he went to his room, he locked up carefully out of the way of harm Clare's papers. To-morrow, perhaps, when his mind was more fresh, he would look them over to please her, or, if not to-morrow, some day soon. He was quite tranquil about them, while she was so anxious. His sister's good-night had soothed him, and so, to tell the truth, had his cigar. He had a peaceful, lovely Sunday before him, and then the arrival of the Thornleighs, and then—Thus it was, with a mind much tranquillised, and the feeling of home once more strong upon him, that Edgar went to rest in his own house.

Next morning was a calm bright summer Sunday, one of those days which are real Sabbaths—moments of rest. It was like the "sweet day, so cool, so calm, so bright," of George Herbert's tender fancy. Nothing that jarred or was discordant was audible in the soft air. The voices outside, the passing steps, were as harmonious as the birds and the bees that murmured all about—everything that was harsh had died out of the world. There was nothing in this Sunday but universal quiet and calm.

Except in Clare Arden's face and voice. She came down stairs before her brother, long before him, as if she had been unable to sleep. Her brow was drawn in and contracted as if by some pressing uncertainty and suspense. Her voice had a broken tone in it, a tone like a strained string. With a restlessness which it was impossible to conceal, she waited for Edgar's appearance, gliding back and forward from the library to the dining-room where breakfast was laid. The round table had been placed for them in the window not by Clare's care, but by Wilkins; a great vase of late roses—red and white—stood in the centre. The roses were all but over, for it was the second Sunday in July; but still the lawns and rosebeds of Arden produced enough for this. How strange she thought that he should be so late. Was it out of mere wantonness? Was it because he had been sitting up late over the enclosures she had given him; was it that he feared to meet her after—She suggested all these reasons to herself, but they did not still her restlessness nor bring Edgar down a moment earlier. She could not control her excitement. How was she to meet him for the first time after this discovery, if it was a discovery? How would he look at her after such a revelation? And yet Clare did not know what manner of revelation it was; or it might be no revelation at all. It might be her fancy only which had put meaning into the words she had seen. They might refer to something entirely indifferent to her brother and herself. Clare said so in her own mind, but she could not bring herself to believe it. The thought had seized upon her with crushing bewildering force. It had left her no time to think. She did not quite know what she fancied, but it was something that would shake her life and his life to their foundations, and change everything in heaven and earth.

Edgar came down at his usual hour, bright and light-hearted, as his nature was. He went up to the breakfast table with its vase of roses, and bent his face down over it. "How pleasant Sunday is," he said, "and how pleasant it is to be at home! I hope you are better this morning, Clare. Could any one help being better in this sweet air and this lovely place? I never thought Arden was half so beautiful. Fancy, there are people in town just now wasting their lives away! I am sure you are better, Clare—"

"I—think so," she said, looking at him anxiously. Had he read them? Had he not read them? That was the question. Her whole soul was bent upon that and that alone.

"You are not looking well," he said, with tender anxiety. "What have you been doing to yourself? I would say I hoped you had missed me; but you don't look so very glad to see me now—not nearly so glad as I am to see you. If you had come with me to town it might have done you good. And I am sure it would have done me good. It is dreary work living alone—in London above all—"

"Not for a man," said Clare. Her voice was still constrained; but she made a desperate effort, and put away from her as much as she could her disinclination for talk. How unlike he was to other men—how strange that he should not take pleasure in things that everybody else took pleasure in; dreary work living alone, for a young man of his position, in London—how ridiculous it was!

"Well, I assure you I found it so," said Edgar; "if you had been with me, I should have enjoyed it. As it was, I was only amused. The Thornleighs are coming back to-morrow. I saw a great deal of them—more than before they went to town—"

Here he paused, and a warmer colour, a certain air of pleasure and content diffused itself over his face. A thrill of pain and apprehension ran through Clare. The Thornleighs!—were they to be brought into the matter too? She half rose from the seat she had taken at the table. "Have you read those letters?" she asked, in a hasty, half-whispering, yet almost stern voice.

"What letters? Oh, those you gave me last night! No, not yet. Do you wish me to do it at once? You said it did not matter, I think; or, at least, I understood there was no haste."

"Oh, no haste!" said Clare, with a certain sense of desperation stealing over her; and then she took courage. "I don't mean that; they have troubled me very much. The sooner you read them, the sooner I shall be relieved, If I am to be relieved. If it would not trouble you too much to go over them to-night?"

"My dear Clare, of course I will read them directly if you wish it," said Edgar, half-provoked. "You have but to say so. Of course, nothing troubles me that you wish. I sent down to ask after poor little Jeanie this morning," he added, after a pause, falling into his usual tone; "and the doctor says she has had a tolerably good night. I must go and see Miss Somers after church. She will have learned all about it by this time, and that story about Arthur Arden and the Pimpernels. Miss Pimpernel, I told you, was thrown out of the carriage as well as Jeanie—"

"I think you told me," said Clare faintly. "I know so little about Miss Pimpernel; and I do not like that other girl. It may be prejudice, but I don't like her. I wish you would not talk of her to me."

Edgar looked up at his sister with grave wonder—"As you please," he said seriously, but his cheek flushed, half with anger, half with disappointment. What could have happened to Clare? She was not like herself. She scarcely looked at him even when she spoke. She was constrained and cold as if he were the merest stranger. She had again avoided his kiss, and never addressed him by his name. What could it mean? Scarcely anything more was said at breakfast. Clare could not open her lips, and Edgar was annoyed, and did not. It seemed so very mysterious to him. He was indeed as nearly angry as it was in his nature to be. It seemed to him a mere freak of temper—an ebullition of pride. And he was so entirely innocent in respect to Jeanie! The child herself was so innocent. Poor little Jeanie!—he thought of her with additional tenderness as he looked at his sister's unsympathetic face.

"I suppose we may walk together to church as usual," he said. It was the only remark that had broken the silence for nearly half an hour.

"If you have no objection"—said Clare formally, with something of that aggravating submission which wives sometimes show to their husbands, driving them frantic, "I think I shall drive—but not if you object to the horses being taken out."

"Why should I object?" he said, restraining himself with an effort, "except that I am very sorry not to have your company, Clare."

Then she wavered once more, feeling the empire of old affection steal over her. But he had turned away to the window, grieved and impatient. It was like a conjugal quarrel, not like the frank differences between brother and sister. And this was not how Clare's temper had ever shown itself before. Edgar left the table, with a sense of pain and disappointment which it was very hard to bear. Why was it? What had he done? His heart was so open to her, he was so full of confidence in her, and admiration for her, that the check he had thus received was doubly hard. His sister had always been to him the first among women. Gussy of course was different—but Gussy had never taken the same place in his respect and admiring enthusiasm. Clare had been to him, barring a few faults which were but as specks on an angel's wing, the first of created things; and it hurt him that she should thus turn from him, and expel him, as it were, from her sympathies. He stood uncertain at the window, not knowing whether he should make another attempt to win her back; but when he turned round he found, to his astonishment, that she was gone. How strange—how very strange it was. As she had abandoned him, he saw no advantage in waiting. He could go and ask for Jeanie, and see how things were going on, at least, if he was not required here. He gave Wilkins orders about the carriage with a sigh. "My sister proposes to drive," he said; and as he said it he looked out upon the lovely summer Sunday morning, and the wonder of it struck him more than ever. She had liked to walk with him down the leafy avenue, under the protecting shadows, when he came home first, and now she changed her habits to avoid him. What could it mean? Could this, too, be Arthur Arden's fault?

Thus it was that Edgar left the house so early, ill at ease. His sister thought that probably the effect of her constraint and withdrawal of sympathy would be that, tracing her changed demeanour to its right cause, he would hasten to read the packet she had given him. But Edgar never thought of the packet. It did not occur to him that a parcel of old letters could have anything to do with this most present and painful estrangement. While he went out, poor fellow, with his heart full of pain, Clare looked at him from the window with anger and astonishment. What did he care? Perhaps he had known it all along—perhaps he was a conscious—But no, no. Not till the last moment—not till evidence was before her which she could not resist—would she believe that. So the carriage came round, and she was driven to church in solitary state—sometimes excusing, sometimes condemning herself. It was a thing which happened so rarely that the village folks were in a state of commotion. Miss Arden was ill, they thought—nothing else could explain it; and so thought the kind old Rector and even Dr. Somers, who knew, or thought he knew, better than any of the others. As for Arthur Arden, who had gone to church with the hope of being invited by Edgar to accompany him home, he was in despair.

Edgar, for his part, walked down very gloomily through the village to ask for Jeanie, and had his news confirmed that she had spent a tolerably good night. "But in a dead faint all the time," said Mrs. Hesketh, who had taken the place of nurse. "She breathes, poor dear, and her heart it do beat. But she don't know none of us, nor open her eyes. It's awful to see one as is living, and yet dead. T'ou'd dame, she never leaves her, not since she was a-talking to you, sir, last night."

"Could I see her now?" said Edgar; but Mrs. Hesketh shook her head; and he could not tell why he wanted to see her, except as some relief to the painful dulness which had come over him. The next best thing he could do seemed to be to walk to the Red House, and ask after Alice Pimpernel. There he found no lack of response. Mr. Pimpernel himself came out, and so did Mrs. Pimpernel, with profuse and eager thanks. "If it had not been for you Mr. Arden, my child might have perished," said the mother. "No, no, not so bad as that," Edgar could not but say with surprise. "And the person who was most to blame never even gave himself the trouble to inquire till all was over," the lady added with a look of rage. They wanted to detain him, to give him breakfast, to secure his company for Mr. Pimpernel, who was going to drive to church with the younger children. But Edgar did not desire to join this procession, and suffer himself to be paraded as his cousin's successor. Somehow the village and everything in it seemed to have changed its aspect. He thought the people looked coldly at him—he felt annoyed and discouraged, he could not tell why. It seemed to him as if the Thornleighs would not come, or coming, would hear bad accounts of him, and that he would be abandoned by all his friends. And he did not know why, that was the worst of it; there seemed no reason. He was just the same as he had been when Clare received him as her dearest brother. What had happened since to change her mind towards him he was totally unable to tell. The sourd and obscure atmosphere of family discord was quite novel to Edgar. For most of his existence he had known nothing about family life; and then it had seemed to him so warm, so sweet, so bright. The domestic life, the warm sense of kindred about him had been his chief attraction to Gussy. His heart was so full, he wanted sisters and brothers and quantities of kinsfolk. And now the discovery that those good things could bring pain as well as pleasure confused him utterly. Clare! his only sister, the sole creature who belonged to him, whom nature gave him to love, to think that without a cause she should be estranged from him! When he fairly contemplated the idea, he gave himself, as it were spiritually, a shake, and smiled. "It takes two to make a quarrel," he said to himself, and resolved that it was impossible, and could not last another hour.

CHAPTER V

Mr. Fielding preached one of his gentle little sermons upon love to your neighbour on that especial morning. The Doctor had been quiet, and had not bothered the Rector for some time back. There had been a good deal of sickness at the other end of the parish, and his hands had been full. It was a sermon which the Arden folks had heard a good many times before; but there are some things which, like wine, improve in flavour the longer that they are kept. Mr. Fielding produced it about once in five years, and preached it with little illustrations added on, drawn from his own gentle experience. And each time it was better than the last. The good people did not remember it, having listened always with a certain amount of distraction and slumberousness; but Dr. Somers did, and had noted in his pocket-book the times he had heard it. "Very good, with that story about John Styles in the appendix," was one note; and four or five years later it occurred again thus—"Little sketch of last row with me put in as an illustration—John Styles much softened; always very good." Next time it was—"John Styles disappeared altogether—quarrel with me going out—old Simon in the foreground; better than ever." The Arden folks were not alert enough in their minds to discern this; but the gentle discourse did them good all the same.

And there in front of him, listening to him, in the Arden pew, were three who needed Mr. Fielding's sermon. First, Clare, pale with that wrath and distrust which takes all happiness out of a woman's face, and almost all beauty. Then, sitting next to her, with a great gap between, now and then looking wistfully at her, now casting a hasty glance to his other side—anxious, suspicious, watchful—Arthur Arden, at the very lowest ebb, as he thought, of his fortunes. He had been as good as turned out of the Red House. He had no invitation nearer than the end of August. Clare had passed him at the church door with a bow that chilled him. Edgar, coming in late, had taken scarcely any notice of him. Nothing could appear less hopeful than his plan of getting himself invited once more to Arden, covering the Pimpernels with confusion, and showing publicly his superiority over them. Alas! he would not look superior, he could not be happy in the Arden Arms. Accordingly he sat, anxious about his cousins, hating all the world besides. Could he have crushed Mrs. Pimpernel by a sudden blow he would have done it. Could he have swept Jeanie out of his way he would have done it. Even underneath his anxiety for their favour, a bitter germ of envy and indignation was springing up in his heart towards his kinsfolk, Edgar and Clare.

And next to him sat Edgar, whose heart was heavy with that sense of discord—the first he had ever known. He had not been the sort of man with whom people quarrel. If any of his former comrades had been out of temper with him, it had been but for a moment—and he had no other relation to quarrel with. The sense of being at variance with his sister hung over him like a cloud. Edgar was the only one to whom the Rector's gentle sermon did any good. He was guiltless in his quarrel, and therefore he had no amour-propre concerned, no necessity laid upon him to justify himself. He was quite ready to say that he was wrong if that would please any one; yes, no doubt he had been wrong; most people were wrong; he was ready to confess anything. And though he was not a very close listener generally to Mr. Fielding's sermons, he took in this one into his heart. And the summer air, too, stole into his heart; and the faint fragrance of things outside that breathed in through the open door, and even the faint mouldy flavour of age and damp which was within. The little village church, when he looked round it, filled him with a strange emotion. What was it to others? What was it to himself? A little break in life—a pause bidding the sleepy peasant rest in the quiet, dropping warm langour on the eyelids of the children, giving to the old a slumberous pensiveness. He saw them softly striving to keep themselves awake—sometimes yielding to the drowsy influence—sometimes open-eyed, listening or not listening—silent between life and death. Such sweet, full, abounding life outside; hum of insects, flutter of leaves, soft, all-pervading fragrance of summer roses. And within, the monuments on the wall glimmering white; the white head in the pulpit; the shadowy, quiet, restful place where grandsires had dozed and dreamed before. What an Elysium it was to some of those weary, hardworking old bodies! Edgar looked out upon them from the stage-box in which he sat with a thrill of tender kindness. To himself it might have been a mental and spiritual rest before the agitations of the next week. But something had disturbed that and made it impossible. Something! That meant Clare.

When they all left the church Arthur Arden made a bold stroke. "I will walk up with you to the Hall if you will let me," he said. Clare was within hearing, and she could not restrain a slight start and tremor, which he saw. Was she afraid of him? Did she wish him to come or to stay away? But Clare never turned round or gave the slightest indication of her feelings. She walked out steadily, saying a word here and there to the village people who stood by as she passed to the carriage, which was waiting for her at the gate.

"I am going to see Miss Somers," said Edgar, "and Clare is driving—but if you choose to wait—"

It was not a very warm invitation, but Arden accepted it. He wished the Pimpernels to see him with his cousin. This much of feeling remained in him. He would have been mortified had he supposed that they knew he was only at the Arden Arms. He would go to the Doctor's house with Edgar, and declared himself quite ready to wait. "I don't think Miss Somers likes me, or I should go with you," he said, and then he went boldly up to Mr. Pimpernel and asked for his daughter. "I am sorry I had to leave so abruptly," he said, "but I could not help myself," and he gave his shoulders a shrug, and looked compassionately with a half smile at the master of the Red House.

"Yes," said Mr. Pimpernel, accepting the tacit criticism with a certain cleverness. "Mrs. Pimpernel expresses herself strongly sometimes. Alice is better. Oh, yes! It was an affair of scratches only—though for a time I was in great fear."

"I never was so afraid in my life," said Arthur, and he shuddered at the thought, which his companion thought a piece of acting, though it was perfectly genuine and true.

"You did not show it much," he said, shrugging his shoulders in his turn, "at least so far as we were concerned. But, however, that is your affair." And with a nod which was not very civil he called his flock round him, and drove away. Arthur followed Edgar to the Doctor's open door. He went into the Doctor's sacred study, and took refuge there. Dr. Somers did not like him he was aware; but still he did not hesitate to put himself into the Doctor's easy chair. Why didn't people like him? It was confounded bad taste on their part!

In the meantime Edgar had gone up stairs, where Miss Somers awaited him anxiously. "Oh, my dear Edgar," she said, "what a sad, sad—Do you think she will never get better? My brother always says to me—but then, you know, this isn't asking about nothing—it's asking about Jeanie. And Alice, whose fault it was—Oh Edgar, isn't it just the way of the world? The innocent little thing, you know—and then the one that was really to blame escaping—it is just the way of the world."

"Then, it is a very disagreeable way," said Edgar. "I wish poor little Jeanie could have escaped, though I don't wish any harm to Miss Pimpernel."

"No, my dear," said Miss Somers; "fancy my calling you 'my dear,' as if you were my own sister! Do you know I begin now to forget which is a gentleman and which a lady—me that was always brought up—But what is the good of being so very particular?—when you consider, at my time of life. Though some people think that makes no difference. Oh, no, you must never wish her any harm; but a little foolish, flighty—with nothing in her head but croquet you know, and—Young Mr. Denbigh has so fallen off. He used to come and talk quite like—And then he would tell my brother what he should do. My brother does not like advice, Edgar. Doctors never do. They are so used, you know—And then about these German baths and everything. He used to tell my brother—and he was not nice about it. Sometimes he is not very nice. He has a good heart, and all that; but doctors, you know, as a rule, never do—And then your cousin—do you think he meant anything?—I once thought it was Clare; but then these people are rich, and when a man like that is poor—"

"I don't know what he meant," said Edgar; "but I am sure he can't mean anything now, for he has left the Pimpernels."

"And I suppose he is going to you?" said Miss Somers, "for he can't stay in the Arden Arms; now, can he? He is sure to be so particular. When men have no money, my dear—and used to fine living and all that—And I don't believe anything is to be had better than a chop—Chops are greasy in such places—And then Arthur Arden is used to things so—But my dear, I think not, if I were you—on account of Clare. I do think not, Edgar, if you were to take my advice."

"But I fear I can't help myself," said Edgar, with a shadow passing over his face—

Miss Somers shook her head; but fortunately not even the gratification of giving advice could keep her long to one subject. "Well—of course Clare is like other girls, she is sure to marry somebody," she said—"and marriage is a great risk Edgar. You shouldn't laugh. Marriage is not a thing to make you laugh. I never could make up my mind. It is so very serious a thing, my dear. Suppose afterwards you were to see some one else? or suppose—I never could run the risk—though of course it can't be so bad for a gentleman—But, Edgar, when you are going to be married—vows are nothing—I wouldn't make any vow—but,—it is this, Edgar—it is wrong to have secrets from your wife. I have known such trouble in my day. When a man was poor, you know—and she would go on, poor thing, and never find out—and then all at once—Oh, my dear, don't you do that—tell her everything—that is always my—and then she knows exactly what she can do—"

"But I am not going to be married," said Edgar with a smile, which did not pass away as common smiles do, but melted over all his face.

"I hope not," said Miss Somers promptly, "oh, I hope not—after all this about the Pimpernels—and—But that was your cousin, not you. Oh, no, I hope not. What would Clare do? If Clare were married first, then perhaps—But it would be so strange; Mrs. Arden—Edgar, fancy! In my state of health, you know, I couldn't go to call on her, my dear. She wouldn't expect—but then sometimes young ladies are very—And perhaps she won't know me nor how helpless—I hope she'll be very nice, I am sure—and—pretty, and—Some people think it doesn't matter—about beauty, you know, and that—It's a long, long time since I took any interest in such things—but when I was a young girl, it used to be said—Now I know what you are thinking in yourself—how vain and all that—but it is not vanity, my dear. You like to look nice, you know, and you like to please people, and you like—of course, you like to look nice. When I was young there were people that used to say—the little one—they always called me the little one—or little Letty, or something—I suppose because they were fond of me. Edgar, everybody is fond of you when you are young."

"And when you are old too," said Edgar; "everybody has been fond of you all your life, I am sure—and will be when you are a hundred—of course you know that."

"Ah, my dear," said Miss Somers, shaking her head. "Ah my dear!"—and two soft little tears came into the corners of her eyes—"when you are old—Yes. I know people are so kind—they pity you—and then every one tries; but when you were young, oh, it was so—There was no trying then. People thought there was nobody like—and then such quantities of things were to happen—But sometimes they never happen. It was my own fault, of course. There was Mr. Templeton and Captain Ormond, and—what is the good of going over—? That is long past, my dear, long past—"

And Miss Somers put her hands up softly to her eyes. She had a sort of theoretical regret for the opportunity lost, and yet, at the same time, a theoretical satisfaction that she had not tempted her fate—a satisfaction which was entirely theoretical; for did she not dream of her children who might have been, and of one who called Mamma? But Miss Somers was incapable of mentioning such a thing to Edgar, who was a "gentleman." To have betrayed herself would have been impossible. Arthur Arden was below waiting in the Doctor's study, and he came out as Edgar came down and joined him. He had not been idle in this moment of waiting. Something told him that this was a great crisis, a moment not to be neglected; and he had been arranging his plan of operations. Only Edgar, for this once thoughtless and unwary, thought of no crisis, until Tuesday came, when he should go to Thorne. He thought of nothing that was likely to change his happy state so long as he remained at home.

CHAPTER VI

"The fact is, I am a little put out by having to change my quarters so abruptly," said Arthur Arden. "I am going to Scotland in the beginning of September, but that is a long way off; and to go to one's lodgings in town now is dreary work. Besides, I said to the Pimpernels when they drove me out—they actually turned me out of the house—I told them I was coming here. It was the only way I could be even with them. If there is a thing they reverence in the world it is Arden; and if they knew I was here—"

"It does not entirely rest with me," said Edgar, with some embarrassment. "Arden, we had a good deal of discussion on various subjects before I went away."

"Yes; you went in order to turn me out," said Arthur meditatively. "By George, it's pleasant! I used to be a popular sort of fellow. People used to scheme for having me, instead of turning me out. Look here! Of course, when you showed yourself my enemy, it was a point of religion with me to pursue my own course, without regard to you; but now, equally of course, if you take me in to serve me, my action will be different. I should respect your prejudices, however they might run counter to my own."

"That means—?" said Edgar, and then stopped short, feeling that it was a matter which he could not discuss.

"It is best we should not enter into any explanations. Explanations are horrid bores. What I want is shelter for a few weeks, to be purchased by submission to your wishes on the points we both understand."

"For a few weeks!" said Edgar, with a little horror.

"Well, say for a single week. I must put my pride in my pocket, and beg, it appears. It will be a convenience to me, and it can't hurt you much. Of course, I shall be on my guard in respect to Clare."

"I prefer that my sister's name should not be mentioned between us," said Edgar, with instinctive repugnance. And then he remembered Mrs. Murray's strange appeal to him on behalf of his cousin. "You have all but as much right to be in Arden as I have," he said. "Of course, you must come. My sister is not prepared; she does not expect any one. Would it not be wiser to wait a little—till to-morrow—or even till to-night?"

"Pardon me," said Arthur; "but Miss Arden, I am sure, will make up her mind to the infliction better—if I am so very disagreeable—if she gets over the first shock without preparation. Is it that I am getting old, I wonder? I feel myself beginning to maunder. It used not to be so, you know. Indeed, there are places still—but never mind, hospitality that one is compelled to ask for is not often sweet."

It was on Edgar's lips to say that it need not be accepted, but he refrained, compassionate of his penniless kinsman. Why should the one be penniless and the other have all? There was an absence of natural justice in the arrangement that struck Edgar whenever his mind was directed to it; and he remembered now what had been his intention when his cousin first came to the Hall. "Arden," he said, "I don't think, if I were you, I would be content to ask for hospitality, as you say; but it is not my place to preach. You are the heir of Arden, and Arden owes you something. I think it is my duty to offer, and yours to accept, something more than hospitality. I will send for Mr. Fazakerly to-morrow. I will not talk of dividing the inheritance, because that is a thing only to be done between brothers; but, as you may become the Squire any day by my death—"

"I would sell my chance for five pounds," said Arthur, giving his kinsman a hasty look all over. "I shall be dead and buried years before you—more's the pity. Don't think that I can cheat myself with any such hope."

This was intended for a compliment, though it was almost a brutal one; but its very coarseness made it more flattering—or so at least the speaker thought.

"Anyhow, you have a right to a provision," Edgar continued hastily, with a sudden flush of disgust.

"I am agreeable," said Arthur, with a yawn. "Nobody can be less unwilling to receive a provision than I am. Let us have Fazakerly by all means. Of course, I know you are rolling in money; but Old Arden to Clare and a provision to me will make a difference. If you were to marry, for instance, you would not find it so easy to make your settlements. You are a very kind-hearted fellow, but you must mind what you are about."

"Yes," said Edgar, "you are quite right. What is to be done must be done at once."

"Strike while the iron is hot," said Arthur, languidly. He did not care about it, for he did not believe in it. A few weeks at Arden in the capacity of a visitor was much more to him than a problematical allowance. Fazakerly would resist it, of course. It would be but a pittance, even if Edgar was allowed to have his way. The chance of being Clare's companion, and regaining his power over her, and becoming lawful master through her of Old Arden, was far more charming to his imagination. Therefore, though he was greedy of money, as a poor man with expensive tastes always is, in this case he was as honestly indifferent as the most disinterested could have been. Thus they strolled up the avenue, where the carriage wheels were still fresh which had carried Clare; and a certain relief stole over her brother's mind that they would be three, not two, for the rest of the day. Strange, most strange that it should be so far a relief to him not to be alone with Clare.

Clare received them with a seriousness and reserve, under which she tried to conceal her excitement. Her cousin had deceived her, preferred a cottage girl to her, insulted her in the most sensitive point, and yet her heart leapt into her throat when she saw him coming. She had foreseen he would come. When he came into church, looking at her so wistfully, when he followed her out, asking to walk with Edgar, it became very evident to her that he was not going to relinquish the struggle without one other attempt to win her favour. It was a vain hope, she thought to herself; nothing could reverse her decision, or make her forget his sins against her; but still the very fact that he meant to try, moved, unconsciously, her heart—or was it his presence, the sight of him, the sound of his voice, the wistfulness in his eyes? Clare had driven home with her heart beating, and a double tide of excitement in all her veins. And then Arthur, too, was bound up in the whole matter. He was the first person concerned, after Edgar and herself; they would be three together in the house, between whom this most strange drama was about to be played out. She waited their coming with the most breathless expectation. And they came slowly up the avenue, calm as the day, indifferent as strangers who had never seen each other; pausing sometimes to talk of the trees; examining that elm which had a great branch blown off; one of them cutting at the weeds with his cane as undisturbed as if they were—as they thought—walking quietly home to luncheon, instead of coming to their fate.

"Arden is going to stay with us a little, Clare, if you can take him in," Edgar said, with that voluble candour which a man always exhibits when he is about to do something which will be disagreeable to the mistress of his house—be she mother, sister, or wife. "He has no engagements for the moment, and neither have we. It is a transition time—too late for town, too early for the country—so he naturally turned his eyes this way."

"That is a flattering account to give of it," said Arthur, for Clare only bowed in reply. "The fact is, Miss Arden, I was turned out by my late hostess. May I tell you the story? I think it is rather funny." And, though Clare's response was of the coldest, he told it to her, giving a clever sketch of the Pimpernels. He was very brilliant about their worship of Arden, and how their hospitality to himself was solely on account of his name. "But I have not a word to say against them. My own object was simply self-interest," he said. He was talking two languages, as it were, at the same moment—one which Edgar could understand, and one which was addressed to Clare.

And there could be no doubt that his presence made the day pass more easily to the other two—one of whom was so excited, and the other so exceedingly calm. They strolled about the park in the afternoon, and got through its weary hours somehow. They dined—Clare in her fever eating nothing; a fact, however, which neither of her companions perceived. They took their meal both with the most perfect self-possession, hurrying over nothing, and giving it that importance which always belongs to a Sunday dinner. Dinner on other days is but a meal, but on Sunday it is the business of the day; and as such the two cousins took it, doing full justice to its importance, while the tide rose higher and higher in Clare's veins. When she left them to their wine, she went to her own room, and walked about and about it like a caged lioness. It was not Clare's way, who was above all demonstration of the kind; but now she could not restrain herself. She clenched her two hands together, and swept about the room, and moaned to herself in her impatience. "Oh, will it never be night? Will they never have done talking? Can one go on and go on and bear it?" she cried to herself in the silence. But after all she had to put on her chains again, and bathe her flushed face, and go down to the drawing-room. How like a wild creature she felt, straining and chafing at her fetters! She sat down and poured out tea for them, with her hand trembling, her head burning, her feet as cold as ice, her head as hot as fire. She said to herself it was unlady-like, unwomanly, unlike her, to be so wild and self-indulgent, but she had no power to control herself. All this time, however, the two men made no very particular remark. Edgar, who thought she was still angry, only grieved and wondered. Arthur knew that she was dissatisfied with himself, and was excited but not surprised. He gave her now and then pathetic looks. He wove in subtle phrases of self-vindication—a hundred little allusions, which were nothing to Edgar but full of significance to her—into all he said. But he could not have believed, what was the case, that Clare was far past hearing them—that she did not take up the drift of his observations at all—that she hardly understood what was being said, her whole soul being one whirl of excitement, expectation, awful heartrending fear and hope. It was Edgar at last who perceived that her strength was getting worn out. He noticed that she did not hear what was said—that her face usually so expressive, was getting set in its extremity of emotion. Was it emotion, was it mania? Whatever it was, it had passed all ordinary bounds of endurance. He rose hastily when he perceived this, and going up to his sister laid his hand softly on her shoulder. She started and shivered as if his hand had been ice, and looked up at him with two dilated, unfathomable eyes. If he had been going to kill her she could not have been more tragically still—more aghast with passion and horror. A profound compassion and pity took possession of him. "Clare," he said, bending over her as if she were deaf, and putting his lips close to her ear, "Clare, you are over-exhausted. Go to bed. Let me take you up stairs—and if that will be a comfort to you, dear, I will go and read them now."

"Yes," she said, articulating with difficulty—"Yes." He had to take her hand to help her to rise; but when he stooped and kissed her forehead Clare shivered again. She passed Arthur without noticing him, then returned and with formal courtesy bade him good-night; and so disappeared with her candle in her hand, throwing a faint upward ray upon her white woe-begone face. She was dressed in white, with black ribbons and ornaments, and her utter pallor seemed to bring out the darkness of her hair and darken the blue in her eyes, till everything about her seemed black and white. Arthur Arden had risen too and stood wondering, watching her as she went away. "What is the matter?" he said abruptly to Edgar, who was no better informed than himself.

"I don't know. She must be ill. She is unhappy about something," said Edgar. For the first time the bundle of old letters acquired importance in his eyes. "I want to look at something she has given me," he added simply. "You will not think me rude when you see how much concerned my sister is? You know your room and all that. I must go and satisfy Clare."

"What has she given you?" asked Arthur, with a certain precipitation. Edgar was not disposed to answer any further questions, and this was one which his cousin had no right to ask.

"I must go now," he said. "Good-night. I trust you will be comfortable. In short, I trust we shall all be more comfortable to-morrow. Clare's face makes me anxious to-night."

And then Arthur found himself master of the great drawing-room, with all its silent space and breadth. What did they mean? Could it be that Clare had found this something for which he had sought, and instead of giving it to himself had given it to her brother, the person most concerned, who would, of course, destroy it and cut off Arthur's hopes for ever. The very thought set the blood boiling in his veins. He paced about as Clare had done in her room, and could only calm himself by means of a cigar which he went out to the terrace to smoke. There his eyes were attracted to Clare's window and to another not far off in which lights were burning. That must be Edgar's, he concluded; and there in the seclusion of his chamber, not in any place more accessible, was he studying the something Clare had given him? Something! What could it be?

CHAPTER VII

More than one strange incident happened at Arden that soft July night. Mr. Fielding was seated in his library in the evening, after all the Sunday work was over. He did not work very hard either on Sundays or on any other occasions—the good, gentle old man. But yet he liked to sit, as he had been wont to do in his youth when he had really exerted himself, on those tranquil Sunday nights. His curate had dined with him, but was gone, knowing the Rector's habit; and Mr. Fielding was seated in the twilight, with both his windows open, sipping a glass of wine tenderly, as if he loved it, and musing in the stillness. The lamp was never lighted on Sunday evenings till it was time for prayers. Some devout people in the parish were of opinion that at such moments the Rector was asking a blessing upon his labours, and "interceding" with God for his people—and so, no doubt, he was. But yet other thoughts were in his mind. Long, long ago, when Mr. Fielding had been young, and had a young wife by his side, this had been their sacred hour, when they would sit side by side and talk to each other of all that was in their hearts. It was "Milly's hour," the time when she had told him all the little troubles that beset a girl-wife in the beginning of her career; and he had laughed at her, and been sorry for her, and comforted her as young husbands can. It was Milly's hour still, though Milly had gone out of all the cares of life and housekeeping for thirty years. How the old man remembered those little cares—how he would go over them with a soft smile on his lip, and—no, not a tear—a glistening of the eye, which was not weeping. How frightened she had been for big Susan, the cook; how bravely she had struggled about the cooking of the cutlets, to have them as her husband liked them—not as Susan pleased! And then all those speculations as to whether Lady Augusta would call, and about Letty Somers, and her foolish, little kind-hearted ways. The old man remembered every one of those small troubles. How small they were, how dear, how sacred—Milly's troubles. Thank Heaven, she had never found out that the world held pangs more bitter. The first real sorrow she had ever had was to die—and was that a sorrow? to leave him; and had she left him? This was the tender enjoyment, the little private, sad delight of the Rector's Sunday nights; and he did not like to be disturbed.

Therefore, it was clear the business must be of importance which was brought to him at that hour. "Your reverence won't think as it's of my own will I'm coming disturbing of you," said Mrs. Solmes, the housekeeper; "but there's one at the door as will take no denial. She says she aint got but a moment, and daren't stay for fear her child would wake. She's been in a dead faint from yesterday at six till now. The t'oud woman as lives at oud Sarah's, your reverence; the Scotchy, as they calls her—her as had her granddaughter killed last night."

"God bless me!" said Mr. Fielding, confused by this complication. He knew Jeanie had not been killed; but how was he to make his way in this twilight moment through such a maze of statements? "Killed!" he said to himself. It was so violent a word to fall into that sacred dimness and sadness—sadness which was more dear to him than any joy. "Let her come in," he added, with a sigh. "Lights? no! I don't think we want lights. I can see you, Mrs. Solmes, and I can see to talk without lights."

"As you please, sir," said the housekeeper; "but them as is strangers, and don't know your habits, might think it was queer. And then to think how a thing gets all over the village in no time. But, to be sure, sir, it's as you please."

"Then show Mrs. Murray in," said Mr. Fielding. He had never departed from his good opinion of her, notwithstanding that she was a Calvinist, and looked disapproval of his sermons; but that she should come away from her child's sick-bed, that was extraordinary indeed.

And then in the dark, much to the scandal of Mrs. Solmes, Mrs. Murray came in. Even the Rector himself found it embarrassing to see only the tall, dark figure beside him, without being able to trace (so short-sighted as he was, too) the changes of her face. "Sit down," he said, "sit down," and bustled a little to get her a chair—not the one near him, in which, had she been alive, his Milly would have sat—(and oh! to think Milly, had she lived, would have been older than Mrs. Murray!)—but another at a little distance.

"How is your child?" he asked. "I meant to have gone to see her to-night, but they told me she was insensible still."

"And so she is," said the grandmother, "and I wouldna have left her to come here but for something that's like life and death. You're a good man. I canna but believe you're a real good man, though you are no what I call sound on all points. I want you to give me your advice. It's a case of a penitent woman that has done wrong, and suffered for it. Sore she has suffered in her bairns and her life, and worse in her heart. It's a case of conscience; and oh! sir, your best advice—"

"I will give you the best advice I can, you may be sure," said Mr. Fielding, moved by the pleading voice that reached him out of the darkness. "But you must tell me more clearly. What has she done? I will not ask who she is, for that does not matter. But what has she done; and has she, or can she, make amends? Is it a sin against her neighbour or against God?"

"Baith, baith," said the old woman. "Oh, Mr. Fielding, you're an innocent, virtuous man. I ken it by your face. This woman has been airt and pairt in a great wrong—an awfu' wrong; you never heard of the like. Partly she knew what she was doing, and partly she did not. There are some more guilty than her that have gone to their account; and there's none to be shamed but the innocent, that knew no guile, and think no evil. What is she to do? If it was but to punish her, she's free to give her body to be burned or torn asunder: oh, and thankful, thankful! Nothing you could do, but she would take and rejoice. But she canna move without hurting the innocent. She canna right them that's wronged without crushing the innocent. Oh, tell me, you that are a minister, and an old man, and have preached God's way! Many and many a time He suffers wrong, and never says a word. It's done now, and canna be undone. Am I to bear my burden and keep silent till my heart bursts, or must I destroy, and cast down, and speak!"

The woman spoke with a passion and vehemence which bewildered the gentle Rector. Her voice came through the dim and pensive twilight, thrilling with life and force and vigour. In that atmosphere, at that hour, any whisper of penitence should have been low and soft as a sigh. It should have been accompanied by noiseless weeping, by the tender humility which appeals to every Christian soul; but such was not the manner of this strange confession. Not a tear was in the eye of the penitent. Mr. Fielding felt, though he could not see, that her eyes, those eyes which had lost none of their brightness in growing old, were shining upon him in the darkness, and held him fast as did those of the Ancient Mariner. Suddenly, without any warning, he found himself brought into contact, not with the moderate contrition of ordinary sinners, but with tragic repentance and remorse. He could not answer for the first moment. It took away his breath.

"My dear, good woman," he said, "you startle me. I do not understand you. Do you know what you are saying? I don't think you can have done anything so very wrong. Hush, hush! compose yourself, and think what you are saying. When we examine it, perhaps we will find it was not so bad. People may do wrong, you know, and yet it need not be so very serious. Tell me what it was."

"That is what I cannot do," she said. "If I were to tell you, all would be told. If it has to be said, it shall be said to him first that will have the most to bear. Oh, have ye been so long in the world without knowing that a calm face often covers a heavy heart! Many a thing have I done for my ain and for others that cannot be blamed to me; but once I was to blame. I tell ye, I canna tell ye what it was. It was this—I did what was unjust and wrong. I schemed to injure a man—no, no me, for I did not know he was in existence, and who was to tell me?—but I did the wrong thing that made it possible for the man to be injured. Do you understand me now? And here I am in this awful strait, like Israel at the Red Sea. If I let things be, I am doing wrong, and keeping a man out of his own; if I try to make amends, I am bringing destruction on the innocent. Which, oh, which, tell me, am I to do?"

She had raised her voice till it sounded like a cry, and yet it was not loud. Mrs. Solmes in the kitchen heard nothing, but to Mr. Fielding it sounded like a great wail and moaning that went to his heart. And the silence closed over her voice as the water closes over a pebble, making faint circles and waves of echo, not of the sound, but of the meaning of the sound. He could not speak, with those thrills of feeling, like the wash after a boat, rolling over him. He did not understand what she meant; her great and violent pain bewildered the gentle old man. The only thing he could take hold of was her last words. That, he reflected, was always right—always the best thing to advise. He waited until the silence and quietness settled down again, and then he said, his soft old voice wavering with emotion, "Make amends!"

"Is that what you say to me?" she said, lifting up her hands. He could see the vehement movement in the gloom.

"Make amends. What other words could a servant of God say?"

He thought she fell when he spoke, and sprang to his feet with deep anxiety. She had dropped down on her knees, and had bent her head, and was covering her face with her hands. "Are you ill?" he said. "God bless us all, she has fainted! what am I to do?"

"No; the like of me never faints," she answered; and then he perceived that she retained her upright position. Her voice was choked, and sounded like the voice of despair, and she did not take her hands from her face. "Oh, if I could lie like Jeanie," she went on, "quietly, like the dead, with nae heart to feel nor voice to speak. My bit little lily flower! would she have been broken like that—faded like that, if I had done what was right? But, O Lord my God, my bonnie lad! what is to become of him?"

"Mrs. Murray! Mrs. Murray!" said Mr. Fielding, "let me put you on that sofa. Let me get you some wine. Compose yourself. My poor woman, my good woman! All this has been too much for you. Are you sure it is not a delusion you have got into your mind?"

The strange penitent took no notice of him as he stood thus beside her. Her mind was occupied otherwise. "How am I to make amends?" she was murmuring; "how am I to do it? Harm the innocent, crush down the innocent!—that's all I can do. It will relieve my mind, but it will throw nothing but bitterness into theirs. The prophet he threw a sweetening herb into the bitter waters, but it would be gall and wormwood I would throw. The wrong's done, and it canna be undone. It would but be putting off my burden on them—giving them my pain to bear; and it is me, and no them, that is worthy of the pain."

"Mrs. Murray," said the Rector, by this time beginning to feel alarmed; for how could he tell that it was not a madwoman he had beside him in the dark? "you must try and compose yourself. I think things cannot be so bad as you say. Perhaps you are tormenting yourself for nothing. My dear good woman, sit down and rest, and compose yourself, while I ring the bell for the lamp."

Then she rose up slowly in the darkness between him and the window, and took her hands from her face. She did not raise her head, but she put out her hand and caught his arm with a vigour which made Mr. Fielding tremble. "I was thinking if I had anything else to say," she said, in a low desponding tone, "but there's nothing more. I cannot think but of one thing. If you've nothing more to say to me, I'll go away. I'll slip away in the dark, as I came, and nobody will be the wiser. Mr. Fielding, you're a real good man, and that was your best advice?"

"It's my advice to everybody, in ordinary circumstances," said Mr. Fielding. "If you have done wrong, make amends—the one thing necessitates the other. If you have done wrong, make amends. But, Mrs. Murray, wait till the lamp comes and a glass of wine. You are not fit to go back to your nursing without something to sustain you. Sit down again."

"I am fit for a great deal more than that," she said; "but no, no, nae lights. I'll go my ways back. I'll slip out in the dark, as I slipped in. I'm like the owls—I'm dazzled by the shinin' light. That's new to me, that always liked the light; but, sir, I thank ye for your goodness. I must slip away now."

"You are not fit to walk in this state," he said, following her anxiously to the door; "take my arm; let me get out the pony—I will send you comfortably home."

Mrs. Murray shook her head. She declined the offer of the old man's arm. "I have mair strength than you think," she said; "and Jeanie must never know that I have been here. Oh, I'm strengthened with what you said. Oh, I'm the better for having opened my heart; but I'll slip out, as long as there are none to see."

And, while the gentle Rector stood and wondered, she went out by the open window, as erect and vigorous as if no emotion could touch her. Swiftly she passed into the darkness, carrying with her her secret. What was it? Mr. Fielding sunk into his chair with a sigh. Never before had any interruption like this come into Milly's hour.

CHAPTER VIII

Edgar went to his own room, with a certain oppression on his mind, to seek those papers which surely his sister gave the most exaggerated importance to. It seemed ridiculous to go upstairs at that hour; he took them out of his dressing-case, into which he had locked them, and went down again to the library. It was true that he would fain have occupied his evening in some other way. He would have preferred even to talk to Arthur Arden, though he did not love him. He would have preferred to read, or to walk out and enjoy the freshness of the summer night. And, much better than any of these, he would have preferred to have Clare's own company, to talk to her about the many matters he had laid up in his mind, and, perhaps, if opportunity served, to enter upon the subject of Gussy. But this evidently was not how it was to be. He must go and read over dull papers, to please his sister. Well, that was not so very difficult a business, after all. It was Clare's interest in them that was so strange. This was what he could not understand. As he settled himself to his task, a great many thoughts came into his mind in respect to his sister. She had been brought up (he supposed) differently from other girls. He could not fancy the Thornleighs, any of them, taking such interest in a parcel of old papers. They must be about Arden somehow, he concluded, some traditionary records of the family, something that affected their honour and glory. Was this what she cared for most in the world—not her brother or any future love, but Arden, only Arden, her race. And then he reflected how odd it was that two of Clare's lovers had made him their confidant—Arthur, a man whom any brother would discourage; and Lord Newmarch, who was an excellent match. The one was so objectionable, the other so irreproachable, that Edgar was amused by the contrast. What could they expect him to do? The one had a right to look for his support, the other every reason to fear his opposition; but what did Clare say, what did she think of either?—even Arthur Arden's presence was nothing to her, compared with these old letters. He seated himself, without knowing it, at his father's place, in his father's chair. No association sanctified the spot to him. Once or twice, indeed, he had been called there into the Squire's dreadful presence, but there was nothing in these interviews to make the room reverent or sacred. He put himself simply in the most convenient place, lighted the candles on the table, and sat down to his work. Clare was upstairs—he thought he heard her soft tread overhead. Yes, she was different from other girls; and he wondered in himself what kind of a life hers would be. Would she—after all, that was the first question—remain in Arden when Gussy came as its mistress?—if Gussy ever came. Would she find it possible to bend her spirit to that? Would she marry, impatient of this first contradiction of her supremacy?—and which would she choose if she married? All these questions passed through Edgar's mind, gravely at first, lightly afterwards, as the immediate impression of her seriousness died away. Then he looked at all the things on the table— his father's seal, the paper in the blotting-book, with its crest and motto. How well he remembered the few curt letters he had received on that paper, bidding him "come home on Friday next to spend a week or a fortnight," as the case might be—very curt and unyielding they had been, with no softening use of his name, no "dear Edgar," or "dear boy," but only the command, whatever it was. It was not wonderful that he had little reverence, little admiration, for his father's memory. His face grew sterner and paler as he turned over those relics of the dead man, which moved Clare only to tenderest memories. Twenty years of neglect, of injury, of unkindness came before him, all culminating in that one look of intense hatred which he remembered so well—the look which made it apparent to him that his father—his father!—would have been glad had he died.

Such thoughts had been banished from Edgar's breast for a long time. He had dismissed them by a vigorous effort of will when he entered upon his life at Arden; it was but those signs and tokens of the past that brought them back, and again he made an effort to begin his task, though with so little relish for it. If it was anything affecting the Squire, Edgar felt he was not able to approach it calmly. A certain impatience, a certain disgust, came into his mind at the thought. To please Clare—that was a different matter. He opened the enclosure slowly and with reluctance, and once more turned over in his hand the inner packet, still sealed up, which had the appearance of having been thrown into the fire, and hastily snatched out again. The parcel was singed and torn, and one of the seals had run into a great blotch of wax, obliterating all impression. As he held it in his hand he felt the place where the envelope was torn across, and remembered dimly that his sister had attributed her interest in it to the words she had read through this tear. What were they? he wondered. He turned the packet round and laid it on the table, with the torn part uppermost. It was his father's handwriting that appeared below, a writing somewhat difficult to read. He studied it, read it, lifted it nearer to his eyes—asked himself, "What does it mean?"—then he held it up to the light and read it over once more. What did it mean? A certain blank seemed to take possession of all his faculties—he wondered vaguely—the powers of his mind seemed to forsake him all at once.

This is what was written, in uneven lines, under the torn envelope, which had driven Clare desperate, and made her brother stupid, in his inability to understand—

"I will take him from you, bring him up as my son, and make him my heir—as you say, for my own ends."

Edgar was stupefied. He sat and looked at it blankly over and over. Son!—heir! What was the meaning of the words? He did not for the moment ask any more. "What does the fool mean? What does the fool mean?" he said, over and over. It did not move him to open the cover to inquire further. He only sat stupid, and looked at it. How long he might have continued to do so it is impossible to tell; but all at once, in the quiet house, there was a sound of something falling, and this roused him. What could it be? Could it be Clare who had fallen? Could it—He roused himself up, and went to the door and listened. He had wasted an hour or more in one way or other before he even looked at his packet, and now the house was at rest, and everything still. Had Clare known the moment at which he read those words—had she fainted in sympathy? His mind had grown altogether so confused that he could not make it out. He stood watching at the door for some minutes, and then, hearing nothing further, shut it carefully, and went back and sat down again. The candles were clear enough; the writing, though difficult, was distinct. "I will take him from you, bring him up as my son, make him my heir." "Perhaps there is something more about it inside," Edgar said to himself, with a faint smile. He spoke aloud, with a sense that he was speaking to somebody, and then started at the sound of his own voice, feeling as if some one else had spoken. And then he laughed. It made a diabolical sound in the silence. Was it he that laughed, or some devil?—there must be devils about—and what a fool he must be to be so easily startled; what a fool—what a fool!

Then he opened the envelope. His hands trembled a little; he came to himself gradually, and became aware that this was no light business he was about. It was the laugh that had roused him, the laugh with which he himself or somebody else—could it be somebody else?—had disturbed the silence. A quantity of letters were inside, some in his father's writing, some in another—a large, irregular, feminine hand. Instinctively he secured that one which had appeared through the tear in the cover, and read it word by word. It was one of the square letters written before envelopes were used, and bore on the yellow outside fold an address half-obliterated and some postmarks. He read it to the last word; he made an effort to decipher the outside; he investigated and noted the yellow date on the postmarks. He knew very well what he was doing now; never had his brain been more collected, never had he been more clear-headed all his life. Twice over he read it, word by word, and then put it down by his side, and arranged the others according to their dates. There were alternate letters, each with its reply. Two minds—two souls—had met in those yellow bits of paper, and gone through a terrible struggle; they were the tempter and the tempted—the one advancing all his arguments, the other hesitating, doubting, refusing—hesitating again. Carefully, slowly, Edgar read every one. There was nothing fictitious about them. Clear and distinct as the daylight was the terrible story they involved—the story of which he himself, in his ignorance, was the hero—of which he was the victim. All alone in the darkness and stillness of the night there fell upon him this awful revelation—a thing he had never expected, never feared—a new thing, such as man never had heard of before.

The business he was about was too tremendous to allow time for any reflection. He did not reflect, he did not think, he only read and knew. He felt himself change as he read, felt the room swim, so that he had to hold by the table, felt new lights which he had never dreamt of spring up upon his life. Sometimes it seemed to him as if even his physical form was changing. He was looking at himself as in a magic mirror, for the first time seeing himself, understanding himself, beholding the mystery clear away, the reality stand out. How clear it grew! A chill arose about him, as of a man traversing a mine, poking through half-lighted dreary galleries, and finding always the blue circle of outlet, the light at the end. He went on and on, never pausing nor drawing breath. He looked like a historical student seated there, regulating his documents with such exactness, reading every bit of paper only according to its date. Some of them were smoked and scorched, and took a great deal of trouble to make out. Some were crabbed in their handwriting and uncertain in spelling. At some words a faint momentary smile would come upon his lips. It was a historical investigation. No family papers ever had such interest, ever claimed such profound study. The daylight came in over the tops of the shutters; first a faint blueness, gradually widening and whitening into light. To see him sitting with candles blazing on each side of him, holding up his papers to them, and the quiet observant day flooding the room around him with light, and the ineffectual barred shutters vainly attempting to obscure it—oh, how strange it was! Edgar himself never perceived the change. He felt the chill of morning, but he had been cold before, and took no notice. How grave he was, how steady, how pale, in the flashing foolish light of the candles! As if that was needed! as if all was not open, clear, and legible, and patent to the light of day.

This was the scene which Clare looked in upon when she softly opened the door. She had not even undressed. She had sat up in her room, thinking that he would perhaps call, perhaps come to her, perhaps laugh, and ask her what her fright had meant, and show her how innocent and foolish these words were which had alarmed her. And then she had dozed and slept with a shawl round her; and then, waking up in the early morning, had stolen out, and seeing her brother's room open, had been seized with sudden terror wilder than ever. Her heart beat so loudly that she felt as if it must wake the house. She stole downstairs like a ghost, in her white evening dress. She opened the door, and there he sat in the daylight with his candles, not hearing her, not seeing her, intent upon his work. Was not that enough? She gave a low cry, and with a start he roused himself and looked up, the letters still in his hand. There was a moment in which neither moved, but only looked at each other with a mutual question and reply that were beyond words. Then he rose. How pale he was—like a dead man, the blood gone out of his very lips; and yet could it be possible he smiled? It was a smile Clare never forgot. He got up from his chair, and placed another for her, and turned to her with that look full of tenderness and pathos, and a certain strange humour. "I don't know how to address you now," he said, the smile retiring into his eyes. "I know who you are, but not who I am. It was natural you should be anxious. If you sit down, I will tell you all I know."

She came to him with a sudden impulse, and caught his arm with her hands. "Oh, Edgar! oh, my brother Edgar!" she said, moaning, but gazing at him with a desperate question, which he knew he had already answered, in her eyes.

"No," he said, gently putting his hand upon hers. A sudden spasm crossed his face, and for the moment his voice was broken. "No—Your friend, your servant; so long as you want me your protector still—but your brother no more."

CHAPTER IX

Arthur Arden felt himself very much at a loss next morning, and could not make it out. The brother and sister had left him to his own devices the night before, and again he found himself alone when he came down to breakfast. The same round table was in the window—the same vase of roses stood in the middle—everything was arranged as usual. The only thing which was not as usual was that neither Edgar nor Clare were visible. In this old, orderly, well-regulated place, such a thing had been never seen before. Wilkins paused and made a little speech, half shocked, half apologetic, as he put a savoury dish under Arthur's nose. "Master's late, sir, through business; and Miss Arden, she's not well. I'm sure I'm very sorry, and all the house is sorry. The first morning like—"

"Never mind, Wilkins," said Arthur. "I daresay my cousin will join me presently. I have been late often enough in this house."

"But never the Squire, if you'll remember," said Wilkins. "Master was always punctual like the clock. But young folks has new ways. Not as we've anything to complain of; but from time to time there's changes, Mr. Arthur, in folk's selves, and in the world."

"That is very true, Wilkins," said Arthur, with more urbanity than usual. He was not a man who encouraged servants to talk; but at present he was on his good behaviour—amiable to everybody. "I am very sorry to hear Miss Arden is ill. I hope it is not anything beyond a headache. I thought she looked very well last night."

"Yes, sir; she looked very well last night," said Wilkins, with a little emphasis; "but for a long time past we've all seen as there was something to do with Miss Clare."

Arthur made no answer. He felt that to enter into such a discussion with a servant would not do, though he would have been glad enough to discover what was supposed to be the matter with Clare. So he held his tongue and eat his breakfast; and Wilkins, after lingering about for some minutes wooing further inquiry, took himself gradually away to the sideboard. Arthur sat in the bow-window at the sunny end, enjoying the pretty, flower-decked table, with all its good things; while Wilkins glided about noiselessly in black clothes, as glossy as a popular preacher's, and as spotless, deferentially silent and alert, ready to obey a whisper, the lifting of a finger. No doubt it was chiefly for his own ends, and for the delight of gossip that life was so ready to obey, for Wilkins generally had a will of his own. But the stillness, the solitude, the man's profound attention, rapt Arthur in a pleasant dream. If he had been master here instead of his cousin. If he had been Squire Arden instead of this boy, who was not like the Ardens, neither externally nor in mind. His brain grew a little dizzy for a moment. Was he so? Was the other but a dream? Should he go out presently and find that all the people about the estate came to him, cap in hand, and that Edgar was a shadow which had vanished away. He could not tell what vertigo seized him, so that he could entertain even for a moment so absurd a fancy. The next, he gave himself a slight shake and smiled, not without some bitterness. "I am the penniless one," he said to himself; "I may starve, while he has everything. If he likes to turn me out to-morrow, I shall have nowhere to go to." How strange it was! Arthur was, of course, a Tory of the deepest dye—he held the traditional politics of his race, which equally, of course, Edgar did not hold; but at this moment it would be vain to deny that certain theories which were wildly revolutionary crossed his mind. Why should one have so much and another nothing? why should one inherit name, and authority, and houses, and lands, and another be left without bread to eat? No democrat, no red republican could have felt the difference more violently than did Arthur Arden; as he sat that morning alone in the quiet Arden dining-room, eating his kinsman's bread.

After a while Edgar came in. He was singularly pale, and his manner had changed in a way which Arthur could not explain to himself. He perceived the change at the first glance. He said to himself (thinking, as was natural, of himself only), "He has come to some determination about me. He has got something to propose to me." Edgar looked like a man with some weighty business on hand. He had no time for his usual careless talk, his friendly, good-humoured notice of everything. He looked like a general who has a difficult position to occupy, or to get his troops safely out of a dangerous pass. His forehead, which had always been so free of care, was lined and clouded. His very voice had changed its tone. It was sharper, quicker, more decisive. He seemed to have made a sudden leap from a youth into a serious man.

"My sister, I am sorry, is not well," he said; "and I was up very late. I think she will stay in her room all day."

"I am very sorry," said Arthur, "Wilkins has been telling me. He says you were kept late by business; and you look like it. You look as if you had all the cares of the nation on your head."

"I suppose the cares of the nation sometimes sit more lightly than one's own," said Edgar, with a forced smile.

"My dear fellow!" said his cousin, laughing in superior wisdom. "Your cares cannot be of a very crushing kind. If it was mine you were talking of—a poor devil who sometimes does not know where his next dinner is to come from; but that is not a subject, perhaps, for polite ears."

"And the dinners have always come to you, I suspect," said Edgar; "good dinners too, and handsomely served. Chops have not been much in your way; whereas you know most people who talk on such a subject—"

"Have to content themselves with chops? Some people like them," said Arthur, meditatively. "By the way, Arden, does it not come within the sphere of a reforming landlord like you to reform the cuisine at the Arden Arms? If I were you, and had poor relations likely to come and stay there, I would make a difference. For you do consider the claims of poor relations. Many people don't; but you—By the way, you said something about Fazakerly. Is he actually coming? I should like to see the old fellow, though he is not fond of me."

"He is coming, certainly," said Edgar, with a momentary flush, "but I think not so soon as to-morrow. I—have something to do to-morrow—an old engagement. And then—my business with Fazakerly may be more serious than I thought."

"As you please," said Arthur, shrugging his shoulders slightly. "You are master, I have nothing to do with it. It was bad taste to remind you, I know. But when one's pockets are empty, and the Mrs. Pimpernels of life begin to cast one off—that was an alarming defeat; I begin to ask myself, Are the crowfeet showing? is the grey visible in my hair."

"I can't see it," said Edgar, with a momentary smile.

"No, I take care of that," said the other; "though a touch of grey is not objectionable sometimes—it makes a man interesting. You scorn such levity, don't you? But then you are five and twenty, and foolish thoughts are extinguished in you by the cares of the estate."

Once more a momentary smile passed over Edgar's face. "Have you noticed any of the changes I have made in the estate—do you like them?" he asked, with something like anxiety. What a strange fellow he is, Arthur thought—if I were he, should I care what any one thought? "I have renewed some leases which it perhaps was not quite wise to renew," Edgar continued, "and lent some money for draining and that sort of thing. Probably you would not have done it. If I were to die now—let us make the supposition—"

"My dear Arden, I am sadly afraid you won't die," said his cousin; "don't tantalise a man by putting such hopes in his head. How can you tell that I may not be prepared with a little white powder? If you were to die I should probably call in your drainage money, for even then I should be as poor as a rat—but I could not change anybody's lease."

"I wonder if you would take any interest in the property?" said Edgar; "there is a great charm in it, do you know. You feel more or less that you have some real power over the people. I don't think much of what people call influence, but actual power is very different. You can speak to them with authority. You can say, if you do this, I will do that. You can rouse their self-interest, as well as their sense of right. I have not done very much more than begin it, but it has been very interesting to me. I wonder if it would have the same effect on you."

He means to offer me the situation of agent, said Arthur Arden to himself. His agent! I! And then he spoke—"I'll tell you one thing I should take an interest in, Arden. I should look after those building leases for the Liverpool people. It would make the greatest possible difference to the estate; it would make up for the loss of Old Arden, which your sister carries off. That was a wonderfully silly business, if you will allow me to say so—I cannot imagine how you could ever think of alienating that."

A curious thrill passed over Edgar. It was quite visible, and yet he did not mean it to be visible. Up to this moment his gravity had been so real, his manner so serious, that his cousin had not for a moment suspected that he had anything to conceal. But this sudden shudder struck him strangely. "Are you cold," he asked, looking at him fixedly with a suspicious, watchful glance, "this fine morning? or are you ill, too?"

"Neither," said Edgar, restraining himself. "We were talking about the building leases. You, who are more of an Arden than I have ever been supposed to be—"

He attempted to say this with a smile, but his lips were dry and parched, and his pallor increased. Was it possible that he could have found anything out—he whose interest, of course, was to destroy any evidence that told against himself? At the thought Arthur Arden's heart sank; for if Edgar's fears for his own position were once raised, it was very certain that there would not long remain anything for another to find out.

"You mistake," he said, "the spirit of the Ardens; they were not a romantic race, as people suppose—they had their eyes very well open to their interests. I don't know what made your father so obstinate; but I am sure his father, or his grandfather, as far back as you like to go, would never have neglected such an opportunity of enriching themselves. Why, look at the money it would put into your purse at the first moment. I should do it without hesitation; but then, of course, people would say of me—He is a needy wretch; he is always in want of money. And, of course, it would be quite true. Has old Fazakerly's coming anything to do with that?"

"It may have to do with a great many things," said Edgar, with a certain irritable impatience, rising from his chair. "Pardon me, Arden, I am going down to the village. I must see how poor little Jeanie is. I have got some business with Mr. Fielding. Perhaps you would like to make some inquiries too."

"Not if you are going," said Arthur, calmly. "The girl was going on well yesterday. If you were likely to see her, I should send my love; but I suppose you won't see her. No, thanks; I can amuse myself here."

"As you please," said Edgar, turning abruptly away. He could not have borne any more. With an inexpressible relief he left the room, and freed himself from his companion. How strange it was that, of all people in the world, Arthur Arden should be his companion now!

As for Arthur, he went to the window and watched his cousin's progress down the avenue with mingled feelings. He did not know what to make of it. Sometimes he returned to his original idea, that Edgar, in compassion of his poverty, was about to make a post for him on the estate—to give him something to do, probably with some fantastic idea that to be paid for his work would be more agreeable to Arthur than to receive an allowance. "He need not trouble," Arthur said to himself. "I have no objection to an allowance. He owes it me, by Jove." And then he strolled into the library, which was in painful good order, bearing no trace of the vigils of the previous night. He sat down, and wrote his letters on the old Squire's paper, in the old Squire's seat. The paper suited him exactly, the place suited him exactly. He raised his eyes and looked over the park, and felt that, too, to be everything he could desire. And yet a fickle fortune, an ill-judging destiny, had given it to Edgar instead.

CHAPTER X

Edgar was thankful for the morning air, the freshness of the breeze, the quietness of the world outside, where there was nobody to look curiously at him—nobody to speak to him. It was the first moment of calm he had felt since the discovery of last night, although he had been alone in his room for three or four hours, trying to sleep. Now there was no effort at all required of him—neither to sleep, nor to talk, nor to render a reason. He was out in the air, which caressed him with impartial sweetness, never asking who he was; and the mere fact that he was out of doors made it impossible for him to write anything or read anything, as he might have otherwise thought it his duty to do. He went on slowly, taking the soft air, the fluttering leaves, the gleams of golden sunshine, all the freshness of the morning, into his very heart. Oh, how good nature was, how kind, caressing a man and refreshing him, however unhappy he might be! But the curious thing in all this was, that Edgar was not unhappy. He did not himself make any classification of his feelings, nor was he aware of this fact. But he was not unhappy: he was in pain: he felt like a man upon whom a great operation has been performed, whose palpitating flesh has been shorn away or his bones sawed asunder by the surgeon's skilful torture. The great shock tingles through his whole system, affects his nerves, occupies his thoughts, is indeed the one subject to which he finds himself ever and ever recurring; and yet does not go so deep as to affect the happiness of his life or the tranquillity of his mind. Perhaps Edgar did not fully realise what it was which had fallen upon him. He was tingling, suffering, torn asunder with pain; and yet he was quite calm. Any trifle would have pleased him. He was so wounded, so sore, so bleeding, that he had not time to look any further and be unhappy. The question what he should do had not yet entered his mind. In the meantime he was gladly silent, taking rest after the operation he had gone through.

He went down to the village vaguely, like a man in a dream. When he got to the great gate he asked himself, with a sort of curious wonder and interest, Should he go and tell Mr. Fielding—resolve all the Doctor's doubts for ever? But decided no, because he was too tired. Besides, he had not made up his mind what was to be done. He had not fully realised it—he had only felt the blow, and the rending, tearing pain—and now the hush after the operation, his veins still tingling, his flesh palpitating, but some soft opiate giving him a momentary, sweet forgetfulness of his suffering. Sufferers who have taken a very strong opiate often feel as Edgar did, especially if it does not bring sleep, but only a strange insensibility, an unexplainable trance of relief. He walked on and on, and he did not think. The thing had happened, the knife had come down; but the shearing and rending were past, and he was quiet. He was able to say nothing, think nothing—only to wait. At the present moment this was all.

And then he went down in his dream to the cottage where Jeanie was. As the women curtseyed to him at their doors, and the school-children made their little bobs, he asked himself, why? Would they do it if they knew? What would the village think? How would the information be received? Those Pimpernels, for instance, who had turned Arthur Arden out, how would they take it? Somehow, Edgar felt as if he himself had changed with Arthur Arden. It was he, he thought, who had become the poor cousin—he who was the one disinherited. We say he thought, but he did not really think; it was but the upper line of fancy in his mind—the floating surface to his thoughts. Though he had not made up his mind to any course of action, and was not even capable of thinking, yet at the same time he felt disposed to stop and speak to everybody, and say certain words of explanation. What could he say? You are making a mistake. This is not me; or, rather, I am not the person you take me for. Was that what he ought to say? And he smiled once more that curious smile, in which a certain pathetic humour mingled. "Who am I?" he said to himself. "What am I?—a man without a name." It gave him a strange, wild, melancholy amusement. It was part of the effect of the laudanum; and yet he had not taken any laudanum. His opiate was only the great pain, the sleepless night—the sudden softening, calming influence of the fresh day.

"She's opened her eyes once," said Mrs. Hesketh, at the cottage door. "You don't think much of that, sir; but it's a deal. She opened her eyes, and put out her hand, and said, 'Granny!' Oh, it's a deal, sir, is that! The Doctor is as pleased as Punch; and as for t'oud dame—"

"Is she pleased?" said Edgar.

"I don't understand her, sir," said the woman; "it looks to me as if she was a bit touched"—and here Mrs. Hesketh laid her finger on her own forehead. "Husht! she'll hear. She won't take a morsel of rest, won't t'oud dame. I canna think how she lives; but, bless you! she's got somethin' else on her mind— something more than Jinny. I'm a'most sure—Lord! I've spoke below my breath, but she's heard us, and she's coming here."

"Will you watch my bairn ten minutes, while I speak to the gentleman?" said Mrs. Murray. "Eh! I hope you'll be blessed and kept from a' evil, for you're a good woman—you're a good woman. Aye, she's better. She'll win through, as I always said. We've grand constitutions in our family. Oh, my bonnie lad! it's a comfort to me to see your face."

Edgar must have started slightly at this address, for the old woman started too, and looked at him with a bewildered air. "What did I say?" she asked. "Mr. Edgar, I've sleepit none for three nights. My heart has been like to burst. I'm worn out—worn out. If I said something that wasna civil, I beg your pardon. It is not always quite clear to me what I say."

"You said no harm," said Edgar. "You have always spoken kindly, very kindly, to me—more kindly than I had any right to. And I hope you will continue to think of me kindly, for I am not very cheerful just now, nor are my prospects very bright—"

"Your prospects no bright!" Mrs. Murray looked round to see that no one was near, and then she came out upon the step, and closed the cottage door behind her, and came close up to him. "Tell me what's wrong with you—oh, tell me what's wrong with you!" she said, with an eager anxiety, which was too much in earnest to pause or think whether such a request was natural. Then she stopped dead short, recollecting—and went on again with very little interval, but with a world of changed meaning in her voice. "Many a one has come to me in their trouble," she said. "It's that that makes me ask—folk out of my ain rank like you. Whiles I have given good advice, and whiles—oh! whiles I have given bad; but its that that makes me ask. Dinna think it's presumption in me."

"I never thought it was presumption," said Edgar; and there came upon him the strongest, almost irresistible, impulse to tell what had happened to him to this poor old woman at the cottage door. Was he growing mad too?—had his misfortune and excitement been too much for him? He smiled feebly at her, as he bewildered himself with this question. "If I cannot tell you now, I will afterwards," he said; and lingered, not saying any more. Her keen eyes investigated him while he stood so close to her. His fresh colour was gone, and the frank and open expression of his face. He was very pale; there were dark lines under his eyes; his mouth was firmly closed, and yet it was tremulous with feeling repressed and restrained. Alarm and a look of partial terror came into Mrs. Murray's face.

"Tell me, tell me!" she cried, grasping his arm.

"There is nothing to tell, my good woman," he said, and turned away.

She fell back a step, and opened the door which she had held closed behind her. Her face would have been a study to any painter. Deep mortification and wounded feeling were in it—tears had come to her eyes. Edgar noticed nothing of all this, because he was fully occupied with his own affairs, and had no leisure to think of hers; and had he noticed it, his perplexity would have been so intense that he could have made nothing of it. He stood, not looking at her at all—gone back into his own thoughts, which were engrossing enough.

"Ay," she said, "that's true—I'm but your good woman—no your friend nor your equal that might be consulted. I had forgotten that."

But Edgar had given her as much attention as he was capable of giving for the moment, and did not even remark the tone of subdued bitterness with which she spoke. He roused himself a little as she retired from him. "I hope you are comfortable," he said; "I hope no one annoys you, or interferes. The woman of the house—"

"There she is," said Mrs. Murray, and she made him a solemn little curtsey, and was gone before he could say another word. He turned, half-bewildered, from the door, and found himself face to face with Sally Timms, who felt that her opportunity had come.

"I don't want to be disagreeable, sir," said Sally, without a moment's pause. "I never was one that would do a nasty trick. It aint your fault, nor it aint her fault, nor nobody's fault, as Jinny is there. But not to give no offence, Squire, I'd just like to know if I am ever going to get back to my own little 'ouse?"

"I am very sorry, Sally," Edgar began, instinctively feeling for his purse.

"There's no call to be sorry, sir," said Sally; "it aint nobody's fault, as I say, and it aint much of a house neither; but it's all as I have for my little lads, to keep an 'ome. A neighbour has took me in," said Sally; "an' it's a sign as I have a good name in the place, when folks is ready o' all sides to take me in. And the little lads is at the West Lodge. But I can't be parted from my children for ever and ever. Who's to look to them if their mother don't? Who's to see as their faces are clean and their clothes mended? Which they do tear their clothes and makes holes in their trousers enough to break your heart—and nothing else to be expected from them hearty little lads."

"I will give you any rent you like to put on your house," said Edgar, with his purse in his hand. "I wish I could make poor Jeanie better, and give you your cottage back; but I can't. Tell me your price, and I will give it to you. I am very sorry you have been disturbed."

"It aint that, sir," said Sally, with her apron to her eyes. "Glad am I and 'appy to be useful to my fellow-creetures. It aint that. She shall stay, and welcome, and all my bits o' things at her service. I had once a good 'ome, Squire; and many a thing is there—warming-pans, and toasting-forks, and that—as you wouldn't find in every cottage. Thank ye, sir; I won't refuse a shillin' or two, for the little lads; but it wasn't that. If you please, Squire—"

"What is it?" said Edgar, who was getting weary. The day began to pall upon him, though it was as fresh and sweet as ever. The influence of that opiate began to wear out. He felt himself incapable of bearing any longer this dismal stream of talk in his ears, or even of standing still to listen. "What is it? Make haste."

"If you please," said Sally, "old John Smith, at the gate on the common, he's dead this morning, sir. It's a lonesome place, but I don't mind that. The little lads 'ud have a long way to come to school, but I don't mind that; does them good, sir, and stretches their legs so long's they're little. If you would think of me for the gate on the common—a poor decent widow-woman as has her children's bread to earn—if ye please, Squire."

A sudden poignant pang went through Edgar's heart. How he would have laughed at such a petition yesterday! He would have told Sally to ask anything else of him—to be made Rector of the parish, or Lord Chancellor—and he would have thrown that sovereign into her lap and left her. But now he thought nothing of Sally. The lodge on the common! He had as much right to give away the throne of England, or to appoint the Prime Minister. A sigh which was almost a groan burst from his heart. He poured out the contents of his purse into his hands and gave them to her, not knowing what the coins were. "Don't disturb Jeanie," he said, incoherently, and rushed past her without another word. The lodge on the common! It occurred to Edgar, in the mere sickness of his heart, to go round there—why, he could not have told. He went on like the wind, not heeding Sally's cry of wonder and thanks. The morning clouds had all blown away from the blue sky, and the scorching sun beat down upon his head. His moment of calm after the operation was past.

CHAPTER XI

Edgar walked on and on, through the village, over the perfumy common, which lay basking in the intense unbroken sunshine. All the mossy nooks under the gorse bushes were warm as nests which the bird has just quitted—the seedpods were cracking under the heat, all the sweet scents of the wild, mossy, heathery, aromatic bit of heath were coming out—the insects buzzing, every leaf of the vegetation thrilling under the power of the sunshine. He went straight across the common, disregarding the paths, through gorse and juniper bushes, and tufts of bracken, and beds of heather. He did not see and he did not care. The lodge was two miles away along a road which was skirted on either side by the lingering half-reclaimed edges of the heath—and if the walk had been undertaken with the intention of making a survey of the beauties of Arden, it could not have been better chosen. The lodge on the common was just within the enclosure of the park. Its windows commanded the long, purple-green stretch of heath, with the spire of Arden church rising over it in the distance, and a white line of road, on which were few passengers; but the lodge windows were closed that morning. The hot sun beat on them in vain—old eyes which for fifty years had contemplated that same landscape were now closed upon it for ever. John Smith had been growing old when he went to the lodge; he had been there before the old Squire's time, having known him a boy. He had lived into Edgar's time, and was proud of his hundred years. "I can't expect to see e'er another young Squire," he had said the last time Edgar had seen him. "Don't you flatter me. Short o' old Parr, and them folks in the Bible, I don't know none as has gone far over the hunderd; but I don't say but what I'd like to see another young Squire." The words came back into Edgar's mind as he paused. He knocked softly at the cottage door, and took off his hat when the daughter, herself an old woman, steady and self-possessed, as the poor are in their deepest grief, came to the door. "Will you come in and look at him, sir," she said; and her look of disappointment when he said no, went to Edgar's heart, full as it was of his own concerns. He turned back, and went in, and looked with awe upon the old, old worn face, which he remembered all his life. That wrinkled pallid countenance might have been a thousand years old, instead of only a hundred. Only a hundred! And poor old John, too, in his time had known troubles such as make years of days. One son had gone for a soldier, and been killed "abroad;" another had been the victim of an accident in the Liverpool docks, and was a cripple for life; another had "gone to the bad;" and there was a daughter, too, who had "gone to the bad"—landmarks enough to portion out the life of any man. Yet there he lay, so quiet after all, having shaken it off at last. Edgar, in his youth, in the first terrible shock of a misfortune which seemed to throw every other misfortune into the shade, looked at the remains of his old, old servant with a thrill of awe. Do your best for a hundred years, suffer your worst, take God's will patiently, go on working and working: and at the end this—this and no more. "He's got to his rest now, sir," said the daughter, putting up her apron to her eyes which shed few tears—"we didn't ought to grumble nor to cry; and I try not. He's safe now is t'oud man. He's with mother and the little ones as died years ago. I can't think as I'll know 'em when I get there. It's so long ago, and I'm so old mysel', they'd never think it was me. But I'll know father, and father will tell them. I can't help cryin' now and again, but I canno' grudge that he's got to his rest."

Edgar went out of the house hushed for the moment in all his fever of wild thoughts. Rest! He himself did not want rest. He was too young, too ardent, too full of life to think of it as desirable; but anyhow there was an end to everything: an end—and perhaps a new beginning elsewhere. His mind was a religious mind, and his nature was not one to which real doubts concerning the unseen were possible. But there is something in a great mental shock which unsettles all foundations. At all events, whatever else there might be in life, there was an end—and perhaps a new beginning. And yet what if a man had to work on through all the perplexities of this sick and vexed world for a hundred years?—a world in which you never know who you are, nor what—where all in a moment you may be thrust out of the place you believed you were born in, and your life, all torn across and twisted awry, made to begin anew. How often might a man have to begin anew?—until at last there came that End.

He walked along through the woods not consciously remarking anything, and yet noting unconsciously how all the big trunks gleamed in the sunshine, the silvery white lines of the young birches, the happy hush and rustle among the branches. Was it sound, or was it silence? The leaves twinkled in the light, which seemed to fill all their veins with joy, and yet they said Hush, hush! at their highest rapture. Hush, hush! said all nature, except here and there a dry bough which cracked under the flying feet of rabbit or squirrel, a broken branch or a pine cone that fell. The dying, the falling, the injured, and broken, sent harsh, undertones into the harmony; but the living and prospering whispered Hush! Did this thought pass articulately through the young man's mind as he threaded these woodland paths? No; some broken shadow of it, a kind of rapid suggestion—no more; and moment by moment his painful thoughts recurred more and more to himself.

What was he to do? It was not the wealth of Arden, or even the beauty of Arden, or the rank he had held as its master, or any worldly advantage derived from it that wrung his heart to think of—All these had their share of pain apart from the rest. The first and master pang was this, that he was suddenly shaken out of his place, out of his rank, out of that special niche in the world which he had supposed himself born to fill. He was cast adrift. Who was he? what was he? what must he do? At Arden there were quantities of things to do. He had entered upon the work with more absolute pleasure, than he had felt in the mere enjoyment of the riches and power connected with it. It was work he could do. He felt that he had penetrated its secrets, held its key in his hand; and now to discover that it was not his work at all—that it was the work of a man who would not do it, who would never think of it, never care for it. This thought overwhelmed him as he went through the wood. It came upon him suddenly, without warning, like a great thunderbolt. The work was to be transferred to a man who would not do it—whose influence would be not for good but for evil in the place. And nobody knew—Hush, hush! oh, heavens, silence it! fresh breeze, blow it away! Nobody knew—nobody but one, who had vowed never to betray, never to say a syllable—one whose loss would be as great as his own. There was so much that could be done for Arden—the people and the place had such powers of development in them. There was land to be reclaimed, fit to grow seed and bread; there were human creatures to be helped and delivered; a thousand and a thousand things came into his mind, some great and some small—trees to be planted even—and what Arthur Arden would do would be to cut down the trees; cottages to be built—and what would he care for the poor, either physically or morally? If Arden could speak, would not it cry to heaven to be kept under the good rule of the impostor, and saved from the right heir? And then the race which had been so proud, how would it be covered with shame!—the house which had wrapped itself up in high reserve, how would its every weakness be exposed to the light! And up to this time nobody knew—The good name of the Ardens might be preserved, and the welfare of the estate, and every end of real justice served—by what? Putting a few old papers into the fire. Clare had nearly done it last night by the flame of her candle. God bless Clare! And she, too, would have to be given up if everything else was given up—he would no longer have a sister. His name, his work, his domestic affections—everything he had in the world—all at the mercy of a lit taper or a spark of fire! If Arden was to be burnt down, for instance—such things have been—if at any time in all these years it had been burnt down, or even the wing which contained the library, or even the bureau in that room—no one would ever have known that there was any doubt about the succession. Ah, if it had happened so! What a strange, devilish malice it was to lock it up there, to throw confusion and temptation upon two lives! Was it Squire Arden's spirit, vindictive and devilish, which had led Clare to that packet? But no (Edgar thought in the wandering of his mind), it could not be Squire Arden; for Clare, too, would be a sufferer. He saw now, so well and clearly, why he had been made to consent to the arrangement which gave Old Arden to Clare. Clare was of the Arden blood; whereas he—

And then it occurred to him to wonder who he was. Not an Arden! But he must be some one's son— belong to some family—probably have brothers and sisters. And for ever and ever give up Clare!—Clare, his only sister—the sole being in the world to whom from childhood his heart had turned. Already he no longer ventured to touch, no longer called her by her name. He had lost his sister; and no other in the world could ever be so sweet.

Edgar's mind was gradually drained of courage and life as he went on. How was he to do it? It was not money or position, but himself and his life he would have to give up. How could he do it? Whereas, it was easy, so easy to have a fire kindled in his bedroom, or even a candle—They had been almost burned already. If they had been burned he never would have known. Nobody would have been the wiser; and yet he would have been an impostor all the same. And as for Arthur Arden, he should share everything—everything he pleased. He should have at least half the income now, and hereafter all—Yes; Edgar knew that such arrangements had been made. He himself might pledge himself not to marry; but then he thought of Gussy Thornleigh, and this time felt the blow so overpower him that he stopped short, and leant against a tree to recover himself. Gussy, whom he was to speak to to-morrow. Oh, good heavens!—just heavens!—was ever innocent man so beset! It is easy to speak of self-sacrifice; but all in a moment, in the twinkling of an eye, that a man should give up name, home, living, his position, his work, his very existence, his sister, and his bride—all because Squire Arden who was dead was a damned accursed villain; and that Squire Arden who was alive might squander so much money, spoil so many opportunities of valiant human service! Good God! was ever innocent man so beset!

And then, as he went on thinking, the horror of it overpowered him more and more. Most men when they are in trouble preserve the love of those who are dear to them—nay, have it lavished upon them, to make up for their suffering, even when their suffering is their own fault. But Edgar would have to relinquish all love—even his sister's—and it was no fault of his. No unborn babe could be more innocent than he was of any complicity in the deception. He had been its victim all his life; and now that he had escaped from its first tyranny, must he be a greater victim still—a more hopeless sacrifice? Oh, God, what injustice! What hateful and implacable tyranny!

And the flame of a candle would set everything right again—a momentary spark, the scented, evanescent gleam with which he lit his cigar—the cigar itself falling by chance on the papers. And were there not a hundred such chances occurring every day? Less than that had been known to sweep a young, fair, blooming, beloved creature, for whose sweet life all the estates in the world would not be an equivalent, out of the world. And yet no spark fell to burn up those pieces of paper which would cost Edgar everything that made life dear. He had been standing all this while against the trunk of the tree, pondering and pondering. He was startled by a gamekeeper passing at a distance, who took off his hat respectfully to his master. His master? Couldn't the fellow see? Edgar felt a strong momentary inclination to call out to him—No; not to me. I have no right to your obeisance, not much right even to your respect. I am an impostor—a man paltering with temptation. Should he break the charmed whispering silence, and shout these words out to the winds, and deliver his soul for ever? No. For did not the leaves and the winds and the tender grass and the buzzing insects unite in one voice—Hush! Hush! Hush! Such was the word which Nature kept whispering, whispering in his ear.

CHAPTER XII

The state of affairs at Arden on this strange day was very perplexing to Arthur. Clare did not make her appearance even at dinner, but there were sounds of going and coming on the stairs, and at one time Arthur could have sworn he heard the voice of Edgar at his sister's door. She was well enough to see her brother, though not to come downstairs. And among the letters which were brought down to be put into the post-bag surely there was more than one in her handwriting. She had been able to carry on her correspondence, then; consequently the illness must be a feint altogether to avoid him, which was not on the whole flattering to his feelings. Arthur felt himself, as he was, in a very undignified position. He had experienced a good many humiliations of late. He had been made to feel himself not at all so captivating, not so sought-after, as he had once been. The Pimpernels had ejected him; and here were his cousins, his nearest relations—two chits who might almost be his own children, and who ought to have been but too happy to have a man of his experience with them, a man so qualified to advise and guide them—here were they shutting themselves up in mysterious chambers, whispering together, and transacting their business, if they had any business, secretly, that he might not be of the party! It was not wonderful that this should be galling to him. He resented it bitterly. What! shut him out from their concerns, pretend illness, whisper and concert behind his back! He was not a man, he reflected, to thrust himself into anybody's private affairs; and surely the business might have been put off, whatever it was, or they might have managed somehow to keep it out of his sight if he was not intended to see it; whereas this transparent and, indeed, vulgar device thrust it specially under his eye. In the course of his reflections it suddenly flashed upon his mind that such conduct could only proceed from the fact that what they were occupied about was something which concerned himself. They were laying their heads together, perhaps, to be of service to him—to "do him good." There was never man so careless yet but the thought that somebody wished to do him good was gall to him. What they intended, probably, was to make him Edgar's agent on the estate. It would be earning his bread honestly, doing something for his living—a step which had often been pressed upon him. He would be left at Arden, guardian of the greatness and the wealth of a property which he was never to enjoy, making the best of the estate for Edgar's benefit; seeing him come and go, enjoying his greatness; while his poor kinsman earned an honest living by doing his work! By Jove! Arthur Arden said to himself; it was a very likely idea, this of the agentship—nothing could have been more natural, more suitable. It was just the sort of thing to have occurred to such a mind as Edgar's, who was naturally fond of occupation, and who would have been his own agent with pleasure. If the truth were known, no doubt Edgar thought he was making a little sacrifice by arranging all this for his cousin. Confound him! Arthur said. And if such an idea had actually entered Edgar's mind, this would have been his reward.

After dinner he went out into the Park to smoke his cigar. It was a lovely night, and strolling about in the fresh evening air was better than being shut up in a melancholy room without a creature near him to break the silence. He took a long walk, and finally came back to the terrace round the house. The favourite side of the terrace was that which lay in front of the drawing-room windows; but the terrace itself ran quite round Arden to the flower garden behind, which it joined on the two sides. In mere wantonness Arthur extended his stroll all the way round, which was an unfrequent occurrence. On the darkest side, where the terrace was half-obscured by encroaching trees, he saw a glimmer of light in some windows on the ground-floor. They were the windows of the library, he perceived after a while, and they were partially open—that is to say, the windows themselves were open, but the shutters closed. As Arthur strolled along passing them, he was attracted by the sound of voices. He stopped; his own step was inaudible on the grass, even if the speakers within had ever thought of danger. He paused, hesitated a moment, listened, and heard the sound more distinctly; then, after a moment's debate with himself, went up to the nearest window. There was no moonlight; the night was dark, and the closest observer even from without could scarcely have seen him. He threw his cigar away, and after another pause seated himself on the stone sill of the window. A great bush of clematis which clung about one side hid him in its fragrant bower. He could have escaped in a moment, and no one would have been the wiser; and the moths buzzed in over his head to the light, and the sound of the two voices came out. It was Clare and Edgar who were talking—Clare, who had been shut up in her room all day, who was too ill to come downstairs; but she had come down now, and was talking with the utmost energy—a tone in which certainly there was no appearance of failing strength. It was some time before he could make out more than the voices, but indignation and despite quickened his ears. The first, whose words he could identify, was Clare.

"Look here," she said, advancing, as would seem, nearer to the window, and speaking with an animation very unlike her ordinary tones. "Look here, Edgar! My father himself meant to burn them. Oh, that I should have to speak so of poor papa! But I acknowledge it. He has been wicked, cruel! I don't want to defend him. Yet he meant to burn them, you can see."

"But did not," said Edgar. "He did not; that is answer enough. Why, having taken all this trouble, and burdened his soul with a crime, he should have left behind the means of destroying his own work, heaven knows! Probably he thought I would find it, and conceal it for self-interest; but yet carry the sting of it for ever. I have been thinking long on the subject: that is what he must have meant."

"Oh, Edgar!" said Clare.

"That must have been his intention. I can see no other. He must have thought there was no doubt that I would in my turn carry on the crime. How strangely one man judges another! It was devilish, though. I don't want to hurt your feelings, but it was devilish. After having bound me, as he thought, by every bond to keep his secret, he would have thrust upon me the guilt too!"

"Oh, Edgar, Edgar!" Clare said, with a moan of pain. From the sound of the voices Arthur gathered that Edgar must be seated somewhere near the table, while Clare walked about the room in her agitation. Her voice came, now nearer, now farther from the window, and it may be supposed with what eager interest the eavesdropper listened. He would not have done it had there been time to think, or at least so he persuaded himself afterwards. But for anything he knew his dearest interests might be involved, and every word was important to him. A long silence followed—so long, that he thought all had come to an end, and with an intense sense of being mocked and tantalised, was about to get up and steal away, when he was recalled once more by the voice of Clare.

"It was I who found them," she said, "where I had no right to look. It was for you to say whether these papers should have been disturbed or not. I thrust myself among them, having no right: therefore I ought to be heard now. Edgar, listen to me! If you make them public, think of the scandal, the exposure! Think of our name dragged in the dust, and the house you have been brought up in—the house that is yours—Listen to me! Oh, Edgar! are you going to throw away your life? It is not your fault. You are innocent of everything. You would never have known if my father had had the justice to destroy these papers—if I had not had the unpardonable, the horrible levity of finding them out. If you will not do what I ask you to do, I will never, never forgive myself all my life. I will feel that I have been the cause. Edgar! you never refused to listen to me before."

"No," he said. The voice was farther off, and Arthur Arden had to bend forward close to the window to hear at all, but even then could not be insensible to the thrill of feeling that was in it. "No; but you never counselled me to do wrong before. Never! You have been like an angel to me—Clare."

There was a pause between the preceding words and the name, as if he had difficulty in pronouncing it; but this was wholly unintelligible to Arthur, whose worst suspicions fell so much short of the truth.

"Oh, no, no," she said: "do not speak to me so, Edgar. This has shown me what I am. I have been more like a devil. I have nothing but pride, and ill-temper, and suspicion to look back upon. Nothing, nothing else! Remember, I might have burned them myself. If I had been worthy to live, if I had been fit for my place in this house, if I had been such a woman as some are—my father's daughter—your sister, Edgar— I should have burned them myself."

"My—sister," he cried, with again a pause, and in a softened tremulous tone. "That is the worst; that is the worst! What are you doing, Clare?"

"My duty now," she said wildly, "to him and to you!"

Then there was a pause. Arthur Arden would have given everything he possessed in the world for the power of looking inside—but he dared not. He sat on the window-sill with all his faculties concentrated in his ears. What was she doing? There was some movement in the room, but sounds of gentle feet upon a Turkey carpet betray little. The first thing audible was a broken sobbing cry from Clare.

"Let me do it! I will go down on my knees to you. I will bless you for it, Edgar! Edgar! You will be more my brother than ever you were in my life!"

Another silence—nothing but the sobbing of intense excitement and a faint rustle as if the girl worn out had thrown herself into a chair; and then a sound of the rustling and folding of paper. Oh, if he could but see! The half-closed shutter jarred a little, moved by the wind; and Arthur, roused, found a little chink, the slenderest crevice by which he could see in. All that he saw was Edgar sealing a packet. The wax fell upon it unsteadily, showing emotion which was not otherwise visible in his look. Then he wrote some name upon the packet, and put it in the breast-pocket of his coat.

"There it is," he said cheerfully; "I have directed it to Mr. Fazakerly, and that settles the whole business. We must not struggle any more about it. Do you think I have had no temptation in the matter? Do you think I have got through without a struggle? The Thornleighs came back to-day—and to-morrow I was going to Thorne to ask her to be my wife."

When he said these words, Edgar for the moment overcome with his conflict, dropped his head upon his hands and covered his face. All the levity, all the ease and secondary character of his feelings towards Gussy had disappeared now. He felt the pang of giving up this sweetness as he had not yet felt anything. All rushed upon him at once—all the overwhelming revelations he had to make. Edgar was brave, and he had kept the thought at bay. But now—Gussy, Clare, himself—all must go—every love he had any right to, or any hope of—every companionship that had ever been his, or that he had expected to become his—"Oh God!" he said in the depths of his overthrow. It was the first cry that had come from his lips.

Arthur Arden, peering in, saw Clare go to him and throw her arms round him and press his bowed head against her breast. He saw her weep over him, plead with him in all the force of passion. "Give it to me; give it to me; give it to me!" she cried, with the reiteration of violent emotion. "You will make me the most miserable creature on earth. You will take every pleasure out of my life."

"Hush, hush!" he said softly, "Hush! we must make an end of this. Come and breathe the air outside? After all, what is it? An affair of a day. To-morrow or next day we shall have made up our minds to it; and the world cares so little one way or another. Come out with me and take breath, Clare."

"I cannot, I cannot," she cried. "What do I care for air or anything. Edgar, for the last time, stop and think."

"I have thought till my brain is turning," said Edgar, rising and drawing her arm within his to the infinite alarm of the listener, who transferred himself noiselessly to the other side of the great clematis bush, which fortunately for him grew out of a great old rose tree which was close against the wall. "For the last time, there is nothing to think about. It is decided now, and for ever."

And immediately a gleam of light fell upon the window-sill where the false kinsman had been listening; and the brother and sister came out, she leaning closely on his arm. They took the other direction, to the spy's intense relief; but the last words he heard inflicted torture upon him as the two passed out of sight and hearing; they were these: "Arthur Arden loves you, Clare."

CHAPTER XIII

Well! He had listened—he had disgraced himself—he was humbled in his own eyes, and would be lost in Clare's, should she ever find it out. And what had he made by it? He had discovered that Edgar had discovered something, which Clare would fain have destroyed—something which evidently affected them both deeply, and to which they gave a probably exaggerated importance. That was all. Whether it was anything that could affect himself he had not found out—not a word had been said to throw any light upon the mystery. The two knew what it was themselves, and they did not stop in their conversation to give any description of it for the benefit of the listener. Such things are done only by people on the stage. The eavesdropper in this case was none the wiser. He was much excited by the allusions he had heard. His faculties were all wound up to observe and note everything. But his knowledge of the world made him incredulous. After the first thrill of excitement—after the intense apprehension and shame with which he watched them disappear into the night, when he began seriously to think the matter over, he did not find in it, it must be said, any encouragement to his hopes. Arthur Arden knew the definite suspicion which all the circumstances of Edgar's life had raised in many minds, and at a very recent time he had seriously nourished a hope of himself finding among the Squire's papers something which should brand the Squire's heir with illegitimacy, and prove that he was no Arden at all, though the offspring of Squire Arden's wife. Only the other day he had entertained this thought. But now, when it would seem that some such papers had been found, the futility of it struck him as nothing had ever done before. A posthumous accusation would have no effect, he saw, upon the law. Squire Arden had never disowned Edgar. He had given him his name, and acknowledged him as his son, and no stigma that he could put upon him, now he was dead, could counteract that acknowledgment. He smiled bitterly to think that he himself could have been so very credulous as to believe it would; and he smiled still more bitterly at the perturbation of these two young people, and how soon Mr. Fazakerly would set their fears at rest. As soon as they had disappeared, he stepped boldly into the library by the open window, and examined the place to see if perchance any relics were left about, of which he could judge for himself; but there was nothing left about. And he had nothing for it but to leave the library, and retire to the drawing-room, of which for most of the evening he had been the solitary inmate. Some time after the sound of windows closing, of steps softly ascending the stairs, made it apparent that Edgar and Clare had come in, and finally separated for the night; though nobody appeared to disturb his solitude, except Wilkins, who came in and yawned, and pretended to look if the lamps wanted trimming. But even when he retired to his room it seemed to Arthur that he still heard stealthy steps about the house and whispering voices. Disturbance was in the very air. The wind rose in the night, and moaned and shivered among the trees. There was a shutter somewhere, or an open door, which clanged all through the night. This, and his suspicions and doubts, broke Arthur's sleep; and yet it was he who slept most soundly that night of all who bore his name.

In the morning, they all met at breakfast as on ordinary occasions. Clare was so pale that no doubt could be thrown upon her illness of the preceding day. She was as white as marble, and her great blue eyes seemed enlarged and dilated, and shone with a wistful, tearful light, profoundly unlike their ordinary calm. And her brother, too, was very pale. He was carefully dressed, spoke very little, and had the air of a man so absorbed in his thoughts as to be partially unaware what was going on around him. But Clare let nothing escape. She watched her cousin; she watched the servants; she watched Edgar's lips, as it were, lest any incautious word might escape them. When he spoke, she hurried to interrupt him, repeating or suggesting what he was about to say. And Arthur watched too with scrutiny scarcely less keen. He might have taken it all for a fit of temper on her part had he not heard their conversation last night. But now, though he felt sure no results would follow which could affect him personally, his whole being was roused—he was ready to catch the meaning out of any indication, however slight.

It had been late before either the brother or sister appeared, to the great dismay of Wilkins, who made many apologies to the neglected guest. "I don't know what's come over them. I don't indeed, sir," Wilkins had said, with lively disapproval in his tone. And the consequence was that it was nearly eleven before breakfast—a mere pretence to both Edgar and Clare, though their kinsman's appetite was not seriously affected—was over. Then Edgar rose from his chair, looking, if possible, paler than ever, intensely grave and self-restrained. "I think I may go now," he said to Clare; "it is not too early. I should be glad to have it over."

"Let me speak to you first," said Clare, looking at him with eyes that grew bigger and bigger in their intense supplication. "Edgar, before you go, and—Let me speak to you first—"

"No," he said with a faint smile. "I am not going to put myself to that test again. I know how hard it is to resist you. No, no."

"Just five minutes!" cried Clare. She ran out into the hall after him; and Arthur, full of curiosity, rose too, and followed to the open door of the dining-room. She took her brother's arm, put her face close to his ear, pleaded with him in a voice so low that Arthur could make out nothing but many repetitions of the one word, "Wait;" to which Edgar answered only by a shake of the head or tender melancholy look at her. This went on till his horse was brought to the door. "No," he said, "no, dear; no, no," smiling upon her with a smile more touching than tears; and then he stooped and kissed her forehead. "For the last time," he said softly in her ear, "I will not venture to do this when I come back." It was a farewell—one of those first farewells which are almost more poignant than the last—when imagination has fully seized the misery to come, and dwells upon it, inflicting a thousand partings. Arthur Arden, standing at the door behind, with his hands in his pockets, could not hear these words; but he saw the sentiment of the scene, and was filled with wonder. What did it mean? Was he going to run away, the fool, because he had discovered that his mother had not been immaculate? What harm would that do him—fantastic-romantic paladin? So sure was Arthur now that it could not do any legal harm that he was angry with this idiotic, unnecessary display. He could be none the better for it—nobody could be any the better for it. Why, then, should the Squire's legal son and unquestionable heir make this ridiculous fuss? It roused a suppressed rage in Arthur Arden's breast.

And Clare, seeing him watch, came back to the dining-room as her brother rode away from the door. She restrained the despair that was creeping over her, and came back to defy her kinsman. Though, what was the good of defying him, when so soon, so very soon, there would be nothing to conceal? She went back, however, restraining herself—meeting his eyes of wonder with a blank look of resistance to all inquiry. "Has Edgar gone off on a journey?" Arthur asked, with well-affected simplicity. "How strange he should have said nothing about it! Where has he gone?"

"He has not gone on a journey," said Clare.

"I beg your pardon—your parting was so touching. I wish there was somebody to be as sorry for me; but I might go to Siberia, and I don't think anyone would care."

"That is unfortunate," said Clare. She was very defiant, anxious to try her strength. For once more, even though all should be known this very day, she would stand up for her brother—her brother! "But don't you think, Mr. Arden," she said abruptly, "that such things depend very much on one's self? If you are not sorry to part with any one, it is natural that people should not interest themselves about you."

"I wonder if the reverse holds," said Arthur; and then he paused, and made a rapid, very rapid review of the situation. If this was a mere fantastical distress, as he believed, Clare had Old Arden and (independent of feeling, which, in his circumstances, he was compelled to leave out of the transaction) was of all people in the world the most suitable for him; and if there was anything in it, it was he who was the heir, and in such a case he could make no match which would so conciliate the county and reconcile him with the general public. His final survey was made, his conclusion come to in the twinkling of an eye. He drew a chair near the one on which she had listlessly thrown herself. "I wonder," he repeated, softly, "if the reverse holds?—when one loves dearly, has one always a light to hope for some kind feeling in return?—if not love, at least compassion and pity, or regret?"

"I do not know what you are talking of," said Clare, wearily. "I don't think I am equal to discussion to-day."

"Not discussion," he said, very gently. "Would you try and listen and realise what I am talking about, Clare? It seems the worst moment I could have chosen. You are anxious and disturbed about something—"

"No," she said, abruptly; "you are mistaken, Mr. Arden"—and then with equal suddenness she broke down, and covered her face with her hands. "Oh, yes, yes, I am anxious and full of trouble—full of trouble! Oh, if you were a man I could trust in, that I dared talk freely to—But you will know it soon enough."

It was a moment at which everything must be risked. "What if I knew it—or, at least, what if I guessed it already?" said Arthur, bending over her. "Ah, Clare, how surprised you look! You were too innocent to know; but there are many people who have known that there was a danger hanging over Edgar. You don't suppose your father's conduct to him could have been noticed by everybody without there being some suspicion of the cause?"

Clare raised her face, quite bloodless and haggard, from her hands. She looked at him with a look of awe and fear. "Then you knew it!" she said, the words scarcely able to form themselves on her lips.

"Yes," said Arthur; "and for your consolation, Clare—though it should be the reverse of consolation to me—I do not think he should fear. Such things as these are very difficult to prove. The Squire never said a word in his lifetime. I don't know if any court of law would allow your brother to prove his own illegitimacy—I don't think they would. He has no right to bring shame on his mother—"

"What do you mean?" said Clare, looking at him suddenly with a certain watchfulness rising in her eyes.

"I am entering on a subject I ought not to have entered upon," he said. "Forgive me; it was only because I wanted to tell you that I don't think Edgar has any just cause for fear. If you would only trust me, dearest Clare. I should ask your pardon for saying that, too—but though you should never think of me, never speak to me again, you are still my dearest. Clare, you sent me away, and I could not tell why. Don't send me away now. I am a poor beggar, and you are a rich lady, and yet I love you so well that I must tell you, whatever your opinion of me may be. Couldn't you trust me? Couldn't you let me help you? You think I would be Edgar's enemy, but I would not. He should have everything else if he left me you."

She looked up at him with a movement of wonder. Her eyes interrogated him over and over. He had wounded her so much and so often—about Jeanie—about the Pimpernels—about—And yet, if he really meant it—could it be possible that he was willing to leave Edgar everything, to give him no trouble, if only she—? Was it a bargain she was going to make? Ah, poor Clare! She thought so—she thought her impulse was to buy her brother's safety with her own, but at the same moment her heart was fluttering, beating loud, panting to be given to him whom she loved best. And yet she loved Edgar. To her own consciousness it was her brother she was thinking most of now—and what a comfort it would be thus to purchase Arthur's promise not to harm him, and to trust everything to Arthur! She wavered for an instant, with her mind full of longing. Then her heart misgave her. She had allowed him to take her hands in his, and to kiss them; while she looked him in the face, with eyes full of dumb inquiry and longing, asking him over and over again was this true?

"Stop, stop," she said faintly; "if it was my own secret I would trust you—if it was only me—Oh, stop, stop! If you will say the same to-morrow—when he has told you—then I will—Oh, if I can survive it, if I am able to say anything! Cousin Arthur, I am worn out; let me go now."

"It is hard to let you go," he said. "But, Clare, tell me again—if I say the same to-morrow, after he has told me—you will—? Is that a promise? You will listen to me—you will give me what I desire most in the world—is it a promise, Clare?"

"Let me go," she said. "Oh, this is not a time to speak of—of our own happiness, or our own concerns."

"Thanks for such words—thanks, thanks," he cried, "I ask no more. To-morrow—it is a bargain, Clare."

And thus she made her escape, half glad, half shocked that she could think of anything but Edgar, and not half knowing what she had pledged herself to. Neither did Arthur Arden know to what he had pledged himself.

CHAPTER XIV

Edgar rode over the verdant country, wearily, languidly, with a heart that for once was closed to its influence. He was tired of the whole matter. It no longer seemed to him so dreadful a thing to give up Arden, to part from all he cared for. If he could but be done with the pain of it, get it over, have no more trouble. Agitation had worn him out. The thought that he would have another day like yesterday to live through, or perhaps more than one other day, filled his heart with a sick impatience. Why could he not ride on to the nearest railway station, and there take any train, going anywhere, and escape from the whole business? The mere suggestion of this relief was so sweet to him that he actually paused at the cross road which led to the railway. But he was not the kind of man to make an escape. To leave the burthen on others and save himself was the last thing he was likely to do. He touched his horse unconsciously with his whip and broke into a gay canter on the grassy border of the road that led to Thorne. Coraggio! he cried to himself. It would not last so long after all. He would leave no broken bits of duty undone, no ragged edges to his past. A little pain more or less, what did it matter? Honestly and dutifully everything must be done; and, after all, the shame was not his. It was the honest part that was his—the righting of wrong, the abolition of injustice. Strange that it should be he, a stranger to the race, who had to do justice to the Ardens! He was not one of them, and yet he had to act as their head, royally making restitution, disposing of their destinies. He smiled a painful smile as this thought crossed his mind. They were one of the proudest families in England, and yet it fell to a nameless man, a man most likely of no lineage at all, to set them right. If any forlorn consolation was to be got out of it at all it was this.

When Edgar was seen riding up the avenue at Thorne it made a commotion in the house. Mary and Beatrice spied him from the window of the room which had been their schoolroom, and where they still did their practising and wrote their letters to their dearest friends. "Oh, there is Edgar Arden coming to propose to Gussy!" cried Beatrice; and they rushed to the window to have a look at him, and then rushed to the drawing-room to warn the family. "Oh, mamma, oh, Gussy! here's Edgar Arden!" they cried. Lady Augusta looked up from her accounts with composed looks. "Well, my dear children, I suppose none of us are much surprised," she said. Gussy, for her part, grew red with a warm glow of rosy colour which suffused her throat and her forehead. "Poor, dear boy!" she said to herself. He had not lost a moment. It was a little past noon, not time for callers yet. He had not lost a moment. She wondered within herself how it would come—if he would ask her to speak to him alone in a formal way—if he would ask her mother—if he would manage it as if by chance? And then what would he say? That question, always so captivating to a girl's imagination, was soon, very soon, to be resolved. He would tell her he had loved her ever since he knew her—he would tell her—Gussy's heart expanded and fluttered like a bird. She would know so soon all about it; how much he cared for her—everything he had to tell.

But they were all shocked by his paleness when he came in. "What have you been doing to yourself?" Gussy cried, who was the most impulsive. "Have you been ill, Mr. Arden?" said sympathetic Ada. They were all ready to gather about him like his sisters, to be sorry for him, and adopt all his grievances, if he had any, with effusion. He felt himself for the moment the centre of all their sympathies, and his hurt felt deeper and more hopeless than it had ever done before.

"I am not in the least ill," he said, "and I have not been doing anything to speak of; but Fortune has been doing something to me. Lady Augusta, might I have half an hour's talk with you, if it does not disturb you? I have—something to say—"

"Surely," said Lady Augusta; and she closed her account-books and put them back into her desk. He meant to take the formal way of doing it, she supposed—a way not so usual as it used to be, but still very becoming and respectful to the fathers and mothers. She hesitated, however, a little, for she thought that most likely Gussy would like the other method best. And she was not so much struck as her daughters were by the change in his looks. Of course, he was a little excited—men always are in such an emergency, more so than women, Lady Augusta reflected; for when it comes to that a woman has made up her mind what is to be the end of it, whereas the man never knows. These reflections passed through her mind as she locked her desk upon the account-books, thus giving him a little time to get by Gussy's side if he preferred that, and perhaps whisper something in her ear.

But Edgar made no attempt to get by Gussy's side. He stood where he had stopped after shaking hands with them all, with a faint smile on his face, answering the questions the girls put to him, but visibly waiting till their mother was ready to give him the audience he had asked. "I suppose I must go and put him out of his pain; how anxious he looks, the foolish boy," Lady Augusta whispered, as she rose, to her eldest daughter. "Mamma, he looks as if he had something on his mind," Ada whispered back. "I know what he has on his mind," said her mother gaily. And then she turned round and added aloud, "Come, Mr. Arden, to my little room where I scold my naughty children, and let us have our talk."

The sisters, it must be said, were a little alarmed when Edgar was thus led away. They came round Gussy and kissed her, and whispered courage. As for the giddy young ones, they tried to laugh, though the solemnity of the occasion was greater than they could have supposed possible. But the others had no inclination to laugh. "It is only agitation, dear, not knowing what your answer may be," Ada said, though she did not feel any confidence that it was so. "He should not have made so formal an affair of it," said Helena; "That is what makes him look so grave." Poor Gussy, who was the most deeply concerned of all, cried. "I am sure there is something the matter," she said. The three eldest kept together in a window, while Mary and Beatrice roved away in quest of some amusement to fill up the time. And a thrill of suspense and excitement seemed to creep over all the house.

Edgar's courage came back to him in some degree, as he entered Lady Augusta's little boudoir. Imagination had no longer anything to do with it, the moment for action had come. He sat down by her in the dainty little chamber, which was hung with portraits of all her children. Just opposite was a pretty sketch of Gussy, looking down upon him with laughing eyes. They were all there in the mother's private sanctuary, the girls who were her consolation, the boys who were her plague and her delight. What a centre it was of family cares and anxieties! She turned to him cheerfully as she took her chair. She was not in the least afraid of what was coming. She had not even remarked as yet how much agitated he was. "Well, Mr. Arden!" she said.

"I have come to make a very strange confession to you," said Edgar. "You will think I am mad, but I am not mad. Lady Augusta, I meant to have come to-day to ask you—to ask if I might ask your daughter to be my wife."

"Gussy?" said Lady Augusta, with the tears coming to her eyes. There was something in his tone which she did not understand, but still his last words were plain enough. "Mr. Arden, I don't know what my child's feelings are," she said; "but if Gussy is pleased I should be more than content."

"Oh, stop, stop," he said. "Don't think I want you to commit yourself—to say anything. Something has happened since then which has torn my life in two—I cannot express it otherwise. I parted from you happy in the thought that as Arden was so near and everybody so kind—But in the meantime I have made a dreadful discovery. Lady Augusta, I am not Edgar Arden; I am an impostor—not willingly, God knows, not willingly—"

"Mr. Arden," Lady Augusta said, loudly, in her consternation, "you are dreaming—you are out of your mind. What do you mean?"

"I said you would think I was mad. It looks like madness, does not it?" said Edgar, with a smile, "but, unhappily, it is true. You remember how my father—I mean Mr. Arden—always treated me?—how he kept me away from home? I was not treated as his son ought to have been. I have never said a word on the subject, because I never doubted he was my father—but I have the explanation now."

"Good God!" said Lady Augusta; she was so horror-stricken that she panted for breath. But she too put upon the news the interpretation which Arthur Arden put upon it. "Oh, Mr. Arden!" she cried, "don't be so ready to decide against your poor mother! A jealous man takes things into his head which are mere madness. I knew her. I am sure she was not a wicked woman. I am a mother myself, and why should I hesitate to speak to you? Oh, my dear boy, don't condemn your mother! Your father was a proud suspicious man, and he might doubt her without cause. I believe he doubted her without cause. What you have discovered must be some ravings of jealousy. I would not believe it. I would not, whatever he may say!"

And she put out her hand to him eagerly in her sympathy and indignation. Edgar took it in his, and kissed the kind, warm, motherly hand.

"Dear Lady Augusta," he said, "how good you are! It is easier to tell you now. There is no stigma upon— Mrs. Arden; that was one of the attendant evils which have followed upon the greater crime. I am not her son any more than I am her husband's. I am a simple impostor. I have no more to do with the Ardens than your servant has. I am false—all false; a child adopted—nothing more."

"Good God!" said Lady Augusta once more. By degrees the reality of what he was saying came upon her. His face so pale, yet so full of lofty expression; his eyes that gleamed and shone as he spoke; the utter truthfulness and sincerity of every word impressed her in her first incredulity. Good God! he meant it. If he were not mad—and he showed no signs of being mad—then indeed it must be true, incredible as it seemed. And rapidly as a flash of lightning Lady Augusta's mind ran over the situation. How unfortunate she was! First Ada, and now—But if this was how it was, Gussy must not know of it. She was capable of heaven knows what pernicious folly. Gussy must not know. All this ran through Lady Augusta's mind while she said the two solemn words of the exclamation given above.

And then there was a little pause. Edgar stopped too, partly for want of breath. It had cost him a great deal to say what he had said, and for the moment he could do no more.

"Do you mean to say this is true, Mr. Arden?" said Lady Augusta. "True! I cannot believe my ears. Why, what inducement had he? There was Clare."

"So far as I can make out, it was thought to be impossible that there should be any children; but that I cannot explain. It is so," said Edgar, insisting pathetically. "Believe me, it is so."

"And how did you find it out?"

Lady Augusta's tones were very low and awe-stricken; but her interrogatory was close and persistent. Edgar was depressed after his excitement. He thought he had calculated vainly on her sympathy. "Clare found the letters," he said, "in my father's—I mean in Mr. Arden's room. They are too clear to admit of any doubt."

"She found them! What does she think of it? It will not be any the better for her; and you such a good, kind brother to her!" cried Lady Augusta in a tone of indignation. She was glad to find some one to find fault with. And then she made a long pause. Edgar did not move. He sat quite still opposite, looking at her, wondering would she send him away without a word of sympathy? She looked up suddenly as he was thinking so, and met his wistful eyes. Then Lady Augusta, without a moment's warning, burst out sobbing, "Oh, my poor dear boy! my poor dear boy!"

Edgar was at the furthest limit of self-control. He could not bear any more. He came and knelt down before her, and took her hand, and kissed it. It was all he could do to keep from weeping too. "Thanks, thanks," he said, with a trembling voice; and Lady Augusta, kind woman, put her arm round him, and wept over him. "If I had been Clare I would have burned them, and you should never have known—you should never have known," she cried. "Oh, my poor, poor boy!"

"I am very poor now," he said. "I thought you would be my mother—I who never had one. And Gussy—you will tell her; and you will not blame me—"

"Blame you!" cried Lady Augusta. "My heart bleeds for you; but I blame Clare. I would have burned them, and never thought it wrong."

"But it would have been wrong," he said softly, rising. "Clare would burn them now if I would let her. She is not to blame. Dear Lady Augusta, good-bye. And you will say to Gussy—"

He paused; and so did she, struggling with herself. Should she let him see Gussy? Should she allow him to say good-bye? But Gussy was only a girl, and who can tell what mad thing a girl may propose to do? "Pardon me! pardon me!" she said; "but it is best you should not see Gussy now."

"Yes," said Edgar; "it is best." But it was the first real sign that one life was over for him, and another begun.

CHAPTER XV

One life over and another begun—one over and another begun: the words chimed in his ears as he rode away. And great was the consternation of the servants at Thorne when he rode away—great the amazement of Mary and Beatrice, who had gone back to their private room, and were waiting there to be called down and hear "the news." "Gussy has refused him!" they said to each other with indescribable dismay. Their countenances and their hearts fell. What! the excitement all over, nothing to inquire into, no wooing to watch, nor wedding to expect? The girls thought they had been swindled, and went down together, arm in arm, to inquire into it. But the succession of events at this moment was too rapid to permit us to pause and describe the scene which they saw when they went down stairs.

In the meantime Edgar rode back to Arden, saying these words over to himself—one life ended and another begun. The one so sweet and warm and kindly and familiar, the other so cold and so unknown. He did not even know what his name was—who he was. The letters in the packet were few in number. They were signed only with initials. The post-marks on one outside cover which was preserved had been partially obliterated; but the name, so far as he could make it out, was that of some insignificant post-town which he had never heard of. At present, however, that question had not moved him much. He knew himself only as Edgar Arden. He could not realise himself in any other character, although at this very moment he had been proclaiming himself to be Edgar Arden no more. How hard it would be to change; to tear up his roots, as it were, to be no more Clare's brother, to enter a world absolutely unknown. Ah, yes! but that was a distant dread—a thing that looked less by being far. In the meantime it was not the passive suffering, but the active, that was to be his. As he rode along, he asked himself anxiously what must be his next step. The Rector must be told, and Dr. Somers. He thought with a little gleam of satisfaction of going to the Doctor, and dispersing all his evil thoughts in the twinkling of an eye. That sweet little gentle face in the picture, the woman who was Clare's mother, not his—it was his part to remove the cloud that had so long been over it. He saw now that everybody had more or less believed in this cloud—that there had been a feeling abroad even among those who defended her most warmly that poor Mrs. Arden required defence. And now it was he, not her son, a changeling, who was to do her justice. "I can clear my mother," he said to himself—and another swift shooting pang went through his heart the moment he was conscious of the words he had used—but he could not disentangle this dreary knot. The confusion would clear away with time. He could not stop using the words he had always used, or turn his thoughts in a moment from the channel they had flowed in all his life.

What Edgar did first was to ride to the station, but not this time with any thought of making his escape. He telegraphed to Mr. Fazakerly, bidding him come at once on urgent business. "I shall expect you to dinner to-night," was the conclusion of his message. What had to be done, it was best to do quickly, now as always. To be sure he had secured it now. He had done that which made it unimportant whether the papers were burned or not: and it was best that all should be concluded without delay. The only thing that Edgar hesitated at was telling Arthur Arden. He was the person most concerned: all that could be affected in any one else was a greater or less amount of feeling—a thing always evanescent and never to be calculated upon; but the news was as important to Arthur as to Edgar. A man (poor Edgar thought) of high and delicate character would have gone to Arthur first, and told him first; but he himself was not equal to that. He did not want to tell it to Arthur Arden. He would rather have some one else tell it to him—Fazakerly—any one. He loathed the idea of doing it himself. He even loathed the idea of meeting his successor, his heir, as he had so often called him; and he could not have told why. It was not that he expected any unkindness or want of consideration from Arthur. No doubt he would behave just as he ought to do. He would be kind; probably he would offer to pension the unwilling impostor. He would be happy, exultant in his wonderful success; and that would make him kind. But yet, the only person to whom Edgar hesitated to communicate his downfall was the one who was most interested in it. The very thought of him brought renewed and growing pain. For there was Clare to be thought of—Clare whom Arthur professed to love—whom, if he loved her, he would now be, so far as outward circumstances were concerned, a fitting match for. Edgar had made up his mind that he must give up his sister. He had decided that, whatever might be said or done now in this moment of excitement and agitation, Clare was lost to him, and that the bond between them could not be kept up. But if she were Arthur Arden's wife the breaking of the bond would be more harsh, more complete, than in any other case. His breast swelled, and then it contracted painfully, bringing bitter tears to his eyes. Never, should he live a hundred years without seeing her, could Clare cease to be his sister. Nothing could make her less or more to him. If it was not blood, it was something deeper than blood. But Arthur Arden's wife!

Poor Edgar! he could not answer for his thoughts, which were wild and incoherent, and rushed from one point to another with feverish speed and intensity; but his actions were not incoherent. He rode from the railway to the village very steadily and calmly, and stopped at Sally Timms' cottage-door to ask for Jeanie, who was better and had regained consciousness. Then he went up the street, and dismounted at the Rectory gate. He had not intended to do it, or rather he had not known what he intended. The merest trifle, a nothing decided him. The door was open, and the Rector's sturdy cob was standing before it waiting for his master. Edgar made a rapid reflection that he could now tell his story quickly, that there would be no time for much talk. He went in without knocking by the open door. Mr. Fielding was not in the library, nor in his drawing-room, nor in his garden. "I expect him in every moment, sir," Mrs. Solmes said, with a curtsey. "He's visiting the sick folks in the village. The horse is for young Mr. Denbigh, please, sir. Master has mostly given up riding now."

Edgar made a nod of assent. He was not capable of speech. If this had been his first attempt to communicate the news, it would have seemed providential to his excited fancy. But Lady Augusta had not been out, and he had been able to tell his tale very fully there. Now, however, there seemed a necessity laid upon him to tell it again. If not Mr. Fielding, some one at least must know. He went across to the Doctor's, thinking that at least he would see Miss Somers, who would not understand nor believe him. He had sent his horse away, telling the groom he would walk home. He was weary, and half crazed with exhaustion, sleeplessness, and intense emotion. He could not keep it in any longer. It seemed to him that he would like to have the church bells rung, to collect all the people about, to get into—no, not the pulpit, but the Squire's pew—the place that was like a stage-box, and tell everybody. That would be the right thing to do. "Simon!" he called out to the old clerk, who had been working somewhere about the churchyard, and who at the sound of the horse's hoofs had come to see what was going on, and stood with his arms leaning on the wall looking over. "Is there aught ye want as I can do for ye, Squire?" said old Simon. "No; nothing, nothing," said poor Edgar; and yet he would have been so glad had some one rung the church bells. He paused, and this gentle domestic landscape burned itself in upon his mind as he crossed to the Doctor's door. The village street lay asleep in the sun. Old Simon, leaning on the churchyard wall, was watching in a lazy, rural way the cob at Mr. Fielding's door waiting for the curate, Edgar's groom going off with his master's horse towards the big gates, and a waggon which was standing in front of the Arden Arms. The waggoner had a tankard of ale raised to his face, and was draining it, concealing himself behind its pewter disk. The quietest scene: the sun caught the sign-post of the Arden Arms, which had been newly painted in honour of Edgar, and played upon the red cap of the drayman who stood by, and swept down the long white road, clearing it of every shadow. All this Edgar saw and noted without knowing it. In many a distant scene, at many a distant day, this came back to him—the gleam of that red cap, the watchful spectatorship of the old man over the churchyard wall.

Dr. Somers met him coming out. "Ah!" said the Doctor, "coming to see me. I am in no particular hurry. Come in, Edgar. It is not so often one sees you now—"

"You will see me less in the future," said Edgar with a smile; "but I don't think there will be many broken hearts."

"Are you going away?" said Dr. Somers, leading the way into his own room. "Visits, I suppose; but take my word for it, my boy, there is no house so pleasant as your own house in autumn, when the covers are as well populated as yours. No, no; stay at home—take your visits later in the year."

"Dr. Somers," said Edgar, "I have come to tell you something. Yes, I am very serious, and it is very serious—there is nothing, alas, to laugh about. Do you remember what you hinted to me once here about—Mrs. Arden. Do you recollect the story you told me of the Agostini—"

"Ah, yes!" said the Doctor, growing slightly red. "About your mother—yes, perhaps I did hint; one does not like to speak to a man plainly about anything that has been said of his mother. I am very sorry; but I don't think I meant any harm—to you—only to warn you what people said—"

"And I have come to tell you that people are mistaken," said Edgar, with rising colour. He felt, poor fellow, as if he were vindicating his mother by proving that he was not her son. She was his mother in his thoughts still and always. Dr. Somers shook his head ever so slightly; of course, that was the right thing for her son to say.

"You think I have come, without evidence, to make a mere assertion," Edgar continued. "Listen a moment—"

"My dear fellow," said Dr. Somers, shrugging his shoulders, "how could you, or any one, make more than a mere assertion on such a subject. Assert what you please. You may be right—most likely you are right; but it is a matter which cannot be brought to proof."

"Yes," said Edgar. This time it was worse than even with Lady Augusta. With her he had the support of strong feeling, and counted on sympathy. But the Doctor was different. A film came over the young man's eyes; the pulsations of his heart seemed to stop. The Doctor, looking at him, jumped up, and rushing to a cupboard brought out some wine.

"Drink it before you say another word. Why Edgar, what is this?"

He put the wine away from him with some impatience. "Listen," he said; "this is what it is—I am not Mrs. Arden's son!"

Dr. Somers looked at him intently—into his eyes, in a way Edgar did not understand. "Yes, yes," he said, "I see—take the wine; take it to please me—Edgar Arden, I order you, take the wine."

"To please you, Doctor," said Edgar, "by all means." And when he had drank it, he turned to his old friend with a smile. "But I am not Edgar Arden. I am an impostor. Doctor, do you think I am mad?"

Dr. Somers looked at him once more with the same intent gaze. "I don't know what to make of you," he said, in a subdued tone. "No more jesting, Edgar, if this is jesting. What is it you mean?"

"I am speaking the soberest, saddest truth," said Edgar. "Clare will tell you; I have no right to call her Clare. I do not know who I am; but Mrs. Arden is clear of all blame, once and for ever. I am not her son."

CHAPTER XVI

To say that the Doctor was utterly confounded by this revelation was to say little. He had not begun so much as to think what it meant when Edgar left him. An impatience which was foreign to his character had come to the young man. He was eager to tell his astounding news; but it irritated him to be doubted, to have to go over and over the same words. He did not show this feeling. He tried hard to keep his temper, to make all the explanations that were wanted; but within him a fire of impatience burned. He rushed away as soon as he could get free, with again that wild desire to be done with it which was the reverse side of his eagerness to tell it. If he could but get away, be clear of the whole matter, plunge into the deep quiet of the unknown, where nobody would wonder that he was not an Arden, where he might call himself anything he pleased! He went up the avenue with feverish speed, noting nothing. Nature had ceased to have power to compose him. He had been swept into a whirlpool of difficulty, from which there could be no escape but in flight; and till his work was done he could not fly.

And it seemed to Edgar a long, long time since he rode down between those trees—a very long time, a month, perhaps a year. With all his heart he longed to be able to escape, and yet a certain fascination drew him back, a wondering sense that something more might have happened, that there might be some new incident when he went back to divide his attention with the old—Perhaps were the bureau searched more closely there might be something else found—something that would contradict the other. All these fancies flashed through his mind as he went on. He was but half-way up the avenue when he met Mr. Fielding coming down. The Rector looked just as he always did—serene, kind, short-sighted—peering at the advancing figure, with a smile of recognition slowly rising over his face. "I know people generally by their walk," he said, as they met; "but I don't recognise your walk this morning, Edgar: you are tired? How pale you are, my dear boy! Are you ill?"

"Didn't she tell you?" said Edgar, wearily.

"She tell me?—who tell me?—what? You frighten me, Edgar, you look so unlike yourself. I have been with Clare, and I don't think she is well either. She looked agitated. I warned you, you remember, about that man—"

"Don't speak of him, lest I should hate him," said Edgar. "And yet I have no cause to hate him—it is not his fault. I will turn back with you and tell you what Clare did not tell you. She might have confided in you, anyhow, even if there had been a chance that it was not true."

The Rector put his arm kindly within that of the agitated young man. He was the steadier of the two; he gave Edgar a certain support by the contact. "Whatever it is that agitates you so," he said, "you are quite right—she might have told me; it would have been safe with me. Poor Clare! she was agitated too—"

This allusion overwhelmed Edgar altogether. "You must be doubly kind to her when I am gone," he said, hurriedly. "Poor Clare! That is another thing that must be thought of. Where is she to go to? Would you take her in, you who have always been so kind to us? I would rather she were with you than at the Doctor's. Not that I have anything to do with it now; but one cannot get over the habits of one's life in twenty-four hours. Yes, poor Clare, I had no right to it, as it appears; but she was fond of me too."

"Of course, she was fond of you," said the Rector alarmed. "Come, Edgar, rouse yourself up. What does it mean this talk about going away? You must not go away. All your duties are at home. I could not give my consent—"

And then Edgar told him succinctly, in the same brief words which he had used before, his extraordinary tale. He told it this time without any appearance of emotion. He was getting used to the words. This time he paid no attention to the incredulity of his listener. He simply repeated it with a certain dull iteration. Mr. Fielding's exclamations of wonder and horror fell dully on his ears. He could not understand them. It seemed so strange that any one should be surprised at a thing he had known so long. "Sure," he said with a smile; "am I sure of my own existence? No, I don't mean of my own identity, for at present I have none. But I am as sure of it as that I am alive. Do you think it would be any pleasure to me to go and spread such news if it were not true?"

"But, Edgar,—" began the Rector.

"That is the curious thing," he said musingly; "I am not Edgar. I suppose a man would be justified in keeping his Christian name—don't you think so? That surely must belong to him. I could not be John or George all at once, after being Edgar all my life. Surely I keep that."

"My poor boy," cried the Rector, in dismay. "My poor boy, come home, and lie down, and let me bring Somers up to see you. You are not well, you have been doing too much in town, keeping late hours, and—You will see, a little rest will set you all right."

"Do you think I am mad?" said Edgar. "Look at me—can you really think so? I know only too well what I am saying. It is a very strange position to be placed in, and makes one talk a little wild, perhaps. Of course, I know nobody wants to take from me my Christian name; that was nonsense. But when one has just had such a fall as I have had, it confuses one a little. Will you come with me to the Hall, and see the papers? Clare should have told you. There is no harm in my calling her Clare, do you think, just for a time? I never can think of her but as my sister. And we must try and arrange what she is to do."

"Edgar, am I to believe you?" cried Mr. Fielding. "Is it madness, or is it something too dreadful to name? Do not look at me like that, my dear boy. Don't smile, for Heaven's sake! you will break my heart."

"Why shouldn't I smile?" said Edgar. "Is all the world to be covered with gloom because I am not Squire Arden? Nonsense! It is I who must suffer the most, and therefore I have a right to smile. Clare will get over it by degrees," he added. "It has been a great shock to her, but she will get over it. I don't know what to say about her future. Of course I have no right to say anything, but I can't help it. I suppose the chances are she will marry Arthur Arden. I hate to think of that. It is not mere prejudice against him as superseding me; it is because he is not worthy of her. But it would be the most suitable match. Of course you know she will lose Old Arden now that I am found out?"

"Edgar, stop! I can't bear it," cried the Rector. "For Heaven's sake don't say any more!"

"But why not? It is a relief to me; and you are our oldest friend. Of course I had no more to do with the entail than you have; all that is null and void. For Clare's sake I wonder he did not destroy those papers, if for nothing else. Mr. Fielding, I have a horrible idea in my head. I wish I could get rid of it. It is worse than all the rest. He hated me, because of course I reminded him continually of his guilt. He wanted me to break my neck that day after Old Arden was settled on Clare. It would have been the most comfortable way of arranging the matter for all parties, if I had only known. But I can't help thinking he carried his enmity further than that. I think he left those letters to be a trap to me. He meant me to find them, and hide them or destroy them, and share his guilt. Of course he believed I would do that; and oh, God! how strong the temptation was to do it! If I had found them myself—if they not been given to me by Clare—"

Mr. Fielding pressed the arm he held. He doubted no longer, questioned no longer. "My poor boy! my poor boy!" he murmured under his breath; and, kind soul as he was, in his heart, with all the fervour of a zealot, he cursed the old Squire. He cursed him without condition or peradventure. God give him his reward! he said; and for the first time in his life believed in a lake of fire and brimstone, and wished it might be true.

"I suppose I have got into the talking stage now," said poor Edgar. "I have had a long spell of it, and felt everything that can be felt, I believe. It was on Sunday night I found it out—fancy, on Sunday night!—a hundred years ago. And I want you to stand by me to-day. I have telegraphed for Fazakerly. I have asked him to come to dinner; why, I don't know, except that dinner is a solemnity which agrees with everything. It will be my table for the last time. Is it not odd that Arthur Arden should be here at such a moment? not by my doing, nor Clare's, nor even his own—by Providence, I suppose. If Mr. Pimpernel's horses had not run away, and if poor little Jeanie had not been in the carriage—What strange, invisible threads things hang together by! Am I talking wildly still?"

"No, Edgar," said Mr. Fielding, with a half sob. "No, my poor boy. Edgar, I think it would be a relief to be able to cry—What shall you do? What shall you do? I think my heart will break."

"I shall do very well," said Edgar, cheerily. "Remember, I have not been brought up a fine gentleman. I shall be of as much use in the world probably as Arthur Arden, after all. Ridiculous, is it not? but I feel as if he were my rival, as if I should like to win some victory over him. It galls me to think that perhaps Clare will marry him—a man no more worthy of her—But, of course, the match would be suitable, as people call it, now."

"Say you don't like it, Edgar," said Mr. Fielding, with sudden warmth. "Clare, you may be sure, if she ever neglected your wishes, will not neglect them now."

Edgar shook his head; a certain sadness came into the meditative smile which had been on his face. "I believe she loves him," he said, and then was silent, feeling even in that moment that it was not for Clare's good he should say more. No; it was not for him to lay any further burdens upon his sister. His sister! "I must think of her as my sister," he said aloud, defending himself, as it were, from some attack. "It is like my Christian name. I can't give that up, and I can't give her up—in idea, I mean; in reality, of course, I will."

"The man who would ask you to do so would be a brute," cried Mr. Fielding.

"No man will ask me to do so," said Edgar. "I don't fear that; but time, and distance, and life. But you are old—you will not forget me. You will stand by me, won't you, to the last!"

The good Rector was old, as Edgar said; he could not bear any more. He sat down on the roadside, and covered his face with his handkerchief. And the tears came to Edgar's eyes. But the suffering was his own, not another's; therefore they did not fall.

Thus they separated, to meet again in the evening at the dinner, to which Edgar begged the Rector to ask Dr. Somers also. "It will be my last dinner," he said, with a smile; and so went away—with something of his old look and manner restored to him—home.

Home! He had been the master of everything, secure and undoubting, three days ago. He was the master yet to the gamekeeper, who took off his hat in the distance; to Wilkins, who let him in so respectfully; even to Arthur Arden, who watched him with anxious curiosity. How strange it all was! Was he playing in some drama not comprehended by his surroundings, or was it all a dream?

It seemed a dream to the Rector, who hurried home, not knowing what to think, and sent for Dr. Somers, and went over it all again. Could it be true? Was the boy mad? What did it mean? They asked each other these questions, wondering. But in their hearts they knew he was not mad, and felt that his revelation was true. And so all prepared itself for the evening, when everything should be made public. A sombre cloud fell over Arden to everybody concerned. The sun looked sickly, the wind refused to blow. The afternoon was close, sultry, and threatening. Even Nature showed a certain sympathy. She would say her "hush" no longer, but with a gathering of clouds and feverish excitement awaited the catastrophe of the night.

CHAPTER XVII

And yet amid all this excitement and lurid expectation, how strange it was to go through the established formulas of life: the dinner, the indifferent conversation, the regulated course of dishes and of talk! Mr. Fazakerly made his appearance, very brisk and busy as usual. He had come away hurriedly, in obedience to Edgar's summons, from the very midst of the preparations for a great wedding, involving property and settlements so voluminous that they had turned the heads of the entire firm and all its assistants. Fortunately he was full of this. The bride was an heiress, with lands and wealth of every description—the bridegroom a poor Irish peer, with titles enough to make up for the money which was being poured upon him; and the lawyer's whole soul was lost in the delightful labyrinth of wealth—this which was settled upon the lady, that which was under the control of the husband. He talked so much on the subject, that it was some time before he perceived the pre-occupied faces of all the rest of the company. The only one thoroughly able to talk was Dr. Somers, whose mind was never sufficiently absorbed by any one subject to be incapable of others, and who knew everybody, and could discuss learnedly with his old friend upon the property and its responsibilities. Edgar, too, did his best to talk. His excitement had run into a kind of humour which was "only his fun" to Mr. Fazakerly, but which brought tears to the Rector's eyes. He meant to die gaily, poor fellow, and make as little as possible of this supreme act of his life. Clare sat at the head of the table, perfectly pale and silent. She made a fashion of eating, but in reality took nothing, and she did not even pretend to talk. Mr. Fielding by her side was as silent. Sometimes he laid his withered gentle old hand upon hers when she rested it on the table, and he looked at her pathetically from time to time, especially when Edgar said something at which the others laughed. "I wish he would not, my dear—I wish he would not," he would murmur to her. But Clare made no reply. He who was no longer her brother was to her the most absorbing of interests at this moment. She could not understand him. An Arden would have concealed the thing, she thought to herself, or if he had been forced to divulge it, would have done it with unwilling abruptness and severity, defying all the world in the action. But the bitter pride which would have felt itself humbled to the dust by such a revelation did not seem to exist in Edgar. If there was in him a certain desperation, it was the gay desperation, the pathetic light-heartedness of a man leading a forlorn hope. He defied nobody, but faced the world with a smile and a tear—a man wronged, but doing right—a soul above suspicion. And Clare was asking herself eagerly, anxiously, what would be the difference it would make to him. It would make a horrible difference—more, far more, than he in his sanguine soul could understand. His friends would drop off from him. In her knowledge of what she called the world, Clare felt but too certain of this. The dependants who had hitherto hung upon his lightest word would become suddenly indifferent, and she herself—his sister—what could she do? Clare was aware that even she, in outward circumstances, must of necessity cease to be to him what she had been. She was not his sister. They could no longer remain together—no longer be each other's close companions; everything would be changed. Even if she continued as she was, she would be compelled to treat Edgar with the ceremonies which are universally thought to be necessary between a young woman and a young man. If she continued as she was? Were she to marry, the case would be different. As a married woman, he might be her brother still. And yet how could she marry, as it were, on his ruin; how could she build a new fabric of happiness over the sacked foundations of her brother's house? Her brother, and yet not her brother—a stranger to her! Clare's brain reeled, too, as she contemplated his position and her own. She was not capable of feeling the contrast between Edgar's playful talk and the precipice on which he was standing. She was too much absorbed in a bewildering personal discussion what he was to do, what she was to do, what was to become of them all.

Arthur Arden was at her other hand. He was growing more and more interested in the situation of affairs, and more and more began to feel that something must be in it of greater importance than he had thought. Clare never addressed a word to him, though he was so near to her. Her eyes were fixed on the other end of the table, where Edgar sat. Her lips trembled with a strange quiver of sympathy, which seemed actually physical, when her brother said anything. She looked too far gone in some extraordinary emotion to be able to realise what was going on. When Arthur spoke she did not hear him. She had to be called back to herself by Mr. Fielding's soft touch upon her hand before she noticed anything, except Edgar. "You seem very much interested in what Mr. Fazakerly is saying. Do you know this bride he is talking of?" Arthur said, trying to draw her attention. "Clare, my love, Mr. Arden is speaking to you; he is asking if you know Miss Monypenny," said the Rector, with a warning pressure from his thin fingers. "Oh, I beg your pardon; I did not hear you," Clare would reply, but she made no answer to the question. Her attention would stray again before it was repeated. And then Mr. Fielding gave Arthur Arden an imploring glance across the table. It seemed to ask him to spare her—not to say anything—to leave her to herself. "She is not well to-night," the Rector said, softly, with tears glistening in his old eyes. What did it mean? Arthur asked himself. It must be something worse than he had thought.

The silence at the other end of the table struck Mr. Fazakerly, as it seemed, all at once. He gave two or three anxious looks in the direction of Clare. "Your sister does not look well, Mr. Edgar," he said. "We can't afford to let her be ill, she who is the pride of the county. After Miss Monypenny's, I hope to have her settlements to prepare. You will not be allowed to keep her long, I promise you. But I trust she is not ill. Doctor, I hope you have been attending to your duty. Miss Arden can't be allowed, in all our interests, to grow so pale."

"Miss Arden is not in the way of consulting me on such subjects," said the Doctor. "She has a will of her own, like everybody belonging to her. I never knew such a self-willed race. When they take a thing into their heads there is no getting it out again, as you will probably find, Fazakerly, before you are many hours older. I have long known that there was a disposition to mania in the family. Oh, no, not anything dangerous—monomania—delusion on one point."

"I never heard of it before," said Mr. Fazakerly, promptly, "and I flatter myself I ought to know about the family if any one does. Monomania! Fiddlesticks! Why, look at our young friend here. I'll back him against the world for clear-seeing and common sense."

"He has neither the one nor the other," said Dr. Somers, hotly. "I could have told you so any time these ten years. He may have what people call higher qualities; I don't pretend to pronounce; but he can't see two inches before his nose in anything that concerns his own interest; and as for common sense, he is the most Quixotic young idiot I ever knew in my life."

"Don't believe such accusations against me," said Edgar, with a smile. "Your own opinion is the right one. I don't pretend to be clever; but if there is anything I pique myself upon, it is common sense. This is the best introduction we could have to the business of the evening. It is not anything very convivial, and it may startle you, I fear. Perhaps we had better finish our wine first, Doctor, don't you think?"

"What is the matter?" said Mr. Fazakerly. "Now I begin to look round me, you are all looking very grave. I don't know what you mean by these signs, Mr. Fielding. Am I making indiscreet observations? What's the matter? God preserve us! you all look like so many ghosts!"

"So we are—or at least some of us," said Edgar, "ghosts that a puff of common air will blow away in a moment. The fact is, I have something very disagreeable to tell you. But don't look alarmed, it is disagreeable chiefly to myself. To one of my guests at least it will be good news. It is simple superstition, of course, but I can't tell you while you are comfortable, taking your wine. I should like you not to be quite at your ease. If you were all seated in the library, on hard chairs, for example—"

"Edgar!" said Clare, in a sharp tone of pain.

Dr. Somers laid a hand on his arm. "Don't overdo it," he said, with something between remonstrance and sympathy. The Rector stood covering his eyes with his hands. At all this Arthur Arden looked on with keen and eager interest, and Mr. Fazakerly with the sharpest, freshly-awakened curiosity, not knowing evidently what to make of it. Arthur's comment was of a kind that made the heart jump in his breast. The secret, whatever it was, had been evidently confided both to the Doctor and the Rector. They were reasonable men, not likely to be affected by a foolish story; yet they both, it was apparent, considered it something serious. A hundred pulses of impatience and excitement began to beat within him. And yet he could not, with any regard to good taste or good feeling, say a word.

"Don't be afraid," said Edgar; "it is not bravado. What I have to say is very serious, but it is not disgraceful—at least to me. There is no reason why I should assume a gloom which is not congenial to myself, nor natural so far as others are concerned. As it has been mentioned so early, perhaps it is better not to lose any time with preliminaries now. Will you come with me to the library? The proofs of what I have to say are there. And without any further levity, I would rather speak to you in that room than in this."

When he had said this, without waiting to hear Mr. Fazakerly's amazed exclamations, Edgar walked quietly to the other end of the table and offered his arm to Clare. Before she took it, she joined her hands together, and looked up beseechingly in his face. He shook his head, with a tender smile at her, and drew her hand within his arm. This dumb show was eagerly observed by Arthur Arden at her left hand. By this time he was so lost in a maze that he no longer permitted himself to think. What was the meaning of it all? Was the boy a fool to give in, and throw up his arms at once? He had not, it was evident, even spoken to Fazakerly first, as any man in his senses would have done. For once in his life Arthur was moved to a disinterested sentiment. Even yet, after all that had been said, he had no real hope that any advantage was coming to himself; and something moved him to interfere to save an unnecessary exposure. A certain compassion for this candid foolish boy—a compassion mingled with some contempt—had arisen in his heart.

"Arden," he said hastily, "look here, talk it over with Fazakerly first. I don't know what cock-and-a-bull story you have got hold of, but before you make a solemn business of it, for Heaven's sake talk it over with Fazakerly first."

Edgar put out his hand, without at first saying a word. It took him nearly half a minute (a long interval at that crisis) to steady his voice. "Thanks," he said. "It is no cock-and-bull story; but I thank you for thinking, and saying that. Come and hear what it is—and, for your generosity, thanks."

"It was not generosity," answered Arthur, under his breath. He was abashed and confounded by the undeserved gratitude. But he made no further attempt to detain the procession, which set out towards the library. Edgar placed Clare in a chair when he had reached it. He put her beside himself, and with a movement of the hand invited the others to seat themselves. The table had been prepared, the lamp was burning on it, and before one of the chairs was already laid a packet of letters directed to B. Fazakerly, Esq. Edgar meant that his evidence should be seen before he told his tale.

"Will you take possession of these," he said, seating himself at the end of the table. "These are my proofs of what I am going to tell you; and it is so strange that you will need proofs. My sister—I mean Miss Arden—now seated beside me—found these papers. They have thrown the strangest light upon my own life, and upon that of my predecessor here."

"Your father?" said Mr. Fazakerly, with a glance of dismay.

"I shall have to go back to the time when the late Squire was married," said Edgar. "I beg you to wait just for a few minutes and hear my story, before you ask for any explanations. It has been commonly supposed, I believe, that the reason for the treatment I received during my childhood and youth, was that Squire Arden had been led to doubt whether I was his son, and to think my mother—I mean Mrs. Arden—unfaithful to him. This was a great slander and calumny, gentlemen. The reason Squire Arden was unkind to me was that he knew very well I was neither his son nor Mrs. Arden's, but only an adopted child."

There was a murmur and movement among the guests. Arthur Arden rose up in his bewilderment, and remained standing, staring at the man who had thus declared himself to be no Arden; and Mr. Fazakerly cried out loudly, "Nonsense; no! no! no! I know a great deal better. The boy's brain is turned. Don't say another word."

"I asked you to hear me out," said Edgar, whose colour and spirit were rising. "I told you I should have to go back to the time when Squire Arden married. He married a lady in very delicate health—or else she fell into bad health after their marriage. Five years afterwards the doctors told him that he had no chance whatever of having any children. His wife was too ill for that; but not ill enough to die. She was likely to live, indeed, as long as any one else, but never to give him an heir. He hated, I can't tell why, his next of kin. I am not here to excuse him, but I believe there were excuses, for that—and after some hesitation he formed the plan of adopting a child, giving it out to be his own, and born abroad. The manner in which he carried out this plan is to be found in the packet in Mr. Fazakerly's hands; and I am the boy whom he adopted. I can't quite tell you," Edgar continued, with the faint smile which had so often during three days past quivered about his lips, "who I am, but I am not an Arden. I am an impostor; and my cousin—I beg his pardon—Mr. Arthur Arden, is the proprietor of this place and all that is in it. He will allow me, I am sure, to retain his place for the moment, simply to make all clear."

"To make all clear!" gasped Arthur. Clear! as if everything in heaven and earth was not confused by this extraordinary revelation, or could ever be made clear again.

"He must be mad," said Mr. Fazakerly, loudly. And yet there went a thrill round the table—a feeling which nobody could resist—that every word he said was true.

"I have not sought any further," said Edgar. "These letters have contented me, which disclose the whole transaction; but everybody knows as well as I do the after particulars. How Mr. Arden slighted me persistently and continuously—and yet how, without losing a moment when I came of age, he made use of me to provide for my—for Miss Arden. The fact that Old Arden was settled upon her, away from me, is of itself a corroborating evidence. Everything supports my story when you come to think of it. It makes the past clear for the first time."

And then there was a pause, and they all looked at each other with blank astonishment and dismay. At least Mr. Fazakerly looked at everybody, while the others met his eye with appealing looks, asking him, as it were, to interfere. "It cannot be true—it is impossible it should be true," they murmured, in their consternation. But it was Clare who was the first to speak.

CHAPTER XVIII

Clare rose up instinctively, feeling the solemnity of the occasion to be such that she could not meet it otherwise. She was paler than ever, if that was possible—marble white—with great blue eyes, pathetically fixed upon the little audience which she addressed. She put one hand back feebly, and rested it on Edgar's shoulder to support herself. "I want to speak first," she said. "There is nobody so much concerned as me. It was I who found those papers, as my brother says. I found them, where I had no right to have looked, in an old bureau which did not belong to me, which I was looking through for levity and curiosity, and because I had nothing else to do. It is my fault, and it is I who will suffer the most. But what I want to tell you is, that I don't believe them. How could any one believe them? I was brought up to love my father, and if they are true my father was a—was a—I cannot say the word. Edgar asks me to give up everything I have in life when he asks me to believe in these letters. Oh, all of you, who are our old friends! you knew papa. Was he such a man as that? Had he no honour, no justice, no sense of right and wrong in him? You know it would be wicked to say so. Then these papers are not true."

"And I know they are not true in other ways," cried Clare, flushing wildly as she went on. "If Edgar was not my brother, do you think I could have felt for him as I do? I should have hated him, had he been an impostor, as he says. Oh, he is no impostor! He is not like the rest of us—not like us in the face—but what does that matter? He is a thousand times better than any of us. I was not brought up with him to get into any habit of liking him, and yet I love him with all my heart. Could that be anything but nature? If he were not my true brother, I would have hated him. And, on the contrary, I love him, and trust him, and believe in him. Say anything you please—make out what you please from these horrible letters, or any other lie against him; but I shall still feel that he is my own brother—my dearest brother—in my heart!"

Clare did not conclude with a burst of tears, solely because she was past weeping. She was past herself altogether; she was not conscious of anything but the decision about to be come to—the verdict that was to be given by this awful tribunal. She sank back into her chair, keeping her eyes fixed upon them, too anxious to lose a single gesture or look. "Bring her some water," said Dr. Somers; "give her air, Edgar; no, let her alone—let her alone; that is best. Just now, you may be sure, she will take no harm."

And then there came another pause—a pause in which every sound seemed to thud and beat against the anxious ears that waited and listened. Arthur Arden had taken his seat again. He was moved, too, to the very depths of his being. He covered his face with his hands, unable to look at the two at the head of the table, who were both gazing at the company waiting for their fate. Edgar had taken Clare's hand, and was holding it fast between his own. He was saying something, of which he was not himself conscious. "Thanks, Clare! courage, Clare!" he was repeating at intervals, as he might have murmured any other babble in the excitement of the moment. Mr. Fazakerly was the only one who stirred. He broke open the seals of the packet with agitated haste, muttering also under his breath. "Parcel of young fools!" was what Mr. Fazakerly was saying. He let the papers drop out in a heap upon the table, and picked up one here and one there, running it over with evident impatience and irritation. Then he tossed them down, and pushed his spectacles off his forehead, and wrathfully regarded the little company around him. "What am I expected to do with these?" he asked. "They are private letters of the late Mr. Arden, not, so far as I am aware, brought before us by any circumstances that call for attention. I don't know what is intended to be done with them, or who produces them, or why we are called together. Mr. Edgar, I think you might provide better entertainment for your old friends than a mare's nest like this. What is the meaning of it all? My opinion is, they had better be replaced in the old bureau from which Miss Clare tells us she fished them out."

But while he said this in his most querulous tone, Mr. Fazakerly picked up the papers one by one, and tied them together. His irritation was extreme, and so was his dismay, but the last was uppermost, and was not easy to express. "If these had come before me in a proper way," he went on, "of course I should have taken all pains to examine them and see what they meant; but unless there is some reason for it— some object, some end to be gained—I always object particularly to raking up dead men's letters. I have known endless mischief made in that way. The chances are that most men do quite enough harm in their lifetime, or at least in a lawful way by their wills and so forth, after their death, without fishing up every scrap of rancour or folly they may have left behind them. Mr. Edgar, you have no right that I know of to go and rummage among old papers in order to prejudice yourself. It is the merest nonsense. I can't, for my part, consent to it. I don't believe a word of it. If anybody else takes it up, and I am called upon to defend you, of course I will act to the best of my ability; but in the meantime I decline to have anything to do with it. Take them away—"

Mr. Fazakerly thrust the tied-up parcel towards his client. Of course, he knew very well that the position he took up was untenable after all that had been said, but his irritation was real, and the idea of thus spoiling a case went to his very heart. He pushed it along the table; but, by one of those curious accidents which so often surpass the most elaborate design, the little packet which had been the cause of so much trouble, instead of reaching Edgar, stopped short in front of Arthur Arden, who was still leaning on the table, covering his face with his hand. It struck him lightly on the elbow, and he raised his head to see what it was. It was all so strange that the agitated company was moved as by a visible touch of fate. Arthur stared at it stupidly, as if the thing was alive. He let it lie, not putting forth a finger, gazing at it. Incredible change of fortune lay for him within the enclosure of these faded leaves; yet he could not secure them, could not do anything, was powerless, with Clare's eyes looking at him, and the old friends of the family around. His own words came back to his mind suddenly in that pause—"Let him take everything, so long as he leaves me you." And Clare's answer, "Say that again to-morrow." To-morrow! It was not yet to-morrow; and what was he to say?

It was Edgar, however, and not Arthur, who was the first to speak. "If it must be a matter of attack and defence," he said, "the papers are now with the rightful heir, and it is his to pursue the matter further.

But I don't want to have any attack or defence. Mr. Arden, will you be so good as to take the packet, and put it in your lawyer's hands. I suppose there are some legal forms to be gone through; but I will not by any act of mine postpone your entrance upon your evident right."

A pause again—not a word said on any side—the three old men looking on without a movement, almost without a breath; and Arthur Arden, with his elbows still resting on the table, and his head turned aside, gazing, as if it were a reptile in his path, at the packet beside him. How he would have snatched at it had it not been for these spectators! There was no impulse of generosity towards Edgar in his mind. Such an impulse would have been at once foolish and uncalled for. Edgar himself had taken pains to show that he wanted no such generosity—and a man cannot part lightly with his rights. Everything would have been easy enough, clear enough, but for Clare's presence and her words that morning. If he were to do what every impulse of good sense and natural feeling prompted—take up the papers before him and make himself master of a question affecting him so nearly—then no doubt he would lose Clare. He would lose (but that was of small importance) the good opinion of that foolish old Rector. He would create a most unjust prejudice against himself if he showed any eagerness about it, even in the eyes of the doctor and the lawyer, practical men, who knew that justice must prevail; and he would lose Clare. What was he to do? It was cruel, he felt, to put him to such a trial. He kept looking at the papers with his head turned, half of it shadowed over by the hands from which he had lifted it, half of it (his forehead and eyes) full in the light. To his own consciousness, an hour must have passed while he thus pondered. The others thought it five minutes, though it was not one. But another train of thought rapidly succeeded the first in Arthur's mind. What did it matter, after all, what he did? He could be generous at Edgar's cost, who, he felt sure, would accept no sacrifice. He gave a glance at the young man who was no Arden, who was looking on without anxiety now, with a faint smile still on his face, and a certain bright curiosity and interest in his eyes. It was perfectly safe. There are some people whom even their enemies, even those who do not understand them, can calculate upon, and Edgar was one of these. Arthur looked at him, and saw his way to save Clare and to save appearances, and yet attain fully his will and his rights. He took the packet up, and put it in Clare's lap.

"Here I put my fate and Edgar's," he said, with, in spite of himself, a thrill of doubt in his voice which sounded like emotion. "Let Clare judge between us—it is for her to decide—"

Before Clare could speak, Edgar had taken back the papers from her. "That means," he said, almost gaily, with a laugh which sounded strange to the excited company, "that they have come back to me. Clare has had enough of this. It is no matter of romantic judgment, but one of evidence merely. Mr. Fielding, will you take my sister away? Yes, I will say my sister still. She does not give me up, and I can't give her up. Arden is little in comparison. Clare, if you could give me a kingdom, you could not do more for me than you have done to-night. Go with Mr. Fielding now—"

She rose up, obeying him mechanically, at once. "Where?" she said. "Edgar, tell me. Out of Arden? If it is no longer yours, it is no longer mine."

"Hush, dear," he said, soothing her as if she had been a child—"hush, hush. There is no cause for any violent change. Your kinsman is not likely to be hard upon either me or you."

"He put the matter into my hands," she cried, suddenly, with a sob. "O Edgar, listen! Let us go away at once. We must do justice—justice. Let us go and hide ourselves at the end of the world—for it cannot be yours, it is his."

She stumbled as she spoke, not fainting, but overcome by sudden darkness, bewilderment, failure of all physical power. The strain had been too much for Clare. They carried her out, and laid her on the sofa in the quiet, silent room close by, where no excitement was. How strange to go out into the placid house, to see the placid servants carrying in trays with tea, putting in order the merest trifles! The world all around was unconscious of what was passing—unconscious even under the same roof—how much less in the still indifferent universe outside. Edgar laughed, as he went to the great open door, and looked out upon the peaceful stars. "What a fuss we are making about it!" he said to his supplanter, whose mind was incapable of any such reflection; "and how little it matters after all!" "Are you mad, or are you a fool?" cried Arthur Arden under his breath. To him it mattered more than anything else in heaven or earth. The man who was losing everything might console himself that the big world had greater affairs in hand—but to the man who was gaining Arden it was more than all the world—and perhaps it was natural that it should be so.

Half-an-hour after the three most concerned had returned to the library, to discuss quietly and in detail the strange story and its evidences. These three were Edgar, Arthur, and Mr. Fazakerly. The Rector sat by Clare's sofa, in the drawing-room, soothing her. "My dear, God will bring something good out of it," he was saying, with that pathetic bewilderment which so many good people are conscious of in saying such words. "It will be for the best, my poor child." He patted her head and her hand, as he spoke, which did her more good, and kept by her—a supporter and defender. The Doctor gave her a gentle opiate, and went away. They were all, in their vocations, ministering vaguely, feebly to those desperate human needs which no man can supply—need of happiness, need of peace, need of wisdom. The Rector's soft hand smoothing one sufferer's hair; the doctor's opiate; the lawyer's discussion of the value of certain documents, legally and morally—such was all the help that in such an emergency man could give to man.

CHAPTER XIX

The others seated themselves once more round the library table. There was a change, however, in their circumstances and position which would have been immediately manifest to any observer. It had been Edgar an hour ago who was the chief person concerned; it was he who had to communicate his story, and to note its effect upon his audience. But now it was Arthur who was the chief; not that he had anything to tell; but all the anxiety had transferred itself to him—all the burden. His brow was heavy with thought and care. He was feverishly eager to read and to hear everything that could be said, and he watched Mr. Fazakerly with the devouring anxiety of one who felt life and death to hang on his lips. "It does not matter what you think or what I think, but what he thinks," he said abruptly when Edgar explained something. His whole attention was bent upon the lawyer. He read the letters in Mr. Fazakerly's look. The chances were he did not himself make out or understand them, but he saw what the other thought of them, and that was enough.

"Softly, softly," said Mr. Fazakerly; "don't let us go too fast. I acknowledge these are ugly letters to find; they make a very strong case against the old Squire. He was a man who would stick at nothing to get his own will. I would not say so before your sister, Mr. Edgar, but still it was true. I have known cases in which he did not stick at anything. And there can be no doubt that it affords an instant explanation of his conduct to you. But the law distrusts too clear an explanation of motives—the law likes facts, Mr. Edgar, and not motives. We must go very gently in this difficult path. I will allow that I think this is the late Mr. Arden's handwriting—for the sake of argument I will allow that; but these letters, you will perceive, all make a proposition. There is nothing in them to prove that the proposition was accepted—not a word—a fact which of itself complicates the matter immensely. We have Mr. Arden's word for it, without any confirmation—nothing more."

"I think you mistake," said Edgar; "there are these other letters which consider and accept the proposal. They are, I think, remarkable letters. The person who wrote them could no doubt be identified. I think they are quite conclusive that the proposal was accepted. Look at this, and this, and this—"

"All very well—all very well," said the lawyer. "Letters signed 'J. M.;' but who is 'J. M.'? I conclude a woman. I don't make out what kind of a person at all. There are errors of spelling here and there, which do not look like a lady; and there is something about the style which is not like an uneducated person. I decline to receive as evidence the anonymous letters of 'J. M.'"

Arthur Arden followed the speakers with his eyes, and with breathless attention. He turned from one to another, noting even their gestures, the little motions of arm and hand with which they appealed to each other. He was discouraged by Mr. Fazakerly's tone; he raised his eyes to Edgar, almost begging him to say something more—to bring forward another argument for his own undoing. It was the strangest position for them both. Edgar had taken upon himself, as it were, the conduct of his adversary's case; he was the advocate of the man who was to displace and supersede him. He was struggling with the champion of his own rights for those of his rival, and with the strangest simplicity that rival tacitly appealed to him.

"I don't understand these matters of detail—" Edgar began.

"Detail, my dear sir, detail!" said Mr. Fazakerly, "they are matters of principle. If letters like these were to be accepted as affecting the succession to a great property, nobody would be safe. How can I tell who this 'J. M.' was? It might be anybody—nobody. She may have written these letters at random altogether. And, besides, there is not a tittle of evidence to connect you with 'J. M.' Even supposing the whole correspondence perfectly genuine, which is a thing requiring proof in the first place, how am I to know—how is any one to know—that you are the child referred to? There is, the contrary, everything against it. You yourself jump at a conclusion. You say you are not like the Ardens, and that your father was unkind to you, and from these two facts you arrive at the astounding conclusion that you are not Mr. Arden's son. Mr. Edgar, I do not wish to be uncivil, but there is nothing in it. We cannot decide such a question on evidence so slight—God bless me! what is that?"

The sound was startling enough; but it was only a knock, though an emphatic and determined one, at the door. Edgar rose to open it, and found Wilkins outside endeavouring to hold back an unlooked for visitor. "She would come, sir," said Wilkins in trouble

"Is it you, Mrs. Murray?" said Edgar, startled he scarcely knew why; yet somehow not feeling her presence inappropriate. "I am very busy at this moment. I hope Jeanie is not worse—"

She made no attempt to enter the room; but standing outside in the imperfect light, looked anxiously in his face. "I came because I couldna help it," she said slowly, "because I was concerned in my mind about yours and you."

"That was kind," he said with a smile. He opened the door wide, and revealed her standing on the threshold—a dark, commanding figure. "We are busy about very important business," said Edgar; "but still, if you have anything to say to me—if Jeanie is worse—"

"Jeanie is better, or I would not have left her," said the Scotchwoman; and then she put her hand suddenly upon his arm, and drew him towards her. "It's you I am troubled about," she said suddenly, with the hoarseness of great emotion. "I've never got you out of my mind since you said you were in trouble. Oh, my bonnie lad! I have no right to speak, but my heart is in sore pain. Oh, if I could but be of some service to you!"

Edgar never knew how it was—perhaps some trick of words like something he had recently seen—perhaps the passion in her voice—perhaps a sudden intuition, a touch of nature, warning him of things unknown and unseen. Suddenly he changed the position of affairs, put his hand on her arm, and drew her into the room. "Come," he said, "I want you. Don't hesitate any longer; I have a question to ask you." He had to exercise almost a little force to bring her into the room. She stopped upon the threshold, resisting the pressure of his hand. "No," she said, "no before these strange folk; it was for you I came, and you alone."

"I have something to ask you," said Edgar. "Come in and help me. I think you can."

He led her in unwillingly up to the table. She gave an alarmed and anxious look upon the two people sitting by. Arthur Arden, whose mind was open to everything, looked up and stared at her; but the lawyer, after one hasty glance, took no further notice. He went on reading the papers, shrugging his shoulders at this absurd interruption. In his own mind it was a proof that the story he had just heard was true as the Gospel, and that the young man who admitted every chance comer into his intimacy could not be an Arden. But externally he paid no attention. It was not his business to see, but to be blind. Arthur Arden was in a very different mood; everything was important to him—he caught at the faintest indications of meaning, and was on the outlook eagerly for any incident. He watched closely, as Edgar led Mrs. Murray up to the table. He perceived how reluctant she was, how she stood on the defensive, watchful, and guarding herself against surprise. What share could she have in the matter, that all her faculties should be thus on the alert? Edgar's demeanour too was very amazing to the spectator. His eye had brightened—a curious air of quickened interest was in his face; he looked as if he felt himself on the eve of a discovery. He led the old woman up to the table, holding her by the arm. It was a strange scene: the lawyer reading on steadily, taking no notice; the other spectator in the shade, looking on so eagerly—the two figures standing between. The woman had the air of going blindfold to encounter some unknown danger, which, whatever it was, she was prepared to resist. Then Edgar spoke with so much energy and impressiveness that even Mr. Fazakerly paused, and pushed his spectacles up on his forehead, and looked up hurriedly. "Look at these," he said, bringing her close to the open packet of letters—"Look at them, and tell me if you ever saw them before."

Mrs. Murray approached, looking straight before her, keeping, with an evident effort, every sign of emotion from her face. But when her eye fell on the papers, an extraordinary change came over her. She came to a dead stop—she uttered a low cry—she looked at them, stooping over the table, and threw up her hands with a wild gesture of dismay. And then all at once she recollected herself, stiffened all over, stood desperately erect, with her hands clasped before her, and looked at them all with a dumb defiance, which was wonderful to see.

"What did you say, sir?" she asked. "I am growing old; I am no so quick at the up-take as I once was. I've been in this room before, in an hour of great trouble and pain to me, and it works upon my nerves to see it again. Sir, what did ye say?"

And she turned from one to another, severally defying them. Her face had become blank of every expression but that one. This was the way in which she betrayed herself. She defied them all. Her face said—Find me out if you can; I will never tell you—instead of wearing, as a more accomplished deceiver would have done, the air of having nothing to find out.

"Have you ever seen these letters before?" said Edgar; and he lifted the papers and put them into her hands. Arthur, who was watching, saw her breast heave. He saw her hand clutch them, as if she would have torn them in pieces. But she dared not tear them in pieces. She looked at them, made a pretence to read, and stood as if she were an image cut out of stone.

"How should I have seen them?" she said, putting them back on the table as if they had burned her. "My cousin, Thomas Perfitt, is an old servant of your house; but how should its secrets have come to me?"

"Look here," said Edgar, in his excitement; "I believe you know; something tells me that you know. Mr. Fazakerly, give us your attention. You will not serve me by pretending ignorance if you know. I have found out that I am not Mr. Arden's son."

"Softly, softly!" said the lawyer, putting his hand on Edgar's arm. "That is mere assertion on your part; there is no proof."

"Hear me out," cried Edgar. "I am speaking from myself only. I am certain I am not Mr. Arden's son, nor Mrs. Arden's son. I am a stranger altogether to the race. To me these letters prove it fully. For his own evil ends, whatever they may have been, the master of this house adopted me—perhaps bought me—"

Here there was another interruption. Mrs. Murray put out her hand suddenly as if to stop him, and gave a cry as of pain; but once more stiffened back into her old attitude, regarding them with the same defiant look. Edgar paused, he looked her full in the face, he put his hand upon her arm. "You injure me by your silence," he said. "Speak! Are you my—Am I—?" His voice shook, his whole frame trembled. "You are something to me," he cried, looking at her. "Speak, for God's sake! Was it you who wrote these letters? You know them—you recognised them. It is for my benefit that you should speak. Answer me!— the time is past for concealment. Tell me what you know."

Mrs. Murray's lips moved, but no sound came; she looked from one to another with rapid eager looks but the defiance in her face did not pass away. At last her voice burst out aloud with an effort. "Let me sit down," she said; "I am growing old, and I am weary with watching, and I cannot stand upon my feet." The three men beside her leant forward to hear these words, as if a whole revelation must be in them, so highly were they excited. When it became apparent that she revealed nothing, even Mr. Fazakerly was so much disturbed as to push his chair away from the table, and to give his whole attention to the new actor in the scene. Edgar brought her a seat, and she sat down among them with an air of presiding over them, and with a strange knowledge of the crisis, and all its particulars which seemed natural at the moment, and yet was proof above all argument that she was not unprepared for the disclosure that had been made to her. There was no surprise in her face. She was greatly agitated, and evidently restraining herself with an effort that was almost superhuman; but she was not astonished, as a stranger would have been. This fact dawned upon the lawyer with curious distinctness after the first minute. Edgar was baffled in his appeal, and Arthur wanted the power to make use of his observations. But Mr. Fazakerly saw, and watched, and had all his wits about him. And neither at that moment nor at any other did the old solicitor of the Ardens, the depository of all the family secrets, forget that the reigning Squire, whether he were the rightful heir or not, was his client, and that he was retained for the defence.

"Mr. Edgar," said Mr. Fazakerly, "and Mr. Arthur, you are both too much interested to manage this properly. You take it for granted that everything bears upon the one question, which this good lady, of course, never heard of before. Leave her with me. If she knows anything—which is very unlikely—she will inform me in confidence. Of course, whatever I find out shall be disclosed to you at once," he added, with a mental reservation. "Leave it to me."

But whether that could have been done or not was never put to the test. As he finished speaking, Wilkins came to the door hastily. "I beg your pardon, sir," he said, "but some folks is come from the village, asking if one Mrs. Murray is here. I beg your pardon, I'm sure, for interrupting—"

The old Scotchwoman rose up suddenly in the midst of them with a cry of fear, which she no longer attempted to restrain.

"Is it my Jeanie?" she exclaimed. "Oh, good Lord, good Lord, I'm paying dear, dear!"

"I must go with her," said Edgar, in his excitement. Something in his face, some strange likeness never perceived before, startled both his companions. Arthur Arden rose too. He did not care about Jeanie. He had forgotten, in this greater excitement, that he was guilty in regard to the girl. All he thought of was to follow this new clue—to see them together—to watch the new resemblance he had found out in Edgar's face.

CHAPTER XX

Jeanie was lying propped up on pillows, struggling for breath. Her face, which had always been like that of an angel, was more visionary, more celestial than ever; the golden hair, which had always been so carefully braided, hung about her head like a halo. It was hair which fell in soft, even tresses, not standing on end or struggling into rebellious curls: everything about her was soft, harmonious, submissive. Her eyes were full of light, enlarged, with that fatal breadth and fulness which generally has but one meaning. A little flush of fever on her cheeks kept up the appearance of health. Her pretty lips were parted with the panting, struggling breath. Dr. Somers stood at her bedside, looking very grave. Sally Timms sat crying in a corner. Mrs. Hesketh came to the door to meet the poor grandmother, with her apron at her eyes. "She was took bad half-an-hour after you went—just about when you'd have got to the Hall; and called and called till it made you sick to hear—'Granny! granny! granny!'—never another word. Oh, I'm thankful, Missis, as you've come in time."

"Half-an-hour after I left!" said Mrs. Murray; "when I was denying the truth. Oh, me that thought to hide it from the Lord!—me that thought she was better, and He couldna go back! And the angel cried upon me, Granny! granny! Lad, do you hear that!—I have lost my Jeanie for you!"

She put her hand upon Edgar's shoulder as she spoke. Her face was white and ghastly with her despair. She thrust him from her, almost with violence. "Oh, let me never see you more! Oh, let me never see you more! I have lost my Jeanie for you!"

"Is there no hope?" said Edgar, clutching Dr. Somers by the arm. He had given way to the mother, to let her approach the bed, and now stood behind with a face so grave and grieved that any answer seemed unnecessary. He shook his head; and then, after a little interval, spoke.

"I know no reason why this should have come on. Some agitation which I cannot explain. There is no hope, unless it can be calmed somehow. The grandmother may do it, or perhaps—"

Dr. Somers turned round and looked the newcomers in the face. Was it possible that the innocent creature dying before his eyes could have loved either of these men? Arthur Arden was the kind of man to pursue an intrigue anywhere, and he had singled out Jeanie. And Edgar was young and well-looking, and the chief object of interest to the village. Could her eye or her heart have been caught by one of them. Why were they both here? The Doctor's mind was full of the one remaining chance. He looked at Edgar again, whose face was full of emotion; he had his heart in his eyes; he was always sympathetic, always ready to feel for any sufferer. The Doctor mused over it a little, watching keenly the approach of the grandmother to the bedside. Mrs. Murray went to her child as calmly as if she had never known a disturbing feeling in her life. She bent over her like a dove over her nest. "My bairn! my bonnie woman! my Jeanie!" she murmured; but the patient was not stilled. The Doctor looked anxiously on, and then he yielded to an impulse, which he could not have explained. He took Edgar by the shoulder and drew him forward. "Go and speak to her," he said. "I!" whispered Edgar, astonished. "Go and speak to her," cried the Doctor, in tones scarcely audible, yet violently imperative, and not to be disobeyed. The young man, deeply moved as he was, went forward doubtfully, longing and yet afraid. What could he say? What could he do? He did not understand the yearning that was in his heart towards this little suffering girl. He had no sense of guilt towards her, had never harmed her, one way or another. He longed to go and take her in his arms, and carry her away to some halcyon place where there would be rest. Dying was not in his thoughts; but Edgar, too, was weary of agitation, and suffering, and distress. He had suffered, and he had not come to the end of his sufferings. Oh, to be able to escape somewhere, to carry away poor Jeanie, to lay her down in some cool valley, in some heavenly silence! Tears were in his eyes. He thought of her, and of Clare, and Gussy, all mingled together—all whom he loved best. He went up to the bedside, behind the old woman who had thrust him away so passionately, yet who somehow belonged to him too. "Jeanie," he said, in a low tremulous voice, "Jeanie, little Jeanie!" The other spectators instinctively fell back, perceiving, they could not tell how, that this was an experiment which was being tried. Jeanie's panting breath was hushed for a moment; she made a distinct effort, half raising herself. "Who was that; who was that?" she cried. ("Speak again," said Dr. Somers, once more, in that imperative, violent whisper behind.) "Jeanie," said Edgar, advancing another step, "Do you know me? Speak to me, Jeanie!"

She gave a great cry. She threw herself forward, opening her arms; her face blazed as with a sudden light of joy. "Willie! Willie! Willie!" she cried, as on the first night when she had seen Edgar from her window, and, leaning half out of her bed, threw herself into his arms.

An awful pause ensued. Mrs. Murray kneeled down by the bedside, and with her face raised, and two big tears flowing slowly down her cheeks, lifted up her clasped hands and prayed. Her eyes were fixed upon Jeanie, but she did nothing to detach her from the arms in which, as the spectators thought, she would certainly die. Dr. Somers held them all back. He held up his hand so that no one moved. He stood watching the pair thus strangely clasping each other, standing close behind Edgar, to give aid if necessary, with one finger laid softly on Jeanie's wrist. Was it for life, was it for death? Even the women, who had been looking on, stole softly forward, with all the interest which attends the crisis of a tragedy, staying the tears which had flowed in a kind of mechanical sympathy at the apparent approach of death. They comprehended that death had been stayed at least for the moment, and they did not know how. As for Edgar, he stood in this unexpected and innocent embrace, feeling the soft weight upon his breast, the soft, feeble arm round him, the velvet-soft lips on his cheek, with an indescribable emotion. "If she lives, I will be her brother. I am her brother from this hour," he said to himself. He held her fast, supporting her, with thoughts in which not a single shade of evil mingled. Jeanie was sacred to him. He did not understand what had moved her. He had, indeed, forgotten, in this sudden change of all his thoughts, the suspicions he had of her mother. He thought only that she had cast herself upon his support and protection, and that henceforward she was to him as the sister he had lost.

"Lay her back gently. Stand by her—her strength is failing," said the Doctor's quick voice in his ear. "Softly, softly! Stand by her. Now the wine—she will take it from you. Edgar, life and death are on your steadiness. Support her—give her the wine—now—now—"

She took it from him, as Dr. Somers said. She smiled on him, and drew his hand feebly with both hers till she had placed it under her cheek. Then she said "Willie!" again in a faint whisper like a sigh, and fell asleep sweetly and suddenly, while they all watched her—fell asleep, not in death but in life, with Edgar's hand supporting her child-like, angel-like face.

Then Mrs. Murray rose from her knees. "I must speak," she said, with a gasp; "if I did not speak now, I would repent and tempt the Lord again. Him that's standing there is Jeanie's near kin—no her brother, as my bonnie lamb thinks he is—but near, near of kin, and like, like to him that's gane. And I am his mother's mother, a guilty woman, no worthy of God's grace. I have made my confession, and now I can tempt the Lord no more."

This strange speech fell upon, it seemed, unheeding ears. The indifferent spectators stared, not knowing what it meant. The Doctor was absorbed in watching his patient; and Edgar, in the new and strange position which he was obliged to keep, did not realise what was said. He heard the words, and was conscious of a vague wonder in respect to them, but was too fully occupied, body and mind, to be able to make out what they meant. Only Arthur Arden took them fully into his mind. He could scarcely restrain an exclamation, scarcely keep himself still, when this confirmation of every hope, and explanation of every difficulty, came to his ears. He went out immediately, in the stupor of his delight, and stood at the cottage door, under the twinkling stars, repeating it over to himself. "Near of kin to Jeanie—near, near of kin." No Arden at all—an alien, of different name and inferior race. And it was he, Arthur, who was Arden of Arden. Could it be true? was it true? The night was dark, relieved only by the stars which throbbed and trembled in the sky. One of them shone over the dark trees of Arden in the distance, as if it were a giant fairy blossom springing out of the foliage. Was the star his, too, as well as the tree? Was all his, really his—the dewy land under his feet, the wide line of the horizon where it extended over the park and the woods—the very sky, with its "lot of stars." His head swam and grew dizzy as the thought grew—all his—house and lands, name and honour. A wild elation took possession of him. All that had happened had been well for him; and there passed across his mind vaguely an echo of that wonderful sentiment with which those who are at ease pretend to console those who suffer. All for the best—had not all been for the best? The accident which almost killed Jeanie—the sudden crisis of illness which had made the watchers send to Arden for her grandmother—all for the best. God had taken the trouble to disturb the order of nature—to wear out the young life to such a thread as might snap at any moment—to wring the old heart with bitterest pangs of anxiety—all for good to him. Thus the egotist mused; and though he was irreligious, said, with a horrible gratitude, and something like an assumption of piety in his heart, "Thank God!"—Thank God! for all but killing Jeanie—for working havoc in her mother's breast. It had been all for the best.

Strangely enough, Mrs. Murray, after an interval, followed him out to the door. She grasped him by the arm in her excitement. "I thought once I was indebted to you," she said. "I thought I should be thankful that you brought my bairn in, carrying her in your arms; but I know now whose blame it was she got her accident. I know now what you would have put into her head if it had not been for her innocence. And it is for you I must ruin my bonnie lad, and cover my name with shame. Oh, the Lord sees if it's hard or no! But mind you this, man, you will never be his equal if you were to labour night and day—never his equal—nor nigh him. And never think that those that have loved him will stoop down to the like of you."

She thrust him away, as she spoke, with a scorn that made Arthur wild. What! he the true proprietor of Arden to be dismissed so? He turned to gaze at her as she disappeared, shutting the door upon him. An impulse seized him to throw a stone at the window—to do something which should show his contempt and rage; but he did not do it. He thought better of it. He could afford to be magnanimous. He left the place where Jeanie's young life had been put in such jeopardy by his fault, and where he had just concluded that it had been for the best, without seeking for any further news of Jeanie. She might die or live for anything he cared. Her brother was with her, or her cousin, or whatever he was—the fellow who had kept him so long out of Arden. Thus he turned away through the dark village, up the dark avenue, and went home to Arden, where the lights were still burning in all the windows, and the master expected home. It was on his lips to say—"I am master now; when that fellow comes, do not let him in;" but in that point too he restrained himself. Fazakerly was in the house, and Clare was in the house. He did not wish to come into collision with either of them. For Edgar, he did not care.

Meantime Edgar stood, fatigued and weakened by the excitement of the day, by Jeanie's bedside, with her cheek resting on his hand. It required all his muscular energy to support him in that strange task. He scarcely ventured to breathe for fear of disturbing her. When he made a little movement, her hands tightened upon his arm as she slept. The Doctor held wine to his lips, and encouraged him. "You are saving her life," he said; and Edgar smiled and stood fast. He was saving her life—at this moment when his own strength was weakest, his own courage lowest; but it was not he who had endangered her life. The man who was to blame was entering Arden, full of elation and selfish joy, while Edgar stood by the humble bedside saving the life of the almost victim. What a strange contrast it was! But there are some men in the world whose lot it always is to be the ones who suffer and save—and their lot is not the worst in this life. The hours were long as they crept and crept onward to the morning. The Doctor dozed in his chair. Even the old mother slept by snatches in the midst of her watch—but Edgar, elevated by weariness, and weakness, and spent excitement, out of the ordinary regions of fleshly sensation, stood by Jeanie's bedside, and did not sleep. He went over it all in his heart—he felt it was now finally settled somehow—everything confirmed and made certain, though he did not quite know how. He thought of all that had to be given up, with a faint, wan smile upon his lips. This time it was not an opiate, it was a numbness that hung over him, partly physical because of his attitude, but still more spiritual because of the exhaustion of his heart. All was over—he was a new being, coming painfully into a changed life through bitter pangs, of which he was but half-conscious. And Jeanie slept with her cheek on his hand, and the other living creatures in the cottage watched and slept, and breathed around him. And life and the great universe moved and swam about him, like scenes in a phantasmagoria—one scene dissolving into another, nothing steady or definite in earth or heaven. Sometimes, as if a stray light had caught it, one scene out of the past would suddenly shine out before him, generally something quite unconnected with his present position; and then a strange gleam would fall over the future, over that unknown waste which lay before. Thus the night stole on, till every minute seemed an hour, and every hour a day.

Arthur Arden went up to the house, which he was now convinced was his own, with the strangest mixture of feelings. He was so confused and overwhelmed by all the events of the night, by the fluctuations of feeling to which he had himself been subject, that the exultation which it was natural should be in his mind was kept down. He did exult, but he did it like a man asleep, conscious that he was dreaming. He went in, and found the house all silent and deserted. Mr. Fazakerly had gone to his room; Clare had retired to hers; the Rector had gone home. Nobody but the solemn Wilkins was visible in the house, which began, however, to show a certain consciousness of the excitement within it. The tea-tray, which nobody had looked at, still stood in the drawing-room, lights were left burning everywhere, windows were open, making the flames flutter. It was not possible to mistake that visible impression of something having happened, which shows itself so soon on the mere external surroundings of people in trouble. "May I make so free as to ask, sir, if ought has gone wrong?" Wilkins asked, standing at the door of the drawing-room, when he had opened it. "Yes, Wilkins, something has happened," said Arthur. It was on his lips to announce the event, not for the solace of Wilkins, but only to assure himself, by putting it into words, that the thing was true; but he restrained the impulse. "You will know it soon," he added, briefly dismissing the man with a slight wave of his hand. Wilkins went downstairs immediately, and informed the kitchen that "somethink was up. You can all go to bed," he added, majestically. "I'll wait up for master. That Arthur Arden is awful stuck up, like poor relations in general; but master he'll tell me." And thus the house gradually subsided into silence. Wilkins placed himself in the great chair in the hall and went to sleep, sending thrills of suppressed sound (for even in his snores he remembered his place, and kept himself down) through the silent dwelling. Arthur Arden was too much excited to sleep. He remained in the drawing-room, where he had allowed himself to be led by Wilkins. He was too self-absorbed to go from one room to another, to be conscious of place or surroundings. For hours together he paced up and down, going over and over everything that had passed, and at every change in the scenes which formed before his fancy, stopping to tell himself that Arden was his own. His head swam; he staggered as he walked; his whole brain seemed to whirl with agitation; and yet he walked on and on, saying to himself at intervals, "Arden is mine." How extraordinary it was! And yet, at the same time, he was only the poor relation, the heir presumptive, in the eyes of the world. Even the declaration he had heard was nothing but evidence which might have to be produced in a court of law, which it would take him infinite pains and money, and much waiting and suspense, to establish, should it be necessary to establish it, in legal form. The letters were still in the hands of those most interested to suppress them. The witness whose testimony he had just heard was in their hands, and no doubt might be suborned or sent away. If it were any one but Edgar, he would have felt that all he had heard to-night might be but as a dream, and that his supplanter might still be persuaded by Fazakerly, by Clare, by some late dawning of self-interest, to defend himself. In such a case his own position would be as difficult as could be conceived. He would have to originate a lingering expensive lawsuit, built upon evidence which he could not produce. If he were himself in Edgar's position, he felt that he could foil any such attack; but Edgar was a fool, a Quixote, a madman; or rather he was a low fellow, of no blood or courage, who would give in without a struggle, who had not spirit enough to strike a blow for his inheritance. By degrees he got to despise him, as he pursued his thoughts. It was want of blood which made him shirk from the contest, not the sense of justice or right, or any fantastic idea of honour. Arthur Arden himself was an honourable man—he did nothing which society could put a mark against, which could stain his reputation among men; but to expose the weakness of his own position, to relinquish voluntarily, not being forced to it, his living and name, and everything he had, in the world!—He calculated upon Edgar that he would do this, and he despised him for it, and concluded in his heart that such cowardice and weakness, though, perhaps, they might be dignified by other names—such as generosity and honour—were owing to the meanness of his extraction, the vulgarity of his nature. No Arden would have done it, he said to himself, with contempt.

At last he threw himself upon a sofa, in that feverish exhaustion which excitement and long abstinence from sleep produce. He had slept little on the previous night, and he had no longer the exuberance of youth to carry him over any repeated shortening of his natural rest. He put himself on the sofa where Clare had lain after her faint; but he was in too great a whirl to be able to think of Clare. He propped himself up upon the pillows, and fell into feverish snatches of sleep, often broken, and full of dreams. He dreamt that he was turning Edgar and all his belongings out of Arden. He dreamt that he himself was being turned out—that Clare was standing over him like an inspired prophetess, denouncing woe on his head—that old Fazakerly was grinning in a corner and jibing at him. "You reckoned without your host," the lawyer said; "or, at least, you reckoned without me. Am I the man to suffer my client to make a fool of himself? Wilkins, show Mr. Arthur Arden the door." This was what he dreamed, and that the door was thrown open, and a chill air from without breathed on him, and that he knew and felt all hope of Arden was gone for ever. The chill of that outside cold so seized upon him that he awoke, and found it real. It was the hour after dawn—the coldest of the twenty-four. The sun had not yet risen out of the morning mists, and the world shivered in the cold beginning of the day. The door of the room in which he was, was standing wide open, and so was the great hall door, admitting the cold. In the midst, as in a sketch made in black and white, he saw Edgar standing talking to Wilkins. It struck him with a certain peevish irritation as he struggled up from his pillow, half-awake. "Don't stand there, letting in the cold," he said, harshly. Wilkins, irritable too from the same reason, gave him a hasty answer—"When a servant as has waited all night is letting in of his master, I don't know as folks as might have been in bed has got any reason to complain." Arthur swore an angry oath as he sprang from the sofa. "By—, you shall not stay in this house much longer, to give me your impudence!" "That's as the Squire pleases," said Wilkins, utterly indifferent to the poor relation. Edgar dismissed him with a kindly nod, and went into the drawing-room. He was very pale and worn out with all his fatigues; but he was not irritable. He came in and shut the door. "I wonder you did not go to bed," he said.

"Bed!" said Arthur, rising to his feet. "I wonder who could go to bed with all this row going on. Order that fellow to bring us some brandy. I am chilled to death on this confounded sofa, and you staying out the whole night. I haven't patience to speak to the old villain. Will you give the order now?"

"Come to the other room and I'll get it for you," said Edgar. "The man wants to go to bed."

"If I don't go to bed, confound them, why can't they wait?" said Arthur. He was but half awake; excited, chilled, anxious, and miserable; altogether in a dangerous mood. But Edgar had his wits sufficiently about him to feel all the unseemliness of a quarrel between them. He took him into the dining-room, and giving him what he asked for left the room with a hurried good night. He was not able for any contention; he went upstairs with a heavy heart. The excitement which had supported him so long was failing. And this last discovery, when he had time to realise it, was not sweet to him, but bitter. He could not tell how that was. Before he had suspected her to be related to him, he had wondered at himself to feel with what confidence he had turned to the old Scotchwoman, of whose noble life Perfitt had told him. It had bewildered him more than once, and made him smile. He remembered now that he had gone to her for advice; that he had consulted her about his concerns; that he had felt an interest in all her looks and ways, which it was now only too easy to explain. He had almost loved her, knowing her only as a stranger, entirely out of his sphere. And now that he knew she was his nearest relation, his heart recoiled from her. What harm she had done him! She had done her best—her very best—she and Squire Arden together, whose name he loathed—to ruin his life, and make him a wreck and stray in the world. By God's help, Edgar said to himself, he would not be a wreck. But how hard it was to forgive the people who had done it—to feel any charity for them! He did not even feel the same instinctive affection for Jeanie as he had done before. And yet he had saved her life; she had called him her brother, and in utter trust and confidence had been lying on his breast. Poor little Jeanie! Yet his heart grew sick as he thought of her and of the mother, who was his mother too. They were all that was left to him, and his heart rose against them. Sadness unutterable, weariness of the world, a sore and sick shrinking of the heart from everything around him, came upon Edgar. He had kept up so long. He had done all his duty, fulfilled everything that could be required of him. Could not he go away now, and disappear for ever from Arden, and be seen of none who knew him any more?

Such was the dreary impulse in his mind—an impulse which everyone must have felt who has borne the desertion of friends, the real or supposed failure of love and honour—and which here and there one in the chill heart-sickening pride of despair has given way to, disappearing out of life sometimes, sometimes out of all reach of friends. But Edgar was not the kind of man to break off his thread of life thus abruptly. He had duties even now to hold him fast—a duty to Clare, who, only a few hours ago (or was it years), had called him—bless her!—her true brother, her dearest brother. If he were to be tortured like an Indian at the stake, he would not abandon her till all was done for her that brother could do. And he had a duty even to the man whom he had just left, to remove all obstacles out of his way, to make perfectly plain and clear his title to Arden. His insolence cannot harm me, Edgar reflected, with a smile which was hard enough to maintain. And then there were his own people, his new family, his mother's mother. Poor Edgar! that last reflection went through and through him with a great pang. He could not make out how it was. He had had so kind, so tender a feeling towards her, and now it seemed to him that he shrunk from her very name. Was his name, too, the same as theirs? Did he belong to them absolutely, to their condition, to their manner of life? If it were so, none in the outer world should see him shrink from them; but at this moment, in his retirement, the thought that they were his, and they only, was bitter to Edgar. He could not face it. It was not pride, nor contempt of their poverty, nor dislike to themselves; but yet the thought that they were his family—that he belonged to them—was a horror to him. Should he go back with them to their Highland cottage?—should he go and desert them, as if he were ashamed? In the profound revulsion of his heart he grew sick and faint with the thought.

And thus the night passed—in wonder and excitement, in fear and trembling of many kinds. When the morning came, Jeanie opened her soft eyes and smiled upon the watchers round her, over all of whom was a cloud which no one understood. "I've been in yon awful valley, but I'm come back," she said, with her pale lips. She had come back; but ah how many hopes and pleasant dreams and schemes of existence had gone into the dark valley instead of Jeanie! The old mother, who had seen so many die, and gone through a hundred heartbreaks, bent over the one who had come back from the grave, and kissed her sadly, with a passion of mingled feelings to which she could give no outlet. "But oh, my bonnie lad!" she said under her breath with a sigh which was almost a groan. She had seen into his heart, though he did not know it. She had perceived, with a poignant sting of pain, one momentary instinctive shrinking on his part. She understood all, in her large human nature and boundless sympathy, and her heart bled, but she said never a word.

The reader may be weary of hearing of nights which went over in agitation, and mornings which rose upon an excitement not yet calmed down. But it is inevitable in such a crisis as that which we are describing that the excitement should last from one day to another. The same party who had met on the previous night in the library to examine the packet of letters, which had occasioned all this distress and trouble, met again next morning at breakfast. Clare did not appear. She had sent for Edgar in the morning, rousing him out of the brief, uneasy slumber which he had fallen into in broad daylight, after his night of trial. She had received him in her dressing-room, with a white muslin wrapper thrown round her, and her hair hanging about her shoulders, as she would have received her brother. But though the accessories of the scene were carefully retained, there was a little flush of consciousness on Clare's cheek that it was not her brother who was coming to her; and Edgar did not offer the habitual kiss, but only took her hand in his while she spoke to him. "I cannot come down," she said. "I will not come down again while Arthur Arden is in the house. That is not what I mean; for I suppose, now you have made up your mind, it is Arthur Arden's house, and not ours."

"It is not mine," said Edgar. "Something else happened last night which confirmed everything. It is quite unimportant whether I make up my mind or not. The matter is beyond question now."

"What happened last night?" said Clare eagerly.

"I will tell you another time. We found out, I think, who I really am. Don't ask me any more," said Edgar, with a pang which he could not explain. He did not want to tell her. He would have accepted any excuse to put the explanation off.

Clare looked at him earnestly. She did not know what to say—whether to obey a rising impulse in her heart (for she, too, was a genuine Arden) of impatience at his tame surrender of his "rights"—or the curiosity which prompted her to inquire into the new discovery; or to do what a tender instinct bade her—support him who had been so true a brother to her by one more expression of her affection. She looked up into his face, which began to show signs of the conflict, and that decided her. "You can never be anything less to me than my brother," she said, leaning her head softly against his arm. Edgar could not speak for a moment—the tears came thick and blinding to his eyes.

"God bless you!" he said. "I cannot thank you now, Clare. It is the only drop of sweetness in my cup; but I must not give way. Am I to say you cannot come down stairs? Am I to arrange for my dear sister, my sweet sister, for the last time?"

"Certainly for this time," said Clare. "Settle for me as you think best. I will go where you please. I can't stay—here."

She would have said, "in Arthur Arden's house," but the words seemed to choke her; for Arthur Arden had not said a word to her—not a word—since he knew—

And thus authorised, Edgar presented himself before the others. He took no particular notice of Arthur Arden. He said calmly, "Miss Arden does not feel able to join us this morning," and took, as a matter of course, his usual place. There was very little said. Arthur sat by sullenly, beginning to feel himself an injured man, unjustly deprived of his inheritance. He was the true heir, wrongfully kept out of his just place: yet the interest of the situation was not his, but clung to the impostor, who accepted ruin with such a cheerful and courageous quiet. He hated him, because even in this point Edgar threw him quite into the shade. And Arthur felt that he might have taken a much superior place. He might have been magnanimous, friendly, helpful, and lost nothing by it; but even though the impulse to take this nobler part had once or twice visited him, he had not accepted it; and he felt with some bitterness that Edgar had in every way filled a higher rôle than himself.

They had finished their silent breakfast when Edgar addressed him. He did it with a marked politeness, altogether unlike his aspect up to this time. He had been compelled to give up the hope that his successor would be his friend, and found there was nothing now but politeness possible between them. "I will inform Mr. Fazakerly at once," he said, "of what took place last night. He will be able to put everything into shape better than we shall. As soon as I have his approbation, and have settled everything, I will take my sister away."

"She is not your sister," said Arthur, with some energy.

"I know that so well that it is unkind of any one to remind me," said Edgar, with sudden tears coming to his eyes; "but never mind. I repeat we will leave Arden to-day or to-morrow. It is easier to make such an arrangement than to break the natural bonds that have been between us all our lives."

Arthur had made a calculation before he came downstairs. He had taken a false step last night when he adopted an insolent tone to, and almost attempted to pick a quarrel with the man who was saving him so much trouble; but in the circumstances he concluded that it was best he should keep it up. He said abruptly, "Miss Arden is not your sister. I object as her nearest relation. How do I know what use you may make of the influence you have obtained over her? I object to her removal from Arden—at least by you."

Edgar gave Mr. Fazakerly a look of appeal, and then made a strong effort to command himself. "I have nothing to keep now but my temper," he said, with a faint smile, "and I hope I may be able to retain that. I don't know that Mr. Arden's presence is at all needed for our future consultations; and I suppose, in the meantime, as I am making a voluntary surrender of everything, and he could not by legal form expel me for a long time, I am justified in considering this house, till I give it up, to be mine, and not his?"

"Certainly, Arden is yours," said Mr. Fazakerly. "You are behaving in the most unprecedented way. I don't understand what you would be at; but Mr. Arthur Arden is utterly without power or capability in the matter. All he can do is to inform his lawyer of what he has heard—

"No power in the matter!" cried Arthur. "When I heard that woman confess last night openly that this— this gentleman, who has for so long occupied the place I ought to occupy, was her grandson! What do you mean by no power? Is Mr.—Murray—if that is his name—to remain master of my house, in face of what I heard with my own ears—"

"You are perfectly entitled to bring an action, and produce your witnesses," said Mr. Fazakerly promptly; "perfectly entitled—and fully justified in taking such a step. But in the meantime Mr. Edgar Arden is the Squire, and in full possession. You may wait to see what his plans are (no doubt they are idiotical in the highest degree), or you can bring an action; but at the present moment you have not the smallest right to interfere—"

"Not in respect to my cousin!" Arthur said, with rising passion.

"Not in respect to anything," said the lawyer cheerfully.

And then the three stood up and looked at each other—Mr. Fazakerly having taken upon himself the conduct of affairs. It was Arthur only who was agitated, Edgar having recovered his composure by renunciation of everything, and the lawyer having fully come to himself, out of sheer pleasure in the conflict which he foresaw.

"There have been a great many indiscreet revelations made, and loose talk of all kinds," Mr. Fazakerly continued; "enough, I don't doubt, to disturb the ideas of a man uninstructed in such matters. That is entirely your cousin's fault, not mine; but I repeat you have no power here, Mr. Arthur Arden, either in respect to Miss Clare or to anything else. Mere hearsay and private conversation are nothing. I doubt very much if the case will hold water at all; but if it does, it can only be of service to you after you have raised an action and proved your assertions. Good morning, Mr. Arthur. You have gone too fast and too far."

And in another moment Arthur was left alone, struggling with himself, with fury and disappointment not to be described. He was as much cast down as he had been elated. He gave too much importance to these words, as he had given to the others. He had thought, without any pity or ruth, that he was to take possession at once; and now he felt himself cast out. He threw himself down in the window seat and gnawed his nails to the quick, and asked himself what he was to do. A lawsuit, a search for evidence, an incalculable, possibly unrecompensed expenditure—these were very different from the rapid conclusion he had hoped.

"My dear young friend," said Mr. Fazakerly solemnly, turning round upon Edgar as they entered the library, "you have behaved like an idiot!—I don't care who tells you otherwise, or if it has been your own unassisted genius which has brought you to this—but you have acted like a fool. It sounds uncivil, but it is true."

"Would you have had me, as he says, carry on the imposture," said Edgar, with an attempt at a smile. "Would you have had me, knowing who I am—"

"Pooh! pooh!" said Mr. Fazakerly. "Pooh! pooh! You don't in the least know who you are. And that is not your business in the least—it is his. Let him prove what he can; you are Edgar Arden, of Arden, occupying a position which, for my part, I think you ought to have been contented with. To make yourself out to be somebody else is not your business. Sit down, and let me hear what you have to say."

Then the client and the adviser sat down together, and Edgar related all the particulars he had learned. Mr. Fazakerly sobered down out of his hopeful impatience as he listened. He shook his head and said, "Bad, very bad," at intervals. When he heard what Mrs. Murray had said, and that it was in Arthur Arden's presence, he gave his head a redoubled shake. "Very—bad—indeed," and pondered sadly over it all. "If you had but spoken to me first; if you had but spoken to me first!" he cried. "I don't mean to say I would have advised you to keep it up. An unscrupulous counsellor would have told you, and with truth, that you had every chance in your favour. There was no proof whatever that you were the boy referred to before this Mrs. Murray appeared; and nothing could be easier than to take Mrs. Murray out of the way. But I don't advise that—imposture is not in my way any more than in yours, Mr. Edgar. But at least

I should have insisted upon having a respectable man to deal with, instead of that cold-blooded egotist; and we might have come to terms. It is not your fault. You are behaving most honourably—more than that—Quixotically. You are doing more than any other man would have done—and we could have made terms. There could have been no possible objection to that."

"Yes, I should have objected," said Edgar; "I do not want to make any terms—"

"Then what do you mean to do?" cried Mr. Fazakerly. "It is all very fine to be high-minded in theory, but what are you to do? You have not been brought up to any profession. With your notions, you could never get on in business. What are you to do?"

Edgar shook his head. He smiled at the same time with a half-amused indifference, which drove his friend to renewed impatience.

"Mr. Edgar," he said solemnly, "I have a great respect for you. I admire some of your qualities—I would trust you with anything; but you are behaving like a fool—"

"Very likely," said Edgar, still with a smile. "If that were all! Do you really suppose that with two hands capable of doing a few things, not to speak of a head and some odd scraps of information—do you really suppose a man without any pride to speak of, will be unable to get himself a living? That is nonsense. I am quite ready to work at anything, and I have no pride—"

"I should not like to trust too much to that," said Mr. Fazakerly, shaking his head. "And then there is your sister. Miss Clare loses by this as much as you do. Of course now the entail stands as if you had never taken any steps in the matter, and Old Arden is hers no longer. Are you aware that, supposing her fully provided for by that most iniquitous bequest, your father left her nothing else? She will be a beggar as well as you."

"You don't mean it!" cried Edgar, with a flush of warm colour rushing over his face. "Say that again! You don't really mean it? Why, then, I shall have Clare to work for, and I don't envy the king, much less the proprietor of Arden. Shake hands! you have made me twice the man I was. My sister is my sister still, and, after all, I am not alone in the world."

Mr. Fazakerly looked at the young man aghast. He said to himself, "There must be madness in the family," not recollecting that nothing in the family could much affect Edgar, who did not belong to it. He sat with a certain helpless amazement looking at him, watching how the life rose in his face. He had been very weary, very pale, before, but this news, as it were, rekindled him, and gave him all his energy back.

"I thought it did not matter much what became of me," he said, with a certain joyous ring in his voice, which stupified the old lawyer. "But it does matter now. What is it, Wilkins? What do you want?"

"Please, sir, Lady Augusta Thornleigh and the young ladies is come to call," said Wilkins. "I'd have shown them into the drawing-room, but Mr. Arthur Arden he's in the drawing-room. Shall they come here?"

Edgar's countenance paled again as suddenly as it had grown bright. His face was like a glass, on which all his emotions showed. "They must want to see my sister," he said, with a certain longing and wistfulness in his tone.

"It was you, sir, as my lady asked for, not Miss Arden. It's the second one of the young ladies as is with her—Miss Augusta I think they calls her, sir," said Wilkins, not without some curiosity. "They said special as they didn't want to see no strangers—only you."

Edgar rose up once more, his face glowing crimson, his eyes wet and full. "Wherever they please— wherever they please," he said half to himself, with a confused thrill of happiness and emotion. "I am at their orders." He did not know what he expected. His heart rose as if it had wings. They had come to seek him. Was not he receiving compensation, more than compensation, for all his pain?

But before he could give any orders, before Mr. Fazakerly could gather up his papers, or even offer to go away, Lady Augusta herself appeared at the open door.

CHAPTER XXIII

Lady Augusta came in with a disturbed countenance and traces of anxiety on her brow. She was alone, and though her good heart, and another pleader besides, had impelled her to take this step, she was a little doubtful as to the wisdom of what she was doing, and a little nervous as to the matter generally. She had her character for prudence to keep up, she had to keep the world in ignorance of the danger there had been to Gussy, and of all the pain this business had cost her. And yet she could not let the poor boy, who had been so disinterested and so honourable, go without a word from her—without once more holding out her hand. She said to herself that she could not have done it, and at all events it was quite certain that Gussy would have given her no peace, and would have herself done something violent and compromising, had her mother resisted her determination. "I will be very good," Gussy had said. "I will say nothing I ought not to say; but he was fond of me, and I cannot, cannot let him go without a word!" Lady Augusta's heart had spoken in the same tone; but the moment she had yielded, the other side of the question appeared to her, and a hundred fears lest she should compromise her child had taken possession of her mind. It was this which had brought her alone to the library door, leaving Gussy behind. She came forward, almost with shyness, with an air of timidity quite unlike her, and held out both her hands to Edgar, who for his part could scarcely repress an exclamation of disappointment at seeing her alone. "I am so glad to see Mr. Fazakerly with you," Lady Augusta said, taking prompt advantage of this fact, and extending her hand graciously to the lawyer. "I do hope you have dismissed that incomprehensible story you told me altogether from your mind."

"Don't be angry with me," said Edgar, gazing at her wistfully; "but was it with that idea you came here?"

She looked at him, and took in at a glance the change in his appearance, the pathetic look in his eyes, and her heart was touched. "No," she said, "no, my poor boy; it was not that. We came to tell you what we felt—what we thought. Oh, Mr. Fazakerly, have you heard this dreadful story? Is it true?"

"I decline to say what is and what is not true," said Mr. Fazakerly, doggedly. "I am not here to define truth. Your ladyship may think me very rude, but Mr. Arden is behaving like a fool."

"Poor boy!" said Lady Augusta; "poor boy!" Her heart was bleeding for him, but she did not know what to do or say.

"You said we," said Edgar. "Some one else came with you. Some one else had the same kind thought. Dear Lady Augusta, you will not take that comfort from me now."

Lady Augusta paused, distracted between prudence and pity. Then she drew herself up with a tremulous dignity. "Mr. Fazakerly has daughters of his own," she said. "I am not afraid that he will betray mine. Yes, Mr. Arden, Gussy has come with me. She insisted upon coming. There has never been anything between them," she added, turning to the lawyer. "There might have been, had he not found out this; but the moment he discovered—, like a true gentleman, as he is—" Here Lady Augusta had to pause to stifle her tears. "And my Gussy's heart is so warm. She would not let him go without bidding him good-bye. I told her it was not prudent, but she would not listen to me. Of course, it must end here; but our hearts are breaking, and we could not let him go without one good-bye."

She stopped, with a sob, and once more held out her hand. Poor woman! even at that moment it was more herself than him she bewailed. Standing there in his strength and youth, it did not seem possible to believe that the world could go very badly with him; but how unfortunate she was! Ada first, and then Gussy; and such a son as he would have been—somebody to trust, whatever happened. She held out her hand to him, and drew him close to her, and wept over him. How unfortunate she was!

"And Gussy?" said Edgar eagerly.

"I put her into the little morning-room, Clare's room," said Lady Augusta. "Go to her for a few minutes; Mr. Fazakerly will not think it wrong of me, I am sure. And oh, my dear boy, I know I can trust you not to go too far—not to suggest anything impossible, any correspondence—Edgar, do not try my poor child too far."

He pressed her hand, and went away, with a kind of sweet despair in his heart. It was despair: hope and possibility had all gone out of any dream he had ever entertained on this subject; but still it was sweet, not bitter. Lady Augusta sat silent for some minutes, trying to compose herself. "I beg your pardon," she said; "indeed I can't help it. Oh, Mr. Fazakerly, could no arrangement be made? I cannot help crying. Oh, what a dear fellow he is! and going away from us with his heart broken. Could nothing be done?—could no arrangement be made?"

"A great many things could be done, if he was not behaving like a fool," said Mr. Fazakerly. "I beg your pardon; but it is too much for me. He is like an idiot; he will hear no reason. Nobody but himself would have taken any notice. Nobody but himself—"

"Poor boy—poor dear boy!" said Lady Augusta. And then she entered into the subject eagerly, and asked a hundred questions. How it had been found out—what he was going to do—what Arthur Arden's position would be—whether there ought not to be some provision made for Edgar? She inquired into all these matters with the eagerness of a woman who knew a great deal about business and was deeply interested for the sufferer. "But you must not suppose there was anything between him and my daughter," she repeated piteously; "there never was—there never was!"

In the meantime, Edgar had gone hastily, with a thrill of sadness and of pleasure which it would be difficult to describe, to the room where Gussy was. He went in suddenly, excitement and emotion having brought a flush upon his cheeks. She was standing with her back to the door, and turned round as he opened it. Gussy was very much agitated—she grew red and she grew pale, her hands, which she extended to him, trembled, tears filled her eyes. "O Mr. Arden!" was all she was able to say. As for

Edgar, his heart so melted over her that he had hard ado to refrain from taking her into his arms. It would have been no harm, he thought—his embrace would have been that of a brother, nothing more.

"It is very, very good of you to come," he said, his own voice faltering and breaking in spite of him. "I don't know how to thank you. It makes me feel everything so much less—and so much more."

"I could not help coming," said Gussy, with a choking voice. "O Mr. Arden, I am so grieved—I cannot speak of it—I could not let you go without—without—"

She trembled so that he could not help it—he drew her hand through his arm to support her. And then poor Gussy, overwhelmed, all her self-restraint abandoning her, drooped her head upon his shoulder as the nearest thing she could lean upon, and burst into tears.

There had never been a moment in her life so sad—or in either of their lives so strangely full of meaning. A few days ago they were all but affianced bride and groom, likely to pass their entire lives together. Now they met in a half embrace, with poignant youthful feeling, knowing that never in their lives would they again be so near to each other, that never more could they be anything to each other. It was the first time, and it would be the last.

"Dear Gussy," Edgar said, putting his arm softly round her, "God bless you for being so good to me. I will cherish the thought of you all my life. You have always been sweet to me, always from the beginning; and then I thought—But, thank God, you are not injured. And thank you a thousand and a thousand times."

"Oh, don't, don't!" cried Gussy. "Don't thank me, Mr. Arden. I think my heart will break."

"Don't call me Mr. Arden; call me Edgar now; it is the only name I have a right to; and let me kiss you once before we part."

She lifted up her face to him, with the tears still wet upon her cheeks. They loved each other more truly at that moment than they had ever done before; and Gussy's heart, as she said, was breaking. She threw her arms round his neck, and clung to him. "O Edgar, dear! Good-bye, good-bye!" she sobbed. And his heart, too, thrilled with a poignant sweetness, ineffable misery, and consolation, and despair.

This was how they parted for ever and ever—not with any pretence between them that it could ever be otherwise, or anything that sounded like hope. Lady Augusta's warning was unnecessary. They said not a word to each other of anything but that final severance. Perhaps in Gussy's secret heart, when she felt herself placed in a chair, felt another sudden hot kiss on her forehead, and found herself alone, and everything over, there was a pang more secret and deep-lying still, which felt the absence of any suggestion for the future; perhaps there had flitted before her some phantom of romance, whispering what he might do to prove himself worthy of her—revealing some glimpse of a far-off hope. Gussy knew all through that this was impossible. She was sure as of her own existence that no such thing could be; and yet, with his kiss still warm on her forehead—a kiss which only parting could have justified—she would have been pleased had he said it, only said it. As it was, she sat and cried, with a sense that all was finished and over, in which there lay the very essence of despair.

Edgar returned to the library while Lady Augusta was still in the very midst of her interrogations. She stopped short at sight of him, making an abrupt conclusion. She saw his eyes full of tears, the traces of emotion in his face, and thanked God that it was over. At such a moment, in such a mood, it would have been so difficult, so impossible to resist him. If he were to ask her for permission to write to Gussy, to cherish a hope, she felt that even to herself it would have been hard, very hard, to say absolutely, No. And her very soul trembled to think of the effect of such a petition on Gussy's warm, romantic, young heart. But he had not made any such prayer; he had accepted the unalterable necessity. She felt sure of that by the shortness of his absence, and the look which she dared scarcely contemplate—the expression of almost solemnity which was upon his face. She got up and went forward to meet him, once more holding out both her hands.

"Edgar," she said, "God will reward you for being so good and so true. You have not thought of yourself, you have thought of others all through, and you will not be left to suffer alone. Oh, my dear boy! I can never be your mother now, and yet I feel as if I were your mother. Kiss me too, and God bless you! I would give half of everything I have to find out that this was only a delusion, and that all was as it used to be."

Edgar shook his head with a faint smile. There passed over his mind, as in a dream, the under-thought—If she gave half of all she had to bring him back, how soon he would replace it; how easy, were such a thing possible, any secondary sacrifice would be! But notwithstanding this faint and misty reflection, it never occurred to him to think that it was because he was losing Arden that he was being thus absolutely taken farewell of. He himself was just the same—nay, he was better than he ever had been, for he had been weighed in the balance, and not found wanting. But because he had lost Arden, and his family and place in the world, therefore, with the deepest tenderness and feeling, these good women were taking leave of him. Edgar, fortunately, did not think of that aspect of the question. He kissed Lady Augusta, and received her blessing with a real overflowing of his heart. It touched him almost as much as his parting with Gussy. She was a good woman. She cried over him, as if he had been a boy of her own.

"Tell me anything I can do for you," she said—"anything, whatever it is. Would you like me to take charge of Clare? I will take her, and we will comfort her as we best can, if she will come with me. She ought not to be here now, while the house is so much agitated, and everything in disorder; and if there is anything to be done about Mr. Arthur Arden—Clare ought not to be here."

She had not the heart to say, though it was on her lips, that Clare ought not to be with the man who was no longer her brother. She caught his wistful look, and she could not say the words, though they were on her lips. But her offer was not one to be refused. Edgar—poor Edgar—who had everything to do—to sign his own death-warrant, as it were, and separate himself from everything that was near to him, had to go to Clare to negotiate. Would she go with Lady Augusta? He spoke to her at the door of her room, not entering, and she, with a flush of pain on her face, stood at the door also, not inviting him to go in. The division was growing between them in spite of themselves.

"Would you come to see me at Thorne?" said Clare. "Upon that must rest the whole matter whether I will go or not."

Edgar reflected, with again that sense of profound weariness stealing over him, and desire to be done with everything. No; he could not go through these farewells again—he could not wear his heart out bit by bit. This must be final, or it was mere folly. "No," he said; "it would be impossible. I could not go to see you at Thorne."

"Then I will not go," said Clare. And so it was settled, notwithstanding all remonstrances. The more she felt that distance creep between, the more she was determined not to recognise or acknowledge it. Edgar went back to the library and gave his message, and stayed there, restraining himself with an effort, while Mr. Fazakerly gave her ladyship his arm and conducted her to her carriage. Edgar would not even give himself that last gratification; he would not disturb Gussy again, or bring another tear to her eyes. It was all over and ended, for ever and ever. His life was being cut off, thread after thread, that he might begin anew. Thread after thread—only one trembling half-divided strand bound him at all to the old house, and name, and associations. Another clip of the remorseless shears, and he must be cut off for ever. One scene after another came, moving him to the depths of his being, and passed, and was over. The worst was over now—until, indeed, his final parting came, and Clare, in her turn, had been given up. But Clare, like himself, was penniless, and that last anguish might, perhaps, be spared.

CHAPTER XXIV

Clare left Arden that same afternoon. She came downstairs with her veil over her face, trembling, yet perhaps hoping to be met upon the way. Even Edgar was not aware of the moment when she took her flight. She had sent her maid to see that there was no one about, and even to herself she kept up the delusion that she wished to see no one—that she was able for no more agitation. So many long hours had passed—a night, a new morning, another day—yet Arthur Arden had not sought her, had not repeated those words which she had bidden him, if he would, repeat. She had made that concession to him in a moment of utter overthrow, when her heart had been overwhelmed by the sense of her own weakness and loneliness—by deepest poignant compassion and love for her brother. She had almost appealed to him to save them all—she had put, as it were, the welfare of the family into his hands. It had been done by impulse—almost against her will—for had she not grievances against him enough to embitter the warmest love? He had deserted her (she thought) for the merest village girl—a child with a lovely face, and nothing more. He had slighted her, making vain pretences of devotion, spending the time with Jeanie which he might have passed at her side. Yet all this she had forgotten in one moment when her heart was desperate. She had turned to him as to her last hope. She had as good as said— "Because I love you, save us." Not in words—never in words had she made such a confession. But could he be an Arden and not know that a woman of the house of Arden never asked help or succour but from a man she loved? And yet twenty-four hours had passed, and he had made no sign. She had thought of this all the night. Her heart was sore, and bleeding with a thousand wounds; there did not seem one corner of it that some sword had not stabbed. She had lost her father for ever; she could no longer think of him as she had once done; his image was driven away into the innermost depths of her heart, where she cherished, and wept over, and loved it, but could not reverence any longer. And her brother was her brother no more. He had done nothing to forfeit her love or her respect, but he was not her brother— different blood flowed in his veins. His very best qualities, his virtues and excellences, were not like the Ardens. He was a stranger to her and her race. Thus Clare was left alone and unsupported in the world. And Arthur! He had wounded her, slighted her, failed to understand her, or, understanding, scorned. Everything seemed to close round her, every door at which she might have knocked for sympathy. Her heart was sick, and sore, and weary with suffering, but not resigned. How could she ever be resigned to give up everything that was dearest to her, and all that made her prize her life?

It was for this reason that she stole out in the dullest hour of the afternoon, when the heart is faintest, and the vital stream flows lowest. She had a thick veil over her face, and a cloak which completely enveloped her figure. She left her maid behind to explain to her brother—whom she still called her brother, though she was forsaking him—how and where she had gone. "He will give you your orders about my things," she said to Barbara, who was in the highest state of restrained excitement, feeling, as all the household had begun to feel, that something strange must have happened. "Oh, Miss Clare, you've never gone and quarrelled with master?" the girl cried, ready to weep. "No; I will never quarrel with him. I could not quarrel with him," cried Clare. "How could you think so. Did you ever see so kind a brother?" "Never, Miss!" cried Barbara, fervently; and Clare paused and cried: but then drew the veil over her face, and set out alone—into a new world.

She paused for a moment, lingering on the steps, and gave a wistful look round her, hoping, she said to herself, that she would see nobody—but rather, poor Clare, with a wistful longing to see some one—to have her path intercepted. But no one was visible. Edgar was still in the library with Mr. Fazakerly. Arthur Arden was—no one knew where. The whole world stood afar off, still and indifferent, letting her do what she pleased, letting her leave her father's house. She stood on the doorstep, with nobody but Wilkins in sight, and took leave of the place where she was born. Had she been called upon to leave it under any other circumstances, her whole mind would have been occupied by the pang of parting from Arden. Now Arden had the lightest possible share in her pain—so little that she scarcely remembered it. She had so many more serious matters to grieve over. She forgot even, to tell the truth, that she was leaving Arden. She looked round, not to take farewell of her home, but to see if there was no shadow anywhere of some one coming, or some one going. She looked all round, deep into the shade of the trees, far across the glimmer of the fish pond. All was silent, deserted, lonely. The moment had come when she must step forth from the shelter in which she had spent all her life.

The avenue sloped gently downward to the village, and yet Clare felt it as hard as a mountainside. She seemed to herself to be toiling along, spending all her strength. For she was so solitary—no one to lend her an arm or a hand; no one to comfort her, or even to say the way was long. She was (she believed) a scorned and forsaken woman. Heaven and earth were made bitter to her by the thought. Once more she looked round, a final double farewell. He might even have been roused, she thought, by the sound of her step crossing the hall, by Wilkins swinging open the door for her, as he always did when any Arden went or came; for others, for the common world, it was open enough, as it stood usually at half its width. Oh, how slight a noise would have roused her, how faint a sound, had it been Arthur who was going away! She bethought herself of an expedient she had heard of—swallowing her own pride in the vehemence of her feelings. She wished for him with all her heart, making a vehement conscious exertion of her will. She cried out within herself, Arthur! Arthur! Arthur! It was a kind of Pagan prayer, addressed not to God, but to man. Such a thing had been known to be effectual. She had read in books, she had heard from others, that such an appeal made, with all the heart, is never unsuccessful; that the one will thus exerted affects the other unerringly; and that the name thus called sounds in the ears of its owner, calling him, wherever he may be. Therefore she did it, and watched its effect with a smothered excitement not to be described. But there was no effect; the park spread out behind her, the avenue ran into two lines of living green before. She was the only human creature on the scene—the only being capable of this pain and anguish. She drew her veil close, and went her way, with an indignation, a resentment, a rush of shame, greater than anything she had felt in all her life. She had called him, and he had not come. She had stooped her pride, and humbled herself, and made that effort, and there had been no response. Now, it was, it must be, over for ever, and life henceforward contained nothing for her worth the trouble of existing for.

It was thus that Clare left Arden, the old home of her race, her birthplace, the place which was, she would have said, everything to her—without even thinking of it or caring for it, or making any more account of it than had it been the veriest hired house. She was not aware of her own extraordinary indifference. Had any one met her, had her feelings been brought under her own notice, she would have said, beyond any dispute, that her heart was breaking to leave her home. But nobody met her to thrust any such question upon her, and the stronger feeling swallowed up the weaker, as it always does. All the way down the avenue not a creature, not even a servant, or a pensioner from the village—though on ordinary occasions there was always some one about—broke the long silent expanse of way. She was suffered to go without a remonstrance, without a question, from any living creature. Already it appeared the tie was broken between her and the dwelling so familiar to her—the place which had known her already began to know her no more.

Mr. Fielding was in his study when Clare went in upon him veiled and cloaked—a figure almost funereal. She gave him a great start and shock, which was scarcely softened when she raised her veil. "Something more has happened?" he said; "something worse—Edgar has gone away? My poor child, tell me what it is—"

"It is nothing," said Clare. "Edgar is quite safe, so far as I know. But I have left Arden, Mr. Fielding. I have left it for ever. Till my brother can make some arrangement for me, may I come here?"

"Here!" cried the good Rector, in momentary dismay.

"Yes—you have so often said you felt me like a child of your own; I will be your child, dear Mr. Fielding. Don't make me feel I have lost everything—everything, all in a day."

"My dear! my dear!" cried Mr. Fielding, taking her into his old arms, "don't cry so, Clare; oh, my poor child, don't cry. Of course, you shall come here—I shall be too happy, too pleased to have you. Of that you may be quite sure. Clare, my darling, it is not like you—oh, don't cry!"

"It is a relief," she said. "Think—I have left Arden, where I was born, and where I have lived all my life; and you are the only creature I can come to now."

"My poor child!" said the kind Rector. Yes, she who had been so proud of Arden, so devoted to the home of her race, it was not wonderful that she should feel the parting. He soothed her, and laid his kind hand on her head, and blessed her. "My dear, you have quantities of friends. There is not a man or woman in the county, far or near, but is your friend, Clare," he said; "and Edgar will always be a brother to you; and you are young enough to form other ties. You are very young—you have your whole life before you. Clare, my dearest child, you would have left Arden some time in the course of nature. It is hard, but it will soon be over—and you are welcome to me as the flowers in May."

She had known he would be kind to her—it had required no wizard to foresee that; and the old man's tenderness made less impression upon her than if it had been unlooked for. She composed herself and dried her tears, pride coming to her aid. Yes, everybody in the county would be her friend. She was still an Arden of Arden, though Edgar was an alien. No one could take from her that natural distinction. Her retirement was a proud one—not forced. She could not be mistaken in any way. If it had been but Arden she was leaving, she would have got over it very soon, and taken refuge in her pride. But there was more than Arden in question—more than Edgar—something which she could confide to no mortal ears.

Then she was conducted by the Rector through all the house, that she might choose her room. "There are none of them half pretty enough," he said. "If we had known we had a princess coming, we would have done our best to prepare her a bower. This one is very bright and sunny, and looks out on the garden; and this is the best room—the one Mrs. Solmes thinks most of. You must take your choice, and it shall be made pretty for you, Clare. I know, I once knew, how a lady should be lodged. Yes, my dear, you have but to choose."

"It does not matter," Clare said, almost coldly. She did not share the good man's pleasant flutter. It was gain to him, and only loss to her. She threw off her cloak and her hat in the nearest room, without any interest in the matter—an indifference which checked the Rector in the midst of his eager hospitalities. "Don't mind me," she said, "dear Mr. Fielding; go on with your work—don't take any notice of me. I shall go into the drawing-room, and sit there till you have finished. Never mind me—"

"I have to go out," the Rector said, with a distressed face. "There are some sick people who expect me. But Clare, you know, you are mistress here—entirely mistress. The servants will be too proud to do anything you want; and the house is yours—absolutely yours—"

"The house is mine!" Clare said to herself, when he was gone, with a despite which was partly the result of her mortification and grief. As if she cared for that—as if it was anything to her being mistress there, she who had been mistress of Arden! She sat down by herself in the old-fashioned, dingy drawing-room—the room which Mr. Fielding had furnished for his Milly nearly fifty years before, and where, though everything was familiar, nothing was interesting. She could not read, even though there had been anything to read. She had nothing to work at, even had she cared to work. She sat all alone, idle, unoccupied—a prey to her own thoughts. There is nothing in the world more painful than the sudden blank which falls upon an agitated spirit when thus turned out of confusion and excitement into the arbitrary quiet of a strange house—a new scene. Clare walked about the room from window to window, trying vainly to see something where there was nothing to see—the gardener rolling the grass, old Simon clamping past the Rectory gate in his clogs, upon some weird mission to the churchyard. Impatience took possession of her soul. When she had borne it as long as she could, she ran upstairs for her hat, and went across the road to the Doctor's house, which irritated her, twinkling with all its windows in the slanting sunshine. Miss Somers could not be much consolation, but at least she would maunder and talk, and give Clare's irritation vent in another way. The silence, the quiet, the peace, were more than she could bear.

CHAPTER XXV

Miss Somers was seated very erect on her sofa when Clare went in—more erect than she had been known to be for many a day—and was at the moment engaged in a discussion with Mercy, which her visitor could not but hear. "I don't believe it was Clare," Miss Somers was saying; "not that I mean you are telling a story—oh, no! I should as soon think—But Clare will break her heart. She was always so—And if ever a brother deserved it—Oh, the poor dear—I don't mean to say a word against my brother—he is very, very—But, then, as to being feeling, and all that—If you are never ill yourself, how are you to know? But, Edgar, oh!—the tender heartedest, feelingest—She never, never could—Oh, can it be—is it—Clare?"

"Yes," said Clare, with her haughtiest look. "And I think you were discussing us, Miss Somers—please don't. I do not like it, nor would my brother. Talk of us to ourselves as you like, but to others—don't, please."

"Mercy," Miss Somers said, hastily interrupting her, "I must have some more wool to finish these little— white Andalusian—Mrs. Horsfall at the post-office—you must run now. Only fancy if I had not enough to finish—and that dear little—Run—there's a good woman, now. O Clare, my dear!" she added, out of breath, as the maid sulkily withdrew; "it isn't that I would take upon me—Who am I that I should find fault? but other people's feelings, you know—though you were only a servant—What was I saying, my dear?—that Edgar was the best, the very best—And so he is. I never saw any one—not any one—so unselfish, and so—O Clare! nobody should know it so well as you."

"Nobody knows it so well as me," said Clare. She had come with a kind of half hope of sympathy, thinking at least that it would be a relief to let her old friend run on, and talk the whole matter over as pleased her. But now her heart closed up—her pride came uppermost. She could not bear the idea of being discussed, and made the subject of talk to all the village. "But I object to being gossiped about," she said.

"Dear," said Miss Somers, in her soft voice, "it is not gossip when—and I love you both. I feel as if I was both your mothers. Oh, Clare! when I used to have my little dreams sometimes—when I thought I had quite a number, you know, all growing up—there were always places for Edgar and you. Oh, Clare! I don't understand. The Doctor you know—he has so many things to think of—and then gentlemen are so strange—they expect you to know everything without—Oh, what is it that has happened? Something about Edgar—that he was changed at nurse—or something. I am not very clever, I know, but you understand everything, Clare. Oh, what is it?—Arthur Arden and Edgar—but it is not Arthur that is your—? It is Edgar that was—and something about that Scotch person and Mr. Fazakerly, and—oh, Clare, it makes the whole house swim, and my poor head—"

"I cannot speak of it," said Clare. "Oh, Miss Somers, don't you understand?—how can I speak of it. I would like to forget it all—to die, or to go away—"

"Oh, hush, my dear—oh, hush," said Miss Somers, with a scared face; "don't speak of such—and then, why should you? You will marry, you know, you will be quite, quite—and all this will pass away. Oh, as long as you are young, Clare—anything may happen. Brothers are very nice," said Miss Somers, shaking her head softly, "but to give yourself up, you know—and then they may marry; the Doctor never did—if he had brought home a wife, I think often—Though, to be sure, it might have been better, far better. But a brother is never like—he may be very nice; and I am sure Edgar—But, on the whole, Clare, my dear, a house of your own—"

Clare was silent. Her mind had wandered away to other matters. A house of her own! The Rector had said that his house was hers, and the thought had not consoled her. Was it possible that in the years to come, in some dull distant time she too might consent, like other girls, to marry somebody—that she might have a house of her own. In the sudden change that had overwhelmed her this dream had come like many others. Was it possible that she could no longer command her own destiny, that the power of decision had gone out of her hands. Bitterness filled her heart; a bitterness too deep to find any outlet in words. A little while ago she had been conscious that it was in her power to make Arthur Arden's life wealthy and happy. Now she had been tossed from her elevation in a moment, and the power transferred to him; and he showed no desire to use it. He was silent, condemning her to a blank of suspense, which chafed her beyond endurance. She said to herself it was intolerable, not to be borne. She would think of him no more; she would forget his very name. Would he never come? would he never come?

"I don't pretend to understand, my dear," said Miss Somers humbly; "and if it distresses you, of course—It is all because the Doctor is so hasty; and never, never will—And then he expects me to understand. But, anyhow, it will stop the marriage, I suppose. The marriage, you know—Gussy Thornleigh, of course. I am so sorry—I think she is such a nice girl. Not like you, Clare; not beautiful nor—; but such a nice—I was so pleased—Dear Edgar, he will have to wait, and perhaps she will see some one else, or he—Gentlemen are always the worst—But, of course, Clare, the marriage must be put off—"

"I don't know of any marriage," said Clare.

"Oh, my dear, I heard—I am not of much account, but still I have some friends; and in town, you know, Clare. They were always—; and everybody knew. Poor Edgar! he must be very, very—He is so affectionate and—He is one of the men that throw themselves upon your sympathy—and you must give him your—Clare, my dear! are they to share Arden between them?—or is Edgar to be Arthur, you know? Oh! I do wish you would tell me, Clare."

"Mr. Arthur Arden has everything," said Clare raising her head. "It all belongs to him. My brother has no right. Oh, Miss Somers, please don't make me talk!"

"That is just what I said," said Miss Somers; "and oh, my dear, don't be unhappy, as if it were death or—, when it is only money. I always say—And then he is so young; he may marry, or a hundred things. So, Arthur is Edgar now? but he is not your—I don't understand it, Clare. He is a great deal more like you, and all that; but he was born years before your poor, dear mamma—Oh, I remember quite well—before the old Squire was married—so it is impossible he could be your—I daresay I shall have it clear after a while. Edgar is found out to be Arthur, and Arthur Edgar, but only not your—And then, Clare, if you will but think—how could they be changed at nurse? for Arthur was a big fellow when your poor, dear mamma—You could not mistake a big boy of ten, with boots and all that, you know, for a little baby—Oh, I am so fond of little babies! I remember Edgar, he was such a—But Arthur was a troublesome, mischievous boy—I can't make out, I assure you, how it could be—"

Again Clare made no reply. She sat and pursued her own thoughts, leaving the invalid in her confused musings to make the matter out as best she could. It was better to be here, even with Miss Somers' babble in her ears, than alone in the awful solitude of the Rectory, with nothing to break the current of her thoughts. Miss Somers waited a few minutes for an answer, but, receiving none, returned to her own way of making matters out.

"If Edgar is in want—of—anything, Clare—I mean, you know—Money is always nice, my dear. Whatever one may want—Oh, I know very well it cannot buy—but still—And then there is that nice chair: he was so very kind—Clare," she said, sitting up erect, "if it is all true about their being changed, and all that, why, it was Arthur's money, not Edgar's; and I am sure if I had been shut up for a hundred years—I am not saying anything against your cousin—but it would never have occurred to him, you know—Clare, perhaps I ought to send it back—"

"I hope you don't think my cousin is a miser or a tyrant," said Clare, flushing suddenly to her very hair.

"Oh, no, no, dear—But then one never knows—Mr. Arthur Arden is not a miser, I know. I should not like to say—He is fond of what belongs to him, and—He is not at all like—My dear, I never knew any one like Edgar. Other gentlemen may be kind—I daresay Mr. Arthur Arden is kind—but these things would never come into his head—He is a man that is very fond of—Well, my dear, it is no harm. One ought to be rather fond of oneself—But Edgar—Clare—"

"Edgar is a fool!" cried Clare, with passion. "He is not an Arden; he would give away everything—his very life, if it would serve anybody. Such men cannot live in the world; it is wicked—it is wrong. When God sent us into the world, surely He meant we were to take care of ourselves."

"Did he?" said Miss Somers, softly. She was roused out of her usual broken talk. "Oh, Clare, I am not clever, to talk to you. But if that is what God meant, it was not what our Saviour did. He never took care of Himself—He took care—Oh, my dear, is not Edgar more like—Don't you understand?"

Once more Clare made no reply. A cloud enveloped her, mentally and physically—a sourd misery, inarticulate, not defining itself. Why should Edgar, why should any one, thus resign their own happiness? Happiness was the better part of life, and ought there not to be a canon against its renunciation as well as against self-murder? Self-murder was nothing to it. To give up your identity, your real existence, all the service you could do to God or man, was not that worse than simply taking your own life? So Clare asked herself. And this was what Edgar had done. He had not considered his duty at all in the matter. He had acted on a foolish, generous impulse, and thrown away more than his existence. Then, as she sat and pursued the current of her thoughts, she remembered that but for her, Edgar, in the carelessness of his security, would never have looked at those papers, would never have thought of them. It was she, and she only, who was to blame. Oh, what fancies had been in her mind—visions of wrong to Arthur, of the duty that was upon herself to right him! To right him who cared nothing for her, who was ready to let her sink into the abyss, whose heart did not impel him towards her, whose hand had never sought hers since he knew—It was her fault, not Edgar's, after all.

"I am not one to preach," said Miss Somers, faltering. "I know I never was clever; but oh, Clare, when one only thinks—What a fuss we make about ourselves, even me, a helpless creature! We make such a fuss—and then—As if it mattered, you know. But our Saviour never made any fuss—never minded what happened. Oh, Clare! If Edgar were like that—and he is so, so—Oh, I don't know how to express myself. Other people come always first with him, not himself. If he was my brother, oh, I would be so—Not that I am saying a word against the Doctor. The Doctor is very, very—But not like Edgar. Oh! if I had such a brother, I would be proud—"

"And so am I," said Clare, rising with a revulsion of feeling incomprehensible to herself. "He is my brother. Nothing can take him away from me. I will do as he does, and maintain him in everything. Thank you, dear Miss Somers. I will never give Edgar up as long as I live—"

"Give Edgar up!" cried Miss Somers in consternation—"I should think not, indeed, when everybody is so proud—It is so sweet of you, dear, to thank me—as if what I said could ever—It is all Edgar's doing—instead of laughing, you know, or that—And then it makes others think—she cannot be so silly after all—I know that is what they say. But, oh! Clare, I'm not clever—I know it—and not one to—, but I love you with all my heart!—"

"Thanks, dear Miss Somers," cried Clare, and in her weariness and trouble, and the revulsion of her thoughts, she sat down resolving to be very good and kind, and to devote herself to this poor woman, who certainly was not clever, nor clear-sighted, nor powerful in any way, but yet could see further than she herself could into some sacred mysteries. She remained there all the afternoon reading to her, trying to keep up something like conversation, glad to escape from her own thoughts. But Miss Somers was trying for a long stretch. It was hard not to be impatient—hard not to contradict. Clare grew very weary, as the afternoon stole on, but no one came to deliver her. No one seemed any longer to remember her existence. She, who could not move a few days since without brother, suitor, anxious servants to watch her every movement, was left now to wander where she would, and no one took any notice. To be sure, they were all absorbed in more important matters; but then she had been the very most important matter of all, both to Edgar and Arthur, only two days ago. Even, she became sensible, as the long afternoon crept over, that there had been a feeling in her heart that she must be pursued. They would never let her go like this, the two to whom she was everything in the world. They would come after her, plead with her, remonstrate, bid her believe that whosoever had Arden, it was hers most and first of all. But they had not done so. Night was coming on, and nobody had so much as inquired where she was. They had let her go. Perhaps in all the excitement they were glad to be quit of her. Could it be possible? Thus Clare mused, making herself it is impossible to say how miserable and forlorn. Ready to let her go; glad to be rid of her. Oh, how she had been deceived! And it was these two more than any other who had taught her to believe that she was in some sort the centre of the world.

Some one did come for Clare at last, making her heart leap with a painful hope; but it was only Mr. Fielding, coming anxiously to beg her to return to dinner. She put on her hat, and went down to him with the paleness of death in her face. Nobody cared where she went, or what she did. They were glad that she was gone. The place that had known her knew her no more.

CHAPTER XXVI

It is unnecessary to say that to one at least of the two people whose behaviour she thus discussed in her heart Clare was unjust. Edgar had neither forgotten her nor was he glad to be rid of her. It was late before he knew that she was gone. All the afternoon of that day he had spent with the lawyer, going over again all the matters which only two months ago had been put into the hands of the heir. Mr. Fazakerly had ceased to remonstrate. Now and then he would shake his head or shrug his shoulders, in silent protest against the mad proceeding altogether, but he had stopped saying anything. It was of no use making any further resistance. His client had committed himself at every step; he had thrown open his secret ostentatiously to all who were concerned—ostentatiously, Mr. Fazakerly said with professional vehemence, feeling aggrieved in every possible way. Had he been called upon to advise in the very beginning, it is most likely that the task would have tried him sorely; for his professional instinct to defend and conceal would have had all the force of a conscience to contend with. But now that he had not been consulted, he was free to protest. When he found it no longer of any use to make objections in words, he shook his head—he shrugged his shoulders—he made satirical observations whenever he could find an opportunity. "Were there many like you, Mr. Edgar," he said, "we lawyers might shut up shop altogether. It is like going back to the primitive ages of Christianity. Let not brother go to law against brother is, I know, the Scriptural rule; though it is generally the person who is attacked who says that—the one who has something to lose. But you have gone beyond Scripture; you have not even asked for arbitration or compensation; you have thrown away everything at once. We might shut up shop altogether if everybody was like you."

"If I were disagreeable," said Edgar, laughing, "I should say, and no great harm either, according to the judgment of the world."

"The world is a fool, Mr. Edgar," said Mr. Fazakerly.

"It is very possible," said Edgar, with a smile. This was at the termination of their business, when he felt himself at last free from all the oft-repeated consultations and discussions of the last two or three days. Everything was concluded. The old lawyer had his full instructions what he was to do, and what to say. Edgar gave up everything without reservation, and, at the instance of Mr. Fazakerly, consented to receive from his cousin a small sum of money, enough to carry him abroad and launch him on the world. He had been very reluctant to do this, but Mr. Fazakerly's strenuous representations had finally silenced him. "After all, I suppose the family owes it me, for having spoiled my education and career," Edgar said, with the half smile, half sigh which had become habitual to him; and then he was silent, musing what his career would have been had he been left in his natural soil. Perhaps it would have been he who should have ploughed the little farm, and kept the family together; perhaps he might have been a sailor, like Willie who was lost—or a doctor, or a minister, like others of his race. How strange it was to think of it! He too had a family, though not the family of Arden. His life had come down to him through honest hands, across the homely generations—not peasants nor gentlefolk, but something between—high-minded, righteous, severe people, like the woman who was the only representative of them he knew, his mother's mother. His heart beat with a strange sickening speed when he thought of her—a mixture of repulsion and attraction was in his thoughts. How was he to tell Clare of her? He felt that nothing which had yet occurred would so sever him from his sister as the appearance by his side of the two strangers who were his flesh and blood. And then he remembered that in the sickness of his heart he had made no inquiry after Jeanie during that whole long day.

When he went out into the hall he found boxes standing about, a sight which struck him with surprise, and Barbara standing, bonneted and cloaked, among them. She turned to him the moment he appeared, with an eager appeal. "Please, sir, Miss Clare said as I was to ask you what to do."

"I will speak to my sister," said Edgar in his ignorance; but Barbara put out her hand to detain him.

"Oh, sir, please! Miss Clare has gone down to the Rectory. She said to me as I was to ask you what to do with all these things. There are a deal of things, sir, to go to the Rectory. The rooms is small—and you was to tell me, please, what to do. Don't you think, sir, if I was to leave the heavy things here—"

"Nothing must stay here," said Edgar peremptorily. He was more angry at this suggestion than at anything which had yet been said. "Take them all away—to the Rectory—where Miss Arden pleases; everything must go." He was not aware while he spoke that Arthur Arden had made his appearance and stood looking at him, listening with a certain bitterness to all he said.

"That seems hard laws," said Arthur. "I am Miss Arden's nearest relative. It may be necessary that she should go at present; but why should you take upon you to pronounce that nothing shall stay?"

"I am her brother," said Edgar gravely. "Mr. Arden, you will find Mr. Fazakerly in the library with a communication to make to you. Be content with that, and let me go my own way."

"No, by Jove!" cried Arthur; "not if your way includes that of Clare. What business have you, who are nothing to her, to carry her away?"

The servants stood gaping round, taking in every word. Mr. Fazakerly, alarmed by the sound of the discussion, came to the door; and Edgar made the discovery then, to his great surprise, that it hurt him to have this revelation made to the servants. It was a poor shabby little remnant of pride, he thought.

What was the opinion of Wilkins or of Mrs. Fillpot to him? and yet he would rather these words had been spoken in his absence. But the point was one in which he was resolute not to yield. He gave his orders to Wilkins peremptorily, without so much as looking at the new heir. And then he himself went out, glad—it is impossible to say how glad—to escape from it all. He gave a sigh of relief when he emerged from the Arden woods. Even that avenue he had been so proud of was full of the heavy atmosphere of pain and conflict. The air was freer outside, and would be freer still when Arden itself and everything connected with it had become a thing of the past. When he reached the Rectory, Mr. Fielding was about sitting down to dinner, with Clare opposite to him—a mournful meal, which the old man did his best to enliven, although the girl, worn out in body and mind, was incapable of any response. Things were a little better, to Mr. Fielding at least, when Edgar joined them; but Clare could scarcely forgive him when she saw that he could eat, and that a forlorn inclination for rest and comfort was in her brother's mind in the midst of his troubles. He was hungry. He was glad of the quiet and friendly peace of the familiar place. Oh, he was no Arden! every look, every word bore out the evidence against him.

"It looks unfeeling," he said, "but I have neither eaten nor slept for two days, and I am so sick of it all. If Clare were but safe and comfortable, it would be the greatest relief to me to get away—"

"Clare is safe here. I don't know whether she can make herself comfortable," said the Rector looking at her wistfully. "Miss Arden, from Estcombe, would come to be with you, my dear child, I am sure, if that would be any advantage—or good Mrs. Selden—"

"I am as comfortable as I can be," said Clare, shortly. "What does it matter? There is nothing more necessary. I will live through it as best I can."

"My dear child," said good Mr. Fielding, after a long pause; "think of Edgar—it is worse for him than for you—"

"No," cried Clare passionately; "it is not worse for him. Look, he is able to eat—to take comfort—he does not feel it. Half the goodness of you good people is because you don't feel it. But I—It will kill me—"

And she thrust back her chair from the table, and burst into passionate tears, of which she was soon ashamed. "Edgar does not mind," she cried; "that is worst of all. He looks at me with his grieved face, and he does not understand me. He is not an Arden, as I am. It is not death to him, as it is to me."

Edgar had risen and was going to her, but he stopped short at the name of Arden. It felt to him like a stab—the first his sister had given him. "I hope I shall not learn to hate the name of Arden," he said between his closed lips; and then he added gently, "So long as I am not guilty, nothing can be death to me. One can bear it when one is but sinned against, not sinning; and you have been an angel to me, Clare—"

"No," she cried, "I am no angel; I am an Arden. I know you are good; but if you had been wicked and concealed it, and stood by your rights, I should have felt with you more!"

It was in the revulsion of her over-excited feelings that she spoke, but yet it was true. Perhaps it was more true than when she had stood by Edgar and called him her dearest brother; but it was the hardest blow he had yet had to bear. He sat down again, and covered his face with his hands. Poor fellow! the little comfort he had been so ready to enjoy, the quietness and friendliness, the food and rest, had lost all savour for him now. Mr. Fielding took his hand and pressed it, but that was only a mild consolation. After a moment he rose, rousing himself for the last step, which up to this moment he had shrunk from. "I have a further revelation to make to you," he said in an altered voice; "but I have not had the courage to do it. I have to tell you who I really belong to. I think I have the courage now."

"Edgar!" she cried, in alarm, raising her head, holding out her hand to him with a little cry of distress, "Will you not always belong to me?"

He shook his head; he was incapable of any further explanation. "I will go and bring my mother—" he said, with a half sob. The other two sat amazed, and looked after him as he went away.

"Do you know what he means?" asked Clare, in a voice so low as to be scarcely audible. Mr. Fielding shook his head.

"I don't know what he means, or if his mind is giving way, poor boy—poor boy, that thinks of everybody but himself; and you have been hard, very hard upon him, Clare."

Clare did not answer a word. She rose from the table, from the fruit and wine which she had spoiled to her gentle host, and went to the deep, old-fashioned window which looked down the village street. She drew the curtain aside, and sat down on the window-seat, and gazed into the darkness. What had he meant? Whom had he gone to seek? An awful sense that she had lost him for ever made Clare shiver and tremble; and yet what she had said in her petulance was true.

As for Edgar, he hastened along through the darkness with spasmodic energy. He had wondered how he could do it; he had turned from the task as too difficult, too painful; he had even thought of leaving Clare in ignorance of his real origin, and writing to tell her after he had himself disappeared for ever. But here was the moment to make the revelation. He could do it now; his heart was very sore and full of pain—but yet the very pain gave him an opportunity. He reflected that though it was very hard for him, it was better for Clare that the severance between them should be complete. He could not go on, he who was a stranger to her blood, holding the position of her brother. Years and distance, and the immense difference which there would most likely be between them would gradually make an end of any such visionary arrangement. He would have liked to keep up the pleasant fiction; the prospect of its ending crushed his heart and forced tears into his eyes; but it would be best for Clare. She was ready to give him up already, he reflected, with a pang. It would be better for her to make the severance complete.

He went into the cottage in the dark, without being recognised by any one. The door of the inner room was ajar, and Mrs. Murray was visible within by the light of a candle, seated at some distance from her child's bedside. The bed was shaded carefully, and it was evident that Jeanie was asleep. The old woman had no occupation whatever. A book was lying open before her on the little table, and her knitting lay in her lap; but she was doing nothing. Her face, which was so full of grave thoughtfulness, was fully revealed by the light. It was the face of a woman of whom no king need have been ashamed; every line in it was fine and pure. Her snow-white hair, her dark eyes, which were so full of life, the firm lines about her mouth, and the noble pose of the head, gave her a dignity which many a duchess might have envied. True, her dress was very simple—her place in the world humble enough; but Edgar felt a sense of shame steal over him as he looked at her. He had shrank from calling such a woman his mother, shrank from acknowledging her in the face of the day; and yet there was no Arden face on the walls of the house he had left which was more noble in feature, or half so exalted in expression. He said this to himself, and yet he shrank still. It was the last and highest act of renunciation. He went in so softly that she was not disturbed. He went up to her, and laid his hand on her shoulder. His heart stirred within him as he stood by her side. An unwilling tenderness, a mixture of pride and shame, thrilled through him. "Mother!" he said. It was the first time he had ever, in his recollection, called any one by that sacred name.

CHAPTER XXVII

Mrs. Murray started violently, and uttered a low cry. She turned to him with a look of sudden joy, that made her dark eyes expand and dilate. But when she saw Edgar's face, a change came over her own. She rose up, half withdrawing from his touch, and signed to him to leave the room, with a gesture towards the bed in which Jeanie lay asleep. She followed him to the door, where they had had so many broken interviews. The silence and the darkness, and the faint stars above, seemed a congenial accompaniment. She put her hand upon Edgar's arm as he stepped across the threshold. "What is your will; what is your will?" she said, in an agitated voice. It seemed to the young man that even this last refuge—the affection to which he had a right—had failed him too.

"My will?" he said. "It is for me to ask yours, you that are my mother. My life has changed like a dream, but yours is as it always was. Do you want nothing of me?"

"Na," said Mrs. Murray, with a voice of pain; "nothing, lad! nothing, lad! You've been good to me and mine without knowing. You've saved my Jeanie's life. But we're proud folk, though we were not brought up like you. Nothing will we take but your love; and I'm no complaining. I bow to nature and my own sin. I've long repented, long repented; but that is neither here nor there; it cannot be expected that you should have any love to give."

"I don't know what I have to give," said Edgar. "I am too weary and heart-broken to know. Can you come with me now to see my sister?—I mean Miss Arden. I must tell her. Don't be grieved or pained, for I cannot help it. It is hard."

"Ay, it is hard," said Mrs. Murray; "Oh, it's hard, hard! You were but a babe when I put you out of my arms; but I've yearned after you ever since. No, I'm asking no return; it's no natural. You are more like to hate us than to love us. I acknowledge that."

"I don't hate you," said Edgar. He was torn asunder with conflicting feelings. Was it hatred or was it love? He could not tell which.

"I'm ready to put my hands on my mouth, and my mouth in the dust," she went on. "I've sinned and sinned sore against the Lord and against you. You were the only one left of all your mother's bairns; and she was dead, and he was dead—all gone that belonged to you but me—and my hands full, full of weans and of troubles. I had the love for you, but neither time nor bread, and I was sore, sore tempted. They said to me there was none to be wronged, but only a house to be made glad. Oh, lad, I sinned; and most I have sinned against you."

He could not say no. His heart seemed shut up and closed against her. He could utter no forgiveness. It was true—quite true. She had sinned against him. Squire Arden was deeply to blame, but she, too, had sinned. There was not a word to say.

"When you said mother, I thought my heart would burst with joy. I thought the Lord had sent to you the spirit to forgive. But I canna expect it; I canna look for it. Oh, no! I wouldna be ungrateful, good Lord! He has his bonnie mother's heart to serve his neighbour, and his father's that died for the poor, like Christ. I maunna complain. He has a heart like his kin though no for me!"

"Tell me what you mean," cried Edgar, with a thrill of emotion tingling to his very finger-points; "or rather come with me, come with me. Clare must know all now—"

"And Jeanie is sleeping," she said. "I'll cry upon that good woman to watch her, and I'll do your bidding. God bless you, lad, for Jeanie's life!"

He stood and waited for her outside with a new life, it seemed, thrilling through him. His father? He had once had a father, then—a man who had done his duty in the world—not a tyrant, who hated him. The idea of his mother did not so much move him; for somehow the dead woman whose reputation he had vindicated, the sweet young face in Clare's picture, was his mother to Edgar in spite of all. He could not turn her out of his imagination. But his father! A new spring of curiosity, which was salvation to him, sprang up in his heart. Presently Mrs. Murray came out again, in her old-fashioned shawl and bonnet. Her dress veiled the dignity of her head. It gave him a sort of shudder to think of Clare looking at this woman, whom she had wanted to be kind to—to treat as a dependent—and knowing her to be his grandmother. She looked a little like Mrs. Fillpot, in her old-fashioned bonnet and shawl—he scorned himself for the thought, and yet it came back to him—very much like Mrs. Fillpot until you saw her face; and Edgar was made of common flesh and blood, and it went to his heart. He walked up the village street by her side with the strangest feelings. If she wanted him, it would be his duty, perhaps, to go with her—to provide for her old age—to do her the service of a son. She had a hold on him which nobody else in the world had. And yet—To be very kind, tender-hearted, and generous to your conventional inferiors is so easy; but to take a family among them into your very heart, and acknowledge them as your own!—Edgar shivered with a pang that ran through every nerve; and yet it had to be done!

He was more reconciled to it by the time he reached the Rectory. Mrs. Murray did not say another word to conciliate or attract his regard, but she began a long soft-voiced monologue—the story of his family. She told him of his father, who had been a doctor, and had died of typhus fever, caught among the poor, to whom he had dedicated his life; of his mother, who had broken her heart; of all her own children, his relations, who were scattered over the world. "We're no rich nor grand, but we are folk that none need think shame of," she said, "no one. We've done our duty by land and by sea, and served God, and wronged no man—all but me; and the wrong I did is made right, oh my bonnie lad, thanks to you."

Thus a certain comfort, a certain bitterness distilled into his heart with every word. He made her take his arm as he entered the Rectory. He had seen the curtain raised from the window, and some one looking out, and felt that it was Clare watching, with perhaps a suspense as great as his own. He led his grandmother into the dining-room, which he had left so suddenly, leaning on his arm. Clare rose from her seat at the window as they entered, and so did Mr. Fielding, who, really unhappy and distressed, had been dozing in his chair. The Rector stumbled up half asleep, and recollected the twilight visit he had received only a few days before, and said "God bless me!" understanding it all in a moment. But

Clare did not understand. She walked forward to meet them, her face blazing with painful colour. A totally different fancy crossed her mind. She made a sudden conclusion, not like the reasonable and high-minded being she desired to be, but like the inexperienced and foolish girl she was. An almost fury blazed up in her eyes. Now that he had fallen, Edgar was making haste to unite himself to that girl who had been the bane of her life. He had brought the mother here to tell her so. It was Jeanie, Jeanie, once more—the baby creature with her pretty face—who was continually crossing her path.

"What does this mean?" she cried haughtily. "Is this a time for folly, for forming any miserable connexion—why do you bring this woman here?"

"You must speak of her in other tones, if you speak of her to me," said Edgar. "I have shrunk from telling you, I can't tell why. It seemed severing the last link between us. But I must not hesitate any longer. Miss Arden, this is Mrs. Murray, who wrote the letters you found in your father's room, who shared with him the guilt of the transaction which has brought us all so much pain; but she is my mother's mother, my nearest relative in the world, and any one who cares for me will respect her. This is the witness I told you of—her testimony makes everything clear."

Clare stood thunderstruck, and listened to this revelation; then she sank upon the nearest seat, turning still her pale countenance aghast upon the old woman, who regarded her with a certain pathetic dignity. Horror, dismay, shame of herself, sudden lighting up of a hundred mysterious incidents—light glimmering through the darkness, yet confounding and confusing everything, overwhelmed her. His mother's mother. Good Heavens! is she mine too? Clare asked herself in her dismay, and then paused and tried to disentangle herself from that maze of old habit and new bewildering knowledge. She could not speak nor move, but sat and gazed upon the Scotchwoman who had been somehow painfully mixed up in all the story of the past two months and all its difficulties. Was this an explanation of all? or would Arthur Arden come in next, and present this woman to her with another explanation? Clare's heart seemed to stand still—she could not breathe, but kept her eyes fixed with a painful mechanical stare upon Mrs. Murray's face.

"Yes, Miss Arden," said the old woman, "he says true. I was tempted and I sinned. He was an orphan bairn, and it was said to me that no person would be wronged by it—though it may be a comfort to you to hear that your mother opposed it with all her might. She knew better than me. She was a young thing, no half my age; but she knew better than me. For all her sweetness and her kindness, she set her face against the wrong. It was him that sinned, and me—"

And then there was a long pause. Clare seemed paralysed—she neither moved nor spoke; and Edgar stood apart, struggling with his own heart, trying not to long for the sympathy of the sister who had been his all his life—trying to enter into the atmosphere of love towards the other through whom his very life had come to him. Mr. Fielding, who was not at the same pitch of excitement, bethought himself of those ordinary courtesies of life which seem so out of place to the chief actors in such a scene. He offered Mrs. Murray a chair; he begged her to take some wine; he was hospitable, and friendly, and courteous—till Clare and Edgar, equally moved, interposed in the same breath—"Oh, don't, please, don't say anything," Clare cried, "I cannot bear it." And Edgar, to whom she had not spoken a word, whom she had not even looked at, came forward again and gave the stranger his arm.

"Thanks," he said, with an attempt at cheerfulness; "but now that all is said that need be said, I must take my mother away."

"My dear Edgar, stop a little," cried Mr. Fielding, in much agitation. "This must not be permitted. If this—lady is really your—your grandmother, my dear boy. Pardon me, but it is so hard to realise it—to imagine; but she cannot be left in that poor little cottage—it is impossible. I am amazed that I could have overlooked—that I did not see. The Rectory is small, and Clare perhaps might not think—or I should beg you to come here—but some other place, some better place."

Mrs. Murray's face beamed with a sudden smile. Edgar looked on with terror, fearing he could not tell what. Was she about to seize this social elevation with vulgar eagerness? Was she about to make it impossible for him even to respect her? "Sir," she said, holding out her hand to the Rector, "I thank you for my lad's sake. Every time I see or hear how he's respected, how he's thought of, my heart leaps like the hart, and my tongue is ready to sing. It's like forgiveness from the Lord for the harm I've done—but we're lodged as well as we wish for the moment, and I desire nothing of any man. We're no rich, and we're no grand, but we're proud folk."

"I beg your pardon, madam," said Mr. Fielding, bowing over her hand as if she had been a duchess. And Edgar drew the other through his arm. "Folk that none need think shame of," he said in his heart, and for the first time since this misery began that heart rose with a sensation which was not pain.

"And good night, Miss Arden," she said, "and God bless you for being the light of his eyes and the comfort of his life. Well I know that he owes all its pleasantness to you. An old woman's blessing will do you no harm, and it's likely that I will never in this life see you more."

Thus Clare was left alone in the silence. Mr. Fielding hastened to the door to attend his visitor out, with as much respect as if she had been a queen. Clare remained alone, her whole frame and heart tingling with emotion. She was ashamed, humbled, and mortified, and cast down. Her brother!—and this was his true origin—these his relations. She, too, had remarked that Mrs. Murray was like Mrs. Fillpot at the first glance—a peasant woman—a farmer's wife at the best. It was intolerable to Clare. And yet all the while he was Edgar—her brother, whom she had loved—her companion, whom she had kissed and hung upon—who had been her support, her protector, her nearest and closest friend. She rose and fled when she heard the sound of the closing door, and Mr. Fielding's return. She could not bear to see him, or to have her own dismay and horror brought under remark. He would say they were unchristian, wicked; and what if they were? Could she help it? God had made her an Arden—not one of those common people without susceptibilities, without strong feeling. Had Edgar been an Arden he never could have done it. He did it, because he was of common flesh and blood; he had not felt it. All was explained now.

As for Edgar, he walked down again to Sally Timms's cottage, with his old mother on his arm. "Lean on me," he said to her as they went along in the dark. He could not be fond of her all at once, stranger as she was; but he was—could it be possible?—proud of her, and it was a pleasure to him to feel that he supported her, and did a son's natural duty so far. And then it went to his heart when he saw all at once in the light of a cottage window which gleamed on her as they passed, that she was weeping, silently putting up her hand to wipe tears from her face. "It's no for trouble, it's for gladness," she said, when he looked up at her anxiously. "I canna think but my repentance is accepted, and the Lord has covered over my sin."

CHAPTER XXVIII

"These are our terms, Mr. Arden," said Mr. Fazakerly. "It is, of course, entirely in your own hands to accept or reject them: a provision such as has been usually made for the daughters of Arden, for Miss Clare; and a certain sum—say a few hundreds—he would not accept anything more—for—your predecessor—These are our conditions. If you accept them, he offers (much against my will—all this surrender is against my will) immediate possession, without any further trouble. My own opinion is quite against this self-renunciation, but my client is obstinate—"

"Your client!" said Arthur Arden, with a tone of contempt. "Up to this time your clients have always been the lawful owners of Arden."

"Understand, sir," said the old lawyer, with a flush of irritation on his face, "that I do not for a moment admit that Mr. Edgar is not the lawful owner of Arden. That rests on your assertion merely; and it is an assertion which you might find it amazingly difficult to prove. He offers you terms upon his own responsibility, against my advice and wish, out of an exaggerated sense of honour, such as perhaps you don't enter into. My wish would have been to let you bring your suit, and fight it out."

Arthur Arden was in great doubt. He paced the long library up and down, taking council with himself. To make conditions at all—to treat with this beggar and impostor, as he called him in his heart—was very galling to his pride. Of course he would have been kind to the fellow after he had taken possession of his own. He would have made some provision for him, procured him an appointment, given him an allowance, out of pure generosity; but it was humiliating to pause and treat, or to acknowledge any power on the part of the usurper to exact conditions. It was astonishing how fast and far his thoughts had travelled in the last twenty-four hours. He had scarcely allowed the bewildering hope to take hold of his mind then—he could not endure to be kept for another hour out of his possessions now. He walked up and down heavily, pondering the whole matter. It appeared to him that he had nothing to do but to proclaim himself the reigning monarch in place of the usurper found out, and to expel him and his belongings, and begin his own reign. But the old lawyer stood before him, vigilant and unyielding, keeping an eye upon him—cowing him by that glance. He came forward to the table again with reluctant politeness. "I don't understand it," he said. "It stands to reason that from the moment it is found out, everything becomes mine as the last Squire Arden's next of kin."

"You have to prove first that you are nearer of kin than his son."

"His son! Do you venture to keep up that fiction? How can I consent for a moment to treat with any one who affirms a lie?"

"Your conscience has become singularly tender, Mr. Arden," said the lawyer, with a smile. "I don't think you were always so particular; and remember you have to prove that it is a lie. You have to prove your case at every step against all laws of probability and received belief. I do not say that you will fail eventually, but it is a case that might occupy half your remaining life, and consume half the value of the estate. And I promise you you should not gain it easily if the defence were in my hands."

"When I did win you should find that no Arden papers found their way again to your hands," said Arthur, with irritation.

Mr. Fazakerly made him a sarcastic bow. "I can live without Arden," he said; "but the question is, can you?"

Then there was another pause. "I suppose I may at least consult my lawyer about it," said Arthur, sullenly; and once more Mr. Fazakerly made him a bow.

"By all means; but should my client leave the country before you have decided, it will be necessary to shut up the house and postpone its transference. A few months more or less will not matter much. I will put down our conditions, that you may submit them to your lawyer. A provision such as other daughters of Arden have had, for Miss Clare—"

"I will not have Miss Arden's name mentioned," said Arthur, angrily; "her interests are quite safe in my hands."

"That may or may not be," said Mr. Fazakerly; "but my client insists absolutely on this point, and unless it is conceded, all negotiations are at an end. Fit provision for Miss Clare; and a sum of money—say a thousand pounds—"

"You said a few hundreds," interposed the other with irritation. Mr. Fazakerly threw down his pen, and looked up with amazement into Arthur's face.

"Good Lord," he said, "is it the soul of a shopkeeper that you have got within you? Do you understand what Edgar Arden is giving up? And he was not called upon to give it up. He was not called upon to say a word about it, to furnish you with any information. What Edgar Arden would have done had he been guided by me—"

"He is not Edgar Arden," said Arthur sharply.

"By the Lord," cried Mr. Fazakerly, wrought up to a pitch of excitement which would have vent, "he is by a hundred times a better man than—" you, he was going to say, but resisted the temptation—"than most men that one meets," he added hastily. And then, subduing himself, sat down and wrote the conditions fully out. He handed them to the other without adding a word, and immediately unlocked a box full of papers which stood on the table by him, and began to work at them, as if he were unconscious of the presence of any stranger. Arthur stood by him for some minutes with the paper in his hand, and then went out with a mortification which he had to conceal as best he could. It was the morning after Clare had left the house, and Edgar, though he had not appeared that day was still master of the house, acknowledged by everybody in it as its legitimate head. It is impossible to say how much this chafed the true heir. He was so angry that he gave Wilkins to understand the real state of affairs, to the private consternation but well-enacted unbelief of that family retainer. Wilkins did not like Arthur Arden—none of the servants liked him. Edgar's kindly sway had given them a glimpse of something better; and the butler and the housekeeper had long entertained matrimonial intentions, and were too well off and too much used to comfort to put up with a less satisfactory regime. "I'll ask master, sir," was all Arthur Arden could elicit from Wilkins. Master!—the word made him almost swear. Arthur went out, with the conditions of surrender in his pocket, and pondered over them like a general who is victorious yet baffled, and whose army has won the external but not the moral victory. Of course there could be no real question as to these conditions; under any circumstances public opinion, or even his own reluctant sense of what was fit and necessary, would have bound him to do as much or more. But he was irritated now, and if he had been able, he would have liked to punish his rival for his usurpation; while, on the contrary, that rival claimed to march out with all the honours of war, his reputation unimpeached, his fame spread. It galled the new Lord of Arden more than it is possible to describe. He gnawed his moustache and his nails as he pondered, and then his thoughts took a sudden turn. The subject which had been uppermost in his mind before this new matter drove everything else out of the question. Come back—Clare! For the moment she had taken Edgar's part; but this at least it was in his power to alter. As much as he had ever loved any one, he loved Clare; but he was come to his kingdom, and the intoxication of the triumph bewildered his faculties. He might marry any one—not any longer a mere heiress, great or small, but anybody—a duke's daughter, a lady of the highest pretensions. Arden of Arden was the equal of the best nobleman in Christendom. So he reasoned from the heights of his new elevation. For a moment ambition struggled in him with love: it was in his power now to give Clare back all, and more than all, that she had lost; and in thus gratifying himself he could inflict the last wound upon his adversary. In reality, notwithstanding a thousand shortcomings, he loved her. He thought over all their intercourse, everything that had passed between them—her last words, to which as yet he had made no response. And the heart began to beat more warmly, more quickly in his breast. The end of his musings was that he took his way down the avenue to the Rectory, with his paper of conditions in his pocket. Again it must be said for Arthur Arden that in any case he would have taken this step; but still the alloy of his nature mingled with all he did. Even in seeking his love, he went with a vengeful feeling of satisfaction that if he won Clare from him, that fellow would not have so much to brag of after all.

Clare was seated in the deep window of the Rectory drawing-room with a book in her hand; but she was not reading the book. She was gazing listlessly out, seeing nothing, going over a hundred recollections. Her life had become far more interesting than any book—too interesting—full of pain and tragic interest. She sat with her eyes fixed on the broad expanse of summer sunshine, the distant gleam of the village street, the Doctor's house opposite, with its twinkling windows. Everything was still as peace itself. The old gardener was rolling the grass with gentle monotony, as if he might go on doing it for ever; Dr. Somers' phæton stood at the door awaiting him; old Simon clamped past on his clogs—all so peaceful as if nothing out of the usual routine could ever happen; and yet in that very room Edgar had stood by the side of the old Scotch woman and called her mother! A deep suppressed excitement and resentment were in Clare's heart. It was not his fault, but notwithstanding she could not forgive him for it. When the door opened she did not turn her head. Most likely it was Edgar, and she did not wish to see him; or Mr. Fielding, with his grieved, disapproving looks. Clare was in such a state of mind that even a look of reproof drove her wild. She could not bear it. Therefore she kept her back turned persistently, and gave no heed to the opening of the door.

"Clare!"

She looked up with a violent start, rising from her seat, and perceived him standing over her—he whom she had tried to put out of her calculations, and think of no more. She had been planning a proud miserable life retired out of sight of all men, specially hidden from him. She had resolved he should not even know where she was to insult her with his pity—neither he nor Edgar should know; for Clare was quite unaware that the discovery which lost her a brother lost her a fortune too. But now at the moment when she was most miserable, most forlorn, forming the most dreary plans, here he was! The sight of him took away her breath, and almost her senses, for the moment. She said, "Is it you?" faintly, gazing at him with dilated eyes and parched lips, as if he had been a ghost. The surprise was so great that it threw down all her defences, and brought her back to simple reality. She was not glad to see him—these were not the words; but his sudden coming was like life to the dead.

And he too was touched by the sight of her utter dejection and solitude. He dropped down on one knee beside her as she reseated herself, and took her hand. "My Clare!" he said, "my Clare! why did you fly from me? Is not my house your house, and my life yours? Is there any one so near to you as me? Even now I have the only claim upon you; and when you are my wife—"

"No such word has ever been spoken between us," said Clare, making an effort to resume her old dignity. "Mr. Arden, rise—you forget—"

"I don't forget anything," said Arthur. "There was one between us that took it upon him to keep me away, that prevented me from seeing you, prejudiced you against me, and has all but beguiled you away from me. But, Clare, you see through it now. Are words necessary between you and me? When I was a beggar I might hesitate to ask you to share my poverty, but now—Don't you know that I would rather have you without Arden than Arden without you—"

Let him take everything else, as long as he leaves me you—these had been the words Arthur Arden had spoken two days ago. They rang in Clare's ears as clearly as if he had just pronounced them, and they had an echo in his own memory. But neither of them referred to that vain offer now—neither of them said a syllable of Edgar. "If he had not so shocked me, so repelled me, brought in that woman," Clare said to herself in faint self-apology—but not a word did she say aloud. She laid down her head on Arthur Arden's shoulder, and wept away the accumulated excitement and irritation and misery of the past night. She did not reproach him for his delay or ask a single question. She had wanted him, oh, so sorely! and he had come at last.

"It is too great happiness," said Arthur, when they had sat there all the bright morning through and made their plans, "that you and I should spend all our lives together in Arden, Clare. To have you anywhere would have seemed too much joy a month ago; but you and Arden! which I have been kept out of, banished from, treated as a stranger in—"

"Do not think of that now, do not think of that now! Oh, Arthur, if you love me, be kind to him."

"Kind to him! when he had all but succeeded in severing you from me, in carrying you away, with Heaven knows what intention. But, my Clare," said the new Squire Arden, with that paper in his pocket, of which he did not say a word to her, "for your sake!"

And Clare believed him, every word—she who was not credulous, nor full of faith, and who prided herself that she knew the world—her own world, in which people were moved by comprehensible motives, not visionary impulses. Clare believed her lover. He would be kind, he would not be too hard or unmerciful. He would forgive the usurper, the Edgar who was Mrs. Murray's son. She stifled every other feeling in that moment of love and intoxication—if, indeed, at such a time there was room for any other feeling towards the Edgar who had been the brother of her youth.

And thus the last link was broken which bound Edgar to his old life. The moment when his sister and his successor clasped hands was the conclusion, as it were, of his career. Had Clare clung to him, and sought to detain him, he might have held on somehow, sadly and reluctantly, by some shadow of the former existence, trying to do impossibilities, and to reconcile the adverse elements. Her sudden decision was a cruel blow to him: it was his final extinction as Edgar Arden; but at the same time, no doubt, it was a relief. It settled her in the position which in all the world was the one most suitable for her, which she herself preferred; and at once and for ever it severed the bond which was now no better than a fictitious and sentimental tie. It was best so, he said to himself, even when he felt it most sorely. They could not have continued together: they were no longer brother and sister. It was best for both that the severance should be complete.

And thus it was that Edgar Arden's life came to an end. Had he died it could not have finished more completely. His life, his career, his very name were gone. He existed still, and might for aught he knew continue to exist for many years, and even make for himself another history, new hopes, new loves, a renewed career. But here the man who has been the hero of this story, the only Edgar known to his friends and to himself—concluded. The change was like Death—a change of condition, place, being, everything that makes a man. And here the story of Squire Arden must perforce come to an end.

CHAPTER XXIX

POSTSCRIPT

Time flies in the midst of great events; and yet it is long to look back upon, doubling and redoubling the moments which have been great with feeling—filling the spectator with wonder that in so short a time a human creature could live so long or undergo so much. But after a great crisis of life, time becomes blank, the days are endless as they pass, and count for nothing when they have gone. Flatly they fall upon the memory that keeps no record of them—so much blank routine, so many months; in ordinary parlance, the fallow season, in which brain and heart have to recover, as the earth has, under her veil of rain and snow—chill days and weeks without a record; or bright days and weeks which are almost as blank—for even happiness keeps no daybook—until the time of exhaustion is over, and life moves again, most often under the touch of pain.

The episode of personal history, which we have just concluded, was fully known to the world only after it was over. Then the county, and almost the country—for the report of such a "romance of real life" naturally afforded food for all the newspaper readers in the kingdom—was electrified by the Arden case. It was rumoured at first that a great lawsuit was to be brought, with an exciting trial and all the delightful exposure of family secrets and human meanness which generally attends a law plea between near relations. Then, Mr. Fazakerly published a solemn statement of the facts. Then somebody in Arthur Arden's interest attempted to prove that Edgar had been in the secret all along; then this imputation was indignantly contradicted by the solicitor of Arthur Arden, Esq. of Arden, but left a sting notwithstanding, and made many people shake their heads, and doubt the romantic tale of generosity, which they held to be contrary to human nature. Then the clever newspapers—those which are great in leading articles—took the matter up, and gave each a little treatise on the subject; and then the story was suddenly suffered to drop, and was heard of no more. At least it was not heard of for a month, when it was all revived by the marriage of Clare Arden to her cousin—a marriage which rent the county asunder, making two parties for and against. "How she could ever do it!" and "it was the very best thing she could do." These two events had a great effect upon Arden parish and village. They aged Mr. Fielding, so that he was scarcely ever able for duty again, and had to devolve almost the whole service on Mr. Denbigh, feebly uttering the absolution only, or a benediction from the altar. They brought upon Miss Somers that bad illness which brought her almost to death's door; and it is said the poor lady cried so much that she never could see very well after, and never was seen abroad more. And they utterly crushed the Pimpernels. Mrs. Pimpernel's face of horror, when she found that she had actually turned out from her house the rightful owner of Arden, was a thing talked of all over the county; and the family never recovered the shock. They left the Red House that summer, and removed to the other side of the county, at least twenty miles away, and conveniently close to a railway station. "After that accident, when my Alice was so nearly killed, I could not bear it," Mrs. Pimpernel said, though people maliciously misunderstood which accident it was.

And Jeanie, the real victim of the accident, after a long illness, recovered sufficiently to be taken home. Dr. Somers believed, with professional pride and a little human sympathy, that he had effected a cure on Jeanie mentally as well as physically; but whether her gentle mind was quite restored was, of course, a matter which time alone could prove. Edgar, who had been absent since the day after he received intelligence of Clare's engagement, returned to take his relations home. But it was not till a month after Clare's marriage that he reappeared finally in Arden to say good-bye to all his friends. The bride and bridegroom had not yet returned, which was a relief to him; and his company was a great solace and consolation to the feeble Rector, with whom he lived. "Ah, Edgar, if you would but stay with me and be my son," the old man would say wistfully, as he leaned upon his vigorous arm. "I have no one now whom I can lean upon, who will close my eyes and see me laid in my grave. Edgar, if it were God's will, before you go away I should be glad to be there."

"Don't say so," said Edgar. "Everybody loves you; and my—I mean Mrs. Arden—you must not withdraw your love from her."

Mr. Fielding shook his head. "She will not want my love," he said. "Never could I give up Clare, however I might disapprove of her; but she will not want me. Nobody wants me; and the last fag-end of work is dreary, just before the holiday comes; but I am grumbling, Edgar. Only I'll be sadly dull when you go, that's all."

"And I cannot stay, you know," said Edgar, with a sigh.

"No," said the old man, echoing it. That was the only thing that was impossible. He could not stay. The Thornleighs were at Thorne, and Lady Augusta had written him an anxious, affectionate note, bidding God bless him, but begging him, by all he held dear, not to show himself to Gussy, who was ill and nervous, and could not bear any shock. Poor Edgar put the letter in his pocket and tried to smile. "She might have trusted me," he said. He was not to go near Thorne; he could not approach Arden; but he went to the poor folk in the village, and received many tearful adieus. Old Miss Somers threw her arms round him and cried. "Oh, Edgar, my dear, my dear!—" she said, "how shall I ever—; and I who thought you would be always—, and meant to leave you what little I have. It is all left to you, Edgar, all the same. Oh, if you would not go! I daresay now they will never return. Though she is your sister, my dear, I must say—If I were Clare I would never more come back to the Hall—"

"But I trust she will, and be very happy there, and that you will be all to her you have ever been," said Edgar, kissing the wrinkled old hand.

"Oh, my dear boy! Oh, Edgar, God will reward—Kiss me, my dear; though you are a gentleman, I am so old, and ill; it can't matter, you know. Kiss me, Edgar! and God bless—; and if ever there was one in this world that should have a reward—"

A reward! Edgar smiled mournfully as he went away. The reward he had was abandonment, banishment, solitude, the love and tears of a few old people for whom he had done nothing and could do nothing, who loved him because they had been good to him all his life. As he drove over to the station in Mr. Fielding's old gig, with Jack, silent and respectful, by his side, he passed all the rich woods of Arden, clouds of foliage almost as rich in colour as were the sunset clouds above them—the woods which he had once looked at with so much pride and called his own. He passed the little lodge on the common where he had seen old John lying dead, and had wondered (he recollected as if it were yesterday) if that was the end of all life's struggles and trials? It was not the end; what a poor joke life would be if it was!—weary days, not few, as the patriarch complained, but oh, so weary, so endless, so full of pain to come, as they seemed to the young man—struggles through which the soul came only half alive. But Edgar felt alive all over as he took farewell of all the familiar places, and remembered the human creatures, much more dear, of whom he could not take farewell. Poor, sweet little Gussy, "ill and nervous"—was it for him? and Clare, who had been silent to him since her marriage, taking no notice of his existence. He brushed away a tear from his eyes as he drove on. He was going he knew not where—to seek his fortune—But that was no grievance; rather his heart rose to the necessity with a vigorous impulse, which would have been gay, had it been less sore. God bless them!—the one who thought of him still, and the one who had cast him off. They were alike, at least, in this—that he loved them, and would never see them more.

Jack had been sent away with a good-bye and a sovereign, and a sob in his throat which almost choked him; and Edgar was alone. The train was a little late, and he stood on the platform of the small country station waiting for it, longing to be gone. He saw without noticing a little brougham drawn up close to the roadside, so as to enable its occupants to see the train as it passed. While he waited, he was attracted by the flutter of a white handkerchief from the window. He went as close as he could reach, and looked over the paling, wondering, yet not thinking that this signal could be for him. There was no expectation in his mind, only a certain sad surprise. Then suddenly Lady Augusta's face appeared at the window, full of anxiety and distress; and, in the corner behind her, a little pale face—a worn little figure. "Good-bye, Edgar!—dear Edgar, good-bye!" cried a faltering voice. "We could not let you go without one word. God bless you!" said Lady Augusta, pulling the check in her hand. The coachman turned his horses before Edgar could approach a step nearer; and at the same moment the train came up like a roll of thunder behind—

Edgar went back with his heart and his eyes so full that he saw nothing. He gathered his small possessions together mechanically. His whole being was moved by the sweetness and the bitterness of this last parting and blessing. There was an unusual stir and commotion on the platform, but he took no notice. What was it to him who came or went? She might have been his bride—that tender creature with her soft voice, which came to him like a voice from heaven. So faithful, so tender, so sweet! It was all he could do to keep the tears which blinded him from falling. He threw his bag into the carriage; he had his foot on the step—

What was that cry? Once more, "Edgar! Edgar!" The party arriving had stopped and broken up. He turned round; through the mist in his eyes he saw who it was. They were standing at a distance in their bridal finery: he with a cloud on his face, with his hand upon her arm holding her back—yet not arbitrarily nor unkindly. And even in Arthur Arden's face there was a certain emotion. They stood looking at each other as if across an ocean or a continent—more than that—a whole world. Then all at once she rushed to him, and threw her arms round his neck. "O Edgar, speak to me, speak to me!—forgive me! I am your sister still—your only sister; don't go away without a word to me!"

"God bless you, my dearest sister, my only Clare!" he cried. The tears rained down on his cheeks. He gave her one convulsive kiss, and put her into her husband's arms.

So all was over! The train rushed on, tearing wildly across the familiar country. And Edgar fell back in the solitude, the silence, the distance, parted from everything that was his; but not without a little of that reward Miss Somers had prayed for—enough of it to keep his heart alive.

Margaret Oliphant – A Short Biography

Margaret Oliphant Wilson was born on April 4th, 1828 to Francis W. Wilson, a clerk, and Margaret Oliphant, at Wallyford, near Musselburgh, East Lothian.

She spent her childhood at Lasswade, near Dalkeith, Glasgow before moving to Liverpool.

Her youth was spent in establishing a writing style so much so that, in 1849, she had her first novel published: Passages in the Life of Mrs. Margaret Maitland based on the Scottish Free Church movement. It met with some success and was a good start to her career.

Two years later, in 1851, her third book Caleb Field was published. It was also now that she met the publisher William Blackwood in Edinburgh and was asked to contribute to his well-received Blackwood's Magazine. It was to be a lifetimes endeavor. Over the course of the relationship she would have well over 100 articles published.

In May 1852, Margaret married her cousin, Frank Wilson Oliphant, at Birkenhead, and they settled at Harrington Square, Camden, London. He was an artist working primarily in stained glass. With the marriage she became Margaret Oliphant Wilson Oliphant.

Their marriage produced six children but three tragically died in infancy.

When her husband developed signs of the dreaded consumption (tuberculosis) they moved, on the advice of doctors, to warmer climes. In January 1859 it was to Florence, and then to Rome where, sadly, he died.

Margaret was naturally devastated but was also now left without support and only her income from her writing. She returned to England and took up the task of supporting her three remaining children by her literary activity.

By now she was being published both as an established novelist and regularly in Blackwood's Magazine, amongst others. Her incredible and prolific work rate increased both her commercial reputation and the size of her reading audience.

Against this her domestic life continued to be tragic, full of sorrow and disappointment.

In January 1864 her only remaining daughter Maggie died and was buried in her father's grave in Rome. Her brother, who had emigrated to Canada, was shortly afterwards involved in financial ruin. Margaret generously offered a home to him and his children, adding another demand to her already heavy responsibilities.

In 1866 she settled at Windsor to be closer to her sons, who were being educated at near-by Eton School. That year, her second cousin, Annie Louisa Walker, came to live with her as a companion-housekeeper. Windsor was now to be her home for the rest of her life.

Her literary career for three decades was one of constant delivery and success. Whether she wrote historical works or across several genres in fiction: domestic realism, historical, romance or supernatural she was successful.

For more than thirty years she pursued a varied literary career but family life continued to bring problems.

The literary ambitions she wished for her sons were unfulfilled. Cyril Francis, the eldest, died in 1890, leaving a Life of Alfred de Musset, incorporated in his mother's Foreign Classics for English Readers. The younger, Francis, who she nicknamed 'Cecco', collaborated with her in the Victorian Age of English Literature and won a position at the British Museum, but was rejected by Sir Andrew Clark, a famous physician. Cecco died in 1894.

With the last of her children now lost to her, she had but little further interest in life. Her health steadily and inexorably declined.

Margaret Oliphant Wilson Oliphant died at the age of 69 in Wimbledon on 20th June 1897. She is buried in Eton beside her sons.

At her death, Margaret was still working on Annals of a Publishing House, a record of Blackwood's Magazine with which she had enjoyed such a successful relationship.

Her Autobiography and Letters, which present a thoughtful picture of her domestic anxieties, was published in 1899. Only parts were written with a wider audience in mind: she had originally intended the Autobiography for her son, but he died before she could finish it.

Opinions on Oliphant's work are split, with some critics seeing her as a 'domestic novelist', while others recognize her work as influential and important to the Victorian literature canon. Critical reception from her contemporaries is also divided. John Skelton took the view that Oliphant wrote too much and too quickly. Writing a Blackwood's article called 'A Little Chat About Mrs. Oliphant', he asked, "Had Mrs. Oliphant concentrated her powers, what might she not have done? We might have had another Charlotte Brontë or another George Eliot." However not all of the contemporary reception was negative. The esteemed M. R. James admired Oliphant's supernatural fiction, concluding that "the religious ghost story, as it may be called, was never done better than by Mrs. Oliphant in 'The Open Door' and 'A Beleaguered City'. Mary Butts lavished praise on Oliphant's ghost story 'The Library Window', describing it as "one masterpiece of sober loveliness".

More modern critics of Oliphant's work include Virginia Woolf, who asked in Three Guineas whether Oliphant's autobiography does not lead the reader "to deplore the fact that Mrs. Oliphant sold her brain, her very admirable brain, prostituted her culture and enslaved her intellectual liberty in order that she might earn her living and educate her children."

Whatever the merits of their cases Margaret Oliphant has been shamefully neglected in modern years. She is now becoming more widely recognised as a leading writer of her day.

A canon of more than 120 works, including novels, travel books, histories, and volumes of literary criticism.

Novels

Margaret Maitland (1849)
Merkland (1850)
Caleb Field (1851)
John Drayton (1851)
Adam Graeme (1852)
The Melvilles (1852)
Katie Stewart (1852)
Harry Muir (1853)
Ailieford (1853)
The Quiet Heart (1854)
Magdalen Hepburn (1854)
Zaidee (1855)
Lilliesleaf (1855)
Christian Melville (1855)
The Athelings (1857)
The Days of My Life (1857)
Orphans (1858)
The Laird of Norlaw (1858)
Agnes Hopetoun's Schools and Holidays (1859)
Lucy Crofton (1860)
The House on the Moor (1861)
The Last of the Mortimers (1862)
Heart and Cross (1863)
Salem Chapel (1863)
The Rector (1863)
Doctor's Family (1863)
The Perpetual Curate (1864)
Miss Marjoribanks (1866)
Phoebe Junior (1876)
A Son of the Soil (1865)
Agnes (1866)
Madonna Mary (1867)
Brownlows (1868)
The Minister's Wife (1869)
The Three Brothers (1870)
John: A Love Story (1870)
Squire Arden (1871)
At his Gates (1872)

Ombra (1872
May (1873)
Innocent (1873)
The Story of Valentine and his Brother (1875)
A Rose in June (1874)
For Love and Life (1874)
Whiteladies (1875)
An Odd Couple (1875)
The Curate in Charge (1876)
Carità (1877)
Young Musgrave (1877)
Mrs. Arthur (1877)
The Primrose Path (1878)
Within the Precincts (1879)
The Fugitives (1879)
A Beleaguered City (1879)
The Greatest Heiress in England (1880)
He That Will Not When He May (1880)
In Trust (1881)
Harry Joscelyn (1881)
Lady Jane (1882)
A Little Pilgrim in the Unseen (1882)
The Lady Lindores (1883)
Sir Tom (1883)
Hester (1883)
It Was a Lover and his Lass (1883)
The Lady's Walk (1883)
The Wizard's Son (1884)
Madam (1884)
The Prodigals and their Inheritance (1885)
Oliver's Bride (1885)
A Country Gentleman and his Family (1886)
A House Divided Against Itself (1886)
Effie Ogilvie (1886)
A Poor Gentleman (1886)
The Son of his Father (1886)
Joyce (1888)
Cousin Mary (1888)
The Land of Darkness (1888)
Lady Car (1889)
Kirsteen (1890)
The Mystery of Mrs. Biencarrow (1890)
Sons and Daughters (1890)
The Railway Man and his Children (1891)
The Heir Presumptive and the Heir Apparent (1891)
The Marriage of Elinor (1891)
Janet (1891)
The Cuckoo in the Nest (1892)

Diana Trelawny (1892)
The Sorceress (1893)
A House in Bloomsbury (1894)
Sir Robert's Fortune (1894)
Who Was Lost and is Found (1894)
Lady William (1894)
Two Strangers (1895)
Old Mr. Tredgold (1895)
The Unjust Steward (1896)
The Ways of Life (1897)

Short stories

Neighbours on the Green (1889)
A Widow's Tale and Other Stories (1898)
That Little Cutty (1898)
The Open Door (1918)

Selected Articles

Mary Russel Mitford (Blackwood's Magazine, Vol. 75, 1854)
Evelin and Pepys (Blackwood's Magazine, Vol. 76, 1854)
The Holy Land (Blackwood's Magazine, Vol. 76, 1854)
Mr. Thackeray and his Novels (Blackwood's Magazine, Vol. 77, 1855)
Bulwer (Blackwood's Magazine, Vol. 77, 1855)
Charles Dickens (Blackwood's Magazine, Vol. 77, 1855)
Modern Novelists—Great and Small (Blackwood's Magazine, Vol. 77, 1855)
Modern Light Literature: Poetry (Blackwood's Magazine, Vol. 79, 1856)
Religion in Common Life (Blackwood's Magazine, Vol. 79, 1856)
Sydney Smith (Blackwood's Magazine, Vol. 79, 1856)
The Laws Concerning Women (Blackwood's Magazine, Vol. 79, 1856)
The Art of Caviling (Blackwood's Magazine, Vol. 80, 1856)
Béranger (Blackwood's Magazine, Vol. 83, 1858)
The Condition of Women (Blackwood's Magazine, Vol. 83, 1858)
The Missionary Explorer (Blackwood's Magazine, Vol. 83, 1858)
Religious Memoirs (Blackwood's Magazine, Vol. 83, 1858)
Social Science (Blackwood's Magazine, Vol. 88, 1860)
Scotland and her Accusers (Blackwood's Magazine, Vol. 90, 1861)
The Chronicles of Carlingford (Blackwood's Magazine 1862–1865)
Girolamo Savonarola (Blackwood's Magazine, Vol. 93, 1863)
The Life of Jesus (Blackwood's Magazine, Vol. 96, 1864)
Giacomo Leopardi (Blackwood's Magazine, Vol. 98, 1865)
The Great Unrepresented (Blackwood's Magazine, Vol. 100, 1866)
Mill on the Subjection of Women (The Edinburgh Review, Vol. 130, 1869)
The Opium-Eater (Blackwood's Magazine, Vol. 122, 1877)
Russian and Nihilism in the Novels of I. Tourgeniéf (Blackwood's Magazine, Vol. 127, 1880)
School and College (Blackwood's Magazine, Vol. 128, 1880)

The Grievances of Women (Fraser's Magazine, New Series, Vol. 21, 1880)
Mrs. Carlyle (The Contemporary Review, Vol. 43, May 1883)
The Ethics of Biography (The Contemporary Review, July 1883)
Victor Hugo (The Contemporary Review, Vol. 48, July/December 1885)
A Venetian Dynasty (The Contemporary Review, Vol. 50, August 1886)
Laurence Oliphant (Blackwood's Magazine, Vol. 145, 1889)
Tennyson (Blackwood's Magazine, Vol. 152, 1892)
Addison, the Humorist (Century Magazine, Vol. 48, 1894)
The Anti-Marriage League (Blackwood's Magazine, Vol. 159, 1896)

Biographies

Edward Irving (1862)
Francis of Assisi (1871)
Count de Montalembert (1872)
Dante (1877)
Cervantes (1880)
Life of Sheridan in the English Men of Letters series (1883)
John Tulloch (1888)
Laurence Oliphant (1892)

Historical & Critical Works

Historical Sketches of the Reign of George II (1869)
The Makers of Florence (1876)
A Literary History of England from 1760 to 1825 (1882)
The Makers of Venice (1887)
Royal Edinburgh (1890)
Jerusalem (1891)
The Makers of Modern Rome (1895)
William Blackwood and his Sons (1897)
The Sisters Brontë. In: Women Novelists of Queen Victoria's Reign (1897)

www.ingramcontent.com/pod-product-compliance
Lightning Source LLC
Chambersburg PA
CBHW072106020726
47501CB00003B/738